Arin stopped her hor
an arrow. Then she took a deep breath and concentrated, and looked through the fog in her *special*
way. And although the mist yet hampered her sight,
she now seemed able to see perhaps twice as far.
Aiko, her swords in hand, remained silent.

Now the horses and ponies began to skit and shy, as
if they, too, sensed an unseen menace. And a faint
stench came through the dampening mist. They
rode forward a few tens of yards, and the reek grew
stronger, foul to the point of gagging.

"It is at hand," hissed Aiko, but Arin still could not
sight any hazard.

A pony squealed and from behind there came a loud
scrape. Arin whirled her horse 'round in time to see
a monstrous form lunge out from a great hole and
hammer a massive fist into the neck of one of the
small steeds, snapping its spine as if it were but a
twig, while the other pony bleated and fled, only to
be jerked up short by the rope tied to Arin's saddle.

"Troll!" shouted Arin as the hulking beast loomed
before her. . . .

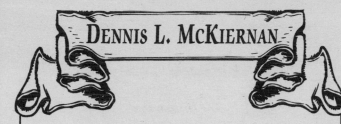

DENNIS L. McKIERNAN

THE DRAGONSTONE

A ROC BOOK

ROC
Published by the Penguin Group
Penguin Books USA Inc., 375 Hudson Street,
New York, New York 10014, U.S.A.
Penguin Books Ltd, 27 Wrights Lane,
London W8 5TZ, England
Penguin Books Australia Ltd, Ringwood,
Victoria, Australia
Penguin Books Canada Ltd, 10 Alcorn Avenue,
Toronto, Ontario, Canada M4V 3B2
Penguin Books (N.Z.) Ltd, 182–190 Wairau Road,
Auckland 10, New Zealand

Penguin Books Ltd, Registered Offices:
Harmondsworth, Middlesex, England

Published by Roc, an imprint of Dutton Signet, a division of Penguin Books USA Inc.
Originally published in a Roc hardcover edition.

First Mass Market Printing, September, 1997
10   9   8   7   6   5

Cover art by Donato

 REGISTERED TRADEMARK—MARCA REGISTRADA

Printed in the United States of America

To my brother
Larry Edward

and

to my friend of more than fifty years
Richard Lee Rose

and to all of our kindred and friends everywhere,
from those we've known the longest
to those we've yet to meet

Foreword

In looking out there, I see a lot of red slippers scattered across the Mithgarian landscape, each just waiting to be examined, for each has a tale to tell if I can but scrutinize it closely.

Red slippers? Red slippers? What in the world is he talking about?

Just this:

Although to my knowledge this never happened, still I can imagine Watson beginning a narrative as follows: "It was soon after Holmes and I had resolved the peculiar case of the singular red slipper, when there came a knock on the door of our quarters at 221-B Baker Street. As I set aside the paper and prepared to answer the summons, Holmes put a finger to his lips and hissed, 'Do not under any circumstance, Watson, open the door without your pistol in hand, for it can be none other than the Bangalian assassin. . . .'"

Watson would then go on to illuminate us as to the fascinating case of the circular cord.

But you know what? We never do find out about the red slipper, the one mentioned in his opening sentence.

Yet, for those of us who avidly followed Watson's narratives, we knew, *knew,* that in between, *in between,* those cases we *did* get to read about, the Great Detective was out there solving other most singular dilemmas, and if we just kept our eyes open, we indeed might see him afoot observing clues obvious to him but completely obscure to us . . . obscure, that is, until explained, at which time Lestrade might say, "Oh, how simple. Why anyone can see that." —Um, you bet.

Now, I repeat, as far as I know, Watson did not chronicle

any *Case of the Red Slipper,* nor did he publish anything concerning a Bengalian assassin or a circular cord . . . but surely such things *should* have been. After all, there *was* the case of the giant rat of Sumatra, and there *was* the account of the Addington tragedy, and the story of the red leech, and the terrible death of Crosby, the banker, and many, many more cases alluded to but never published . . . each a red slipper dropped upon the Holmesian 'scape.

And there are red slippers lying all across Mithgar, and every now and again I pick up one that somehow was dropped, and in my best Sherlockian manner I examine it closely and tell you what I see.

Some Mithgarian red slippers have been: a small silver horn found in the hoard of Sleeth; a logbook entry concerning a crystal spear; a mention of the long-held secret of the Châkkia; a stone knife which disappeared in an iron tower; a silver sword taken from the hand of a slain Elven prince; and so on.

Some red slippers are enormous, such as a tapestry depicting a key moment in the Great War of the Ban. Some are small but have great impact, such as a stone ring given to an impossible child. These and more hold the most intriguing tales, and they are red slippers all, slippers which I may take up someday and see what they can tell you and me.

There is a problem in examining red slippers, though, for every time I take one up to tell its story, it seems more red slippers fall out.

Oh, well . . .

In any event, come with me as I pick up another one of these crimson shoes from the 'scape and let us not only see what we find but also what other red slippers might fall out.

—Dennis L. McKiernan
May 1995

Author's Notes

The Dragonstone is a tale which takes place before the Separation, when mystical and mythical peoples and creatures yet lived within this world.

It is a story which begins 323 years before the events chronicled in *Voyage of the Fox Rider,* hence *The Dragonstone* is a tale which takes place *before* the Great War of the Ban, thus, the *Rûpt* are free to roam about in daylight as well as night, although it is told that they prefer to do their deeds in darkness rather than under the sun.

The story of the Dragonstone was reconstructed from the fragments of a lengthy lay attributed to a bard named Delon. I have in several places filled in the gaps with notes from other references, but in the main the tale is true to its source.

As I have done in other of my works, I have used transliterated archaic Greek to represent the magical language of the Black Mages, and Latin to represent the magical words of all other Magekind.

There are many instances where in the press of the moment, the humans, Mages, Elves, and others spoke in their native tongues; yet to avoid burdensome translations, where necessary I have rendered their words in Pellarion, the Common Tongue of Mithgar. However, some words and phrases do not lend themselves to translation, and these I've either left unchanged or, in special cases, I have enclosed in angle brackets a substitute term which gives the "flavor" of the word (i.e., <see>, <fire>, and the like). Additionally, sundry words may look to be in error, but indeed are correct—e.g., DelfLord is but a single word though a capital L nestles among its letters.

The Elven language of Sylva is rather archaic and

formal. To capture this flavor, I have properly used thee and thou, hast, dost, and the like; however, in the interest of readability, I have tried to do so in a minimal fashion, eliminating some of the more archaic terms.

For the curious, the *w* in Rwn takes on the sound of *uu* (w *is* after all a double-u), which in turn can be said to sound like *oo* (as in spoon). Hence, Rwn is *not* pronounced Renn, but instead *is* pronounced Roon, or Rune.

"Perhaps, Ferai, you are along to make us believe that we indeed have free will."

"And perhaps, Burel, you are along to make us believe we do not."

Northern Sea

Leut

Kairn · Rvn

Arbor

Thok

Jillian Tors

Dalara Rian

Atala · Anster

Geten

Königreich Jute

Wellen

Trellinath

Gothon

Hoven

Tugal

Weston Ocean

Basq

Portho

Vancha

Castilla

Kistan

Ulan Koy

Straits of Kistan

Khalish

Hyree

Talak Mesa

Barrens

Untended
Lands

Boreal
Sea

Black Mtn.

Grey Mtns.

Fjordland

Morkfjord

Roth

Dragon's
Roost

Great
Maelstrom

Grimwall Mtns.

Seabane
Is.

Steppes
of Jord

Rian

Rood

Xian

Khal

Kandor
Pass

Wolfwood

Gron

Aven

Aralan

Garia

Landover Road

Riamon

Jallor

Ganar

Rell

Galion
Vancha

Alban

Valon

Harth's
Crucible

Jugo

Dellin

The Lands
of Stone

Hurn

Arbalin
Is.

Thell
Cove

Caer
Pendwyr

Voran
Is.

Avagon Sea

Sarain

Aban

בוכ הַשָׂה

Gjeen Is.

Chabba

Thayra

Sabra

The Karoo

Khem

Nizari

Scale

0   200   400
Miles

N

W   E

S

THE
DRAGONSTONE

CHAPTER 1

Lightning stroked the night, the glare flaring through the narrow windows, thunder rolling after. As if summoned by the flash, a blast of rain hammered down on the small, ramshackle, dockside tavern, while the wind rattled door and sideboards and slammed a loose shutter to and fro, and waves roared against the pilings 'neath.

Inside the weatherworn building the sound of the storm was muted somewhat, and Olar, his sharp elbows on the rough broad plank which served as a bar, leaned forward and hissed to Tryg, "Wha' be them two women doin' here, eh?" He thrust his narrow chin sideways toward the shadow-wrapped corner where the two strangers sat just beyond the yellow light of the single tavern lantern hanging above the bar. "Mayhap a couple o' doxies come t' ply their trade when th' raiders return, aye?"

Tryg, proprietor of the Cove, snorted at Olar's remark, then leaned forward and said in a voice just loud enough to be heard above the moan of the wind and drum of the rain and the rattle and bang and swash, "Ye'd better not let them hear ye call 'em doxies, laddie, else ye're like to come up missing y'r balls."

Yngli, the only other person in the tavern, slapped the plank and laughed at this remark, but Olar looked at Tryg in surprise. " 'N' j'st why d'ye say that?"

" 'Cause one o' them be an Elf, 'n' t'other's a, a, well I don't rightly know her kind, yet she be th' one wi' th' gleamin' swords."

Olar drew his breath in through clenched teeth and glanced toward the shadows of the darkened corner as lightning again stroked nearby, thunder slapping after.

The flare briefly illuminated the outsiders' faces: delicate,

strange, exotic. The one on the left was fair skinned—
ivory and alabaster—and she had hazel eyes aslant and
chestnut locks falling to her shoulders, with pointed-
tipped ears showing through. The one on the right was
saffron skinned—tawny, ivory yellow—her tilted eyes
glittered onyx, her short-cropped raven-black hair shone
glossy . . . but this one's ears were not tipped.

The strangers sat in the corner with their backs to the
wall, silent, impassive, as if waiting. On the table before
the yellow one lay two unsheathed swords, one long, one
shorter, each slightly curved; the blades glinted wickedly
as lightning flared.

Olar blenched and quickly faced forward once more.
After a moment he said, "Then wha' think ye be th'
reason brought them two t' Mørkfjord, eh?"

Tryg shrugged his beefy shoulders as he tipped the
pitcher to replenish the mug sitting before the gaunt
fisherman. "Seekin' passage, I would think, now, aye?"

Olar cocked an eyebrow, but Yngli shook his head. "I
think they ha'e come t' hire a Dragonship and crew—a
raid on enemies, aye? They be waiting for the return o'
one o' them anow—likely Orri's craft, since he fared out
first and should come back soonest, I would say."

Rain hammered down as again Olar cast a quick sideways glance toward the enshadowed corner. Then he
leaned forward and slurped at the foam in his mug.
Wiping the back of his hand across his lips, "Th' Elf," he
hissed, "d'ye suppose she be one o' them Lian, one o'
them Guardians?"

Tryg shook his head. "Too short. More like them what
lives in th' deep woods—"

"Dylvana, ye mean?" interjected Yngli.

"Like as not."

Yngli smiled. "Then she be my size."

Tryg looked at the grin on Yngli's face. "P'rhaps y'r
size, my smallish friend, but I wouldn't go about getting
ideas, else ye, too, are like t' lose y'r hopes f'r future offspring, from what I hear about Dylvana females."

"Wha' about th' yellow one?" sissed Olar. "D'ye suppose she be an Elf, too?"

Tryg shrugged.

"She ha'e got slanty eyes," muttered Yngli.

"But her ears don't be pointy," responded Tryg.

Yngli eyed the swords. "D'ye think they be here t' stir up trouble? Mayhap t' kill some'n' who did 'em wrong?"

"Or t' cut off their balls?" groaned Olar, shivering.

Tryg opened his mouth to say something, but in that moment the rattling door flew open, admitting wind and rain and a scrawny old man who came lurching in, water runneling down through drenched strings of unkempt, long hair fringing 'round his glistering wet bald pate, his scraggly beard and his ragged cloak dripping.

"Get out, Alos!" shouted Tryg above the blow. " 'N' shut th' door behind as ye go!" The old man staggered a few more feet, a trail of wetness following. "I told ye before, I don't want ye in here, Alos!" The tavernkeep started around the end of the bar as the old man inarticulately whined something and turned his head aside and threw up a warding hand and fled stumbling among the few tables, seeking refuge. Behind him the door whipped to and fro, banging against the wall in counterpoint to the loose shutter, and rain gusted inward and the tavern lantern swung on its chain in the swirling blow to set the shadows swaying.

Muttering curses, Tryg started for the old man. "Get th' door for me, Yngli," called the beefy tavernkeep, "while I throw this good-for-nought out."

Yngli leapt to his feet and stepped to the banging door, pushing it to and standing ready at the latch while Tryg went after the whimpering old man.

Ineffectually, the oldster scrabbled among the tables, trying to evade Tryg, finally cowering under one to no effect, for the tavernkeep swiftly caught him by the cloak collar and jerked him up to his feet. "Alos, I told ye I don't want ye in here ever."

In the swaying lanternlight, the old man looked up at Tryg, one eye watery brown, the other, the right one, blind, the entire cornea white. "Just one drink, Master Tryg"—his voice was a whine—"one is all I need."

Left hand on Alos's collar, the right gripping a fistful of breeks through the sodden cloak, Tryg yanked the old man up on tiptoes and propelled him mewling toward the door, where Yngli stood waiting. But Yngli's eyes widened and he gasped hoarsely and scuttled backwards, away, his gaze beyond Alos, beyond Tryg.

" 'Ware, Tryg," sounded Olar's call, more of a squawk than a shout.

At the same time—"Hold!" came a command from the shadows.

Tryg jerked his head 'round and he sucked in air between clenched teeth, his grip on Alos all but forgotten, for there just behind stood the yellow lady, her swords in hand, the blades viciously gleaming in the shifting light. She had left her cloak behind, and for the first time Tryg could see that she was not wearing a *proper* dress like a *proper* lady should, but instead was garbed in brown leather—vest and breeks and boots. Hammered bronze plates like scales were sewn on the vest; underneath she wore a silk jerkin the color of cream. A brown leather headband incised with red glyphs held her raven-black hair back and away from her high-cheekboned face. She stood in a warrior's stance: balanced, ready. *Like one o' them Jordian warrior maids . . . 'cept she ain't no Jordian, being slanty-eyed and yellow and all.*

Armed and armored and standing perhaps but five feet two, she looked at Tryg, her tilted eyes black and impassive. "*Kanshu,* my mistress would speak with this one," she said quietly in a strangely accented voice as she canted her head toward Alos. The old man smiled a snagtoothed grin at her, his few remaining teeth yellow-brown.

Tryg glanced at the Dylvana in the corner then back at the yellow woman. "Lady, he be nought but a derelict, a beggarly drunk, and no good'll come o' this."

The swords shifted slightly, glimmering.

Tryg released Alos. " 'Tis all on y'r heads," he muttered under his breath, backing away from this female. "Don't say I didn't warn ye."

With a great show of dignity, Alos stood erect and gripped the lapels of his sodden cloak and straightened the garment, stretching his dirt-encrusted wet scrawny neck as he did so; then he turned his white eye toward his rescuer and bobbed his head and grinned a mindless, gap-toothed, ocherous smile. "First we'll have us a drink, aye?"

For a moment the yellow lady eyed him impassively ... then with a quick turn of her hands she reverse-gripped her swords and fluidly sheathed them. Then she spun on her heel and stepped toward the shadows where the Dylvana waited, the old man trailing water and licking his lips in anticipation as he lurched after.

CHAPTER 2

Even before Tryg could leave the table the sodden old man slurped down his ale, running his grimy finger about the rim of the mug to pick up the remaining light froth of foam then licking the finger clean, dirt and all. He looked up at Tryg expectantly and then over at the two ladies and smiled his brown-stained gap-toothed grin at them and bobbed his head eagerly.

The saffron-skinned, black-haired female warrior merely stared back at him impassively. The Dylvana sighed and looked into the blind white eye of the oldster as if considering her options.

Tryg cocked an eyebrow at the Dylvana. She, too, was dressed somewhat like a man: a long-sleeved pale green silk jerkin and tan breeks and brown boots. Her chestnut hair was held in place by a green silk ribbon bound 'round her head. He guessed she was shorter than the yellow woman by as much as seven or eight inches—perhaps no taller than four feet six or seven—though it was difficult to judge with her sitting down. As far as he could tell, unlike her companion she was unarmed. He cleared his throat. "Lady?"

She turned her tilted hazel eyes his way and nodded, and Tryg took up the empty mug and headed for the bar, the old man's full attention now locked upon his retreating back.

"The taverner seems a decent sort, Aiko," said the Dylvana. "I do not think thou didst need show him thy swords to have him release our guest."

Aiko's almond-eyed gaze followed Tryg as well. "Even at rest a sword in the hand speaks with a loud voice, Dara."

The Dylvana smiled, then turned to Alos, but the oldster was totally absorbed in watching Tryg refill the mug. The Dylvana sighed but said nothing, instead studying the old man's face, her gaze returning ever again to his white eye.

Shortly the tavernkeep came back to the table, and Alos avidly reached out both of his liver-spotted hands to eagerly take the mug. Again he quickly drained it and once more fingered up the remaining froth of foam. He ardently looked at the Dylvana in anticipation and smiled his yellow-brown snag-toothed smile, but his face fell as she shook her head and waved Tryg away and said, "We will talk first and then perhaps have some more ale."

"But, mum, I could talk better if—"

Aiko's hand struck viper-swift across the table and snatched the old man by his still damp wrist. "*Kojiki,* you will address her as 'Lady' or as 'Dara,' " she hissed. As if to underscore her words, a thunderbolt cracked the night sky, light flaring through the window, Aiko's face standing out in bold relief.

The old man whined and tried to pull back, to no avail.

"Aiko," came the Dylvana's soft words. "Let be."

Roughly, Aiko pushed Alos's arm away, and the old man pulled back his sleeve and rubbed his age-marked skin and looked for damage, finding none.

"This unclean *yodakari* cannot be the one," said Aiko, turning her dark gaze to the Elf.

The Dylvana shook her head. "Aiko, we know it not."

After a moment Aiko looked away, her black eyes impassive again.

The Dylvana reached across to pat Alos's hand, but the old man flinched back. She withdrew the gesture and instead took up her wine cup and stared into its depths as if seeking something within. At last she lowered the cup to the table and said, "I am called Arin, and my companion's name is Aiko. We have journeyed far to reach Mørkfjord . . . perhaps to see thee."

Alos nodded, but his one good eye was on her nearly full wine cup as she absently turned it about and about.

"Tell me, Alos, art thou the only one-eyed person in the steading?"

Momentarily taken aback, he looked up at her, his white eye seeming to glare. Then he grinned gap-toothed and said, "As far as I know, mu—er, Lady Arin."

At this answer, Arin glanced at Aiko, but the warrior woman just shook her head and said nothing. Arin gazed back at Alos. The old man's good eye was once again locked on her wine cup. Arin put her palm down over the top, and a look of resigned disappointment fell upon Alos's face as he blew out through his lips and looked up at her.

Arin leaned back in her chair, away from the oldster. *He smells like a wet goat and his rank breath could knock a camel off its feet. He is filthy and dirt smeared and probably hasn't seen soap and water in a year or more. Even so, he could be the one, for there seems to be no other choice, at least not in this village.*

"Dost thou know of any other one-eyed person living nearby? Mayhap in another steading?"

He shook his head and muttered, "None I know, Lady Arin."

"Thy blind eye, Alos, there is scar tissue all about, as if burned long past. Pray tell, if it bothers thee not to speak of it, how came thee to be blind?"

Flinching, Alos looked down and covered his white eye with his right hand. "I take it you are looking for someone one-eyed, mu—er, Lady Arin, true?" He lowered his hand to the table and stared at her with his white eye. "If it's to give a reward, then I'm your man; if it's to reap one, I'm not him."

Arin smiled. "Thine accent, Alos, it does not sound Fjord-lander to mine ear."

"I'm Tholian by birth, from th' Long Coast." Alos glanced at his empty mug and at Tryg, then asked in a plaintive voice, with a hint of whine in overtone, "Lady, could we have another nip?"

His eyes widened as Arin pushed her cup across to him, for seldom did wine come his way. He held the nearly full cup to his nose and savored the aroma; perhaps it was some of Tryg's best, her being a Lady and all, and an Elf at that. In two gulps it was gone, its warmth filling his belly and spreading outward. Smacking his lips he ran his licking-finger around and down into the bottom of the cup, searching for a leftover drop or two.

Her black eyes glittering in the lamplight, Aiko stared impassively at the dirt-streaked old man as he slurped at his digit, grime embedded under the split nail.

"Ah. From the Long Coast of Thol," said Arin. "Yes, I recognize thine accent now. But how came thee to be here in Mørkfjord?"

Alos blew out a long breath and leaned slightly up on one hip and noisily passed gas, then peered about as if to find the miscreant. A look of disgust fell across Aiko's face and she wrinkled her nose and glanced at Arin and raised an eyebrow, but Arin merely shook her head slightly.

"My ship, uh . . . foundered," replied Alos. "Yes . . . foundered."

Arin waited for him to continue, to elaborate, but he said no more.

Lightning flared as Alos looked into the wine cup, searching, and thunder rolled as he shoved the empty cup aside and shifted his gaze to his leftover ale mug. His good eye widened and he tilted the mug up to catch one more drop of brew on his tongue, while rain drummed on the roof of the tavern. He smacked his lips and emitted a belch—a bubble of frothy spittle appeared at the corner of his mouth, which he quickly sucked back in.

Aiko looked away in disgust, but Arin took a deep breath and leaned forward. "Alos, 'tis no accident we are here with thee."

"Here? In the Cove? With me?" Alos's good eye widened then narrowed. "How did you know I would be here?"

Arin shrugged. "We asked about. They said thou wouldst likely be making the rounds of the taverns and there are only three. This one is closest to thy . . . sleeping place."

Alos finger-combed at the long wet strings of white hair fringing his bald top and he smoothed his scraggly beard. He tugged at the lapels of his damp cloak, straightening it. Then he looked at Arin. "Well now, you came to talk with me personally?"

Arin nodded. "Perhaps." She glanced at Aiko, then back at Alos and said, "We come on a mission, and it seems as if thou art part and parcel of it."

Aiko sighed.

The oldster's watery brown eye widened, and he glanced Tryg's way. Then he smiled his yellow-brown grin and turned toward Arin. "A mission, you say? And with me in it? Well anow, let's have some more wine—or even brandy, eh?—while you tell me about this mission, aye? It needn't be the best brandy, or even the best wine. In fact, it could be mere ale, what with—"

There came above the storm the cry of voices, and the dock shuddered as if struck a blow. Tryg stepped 'round the end of the bar and toward the door, but both Olar and Yngli were there before him.

" 'Tis a ship," called Yngli, peering out into the rain. "Tyin' up now."

"Who be it, eh?" asked Tryg.

"Ship's lanterns or no, I can't tell," replied Yngli. "Too dark in this blasted rain."

"Some o' them be comin' this way," said Olar, "carryin' somethin' or some'n on a litter."

"Here now, step back," commanded Tryg. "They be comin' to th' Cove."

Aiko was on her feet, her swords in hand. Arin, too, was standing, though her hands were empty. Behind them Alos scrabbled back and away and crawled under a table in a far dark corner.

Through the door came a large, burly man, helmed and cloaked, fleece vest and leather pants and buskins beneath. He carried a lantern and behind him came two more men, these bearing an unconscious fourth.

"Orri!" cried Yngli. "Y'r back."

"Some'n fetch th' healer," called the burly man as he set aside the lantern and swept the mugs from the bar. "Lay him here, lads," he ordered the two bearers. As they hefted the litter to the plank, the large man's gaze fell upon Yngli. "You, Yngli. Run get Thar. Damned Jutes; Egil took a sword cut from th' duke's brother—killed him dead for it, though—but th' wound ha' fevered him."

"Right, Orri!" Yngli gulped down the last of his ale,

then snatched up his cloak and Orri's lantern and dashed away on his errand.

As the Dragonship was secured, more men came through the door and into the Cove, a few with bandaged wounds, but most hale though wet from the storm. Orri glanced about as the place began to fill, then he cast a handful of silver coins onto the counter and called out to the taverner: "These men fought like wild wolves, Tryg, 'n' worked up a mighty thirst, so open y'r taps wide 'n' start th' ale t' flowin'."

There was a glad whoop and men surged toward the bar. "But what about Egil?" cried Tryg, shouting to be heard.

"Ar, there's nought can be done till Thar arrives," bellowed Orri above the clamor. "Besides, wound or no, fever or no, should Egil wake he'll want an ale o' his own."

As men crowded forward to get one of the mugs of brew being served across Egil's prostrate form, Olar wormed his way through the press to get one of his own. As he stood behind Orri, he craned his neck up and looked over the raider's shoulder at the wounded man. "Adon's daughter Elwydd," Olar burst out atop the milling din, "Egil's lost an eye!"

At these words, Aiko, standing unnoticed in the shadows along the wall, drew in her breath and glanced at Arin just as the Dylvana started forward.

CHAPTER 3

Hoy! What th'—?" Men on the fringe of the clamoring crowd turned 'round to see—

"Make way for the Dara."

—a small, yellow woman in bronze scale pressing her way through the ranks to make a path for—

"By gar, 'tis an Elf or two."

—the even smaller female who followed.

The tall warriors stepped aside, for here come among them were two the likes of which they had never seen: an ebon-haired, armed and armored woman of saffron skin and slanted eyes of black—

"Adon's foam, but she's yellow."

"Top o' her head won't even reach my chin."

"But th' one behind her—"

—and a chestnut-haired Elf of ivory and alabaster, her tilted eyes hazel—

"—why, she can't be no more'n chest high t' me."

—both females dressed manlike, as if they had traveled far.

A quietness fell upon the raiders as they parted ranks to form a corridor for these exotic strangers to pass through, the stillness broken only by the drumming of the rain on the roof and an occasional thunderbolt. Aiko's hands rested on the pommels of her two swords and her dark eyes scanned these warriors as she led Arin toward the unconscious man on the bar.

Wide-eyed, Orri, the last raider between the females and their goal, stepped aside. Aiko, too, stood away as Arin came to the bar and gazed at the man lying there. Slender and tawny-haired, he was perhaps in his early thirties, and his fair skin was flush with fever. As others crowded near, Arin laid a hand to the man's forehead, then gasped, "*Vada!*" She turned to make her way around to the other side; men stood in her path.

"Out o' th' way, Svan, Bili!" bellowed Orri. "Can't y' see she needs t' pass?"

Svan stumbled back into Bili just behind, and they both nearly fell, spilling splashes of ale from their mugs. Tangle-footed, they managed to move aside to let Arin by.

With dark gaze Aiko looked up at Orri, the warrior woman seeming taller than her five feet two. "Captain?"

Orri nodded, his ear catching the hint of a lilting accent in her spoken word.

"Have your warriors give back, Captain. The Dara will see to your wounded comrade . . . if it is not too late."

As Orri bellowed for his men to move hindward, the door banged open and Yngli came splashing in, wind and rain following, a white-haired man coming after and carrying a leather knapsack.

"Here be Thar!" cried Yngli, closing the door with a flourish to shut out the storm. "Now we'll get Egil tended to, good and proper."

Yngli's words were greeted with a cheer as the white-haired man set down his knapsack and stripped off his wet cloak.

Arin, now on the far side of the bar, paid no heed to the uproar, but instead scanned Egil's face. An angry red gash sliced downward from his forehead to his cheek, his left eye completely destroyed. Arin glanced up at Orri. "Hadst thou no bandage?"

Orri spread his hands wide. "He ripped it off in his nightmares, Lady, in his fever."

"Hadst thou no healer with thee?"

"We bind our own wounds, Lady, just as we bound his," bristled Orri. "But we were too busy fighting off Duke Rache and his men most o' th' way back—flaming arrows and quarrels and sling bullets and such—till finally we managed t' set fire t' their sails and left them cursing behind, then lost 'em in th' dark. But as t' Egil, every able man was needed and none were free t' see t' his hurt. 'Sides, he was fightin' th' Jutlanders as well, even though he was wounded and fevered and could see but from one eye. And when th' fight ended, well then we tended him—salt water on his wounds t' keep 'em free o' fester, bandages. But Egil ha' ill dreams, Lady, mayhap made worse by th' fever, and he j'st kept pullin' free th' dressin', and finally we let be."

As Arin acknowledged Orri's words, Thar came to the side of the wounded man. The old healer's eyes widened slightly at the sight of the Dylvana and her yellow-skinned companion, but he shook his head as if clearing it of vagaries and then began examining Egil.

Arin glanced up at Thar. "The eye, what remains, it must come out."

Thar nodded. "Be ye a healer, Lady?"

"I have some skill at it," replied Arin. "Yet I have no herbs and simples at hand, nor tools."

"I ha'e mine," said Thar, gesturing at his leather knapsack. "But he be y'r patient, Lady. J'st tell me—or whoe'er else—what it might be ye need."

Arin canted her head in acceptance, then turned to Tryg, the taverner, filling mugs. "Hast thou a crate on which I can stand? I need be at a level to work on his wounds."

Tryg motioned for Olar to take over the duty of dispensing ale, then with a practiced eye, measured the Dylvana's four feet eight inches of height. He stepped into the storage room, emerging moments later with a wide wooden box and set it to the floor. The Dara smiled as she stepped upon the crate, then said, "I will need a knife, glowing red with heat. Two, if thou canst provide. —And a bottle of thy strongest brandy."

Tryg reached under the counter and pulled forth a flask and set it at her side, saying, "This be th' best I ha'e." Then he caught up two knives and stepped to the small charcoal burner he used to heat the poker for mulling wine.

Arin uncorked the brandy and sniffed. Satisfied, she poured some in her palm and washed her hands with it and looked across at Thar. "Hast thou wire nips? Something to pluck away the flesh when seared? And a needle and gut to sew up the sword gash? And clean cloth for bandages and other needs?"

Thar rummaged through his knapsack and pulled forth

a curved bronze needle and thin strand of gut thread and pair of bent-wire tweezers. Too, he fetched out a rolled length of washed muslin.

Under the bar Arin found a candle and holder and soon had the taper lit. She then began passing the bronze needle back and forth through the flame.

"Ah," murmured Thar, his eyes taking in all she did. "Burnin' away th' bad vapors, aye?"

Arin nodded. "I'll need a piece of clean white cloth to lay these on."

Thar took up the muslin and tore off a square and spread it out. Arin placed the flame-cleansed needle and gut thread on it, then took up the tweezers and began passing them through the flame. "How be the knives?" she called out to Tryg.

The taverner looked into the fire, then held up a hand palm out. "Soon."

"We're goin' t' need t' set th' leeches on him, too, y'know," said Thar.

"Leeches?"

"T' bleed th' fever away, Lady."

Arin shook her head. "Nay, healer. Leeches will but weaken him at a time he will need his greatest strength."

"But we always bleed for fever," protested Thar.

Arin fixed him with an eye. "Dost thou oft cure the ill by doing such?"

"A good half o' them," responded Thar with some pride.

"Then that means thou loseth half as well, neh?"

"We lose a share o' them, aye, but that's t' be expected."

"Nay, healer. By bleeding, thou weaken the afflicted when they can least spare strength. Instead thou shouldst fortify the blood of the sick and not drain it away."

"Fortify?"

"Aye."

"How?"

"They be borderin' on ruddy red!" called Tryg.

"How?" Thar asked again.

"Thou hast the means nearby," said Arin, and she beckoned to Aiko.

"Dara?"

"Ride swift to the high fell and gather a handful of the blue flowers we saw at the foot of the glacier. Take up as well some pure snow and pack the flowers therein. Then return within a candlemark."

Aiko glanced left and right and then leaned forward and hissed, "Dara, I would not leave you alone among these *iyashii* men."

The Dylvana made a sharp gesture of negation. "Go now, Aiko. I will be safe, and this man needs aid else he will die, and he is perhaps the one we need."

Yngli took up his cloak as well as Orri's lantern and stepped to Aiko's side. "Though I don't own a horse, I'll ride wi' ye, double that is, t' light y'r way if ye'll ha' me. I know a shortcut t' th' fell."

Aiko looked at Yngli, then at Arin. At the Dylvana's nod, Aiko strode back to the table and donned her own cloak while Yngli lighted the lantern, then she gestured for Yngli to follow.

As they left the room, Thar turned to Arin and raised a questioning brow.

Arin set the flame-cleansed tweezers down next to the bronze needle, then wetted her fingers and snuffed out the candle. "When we rode down into Mørkfjord, we saw in the high fell at the foot of the glacier small blue flowers nodding on their stems."

"Blue flowers? . . . Ah, blue-eyed ladies."

"Blue-eyed ladies in thy tongue; arél in mine. Yet by any name a tea brewed from their fresh petals is a potent foe of fever."

"Th' knives be cherry red and some, m'Lady," called Tryg.

Arin took a deep breath and slowly let it out as she looked down at Egil. "Hast thou a sleeping draught, Thar?"

The man shook his head. "Nay, Lady. Egil'll j'st ha'e t' bear up."

Arin sighed and then turned to Orri. "I shall need six of thy strongest."

"Six?"

"One on each limb and two t' hold his head, Orri," said

Thar. "Can't ha'e him jerkin' about when th' burnin' knife goes in."

"Aye." Orri gestured to five more men, then stepped to the bar himself.

"A moment, Captain," said Arin, and she took up the flagon and again used brandy to wash her hands, indicating for Thar and Tryg to do likewise. Then she turned to Orri. "Now, Captain, take hold."

"Arms and legs, lads, and hold hard. He'll thrash quite a bit. Bili, help me up here."

The men grasped Egil's limbs, and Orri and Bili stood opposite one another and braced his head by jaw, temple, and pate.

Arin glanced across at Thar. "Art thou ready?"

At the healer's nod, Arin held out a hand to Tryg, and using a square of clean cloth he took up a knife by the handle and carefully handed it to the Dylvana, its blade glowing yellow-hot.

Arin grasped the handle through the cloth and picked up the tweezers, then said, "Peel back his eyelids, healer; the rest of ye hold firm."

In the stable at the Blackstein Lodge, by Yngli's lanternlight Aiko pulled tight the saddle cinch. She drew her cloak hood over her head, and with Yngli following, led the steed outside, where rain fell in torrents and lightning strode across churning skies. She mounted up and then gave a stirrup and an arm to Yngli, and he swung up behind her. As he did so there came the faint sound of agonized screams muted by the storm and distance. Yngli shuddered and looked far downslope at the light shining out from the windows of the Cove. And then Aiko put spurs to the horse and they rode away through the black night.

CHAPTER 4

Within a candlemark of plucking the flowers, drenched and mud spattered, Aiko and Yngli returned to Mørkfjord, Yngli bearing a leather sack filled with snow, the blue-petaled blossoms within. As they strode to the dock, the rain pattered down gently, the rage of the storm having moved off to the east, though now and again the sky was lit by the backflare of distant lightning. Yngli opened the door to the Cove and followed Aiko in, the small man holding up the bag and declaring to one and all, "Hoy, everyone, we're back wi' our bouquet." A shout greeted the announcement as Yngli and the yellow woman shed their dripping cloaks.

"Ah, good and well done, Aiko. Good and well done, Yngli," said Arin, looking up from her red stitchery as she sewed Egil's sword gash shut. She'd had to cut the flesh anew so the wound would grow back together, and her fingers and hands were slathered with his fresh blood. "Thar, separate the flowers from the snow. Tryg, put a kettle over the charcoal. We'll use pure melt to make the tea."

Yngli stepped up to the bar and handed the bag to Thar as Arin continued to stitch. Then he slapped himself on the chest and gestured to Aiko and called out, "Hoy, Tryg, give me and her a tot o' brandy. We're soaked t' th' bone and dead chill."

Tryg grunted at Olar, and the fisherman fetched a flask and two cups and filled them nearly to the brim.

The small man took up both cups and handed one to Aiko, then he quaffed a stiff drink from his own. "Whuk!" he choked, then began hacking and coughing. Bili pounded him on the back repeatedly till he caught his wind and voice again. With his eyes watering he looked 'round the Cove and finally declared, "*Whoo!* Good stuff."

As the laughter died down, Yngli glanced at Egil, then turned to Orri. "How were it, Captain? Egil, I mean."

Orri shook his head, and for the first time Yngli saw that the raider had a bloody nose. "By gar, he woke up when we put th' hot knife t' him. Berserk he was. It took eleven o' us j'st t' hold him down. Broke my nose, I think. Then she"—Orri nodded toward Arin—"soothed him with a song and got him drunk on brandy till he passed out. Adon's blood, Yngli, look at him: he's happy as a clam, drunk as he is, or would be if he were awake."

"I think not," said Thar, shaking his head. "Were he awake he'd be in pain, no matter th' brandy."

Arin cinched the final stitch and tied off and clipped the gut. "There. It is done. Thar, wouldst thou bandage this man's hurts?"

Thar took up the muslin to swathe Egil's wounds; as he did so he examined the work. "As fine a job o' tackin' as could be, Lady—tight, close, tiny—I c'd ne'r do as well. He'll ha'e a scar, though a fine one, what wi' th' splendid work ye ha'e done." He began carefully wrapping cloth about Egil's head, covering forehead, eye, and cheek, leaving the man's mouth and nose and good eye free.

"He will be in pain for some days to come," said Arin as she washed her crimson hands and arms in the basin Tryg had brought. "Hast thou no sleeping draughts at all? Nought to relieve the ache?"

Thar shrugged and muttered, "Nought," as he finished with the wrapping.

Arin sighed. "Then we must needs make some, can we find the ingredients."

"What is it ye need?" asked Thar, tying the last knot.

Above the glowing charcoal the teakettle began to hiss and steam.

"At the moment, healer," said Arin, looking 'round while toweling off her hands and forearms, "I need to make the arél tea. As to the draughts, we will speak of them after."

The Dylvana turned to Tryg. "Hast thou a teapot? No? Then an earthenware vessel will do."

With Thar watching, Arin plucked blue petals from the flowers and cast them in one of Tryg's wide-mouthed mulling jugs. When she judged she had enough, she poured the boiling snowmelt in as well—sufficient to make a bit over a quart of tea altogether. A sweet fragrance wafted up from the jug, heartening all those nearby.

"Aiko, Yngli," she called to the two as the beverage steeped, "ye need both drink a cup of this as well, for I would not have ye come down with fever, drenched as ye were."

Moments passed and moments more as the benefit of the petals infused throughout the hot melt. Finally Arin dipped up a spoonful of the steaming liquid and blew on it and then tasted it. With a nod, the Dylvana filled a cup and motioned Aiko to do likewise and to pour one for Yngli too. As Aiko complied, Arin stepped upon the crate to stand at Egil's side. She waited long moments for the steaming tea to cool down, testing it now and again. Finally, slowly and carefully, a bit at a time, she began spooning small sips of the clear liquid into Egil's mouth as he reflexively swallowed. After a while she gave over the task to Thar.

Arin turned to Orri. "Captain."

"Lady."

"The wounds of thine other men—"

"Ar, nothin' as bad as Egil's, them what wasn't killed outright. We patched up most aboard."

Thar looked up from his task. "Ye've done enough, Lady. I'll see to their scratches."

Arin smiled at the healer and turned again to Orri. "Is Egil married, betrothed, promised?"

"Ha!" Orri barked a laugh. "Nay, Lady. He be free wi' th' women, and they be free wi' him."

"Then, Captain, when he has had his cup of tea and another, I would have thy men bear him to my quarters at Blackstein Lodge where I may tend him in the days to come."

Orri's eyes widened, but he said, "Aye, Lady."

Arin poured herself a cup of arél tea and then moved to where Aiko sat with Yngli. As the Dylvana took a chair, she said to Aiko, "Egil will be moved to our quarters at Blackstein Lodge."

Aiko's dark eyes betrayed no hint of approval or censure. Instead with a faint nod of her head, Aiko acknowledged Arin's words.

"We cannot afford to lose him," added the Dylvana.

Again Aiko faintly nodded.

Yngli turned to Aiko. "I'd ask ye t' come t' my home, but I think my wife w'd take an axe t' me."

Aiko looked at him impassively, then said, "If I did not take my sword to you first."

Yngli laughed, heartily to begin with but fading to silence as he looked into the warrior woman's eyes. He shuddered, dropping his hands to cover his crotch. "Why, I b'lieve y'would at that." Abruptly, Yngli downed the last of his arél tea, then stood. "As long as Captain Orri's buying, I be thinkin' I'll ha'e me some ale." He turned to Arin. "Thank ye f'r th' tea, Lady."

"I thank thee for thy help, Master Yngli," she replied.

Yngli bowed to them both—"Ladies"—and spun on his heel and shouted, "Hoy, Tryg, set me up a mug o' ale!"

For long moments Arin sipped her tea in silence, then turned to Aiko. But before she could say aught, Thar called, "Lady Arin, Egil's had his two cups o' tea."

Wearily, Arin pressed her fingers to her eyes, then stood. "Captain Orri?"

"Har there, Bili, Svan, Angar, Rolle ... take up Egil's litter and bear him t' th' Blackstein, t' Lady Arin's quarters."

"Cover him wi' a cloak or two," added Thar, "it still be rainin' out."

As they carried the unconscious man away, Aiko got to her feet and donned her still wet cloak and said in a low voice, "Then you think, Dara, as do I, that this is the man of your Seeing?"

Arin caught up her own cloak and turned to the warrior. "Art thou forgetting Alos?"

The corners of Aiko's mouth turned down. "Dara, how can you think of Alos when Egil is the one?"

"Alos, too, has but one eye," responded Arin, the Dylvana,

looking about. "And speaking of Alos, where has he gotten to?"

They found the scraggly old man lying under a table in the corner, surrounded by empty ale mugs and clutching an empty brandy flagon and sleeping in his own vomit.

Aiko covered her nose in disgust, but with a sigh Arin said, "We must take him, too."

Aiko's eyes widened, then she said, "To the boathouse where he sleeps, neh?"

"Nay, Aiko. To our quarters in the lodge."

Aiko looked down at Alos in disgust. "But, Dara, he is foul, *fuketsuna,* unclean."

Arin settled her cloak about her shoulders. "Then we will have to bathe him."

"Huah!" Aiko shook her head. "Scour him, you mean. And pumice his teeth and mint his breath and burn his clothes as well."

"Enough, Aiko," admonished Arin. "He has but one eye, and we must discover if he is the one."

"Jikoku," growled Aiko . . . then sighed. "If it is your will, Dara."

With that, Aiko reached beneath the table and dragged Alos by his ankle out from under, ale cups rattling in his wake, the flagon lost to his grip. Then with a grunt she hefted him up and across her shoulders. And with Orri and his raiders looking on in wonder, she followed Arin across the floor and out into the dank night, a thin thread of vomit-tainted drool dribbling from Alos's slack jaw and leaving a wet trail behind.

CHAPTER 5

It was well past mid of night as Arin sat staring into the flames, trying to <see> just who the one-eyed man was, to no avail. Behind her, Egil now slept in the bed, the brandy coursing through his veins keeping him unconscious. From the next room came an agonized howling as Aiko scrubbed the old man, hauling him shrieking from tub to tub as the water in each became too filthy, the lodge boy running back and forth, bearing fresh hot water after dumping the old out through the trough of the bathing room. Perhaps it was this caterwauling which kept the vision from coming—Arin did not know, yet she continued to fix her gaze deep within the fire.

As the lodge boy passed through the room carrying the old man's clothes out to the greatroom hearth to be burned, in through the door came Thar, the healer bearing a bulging leather sack. He momentarily paused and frowned at the ruckus in the next room, then a look of understanding crossed his face. He stepped to the Dylvana's side and raised his voice above the howls and said, "Right, Lady, I ha'e th' herbs and stones and powders ye asked f'r, though th' gettin' o' some o' them were a fair quest i' itself. Ha' t' look through all me goods. Ha' t' get old Maev up f'r some o' 'em." He set the bag on the small table next to the chifforobe.

From the next room there came a sodden *thunk!* and the yowling ceased.

"Aiko?" called Arin.

"He tried to get away, Dara, but slipped and hit his head" came the reply.

Arin raised a skeptical eyebrow but did not question Aiko further. Thar pointed to the leather bag. "Ye look at what I ha'e brought and make certain I got all that be needed. I'll go peer at Alos, see if he be truly injured or no. But, Lady Arin, do not start mixing the medicks wi'out me. I c'n use th' knowledge o' th' sleepin' draught t' aid them what need such."

"A sleeping draught and a potion to ease pain, Thar. I shall show thee the making of each."

Thar bobbed his head and then stepped into the next room as Arin began laying out the contents of the bag: harf root, laka reed, soda stone, oil of cod . . .

The lodge boy came back through carrying a fresh pail of steaming water. Moments later he stood shuffling from foot to foot at Arin's side. "Beggin' y'r pardon, Lady, but"—he swallowed—"*she* wants th' chewin' stick, th' p-p-pumice, 'n' th' mint leaves, er, 'right now,' she said, she did, Lady, beggin' y'r pardon."

Arin unloaded the rest of the bag and found the requested items and gave them to the lad.

Back to the other room he sped as Thar returned. "Alos, he be no th' worse f'r th' havin' o' a knot on top o' his head, though how it came about from a slip, I nae c'd say."

Arin sighed and cast a glance toward the room where Aiko could be heard muttering words in her native tongue. As the Dylvana turned her attention back to the goods on the table, soft moans from Alos began as well.

"This is the way of a sleeping draught, Thar," began Arin.

From the bathing room Alos's moans became a feeble yowling only to be choked into muted squawks as if something had been jammed in his mouth.

Arin heaved a sighing breath of resignation . . . and then took up the mortar and pestle. "First thou must grind the soda stone into fineness, thus. . . ."

Once again Arin sat before the fire and gazed intently into the flames, yet the vision simply would not come to her. Which of these two—the scrubbed and scoured, flatulent old man whimpering in his sleep on a pallet on the floor, or the bandaged younger man in the bed— which of these two was the one-eyed person of her vision, she could not say.

In one corner with her back to the wall Aiko sat in a lotus position on a square of tatami, the woven straw mat from her family home in Ryodo and borne with her throughout her travels. Her hands curled laxly on her thighs; her eyes were closed, though she was not asleep but resting in deep meditation. She was dressed in a black silken chemise, and the tattoo of an ornate red tiger could just be seen glowering balefully out from between her breasts. Her leather-and-bronze armor was racked in the chifforobe, but on the mat before her lay her two gleaming swords. Her hair was still wet from her own bath, and her glowing skin held the sheen of gold, for she had needed to scour herself free from the taint of the old man's layers of filth.

An anguished groan brought Arin to her feet. Egil began to stir, and then to thrash and shout, his hands clawing at the bandages. She hurried to the bedside and tried to hold him still, but in spite of his weakened state, she had not the strength to do so. Aiko appeared at the opposite side of the bed and grabbed an arm. Egil's good eye was wide open and filled with berserker madness, and he hissed in muted rage, yet drugged as he was he could not overcome the two of them. Of a sudden he slumped and began to weep and mumble men's names—"Ragnar, Argi, Bram, Klaen . . ."—his voice fading as he spoke, and then he closed his eye and fell unconscious once more. Arin felt for his pulse. It was strong and steady.

An unspoken question in her eyes, Aiko looked across at the Dylvana. "Orri said he had ill dreams," whispered Arin.

"Is it safe to let him be, Dara?"

Arin nodded. "He seems to be sleeping again." She glanced at the window. It was yet night. "Return to thy rest, Aiko. I will remain on watch."

As the first light of day seeped through the lodge windows, Arin stood and stretched, then stepped to the bedside and again measured Egil's pulse. As she did so she looked down at his face only to find his good blue eye fixed upon her, his gaze now filled with sanity and not berserker madness.

"Am I dead, Lady? Gone beyond the sky?"

Arin smiled. "Nay, Egil, thou art yet in Mithgar."

Egil put his hand to his bandaged head. "I should have suspected. I am in too much pain to be dead. Though you are the vision of an *engel*."

"*Engel?*" Arin's face clouded momentarily. Then she laughed. "Oh, I see: one who lives beyond the sky."

A faint smile crossed Egil's features, then he grunted and struggled to a sitting position. "Where am I? Who are you? Last I remember, the damned Jutes were pursuing and flaming arrows were thick as flies on a dung pile."

Arin began preparing a potion, adding tepid water to a white powder in a cup and then stirring. "Thou didst fall to thy fever."

Once more Egil touched the wrappings passing 'round his head and down his cheek and under his chin only to go back up and 'round and down again several times. "Poisoned blade, I wonder?"

Arin shook her head. "I think not. Unclean, mayhap, even foul, perhaps from grume long past, but not poisoned. Thy comrades did well to treat the gash with salt water, for it washed the wound free of filth, but not ere some of the foulness tainted thine own blood and thou didst succumb to the ill vapors. But thou art now on the journey to wellness, for Thar and I treated thy wounds and thy fever."

"Thar? Healer Thar? Then, Lady, I am in Mørkfjord?" Egil looked 'round the room.

"Aye. In Blackstein Lodge."

Egil's eye widened at the sight of Aiko sitting as still as a statue of gold and of an old man snoring on the floor, his fingers scrabbling at the pallet as he dreamed. "Again I ask, Lady, who are you, and who are your companions?"

"I am Arin, Dylvana of Darda Erynian, the Great Greenhall to the south."

For the first time Egil saw what she was. "Elf," he whispered half to himself.

Arin canted her head toward Aiko. "My companion is

Aiko, Ryodoan by birth, past Warrior of the Mages of Black Mountain, but now in service to me."

Egil started, and stared at the meditating woman. "Warrior? Mages? Black—?"

"The old man thou shouldst know, for he is Alos of Mørkfjord."

"Alos?" Egil slowly shook his head, then winced with the movement of it. "I would never have recognized him as the beggarly old man who sleeps in Norri's boathouse. Why, he's clean for a change."

Arin smiled faintly. "Scrubbed to a fare-thee-well by Aiko." The Dara set the spoon aside and held out the cup to Egil. "Drink. It is a potion to relieve thine aches."

"Good," grunted Egil. "My head is pounding and my stomach churns as if I'd been on a ten-day drunk; my forehead and cheek are sore to the touch; and my left eye burns as if it has been dipped in a molten pit of Hèl."

"Thy head pounds loudly for we had to fill thee with brandy ere we could work on thy wounds. Thy stomach suffers for it."

Egil smiled above the rim of the cup.

"Thy forehead and cheek ache from the sword slash; it is yet a raw wound, though now sewn shut. It will hurt for some days and leave a scar."

"A handsome scar, I hope," said Egil. "What about my eye?"

Arin did not immediately answer, but waited until he had downed the potion, then said, "Egil, thy left eye is gone, destroyed by a reaver's sword."

Egil took a deep breath and gradually let it out, and handed her the empty cup. "Then it is as I feared: I am now Egil One-Eye."

Slowly Arin nodded.

As morning drew upon the land 'neath overcast skies, Egil slipped back into a restless sleep. Arin returned to her seat by the fire, and time passed.

There came a tapping on the door.

Golden Aiko opened her eyes.

Again came the tapping.

Taking swords in hand, Aiko rose to her feet. She

looked at Arin staring intently at the flames, for the moment completely oblivious to her surroundings. Aiko padded to the door and opened it. Thar stood there, a serving girl behind him bearing a great tray on which was piled eggs and rashers, tea and toast, jams and butter.

Thar looked at the yellow woman in black chemise, a baleful red tiger staring out, then said, "Would ye break y'r fast wi' me?"

Aiko stepped aside and gestured him in with her shorter blade.

Thar crossed to the bed and took Egil's pulse as the serving girl, amid rattling crockery, scurried into the room and set the tray on the sideboard table and distributed the dishes along its length while darting quick glances at the golden warrior and her gleaming swords. When she had finished, she excused herself with a hurried bounce of a curtsey and fled from the chamber.

By this time Arin was on her feet. Aiko glanced at her, one eyebrow raised. Arin shook her head, *No,* and moved to the side of Egil's bed opposite Thar.

"Strong and steady," said Thar, lowering Egil's hand back to the cover. He felt Egil's forehead. "Fever's down and he seems t' be resting well enough." Thar looked up at Arin. "But ye, ye look drawn; did ye get any sleep at all, my dear?"

At this familiarity of address, Aiko growled, *"Bureina yabanjin,"* low in her throat and started forward, but with a gesture of negation, Arin waved her back.

As they sat in the midst of breakfast, Alos awoke, the old man gummily smacking his lips and blearily staring about. When his good eye fell upon Aiko, he shrieked and scrambled away from her, crawling on hands and bony knees toward the door to escape, only to scrawk and clutch his hands to himself when he discovered he was naked. "My clothes! Someone has stolen my clothes!" he sniveled. Ineffectual in his modesty and still on his hands and knees, back to the pallet he scuttled, where he snatched up his blanket and, struggling, wrapped it 'round his scrawny self, all the while keeping his one good eye on Aiko, as if she would attack.

Thar cackled in glee; Aiko stared in loathing. Smiling, Arin stood, and at this movement the oldster cowered down and threw up a warding hand. "Don't hit me!"

"I was not thinking of striking thee, Alos, but instead of inviting thee to break thy fast with us." She gestured toward the laden table.

Anticipation flickering across his face, Alos craned his neck up and peered at the food on the sideboard. "Be there any morning ale? No?" His countenance fell, then perked up again. "Wine? A hearty breakfast wine perhaps?"

Aiko snorted in disgust, but Arin said, "Nay, Alos. Neither ale nor wine nor brandy nor spirits of any sort. Yet there is food aplenty and tea to drink."

Alos sighed and muttered, "Tea? Just tea?"

"Wilt thou join us, friend?"

"Friend?" Alos looked up at her in surprise.

Arin smiled.

"Well"—Alos struggled to his feet and hitched the blanket tighter about—"perhaps I will have a bite to eat." He cast a glare at Aiko and ran a hand over his bald pate, wincing when he discovered the sore knot atop his head. "But only if you keep that yellow demon off, her and her torturing ways."

Aiko bristled—"*Inu!*"—and started to gain her feet, and Alos cowered hindward, but at a sharp word from Arin, Aiko settled back. Then the Dylvana turned her gaze upon the old man and smiled, and Alos, taking that as a promise of protection, stepped to the table and took up a plate, all the while muttering under his breath: ". . . like to have rubbed me raw, she did . . . like to have torn my balls off, too . . . and gouged loose my teeth. . . . — And another thing . . ."

Quiet laughter came from the bed, and then an "Ooo, but it hurts to smile." Arin turned. Egil was awake.

"Wouldst thou break fast with us, Egil?"

Egil nodded. "Aye, I would at that. But first I've got to relieve myself." He started to swing his feet out from under his blanket and to the floor.

"Egil, wait!" Arin hurriedly stepped to the bedside. "Aiko, aid me."

"Adon," exclaimed Egil, clutching the mattress. "The room reels."

" 'Tis the dregs of the fever," said Arin as she slipped his left arm over her shoulders and Aiko did the same with his right. Together they got him to his feet and slowly led him toward the private bathing room adjoining. Blinking, he looked side to side and down at them: Egil at five feet ten, stood fully eight inches taller than Aiko and fourteen taller than Arin. They were scanty compared to him, though at a lean eleven stone six he was by no means heavy. To the contrary, he was slender and lithe and muscled well enough.

They stood him before a chamber pot on a pedestal and braced him as he fumbled at his breeks. He looked at them. "Are you going to stand and watch?"

Aiko sighed. "Would you rather collapse, *orokana ningen*?"

Egil snorted and braced one hand against the back wall. "There."

Reluctantly they released him and turned the other way.

Moments later he desperately clutched at them to keep from falling down. Modesty would have to wait for another day.

Following breakfast Egil fell asleep again, and Thar was called away by a message from the widow Karl. Shortly after the healer had gone, fresh clothes were delivered to Alos, clothes ordered by Arin last eve: soft woolen brown breeks, a tan linen jerkin, tan woolen hose, pale linen underwear, new brown boots, a brown leather belt with a black iron buckle, a dark brown woolen jacket, and a tan linen pocket kerchief. He slipped the new garments on his gaunt frame and strutted and preened in front of the small chiffonnier mirror, standing in profile and sucking in his tiny potbelly, more sag than fat.

"A fine figure of a man," he declared, brushing with his palms the long thin strands of straggling hair fringed 'round his bald pate; and he ran his fingers through his scraggly white beard and smoothed it. Then he turned to Arin and smiled, his wanting teeth somewhat less yellow coated, though still brown stained. "And now, m'Lady, I must be going. Much to do, you know."

Aiko shook her head in disgusted disbelief, but Arin said, "Nay, Alos, I would have thee stay."

"Stay?"

"Aye. There's a tale I would tell thee, but after Egil wakens, for I would have him hear it as well."

"But there's one or two down at the Stag who'll buy me a mug of ale, I'm sure of it, and I mustn't keep them waiting."

"Yopparai," muttered Aiko, loathing in the word.

Arin took a deep breath and then let it out. "If thou wilt remain, Alos, I shall have ale brought to the room."

Briskly, Alos rubbed his hands together and smiled his missing-toothed brown grin. "Well, now that you put it that way, I suppose the Stag can wait."

Arin stood at the window watching Aiko in the court-yard below. The Ryodoan warrior was now dressed in her armor and she slowly stepped through an intricate drill, her gleaming swords in hand. Across the way the stableman stood and watched, his jaw agape. Likewise, down below stood the cook and the lodge boy, equally fascinated.

In the near distance down the steep slopes Arin could see the deep waters of the narrow fjord. Mørkfjord was well named, for the waters were truly dark, nearly ebon.

"I say again, Lady, my mug seems to be empty," whined Alos behind.

"Thou hast had three, Alos," replied Arin without taking her eyes from Aiko's morning exercises. "I shall have the 'keep fetch another as soon as Egil awakens."

Disgruntled, Alos blew his nose into his new kerchief. As he examined the result, he said, "But I'm certain that my friends at the Stag would surely have given me four or five by now."

Arin turned about. "Alos, thou canst go and chance that thy friends at the Stag will serve thee up with all the ale thou dost desire, or thou canst stay here and take the ale certain to come when I choose to call for it."

Sighing, Alos rolled up his sodden kerchief and jammed it into his pocket. Then he peered into his mug once again, searching for an overlooked drop or two, drops that were not there.

Time passed . . .

Aiko returned and stepped into the bathing room and stripped and washed the sheen of sweat from her body and wiped down her armor as well.

At last Egil stirred and opened his eye. Momentarily he seemed to be at a loss. Arin stepped to his side. "Ah," said Egil. "My *engel*."

At the sound of Egil's voice, Alos looked up from his mug. "Good. He's awake. Now we call the 'keep, aye?"

"In a moment," replied Arin as she felt Egil's forehead and took the measure of his pulse. "Thou art strengthening, Egil."

"I need to use the privy again, and I could do with a drink."

"Me too," chimed in Alos. "Use a drink, that is."

Again Arin and Aiko aided Egil to the chamber pot, but this time he stood on his own.

When Egil was safely back in the bed, Arin unwound his bandages to examine the wound.

"I would see, Lady Arin," said Egil.

"Alos, bring the hand mirror from the chiffonnier, please."

Alos stopped sliding his ale cup back and forth on the table and fetched the mirror, then stood nearby holding his mug and shifting from foot to foot.

Egil looked at the raw sword wound. "Ugly."

" 'Twill subside, leaving a white scar behind."

Egil glanced up at Arin. "A patch. I need an eye patch. What color would you say? Red? Yellow? Something bright, regardless. Something the Jutes will not forget when Egil One-Eye returns and wreaks his vengeance on them."

"Mayhap thou wilt postpone thy vengeance once thou hast heard a tale I will tell."

"Ha! Not likely," barked Egil. "As the Dwarves say, vengeance delayed is vengeance denied."

Arin did not reply as she swathed his head with fresh bandages.

The moment she stepped back, Alos said, "Now for the ale, aye?"

Egil looked at the old man. "I wouldn't mind a mug myself, Alos. I've worked up a thirst, getting hacked by the Jutes and all." He turned to Arin. "Lady Engel?"

Aiko rose up from her tatami and stalked over to Egil's bedside. "Wounded you may be, perhaps still fevered, yet you will give the Dara her proper due and address her accordingly."

Egil fixed her with his blue eye. They locked stares for a moment, then he laughed. "All right, lady warrior, polite I shall be and forgo calling her my *engel*."

Only Alos was in position to see the glimmer of disappointment flicker across Arin's face, but the old man was too busy looking into his empty ale mug to notice aught.

Arin started toward the bathing room to wash the blood from the used bandages. "Alos, call the lodge boy. Order a pitcher of ale and an extra mug, one for Egil."

Alos was out the door and yelling for service before Arin took two more steps.

With Aiko rationing out the ale to Alos, much to his dismay, Arin took a chair by Egil's bedside and motioned for Alos to sit near. "I have a tale to tell and I would have ye both hear it, for it has to do with the very fate of Mithgar, or so I deem."

With a sigh the old man hitched his own chair near.

"Aiko and I have traveled far to come unto Mørkfjord to look for a one-eyed man—"

"Or woman," interjected Aiko.

"Aye, or woman," amended Arin.

Both Egil and Alos unconsciously moved a hand to their faces, Alos to his blind white eye, the right, and Egil to his bandaged left.

"You came looking for us?" asked Egil, glancing over at Alos.

"Looking for one of thee, it would seem."

"Which one?"

Arin shrugged. "That I know not . . . for the moment." She glanced at the fire. "But perhaps I will in the days to come."

Slowly Egil shook his head. "But why, Dara? Why would you come looking for a wounded raider or a . . . a . . ." Egil gestured at the oldster.

"A *fuketsuna yopparai*," supplied Aiko, looking at Alos in disgust.

Arin shot Aiko a glance of disapproval, but the warrior woman merely stared impassively back.

Alos looked up from his cup. "What's this all about, m'Lady? This fate of Mithgar?"

" 'Tis about a green stone, Alos, the Green Stone of Xian."

Egil looked at Aiko. "Xian? Why, that's where Black Mountain is said to lie. That's where the Mages live."

"There and on the Island of Rwn," replied Arin.

"M-mages?" stuttered Alos. He turned to Aiko. "I need another drink."

Aiko looked at Arin, and at a nod replenished the old man's mug.

"Perhaps," said Egil, bringing his own cup to his lips and taking a sip, "perhaps your tale would go swifter if you told us the whole of the story and we did not interrupt."

Arin nodded " 'Tis a long tale, yet one worth the fullness of it, else ye will not be able to judge if ye will join us in our mission."

"Mission?" squawked Alos.

"Silence, *inu*!" commanded Aiko.

Flinching, Alos cowered in his chair and took a quick gulp of ale.

As Arin stared at the flames of the fire, gathering her thoughts, quietness descended, and only the muted sounds of the lodge broke the still: dishes clattering in the kitchen; laughter from the greatroom; an axe hewing wood outside; and other such. In the room a burning knot in the fireplace popped, and at last Arin shook her head and began:

"I am a flame seer, and at times divinations come as I peer deeply into fire: visions, redes, oracular pronouncements. They herald that which has happened, that which is happening now, and that which will happen someday. These Seeings are most often significant, as if only things of importance are great enough to be Seen. At times I See events which are joyous and at other times quite grim—calamitous, a catastrophe of great scope. But my visions are mysterious, cloaked in confusion, and to fathom their meanings is most difficult; they are riddles to resolve, and oft I fail. I cannot command what I will See, for these divinations all come at their own whim; I govern them not. Most of the time when I gaze into the flames, nothing at all will appear; yet occasionally in the burning I will glimpse something of import—something from the past, long gone or recent; something from the present, at hand or afar; or something from a future yet to come.

"Such was I doing, staring into the flames, when I beheld the horror of the Green Stone. . . ."

CHAPTER 6

Bordered on the north and east by the Rimmen Mountains, on the south by the River Rissanin, and on the west by the mighty River Argon, there lies a vast forest named Darda Erynian, the Great Greenhall, or Blackwood of old. Through the northern quadrant of this hoary weald runs an ancient east-west trade route, the Landover Road, and along this wooded way merchants and travelers fare. By no other path do common folk journey across this forest realm, for it is said that these woods are . . . occupied . . . by fierce Elves and huge men and, worse yet, by the Hidden Ones—all lurking back among the dense green foliage, in the shadows, in the shade. And of the merchants and travelers, caravans and groups, riders and walkers who pass this way, seldom do any stray far from the road, but instead they hie along its length till they are quit of these looming, foreboding woods.

Even in winter when the leaves are fallen and nought but desolate trunks crowd 'round and exposed branches slash at the sky, even then the woods are filled with trepidation, perhaps more so than in summer, for the barren tangle then looks dead and grasping, as if its harsh woody claws would seize any living fool within reach and rend him asunder.

With its whispered reputation it is not surprising that common travelers are apprehensive when passing through the forest; one of its names is, after all, Blackwood, so called because of the dark unease permeating the vast forest. Some say these woods are indeed warded by the Hidden Ones—Angry Trees and Living Mounds and Groaning Stones and Pysks and Giants and other creatures of lore and legend, all with arcane ways of turning aside those who are unwelcome—and woe betide the unfortunate soul who ignores the warnings and intrudes too far into this shadowy domain, for he will never be seen alive again . . . or so it is said.

In spite of the lore and legend, here it is the Dylvana dwell, here in Darda Erynian, for the Elves know the truth of these woods.

CHAPTER 7

In a green glade in Darda Erynian, Arin sat staring deeply into the flames. She did not hear the remote belling of the stag horns nor the thudding of distant hooves as Rissa and Vanidar and the others reveled in the hunt. Nay, she heard them not, nor was she among them, for her own bow lay beside her—unstrung, unnocked with arrows, unnoticed in her mystic abstraction—for she was attempting to <see>.

For days she had felt the pull of the flames, as if the very essence of fire were calling out to her to seek within and find. And so when the others at the campsite had mounted up, she had waved them on. Now in the solitude of the glade under wheeling stars above, and below the gliding moon, she fed tiny twigs to the small blaze and looked deeply into the flames as a far-off stag ran desperately for its life and belling hunters ahorse plunged behind.

But as to the seer alone by the fire, she was a rarity among Elves, was Arin, for at times she glimpsed events—at hand and afar, past, present, and future—events known and unknown. And for those who are not of Magekind, *any* exercise of what common folk call *magic* is very rare indeed. But Arin's glances across seasons and spans seemed random and sporadic and very obscure, and they came only when she peered into flames, and even then but seldom.

Arin had heard of only one other Elf who could <see>: Rael, a Lian who currently resided in Darda Galion, the great Eldwood to the south and west. She, too, could glimpse events beyond perception, though it is said she used a crystal as a focus instead of fire as did Arin.

Females, two females among all of Elvenkind, two females who could <see>. Was it that males of her Kind had not the power? Or was it instead that only females among the Elves had the patience? Arin did not know.

She shook her head to clear it of these vagaries, to empty her mind and give it over wholly unto the flames. Yet the vision would not come . . . and not come . . . and not come . . . though the fire beat deeply within her soul.

Arin did not know how long she had been staring into the modest blaze, but she was brought out of her transfixion by the ringing of bugles across the clearing and the drum of approaching hooves. *"Hai roi!"* called a voice as Arin got to her feet, and an Elf rode into the light of the fire—it was Vanidar, known as Silverleaf, one of the Lian. Perin and Biren followed behind with the others coming after. And across the withers of Silverleaf's horse was draped a stag, slain no doubt by an arrow loosed from Vanidar's white-bone bow, for it is given to the successful hunter the right to bear the kill.

Stopping his lathered mount with nought but a word, Silverleaf swung his leg up and across the buck and sprang to the ground, landing with the grace of a cat. As with all of immortal Elvenkind, Vanidar appeared to be no more than a lean-limbed youth, though his actual age could have been one millennium or ten or more. He had golden hair cropped at the shoulder and tied back with a simple leather headband, as was the fashion among most Lian and Dylvana. He was clad in grey-green and wore a golden belt which held a long-knife. His feet were shod in soft leather and he stood perhaps five feet nine or ten— more than a full head taller than Arin. In fact, compared to all the Dylvana, Silverleaf outstripped them in height, for Dylvana males typically range from four feet eleven to five feet five, while females span four to six inches less.

Behind Vanidar the others dismounted as well—Rissa and Perin and Biren and Ruar and Melor—their horses sweat-foamed and blowing. The Dylvana were dressed much the same as Silverleaf in their loose-fitting jerkins and close-fitting breeks, though for the most part they favored earth tones—brown and russet and umber—all but beautiful, dark-eyed Rissa, who wore a deep blue, nearly black.

As he turned to haul down the stag, Vanidar glanced over his shoulder at Arin and flashed her a smile, his pale grey eyes atwinkle. "Thou shouldst have been with us, Ring. 'Twas a glorious chase. We almost lost him in the grove, but Rissa"—Silverleaf gestured toward the black-haired Dylvana loosening her cinch and pulling off her saddle—"jumped him up and the chase was on again."

Arin smiled. "Tend the buck, Silverleaf; I will tend thy horse."

Vanidar hefted the stag 'cross his shoulders and strode to a nearby oak. He laid the buck down and fetched two lengths of rope. "We didn't dress him in the field; I'll bleed him out here." He stepped back to the stag and squatted, tying the lines 'round the buck's rear shanks just above the hooves.

By this time Arin had the saddle off Vanidar's mount and was using twisted grass sheaves to rub the animal down. "Do I need walk him?" she called as she stroked along its left flank.

"I think not," said Ruar nearby. "We rode at a walk most of the way back . . . until we reached the clearing."

Rissa strode past, heading for Vanidar as he looped the lines over a sturdy low limb. "Let me give thee a hand with that, *chieran*."

Together the two of them haled the stag by its hind legs up off the ground, and it hung there upside down, its rack of antlers swinging just above the grassy loam.

As Arin worked her way 'round to the other side of Silverleaf's horse, Vanidar unsheathed his razor-sharp long-knife and slit the dead buck's throat.

Blood gushed out, staining the earth.

Arin glanced over at the scarlet pour, free-flowing blood runneling down neck and chin and onto the sward and into the soil below.

She glanced away from this sanguine sight and looked into the fire at hand.

Her eyes flew wide and she gasped in distress, and harsh breath hissed 'tween clenched teeth. Horse, stag, Elven companions: all were forgotten as the vision took her.

Tears flooded her eyes and streamed down her cheeks and she cried out in torment, but she couldn't tear her gaze away from the Seeing.

And then her mind fled from her and she fell senseless to the ground.

CHAPTER 8

Dara . . . Dara . . ."
Who calls from afar?
"Dara . . ."
Nearer.
"Dara . . ."
Closer still.
"Dara."

Arin opened her eyes. Ginger-haired Biren knelt beside her, concern in his face as he chafed her wrists and said once again, "Dara." The others stood back, disquieted.

Muzzily Arin nodded in acknowledgment, then struggled to rise, but Biren shook his head and held her back. "A moment more, Dara."

She took a deep breath. "What happened?"

"Thou didst faint."

Of a sudden the vision came flooding back. "Oh, Adon, let it not be," she exclaimed, distress in her voice.

"What?" Perin, Biren's twin, now knelt opposite, consternation in his pale brown eyes. "What is it that should not be?"

"Slaughter, Perin," she replied, "bloody slaughter. War sweeping o'er all." Arin pushed Biren's staying hand aside and sat up. She glanced at the fire. "I Saw."

Elves looked at one another, alarm upon their faces, for they all knew the truth of Arin's visions.

Rissa reached out to take Vanidar's hand in hers. "Mayhap it is a sight from the past," she said, hopefully.

"Aye," said Silverleaf. "Mayhap a war from the elder times, a war long gone."

Arin shook her head. "It cannot be a past happening, Rissa, Vanidar, at least I think it cannot, for it seems too great to be obscure, and I did not recognize it."

Melor handed Arin a cup of water, a crushed mint leaf swirling within. She nodded her thanks to the russet-haired Dylvana and drank it down, then reached up and took Ruar's offered hand and stood. Melor refilled the cup.

"Exactly what didst thou see, Dara?" asked Ruar.

Arin drew a deep breath. "Steeds thundering 'cross the land, reaving swords slashing down, hacking off legs and arms and heads and gutting the innocent, spilling their intestines out on the ground. Day sky dark as night with the smoke of burning cities. Forests hewn. Fields salted. Rivers running red with blood. Gorcrows and vultures by the thousands feeding upon the slain multitudes, slashing beaks plucking out eyes, rending flesh, gulping down gobbets of rotting meat. Great dark winged shapes wheeling in the sky, flame roaring from their throats—"

Rissa gasped. "Dragons?"

Arin nodded. "Aye, Rissa. Dragons."

Biren held out a negating hand. "Dragons in a war on Mithgar? This has never been."

"Mayhap a local war?" conjectured Perin.

Arin shook her head. "Nay, Perin, 'tis more than that, for I have not told all."

"There's more?"

"Aye: I beheld a map of Mithgar, a great stain of blood spreading wide, covering the whole of the land."

Vanidar's jaw clenched and his hand went to his long-knife. "Then it is a great doom thou hast foreseen, mayhap the doom of the world."

Ruar sighed and looked at Silverleaf. "Then thou thinkest it is yet to come?"

Vanidar nodded. "Aye, Ruar. I agree with Dara Arin. A war sweeping across the face of Mithgar, a war with Dragons involved, a doom entangling the whole of the world . . . it has never been."

"Who would be so mad as to do such?" asked Perin.

All eyes turned to Arin. She turned up her palms in distressed uncertainty, then said, "There is more."

Ruar's eyes widened. "More to thy vision?"

"Aye, I have not told all."

"Then say on."

Arin glanced at the fire. "Riding in the train of war comes plague, pestilence, and famine, for long after the crush of cruel iron has swept past, tens of thousands will continue to die—nought but skin and bones with great pustulant black buboes bursting forth and spewing out yellow poison. And scuttling among the stricken to feed upon the dead come rats and beetles and many-legged crawlers and other creeping vermin."

Arin paused to take another drink, and none said aught but waited in silence instead. Melor started to replenish the water, but she shook her head. "There is one last thing central to the vision: a stone . . . a green stone—"

"A rock?" asked Perin.

"A gem?" added Rissa.

"Hush," said Silverleaf. "Let her speak and she will tell us."

"It was pale green, a lucent jade," said Arin. "Smooth and egglike it was, yet how big I cannot say, for there was nought to judge it against. But I do know that it is key to the vision, for all the other images whirled 'round and 'round the stone, as if it were the eye of a maelstrom, the anchor of the doom."

Silence fell among them, broken at last by Perin. "How knowest thou that this thing is a stone? Could it not be a plain egg?"

Arin shook her head. "Plain it is not, Alor Perin, nor is it an egg. How I know I cannot say, yet it *is* a green stone."

They looked at one another, mute in their consternation. Then Melor asked, "Is there aught else to thy Seeing?"

Arin frowned in concentration, and she stared at the ground as if trying to capture an elusive thought. Finally she said, "I am not certain. Mayhap there was more, but my mind fled from the <see>ing and the blackness took me."

Again silence fell. At last Rissa glanced up at Silverleaf. "What shall we do with this Seeing, *chieran*?" He did not answer but stood pondering, unaware that he had been addressed. Rissa's gaze then swept across the others, stopping at last with Arin. "Has any a suggestion?"

Now all eyes looked to Arin. She sighed. "We need consult with others: the Dylvana Coron and his Court, the Lian Coron, too. Mayhap someone will know what to do."

Silverleaf slowly nodded, then said, "There is another we can consult: Dara Rael, for like thee, Dara Arin, she, too, can <see>."

The next day south they rode, heading for the central glades of Darda Erynian, where the Coron of the Dylvana dwelled. They passed the cottage of a Baeron family—a man and wife, with two daughters and a son—living in the northern reaches of the Great Greenhall. Unlike other humans—nearly all of whom are barred from these woods—the Baeron clans dwell within the bounds of Darda Erynian—as well as the Greatwood to the south— for it is said that in the past they had greatly aided the Hidden Ones and so were welcomed herein. The band of Elves paused long enough for a cool drink of water and they gave the bulk of the stag meat over to the Baeron household as well as the hide, though Vanidar kept the antlers from which he would fashion handles for knives and perhaps other utensils as well. The family received the meat and the pelt graciously, though Baeron are adept at fetching their own game. As the man hung the venison in the smokehouse, and the son and daughters stretched out the hide on a tanning rack, the wife carried two meat pies to the Elves, which they accepted gladly.

"Is there no more?"

A look of concentration fell upon Arin's face and for long moments she did not answer, but then she sighed and shook her head. "Some vague images, my Coron, but try as I might, I cannot recall them. It would seem the vision ended when I . . . fainted."

Slowly Remar, Coron of all Dylvana, looked from one to the other of those who had accompanied Arin to the court at Bircehyll, and as his gaze fell upon each, one by one they shook their heads, for they had nought to add to that which Arin had said. Last, Remar's scrutiny fell upon Vanidar, the only Lian among them. "What sayest thou, Guardian?"

As the gentle wind sighed among the silver birch, Vanidar considered his answer. Finally he said, "This portent cannot be ignored. If there is a way to prevent this calamity, then we must take steps to see that such a fate does not befall the world."

Remar looked at Arin. "Thinkest thou that these events can be set aside?"

Arin turned her palms up. "I know not, Coron. Yet Vanidar is right: if there is a way . . ."

She did not finish her words, but all knew what she meant.

Silence fell for a moment, until Rissa cleared her throat. The Coron turned to her. "Hast thou aught to add?"

"Only a question, my Coron."

"Question?"

"Aye. I was pondering whether or not a fate foreseen can be changed at all . . . or is it fixed, immutable, no matter what we may do?" She took Arin's hand in hers. "Dara, hast thou e'er tried to change the course of one of thy Seeings?"

Arin shook her head. "Never. Many were in the past and beyond changing. And as to those in the present or future, for the most they concern events I would not try to alter or turn aside. But this Seeing, this Seeing . . ."

Rissa squeezed Arin's hand to comfort her.

Silverleaf turned to Remar and said, "I suggest we seek the advice of Dara Rael in the Eldwood. Mayhap she will know whether events foreseen can be averted. If so, then there may be prospect of shunting this dire fate away from the world."

Remar ran his fingers through his auburn hair and quiet fell on the greensward. In deep thought he looked downslope at the vale below. At last he shook himself out of his reflection. "This then is what we shall do: Dara Arin, as Alor Vanidar has suggested, thou shalt seek the counsel of Dara Rael. She indeed might know whether destiny is immutable or is instead pliable, subject to change. Seek as well the advice of the Lian Coron, for Aldor is wise and may have much to offer." Remar turned to Vanidar. "Silverleaf, thou shalt escort Dara Arin unto Darda Galion. . . ." Remar paused and then made a wide sweeping gesture, taking in the others. "Indeed, I would have it that all ye accompany the Dara to the Eldwood on this mission, for ye were her companions when the vision came upon her, and mayhap ye have a part to play in events to come." The Coron looked from one to another, then asked, "What say ye?"

Arin tilted her head in silent assent, as did they all. But to his acceptance Biren added, "Alor Remar, should aught of this Seeing be told to others—men, Dwarves, Mages, Hidden Ones, the scattered Waerlinga? A fair warning so that they may prepare?"

"But we know not when it falls due," protested Perin. "Today, tomorrow, or seasons hence—Arin's vision did not say."

Biren turned to his twin. "For all we know, somewhere upon Mithgar the devastation even now thunders forth. Fair warning is the least we should do."

Perin held up a cautionary hand. "Brother of mine, we know not that aught has started or is even poised. Perhaps we will but cause alarm when none is yet warranted."

Biren clenched a fist. "But perhaps it is the very act of waiting that will cause the doom to fall."

"And mayhap it is the very act of mustering for war which will cause it to fall instead," retorted Perin.

"Akka!" spat Melor. "Doomed if we do; doomed if we don't."

Remar shook his head. "Ai, that, I deem, is a trouble with Seeing this future, for I know not whether I would cause it to unfold by my response to the knowledge or allow it to occur by doing nought." He turned to Biren. "But this I will do, Alor Biren, Alor Perin: if Dara Arin and Dara Rael deem it wise, I will send emissaries unto all the Lords of the Free Folk to give fair warning. Until then I'll say nought."

Both canted their heads in assent at Remar's declaration, but Biren added, "And I will pray to Adon that should a warning be called for, we will have enough time to do so ere the doom arrives."

The next day they set forth, riding westerly through the forest, angling to quickly reach the open wold alongside

the Great River Argon. And as they rode through Darda
Erynian, shadows flitted among the boles of the trees, as
if an unseen convoy paced alongside their way. This did
not disturb the Elven band, for they were used to the
Hidden Ones escorting them through the sun-dappled
woods—Fox Riders and Loogas and Sprygt and others,
curious, warding, or driven by motives unknown.

Two days later in the afternoon they emerged from the
marge of the Great Greenhall to come to the wold, the
unforested rolling plain stretching from Darda Erynian to
the River Argon lying some ten miles to the west.
Southerly they turned, angling slightly sunward, paral-
leling the course of the distant river.

All the next day, as in the days before, they rode and
walked and paused to eat and to relieve themselves, or to
rest the horses or feed them grain or stop at a stream
crossing to let the steeds drink. But always they
remounted and took up the trek again until the day came
to an end, when they would set camp and care for the animals and finally take their own rest.

Just after dawn of the third day upon the open wold
they came into sight of the trees bordering the wide
Argon. Here in this place a morning fog reached out from
the placid waters and onto the open moor, and the Elves
were content to stay on the high ground above the layers
of mist, pacing alongside it instead. But as the sun rose
into the sky and the fog slowly burned away, down the
slopes the riders angled, eager to see the mighty flow.
Finally the tendrils of mist withdrew down among the
trees, and of a sudden seemed to vanish entirely as the
clear morning sun glared brightly into their refuge. And
now the glint of the river sparkled in the light of day, the
broad waters flowing gently toward the far-off sea.

Along this course rode the Elven band of seven,
heading ever southerly, making their way toward distant
Olorin Isle, where they planned on crossing the mighty
Argon by way of the ferry there. The isle itself sat in the
river some thirty leagues hence, near the point where
Darda Erynian on the east of the river ended and Darda
Galion on the west began. And given their pace and the

terrain between, it would take them some three or four days to traverse the ninety-one miles.

All during the morning trek the land gently rose, until the band rode along a portage-way atop steep eastern bluffs well above the level of the river. Down at the base of the palisades the water itself swept downstream at an ever increasing pace, for as the land had risen the watercourse had narrowed and the riverbed had gradually angled down. The ravine below was known as the Race, the current swift and strong. Here northbound river travelers must abandon the water and portage overland along the eastside way, but pilots of southbound traffic—if they are skillful enough and if they dare—need only stay in the rushing center of the river and away from the jagged rocks.

As the midday sun reached toward the zenith, the Elven band came to where the high-walled canyon pinched inward to form a long, tight gorge, and from the depths of the cleft roared the thunder of water as the constricted Argon hurled through the narrowest part of an already narrow channel. Here was the deadliest stretch of the perilous strait, for here it was that the water plunged apace between the close-set ramparts, cresting and rolling and breaking over hidden barriers, smashing around massive rocks to leap and fall crashing back only to drive into the next great stone and the next and next, and the least mistake in the hurtling current could cause a pilot to lose boat and cargo to the rocks and water, as well as lose life and limb.

Above the reach of this thundering hazard rode the seven, while down in the roaring gorge the waters impotently raged. They came to the narrowest pinch atop the walls of the gorge, the western rampart but a stone's throw away, and here, of a sudden, the constriction came to an end as the cliffs to either side began to diminish in height and to recede from one another, and the water below slid down a long ramp into a deep trough and shortly thereafter the river widened.

Onward rode the Elven band, down the sloping land, and soon the thunder in the Race behind became a rumble and then a distant grumble . . . and when they set camp that night not even a whispering echo remained.

All the next day they rode on the wold alongside the wooded river vale, now angling a bit easterly as the south-bearing river swung over that way. Once again they made camp as twilight drew upon the land.

It was near mid of day the day after when they sighted the northern end of Olorin Isle, where they could see smoke rising from the dwellings of the Rivermen. Down from the wold rode the Elves and through a narrow marge of woods bordering the Argon to come to the river itself, and following an overgrown trail, a quarter mile downstream they reached the ferry dock. From the pier a well-beaten path bore southward alongside the stream. They all dismounted and stretched their legs and then Vanidar haled on the pull-rope to ring the summoning bell.

After a while they could see the ferry, with four men rowing, leave the island pier; a mule stood in their midst. As they crossed the quarter-mile stretch, the river current carried the float southerly; it would land downstream below the Elves at the dock.

"Should we ride down to meet it?" asked Melor.

Silverleaf shook his head and pointed at the path along the bank. "The mule will haul it here, else on the journey back we could miss the island altogether."

Arin raised an eyebrow. "Why should we go to the isle? It's the far side we would reach and not some point midriver."

Rissa laughed aloud, for she had been this way before, and Vanidar said, "Ah, 'tis the scheming of the Rivermen which makes it so: one ferry to carry us to the isle for a fee; another ferry to take us on to the far shore . . . for a second fee, of course." Now Vanidar joined Rissa in her laughter.

"Huah! Waterway robbery," declared Ruar, yet he was smiling as he said so.

Melor growled, "Outrageous," but Perin and Biren looked at one another and shrugged.

Some time later, harnessed to the ferry, the mule came plodding along the pathway, one man leading the animal while the three other men fended with poles to keep the float from grounding against the shore.

"Y'could help we'ns row," said the Riverman, spitting into the Argon, then jerking his stubble-clad chin toward spare oars as he and his comrades rowed.

"Oh no, my good man," responded Ruar. "For the exorbitant fee paid ye we shall ride in luxury."

"Wi' this load we c'd miss th' isle alt'gether, y'know," replied the Riverman. "Go over Bellon hisself 'n' inter th' Cauldron herself."

"Oh, please do," said Ruar gaily, for he knew full well that mighty Bellon Falls was a full hundred miles downstream, where the Argon plunged over the rim of the Great Escarpment to plummet a thousand feet to the thundering churn below. "I have always wanted to swim in the roar of the Cauldron at the foot of He Who Shouts."

The Riverman growled but said no more and hauled mightily on the oar, for he knew that if they did indeed miss the island they would collect no double fee.

The barge landed on the long shores of Olorin Isle some three miles downstream, where the Elves offloaded and mounted up and rode along the tow path toward the northern point of the isle where the second ferry was docked.

As they cantered along the shoreline, they saw boats put out from the island shore and row into the stream, where the boatmen began fetching up flotsam bobbing in the river.

Vanidar slowed his steed to a walk and stood in his stirrups and shaded his eyes. The others slowed also. "Umh," grunted Silverleaf. "Looks as if a vessel has come to disaster upstream."

"The Race?" asked Arin.

"Most likely," he answered, then sighed. "This is another way the Rivermen make their living: from the misfortune of others." He spurred into a canter again, the rest following his lead.

Shortly they reached the north end of the island and rode in among the sparse dwellings, ramshackle cabins for the most part, though here and there stood an adequate

cottage. No adults were about, yet a few small children—
dirty and ill-clothed—stood on the docks and gazed out at
the boatmen snagging the floating wares. The children
turned and watched as the Elves rode past, and then
resumed their river vigil once the strangers had gone on.

When the band reached the west ferry and dismounted,
only a mule was there to greet them.

"Where is the crew?" asked Melor, looking about but
seeing no one.

Arin gestured at the river. "Salvaging wreckage, I
would imagine." She looked at Vanidar, who nodded in
confirmation.

"Then we wait?" asked Perin.

"That or steal the ferry," answered Biren.

It was nearly twilight when the Rivermen returned from
their "gleaning o' th' waters," as they called it. A ferry
crew was assembled for the trip across, and full night had
fallen by the time they reached the opposite shore.

As the Elven band led their horses from the grounded
barge, a voice rang out from the darkness: *"Kest!"*

"Vio Vanidar!" called Silverleaf in response. *"Vi
didron enistori! Darai Rissa e Arin, e Alori Ruar, Melor,
Perin, e Biren."*

Stepping out from the shadows and into the light cast
by the ferryboat lamps there came a tall Lian. *"Vio Tarol.
Vhal sa Darda Galion."*

Silverleaf turned to the others and smiled. They had
come at last unto Darda Galion. In two days, mayhap
three, they would come to Wood's-heart, where Rael
dwelt. And then perhaps she would tell them how to set
aside the terrible destiny Arin had seen in the fire.

CHAPTER 9

Alos smacked his lips and peered at his mug and then at the ale flagon, both empty. "You tell a powerful tale, Lady Arin. Works me up a great thirst, you know. And there's none left in the pitcher, what with Egil here drinking, too."

Egil smiled and glanced at his mug, his first, and still half full.

Aiko stared impassively at the old man.

Alos peered into the empty pitcher once again and then looked at Arin. "Is the story done? Surely not. And don't you think that Egil here needs some more ale to last him through the rest of the tale? I know I've worked up a great thirst, or did I say that already?"

Arin sighed. "Nay, Alos, my tale is not yet complete; there is more to tell. Much more."

"W'll, if that's the case, then I say we'll need another flagon or two, eh?"

Aiko stalked to the window and stood peering out at the growing day, her fists clenched behind her back.

Arin stepped to Egil's side and felt his brow and took the measure of his pulse. "Art thou able to listen to more? I would not overtire thee."

Egil flashed a smile at her. "I am well enough." Then his face grew somber. "I would hear further of this doom you have foreseen and why it brought you to this place."

Alos took up the pitcher. "But first we get some fresh ale, Lady Arin. Right?"

The Dylvana shook her head. "Nay, Alos. First I shall tell more of the tale and then shall I let thee see to the replenishment of the flagon."

The old man's face fell, and he peered wanly into the empty pitcher.

Egil smiled and held out his half-full mug. "Here, Alos, perhaps this will hold you a moment more."

With alacrity, Alos stepped to Egil's bedside and took the offering, grinning his brown-stained smile. He bore the precious cargo to the table and eased down in his chair.

Aiko remained standing and staring out the window as Arin returned to her seat by the fire and took up the thread of her tale once again:

"We had just come unto the marches of Darda Galion . . ."

CHAPTER 10

Bordered on the north by low-running foothills and an open windswept wold, on the south by the Great Escarpment falling a thousand feet sheer, on the west by the jagged fangs of the towering Grimwall Mountains, and on the east by the ever-flowing mighty River Argon, there lies a twilight land, an Elven land, a land known as Darda Galion, as the Eldwood, as Larkenwald, as the Land of the Silverlarks. It is a vast forest of gigantic trees, Eld Trees, trees not native to Mithgar but borne one by one as seedlings from the Hôhgarda to the Mittegarda, from the High Plane to the Middle, and planted in this rich land of many rivers. A weald from Adonar borne as seedlings yet now they are giants; the scale of the work undertaken by the Elves to bring an entire forest of these trees to Mithgar is truly staggering.

And the trees now tower hundreds of feet into the air; and the girth of each bole is many paces around. The ages needed for them to reach this height? . . . only the Elven foresters know.

Yet the enormous reach of time required is of no moment to the Elves. After all they are an immortal Folk whose lives are forever just beginning, no matter the span of their age. And so what matter that it had taken a thousand years or ten thousand for the forest to be born and soar upward hundreds of feet toward the sky? . . . What matter? Why, none at all to the Elves; the only thing that matters is that the presence of the Eld Trees reminds them of home.

The wood of these forest giants is precious—prized above all others—but none of these trees has ever been felled by any of the Free Folk. Yet at times a harvest of sorts is made in the soaring timberland, for occasionally lightning or a great wind sweeping up from the wide plains of Valon below the escarpment in the south will cause branches to fall; and these are collected by the Lian storm-gleaners and the wood cherished, each priceless limb studied long ere the carver's tools touch the grain. And gentle Elven hands make treasures dear of this precious debris.

It is said that time stands still in the lofty silence of this twilight land, yet that cannot be, else the trees would still be nought but seedlings.

And to the edge of this vast forest came Arin and six others, their mission urgent.

CHAPTER 11

As the ferrymen hitched the mule to the barge, the Elven warden—Tarol—continued speaking in Sylva: "Tonight ye shall stay in our campsite, and tell us whatever news ye have." He glanced at the men now ready to hale the float upriver along the tow path. Turning to the Elven band he lowered his voice and said, "But first we shall follow these Rivermen and make certain they gather no wood but return instead straightly to Olorin Isle."

Silverleaf raised an eyebrow. He canted his head toward the men. "Is there some cause for distrust?"

"Rumors," answered Tarol. "We shall speak of them once the boat is away."

The Riverman on the shore called to the men on the barge, and upon receiving their grunted replies, he began leading the mule upstream and towing the ferry by a long rope behind. On the boat turn by turn each of the three men stepped to the bow and set his pole against the bank and pressed away from the shore, all the while keeping his place by slowly walking toward the stern, only to do it all over again when he reached the end of the deck; in this way the three men kept the boat from grounding. Pacing along the tow path behind came the Elves, Tarol leading, seven following, horses in hand. Stars wheeled up into the spangled sky and traveled nearly a third of the way across the vault ere the ferry arrived at the west-shore dock somewhat north of the northern extent of the midriver isle. The Rivermen took a short rest. Then they unharnessed the mule and walked it aboard and coiled the rope and stowed the poles and unshipped the oars. One of the men hawked and spat in the Argon and they shoved off for Olorin, torchlight along the far dock glimmering in the distance.

* * *

The Elven band sat at the campfire in the march-ward camp down among the enormous Eld Trees and took a late meal along with members of the Lian border patrol. The seven had arrived at the change of shift, and Lian drifted in and out, some departing for their posts, while others, now relieved of duty, came to the fire and a warm meal. Some spoke briefly with Silverleaf and the Dylvana Elves, looking for news from Darda Erynian, trading news of Darda Galion. Of their mission, the seven held tongue, saying instead that they would speak of it to Coron Aldor first.

During a lull in conversation, Melor gestured at the camp and turned to Tarol and asked, "Why is it ye need a border patrol?"

Tarol smiled. "Two reasons, my friend: first, we protect the Eld Trees. They are precious and we would not have any come unbidden to steal the wood away—such as at times the Rivermen try to do.

"Second, unlike Darda Erynian, this mighty forest harbors no Hidden Ones—not that they would be unwelcome; nay, they would be greeted with open arms."

"Oh," exclaimed Melor. "Do they shun Darda Galion? If so, why?"

Tarol sighed and shook his head. "They do not, as you say, *shun* these woods. Instead, none dwell herein because this forest was not in existence when the Fey came unto Mithgar; they put down their roots elsewhere."

Silverleaf nodded in agreement. "Aye. 'Tis true. They were well settled in Darda Erynian even as we began riding the dawn to bring the seedlings from the High Plane to this land of many rivers. As Coron of the forest aborning, I sent emissaries unto the Hidden Ones to welcome them to abide herein. They declined. —Not out of malice or dislike, but simply because they were favorably set in their own warded wood."

Tarol turned to Silverleaf. "Thou wert Coron of Darda Galion?"

"Aye, once, long apast, when the forest was but yea high." Vanidar held his hand a foot or so above the ground. "But then my interest was drawn elsewhere and Elmaron took on the task."

Tarol looked 'round at the immense trees, then canted his head to Vanidar. "Well done, Silverleaf. Well done."

Vanidar smiled but said nought.

Melor peered deeply into the shadows of the Eldwood, then said, "Hm. No Hidden Ones. It must be . . . lonely."

Tarol shrugged. "Mayhap. I cannot say, for I have dwelled only in Darda Galion since riding the dawn."

Melor reached out and clapped Tarol on the shoulder. "Wert thou to come among the Fey, thou wouldst discover they are boon."

In the aftermath of their meal, while taking tea and bits of mian, Vanidar asked, "Tarol, what are these rumors concerning the Rivermen?"

Tarol replenished his cup and Melor's as well. As he set the pot back on the grille—"Ill words, my friend, ill words. It seems that too many merchant boats may be finding the rocks in the Race."

Biren stopped chewing on a last bit of bread. "What has this to do with the Rivermen?"

Perin turned to his twin. "Didst thou not see? The Rivermen salvage wrack downstream from the Race."

Biren shrugged. "Aye. Yet the Race is perilous, and wrecks occur."

They looked at Tarol. He sipped from his cup, then said, "Of recent, too many good pilots have been lost, or so the merchants say—pilots who have run the Race many times."

Ruar helped himself to a small portion of mian. "And thou thinkest foul work is afoot and the Rivermen are to blame?"

"We know not," answered Tarol.

Arin paused in thought, then said, "It would take someone either in the Race or somewhere upriver to set the boats to ruin in those hazardous waters."

Tarol nodded. "Exactly so, Dara. Forget not that thirty-five leagues north of the Race the Rivermen occupy their fort on Great Isle—Vrana, or some such, I think they name it, and River Guardians they style themselves . . . and collect tolls as protection fees."

"That nest of Rivermen was in my mind," replied Arin. "Say on."

Tarol shrugged. "One possibility is that the River Guardians found that more profit is to be made in so-called river salvage, and with their kindred on Olorin Isle they make certain that salvage enough occurs."

"Hai!" exclaimed Perin, leaping to his feet and flashing his blade on high. "But I would like to catch them at it."

Biren clenched his fist and sharply nodded at his twin in agreement.

As Perin sat back down, Rissa asked, "Is aught being done to confirm or lay to rest these rumors?"

Tarol nodded. "The woodsmen of the vales—the Baeron—now set watch on both the Race and the fortress isle, while we keep an eye on Olorin."

"Huah, Baeron on watch upriver?" exclaimed Ruar, cocking a skeptical eyebrow. "We saw them not."

Vanidar smiled. "That is because they did not wish to be seen, my friend."

Soon the change of shift was complete; the returning Lian took their meals and conversed a bit, and then settled down to sleep. At last the seven took to their bedrolls as well, guarded this night by others.

A sweet caroling heralded dawn as the *Vani-lêrihha* sang high in the boughs overhead, the Silverlarks having flown *in-between* with the coming of the sun.

Arin yawned and stretched and rubbed her eyes and peered up among the shadowy leaves of the enormous trees, trying to espy one of the warblers. *Where art thou, little Silverlark? Thou hast ridden the dawn from the High Plane to here and I would see thee ere thou return to Adonar with the setting of the sun.* A silvery grey flash caught her eye as one of the larks darted away. Arin sighed. *Aye, little bird, thou hast the right of it, flying off on a venture of thine own. 'Tis time we, too, set forth.* She sat up and looked 'round at the others, most of whom were awake as well.

After the breaking of fast, the seven set forth amid fare-thee-wells from the march wardens, Tarol wishing them fortune on their mission. And into the towering forest they rode at a canter.

Through the soft shadows of the great trees wended their trail, the hoofbeats of the horses muffled by moss underfoot, and what little sound they made was lost in the dimlit galleries below the umbrous interlace high overhead.

As they passed among the massive boles, Arin studied the Eld Trees: mighty were these great-girthed sylvan giants, soaring into the sky. And even though the morning sun shone brightly, down below in the forest the world took on the cast of twilight . . . for these were Eld Trees from the High Plane, from Adonar, and Elves lived among them, and so the leaves turned dusky green and *gathered* the gloaming.

At one point when the Elves had dismounted to walk the horses through the quiet of the woods, Arin turned to Rissa and asked, "How tall wouldst thou say these stand?"

"The trees?"

"Aye."

Rissa looked into the branches above, gauging. "Vanidar says out here near the marge they are not as tall as those deep in the central woods, for these were planted last." Rissa raised her voice and called out to Silverleaf: "*Chier*, what is the measure of these trees . . . their height?"

Without turning, Vanidar called back, "I would judge that if we could step up their sides, one hundred or so Lian strides would pace the full length of each; yet the first ones we planted nigh Wood's-heart stand at least a hundred and eighty paces tall."

Arin glanced ahead at Silverleaf walking and judged what his stride might be—a bit less than a yard when stepping out a measure. "Then it is as I thought: these are not yet as great as the trees in Adonar."

With his free hand, Vanidar made a negating gesture.
"Nay, they yet have tens of millennia to grow ere
reaching their full height."

Arin gazed into the twilit galleries. "The trees, Vanidar,
they gather twilight in the presence of Elvenkind. Dost
thou know how they do such?"

Silverleaf turned and smiled and shook his head. "Nay,
Ring. I can only say that somehow the trees sense
Elvenkind. Somehow we are connected."

Arin glanced at Rissa, but she tilted her head and
shrugged. "If someone knows, 'tis not I."

Arin nodded and fell into silence as onward they strode.
At last they mounted again and continued riding southwesterly, Vanidar aiming for a ford across the River
Rothro some thirty miles hence. The Eldwood was a land
replete with rivers—the Rothro, the Quadrill, the Cel-
lener, and the Nith, and all of their tributaries—their
sparkling waters flowing down from the wold and from
the nearby Grimwall Mountains to course easterly
through the forest and issue at last into the broad rush of
the mighty Argon. In all, the Elven band would have to
cross two of the great forest's primary rivers—the Rothro
and the Quadrill—though they would splash through
many of the lesser streams.

They had not yet reached the ford when the sun sank
into the horizon and dusk stole over the twilight woods.
Now the Silverlarks took up their evensong, and surrounded by this glorious caroling, Arin's heart swelled
and joyous tears ran down her face. Of a sudden there was
a flurry of wings and the songs rose in crescendo as the
Vani-lêrihha took elegant flight among the trees . . . and
disappeared, songs vanishing in midnote, as the larks
crossed the *in-between* to return to Adonar.

Arin's heart fell in the sudden absence, and she sighed
and wiped her cheeks with the heels of her hands, and saw
through the lattice above that the early stars had begun to
shine. Under their scintillant light the seven made camp,
for none felt like traveling farther.

* * *

That night Arin, gasping, bolted upright, wrenched from her sleep. She was covered with a sheen of perspiration.

Rissa, too, moaned in her slumber, but did not awaken.

Perin on watch asked, "What is it, Dara?"

"I thought I heard screams," replied Arin.

They held their breath and listened.

Nothing.

Stillness.

Nothing but the soft sound of a gentle breeze high in the branches of the Eld Trees.

At last Perin said, "Mayhap 'twas nought but an ill dream."

Arin sighed as if in doubt, but lay back down and closed her eyes. Yet sleep was long in coming and she dreamed of flashing blades.

Once again Arin was awakened at dawn by the singing of Silverlarks. *Ah, my little* Vani-lêrihha, *no wonder mortals call this forest the Larkenwald—how could any hear your songs and not name it so?* But even in her joy of the larksong, still the dregs of last night's dreaming filled her with unease.

By midmorn they reached the shallow crossing on the Rothro and splashed into the crystal waters, pausing in midriver to let the horses drink.

"Now we go south," said Vanidar as he watched his steed take water, "to ford the Quadrill."

"As planned," said Arin.

"How far is Wood's-heart?" asked Ruar.

"Eight leagues or nine," responded Silverleaf, tugging on his reins. "We will be there early next morn, if not this very eve."

Horses watered, they surged on across and up the far bank and into the twilight beyond.

Just after the mid of day they reached the north shore of the swift-running Quadrill. Westerly turned Vanidar, faring upstream along the bank, the others following. The sun had crossed two full handspans of sky ere the riders came to the eastern end of a midriver isle where the water danced broad and shallow. Here they forded to the opposite shore.

Wood's-heart lay some twenty miles due south.

On they rode among the massive trunks towering upward, the dusky leaves interlaced overhead, the land below fallen into a soft gloaming though the sun stood on high.

True twilight came and went, and along with it the carols of the Silverlarks came and went as well, as the *Vani-lêrihha* sang and flew and vanished.

Full night had fallen when the seven passed through a picket of Lian warders. They had come at last to the Elvenholt of Wood's-heart to find a peaceful thorp. They rode into a village of softly lighted dwellings nestled amid the giant Eld Trees. South they fared, past thatch-roofed cottages here and there, glowing with lanternlight, yellow gleaming out through unshuttered windows.

Along the mossy ways they rode until they reached a large, low building in the midst of the others. It was the Coron-hall, where a warder asked their names while attendants took charge of their steeds.

"Vio Vanidar," replied Silverleaf. *"Vio ivon Darda Erynian,* as do my comrades. We would speak with the Coron."

"The Coron and Consort are at banquet with much of the Court, Alor Vanidar, Coron apast," replied the warder, stepping aside. "They celebrate the trothing 'tween Dara Rael and Alor Talarin. Thou and thy comrades are surely welcome."

The warder summoned an Elven page, who escorted them across a foyer and into the lambent Coron-hall, where vivid colors and the smells of food and the ebb and flow of conversation assaulted their senses. Bright Elves turned as Silverleaf and the Dylvana entered. Talk fell to whispers and laughter stilled, for with but a few exceptions the Dylvana were reclusive and seldom visited Darda Galion, and for six Dylvana to simultaneously appear at the Coron-hall, well, something must be afoot. Led by Silverleaf, the Dylvana threaded their way among the Lian seated at the long, food-laden boards. Nodding now and again to acquaintances, Vanidar moved toward the dais, where sat Coron and Consort at the head table, and as was the custom at Lian betrothal banquets, they were flanked left and right by the pledged pair and their two attendants-of-honor.

Aldor smiled when he saw Vanidar, and he stood in greeting. "Silverleaf, welcome again to the land of the Silverlarks and unto this hall." Aldor's hair shone like burnished bronze, and he was dressed all in dark brown, with tan insets in sleeve and breast and legging. His eyes were hazel.

Vanidar bowed in acknowledgment. "Coron Aldor, I bring thee Dylvana from Darda Erynian: Darai Rissa and Arin, and Alori Ruar, Melor, Perin, and Biren." As each was introduced they acknowledged the Coron with a brief bow of the head, for that is the Dylvana way.

Before Aldor could respond, a golden-haired Dara leaned forward, her eyes a deep blue. Dressed in green she was, with green ribbons twining through her long tresses. "Dara Arin? The flame seer?" At Arin's nod, the Lian said, "Long have I wanted to meet thee. I am Rael."

"And I thee, crystal seer," responded Arin.

Aldor laughed. "It seems conversation precedes introduction, yet ere it runs away, let me name names: *Darai Elora e Rael e Irren, Alori Talarin e Rindor.*" As the Consort and betrothal party acknowledged Vanidar and the Dylvana, Aldor asked Silverleaf in a low voice, "Hast thou come on a mission?"

Vanidar nodded.

"Urgent?" asked Aldor.

Before Vanidar could respond, Arin said, "I have come to seek Dara Rael's counsel, yet I deem it can wait till the morrow."

Aldor cocked an eyebrow. Vanidar looked at Arin, then said, "Aye. Tonight we shall eat and drink with ye all and join in the celebration of troth."

Aldor looked from Silverleaf to Arin. "So be it," he declared, then called out, "Make room for our Dylvana guests."

As they made their way toward the tables, again conversation and laughter filled the Coron-hall, and Arin gazed about at the joyous assembly and wondered if this merriment was perhaps the last the hall would ever see.

CHAPTER 12

Elora leaned forward, her black hair unbound and brushing against her face. "And thou didst <see> no more?"

Arin shook her head. "I seem to recall there were other images, yet what they were I cannot say."

They sat at breakfast in the common room of the guest lodge did Consort Elora and Coron Aldor and crystal seer Rael. Arin and the rest of the Dylvana band were ranged 'round the long table. There, too, were Silverleaf and Talarin.

Aldor sipped his breakfast tea. " 'Tis a wicked vision thou hast seen." He turned to Rael. "Hast thou beheld its like?"

Rael shook her golden locks. "Nay, Coron."

Sitting beside Rael was Talarin, the tall Elf now dressed in grey. Like Rael, he, too, had golden hair, but his eyes were green. He placed a hand on Rael's shoulder. Briefly she smiled at him and then turned back to Aldor. "That I have seen none of this is of no moment, my Coron, and does not make it less true, for Visions are heedless as to whom they show their sights. 'Tis likely no two seers in a thousand will view the same image, or so said Elgon the Mage."

"Not even events of this import?"

Rael turned up her hands. "Not even."

Arin cleared her throat. "Dara Rael, can Seen events be set aside, avoided?"

Rael's brow furrowed in thought. Melor poured himself another cup of tea. "I have never tried," answered Rael at last. "To do so would be to tamper with Fate . . . and who knows what would happen then? Mayhap the Wizards . . . but not I."

Arin sighed. "Like thee, Dara, I too have never tried. Yet this vision of mine, it seems as if *something* must be done to negate the oncoming doom."

Arin paused a moment and then asked, "What about the green stone, then? Has any here heard of such?"

The Lian looked at one another and all shook their heads.

"Not even rumor?"

"Perhaps it is a thing of the Drimma," conjectured Talarin. "They work gem and jade and stone, and from thy description it could be any of these."

"True," replied Arin. "Yet I have not seen its like among any artifacts of the delvers."

"It just struck me: mayhap it is a creation of Magekind," volunteered Perin.

Biren turned to his twin. "Why would they do such? To what end?"

Perin shrugged. "Who knows the ways of Wizards?"

Aldor slowly shook his head. "Whatever it is—Drimmen or not, Wizards or not, or even the gods themselves—this green stone would seem to be a true token of power."

"Nevertheless," said Elora, "Perin's suggestion is as valid as any other. Surely someone in the world knows of this particular thing."

Aldor set down his teacup. "I shall have discreet enquiries made among the Lian. Too, I shall send emissaries unto Drimmen-deeve to ask the DelfLord as to knowledge of the artifact. But as to the Wizards . . ."

"As to the Wizards," said Rael, picking up Aldor's thread, "I would suggest that Dara Arin seek out one of Magekind."

Arin turned to the crystal seer. "Thou didst speak of a Mage, Dara Rael—Elgar?"

"Elgon," replied Rael.

"He knows of seers and seeing?"

"Somewhat . . . though it was not his, um, specialty."

"Perhaps I should seek him out, then," suggested Arin.

Rael shook her head. "I know not where he dwells."

"Rwn? Black Mountain?"

Rael shrugged. "Mayhap. Yet there is one closer than

either of those two places: Dalavar in Aralan. He dwells in Darda Vrka, or so I am told."

"The Wolfwood?" Rissa raised an eyebrow. "I know it. Dalavar, too."

The others looked at her. "Aye—Dalavar Wolfmage. I met him once when I passed through in other days," she explained. "His is a shaggy forest . . . and warded."

Rael frowned. "Warded?"

"Aye. By the Draega, by the Silver Wolves."

"Draega in Mithgar?" exclaimed Ruar. "I thought they all dwelt in Adonar."

"Evidently not," said Silverleaf, smiling at Rissa and reaching out to take her hand.

"This Darda Vrka, where lies it?" asked Arin.

"East and north in Aralan," replied Rissa, "some eight hundred leagues as the hawk flies, longer by the route we would take."

Biren looked at Perin. "Eighty to a hundred days by horse at a goodly pace."

"A great deal less if using remounts," replied his twin.

Arin sighed. "And Black Mountain—where does it lie?"

"Beyond Darda Vrka," said Rissa. "Another two hundred leagues or so. In the realm of Xian."

Arin thought a moment. "Can we save time by riding the dusk and the dawn?"

The Elves looked at one another, but none had aught to volunteer. Finally Silverleaf said, "I know of no *in-between* crossings shorter than direct."

Arin groaned. "I was hoping to save time by riding into Adonar and then back unto Mithgar—crossing several times, if necessary."

Ruar cleared his throat. "Would it not be swifter to go to Rwn? We could ride down to the Avagon Sea and take passage on an Arbalinian merchant ship."

Aldor shook his head. "The Rovers of Kistan have the straits blocked, or so I am told. No ship but the *Eroean* is said to have made it through."

"Aravan's ship," said Arin, her eyes brightening. "He would give us passage."

Aldor shook his head. "The King's herald said Aravan

is no longer in port but has sailed through the blockade and beyond again. The herald also said even now the High King is assembling a fleet to break the stranglehold. Yet that could take awhile, perhaps months."

"We could ride north and sail from the Boreal . . . or west to the Ryngar," suggested Melor, "and hope to catch a trader going our way."

"Or engage one," added Ruar.

"Rwn or Darda Vrka or Black Mountain in Xian," said Arin, sighing, "no matter our choice, it will take time."

"There is this," said Rael. "If ye go to Darda Vrka to find answers with Dalavar, if he knows not how to aid ye, then Black Mountain lies just beyond."

Rissa nodded. "Aye, Darda Vrka *is* on the way to Xian."

"I would suggest, then—" began Aldor, but his words fell short as there sounded the distant belling of a bugle echoing among the Eld Trees. "An alarm?" muttered Aldor. He stood and stepped to the front window of the lodge.

Again the bugle sounded, closer this time.

Now all the Elves got to their feet.

Silverleaf girted on his long-knife. The visiting Dylvana took up swords and bows. Elora retrieved Aldor's sword from the table and carried it to him.

Aldor turned from the window and received the weapon and began girting it about his waist. As he did so he looked up at Arin. "Let me say this to thee, Dara, ere it is pushed from my mind by this clarion call: I would suggest that thou and thy companions follow the counsel of Dara Rael and hie to Darda Vrka. Seek out this Dalavar and ask his advice. And if Dalavar cannot help ye, then go on to Black Mountain beyond, for none—"

Now the ringing of the bugle became strident.

"—none here knows of the green stone, but the Wizards may. Meanwhile, I will do all in my power to uncover its import."

A horse and Elven rider came thundering into the thorp, a brace of remounts running behind on long tethers. Again the rider sounded the bugle.

Aldor stepped out the door, the others following after.

The rider and horses skidded to a halt at the Coron-hall, and the rider flung himself from the blowing, lathered steed and raced up the steps, only to be redirected toward the oncoming band by the warder at the door.

His bugle still clenched in his fist, the rider met them halfway between the hall and the lodge and gritted, "My Coron, the *Rûpt* along the Grimwall, they have felled in malice nine of the Eld Trees."

"Kha!" Aldor clenched his fist in rage as cries of dismay rose up from the others. The Coron took a deep breath and blew it out, then asked, "And the *Rûpt,* Loric, what of the *Rûpt*?"

"Dead. Slain by the march warders."

"Blæ!" spat Elora, her look grim. "Too easy. They should have suffered."

Aldor ground his teeth. "The *Rûpt:* Rucha, Loka, Ghûlka, what?"

"Rucha in the main, though two Loka were among them."

"How many?"

"A score and two."

"When?" asked Aldor.

"Yesternight," replied the rider. "Nay, wait, I rode all yesternight, so two nights back it was."

Arin's eyes flew wide. *Two nights back? My dream, the screams, the flashing blades.*

Arin looked at Perin and silently mouthed, *My dream.* He nodded, and then both looked at Rissa, remembering that she had moaned in her sleep that same night as well, but Rissa seemed unaware.

Arin now glanced at the Eld Trees nearby. *Vanidar said we are somehow connected, and connected we are: they sense our presence; I sensed their pain.*

"These *Spaunen,* who sent them?" asked Silverleaf.

"We know not," replied the rider. "We were bloodlust mad with grief and the *Rûpt* were all dead ere we thought to take prisoner."

Silverleaf slapped his leg and said to Aldor, "More than simple killings need answer this rape."

"Of that I am aware," replied Aldor, his eyes narrowing.

"We must uncover the ones behind this vile deed and bring a hard message home unto the Foul Folk."

"Retribution," growled Elora, baring her teeth. "Swift and hard. This must never happen again."

Arin's eyes widened at the Consort's bloodthirsty visage. *Is this how it begins? The war of my vision?*

Vanidar took a deep breath and said, "Aye, retribution for my trees."

"Thy trees?" asked Talarin.

Vanidar nodded. "I was Coron when this forest was first set in the ground."

Now Talarin's eyes widened, and he said, "Then the claim of this Darda upon thee is greater than most here. I would be honored to ride at thy side when we wreak vengeance upon the *Rûpt*."

Aldor made a sweeping gesture, taking in Lian and Dylvana and all of Wood's-heart. "We would all be honored to ride at thy side, Silverleaf. Wilt thou be my warleader?"

Vanidar looked from one to the other of the company, but when his gaze passed to Arin, she shook her head. "Silverleaf, as much as this felling of the nine pains me, I cannot sheer away from my first duty." She turned to the others. "Ye all go with Vanidar and the Lian to render vengeance for this terrible thing the Foul Folk have done; thy presence will let the *Rûpt* know the Dylvana, too, will not allow such deeds to go unpunished. But I . . . I must instead fare to Aralan, fare to Darda Vrka to seek the advice of the Wizard Dalavar. It was the charge of mine own Coron for me to follow the trail of the green stone and try to set aside its doom."

Vanidar clenched his fists so tightly his knuckles shone white. Then he turned to Aldor. "Arin is right. As much as I grieve at the felling of the nine, as much as I crave retribution, I cannot be thy warleader. We were charged by Coron Remar in Darda Erynian to accompany Arin on her mission, and accompany her I will."

Silverleaf looked at the others, and one by one they sighed and nodded their heads.

Aldor's gaze swept over them all. "So be it," he declared. He turned to the rider. "Loric, sound the muster. I would ride in force unto the Grimwall marches."

As Loric's bugle sounded the call to arms, Arin stepped to Silverleaf's side. "I am sorry, Alor Vanidar, for thou didst engender this woodland, and if any should seek vengeance for the slaying, it should be thee."

With all of her goods packed, Arin took one last sweeping look about her quarters in the guest lodge to make certain she had left nothing behind. Then she stepped through the open doorway and onto the porch of the long, low, thatch-roofed lodge, where her companions waited. Little was said as slowly they walked toward the stables, passing Lian dwellings, where inside they could see Elven warriors—male and female alike—girting themselves for war. Now and again a rider thundered past on an urgent mission, and Arin's heart hammered in her chest. *Is this clamor in any way tethered to my Seeing?* She sighed and continued walking, her question unanswered, for at this time there was no way of knowing.

The stables were practically empty—few horses and little tack remaining. As did the others, Arin bridled and saddled her own mount and filled her saddlebags with grain and affixed her traveling gear to the ties behind the rear cantle. At last all was ready and Arin and her escort slowly rode out and away from Wood's-heart and into the twilit forest, while behind Rael watched them go, a troubled look on her face.

Into the airy silence of lofty Eldwood they rode, the horses' hooves making little sound on the mossy way. After a while Arin looked back; nought but towering trees met her gaze. She faced front once more, following behind the others, heading for the ferry at Olorin Isle and to Caer Lindor beyond. At that fortress on the Rissanin River they would provision themselves for the long journey to the land of Aralan and shaggy Darda Vrka within. There they would seek out Dalavar to see if he knew aught of the green stone, aught of that token of power, and whether or not he knew of a way to avert its terrible doom.

CHAPTER 13

"Token of power?" Despite the amount Alos had drunk, his speech was not slurred by ale. "And just what might one of these tokens be, hey?"

Aiko snorted, but Arin said, "Something empowered to fulfill a destiny."

"Eh?" Alos shook his head. "Empowered? Destiny? You speak in riddles, and I need another drink." He held out the empty pitcher, his blind white eye fixed on Arin.

Aiko growled and shifted a sword, its blade glinting wickedly. Alos hurriedly thunked the empty pitcher back to the table and held out his hands and whined, "No offense, Lady. I meant to give no offense. It's just that posers work up a thirst . . . and tokens of power are posers all right, what with their destinies and dooms and all."

Egil shifted in his bed. "I would also like to hear more about these tokens. From what you say, my *engel*—my Lady, it seems they, too, carry wyrds . . . as do we all."

"Wyrds?" Aiko raised an eyebrow.

"Aye," answered Egil, his good blue eye glittering in the lamplight, for eve had fallen during Arin's telling and the room was now illuminated by a soft, yellow glow. "Wyrds: that which drives men in the deeds they do . . . or the thing that awaits them in the end."

"Hmph. Just men? You grunt like the priests of Hodakka. *Baka-gojona dokemono*." Aiko turned her face and stared out the window.

"Dost thou believe thou hast a wyrd, Egil?"

"Aye, Lady Arin: a spear through my heart, a sword thrust, a death at sea, or some such. What it is I cannot say, but surely a wyrd awaits me."

Aiko again fixed him with her dark gaze. "And what if you die of old age in bed?"

Egil barked a laugh. "Me? Die in bed? Not likely."

Arin cast a glance at Aiko and then turned to Egil. "Mayhap thy wyrd has already come to pass, Egil. Mayhap it did so in Jute."

Egil raised a hand to his bandages but did not reply.

Alos peered into his empty mug and sighed. "Wyrds I understand. —Oh, not that I believe in them. . . . But these tokens of power, well, they seem to be another thing altogether." He looked up at Arin. "Just what are they and how do you know?"

All eyes shifted to Arin. She turned up a hand and said, "Tokens of power—at times hard to recognize, at other times known to all. They can be for Good or Ill: Gelvin's Doom was a token of power for Evil—a feartoken. So, too, was the Black Throne of Hadron's Hall. Those for Good are sometimes known: one is the Kammerling, Adon's Hammer, destined to slay the greatest Dragon of all—though where the Kammerling is, none can say. Too, there is a sword in Adonar, Bale by name, and it would appear to fit the mold, though what its destiny may be, none can say. Others are unknown and seem to be one thing—jewels, poniards, rings, a trinket—but are truly something else altogether. Many look as if they hold no power at all, until, that is, they manifest their doom."

Alos took a deep breath and blew it out and shook his head in puzzlement. But Egil said, "What if I bore one of these tokens of power—say, a ring or some such—but when the time came I did not know how to use it, or tried to use it but failed? What then of the destiny?"

"Aye," blurted Alos, "what if Egil failed?" Alos held out an apologetic hand of denial toward the younger man abed. "Not that you are likely to fail, Egil. No offense. No offense."

They both looked at Arin.

The Dylvana returned their gazes. "What then of the destiny if thou didst fail to use a token as it was meant to be?"

They both nodded.

"A token of power seems to have ways of fulfilling its

own destiny," answered Arin. "If thou didst fail, still would the token strive to achieve its doom. By another's hand, if not by thine.

"Aye, I'll grant thee, tokens of power are mysterious things, perhaps guided by Adon from afar, or by Gyphon . . . or Elwydd or Garlon or any of the others—who can say? Yet none but perhaps the gods know for certain which things are tokens . . . until their ordained work comes to pass.

"Hear me, though, for this I do believe: the green stone is a token of power, yet one which I pray never fulfills its destiny."

Silence fell over them all, the stillness broken only by the scrape of Alos turning his empty mug around and around on the tabletop. At last Egil said, "If you are right, then it would seem that we all are driven to fulfill the destinies of these tokens of power. What then does it matter that we strive to reach our own ends? For whether or no we wish it, we are compelled by these things. —I hope I never come upon one of them."

Aiko looked at Egil. "Think on this: perhaps it is your wyrd to, as you say, come upon one of them. Perhaps you have no choice."

Egil gazed back at her. "What do you believe, Aiko? About tokens of power, that is, and whether or no they compel us to pursue their destinies?"

Aiko took a breath and said, "If I were to come upon one, then perhaps I would choose the token for it would suit my aims, and perhaps the token would choose me for the selfsame reason."

"Then you believe that you could also reject the token if it did not suit your aims?"

Aiko nodded.

"Then, Lady Warrior, you believe that the paths of the tokens and their bearers happen to be going in the same direction, aye?"

"Yes, Egil One-Eye, I do. I have free choice, all things being equal."

"All things being equal? What do you mean by that?"

"Just this: the gods may will it otherwise that I do a

thing I would rather not. Then I would have no choice at all in the matter."

Egil nodded. "Except for my wyrd, I, too, believe I have unfettered choice in all things. But as to my wryd, I have no choice whatsoever. No matter the path I freely take, in the end I will meet the blade with my name on it, or the ship or spear or come what may; as it is with all men, I cannot escape my wyrd. The power that rules even the gods makes it so, though the gods themselves may have a hand in it."

"Pfaugh!" snorted Alos. "The gods are capricious and visit nought but afflictions down on mankind." He lowered his head and put a hand over his scarred, blind white eye . . . and of a sudden began weeping. Concerned, Arin stepped to the oldster and laid a hand on his shoulder. Sobbing uncontrollably, Alos looked up at her, his face twisted in anguish. Long strings of tear-driven clear mucus dangled down from his nose. Feebly he groped for his kerchief, blubbering all the while.

Aiko glanced at the old man in disgust. Then she turned back to Egil and asked, "Only men have wyrds? What of women . . . and what of the Dylvana and Lian and Dwarves and all other of Elwydd's creations? And what of the Foul Folk made by Gyphon? Am I and all of these others completely bereft of wyrds?"

As Alos blew his nose, Egil looked at Aiko in astonishment. Then he cocked his head in inward reflection. Still Alos blew and blew. At last Egil said, "Yes, Aiko, all have wyrds. It's just that I—"

"It's just that you had never considered anyone or anything other than men. *Rikotekina otoko!*" She turned her back to him in disgust.

Alos finished blowing and held up his sodden handkerchief and peered at it blearily, then wadded it up and squished it into his pocket. Still tearing, he smiled his gap-toothed, ocherous grin at Arin and said, "Let's all have us a drink, aye?"

Arin did not tell more of her tale that night, for Egil was weakened and weary, and she insisted that he get some sleep.

Alos was all for making his usual rounds of the taverns, but decided to stay after Arin told him that there was more of the tale to tell, and that ale would be served on the morrow and she'd rather he stayed in the room. He pondered for a moment and glanced at the door, then smiled to himself and agreed.

And so all settled down for the nighttide: Egil asleep in his bed; Aiko in cross-legged meditation in front of the door, her swords lying on the tatami before her; Alos prostrate on his pallet, disgruntled, unable to get out without awakening the yellow warrior, if indeed she was truly asleep; Arin sitting by the fire, staring deeply within.

Sometime ere dawn, Egil began thrashing abed, crying out men's names, cursing, a berserker look in his open but unseeing eye. Arin stepped to his bedside and tried to soothe him, to no avail. Aiko stood at hand in case there were a need. Still shouting and cursing, he awakened at last and looked wildly about . . . then buried his face in his hands and wept. Arin sat on the edge of the bed and sang a soft Elven song, and Egil lay back down weeping. After a while he fell deeply asleep. Arin returned to her chair and Aiko to her tatami mat. The Dylvana stared into the fire, but she soon looked away, unable to focus, for her thoughts kept reverting to the man in the bed. *Ill dreams, indeed.*

The next morning at break of fast, Healer Thar came by to check on the patient, and after the Dylvana applied an unguent to the raw wounds, he and Arin laid on fresh bandages.

Thar stayed long enough to have a bite to eat, but then went onward to make his daily rounds.

Orri came right after—bluff and full of cheer—and he brought with him a leather eye patch, dyed the brightest scarlet with a small golden symbol scribed thereon. " 'Tis a gift fr' th' crew. They wanted ye t' ha'e it. Ach, ye'll make a fine figure o' a Fjordsman when we go back at th' Jutes, lad, and ye take y'r revenge. We e'en had it scribed wi' Adon's sign—th' war-hammer one, it be: th' Kammerling, or so they say 'tis. Right fitting, too, for what

better symbol to bear on a raid of vengeance than th'
thing the Dwarves call the Rage Hammer, aye?"

Orri stayed till midmorn, sharing a pitcher of ale with
Alos, much to the oldster's dismay, for Orri got the most
of it before he left.

It was nigh mid of day when Arin took up her tale once
again. . . .

CHAPTER 14

B ack through Darda Galion they rode—Arin and her companions—back through the soft shadows of this dimlit wood. Across mossy swales they fared and alongside and through the streams of the forested land—some quick running, where the water foamed white and tumbled loudly among rocks; others gliding quietly between low ferny banks, or high stone walls, and whispering a fluid song of flow.

The hush of the soaring Eldwood stole over Arin even as she rode, and she nodded in a doze and lost track of time in the timeless twilight.

And morning and eve the argent songbirds sang their melodies of dawn and dusk and caroled beauty throughout the land, filling the forest with song.

Across the swift-flowing Quadrill they fared, and then the slower Rothro, as they made their way back along the route they had ridden just days before.

At last they came to the march-ward camp, where they spent the night . . . and Silverleaf told of the felling of the nine. The warders shouted in dismay and railed at the vile deed wreaked by the *Spaunen* there along the Grimwall flank. Many would have ridden straightaway to join Aldor's force of retribution, but they could not abandon their posts, and so they seethed with impotent rage.

The next morn dawned to a steady rain and glum Tarol accompanied the seven to the dock where they summoned the ferry of Olorin Isle, barely seen in the blowing mist.

They transferred from one Riverman ferry to the other and finally reached the eastern bank of the mighty Argon.

Northeastward they rode through the southernmost tip of Darda Erynian to come that rainy eve to the banks of the River Rissanin.

The next day dawned to overcast skies, but the rain had ceased. Up the westward bank of the river they fared, and the day slowly cleared as they rode. And just as eve drew nigh they sighted in midriver the grey stone towers of Caer Lindor glowing orange in the setting sun.

They crossed the western pontoon bridge to come to that fortress isle, a legacy of the Elven Wars of Succession, a relic of the elder days, when neither man nor Fey nor Dwarf nor Mage nor aught other bestrode the world of Mithgar, and only the Elves walked the land, and they yet filled with madness. But those days were long past and the Elves now sane, yet the huge, square fortress still remained. It was an outpost in event of future want, but served these days as a way station for travelers in need. Yet located where it was, on the border between the warded Blackwood to the north and the Greatwood to the south, seldom did many come this way, and they mostly Elves or Baeron, though now and again a venturesome soul or two would come trekking past.

On this eve six Dylvana and a Lian came across the bridge seeking mules or pack horses as well as provisions for a long journey to the east. But of their mission they said nought, though they did tell the warriors of the Elven garrison of the felling of the nine.

That night, in spite of the grim news, they were cheered somewhat by two Waerlinga, whom, it seems, were on a float trip down the Rissanin and then the Argon beyond—"On our way to look at the Avagon," said Tindel, the tall one, standing some three feet three, simply towering over Brink by a full two inches.

"Going to see the sea," added Brink, his tilted sapphirine eyes atwinkle, "and perhaps ship out on an Arbalinian trader."

"He wants to go as cabin crew," said Tindel, disparagingly, jerking a thumb toward Brink.

"W'll it's not likely they'll take us on as pilots, y'ninny," responded Brink. "Nor as loaders or haulers or any other such. —Or would you be the captain?"

"We c'd be lookouts, I say," said Tindel, pointing a finger toward one of his own gemlike eyes, amber in the lanternlight. "Especially at night."

"What, and get up on one of those tall masts? Not me, bucco. If you want to climb atop a high swaying pole, well, that's your own doings. But as for me . . ."

And so it went between these two, squabbling, the best of friends.

And the Elves smiled at their antics.

The next morning, towing six mules laden with supplies, Arin and her companions prepared to set forth. As they came to the eastern pontoon bridge leading across the Rissanin and into the Greatwood, they saw the Waerlinga readying to cast off their cargo-laden float.

Arin handed over the tether of her mule to Melor and then rode down to the raft. "Beware of Bellon Falls, wee ones; ye wouldn't want to get swept over."

"Bellon Falls?" asked Brink.

"Aye. On the Argon—some twenty leagues south of where the Rissanin joins that river."

Brink scratched his head. "Twenty leagues? Sixty miles?"

"Yes, you ninny," answered Tindel. "Twenty leagues; sixty miles." Tindel then turned to Arin. "But what's this about a falls?"

"Where the Argon flows over the Great Escarpment. It plummets a thousand feet into the Cauldron below."

"A thousand feet!" exclaimed Brink. He reached into a map case and hauled out a roll of parchment and peered at it a moment, then shook his head and said, "No falls. No escarpment. No Cauldron. We're going to have to get this map corrected, Tin."

Arin's eyes flew wide in astonishment. *Imagine these two setting out on a float trip without knowing the perils of the river before them.*

"Thank you, Lady Arin," said Brink.

"Ar, yar, thanks," added Tindel. Then he jerked his head toward the fortress. "Come on, Brink. Daylight's aburning."

As the Waerlinga trudged back toward the caer, Arin could hear Tindel proclaiming, "I told you you couldn't trust a Riverman, Brink. Why, we almost drowned in those rapids upstream, and now we discover the map we bought also doesn't show the falls or escarpment or . . ."

Arin rejoined her comrades across the pontoon bridge, and just before entering the woods she looked back at the Waerlinga. They waved a cheery good-bye, then disappeared under the raised portcullis and through the gateway beyond.

Arin turned and followed her companions into the green galleries of the Greatwood. Swiftly Caer Lindor was lost in the foliage behind. And as they entered the timberland, Arin wondered what unexpected rapids and cataracts sheer and unknown perils lay on her own path ahead.

CHAPTER 15

Bounded on the north by the River Rissanin, on the east by the plains of Riamon, on the south by the Glave Hills, and on the west by the broad Argon and a portion of the Great Escarpment, there lies a vast timberland stretching some seven hundred miles in length and two hundred in width. It is the Greatwood, one of the mightiest forests in all of Mithgar.

In this woodland dwells the race of men known as the Baeron. Huge they are, the males growing to six feet ten or more, the females to six feet six. And like their kindred in the Great Greenhall to the north, they revere and husband the land and all it brings.

In the Greatwood, too, it is rumored that Hidden Ones dwell, yet this forest does not have the warded air of Blackwood, Darda Erynian, the Great Greenhall. If Hidden Ones dwell within, they signal it not.

In the midst of the northern half of the Greatwood there exists an immense area where only grass grows; trees encroach not upon this mighty meadow, some eighty miles by forty. It is simply called The Clearing, and here it is that the Baeron gather the week preceding and following each Mid-Year's Day to sing of the deeds of their kindred and to seek wives or husbands. These are powerful days of kinship and courtship and celebration, there in The Clearing, and when they are over, the Baeron men and women, some newly mated, fade back into these wide woods, returning unto scattered thorps or to isolated dwellings . . .

. . . there in the vast Greatwood.

CHAPTER 16

It was not the time of the solstice when Arin and her companions rode through the Greatwood; it was instead July, and the sun shone down bright and hot. Yet under the sheltering bower of the leafy forest canopy, the dappled shade remained temperate throughout the long days as the Elven band slowly made their way through the dense woodland. They did not meet any Baeron during the easterly trek, nor did they see at the corner of the eye any evidence of the Fey. Hence only woodland birds and forest animals saw them passing through—or so it seemed—as they picked their way among the trees by day and camped in the forest by night. And one late afternoon some seven days after entering the Greatwood they emerged onto the rolling plains of Riamon.

The following day dawned to a mizzling rain as the Elves set out across the open wold on their eastward course, bearing a point or two northerly. In the distance to their left they could see through the drizzle the low crests of a spur of the Rimmen Mountains. They rode parallel to this spur for the next four days ere the mountains swung away to the north to join the main chain running east and west.

In the days that followed, the mountains remained in view 'gainst the distant northern horizon, as the Elves made their way across open rolling land. And another fifteen days elapsed ere they came in mid of day to the village of Bridgeton, there where the Landover Road crossed over the Ironwater River. There, too, the Sea Road began, following southward alongside the Ironwater all the way to Rhondor, a city in the foothills above the great basin known as Hèl's Crucible. The road then followed alongside the foothills and the river and down to the shores of the ocean, rather than go through the Crucible itself, for that place was aptly named: hot, barren, arid, it was a deep bowl stretching a hundred miles onward to abruptly fetch up against a high stone barrier between it and the Avagon Sea.

Arin and her companions put up in the Red Goose in Bridgeton, in this traders' town, and rested the remainder of that day and all the next, replenishing their diminished supplies and enjoying as well hot baths and hot meals and cool ale and rich red wine . . . and sleeping on soft featherbeds. And they sang sad and sweet and rousing songs in the common room of the inn, to the delight of the townsfolk and guests alike, for although bards came through now and again, it was well known that Elven songs and Elven singers were the best of them all . . . or so it was said. Regardless as to whether or not this belief is true, the tavern was packed to overflowing when the news spread that "Elves, real Elves, are singing in the Goose."

The following day Arin and her comrades crossed the stone bridge above the Ironwater, and as they did so, two men on a great, rough, rope-bound raft of logs waved gaily up to them as they floated below downstream, perhaps logger-merchants from Dael riding the timber to Rhondor, a city of tile and clay and brick, where wood is precious.

Eastward fared the Elves along the Landover Road, intending to follow the tradeway all the way to the town of Vorlo on the border of Aralan. Steadily they wended along the road, an arc of the Rimmen Mountains in the distance to their left, the miles passing dustily beneath the shod hooves. They rode by day and stayed in crofters' haylofts or in wayside inns or in open-air camps by night. On the ninth day after leaving Bridgeton they rode up a long slope toward a low set of hills, and late on the following day they crossed over this running ridge connecting the Rimmen Mountains in the north to the Skarpal Mountains in the south. They had come into Garia and they rode down onto the broad plains of this land. It was the twentieth day of August, and they had yet some eighteen hundred miles to go to reach Darda Vrka.

On they rode easterly, along the Landover Road, now running parallel to the Skarpals in the south. And as they rode, there were signs all about that the summer was beginning to wane as farmers in their fields harvested grain and drovers with dogs rounded up livestock and herded them down from the mountain meadows and toward their winter pastures. And at these signals of the passing seasons Arin fretted, for she had had her vision on the first day of July, and now it was nearing September. She chafed at the pace she and her comrades maintained, yet they could go no faster for they had to spare the horses and mules. And so past ripened crops and fresh-cut fields they rode, and herds coming down from the mountains, and all the while Arin wondered if the terrible doom were rushing pell-mell toward them all and if it would fall ere she or any could do aught to avert its horror, if indeed it could be averted at all. And slowly the miles receded behind them as they crept across the face of the world.

Late in the evening of September thirteenth they finally arrived at Vorlo, the city along the west bank of the River Venn. And across the water on the opposite shore lay the realm of Aralan.

They spent that night and all the next day and night in this border town, resting and replenishing their depleted supplies, just as they had in Bridgeton, some eight hundred and fifty miles and thirty-four days behind. Eight leagues a day they had been riding, twenty-four miles each dawn to dusk, and another three hundred thirty or forty leagues lay before them, a thousand miles or so to Darda Vrka. Arin sighed. *Surely we could have reached Rwn ere now, but for the rovers' blockade. Damn the Kistani pirates!*

The following morn they led their animals down to the Vorlo Ferry, and across the river they fared and into Aralan. They followed the Overland Road another mile or so and then veered off to the left, heading northeastward across the open land, riding parallel to the River Venn, whose distant headwaters lay in the far-off mountains of the Grimwall. On the way to the Venn, down from these stark heights course a multitude of streams which converge in the vast Khalian Mire, where the turgid waters slowly ebb southward to ultimately seep into the Lesser Mire whose outflow in turn becomes the River Venn. And alongside this waterway rode the Elven band, at least for the next several days, for they were not bound for either the mires or the Grimwall, but for the Wolfwood instead.

Two weeks or so did they keep the valley of the Venn in sight, the trees along the river vale gradually changing color as the summer slowly waned. Deliberately their course and that of the channel diverged, till at last they could see the river vale no more as into the heart of Aralan they fared, still heading northeastward, following Rissa as she led them toward Darda Vrka.

It was during these same two weeks that the autumnal equinox came and went, and on the eve of the day when light and dark exactly balanced one another, near mid of night and in the western light of a yellow gibbous moon, the Dylvana and Silverleaf solemnly paced out the Elven rite celebrating the harvest and the turning of the seasons.

They dressed in their very best leathers and took their starting places, Darai facing north, Alori facing south, and then singing, chanting, and pacing, slowly pacing, they began a ritual reaching back through the ages. And enveloped by moonlight and melody and harmony and descant and counterpoint and the rustling brush of leather, the Elves trod gravely . . . yet their hearts were full of joy.

Step . . . pause . . . shift . . . pause . . . turn . . . pause . . . step.

Slowly, slowly, move and pause. Voices rising. Voices falling. Liquid notes from the dawn of time. Harmony. Euphony. Step . . . pause . . . step. Arin turning. Rissa turning. Darai passing. Alori pausing. Counterpoint. Descant. Step . . . pause . . . step. . . .

When the rite at last came to an end—voices dwindling, song diminishing, movement slowing, till all was silent and still—Darai and Alori once again stood in their beginning places: females facing north, males facing south. The motif of the pattern they had paced had not been random, but had had a specific design, had had a specific purpose, yet what that purpose was and is, only the Elves could say.

Comforted somewhat by the ancient ritual, Arin glanced at the starlit sky—the pale yellow moon had fallen nigh the western horizon, having covered a quarter of the spangled vault in its silent journey downward during the arcane dance. Its movement only served to remind her that time was irretrievably flowing into the past.

On the eve of the sixteenth of October they sighted the Skög, that hoary forest in the northern extent of Aralan. Autumn had fully come upon this woodland, for its leaves were now all golden and shimmering in the crisp wind blowing down from the distant Grimwall Mountains. And this wind carried with it the hint of the winter to come, and, gauging by the shag the horses and mules had taken on, it would be a brutal season.

Arin and her companions rode along the forest flank for nearly eight days as the gilded leaves turned scarlet and the nights grew even more chill, but at last they came to the margins of Darda Vrka.

Led by Rissa, they had reached the Wolfwood at last, and somewhere within they hoped to find Dalavar the Mage.

CHAPTER 17

Bounded on the north by the towering Grimwall Mountains, on the east by the swift-flowing Wolf River, on the south by the rolling plains of Aralan, and on the west by a broad, open stretch of prairie reaching across to the Khalian Mire, there lie two vast timberlands, joined flank to flank by a wide strip of forest running between. They are the Skög and Darda Vrka, and together they span four hundred miles west to east and two hundred and fifty north to south.

It is said that the Skög is the oldest forest in Mithgar, and perhaps this is true, for the Elves call it by no other name. They do not even call it Darda, but merely refer to it as the Skög. And so perhaps there is something to the tale that the Skög is the eldest . . . yet joined as it is to Darda Vrka, it is difficult to separate the age of the two.

Yet of the twain, it is Darda Vrka, the Wolfwood, captured forever in the songs of bards: songs which fill the very soul to the brim with a longing for the times of legend; songs that bring a glitter to the eyes of all who hear; songs of the Wolfwood where beasts of the elden days once and perhaps yet may dwell: High Eagles, White Harts, horned horses named Unicorn, Bears that once were Men, and more, many more of these mystical, mythical creatures . . . the forest ruled o'er by great Silver Wolves— the Draega of Adonar—or mayhap the Wizard some say dwells within. Aye, it is the Wolfwood bards sing of: a wide forest, an ancient forest, an enchanted forest, a warded forest shunned by those who would do evil.

But the bards neither sing songs nor tell tales of the ancient, hoary Skög, nor speak a word of who or what dwells deep in the shadows therein.

CHAPTER 18

Rissa rode splashing across a swift-running stream and in among the gold and scarlet of the trees, Arin and the others following, and over the next two days they fared north and east, seeking the heart of Darda Vrka, covering forty miles in all. And yet by no earthbound sign could they tell that a Wizard lived herein, though for those same two days high in the cerulean sky above and nearly beyond the eye to see a snow-white falcon circled and circled, always overhead.

"Dalavar's eyes, I would imagine," said Biren when he first spied it.

"Dost thou really think so?" asked Perin, shading his brow and peering upward.

"It never stoops," replied Biren. "Besides, when hast thou ever seen such a bird? White as the driven snow. Falcons are never such, save gyrfalcons."

"Mayhap 'tis a gyrfalcon."

"I think not, brother. It seems too small and too far south. Too, if it were a gyrfalcon, this time of year its plumage would be grey, neh? And this one is white."

"Ghostly, one might say," added Perin.

"Dalavar's eyes," repeated Biren. "Mayhap we'll see him on the morrow."

"Mayhap," agreed Perin.

And onward they rode, following the others into the Wolfwood, while overhead a pale raptor soared.

Early next morn Arin on watch kicked up the smoldering ash and added twigs and broken branches to the newly exposed embers. As small ruddy tongues began licking over the laid-wood, she glanced through the morning fog toward the dimly seen mere at hand, where the mist rose up from the water to coil outward among the surrounding trees and envelop the entire woodland in its obscuring silvery clasp. Taking up a kettle, she stepped to the edge of the clear pond and filled the vessel with limpid water. She heard a splash off somewhere in the fog. *Another of those delicious fish . . . or a frog.* Behind her she heard a mule grunt and one of the horses snort. In a handful of running steps she was back at the campsite, where she roused the others.

"Tsst," she hissed, "something or someone comes."

"Where away?" whispered Vanidar, taking up his silver-handled white-bone bow. There was the soft scrape of steel as the other Elves drew weapons. Tethered to a line strung between two trees, the horses and mules edgily shifted about, their eyes wide and ears upright, their focus an unseen point across the mere.

"Yon," breathed Arin, pointing with her chin toward the pond as she doused the growing campfire with water from the kettle, the ruddy coals softly sissing and adding steam to the mist as they were quenched. "Something opposite caused a frog to jump. And the horses are uneasy. Something steals upon us." Arin set aside the kettle and took up her quarterstaff.

"This is Darda Vrka," hissed Rissa in protest even as she moved to a position along the defensive perimeter, her sword in hand. "Nothing evil should be about."

Silverleaf nodded, stabbing his long-knife into the earth before him, the weapon in easy reach, and he nocked an arrow to string. "Nevertheless, *chieran,* 'tis better to—"

"Yon," breathed Melor, using his spear to point through the fog to the right of the mere. "They come."

Obscured by the mist, blots of darkness slipped among the trees and toward the campsite, dense fog swirling about their vague forms.

Arin stared at the oncoming shapes and cocked her head and focused, as if she were looking into the flames of a fire—a trick of sight which had led her on more than one occasion to espy something otherwise hidden. But as surely as water quenched flames, the mist defeated her.

"Over here," sissed Ruar, gripping his saber and pointing to the left. "More come."

Horses and mules snorted and pulled back against their tethers.

"How many altogether?" hissed Vanidar.

"Four. —Nay, five . . . six," responded Ruar as the shapes in the mist drew closer.

"And six here," added Melor, taking a step or two outward. "They move as a pack and trot on four legs and are—"

"Draega!" called Rissa in glee as one of the great Silver Wolves could clearly be seen at last. Each as large as a pony, they came trotting out from the mist and into the campsite, their mouths grinning and tongues lolling over glistening white fangs.

Sheathing her sword, Rissa clasped the first of the great Wolves about the neck and buried her face in its soft white fur; it suffered the embrace in silence.

As Biren and Perin calmed the snorting horses and grunting mules, altogether twelve Draega gathered 'round the campsite.

Breathing a sigh of relief, Arin turned to set aside her quarterstaff, when there came a flickering in the corner of her eye, yet when she looked, nothing was there. *A trick of the fog?* As she had done before, she cocked her head and focused, attempting again to <see> something otherwise hidden . . . and of a sudden she saw a Mage standing at the extinguished fire.

Six feet or so in height he was—taller than most Elves—and as with all of Magekind his eyes held the hint of a tilt, and his ears were pointed, though less than either Dylvana or Lian. His hair was long and white, hanging down beyond his shoulders, its sheen much the same as Silver Wolf fur, though somehow darker; in spite of his white hair, he did not look to be worn by age. He was dressed in soft grey leathers, black belt with silver buckle clasped at his waist. His feet were shod with black boots, supple and soft upon the land. His eyes were as piercing as those of an eagle, their color perhaps grey, though it was difficult to tell in the mist. At his throat was a glimmer of silver, mayhap an amulet upon leather thong, and to Arin's eyes it seemed to gently glow.

None of the other Elves seemed to note him at all, and in fact looked everywhere but at him. The Draega, though, seemed to know he was there, for now and again one or another would glance at the Mage as if expecting a command, and then look away when none was forthcoming.

He looked straight at Arin and smiled. "Do you see me, hear me?" At Arin's nod, his smile broadened. "Then you must be a wielder of the wild magic."

Rissa at last released the Wolf and looked up and about. Not finding who or what she sought, she turned to the animal at hand and said, "Thou must be one of Dalavar's. Where then is thy master?"

"I am here—" said the Mage.

"Vada!" cried Ruar, startled—as were all but Arin— for seemingly from thin air a Wizard appeared: first he wasn't, and then he was.

"—yet no master of these Draega am I," continued Dalavar. "Instead I would name them my friends."

Recovered from her shock, Rissa stepped forward smiling and embraced the Mage. " 'Tis meet to see thee again, Dalavar Wolfmage."

The Wizard smiled down at her and returned her embrace. Then he looked at the others questioningly.

Rissa turned. *"Dalavar Wolfmage, vi didron enistor: Dara Arin, e Alori Vanidar, Ruar, Melor, e Perin e Biren."* As Elves and Wizard canted their heads to one another in acknowledgment, Rissa turned back to the Mage. "We come on a mission of some urgency and seek thine aid."

The sun had burned away the morning mist during Arin's telling of her vision. Slowly Dalavar shook his head when her tale came to an end. He took a sip of his bracing hot tea while the Elves waited in silence. They sat in the campsite, and all about Draega lay but for the three on perimeter ward. At last Dalavar said, "I know nothing of this green stone."

Perin and Biren groaned together, and Arin sighed, crestfallen.

The Wolfmage turned up his hands. "It has been long since I have stepped from these woods . . . long since I've conferred with my Kind. Yet this I can say: if there are those among the Free Folk who know aught of such a thing as this green stone, you will find them at the Mageholt of Black Mountain."

Silverleaf tilted his head. "Not at Rwn?"

Dalavar grunted. "Ah yes, Rwn too. It is a place of much lore, for there sits the Academy, and the libraries are extensive."

"Libraries?" asked Arin.

"Yes. At the Academy of Mages in the city of Kairn on the west coast of Rwn."

"Hmm," mused Arin. "Would that we could have gone there."

"The blockade," growled Ruar.

"*Kha* on all Kistani!" spat Rissa.

Dalavar raised an eyebrow. "Blockade?"

Ruar nodded. "Aye. They hold hostage the Straits of Kistan."

Dalavar sighed. "So the humans are still at it."

Ruar nodded, and Silverleaf added, "As bad as mankind is, the *Spaunen* are worse. At least there is some hope for the humans, but for the *Rûpt* . . . —Let me tell thee of their latest vile deed."

"Vile deed?"

"Aye: the Felling of the Nine."

They spent a sevenday with Dalavar at his cottage in a central glade: resting, for they had journeyed far with little letup, and the horses and mules needed time to regain vigor. Too, they replenished their supplies from Dalavar's stores, for they had spent awhile out on the open plains, where there were few crofters and no villages to speak of. And during this time they told Dalavar what news they held, for the Magus had not been out in the world for nearly a hundred seasons. In turn he told them of the Wolfwood and of the creatures therein, but what he said is not recorded, and the Elves spoke to no one thereafter regarding his words.

And while they rested, the forest changed in color from

gold and scarlet to russet and bronze and umber, and when it rained, barren branches were left starkly behind here and there.

On November third, one hundred and twenty-six days after Arin had had her vision, she and her companions said good-bye to Dalavar and set out for Black Mountain, the Wizardholt in Xian. And as they fared through the forest, a pair of Draega padded nearby, while brown leaves fell all around, the two Silver Wolves trailing, leading, and warding on distant flanks.

In midafternoon of the following day, Arin and her companions splashed out across a river ford and left the Wolfwood behind. Dalavar stood back among the barren trees and watched them ride away, and at his side sat a single Silver Wolf. When the Elves passed beyond sight 'round the flank of the hill, the Wolfmage turned toward the Draega beside him. "Come, Greylight, let us run." A dark shimmering came over Dalavar, and then two Silver Wolves loped away toward the heart of the wood as snow began to fall.

CHAPTER 19

L ight!" Ruar shouted the single word to Arin riding
double behind, his voice barely heard above the howl
of the blizzard.

Arin slipped back the cowl of her cloak and peered over
Ruar's shoulder. Ahead up the mountain vale she, too,
could see a flicker of yellow light glimmering through the
shrieking darkness. Turning to the others strung out
behind and barely glimpsed in the hurling snow, she beckoned to them and pointed ahead and called out, "Lanternlight! Mayhap a village!" but her words were shredded by
squalling wind and lost in the yowl.

Struggling, up the vale labored the six horses, deep
drifts barring the way. The seventh horse, Arin's, lay dead
a hundred miles and twelve days arear; even farther back,
nearly five hundred miles, were the corpses of the two
mules. The mules had been blizzard-slain, having broken
away from the campsite and gotten lost in the second of
the howling winter storms. Their corpses had been found
three days later when the blast had finally expired. Arin's
horse, on the other hand, had simply collapsed and died;
her heart had given out as she had labored in the deep
snow left behind by another blizzard and another. And
now the fifth winter blow whelmed upon the Elves, and
they struggled through the thundering dark to find
shelter. . . .

. . . And up ahead they saw lanternlight, or so Arin
believed.

But Ruar's horse had stopped, unable to go farther, its
energy gone. "Down!" he called to Arin, and together
they dismounted.

Floundering through a deep drift, Arin worked her way

to the fore, and together, she and Ruar pulling and calling to the steed, they managed to get the horse moving again, the other Elves doing likewise in the track behind.

And with wind and snow battering at them, into the tiny mountain village of Doku they finally came, eight hundred miles and fifty-three days from the cote of Dalavar the Mage, fifty-one days of which had been through driven drifts of snow.

It was a village of huts and hovels, though it had a town square in the center of which stood the community well. All this they discovered as up the snow-covered frozen-mud streets came Arin and her band, while the unrelenting wind raged and clawed and battered at them with stinging ice crystals and tried to steal their heat away.

Since there didn't seem to be an inn or tavern, Arin chose one of the larger huts and bearing her quarterstaff knocked on the door, loudly, to be heard above the wind.

Nothing.

No response.

Again Arin knocked, this time with the butt of her staff.

Moments later the door slid aside, revealing a small yellow man. Surprised that he had a visitor, his gaze took her in—chestnut hair, alabaster skin, tilted hazel eyes, pointed ears, holding a big stick—

"Waugh!" he cried and leapt backwards, for surely this was a snow demon come to claim him, for who else would ride a howling blizzard down from the mountain and come to his very own door?

The demons spent two days sheltered in Doku, until the storm died, and when they left, the one who had ridden the blizzard was now mounted on a rugged mountain pony, with four more of the sturdy animals laden with supplies and trailing on tethers after.

The villagers behind were glad to see these demons go, even though they had not slain a single person, nor had _changed_ a single time into the hideous monsters they truly were. Instead the demons had been polite and had enriched the village exceedingly with two gemstones in trade for the supply of food and five ponies and grain. Nevertheless, it was a great relief to see the seven demons gone.

Down the frozen path they went, the great demon horses broaching the drifts of snow; then leftward they turned, heading perhaps for the col to gain entrance into the realm of the towering Grey Mountains to the east, where other demons dwell.

And when they had passed from sight, the entire village celebrated.

On the fourth day after leaving Doku, Arin and her companions found themselves moving upslope between grey stone ramparts looming left and right, perpendicular slabs soaring up, immense somber massifs, towering dark giants overlooking their progress, and clad with ice and snow.

And although the sun shone down upon the Elves, little warmth did they gather from its light, for it was the dead of winter—just seven nights past they had celebrated Year's Long Night, stepping through the Elven rite of the winter solstice ere the blizzard had struck. And now although the day was clear and the sun rode low in the southern sky, it was small and diamond bright and cast no heat unto them or to the grey mountains at hand.

Up through this windswept frozen hard land of dark unyielding rock plodded horse and pony, led by the Elves afoot, the air thin about them. And as they came through the col, in the distance before them they could see peak upon peak without number marching beyond an unseen horizon.

Yet, to the north and east stood one snow-covered crest above the others, and where the stone shone through it was ebon as the night.

"There," said Rissa, pointing, "there lies our goal."

"Black Mountain," murmured Perin.

"The Wizardholt," added Biren.

Arin shook her head. "We know not whether this is our goal. If the green stone lies within, then perhaps it is. Perhaps all I need do is deliver my vision to the Wizards and then we are done. Yet perhaps this is but a way station along a predestined route."

The other Elves looked at her and somberly agreed, and Silverleaf said, "If that is what Fortune has in store, then so be it," and he turned his eyes once again toward the mountain of black.

They stood and gazed out across the bleak range for long moments more, then, still leading the horses and ponies, down through the col they continued, the way turning northeasterly, heading for a winding vale below that led toward the ebony stone. Night fell ere they came down from the heights, and weary, they made camp in the curve of a mountain wall.

As they sat huddled with their backs against the chill stone rampart, no fire warmed them, for there was no wood to burn among this sterile rock.

The wan light of the dawn of Year's End Day found the Elves ready to move onward, for they had not rested well in the frigid night, for even Elves get cold, though not as easily as Men. Down from the col they fared, and as they rode toward the twisting barren valley below, the sun rose up into the sky, remote and chill, its hard, bright rays lacking comfort. And still the silent grey stone of the high bleak mountains of Xian frowned down upon them, as if this band now intruded where none were meant to go. Yet the dark mountain ahead drew them onward until night fell and they halted travel.

Four more days they fared down within the folds of the harsh grey land, struggling through the deep snow, the horses taking turns breasting the drifts and breaking trail for all others. And for those same four days they gradually drew closer to the dark spire, though to Arin it seemed as if they made little or no progress at all.

The following day, onward they struggled, and nigh the noontide, as Arin eyed the great black mountain towering upward in the near distance, "Huah!" exclaimed Melor, his voice echoing and slapping along the high, bleak stone. Moving afoot to a patch where snow lay in but a thin scattering, he squatted and brushed the white aside, revealing a pavestone. "This is a tradeway."

"Tradeway?" asked Rissa. She stepped to Melor and knelt beside him and helped brush even more snow away, exposing additional pavestones covering the canyon floor.

She turned to Silverleaf. "Vanidar, he's right—it *is* a roadway."

Perin turned to his twin. "Perhaps this leads unto the very Wizardholt itself."

"Most likely," replied Biren. "They would need to bring in supplies: food and clothing and other such, including Wizardly things."

Perin's eyes widened. "Wizardly things?"

Biren shrugged, and as he did so he heard the *chrk!* of a ptarmigan, then the hammer of wings, and looked up to see the bird in white winter plumage flying away to the north.

All the rest of that day, the band pressed northeasterly, drawing nearer and nearer to the great black slopes. And the deeper they fared into the mountains, the more certain they became that they were upon the correct path, for frequently could they see signs that this indeed was a road. Pavestones running in unbroken stretches for up to a furlong ere they disappeared again under the drifts of snow; a hundred yards of stone curbing revealed along one stretch upon the right; a bridge over a frozen stream; stone slopes carved away to provide passage alongside sheer rises: by these indications and more did they see that this was a well-traveled route, a path of commerce.

Now the land began to rise, and they rode and walked up and over ascensions and down again into the folds of the earth, slowly gaining elevation. And as they topped each crest they could see far and wide, peaks rising up beyond peaks, to the limit of the eye's seeing. But always the dominant view was of the great black mountain in the foreground reaching upward toward the sky.

And now the stone about them began to darken, and the deeper they rode, the deeper the shading became. "It is the dark of the Wizards' mountain," noted Vanidar Silverleaf, "reaching outward to touch even this."

The meager sun passed low across the sky and fell beyond the distant mountains and night came upon the land. And once again the band made a fireless camp, settling against the cold, dark stone while remote stars wheeled overhead throughout the icy nighttide, and just

ere dawn the thin pale crescent of the waning moon pre-
ceded the sun into the sky.

They rode all that day and the one following, drawing
unto the very flanks of Black Mountain. And each day
near the noontide they saw a ptarmigan winging north.

"Wizards' eyes?" asked Perin.

"Mayhap," replied Biren. "Just as I suspect the white
falcon was the eyes of Dalavar Wolfmage."

Perin nodded, and together they watched as the snow-
white bird flew toward the black stone ahead.

Just after setting out the next morn they arrived at
road's end. And before them recessed and embedded in
the jet black stone stood two massive, shadow-wrapped,
frost-rimed iron gates.

They had come to the Wizardholt at last.

CHAPTER 20

Alos shivered and gulped down his glass of wine. He turned his face toward Arin. "This talk of Wizards and of Foul Folk, I don't like it."

"Hast thou aught against Magekind? Against the *Rûpt*?"

Again Alos trembled. He opened his mouth as if to say something, his one good eye, watery and pale, staring at the Dylvana.

Arin leaned forward. "Alos?"

He looked at her, pain on his face, as if struggling to release even a single word . . . and in that moment there came a tap at the door.

The old man glanced at the entryway and slumped back in his chair and let out a long breath, then smiled his gap-toothed brown-stained grin and said, "Let's have some more wine, eh?"

As Aiko stood and stepped to the door, the Dylvana sighed and replenished Alos's glass, then looked to Egil, but he seemed lost in his own thoughts—or in his memories—a bleak look on his face. "Egil?"

He glanced up at her.

"More wine?"

Frowning, he shook his head, *No,* and then his gaze dropped as his thoughts turned once again inward.

Again came the tapping on the door just as Aiko opened it. "Oh my!" exclaimed the serving girl, catching her breath at the sight of the yellow warrior, crockery rattling on the tray. "I've come wi' th' noon meal, m'Lady." The girl edged past Aiko and then moved hastily to the sideboard and began laying out the food.

As Aiko resumed her seat on the floor, Egil shook his

head as if to cast away ill memories, and he took a deep breath and seemed to come to himself. Then he turned to Arin and smiled. "I would hear more of this tale of yours for I am curious as to what brought you to Mørkfjord. But first I would see"—he canted his head toward the bathing room and privy—"if I can make it in there and back on my own. And then let's eat; I'm famished."

The noon meal done, Egil leaned back against propped pillows and said, "Now tell us more of your story, Lady Engel, for—"

Aiko growled and started to stand, but Arin held out a staying hand toward the warrior woman, and the Ryodoan settled back, a dour look on her face.

Egil laughed, then sobered. "I'm sorry. I gave my word. And I have broken it twice in this day alone. It's just that . . . just that"—he took a deep breath and then plunged on—"you *are* my *engel,* Lady Arin."

Of a sudden Arin felt her heart racing, and she turned her face from him and stared into the hearth as if seeking a portent, though no fire burned this warm day.

Egil, seeing that he had disturbed her, started to hold out a hand in supplication, but instead dropped it to the coverlet. He cleared his throat and said, "Well now, the meal is finished. Pour me an ale, Alos, and pour one for yourself. And then, Lady Arin, if it pleases you, I would hear more of your tale. Why did you come to Mørkfjord? Too, where are your Elven companions? —Nothing ill has befallen them, has it?"

Arin turned away from the hearth and glanced at Aiko.

Egil's gaze followed her glance, but Aiko's face revealed nought. He looked back to Arin and added, "Tell us, too, of your visit with Wizards and of their sorcerous ways."

With a *clang!* Alos dropped the pewter pitcher a few inches to the table, but it landed upright on its bottom, and although ale sloshed, none spilled out. Shakily the old man handed Egil a full mug and took up his own and gulped full half of it down.

CHAPTER 21

As Arin looked into the deep shadow veiling the massive gates, a thought came upon her unbidden: *Tonight is the full dark of the moon. Is it an ill omen touching our arrival this day?*

"The ironwork—it looks to be Drimmen made," declared Perin, staring at the massive portals recessed deeply in solid black rock.

"Aye," agreed Biren, "as does the stonework. Is this a Mageholt or no?"

For some reason all eyes turned to Arin. She shrugged. "There's nothing for it but to knock on the door and ask."

Arin dismounted and led her pony among the horses and across the wide foregate court embraced by the broad recess, the sheltered smooth stretch of stone covered with but a dusting of snow. The other Elves dismounted as well and, flanking left and right, also moved forward, spreading out as they went. Stepping through shadow, they came to the great gates, the iron rimmed with hoarfrost.

"Hoy, over here," called Ruar. "Runes. They seem to be written in the Drimmen manner, with another style below. I can read neither."

Vanidar Silverleaf moved to Ruar's side, then laughed. "Leave it to a Drimm to brag so."

"What does it say?" asked Perin.

Silverleaf turned, smiling. "Although I cannot read the runes of the Drimma, the ones below them are written in a Vadarian script, one of the Mage tongues, and say, 'I, Velkki Gatemaster, made this.' "

"Then it *is* the work of the Drimm," declared Biren.

Silverleaf nodded, smiling. "Given this translation I would deem it so."

Rissa cleared her throat. "Drimmenholt or no, I say we knock for entrance and leave the cold behind."

Just as Arin raised the butt of her quarterstaff to rap on the great iron gate, a side postern in what had seemed to be solid stone opened and an armored figure stepped out and beckoned to them.

It was a Dwarf.

Irunan laughed and glanced at the armored Dwarf standing next to his chair, then gestured about the lantern-lit chamber, the stone black but hung with bright tapestries. "Yes, my friends, I suppose you could call this place entire a Dwarvenholt, though it was made for us."

Through the archway and into the chamber came a Mage wheeling a tea-service cart. As he rolled the refreshments to the table where the Wizard and the Elves sat, the bearded, broad-shouldered Dwarf turned to Irunan. "Wizard, if you have no further need for me, I shall return to my post."

"Well and good, Boluk," replied the Mage. "And on your way, if you would, send someone to the stables to see that the horses and ponies of this Elven band have been watered and fed and groomed. The journey has been long and hard on the animals, and they deserve a lengthy, well-cared-for rest."

Boluk bowed and then spun on his heel and left.

"Huah," grunted Ruar, his gaze following Boluk as the Drimm passed through the archway. "The journey has been long and hard on us as well."

Irunan smiled, his grey eyes atwinkle. "Yes. We know. Struggling through all that snow. We've been expecting you for some days now."

"The ptarmigans?" asked Biren.

"So you saw," replied Irunan, somewhat surprised.

"Yes," replied Perin. "For the past three days."

"Hmm," mused Irunan, then smiled. "Very observant." He turned to the Mage at the cart. "We shall have to take steps, Gelon, to exercise more stealth in the future."

The other Mage nodded and began setting out porcelainware along with two pitchers of clotted cream and plates piled high with scones. As Gelon did so, Irunan canted his head, his pale yellow hair falling across his shoulder. "Very rarely do we have visitors come through the hard mountain winter to our holt."

Rissa reached for a scone. "Given thy winters, I can see why. —Have any others come this winter?"

"Oh no," said Gelon, setting out cups. "People must be driven by great need to brave such brutal cold. Our last winter visitor came two years back. A woman from the east. A warrior woman who now serves in our guard. From Ryodo, I believe. Said her tiger brought her here."

Perin's eyes widened. "Tiger? She rode a tiger?"

"Brother of mine, perhaps she merely followed it," said Biren.

"Oh . . . mayhap thou art right," said Perin, "though even to follow a tiger is no mere thing."

Both Perin and Biren turned to Irunan. *Ride or follow?* they both asked simultaneously.

Irunan laughed. "Neither. She came ahorse. And no tiger at all was in evidence."

"Hmm, a mystery," said Perin.

"Indeed," agreed Biren.

Now Gelon began serving tea, and Irunan asked in a polite tone, "And what, pray tell, brings you through such harsh weather unto the Mageholt of Blackstone? Not the whisperings of another tiger, is it?" He smiled.

Arin accepted a full cup from Gelon, then said, "I have had a vision."

"Oh?"

"Aye. A vision of war and famine and pestilence and disease, and slaughter, bloody slaughter, and Dragons roaring down and spewing flame—"

"Dragons?" Gelon blurted, slopping tea.

Arin nodded. "Aye, Dragons. Whelming down among masses of people and rending and tearing and burning— just one of the many images revolving about a pale green stone."

"What!" exclaimed Irunan in disbelief, and Gelon dropped the porcelain teapot to smash on the stone floor.

His eyes wide in startlement, Irunan leaned forward and fixed Arin with his gaze. "Did you say a pale green stone?"

Arin looked from Gelon to Irunan and nodded.

Irunan held his hands somewhat apart, fingers curved and nearly touching, as if holding something oblong. "Jadelike? Egg shaped?"

Again Arin nodded.

Irunan leaped to his feet in agitation and turned to Gelon. "But surely this cannot be!"

Arin and her comrades were completely lost by the time they reached the High Council Chamber; they could no longer tell where they had begun, where the stables were, nor the location of the main gates. Discomposed and muttering to himself, Irunan had hurriedly led them through a labyrinth of black stone corridors to reach the forum hall as the echoes of a gong rang throughout the Wizardholt.

"I think they've deliberately designed this place to tangle the unwary mind," hissed Melor as he strode alongside Ruar through the archway and into the council room. "A dark, confusing maze."

Ruar nodded in agreement.

The chamber they had entered was circular and held a great, polished black-granite table, horseshoe shaped and filling half of the room. Chairs padded with red velvet ranged 'round its outer perimeter. Red-velvet-padded chairs stood against the curved black walls all the way 'round the room, except where stood the two arched doorways left and right. At the apex of the table—presumably its head—a dark wooden gavel and gavel block lay on the lustrous surface. In the open space and precisely centered between the two ends of the table arc stood a lectern, which Irunan set aside, and he moved one of the chairs from the wall to take its place.

He motioned the Elves to sit in the chairs against the wall at the foot of the council table and facing into the open arc, then he set about lighting additional lanterns to brighten the room. When he finished, he began pacing back and forth and eyeing the two doorways.

Arin, who had held her tongue till now, asked, "Irunan, what is it? Why art thou so disturbed? Yes, the full of my vision is terrible to contemplate, and I gave thee but a sketch, yet thou dost seem to believe that what I have seen is not possible at all."

Irunan stopped pacing and faced her. "Forgive me, Lady Arin, but what you say is true: it is not possible for you to have seen what your vision has shown you."

"Not possible? But I *did* <see>."

"That I do not doubt. Yet what you saw . . . you should not have been able to <see> at all. That is why I sent Gelon running to fetch the Council. —I must say no more, for it would be nothing but rash speculation on my part. Instead, I will let Arilla and the Council listen to your tale and decide what is at work here, and what it portends."

Arin started to speak, but Irunan held out a staying hand. "Truly, Lady Arin, it is not my place to counsel you. However I will tell you this: you were wise to bring this matter to Black Mountain. Now let us wait for Sage Arilla and the others."

The Mage resumed his caged pacing, and with a sigh, Arin fell silent, leaving her questions unspoken, and none of the other Elves said aught as they sat with their backs to the wall.

By threes and ones and twos, Mages entered the chamber, male and female alike, some to sit at the oval table, others to take places in the chairs along the curved wall. But each and every one fixed the Elven band with stares of speculation, and some seemed to especially eye Arin, as if trying to fathom an enigma beyond grasp.

The chamber slowly filled with a murmur of conversation as more and more Mages arrived. Like Irunan, they were dressed in robes, some blue, as was his, but of many other colors as well. Most of the entering Magefolk seemed to be of indeterminate ages, just as were the Elves, but unlike the Elven band, some of the Wizards were silver haired and bowed under the weight of years, having spent their vigor in the casting of spells. As with all of their kind, however, these "old ones" could recover their vitality by resting in a special way; many had done so before by sailing to Rwn, where they crossed *in-between* to Vadaria, for there in their home realm the return to youth came much faster than anywhere else within the Planes.

Among the last to enter the council hall were Gelon and a female Mage. Gelon looked 'round the chamber to find Irunan and, seeing him, took an adjacent seat. The female on the other hand stepped to the apex of the table and sat.

She was tall and dressed in a yellow robe. Her hair was light brown and fell nearly to her hips, her eyes light brown as well. In this cycle of casting, she had spent some of her youth, though she was not yet at the point where she needed to <rest>.

After taking in the Elves with her piercing gaze— peering long and hard at Arin—she glanced 'round the room, noting who was present and absent, and waited some moments more as a few latecomers hurried in. Soon all the chairs were filled, and Mages stood in the archways as well.

Finally she took up the gavel and rapped it on the block a time or two. A hush settled over the congress.

"Irunan, would you advise the Council as to why you called this meeting."

Irunan moved to the empty chair at the foot of the arc, and stood behind it, grasping high on the sides of its red velvet back. "Sage, this Dylvana"—he turned and gestured toward Arin—"Dara Arin of Darda Erynian, Blackwood, the Great Greenhall, has had a vision of the Dragonstone, of the Green Stone of Xian."

An uproar filled the chamber as Wizards turned to one another, or leaped to their feet or leaned forward and peered at Arin in shocked disbelief.

Impossible.

This cannot be.

The Green Stone?

How do you know?

The babble continued even though the Sage pounded her gavel for order.

Irunan stepped to Arin's side. "My Lady." He held out a hand and Arin took it, and the Mage led the diminutive, four-foot-eight Dylvana to the focal chair. When she was seated, finally the congress began to settle. And the hammering of the gavel at last caused a hush to fall.

"Lady Arin, I am Arilla, Sorceress"—she spread her hands wide, palms upturned—"and Sage of this Council." As Arin canted her head in acknowledgment, Arilla continued: "I understand that you and your companions have traveled far to bring us word of your vision, and as you can see by our outburst, a vision of the Green Stone is cause for much concern."

Again Arin canted her head in acknowledgment.

"And now if you would, Lady Arin, tell us of your Seeing." Arilla took up her gavel and rapped it hard on the block, and her hawklike gaze swept about the room. "And I would have complete silence until her story is done."

Arilla faced Arin once again and lay down the gavel. "If you would begin, my Lady, and please, leave nothing out."

Arin took a deep breath and her soft words fell into the silence of the chamber as the Dylvana recounted her vision in all its bloody detail.

"Without a doubt, it is the Dragonstone," said Arilla in the stunned silence that followed.

"But how can that be?" protested a red-robed Mage. "The Dragonstone defies all scrying. Even the Dragons themselves cannot sense it."

"Or so they said, Belgon," replied Arilla. "Or so they said."

"Well, *we* cannot find it," declared another Mage, an oldster dressed in blue. He turned to a fellow Wizard. "And we looked long and hard."

As the other Mage nodded in agreement, Arilla murmured, "True."

Arin cleared her throat. "If the pale green stone I saw in my vision is indeed this unscryable Dragonstone, then how could I have seen it at all?"

Wizards looked at one another. Some shook their heads. Others shrugged. But Belgon stroked his chin in deep thought then looked up and said, "It must be the 'wild magic.' "

Arin turned to the red-robed, black-haired Wizard.

" 'Wild magic'? That's the term Dalavar Wolfmage used. What does it mean?"

Belgon shook his head. "It means, Lady Arin, that you exercise an unknown power in a way we do not understand, for it requires no manipulation of the astral <fire> or any of the five elements. It seems to be a power of neither earth nor water nor air nor fire nor aethyr. Instead it is something else—something 'wild' and unpredictable. Whence it comes, who knows? Who understands? Certainly not we."

Again a silence fell upon the Council. At last Arilla said, "As you can see, Lady Arin, we are stunned by your vision, not because we know what it means, but instead because you had a vision at all, for the Green Stone of Xian defies scrying of any sort . . . except perhaps that of the 'wild magic.' "

A white-haired female Mage dressed in a white robe leaned forward in her chair and held up a finger. Arilla glanced her way. "Yes, Lysanne."

"Sage, we have not heard all of Lady Arin's vision."

"I know," replied Arilla.

"But I've told ye all," protested Arin.

Lysanne held out a calming hand. "Yes, you have said all you remember, Lady Arin, but you spoke of vague images you cannot recall."

Arin turned up her hands in a wordless response.

"What Lysanne means," said Arilla, "is that perhaps she can help you summon those lost images to mind. If so, then they may give us some clue as to where the Green Stone now lies and what to do about it."

Silverleaf stood and stepped to the side of Arin's chair. Arilla raised her gaze to him.

"I am Alor Vanidar, past Coron of Darda Galion, the Eldwood, the Land of the Larks." Soft exclamations murmured 'round the chamber. Raising his voice slightly, Silverleaf said, "I"—he turned and gazed at Rissa and the other Elves, and then looked down to Arin—"that is, *we* would hear more of this Dragonstone, more of this Green Stone of Xian. Too, we would hear if there is a way to avert its terrible doom."

Arilla nodded. "Yes, we owe you that much." Now her

gaze swept about the chamber. "If there are no objections, I will adjourn the Council for the time being to tell these guests the history of the Dragonstone, inasmuch as we know it. Too, I propose that Lysanne try to recover the lost part of Lady Arin's vision. But although we adjourn for now, be ready to reassemble on short notice."

Again her gaze swept 'round the chamber, and hearing no protest, she looked at Lysanne. "Stay, Lysanne." Then she gestured to Arin and Vanidar and their comrades. "All of you stay as well."

But before she could bang her gavel down, there came a commotion at the doorway, and pressing through the gathered Mages came an armed and armored figure. Small she was, compared to the Mages, five feet two at most. She was garbed in brown leather—vest and breeks and boots—and hammered bronze plates like bronze scales were sewn on the vest; underneath she wore a pale cream silk jerkin. Her skin was the color of saffron, and a brown leather headband incised with red glyphs held her short-cropped raven-black hair back and away from her tilted eyes and her high-cheekboned face. And at her waist were sheathed two slightly curved swords: one barely longer than a long-knife, the other with a full-length blade.

She marched 'round the table, Mages turning to see. Ignoring the murmurs and the stares, she stepped into the open space before Arin and faced the Dylvana, her eyes of onyx staring into the hazel of Arin's, and in a ringing voice declared, *"Watakushi wa tora desu!"*

Now she grasped the hilts of her swords and, steel whispering, drew them both in a flash and held them on high, calling out, *"Kore wa watakushi no kiba desu!"*

Viper swift, at Arin's side, Silverleaf's own blade sprang to hand, and as he started to step forward, the yellow warrior knelt on both knees before Arin and placed the gleaming swords on the black floor. *"Watakushi no kiba wa anata no meirei ni shitagai masu,"* she said in a soft voice, and then bowed forward and down, her forehead to the dark stone.

Arin looked at her in bewilderment, and then up and about at the Mages. "Do any of ye know—?"

Seated at the table, a white-haired Magus, at the end of

his current casting cycle, said, "I will translate for you, Lady Arin. First she said, 'I am a tiger.' And then, when she drew her swords, um, 'These are my fangs.' And lastly, when she lay them at your feet, she said something to the effect of, 'They are yours to command.' "

"Mine to command?"

"Yes."

"Her swords?"

"Yes, her fangs."

"But I—"

"If you do not accept, she will be dishonored."

Arin sighed. Stepping from her chair, Arin knelt on her own two knees before the abased warrior and took up the blades. Then she sat back on her heels and softly said, "Rise . . ."

"Aiko," supplied the white-haired Mage.

"Rise, Aiko," said Arin.

The yellow warrior raised up, and her eyes widened to see the Dylvana on her knees before her. Arin smiled, and reversed the swords and handed them to Aiko hilt first. "I will accept thy friendship and thine aid, Aiko, and yea, even thy service. Yet heed, thou art thine own woman, free to choose as thou wilt, yet should our paths run together awhile, then I welcome thee."

Confusion lurked deeply in Aiko's dark eyes, but she took the swords and sheathed them.

Arin stood and held out a hand to Aiko. Hesitantly, the warrior reached up and took it and stood as well, then she looked at Arin and grinned, her entire face lighting up, and Arin returned her smile. The Dylvana turned to Vanidar and said, "I believe thou canst put that away now," gesturing at the long-knife still in his grasp. Vanidar grinned and slipped the blade back into its scabbard.

"Ahem!" Arilla harrumphed. All eyes turned her way. She glanced 'round the chamber. "If there is no more business . . ."

She banged the gavel down.

After the close of the session, accompanied by Lysanne, Arilla led the Elves and Aiko through the labyrinthine passages of the Wizardholt.

Aiko, striding at Arin's side, was silent.

"Dost thou speak common?" asked Arin.

"Yes, Lady," replied Aiko, the hint of a strange accent overlaying the words.

"I must ask: why didst thou pledge unto me?"

"My tiger told me so."

"Thy tiger?"

"Yes."

Perin, walking behind, said, "Thou must be the one we heard about, the one who came through the winter to Blackstone."

"Two winters past," added Biren.

Without turning, Aiko said, "I did."

Arin glanced at the striding warrior. "And thy tiger told thee to do that as well, to come unto Blackstone?"

"Yes."

"If it is no secret, why?"

"To pledge to you, my Lady."

"To pledge to me?"

"Yes."

Arin looked questioningly at Rissa, but she just shrugged.

"This, um, tiger of thine," said Ruar, "just what is it and how does it tell thee of these things?"

Aiko strode onward in silence, answering not.

Arilla said, "She came to us two winters back. Said she had a purpose for coming, but until this day we knew nothing of it or of its import. She has been in service as a Warrior of Blackstone Mountain . . . until now, that is."

"But this tiger of hers . . ." Ruar probed again.

"She does not explain it," said Lysanne.

"Mayhap it is more 'wild magic,' " volunteered Melor.

"Perhaps," replied Lysanne.

They came to a large room with wooden doors—of various subdued colors—uniformly spaced 'round the walls. There were comfortable chairs and lounges arranged in clusters all about the chamber, with tables here and there. On one of these tables in the center of the room the Elves found their personal equipment piled; someone in the stables had unladed the horses and ponies and had brought their gear to the common room. "Those are the guest quarters," said Arilla, gesturing to doors. "Choose any room you like, at the moment all are unoccupied. Perhaps you need to freshen up—there are bathing facilities within." She glanced at an elaborate waterclock on the wall. "What say we meet here in four marks, yes? At that time I will relate what little I—what little *we* know of the Dragonstone. And then we shall have a midday meal, after which Lysanne will tell you, Lady Arin, how you and she working together will attempt to find your lost memories."

"Mayhap we don't have time," said Perin as he moved to the pile of gear.

"Time for what?" asked Biren, helping his brother sort.

Perin stopped and looked at his twin. "Mayhap every moment counts, and if we stop to refresh ourselves, we will have missed whatever opportunity there is to do whatever it is that can be done."

"But, Perin, we have already been on this, um, mission since midsummer, and now is the dead of winter. What count another four watermarks, eh?"

"*Hai!* In four watermarks I can run three full leagues and some, and mayhap whatever it is that's to be done, wherever it is that we have to go, we will be just three leagues short when the doom falls."

Arilla cleared her throat. "You assume, my friends, that it is you who must carry on with whatever it is, if anything, that can be done. Yet perhaps your only part in this affair was to bring word of the vision to us."

"But mayhap not," said Rissa, taking the gear handed to her by Perin. "The vision, after all, came to Arin, hence mayhap it is we who must avert this thing, if it can be averted at all."

"Please," said Lysanne, her voice soft. "Let us neither argue nor speculate. When we discover what else it is that Lady Arin saw, then we may have a better grasp on exactly what is to be done. Till then, I suggest we all do as Arilla says, for I need Lady Arin well rested before I can begin." She looked at Arin. "You must sleep well tonight, my dear, for tomorrow we shall make our first attempt at uncovering what else you may have seen."

"Tomorrow!" exclaimed Arin, dismayed.

Lysanne nodded and smiled, tiny crow's feet crinkling about the corners of her eyes.

Arin shook her head. "But what if Perin is right and we have no time to spare?"

"Then, my dear, we will simply be too late. Yet I cannot do this sooner, for I can see your <fire> is too low."

"<Fire>?"

"Energy, durance, vigor. Your vitality has been sapped by your long, hard journey. But a good night's rest will restore much of what we will need."

"Enough!" snapped Arilla. "You must do as Lysanne says, else you may never reveal that which is now obscured."

Arin sighed and nodded in glum resignation.

Satisfied, the Sage glanced at the waterclock. "Four marks, and we shall return."

As Arilla and Lysanne left, gloomily Arin watched them go. Biren handed Arin her gear, and, fretting, she chose a muted-green guest-room door and moved toward it, Aiko at her side.

Bathed and somewhat rested, four marks later Arin stepped into the great common room. Waiting were Arilla and Lysanne, pouring tea from a service. Ruar and Melor were already there, as were Biren and Perin. Aiko was there as well, the warrior having moved her gear in the interim to the red-doored room adjacent to Arin's green. As Arin took a cup from Lysanne, Vanidar and Rissa emerged from their room, Silverleaf laughing.

When all were arranged in comfortable chairs, tea in hand, Arilla cleared her throat. All eyes turned her way. She took a deep breath and began: "Let me tell you of a day long past at the gates of Blackstone when the Dragons came to call."

CHAPTER 22

The air over the Grey Mountains of Xian was filled with bellowing roars and the thunder of leathery wings. Dragons, mighty Dragons—glittering red and silver and black and green and other sheens—filled the summer sky. Down they came, spiraling and spiraling, 'round the towering Black Mountain where Wizards dwelled. Gate guardians cried out in fear and fled inside, slamming the great portals to. But still the Dragons descended, to land on mountain crests all 'round, settling like weighty, gleaming monoliths atop the lofty spires ... all but three of the mighty Fire-drakes, and these came to rest before the shut iron gates of the Wizardholt. Two of these Dragons were massive and black, deep violet glints shimmering as they shifted about, and they had ebony claws like sabers which scored the dark stone of the foregate court. And they flanked a third Dragon, small by Dragon measure—if any Dragon could be said to be small. Green, he was, with a yellow cast, and seemed cowed by the other two. And in one claw he held a leather bag, tied tightly at the top by a thong.

"Wizards, we would parley!" bellowed the monstrous black Drake on the left.

The Drake on the right turned and hissed in rage and spoke in a tongue from the dawn of time, the words sounding like great brass slabs grinding heavily upon one another. ["*I* shall be the speaker here, Daagor, for *I* occupy the highest ledge!"]

Daagor's massive tail lashed furiously. ["Only because *I* was in Kelgor, Kalgalath, at the time of the mating."]

The green Drake in between crouched lower.

At that moment a postern gate opened and out stepped a Mage dressed in a dark red robe.

Black Kalgalath eyed the Wizard, and then turned to Daagor. ["We shall settle this once and for all at the time of the testing. But for now it is *I* who will speak for all of Dragonkind."]

Daagor roared in challenge, shifting his bulk to face his nemesis. Black Kalgalath bellowed in response.

The green Drake scuttled backward, out from between these rivals, and the Mage at the gate clapped his hands over his ears in pain.

But from the mountains all 'round, a hundred or more Dragon voices were raised, thundering bellows of their own blaring through the air, and the mountains entire shook and boomed with the echoes of Dragon shouts.

Warily, Black Kalgalath took his eye from Daagor and scanned the crests above, and Daagor did the same. Then Daagor hissed, ["The ledge was and is rightfully mine, Kalgalath, yet even we together cannot defeat all of them, hence *I* will permit you to speak to this Mage."]

["*I* need no sanction from you, Daagor, for that which is rightfully mine."]

Now Kalgalath turned to the Wizard and spoke in the common tongue, though his voice still sounded as great brazen slabs dragging one upon another. "Mage, we have come to parley."

The Wizard stepped forward. "Parley?"

"Yes, we have a small favor to ask."

"A favor?"

"The tiniest of things."

The Mage barked a laugh and flung his arms wide, taking in the entire assembly of Drakes. "The whole of the Dragon nation comes knocking on my door and then requests the tiniest of favors? I think not, Kalgalath."

"You know my name?" Black Kalgalath turned his head and gloated at Daagor.

"Yes, and Daagor's as well."

Now it was that dark Drake's moment to exult.

"Who would not know the names of the two mightiest Dragons in Mithgar?" asked the Mage rhetorically. "Dragons visit woe unto the world—Kalgalath and Daagor most of all."

Both Drakes raised their heads and arched their necks

in high conceit; had there been a great mirror at hand they would have pridefully gazed at their reflections within . . . though truth to tell, Kalgalath and Daagor were so nearly identical that they merely need look at one another to see the image each sought.

"Yet you did not bring all of Dragonkind here merely to hear me sing your praises," said the Mage. "Instead you came to parley. —This favor, this tiniest of things, just what might it be?"

Kalgalath glanced back at Quirm and the leather bag he held, and then at Daagor and finally up at the perched assembly of Drakes. "We would have you hold a thing for us."

"A thing?"

"Yes, but first, all of Magekind must swear an oath."

The Mage grunted in surprise. "An oath, eh?"

"An unbreakable oath," said Daagor.

Kalgalath glared at his rival. "An unbreakable oath," repeated Kalgalath. "A pledge to hide this thing away forever and leave its secrets unlearned . . . and to ward it from all who would do otherwise."

"And just what do you propose to exchange for the keeping and warding of this thing, sealed with an 'unbreakable oath'?"

Black Kalgalath nonchalantly examined the saberlike claws of his right forefoot. "For the keeping and the oath we would pledge to leave your Mageholt alone, unplundered by Dragonkind."

"Ha!" barked the Wizard. "You pledge to leave undone that which you never had the power to do in the first place."

"Take care, Mage," hissed Daagor, "else you will see what Dragonkind can do."

Again Kalgalath shot Daagor a vitriolic glare, then turned to the Wizard. "Only *I* am the voice of all Dragonkind, Mage, yet in this case Daagor speaks true."

The Mage shook his head and gestured at the Wizardholt behind. "First, I do not speak for all of Magekind. There are those of us within Black Mountain, and those on the island of Rwn, and yet others scattered across the face of this world. Too, there are many in the world of

Vadaria and a few on the other Planes. I can only promise
to bring the matter before the Council here at Black
Mountain. And even then the pledge would only concern
the Mages of this Wizardholt.

"Second, ere we promise to speak oaths and receive
oaths in return, we would know just what this thing is that
we are to ward for Drakedom, for we would not give
value without knowing the value of what we give.

"And so, my friend Dragons, I would see this thing you
would have us safeguard."

With a jerk of his head and a hiss of ["Quirm,"] Black
Kalgalath summoned the green Drake forward to stand
once again between him and Daagor. Kalgalath glared
down at Quirm and hissed, ["Let the Wizard heft it."] The
green Dragon set the leather bag onto the forecourt stone.

The Mage raised an eyebrow. "You would have me
walk within reach of your claws?"

Daagor hissed, "Wizard, you are within reach of our
claws even where you stand."

The Mage looked left and right and fore . . . and
shrugged.

Kalgalath snarled at Daagor, then turned to the Wizard.
"If you would feel the weight of this thing, come heft it."

The Mage stepped forward to where the bag lay
between Quirm's flexing claws. He stooped and took up
the leather sack. "Hmm. Rather heavy for its measure.
Something rounded inside. Ovoid. Perhaps the size of a
melon." He squatted and set the bag in front of him and
began plucking at the thong. "What's in here? A mal-
formed crystal ball?"

"You cannot open it, Mage," said Black Kalgalath.

"Ha!" barked the Mage. And he looked at the tightly
lashed strip and muttered, *"Laxa!"* and the thong fell
loose to the forecourt, and the bag slid open and down,
revealing an oblate spheroid of translucent, jadelike
stone, flawless and pale green and lustrous—some six
inches through from end to end, and four inches through
across—and it seemed to glow faintly with an inner light.

All three Drakes roared and backed away and turned
their heads aside, just as did the Dragons all about on the
crests above, the mighty bellows reverberating among the

jagged peaks. Whelmed by the sound, the Mage slapped his hands to his ears in agony, and blood seeped from his nose.

"Put it away," cried Black Kalgalath. "Put the abomination away."

But gritting his teeth, the Mage hefted up the egglike stone, its weight nearly twenty pounds.

Risking short glances, Black Kalgalath slithered forward and reached outward with his great black claws and hissed, "I said, put it away . . . else I'll shred you where you stand."

The Mage squatted and set the stone in the leather sack, and then he drew the bag up and about and retied the thong. As he did so, he asked, "Whence came this stone?"

Now recovered, Black Kalgalath glared full at him. "That is not for you to know."

The Mage stood. "What are its powers?"

Daagor roared. "Fool! Did we not say that was not for you to know?"

Undaunted, the Mage said, "This I do know: here we have a mighty token, one that even Dragons fear. If you would have our pledge of warding, then we need to know something of it, else you can go from here unsatisfied, the stone yet in your grasp."

Daagor and Kalgalath exchanged glances, but Quirm blurted, "We cannot sense it, Mage, and he who holds it and learns of its powers will command—"

["Silence!"] roared Kalgalath in the ancient tongue, turning on Quirm in fury. Yet at the same time flame roared forth from Daagor, and his claws slammed against the green Drake's skull, driving him hindwards. ["Yield nothing, nothing, to these Mages!"]

["Daagor, cease!"] bellowed Black Kalgalath. ["We can trust none but the weakest of us to bear the stone."]

Reluctantly, Daagor lowered his claws and muted his flame and stepped back from the cowering green Drake.

The Mage had scrambled away from the fury of the Dragons and now stood near the gate, ready to flee through the postern at need. But when he saw that the fighting was done, he called out, "I will bear your request to my fellow Mages. We will confer, and I will bring you our answer tomorrow."

But Magekind debated for three days instead of but one, for such a critical issue could not be decided overnight. They speculated on the powers of the green stone and mulled over the reaction of the Drakes. And they considered Quirm's words and the attack of Daagor upon the green Drake for revealing what little he did.

It was of no moment that the Dragons at times had spoken in their ancient tongue, for the seers within had understood their every word. Given the import the Drakes placed upon the stone—now referred to as the Dragon-stone—they debated what they would ask in return for their own unbreakable oath. The debate was long and heated, for there were many who vowed to make no pledge whatsoever unto Dragonkind, and a few who called for all to pledge falsely and study the stone and its hold over the Dragons, to use it to force them into abject submission, if indeed it held that power.

In the end they came to their conclusions and took a binding vote, and only a few renegades refused to stand by it, and these would be no longer welcome in the Wizard-holt should the Dragons agree to the Mages' demand.

When the bargaining Wizard finally returned to stand before the gate, Black Kalgalath and Daagor and Quirm— and the green stone—were yet there, as were the Drakes on the peaks above.

And the Wizard said, "We will ward your Dragonstone, and take the pledge you require, but this we demand in return:

"Dragonkind will no longer plunder at will but instead will let the world be: all cities, towns, dwellings, farms, ships at sea, ports, forests, Mageholts, Elvenholts, Dwarvenholts, human habitations . . ." The Mage droned on and on, naming and restricting, proscribing and banning, describing and detailing, but in the end finally saying, ". . . and if you do not agree, and swear a binding oath on it, then you can take your stone and fly away."

All the while he had been speaking, Daagor and Kalgalath and even Quirm had lashed their tails and flexed their claws as their fury had grown, and even at times had roared, for to command compliance, obedience, in a Dragon was intolerable, insufferable, not to be borne.

Yet in the end Black Kalgalath glanced once more at the leather bag in Quirm's possession and said, "We will consider your despicable demands and give you our answer on the morrow."

But the Dragons debated for nearly two weeks, and the mountains roared with wrath and rage. And some flew off in fury—Sleeth and Redclaw and Skail and others, Daagor among them.

At last Black Kalgalath and Silverscale came to the Wizardholt, Quirm between the two, the green Drake yet bearing the bag.

"This we will agree to, Mage," said Kalgalath.

"We will remove ourselves to remote places and limit our raids to that which is needed for sustenance—a horse, a cow, or other such now and again.

"We will not plunder unless we are plundered ourselves, though I cannot imagine a creature who would even attempt to do so.

"We will not seek to take treasures owned, yet treasures abandoned are fair game.

"We will not mix in the affairs of humans, Dwarves, Mages, or aught others, unless they first meddle in the affairs of Dragons, in which case we will be free to take our just retribution."

Black Kalgalath continued to detail that which the Dragons would accept and that which they would reject, and the Mage took their proposal back unto the Council.

The haggling lasted for another month, demands made and accepted or rejected, omissions and ambiguities clarified, wordings made just so . . . but in the end the agreement was struck, both sides pledging, and those among the Wizards who would not pledge were banished from the holt. There was some haggling over the fact that not all Dragons pledged, but the Dragons countered that all

Mages had not sworn the oath either—each side had their renegades. And so it was settled at last.

And the pledged Mages took the Dragonstone into the darkness of Black Mountain and locked it away in a deep vault, and as they had sworn they did not probe into its secrets at all . . . though some Mages beyond Black Mountain, Mages who had not taken the oath, would now and then meddle in the affairs of the Drakes.

And the oathbound Dragons took to their remote fast-nesses and for the most part let the world be—but for an occasional stolen cow or horse—and peace reigned for millennia . . . except for the scattered ravages of the unpledged renegade Drakes, Daagor's savage plunderings among the worst.

But then one day it was discovered—virtually by acci-dent—that the Green Stone of Xian had vanished, had dis-appeared from the vault; just when this might have occurred, none knew. And when they plied their Wizardly talents to reveal what had happened, and where the missing green stone now lay, to their dismay they discov-ered that the Dragonstone was completely unscryable, hence anything concerning it—past, present, or future—stood beyond the reach of their arcane arts.

And thus things stood until Arin of Blackwood came.

CHAPTER 23

They sat in a small, remote, darkened chamber, where nought but a single candle burned, and that but a scanty taper. Arin's eyes were fixed on the flame as Lysanne spoke softly to her. Aiko knelt nearby on the dark stone floor. None else were present. Arin's eyes were heavy-lidded as Lysanne murmured gently, and at last they closed.

Lysanne set the candle aside, then turned to the Dylvana deep in an unforced trance.

"Can you hear me, Dara Arin?"

"Mmm," replied Arin.

"You may speak, Lady."

"Vi oren ana."

"Speak in the common tongue, Dara. Can you hear me?"

"I hear thee."

"Good." Lysanne glanced at Aiko. "Remember, child of Ryodo, all that you see and hear."

Aiko's black eyes glittered, and she nodded sharply once.

Now Lysanne turned back to Arin. "Dara, you too shall remember all that passes within. Do you understand?"

Slowly, Arin nodded.

"Good." Lysanne leaned back in her soft, padded chair and steepled her fingers. "I want you to return to that night in the glade when you saw the vision."

Arin shifted uneasily and her breathing sharpened.

"It is all right, Dara," soothed Lysanne. "I am here, as is Aiko, and nothing evil is at hand."

There came the whisper of steel being drawn as Aiko slid her swords from their scabbards. "I will protect you, my Lady."

Lysanne frowned at the yellow warrior, but Arin

seemed to relax slightly, though her breathing was yet sharp.

"What do you see and hear, Dara?"

"I see the flames. I hear the horns."

"Horns?"

"The hunting horns. I know the stag now runs."

"Ah." Lysanne nodded. "I understand. But now, Dara, I would have you move forward in time, to when the hunt is done and the hunters returned, to when the vision comes. Tell me now what you see."

"Blood."

"Blood?"

"The slain stag is bleeding."

"And . . . ?"

"And I look away, into the flames. —Oh, oh, oh." Arin began weeping and her breath came in harsh gasps.

Lysanne leaned forward and took Arin's hand and winced in pain at her grip. "Stay calm, my dear. Stay calm."

But Arin squeezed tighter and called out, "Oh, Adon, let it not be."

"Dara Arin?"

"Slaughter. Bloody slaughter."

"Dara Arin!"

"Dragons . . ."

"Dara, listen to me!"

"Oh, the children. Oh, oh, oh . . . I cannot, I cannot, I cannot . . ."

Now Lysanne called out sharply, "Lady Arin, listen to me! Step beyond these vile seeings, past the slaughter, past the famine, past the disease, past the pestilence. Find a place of calm."

Arin jerked her head one way, then another, and back and forth again. "There is, there is no, no place."

"Then listen to me, Arin. Listen to my voice. Hear me. Time stands still! All is frozen in a single moment! Nothing moves! Nothing at all. Nothing. It is arrested as if in a painting, as if in tapestry."

Gradually, Arin slowed her thrashing until she was still, though she continued breathing in rapid puffs. She relaxed her grip, but Lysanne did not take her own bruised hand away.

"Arin, I want you to step past these frozen images until you come to that place where you could endure no more of these sights, where your mind and soul had to flee from the seeing of them. Go to the place where the vision you told to the Council comes to an end, but go no further, for here it is we would see that which was heretofore forgotten by you."

Arin groaned. "Horror," she murmured. "Between here and there."

"Past them, Dara, past them. To the end of your clear telling."

Again Arin moaned, and it seemed as though she were laboring to cross rugged land. At last her breathing slowed.

"Have you come to the place where your remembered vision ends?"

"Yes."

"Good. Heed me, I want you to tell me what you see."

Arin did not speak.

"Tell me," demanded Lysanne.

Arin shook her head and muttered, "Nothing. I see nothing. All is darkness."

"Darkness?"

"Aye."

"And you see nothing whatsoever?"

"Nothing."

Lost in thought, Lysanne glanced 'round the room, unperceiving. Now she turned back to Arin. "Are there memories from this darkness?"

Arin's breathing increased. "Yes."

"Memories of what?"

"Something. A voice, runes, knowledge, I don't know."

Lysanne leaned forward and placed a hand to Arin's forehead. *"Recodare!"* she demanded.

Arin sat up and her eyes snapped open, but they were focused on a point beyond time and space. And in a voice hardly her own she intoned:

"The Cat Who Fell from Grace;
One-Eye in Dark Water;
Mad Monarch's Rutting Peacock;
The Ferret in the High King's Cage;
Cursed Keeper of Faith in the Maze:
Take these with thee,
No more,
No less,
Else thou wilt fail
To find the Jaded Soul."

And then Arin slumped forward as Lysanne caught her, the Dylvana unconscious to the world.

CHAPTER 24

A nd that is the whole of the rede?" asked Sage Arilla.
"Yes," replied Lysanne. "Or so I think." She glanced
at Arin.

The Dylvana nodded. "I remember it all, now. Why I
forgot it, I cannot say."

"Chide not thyself, Arin," said Rissa. "It was a grim
vision. Enough to shake all souls."

"Rissa is right, Dara Arin," concurred Lysanne. "When
the vision first came upon you, it was too much for your
soul to bear, and that's why you fled from it and did not
remember all. Yet listen to me, whether or not I helped
you to recover that which was hidden, you would have
succeeded on your own, given time."

"Mayhap time is what we have little of," said Vanidar
Silverleaf.

"Perhaps it is too late even now," agreed Arin glumly.

Lysanne sighed. "Wild magic is vexing."

Rissa turned to her and frowned. "Vexing?"

Lysanne nodded. "This vision of Lady Arin's—wild
magic does not tell us when it is to happen. The vision
could tell of events occurring at this very moment, or that
which is soon to occur, or that which might occur ten
thousand years in the future."

Arin held out a negating palm. "We cannot gamble on
the chance that the doom lies years in the future, for if we
are wrong the consequences are too great. Instead we
must believe that even now events are moving apace. Else
why would the vision have come to me now?"

Lysanne turned up her hands, for she had no answer to
Arin's question.

They sat in a cluster of comfortable chairs in the

common room of the guest quarters, the Elves and the two Mages. The Ryodoan warrior, Aiko, sat against a wall some distance from them and directly behind Arin.

"But the rede," said Perin, "what does it mean?"

"A complete mystery, that," added Biren.

Lysanne shook her head. "No, Alor Biren, not a complete mystery. Even now there is some we can glean from it, but not all."

Melor looked at the white-haired Mage and said, "I agree."

Biren turned to Melor. "And that is . . . ?"

"Yes, do tell," added Perin.

Melor shrugged, then said, "Dara Arin has been given a mission."

"Mission?" asked Biren.

"To do what?" asked Perin.

"To find the Jaded Soul," said Melor.

Both Lysanne and Sage Arilla nodded in accord.

Biren glanced from one to the other. "And this so-called Jaded Soul. . . ?"

"The Green Stone of Xian," said Arilla.

"The Dragonstone," said Lysanne.

"Hmm," mused Perin.

"But why would it be called the Jaded Soul?" asked Biren.

"It looks like jade," replied Perin.

"Mayhap there's more to it than that," responded Biren.

"And mayhap not," said Perin.

Arin took a deep breath and exhaled. "If we only knew something of the stone and why the Dragons fear it."

"There is a legend," came a voice from behind. It was Aiko. She sat in a lotus position, her back against the wall, her eyes closed.

Arin turned about. "Legend, Aiko?"

Aiko opened her dark, almond eyes. "To the west and north of Ryodo lies an ancient land called Moko. The *soshoku* of Moko, all *onna,* say one day a *mahotsukai yushi odatemono* will come and will bear the mark of the Dragon. He will lead the people of Moko in conquest of all the world. And he will possess a mighty talisman and Dragons shall bow to his will."

Arin held out a hand to stay Aiko's voice. "Aiko, thou didst use words in a tongue I speak not."

"Forgive me, my Lady." Aiko paused in reflection, then said, "Ah. Yes. 'The *soshoku* of Moko are all *onna*,' means, the priesthood of Moko are all women; and a *mahotsukai yushi odatemono* is a Mage warrior-king."

Arilla said, "And the people of Moko believe that a Mage warrior-king will one day lead them in the conquest of the world, and he will have Dragons at his command?"

"Forget not the talisman," said Lysanne. "It could be the Dragonstone."

"The missing Dragonstone," growled Rissa.

Lysanne nodded and looked at Aiko, but the Ryodoan warrior shrugged and said, "If the legend is true."

"Perhaps it is just fancy," said Biren.

"Mage warrior-king or no," said Perin, "we've got to find the Dragonstone and keep it from the hands of those who would use it for ill, whatever it may do." He turned to Arin. "Where will we start? In Moko?"

Vanidar Silverleaf leapt to his feet and paced back and forth in agitation; he clenched his fists white-knuckle tight and he shook his head in ire. "Perin," he gritted, "*we* do not start at all."

"Not start at all?" asked Biren, shocked. "Whatever dost thou mean, Vanidar?"

Silverleaf stopped and turned, his gaze sweeping over everyone there. "The rede. Arin's rede. If we go with her, she will fail."

"What?" barked Ruar.

Silverleaf looked at Arin. "Say the rede again, Dara."

Arin spoke quietly:

> *"The Cat Who Fell from Grace;*
> *One-Eye in Dark Water;*
> *Mad Monarch's Rutting Peacock;*
> *The Ferret in the High King's Cage;*
> *Cursed Keeper of Faith in the Maze:*
> *Take these with thee,*
> *No more,*
> *No less,*
> *Else thou wilt fail*
> *To find the Jaded Soul."*

Now Silverleaf turned to the others. "Heed the words of her vision: 'Take these with thee, no more, no less, else thou wilt fail to find the Jaded Soul.'

"Dara Arin's mission is to find the Jaded Soul, and she must take with her only those who meet the terms of the rede and none else. And although I know not the answer to the conundrum of her vision, this I can say: not a single person among us suits the riddle of the rede."

"Not true," called Aiko. All eyes turned her way. She had a peculiar look on her face, something akin to guilt, as she stood and moved to come before Arin. Aiko knelt at Arin's feet and lowered her gaze and would not meet the Dylvana's eyes. Then she buried her face in her hands and lowered her head to the floor in shame, and her voice could but barely be heard. "Forgive me, my Lady, but this you must know: I am the cat who fell from grace."

CHAPTER 25

Arin leaned down and took Aiko by the shoulders and raised her to a kneeling position, but the Ryodoan kept her eyes downcast and would not meet the Dylvana's gaze.

Perin said, "Aiko, thou art no cat."

"Aye," added Biren. "How couldst thou be the cat of Dara Arin's vision, the cat who fell from grace?"

Her eyes focused on the floor, Aiko bleakly said, "I betrayed my father."

Hiroko died giving birth to Aiko, and Armsmaster Kurita was left with the care of her, his only child. Grieving, he departed the *shiro* of Lord Yodama and took his newborn and household to live in his home in the Kumotta Mountains.

The Armsmaster had always wanted a son to follow the warrior tradition, and in spite of the fact that Aiko was a girl and in spite of the law of the land, he raised her in the ways of *senso o suru hito*. He taught her the bow and stave and spear, and the way of the two swords; he taught her the throwing of daggers and of shiruken, the riding of horses and the ways of the lance; and he taught her the art of unarmed combat as well—for in Lord Yodama's *shiro,* Kurita had been master and mentor in all these things.

When she had reached but sixteen summers, war came unto the province, and a messenger rode to the mountain, and Kurita once again donned his armor to fight at the side of Lord Yodama. He rode away that day and left his daughter behind.

Yet the moment he was out of sight, Aiko donned her own armor, leather and scaled with brass, and took up her

weapons and mounted her horse and followed slowly
after, her face hidden behind a silken mask.

She rode down to the valleys below and overtook her
father's *rentai* marching in the army north to meet the foe,
and she merged her horse into Lord Yodama's Red Tiger
cavalry ranks.

The men of the mounted regiment said nought as they
were joined by this anonymous youth, for it was the
custom of untried young men to come to war wearing
silken masks so that no dishonor would fall upon them or
their families should their services to the Warlord prove
to be undistinguished in any way. Yet should they show
valor in battle, then according to form the mask would be
ceremoniously removed and the warrior and his family
honored. Regardless, at least for now Aiko remained
anonymous as Yodama's brigades passed across the land.

In the days that followed, Aiko was careful never to
expose herself to the men when she relieved herself or
when she washed or bathed, else they would discover she
was female.

At last Yodama's army came face to face with Hirota's,
and they amassed in drawn up ranks on opposite sides of a
shallow valley, a sparkling stream coursing through at the
bottom, a stream which soon would run red.

In the first battle with Hirota's army, Aiko was a
savage reaper, for her father had taught her well.

In the second battle, she and three others broke through
a ring of the foe and rescued the entrapped Lord Yodama
himself. She and Yodama were the only ones to escape
alive, and this primarily because of her flashing steel.

In the ceremony that followed, Aiko did not remove her
silken mask even though it was custom. Lord Yodama
was surprised at her desire to remain anonymous, yet in
the historical past others had also retained their masks,
and so Lord Yodama did not insist. Instead he named her
to the Order of the Red Tiger and sent her to the tent of
the *onna-mahotsukai* and commanded the witch to give
this warrior his requisite tattoo. This Aiko could not
refuse.

The witch was ancient, and when she insisted that Aiko
remove her armored jacket and silken undershirt, the old

woman's eyes widened at what was exposed. Even so, she said nought, but instead muttered over her needles and inks, adding potions and powders to the mix.

The crone carefully etched a baleful red tiger glaring out from between Aiko's breasts, the witch whispering and sissing all the while unto the crimson cat slowly revealed, as if it were a creature alive. When the old woman was done she winked up at Aiko and grinned a toothless smile, sharing the warrior's secret. And as Aiko started to don her silken undershirt and leather jacket, the witch reached out and touched the sanguine image between Aiko's breasts and said, "I have given you a special *tora,* child; listen to her closely; heed her guidance and warnings, for you are in her care."

In the third and fourth battles of the war between Yodama's Red Tigers and Hirota's Golden Dragons, Aiko distinguished herself time and again.

And still she declined to reveal her face to Lord Yodama.

In the fifth and final battle, Lord Yodama was arrow-slain, and his son, Yoranaga, took command. They routed Hirota's Golden Dragons, and no mercy was shown.

In the ceremonies that followed, Lord Yoranaga commanded Aiko to remove the mask. She respectfully declined, but Yoranaga insisted. Reluctantly she did so. Armsmaster Kurita, standing at Yoranaga's side, gasped, "Aiko," for he saw that this gallant warrior was none other than his very own daughter.

Now all was revealed—Aiko was female!—and Lord Yoranaga was harsh in his judgement, for Armsmaster Kurita had broken the law of the land. Kurita was stripped of his weapons and properties and titles and commanded to live all the rest of his days in poverty and disgrace. Aiko, hero—nay, heroine of the war, savior of Lord Yodama, gallant warrior in the Order of the Red Tiger— was banished from Ryodo altogether.

With her eyes still downcast, Aiko said to Arin, "Because of me my father is dishonored. I betrayed him and his lord and my country." Aiko unbuttoned her jacket and silken undershirt to reveal the glaring red tiger. "I am *yadonashi*—outcast. I am the cat who fell from grace."

Arin shook her head and stood and lifted Aiko to her feet. "No, Lady Aiko, thou didst not betray aught. 'Twas but outmoded custom thou didst break."

"Aye," said Rissa. "A custom we Elves abandoned long past. If females bearing arms and engaging in combat is dishonorable, then nearly half of all Elves are so disgraced." Rissa drew her sword and flashed it on high. "Here's to the sisterhood of such dishonor—long may we reign."

Laughing, Vanidar raised up his long-knife and clanged his blade against hers. "So be it."

So be it! echoed Melor, Ruar, Perin, and Biren.

"So be it," whispered Arin in Aiko's ear. Then Arin held Aiko at arm's length and said, "Thou didst no dishonorable thing, Aiko; nevertheless, I do accept thee as the cat who fell from grace."

CHAPTER 26

Councilmage Belgon grasped the lapels of his overrobe and said, "Warrior Aiko may indeed be the so-called 'cat who fell from grace,' Lady Arin, but what of these other references in your rede? Who or what might they be? Given the nature of the Green Stone, I am quite in the dark."

The other Mages 'round the Council chamber muttered and nodded in agreement. Sage Arilla rapped for order, and when quiet fell, she said, "All of us are quite in the dark, Wizard Belgon. Yet perhaps if we reason together we may shed some light on this mystery. In particular, we should strive to resolve the riddle of just who these others are whom Lady Arin must find to aid her in her mission."

A murmur whispered around the Council Chamber, but fell to silence when Lysanne said, "Forget not the legend Warrior Aiko recounted, for it, too, may have some bearing—being, as it is, a tale of a Wizard warrior-king who is to raise the nation of Moko to conquer the world, and who will wield a mighty talisman before which even the Dragons must bow."

"Do you believe it is the Dragonstone?" asked Irunan from his seat against the wall.

Arilla raised a negating hand. "Leap to no conclusions, for the whole tale smacks of but a fable and may have no bearing at all on the Dragonstone or on Dara Arin's mission."

"And then again perhaps it is very relevant," said Belgon, "coming as it does at this particular time. It speaks of war and Dragons and of a Wizard warrior-king."

Gelon, at Irunan's side, called out: "But who among Wizards would do such a thing?"

"Renegades, Black Mages, others," replied Belgon. "Anyone consumed with ambition to rule, no matter the cost to those who get in the way." He paused and looked about the chamber, then said, "Perhaps someone in this very hall."

Shouts of denial followed Belgon's words, and Arilla rapped the gavel hard and long ere order was restored. The Sage fixed Belgon with a cold stare. "There was no cause for that accusation, Belgon."

Belgon sketched a seated bow and said, "I do apologize to this entire assembly, Sage."

Arilla looked long at him and finally said, "Well and good, Belgon. Well and good." She turned to the others and rapped once with her gavel. "And now, Council, let us get to the matter at hand: Lady Arin solicits our advice as concerns the words of her vision. Specifically she desires suggestions as how to find those who are to aid her in her mission." Arilla leaned back in her chair and spoke to Lysanne. "Would you repeat the list?"

"These are the remaining ones she seeks," said Lysanne, holding up her fingers and ticking them off one by one: "One-Eye in dark water; mad monarch's rutting peacock; the ferret in the High King's cage; a cursed keeper of faith in the maze."

A dark-haired Mage raised her hand. "Yes, Ryelle," acknowledged Arilla.

Ryelle looked back and forth between Arin and Lysanne and asked, "Do you think that all these are people, or could some truly be the thing described: a peacock, a ferret, even a cat?"

Arin slowly shook her head and shrugged, and Lysanne said, "All we know, Ryelle, is what the recovery of her vision revealed."

"Well then," said Ryelle, "all I can think of concerning one of the lines of the rede is that the High King's cage could be anywhere . . . though Caer Pendwyr is most likely to be the place, but I do not know if Bleys keeps ferrets. As to the other lines . . ." She turned up her palms in surrender.

"Ha! If you ask me," said white-haired Halorn, "there

are mad monarchs aplenty about the world. Peacocks, too."

"I say," called Perin from his chair against the wall, "cannot one of ye Wizards use thy powers to help narrow the field?"

"Point the way, so to speak?" added Biren.

A tall, gaunt Mage shook his head. "When it comes to the Dragonstone, we are helpless. It blocks all attempts."

"It did not block Lysanne," said Arin.

"No, child," replied the Mage, ignoring the fact that Arin was perhaps many times his elder, "you are mistaken. Your own wild magic had already succeeded in doing what we cannot, and Lysanne did but help you unlock memories hidden away."

Arin glanced at Lysanne, and she smiled and nodded, confirming what had been said.

Arin sighed, then asked, "Do ye think I must find these others—be they peacocks, ferrets, or aught else—in the given order of the rede?" She gestured at Aiko kneeling on the stone floor behind. "First the cat, next the one-eye, then the rutting peacock and so on?"

Mages looked at one another, unable to answer out of knowledge. Then old Halorn said, "I would guess that since you found the cat first, you should go after the one-eye next, and so on down through the slate."

"Then I say," declared Arin, "let us debate as to what each of the phrases of my vision mean, for I would value whatever advice ye can yield."

The debate lasted for tens of candlemarks, and in the end they were no closer to knowing the truth than they were at the beginning, though many options had been proffered as to the meanings of the prophetic words.

It was Vanidar Silverleaf who finally said, "Enough! We are now chasing our own tails."

Arilla agreed, and after minor additional discussion, adjourned the meeting.

As they headed back toward their quarters, Aiko, who had remained silent throughout, said, "Perhaps dark water is a village rather than—"

"*Vada!*" exclaimed Vanidar, slapping a palm to his

forehead. "Aiko could be right! Mayhap it isn't a lake, a pond, a stream, a place in the sea." He turned to Rissa. "Mayhap it *is* a village."

Rissa frowned in concentration. "Let me think, I seem to recall . . ." They strode down the hall, Rissa staring at the passing floor and mumbling to herself. At last she looked up and said, "There is a place in Fjordland, a town named Darkwater, only in their tongue they call it Mørkfjord."

"But there could be hundreds of towns named Darkwater, Mørkfjord, or the like," protested Biren.

"Throughout Mithgar," added Perin.

"Nevertheless," said Silverleaf, grinning and casting an arm about Rissa, "it is a place to start."

"Too," added Ruar, "the towns and villages named after dark water must certainly be fewer than the places throughout the world where water lies dark—every shadow o'er a stream, every dark hole in a pool, every overhanging rock, every deep in the ocean . . . all have dark water and are, I think, without number. Nay, I deem Lady Aiko has the right of it: the dark water of the rede is most likely to be a town . . . or other place so named."

"Where dwells a one-eyed person," added Melor, raising a finger, "or so I would believe."

"A person who will aid in this mission," appended Silverleaf, nodding.

Arin looked across at Rissa. "Where lies this Mørkfjord?"

"In Fjordland along the Boreal Sea."

"I know neither the sea nor the land nor the town, Rissa, for I have not traveled widely as hast thou."

"I will guide thee there," replied Rissa.

"Nay," said Silverleaf. "Thou cannot."

"Oh?"

"Recall the words of the vision, *chier:* 'Take these with thee, no more, no less, else thou wilt fail to find the Jaded Soul.' Neither thou nor I nor anyone here save Lady Aiko may go with Dara Arin."

"*Kha!*" gritted Rissa. "The rede."

"Regardless, Aiko and I still need to know the way to this town of Darkwater," said Arin.

Rissa turned to Mage Lysanne, who strode alongside. "Hast thou a map broad enough to show the way?"

Lysanne smiled and said, "Follow," and led them through corridors and upward, climbing stair after stair within Black Mountain. At last they came to a great spherical chamber in the middle of which was a huge globe rotating slowly on a tilted axis. A catwalk led to a sturdy, latticed framework enclosing the globe, and on one wall of the chamber was a lensed lantern in a housing affixed to a track marked with days and seasons running full 'round the room.

"There is your map of Mithgar," said Lysanne, pointing to the globe. "And the lantern is the sun. We have not yet added the moon, but will someday."

Aiko, who had never been in this particular chamber in all of the months she had served as a warrior of the Mages, cocked an eyebrow. "That is Mithgar?"

Lysanne nodded.

"But it is a ball!" protested the Ryodoan.

Again Lysanne nodded, adding a smile.

Rissa stepped onto the catwalk and to the sphere. She clambered up the framework and across the globe, using the lattice as it was intended. She studied the painted surface and moved about, and finally called to Arin, "Here, Dara, here is the place where Mørkfjord lies, and over here are the Grey Mountains and Black Mountain within."

Arin joined her as did the others, and they pondered long on what route Arin would take. Traveling north through the Grey Mountains and then west to Fjordland was the shortest, but nearly all of it would be through the Untended Lands, where few if any lived. Too, for the next month or so the winter on the polar side of the mountains was entirely too brutal to bear. Following an old trade route west along the southern flank of the Grimwall seemed a better choice—at least there were villages along this way—though there were no passes through that grim range until Kaagor north of the Silverwood, leading from Aven in the south to the Steppes of Jord in the north. In the end, this was the way they decided to go and Rissa called for pen and parchment to sketch a map.

As Rissa charted their route, the others clambered

about upon the framework, looking at the map of the entire world. It was Aiko who asked, "These glints within—what are they?"

"They mark where Mages dwell," replied Lysanne.

"And the dark sparkles? —My tiger murmurs of danger."

"Yes," replied Lysanne. "They, too, are of Magekind, though I would they were not. And your tiger is right: vile they are, renegades, and they walk in darkness. A few were among the Mages who wanted to use the stone to control the Dragons and did not swear the oath. Others are just plain evil. Black Mages we name them—Durlok, Modru, Vegar, Belchar, others." Lysanne fell silent and would say no more.

As they walked back to their quarters, Arin turned to Lysanne and said, "I have a question to ask concerning seers' visions, Wizard Lysanne."

"I will tell you what I can, though one trained in that art could tell you more. In fact, rather than muddle the waters, why don't I ask, um, Seer Zelanj to join us for tea? He can certainly answer your questions better than I."

They sat at afternoon tea, eating sweet breads daubed with honey and sipping the dark brew. Zelanj looked to be ancient, supported by his staff as he hobbled into the chamber. White-haired and wrinkled, he was, and his eyes a faded blue, his skin nearly transparent with age where it was not liver spotted. "Heh," he grumbled as he sat down. "It was a long walk and took much from me. I may have to <rest> right here in Black Mountain, drat! . . . at least long enough to gain some strength for the voyage to Rwn."

He accepted a cup of tea and called for a honeycake, and when it was delivered to his palsied hand, he fixed Arin with a gimlet eye and said, "Now what's all this about visions and such?"

"Just this, Wizard Zelanj: I want to know whether visions foretell things which *must* be, or instead speak of those things which merely *might* be. Are we locked into a future which we cannot change . . . or do we have some choice in the matter?"

"Heh, you've asked one of the oldest questions of all: is destiny immutable, where nothing can be changed, or do we have the freedom to choose? As to the truth of the matter, the debate still goes on. Certainly I don't know what it might be."

"Oh." The small disappointment escaped Arin's lips.

"There, there, my dear, it's not all that bad."

"But I was hoping—"

"Hoping that I could answer the unanswerable?"

Arin nodded. "Some such."

The aged Wizard shrugged and took a bite of his honeycake and chewed slowly and thoughtfully.

Arin set her cup aside, then turned to the seer. "Tell me of visions, Mage Zelanj. Can they be altered? Changed? Their dooms averted? Can the events of my vision of the Dragonstone be changed?"

The ancient seer took a sip of his tea. "Perhaps, child. Perhaps."

Rissa looked at the old Mage. "Hast thou ever known of a vision whose outcome was altered?"

"Certainly," said the oldster. "In my manipulation of the aethyr I have seen many things which could be or were changed."

"A moment, Wizard," protested Perin. "If things can be altered, then hast thou not answered the oldest question of all?"

"*Hai,* brother," exclaimed Biren, clapping his twin on the shoulder, "I think thou hast hit upon it." Biren turned to Zelanj. "If things can in truth be changed, doesn't that say there is indeed free choice?"

"Aye," appended Perin. "Doesn't that say we are not marching along in lockstep at the behest of fixed Destiny into an unchangeable future?"

"Aye. Doesn't it?" echoed Biren.

"Oh, no, not at all," replied Zelanj, waving his half-eaten honeycake at them. "You see, let us say instead some visions are true and some are false, and that the false ones can be changed, proving they were false in the first place. Even so, we may have no choice in the matter and be predestined to prove them false, and therefore we take steps to change them, and in fact do. On the other hand, if we are truly free to choose, and if our choice is to try to alter the vision, if we succeed in changing the outcome then once again we will have proved the vision false. Conversely, if we took no steps, or took steps but failed, then would it not be the case that this vision was true? One destined to be fulfilled? In either instance, true vision or false, changed or not, neither outcome answers the question as to whether we have free choice in the paths ahead or are stuck to following a predestined course." He looked at the twins. "Do you follow what I am saying?"

The twins looked at one another, and then both shook their heads, *No,* and Perin said, "Uh, thou didst take one turn too many for me to step through thy logical maze." To which Biren added, "Aye, I deem I stepped to the left when thou turned right somewhere along the way."

"Huah!" grunted Ruar. "I followed thee, Wizard, and if such is the case, then I would ask thee this: what good are visions at all if they may or may not be true?"

"Why, boy, they are to get us to *do* something, or so I suspect. If we have free choice, then they ennoble us to action; if we have no free choice, then they make us *think* we are ennobled to action. In either case we feel a sense of purpose, a reason for being."

"But, Wizard Zelanj," said Arin, "is it not also possible that a vision shows us what merely might be, and if we strive to change the outcome we can at times alter the course?"

"Certainly, my dear, that is one view: the notion that free choice can overcome predestination. On the other hand, the reverse could be argued as well . . . that no matter what we believe, the outcome is already fixed."

Arin sighed. "And in the case of my vision, hast thou any advice?"

"Why, go out there, girl, and *do* something," replied the ancient Mage. "Perhaps you'll prove it false, changeable; then again, perhaps not. Heh, the test is in the striving . . . or not."

* * *

On the ninth day after arriving at Black Mountain, the Elven band prepared to depart, Aiko now in their ranks. The Mages had reprovisioned them and had provided Arin with a horse to replace the one storm-slain. The sturdy mountain ponies were laden with the supplies for the long journey ahead. Silverleaf and Rissa and the others planned to ride with Arin and Aiko along the old trade route as far as the Silverwood and Kaagor Pass but no farther, for to continue with them might jeopardize the mission. And so, when Arin and Aiko would turn north to fare through the Grimwall and head for Fjordland beyond, the remainder would set out southerly, to report on the mission unto Corons Remar and Aldor, and to perhaps bear the word onward to High King Bleys and others.

"Tell all to aid Dara Arin and Lady Aiko, should they come their way," said Sage Arilla.

"We shall do so," replied Rissa, smiling briefly at Arin, then frowning, "for I deem aid will be needed to stave off the doom ahead."

"Assuming it can be staved," grumbled Ruar.

Following Arilla and the Dwarf, Boluk, they led the horses and ponies out through the postern gate to come to the snow-dusted courtyard before the great iron gates. As Arin mounted up she glanced at the mighty portals where Dragons had come long past. "There is a thing thou never told us, Arilla," said the Dylvana to the Sage.

Arilla looked up at her. "And that is. . . ?"

"Thou didst never speak the name of the Mage who stood before these very gates and parleyed with the Drakes."

"Oh, he is no longer with us, and where he is I cannot say. Perhaps on Rwn. Perhaps in Vadaria. He could be anywhere among the worlds of the Planes."

"And his name. . . ?"

"Ordrune."

CHAPTER 27

"Ordrune!" exploded Egil, lunging up and forward in his bed, his face distorted in fury and flaming with wrath.

"Waugh!" shrieked Alos, pitching over backwards and crashing to the floor, scrambling across the boards on hands and knees to be away from Egil's mad rage. Arin gasped in shock, frozen for the moment, but Aiko, her swords in hand, stepped between the wroth man and the startled Dylvana. Then Egil cried out in agony and clutched his head and face, the violent outburst hammering his savaged forehead and eye and cheek with intense pain, and he fell back prostrate on the bed, air seething in and out between clenched teeth as he gritted, "He is the one. He is the one."

Arin rose and moved past Aiko and her glittering swords and stepped to the wounded man's side. Against a far wall, Alos whimpered, his one-eyed gaze wide, and switching back and forth between the bed and his ale mug still rolling in small circles on the floorboards, the untasted brew seeping down into the cracks between.

Now Arin poured water into a cup and stirred a white powder in. "Here, Egil. Drink."

Mutely, Egil took the cup and drank the contents down.

Seeing that Egil seemed rational again, Alos crawled back across the floor and retrieved his mug and tipped it up for the remaining few drops to fall on his waiting tongue. Then shakily he stood and uprighted his chair at the table once more, and from the pitcher he poured another mugful and gulped a great swallow down.

Arin took the empty cup from Egil, and asked, "What dost thou know about Mage Ordrune, Egil? What is it that lies between the Wizard and thee? Does it bear on our mission?"

His one good eye filled with anguish, Egil looked up at her and shook his head, then covered his face with his hands.

With a sigh, Arin set the cup amid the powders and herbs and simples on the small bedside table. She turned once again to the wounded man. "There is a tale here for the telling, Egil, yet I will not press thee for it anow. Even so, it may have a bearing upon what it is we are to do. There will come a time in the morrows ahead when I will ask thee to speak of whatever it is that lies between thee and that Mage."

"Mages," growled Alos. "They're all bad." He gulped down another great swallow of ale and turned his blind white eye toward Arin. " 'Tis a good thing you left them all behind, my Lady. A good thing."

As Arin resumed her seat, Aiko sheathed her blades and knelt once again upon her tatami.

The Dylvana turned to Alos. "Though there are some who will agree with thee, Alos, not all Mages are sinister. Certainly those we left behind at Black Mountain are no better or worse than thee or me."

"Hah!" barked Alos.

Aiko growled at the old man.

He shot a swift glance at the warrior and blurted, "No offense, my Lady. No offense at all. Ah, what I meant was, it's a good thing you left them behind to come here . . . to Mørkfjord . . . a good thing, yes, a good thing." He snatched up the pitcher and poured himself the last of the ale, then looked with dismay into the empty vessel. Sighing, he sucked a slurp from his mug, then turned to Arin and smiled his ocherous, missing-toothed smile, foam coating the scraggly hair on his upper lip. "Did anything interesting happen after you left them? Egil and I really want to know . . . indeed." He fingered the froth from his stringy mustache and licked the digit clean. "What say we get us another pitcher of ale and then you can tell us, aye?"

Arin now looked at Egil, the man once again in control of his emotions. She raised an eyebrow; he nodded; she gestured for Alos to go after the brew.

CHAPTER 28

The Elves rode back the way they had come, Aiko now in their band, following the trade road south and west and leaving Black Mountain behind. The way was yet covered by snow and the going hard, and riders and horses took turns breaking trail for one another, as well as for the ponies following after. They wended their way through the Grey Mountains, moving ahead by day and resting by night among the cold cheerless stone. And the moon on the nights it could be seen slowly waxed from half to full and then waned to half again ere they came once more unto the village of Doku.

The trembling villagers were dismayed that the demons had returned, their ranks strengthened by one, and that one disguised yellow as if she were a villager herself—a deception which fooled no one. Yet the people of Doku were heartened when the demons traded gold for supplies: food, grain, and charcoal for cooking. And when they left two days later, again the villagers celebrated, hoping that this time the demons were gone for good . . . though some in Doku counted their newfound wealth and wondered whether dealing with demons was all that bad . . . yet knowing all the while deep in their hearts that if any of these strange beings had ever *changed* into the monsters they truly were, no amount of gold would suffice.

West they rode, did Arin and her companions, breasting through the snow, and days passed and some days more, until in all a week after leaving Doku they came to the broad flat between where the Grey Mountains ended and the Grimwall Mountains began. Some two hundred miles wide it was, with little shelter between, and on the day they arrived at its edge, a brutal polar wind thundered south through the great gap from the icy Barrens above.

"We cannot venture out in that," called Melor above the yowl. "The horses and ponies will die in a matter of strides."

From the shoulder of the foothill the travelers looked out at the howling, brumal blow, snow and ice flying horizontally across the stony flats. With a sigh of resignation, Arin turned her horse back toward a sheltering ravine they had passed but a quarter-mile arear.

On the edge of this gap they huddled some four days waiting to risk a crossing. At last the wind faded and they rode pell-mell northwesterly, the way before them nearly swept clean by the savage polar blast, and they covered the span in just over six days altogether. And Dame Fortune smiled down upon them, for no sooner had they reached the protection of the foothills of the Grimwall on the far side than the wind rose up in fury, as if raging at missing easy prey, and snow rode in on its angry wings.

Now they fared along the southern flank of the Grimwall, following the old trade route, no longer used this far west, or so they deemed.

Nearly a month later, on March nineteenth, they espied the Wolfwood to the south and west and rode along its northern marge, where the abandoned path wended its way through the foothills above.

The next night in a freezing rain they celebrated the vernal equinox by stepping through the Elven rite, with Arin and Rissa guiding Aiko through the intricate steps. Before they were finished, the rain turned to sleet and then to snow. Springday had come at last.

West they rode, passing beyond the bounds of the Wolfwood, and although they kept a sharp eye out, they neither saw Dalavar nor his Draega nor aught else in the yet wintry woods.

They passed north of the Skög and some days later forded one of the rivers flowing south to the Khalian Mire, the river waters on the rise with the coming of the snowmelt and the spring floods.

They camped in a thicket that night, and just ere bedding down, of a sudden Aiko hissed, "Quench the fire. Muzzle the horses. Peril comes."

Without question the Elves extinguished the blaze and drew their weapons and stepped in among the animals, soothing the steeds while all waited in the slender shadows. Overhead a waxing gibbous moon shone down on the land. And ere it had moved a handspan, Arin could hear the ching of armor and the distant thud of boots jogtrotting through the night. Now and again there came a snarl of language, but in a tongue she did not speak. Moments later in the moonlight, a jostling band of Rucha trotted into view, coming from the north, heading to the south.

Still the Elves stood silently as the *Spaunen* loped toward them and past and onward into the night beyond, and slowly the sounds faded in the distance. At last Aiko said, "It is safe once more. They are gone."

Arin turned to the Ryodoan warrior. "Until now I had thought that Elves had the keenest senses of all. How didst thou . . . ?"

"My tiger told me," answered Aiko.

Arin looked at Aiko closely and wondered if it were true. Was it indeed wild magic that had warned her, or was it merely instead Aiko's heightened senses? Arin could not say . . . but in the end, she reflected, did it matter?

On the twentieth day of April they came to the stockaded village of Inge in the land of Aralan, where they spent that day and the next in the Ram's Horn, resting, relaxing, and replenishing their depleted supplies.

They traded news and songs and were told "Somethin' be afoot in th' Mire, what wi' droves o' Rutches and such movin' down from the Grimwall. Either that or somethin' in th' mountains be drivin' them out." What that something might be—either down in the Khalian Mire below or up in the Grimwall above—none could say. But whatever it was, it had to be bad, or so opined the elders.

The next day Arin and their band rode onward, passing through Stoneford, where the single family of that hamlet helped them across the spring-flooded river . . . for a small fee, of course.

Westerly they fared, ever westerly, along the southern flank of the Grimwall, following the old tradeway, riding through rain and occasional light flurries of snow as well as through lengthening sunny days as spring drew across the land. They forded rivers and streams, and passed through foothills and mountain spurs, and camped in thickets or in open rolling land. Now and again they stopped in villages or hamlets or towns and took rooms at an inn. At other times they stayed overnight with wood-cutters or crofters or hunters. But always the next day or so they took up the trek westerly once more . . . until on the fourth day of June they came at last to the foot of Kaagor Pass where stood the Silverwood.

CHAPTER 29

Embraced on the north and west and south by an enfolding arm of the Grimwall Mountains, and on the east by the trail leading upward into Kaagor Pass, there lies a woodland of silver birch and trembling aspen and splendid high pine. It is modest as Mithgarian forests go, measuring but some forty miles north to south and thirty east to west, yet it sits like a jewel in a cup, a small treasure to be cared for, cherished, loved. It is the Silverwood.

It has existed for unknown millennia, here in this sheltered mountain bowl. And in the year that Arin camped in these woods—1E9253—the Drimm had just begun delving the Drimmenholt called Kachar at the end of a vale of the Silverwood along its northwestern flank.

This fact would not be mentioned at all but for what was to come. For in the year 3E1602, some four thousand one hundred twenty-four years after Arin passed along its eastern flank, in a war between Drimm and humans, this Silverwood, this precious jewel, would be all but destroyed by raging Dragon fire.

CHAPTER 30

"Hist," cautioned Perin, cocking his head to one side.
"What?" Biren stopped filling the canteens and looked at his brother.

"Hush," admonished Perin. "Listen."

They stood in the twilight silence of the Silverwood and from the north and west there came a faint tapping, nearly rhythmic, as of a hammer on stone.

" 'Tis no bird, my brother," said Biren after a while.

"Nor an animal," added Perin.

"Delving?" asked Biren.

Perin frowned and listened as the gloaming deepened. "If so, 'tis far off."

They finished filling the canteens, then stepped back to the campsite and told the others of the sound, and Arin looked at Aiko and asked, "What says thy tiger?"

Aiko shook her head. "She is silent, my Lady."

"Come," said Rissa, "I would hear this tapping."

They walked away from the sounds of shifting horses and ponies, following the twins back to the nearby snow-melt pool, where they stood quietly and listened, but all they heard was the soft purl of a distant stream.

"Hmm," mused Perin. "It is gone."

"Vanished," added Biren.

"Mayhap it was but sliding rock on the slopes," said Melor, glancing up at the embracing Grimwall. "The spring melt bringing it down."

"It seemed too measured," protested Perin, "purposeful."

"As of a hand at work," agreed Biren.

Silverleaf turned to Rissa. "Is there Drimmenholt nigh, *chier*?"

Rissa shrugged. "None that I know, Vanidar, yet it is long since last I was here."

"It could be *Spaunen*," growled Ruar. "They teem in the Grimwalls."

Again all eyes turned to Aiko, but she shrugged and said, "My tiger warns of no peril. If the *Kitanai Kazoku* are in these mountains, they are not at hand."

"Nevertheless," said Silverleaf, "I think we should build no fire this night . . . and our watch should be extra vigilant."

Melor turned to Aiko. "Does thy tiger sleep?"

Aiko shook her head.

"Good."

There was no moon in the darktide, not even a hair-thin crescent near dusk, and without a fire only the stars lighted the camp. But then the night turned chill and an overcast from the north drew entirely across the sky and not even starlight shone down. And so, even the Elves with their vaunted eyesight could see little in the resulting dark, and all the warders had to depend on their hearing as they each stood watch . . . all but Aiko, who on her turn listened to her tiger instead. Yet the night passed uneventfully, and no danger came through the blackness to threaten the camp.

Dawn found the Elves and Aiko breaking fast beneath lowering skies, the dark grey stretching from horizon to horizon. They ate in gloomy silence, none saying aught, but as they took their utensils down to the pool, again came the faint tapping from the distant northwest.

After listening awhile, "I deem it *is* delving," said Vanidar Silverleaf, "yet whether Drimm or *Rûpt,* I cannot say."

"Shall we go see?" asked Perin.

"Whatever for?" queried Biren.

Perin shrugged. "Mayhap it is important."

"And mayhap not," replied Biren.

Rissa glanced at Silverleaf. "I ween our separate missions are more urgent than discovering some Drimm delver or aught else hacking away at stone. And though I would rather accompany Dara Arin on her mission, to do so risks failure of all. Hence, I say we have come to the parting of the ways: we to ride south and bear the words of Arin's vision to Coron and DelfLord and King; she and the the cat who fell from grace to ride north—and beyond—to discover the one-eye in dark water and all the others entangled in her words . . . and to find the Jaded Soul."

Ruar growled deep in his throat and glanced across to Arin. "Would that I could ride with thee, Dara, yet to do so indeed risks all. I must agree with Dara Rissa—we have come to the parting of the ways."

Arin looked into the eyes of each of her companions, and one by one they nodded. And so, ignoring the tapping, they washed their utensils and returned to the campsite, where they saddled the horses and tied on their gear. They evenly shared out the remainder of the supplies and laded them on the ponies, two of which were given over to Arin and Aiko.

Rissa turned to Arin. "Thou hast the map, neh?"

Arin patted the breast of her leather jacket. "Aye, Rissa, it is yet here."

Silverleaf glanced to the north and west whence came the delving sounds. "Take care, Arin, for Ruar is right: *Spaunen* teem in the Grimwall, and thou and Aiko are about to pass through."

Arin nodded and touched her sword and gestured at the bow tethered behind her saddle, and she waved a hand at Aiko's weaponry, too. "Fear not, for we are prepared."

One by one the Elves embraced Arin, and embraced Aiko as well, the Ryodoan's eyes flying wide at this show of affection, though she embraced them back. Then, as a cold draught blew down from the heights above, all mounted up and with hails of "Fare ye well" and of "Go with Adon" they rode their separate ways—Arin and Aiko into the teeth of the chill wind, up the trail and north, the others south and down, the cold at their backs.

As they entered the pass, Aiko looked up at the steeps to the left and right and at the strait ahead. "I like this not, Lady Arin," she growled. "It is a place of ambush."

"What does thy tiger say?"

"Nothing . . . yet."

On they rode and upward, beneath the leaden skies, the horses and trailing ponies maintaining a good pace. The pass itself was some twenty-one miles through, half upslope, half down, and they planned to cross in a single day, for even at this time of year the nights were frigid and the days chill and sudden snowstorms could still rage at these heights.

On they fared, up and up, toward the dismal sky. The way was narrow and stone-strewn, the walls sheer and high, with dark crannies looming left and right; Aiko's gaze ever searched the gloomy depths, her weapons never far from hand. And still they went onward, at times riding, at times walking, at other times resting the steeds, or feeding them some grain, or watering them at pools of melt after breaking through a thin crust of ice. Yet always they stopped but briefly and soon took up the journey again, pressing ahead.

Now they came into an encloaking mist, where the clouds rode low as they drifted across the Grimwall, grey fog enveloping all. Vision was shortened, ten strides at best, and boulders lying in the slot ahead loomed dark and menacing. Steps were muffled on the mist-wet rock; iron-shod hooves seemed deadened though they trod on stone.

And onward pressed the pair.

Another mile they rode, and of a sudden, "Dara Arin," hissed Aiko, riding behind, "my tiger whispers of danger."

"Where away?"

"I cannot say," replied Aiko. "Only that peril draws near."

Arin stopped her horse—Aiko, too—the Dylvana stringing her bow and nocking an arrow. Then she took a deep breath and concentrated, and looked through the fog in her *special* way . . . and although the mist yet hampered her sight, she now seemed able to see perhaps twice as far.

Up the slot she looked, as well as behind and down, scanning the walls above as she searched. "I see nought," she whispered.

Aiko, her swords in hand, remained silent.

Still they stood long moments more.

At last Arin asked, "Does it draw nearer?"

"No, Dara."

"Then let us proceed . . . but at a walk."

Slowly they began moving ahead and up, nearing the crest. Aiko spurred her horse forward to ride alongside Arin.

"The peril grows," said the Ryodoan.

"Then the danger must lie to the fore," muttered Arin, concentrating on her sight.

They came to the crest and started down, still trapped between crevice-raddled vertical walls rising fifty feet or more. And grey vapor swirled about.

Now the horses and ponies began to skit and shy, as if they, too, sensed an unseen menace. And a faint stench came through the dampening mist. They rode forward a few tens of yards, and the reek grew stronger, foul to the point of gagging.

"It is at hand," hissed Aiko, but Arin still could not sight any hazard.

A pony squealed, and from behind there came a loud scrape. Arin whirled her horse 'round in time to see a monstrous form—Ruchlike but hulking and tall—lunge out from a great hole and hammer a massive fist into the neck of one of the small steeds, snapping its spine as if it were but a twig, while the other pony bleated and fled, only to be jerked up short by the rope tied to Arin's saddle.

"Troll!" shouted Arin, as something spun upward through the mist to strike the huge Ogru in the eye.

"*RRRAAAAWWW!*" roared the Troll in agony, and Arin's horse shied back and down, almost as if struck by a blow. And just as Aiko hurled another shiruken at the twelve-foot-high monster, her horse whirled and bolted and the bladed star merely clanged off the great Ogru's stonelike hide. Caught off balance by the sudden move, Aiko was thrown, and she struck the ground hard but managed to roll to her feet, coming up with her swords in hand. And her horse, squealing in panic, tried to escape, but the dead pony roped to the saddle acted as a massive drag and the horse could not run.

Still the Troll howled in anguish, clutching at its pierced eye and trying to pluck the weapon out. Yowling and thrashing, it lurched between Aiko and Arin.

Arin knew that Aiko's blades, keen as they were, would not cut through the creature's hide, and without a second thought, the Dylvana leapt from her own skitting horse and moved in below the towering monster and took a fixed aim. And as the Troll bellowed in agony, Arin loosed an arrow upward, the shaft to flash into the brute's gaping, yowling maw, punching through the soft inner flesh and driving up into the Ogru's brain.

"*GHAAAA . . . !*" howled the monster, and then toppled backward to land with a thunderous crash, the nearly invincible creature dead, slain by nought but a five-bladed star and a steel-tipped wooden shaft.

Her heart yet hammering, Arin nocked another arrow and surveyed the surroundings with battle-wide eyes as Aiko cautiously edged a step at a time toward the monster, her swords at the ready, the warrior moving in to make certain the creature was dead. Finally she reached the Ogru's side. After a moment, her swords yet at the ready, her flared gaze now surveying the field, she hissed, "It is dead."

"I think there are no more," declared Arin in a voice tight with tension. Even so, she did not lower her bow.

They listened long, their eyes wide and scanning, their air coming in short gasps. No other peril hove into view and all they heard was the sound of Aiko's yet frightened horse clattering at the end of the rope tied to the slain pony. Of Arin's horse and pony there was no sign, both having fled on down the pass, away from the hideous Troll.

"My tiger is silent," hissed Aiko.

Arin took a deep breath and slowly let it out and then lowered her bow. After a moment Aiko sheathed her swords and stepped to the side and picked up the wicked-bladed throwing star, the one that had bounced off the Ogru's stony hide. She turned to the Dylvana. "You should have fled, my Lady," said the yellow warrior. "We both should have fled." She gestured at the fallen Troll. "Such a *Hitokui-oni* cannot be defeated with ordinary weapons."

Arin glanced at the dead Ogru and then back at Aiko.

"Mayhap thou shouldst tell that to the Troll." Then Arin broke into gales of laughter as the battle tension shattered at last, Aiko joining in, covering her own giggles with both hands.

Taking a deep breath and holding it, the Ryodoan stepped to the dead Troll and bent down to retrieve the shiruken embedded in the creature's left eye.

"Take care, Aiko," warned Arin. "Troll's blood is scathing and will burn unprotected flesh."

As Aiko straightened and pulled on a pair of leather gloves, Arin fetched a canteen and handed it to the Ryodoan. "Here, wash any blood away."

Again the yellow warrior bent over the Troll and reached for the embedded shiruken. As Aiko did so, Arin's gaze widened. "Oh, Aiko, I've just had a thought: here we stand in a gloomy mist, and thou dost pluck a blinding thorn from a monster's eye. Could this be the one-eye in dark water? Have we slain our hope?"

With a *thuk!* the shiruken came free and Aiko, yet holding her breath against the Troll stench, straightened up, her dark eyes wide with Arin's question. Then she shook her head and turned up her hands and said, "I do not know." She looked about. "Perhaps the mist does serve as dark water, and the monster as a one-eye; yet whether or no this fits your vision, I cannot say." She washed the star blade free of grume and dried it, then slipped it back into her belt next to the other. She glanced at Arin and then turned toward the Troll. "Should I cut out the eye of the *kaibutsu* so that we may take it with us?"

Take these with thee, no more . . . Arin scrunched her face into a squint of disgust, but turned up a hand and said, "If we find a one-eyed person in Mørkfjord, we can always cast this one away. —'Ware the blood."

Aiko nodded and drew her dagger and bent down, but then straightened up and said, "Which eye should we take—the pierced one or the other?"

"Oh," said Arin. She pondered a moment. "The pierced one, I deem, for it is the one which makes him a one-eye."

"But then, Dara, does not the damaged orb make the other one the true one-eye?"

"Aye, it does at that. Yet redes are things of twists and turns, and oft depend on the unusual."

Aiko nodded. "And a pierced Troll's eye is unusual?"

"Indeed," replied Arin. "For had the Ogru but blinked, thy star would not have cloven through and we would now be the ones lying dead instead of the monstrous Troll. But this one lies slain, all because of a damaged eye, and that is what makes this Ogru different from others of its Kind."

And so, Aiko began hacking out the pierced orb, and where Troll's blood struck stone, it sizzled and popped, and threads of dark smoke rose up. Meanwhile Arin retrieved the goods from the slain pony and stripped it of salvageable tack, and laded all on Aiko's still skittish horse. They washed the blood from the damaged eye and wrapped it in the cloth of an empty grain sack and tied it up in another, then slung it with the other goods. Aiko washed and dried her dagger and sheathed it back in its scabbard. And then walking and leading the horse, they started down the mountain pass, going after Arin's runaway steed and the pony tethered after.

Down they went and down, leaving a dead horseling and a one-eyed slain Troll behind.

Chapter 31

Leading the horse, Arin and Aiko walked down the stony way, fog curling about them and swirling after as they passed through the mist-laden air. A mile they went and a mile more and onward, until in all they covered just over a league, and at last they came upon the runaway steeds, horse and pony nibbling on new spring grass at the foot of a modest slope of slow-melting snow banked against the north face of a great sheltering boulder. The animals looked at Arin and Aiko as if asking "where have you been?" Cooing softly, Arin gathered them in.

As the Dylvana fed the steeds each a cup of grain, Aiko transferred the salvaged goods from her horse to the pony. Shortly they continued onward, Arin and Aiko now mounted.

Down through the blowing mist they rode, the cloud thinning as they descended, until only vague tendrils grasped at them, and soon even these were gone. Another league they fared and the pass debouched onto wide grassy plains. They had at last ridden down from the clouds to come to the Steppes of Jord.

They set up camp in the lee of a hillside at the foot of Kaagor Pass. They had just built a fire to have some hot tea when the rain began to fall.

The next morning, thoroughly drenched, Arin and Aiko studied the map. They decided to follow an old road alongside the Grey River, then cross over to Arnsburg and rest awhile, after which they would push onward, fording the Judra into Naud where they would turn north and follow the banks of that river through Naud and Kath to

Fjordland, where they would turn away easterly to ride to Mørkfjord within, the entire route some six hundred miles altogether.

"If we press," said Arin, studying the way, "we should arrive within a month."

North they started, bearing slightly west, following the road down from Kaagor Pass as a thin dawn mist seeped up from the dank ground, and within two leagues, just this side of a thicket straight ahead, they sighted a fork in the road—one route turning westerly toward Jordkeep, the other bearing northward to Arnsburg. Yet as they came toward the split, a chariot drawn by four horses abreast rumbled out from the copse, two riders within, one driving, one bearing a spear and buckler. The two-wheeled war-wagon trundled to the junction, where it stopped and waited.

Arin glanced at Aiko. "What says thy tiger?"

"She whispers only caution, Dara."

"As I, too, thought," said the Dylvana.

Arin turned her attention back to the chariot and the warriors within. The wagon itself seemed made of wood and covered with a hide—armor of sorts. The wheels were large, the iron rims wide, the better to run over rough ground. A cluster of spears—perhaps ten or twelve in all—stood to the right side and rear, and Arin could see what she deemed was a readied bow racked on the right-side hand rail.

As they rode closer, Arin turned her attention to the warriors: they were women, tall and fair, fierce warrior maidens of Jord. Steel helms they wore, dark and glintless, one sporting a long, tailing gaud of horsehair, the other bearing wings flaring. Fleece vests covered chain-link shirts, and long cloaks draped from their shoulders to ward away the icy chill of the early morning mist.

They looked proud and hard, standing as they did, their weapons at the ready, their visages resolute and framed by coppery hair, their clear eyes flinty as these strangers came into the realm of the Vanadurin. And when Arin and Aiko reached the juncture . . .

"Stanse!" commanded the spear-wielding warrior,

speaking in a tongue neither Arin nor Aiko knew, yet the meaning was clear and they halted their steeds.

"Hva heter Da? Hvor skal du fra? Hvor skal du hen?"

"We do not speak thy tongue," said Arin, casting back her hood.

The warrior maidens' eyes widened slightly at the sight of an Elf. The charioteer holding the four-in-hand said, "My Lady, these are suspicious times, for the realm of Jord is at war. Hence we need know your names and where you are from and where you are bound."

"At war?" asked Arin.

"Aye. With the Naudrons." The maiden waved a hand vaguely to the east.

Now Aiko cast back her own hood, and again the eyes of both maidens widened, for never had they seen a yellow-skinned person before.

"I am Dara Arin of Darda Erynian. My companion is Lady Aiko of Ryodo. We are bound for Fjordland."

The charioteer spoke rapidly, translating Arin's words to the other.

"Hvorledes kommen de til den Jordreich?" asked the warrior holding the spear.

The driver turned to Arin. "How did you come to the Jordreach? Surely not . . ." She glanced up the road at the col.

Arin turned and waved a hand toward the Grimwall. "Through Kaagor Pass."

"Umulig!" snorted the spear bearer.

"That cannot be!" declared the charioteer. "There is a *vanskapnig*—a monster—living there."

"The monster, the Troll, is dead," said Arin.

"Dod? The Troll is *dod*?"

"Aye," replied Arin. "We slew it: by five-bladed throwing-star and bow and arrow."

"Now it is *I* who will say impossible!" proclaimed the driver.

Aiko shifted in her saddle and her hands went to the hilts of her swords. Her voice came low, dangerous: "Call you my Lady a liar?"

"Aiko, no!" snapped Arin. "These are allies. And we are now in their realm. —Show them the eye."

Reluctantly, stiffly, her glare never leaving the eyes of the offending warrior maiden, Aiko dismounted.

The chariot driver murmured a word to the other maid, and that warrior grudgingly leaned her spear away.

Aiko then turned and stepped to the pony and undid the grain sack holding the Troll's eye. She moved to the fore and squatted, setting the sack to the ground and unwrapping the grisly orb.

Both warrior maidens gasped, and a string of words rattled between the two. At last they turned to Arin and Aiko, and the driver said, "We apologize for our doubt, Lady Arin, Lady Aiko, but such a thing has never been."

"We were guided by the hand of Fortune," replied Arin, "else we would not be here speaking with ye."

"Where is the Troll?"

"We left it lying where it fell," growled Aiko, hardly mollified, wrapping up the eye again. "It's not as if we could have hauled such a monster down from the heights on the back of our pony."

Now the charioteer laughed. "Of course, how foolish of me to ask." She turned and translated for the other, and then both broke out in laughter.

"Come," said the driver, smiling. "Come to our camp, and we shall all have some tea and celebrate your astounding deed."

Later that morning, Arin and Aiko pressed onward, now riding cross-country northward, their plans and their route changed by the war. For it seemed as if Arnsburg lay in disputed land, the area between the Judra River on the east and the Grey on the west, territory claimed by both Jord and Naud. And so the Dylvana and the Ryodoan aimed to pass 'round the western edge of a set of hills some two hundred miles to the north, where rise the waters of the Little Grey. Then they planned to swing northeastward and ride across that corner of Jord to reach the realm of Fjordland, crossing the Judra at the wide shallows near the foothills of western Kath. By this route they would avoid the war altogether, or so they hoped.

"I would not entangle myself in the disputes of men," declared Arin.

"Nor I in wars I know not," said Aiko.

And north and west they fared.

A week they rode and another, and the stench from the rotting Troll's eye became unbearable. And so in a small Jordian hamlet, they sealed the putrescent orb in melted beeswax and honey in a tarred leather bag tightly wrapped.

The days had grown long with the coming of summer, and finally the solstice arrived. And a full moon shone down on Arin and Aiko as they stepped out the Elven rite of celebration, the Dylvana singing and guiding the Ryodoan through the intricate paces of the stately sacrament.

On the twenty-fifth day of June they forded the lower Judra, and over the following two days they rode north until they came to the sheer cliffs above the Boreal Sea. Now they turned along the coastline and rode east-northeast as the surf pounded below, the horses and pony clattering along shieldrock bared in an earlier time.

On the twenty-ninth of June they came to a mighty fjord and turned inland to reach its far tapered source, and they rode up onto mountainous slopes, canted land where their journey was slowed.

The air grew colder the higher they went, and in the twilight of the following day they rode past the foot of a glacier, where small blue flowers nodded in the wind. It was now the thirtieth day of June, and morrow night would mark a full year since Arin had had her vision. And as this penultimate evening fell, they espied the lights of a town down by the water's edge.

Arin gazed at her map and nodded, then turned to Aiko and said, "Let us go down and find a suitable inn. . . ."

They had come to Mørkfjord at last.

CHAPTER 32

Egil gazed back and forth between Arin and Aiko, his one good eye wide in amazement. "Together you slew a stone-hided Troll?"

Alos shuddered and seemed to shrink within himself.

Arin glanced at Egil, her heart racing suddenly. *Why does it please me so that he finds it astonishing?* "Aye," she managed to say, "though 'twas mostly by Fortune's favor."

Aiko shook her head. "Fortune may have smiled down upon us, yet even had that Dame been looking elsewhere, or not looking at all, Dara Arin's aim was true, else we would have filled the *Hitokui-oni*'s cooking pot."

"My arrow flew no truer than thine own cast, Aiko."

"Fortune or no," declared Egil, "the fact is, you slew a Troll."

With shaking hand, Alos poured himself a mug of ale and hurriedly gulped it down, brew running adribble from the corners of his mouth.

Egil rubbed his whiskery jaw. "I thought Trolls nearly indestructible. The stories say that only by a high fall, or by a great rock dropping on them, can they be killed."

Arin held up a hand. "A finely placed thrust, in eye, ear, or mouth, will do them in as well, Egil. Too, it is said they are tender of the sole of foot; a heavy caltrop will pierce them there, should they tread upon one."

Alos groaned and buried his face in his hands.

Arin looked at him. "Art thou well, Alos?"

"Leave me be," he moaned.

Arin looked at Egil questioningly, but he turned up his hands and shrugged, for Egil did not know why the old-ster was distressed.

Finally Egil said, "I would hear once again the words of your vision."

Arin intoned:

> *"The Cat Who Fell from Grace;*
> *One-Eye in Dark Water;*
> *Mad Monarch's Rutting Peacock;*
> *The Ferret in the High King's Cage;*
> *Cursed Keeper of Faith in the Maze:*
> *Take these with thee,*
> *No more,*
> *No less,*
> *Else thou wilt fail*
> *To find the Jaded Soul."*

She looked at Egil. "Canst thou help us winnow the answers?"

Slowly Egil shook his head, lost in thought, his lone eye staring at a point unseen. At last he said, "You deem the Jaded Soul to be the green stone, aye?"

Arin nodded but did not speak.

"And to find it you need all the others named in the rede to go at your side . . . one of whom you believe is now with you: Aiko: the cat who fell from grace."

Again Arin nodded silently.

"And the one-eye in dark water you deem is either Alos or me, right?"

Alos groaned. "This talk of finding green stones and of Wizards and T-trolls—I'm not going!" Quickly he poured a mug of ale, slopping some onto the table in his haste. "The one-eye, it's Egil. Egil, y'hear. Not me. Egil's the one-eye you want."

"It could be this," said Aiko, stepping to Alos and thumping a tightly wrapped leather bag onto the table before him. "The rotting pierced eye of a Troll."

Alos shrieked and recoiled from the bag, and leapt up and bolted for the door, banging it open and stumbling out before any could stop him; and the measure of his desperation to be quit of this mad Elf and her yellow cohort was plain for all to see, for he had left his mug of ale behind and a nearly full pitcher as well.

* * *

"Aiko, that was unwarranted," said Arin. "Alos may be the one we need to obtain the green stone."

Unchastened, Aiko shook her head and gestured after the vanished old man. "Dara, for once I agree with that *fuketsuna yodakari:* Egil is the one we came here to find."

"We cannot be certain, Aiko. We cannot even be certain whether or no it is Alos or Egil or the Troll's eye we need."

Aiko sighed. "If it is your will, Dara, I shall fetch him."

Arin looked at the doorway, the door itself slowly swinging shut on its uneven hinges. She waved a negating hand. "Let be for now, Aiko. 'Tis plain to see he is frightened. Let him ponder it some days, then we shall see."

Aiko returned to her tatami mat, but she left behind on the table the bag holding the Troll's pierced eye.

"What is a, um, peacock?" asked Egil, looking up from his supper.

"A bird," replied Arin, "from far lands to the south and east. I have never seen one."

"I have," said Aiko. "They live in Ryodo and Chinga and Jûng . . . and in the islands to the south. They have long, iridescent green tail feathers which they can fan upright in brilliant display. Each feather is marked with an eye."

"An eye?"

"The likeness of."

"Oh," said Egil, stirring his spoon in his bowl of stew.

Arin waited, but Egil did not speak. At last she asked, "Hast thou a thought?"

Egil shook his head. "I just wondered what they were, for like you, I have not seen such a bird."

He fished up a spoonful of beef and sat in thought a moment, then tipped the meat back into the bowl. He got up from his bed and went to the window and looked out over the courtyard and downslope at the fjord beyond, two longships at dock. "The Queen of Jute," he said.

"What?" responded Arin.

Egil turned. "They say she is mad, my *engel,* just as was her ancestor."

"Mad? How?"

"I know not."

"What of her ancestor? Mayhap there lies a clue in the past."

Egil shrugged. "The tales say she once . . . um." Egil stopped, as if reluctant to speak further; his eyes were downcast in embarrassment.

"Say on," Arin urged. "Whatever thou knowest, I would hear."

Egil looked up at her, then took a deep breath and blurted, "They say she once took a horse to her bed."

Aiko raised one eyebrow skeptically as Egil turned back to the window, unwilling to meet Arin's gaze.

"Um," mumbled Egil to the windowsill. "There's even a chanty about it."

Aiko sighed. "Has it come to this, that we are to believe the ribald songs of sailors?"

"Many songs are rooted in truth," said Arin, then asked, "How old is this song?"

"Ancient," replied Egil. "That Queen of Jute is long dead. But they say that madness runs in families, especially in that royal line," responded Egil.

"Has there always been bad blood between Fjordlanders and Jutlanders?"

"Aye, but—"

"What is to say this is not but more bad blood?"

"Nothing, my *engel*. Nothing at all. . . . But true or no, rumor or no, she is the only mad monarch I have an inkling of." Egil turned and faced her again.

"Is there more?" asked Arin.

Egil shrugged. "Only this: they say animals roam in the royal gardens at the court of Jute, yet whether or no any of these are rutting peacocks, I cannot say."

Evening fell, and Egil slipped into slumber. And even though his fever was gone, once again in the middle of the night he suffered ill dreams.

Days passed and days more, and each day Egil's wounds were better than the day before. Every day, Thar came and watched as Arin laid poultices and medicks on

Egil's face and marveled at how fast he mended, swift by the healer's standards, slow by Egil's own.

Every day as well, members of the ship's crew came and visited awhile, including Captain Orri, who always brought laughter to the room.

But every night, Egil woke up weeping, calling out men's names.

There came a day, however, when he sat in a chair facing Arin and said, "My *engel,* I would tell you what I can of the vile Wizard Ordrune."

CHAPTER 33

I cannot . . . there is . . ." Struggling to speak, Egil shook his head, confusion in his eye. He took a deep breath and slowly let it out and stared down at his hands.

Arin drew her chair close, until she sat knee to knee with Egil.

He looked up at her and gritted, "I remember all he did to us in his tower, in his dungeons, in his . . . pits, but as to . . . concerning"—a look of fierce concentration drew over Egil's features—"the other . . . before . . . after." Egil slammed a fist onto open palm. "He stole thoughts. Took memories. Left confusion. Cursed me."

Remaining silent, Arin reached out and took his hand and gently unclenched his fist, and held it softly while smoothing out his fingers.

Egil watched, as if somehow detached from his own hand, yet slowly he relaxed. After a moment he took her fingers in his and lightly kissed each one. She lowered her eyes, and he released her, yet she did not draw away, but instead she reached out and took his hand again. They sat in still comfort, neither speaking. Through the open window they could hear the cook calling for the yard boy to bring more wood, while within the room there sounded only the whisper of whetstone against steel as Aiko sharpened her blades. At last Egil took a deep breath and slowly let it out, and then quietly, calmly, he began again. "This I do remember."

"Ragnar! Ragnar!" Egil scrambled down the slope toward his armsmate. The young man stopped and waited as Egil came scurrying. Egil dropped to the footpath, calling out, "We have it!"

Ragnar's eyes widened. "Your father's ship?"

Egil laughed hugely and shouted, "Yes!"

Ragnar whooped and clapped Egil on the shoulders. "By Garlon, at last! A ship of our own." Suddenly, Ragnar grew sober. "Your father, is he . . . ?"

"It's the ague. He can't seem to cast it off. But he said he didn't want to miss the raiding season altogether, so he gave me command of the ship. 'You are only twenty summers old, my son, yet I was no older when I built her. Besides, 'tis time to see if you can fly on your own.' That's what he said, Ragnar—fly on my own—and me with four unblemished raids under my belt. Ha! I'll show him just how well I can fly. I'll swoop like an eagle, my friend, for is it not my name?"

"*Hai,* Egil, like hawks and falcons and other such we'll all swoop down upon our prey, and no matter how they twist and turn we'll run them to ground." Ragnar paused, then said, "Your very own ship at last."

Egil grinned. "At least for one raid. Come, Ragnar, let us go look her over."

Egil and Ragnar set off down the path toward the docks below, where tethered was the *Sjøløper,* a modest ship by Fjordlander standards—being just seventy feet long and carrying but fifteen pairs of oars—yet to Egil and Ragnar she seemed the greatest of all the Dragonships sweeping across the seas.

They strode along her length, stepping over thwarts, examining the overlapping oaken strakes that yielded the hull its serpentine flexibility, causing the craft to cleave sharply through the waters, giving the ship a nimbleness beyond that which its narrow keelboard could bestow alone. They scrutinized the mast and unpacked the square sail from its protective tarpaulin, unfurling and inspecting the dyed cloth, along with the beitass poles. They checked the steerboard and each of the spruce oars racked amidships in oaken trestles, the oars trimmed to differing lengths so that when plied in short choppy strokes they would all strike the water simultaneously.

Having gone over the ship from stem to stern, Egil said, "She needs a minor bit of work, but the crew will make short shrift of that."

Ragnar leaned against a wale and looked out over the water as if to see lands afar. "When do we sail?"

"As soon as we can," replied Egil.

Ragnar now turned and leaned back, his elbows on the wale. "Where are we bound? What shores? Leut? Thol? Jute? Where?"

Egil shook his head. "Father says those places are already picked over. He suggests West Gelen."

"Ungh," groaned Ragnar, his face twisting sourly. "Fisher villages. We'll find naught but old men to fight and cod to win."

"My thoughts exactly, Ragnar. But you see, I have a plan."

"A plan?"

"Aye. To go where Fjordsmen have not been."

Ragnar cocked an eye at Egil. "Where?"

Egil glanced 'round. No one stood nearby, though a few lads fished from the end of the dock. He slipped his jerkin loose and reached under to take a flat oiled-leather pouch from his belt. From the packet he extracted a tattered fold of parchment, doubled over several times, and said, "I bought this from a seaman in Havnstad in Thol." Slowly he opened the parchment, fanning it out on a thwart. It was a map, rather large.

Ragnar's eyes widened as he scanned the unfamiliar shores. "Where are we going? What will we do?"

"What else, Ragnar, but raid, that's what: towns, towers, ships, villages—we are Fjordlanders! Wolves of the sea! As to where . . .? Here!" Egil stabbed a finger down on the map.

Egil and Ragnar rounded up a crew, mostly younger men, men of their age, men eager for adventure, for Egil would not reveal where he was bound, and many of the older warriors would not go without knowing the destination. Yet the young men had no qualms about setting out on a venture with nought more than the promise it would be exciting. Besides, Egil had named them Hawks of the Sea, though Young Wolves of the Sea would have been more accurate. Hence, with nought but promises of adventure and of deeds of derring-do and of fortune awaiting, Egil and his Hawks set sail on a midsummer's day, leaving behind a puzzle as to where he was headed, and only Egil's father knew whence ship and son were bound, a destination he kept to himself.

In the dark, moonless night, clouds covering the stars, the *Sjøløper* slipped through the blackness to come alongside the unwary craft, and Egil and his Hawks quietly clambered over the wales and up.

Filthy and athirst, with whips flailing against their backs, all the men stumbling in chains, Egil and his crew were driven along the twisting passageway through thick, stone bulwarks and into the courtyard beyond. Behind them, hinges shrieking, the massive main gate slowly swung to and slammed shut, and a huge bar ponderously rumbled across to thud home in a deep recess embedded in the high, buttressed ramparts. And with gears clattering and ratchets clacking and iron squealing, a mighty portcullis screeched downward in its track, its iron teeth grinding down to bottom out in deep socket holes drilled in the stone pave below.

Straight before the captives stood a large, dark building—the main hall—a hundred or more feet wide and three storeys high. To the left and against the stone bulwark were stables and a smithy and outbuildings. To the right, in the northwest corner and abutted against the wide ramparts stood a tall tower. Little of this did Egil get to see as he was shoved forward by his Drôkken guard, yet he saw enough to know that he and his Hawks were caged.

They were driven shuffling across the courtyard and into the large building and down, their chains rattling and manacles clacking, as down the narrow stairwell they floundered to come at last to the foul mews below.

"So, you are the captain of the raiders."

Egil remained silent.

The Mage turned from the window and stared at Egil. "And you would have the wealth of my ship?"

Again Egil said nothing.

"Fool," hissed the Mage.

Egil had been wrenched from the cell and shoved roughly up and across the courtyard and into the tower. Up a spiral stairwell round the walls he had been driven, two Drôkha and a swart man taking turns ramming a prod into his back, sniggering as they did so. They had driven him up the twisting stairs and into the room at the top, the room where awaited the Mage. Tall he was and gaunt and pale, with no hair whatsoever on his head— neither locks nor eyebrows nor lashes nor moustache nor beard. His nose was long and straight, and his eyes dark, obsidian, his lips thin and bloodless, and his fingers long and grasping and black nailed. He wore a bloodred robe.

This was the Mage whose ship Egil had boarded.

This was the Mage who had caused his defeat.

And now they stood in a room high atop the tower in the stronghold of the Mage, in the fortress where Egil and his crew had been dragged in fetters.

The Drôkha and the swart man had chained Egil to a ring in the floor and then had left him alone with his captor, and now Egil and the Mage faced one another— one silent, the other sneering.

"I am Ordrune, Captain. And your name . . . ?"

Egil said nought.

"Your silence is of no moment," said Ordrune. "I will have your name shortly. You will be eager to speak." The Mage turned aside and made his way across the room.

The chamber itself was completely circular, perhaps thirty feet in diameter, and here and there stood tables laden with arcane devices: astrolabes and geared bronze wheels and alembics and clay vessels, mortars and pestles, clear glass jars filled with yellow and red and blue and green granules, braziers glowing red . . . with tools inserted among the ruddy coals. Small ingots of metal lay scattered here and there: red copper, yellow brass, white tin, gleaming gold, argent silver, and more. And 'round the walls there were casks and trunks and cabinets of drawers and a great, ironbound, triple-locked chest, and desks with pigeon holes above, jammed with scrolls and parchments and papers. And four tall windows equipped with drapes were set in the stone at the cardinal points.

Elsewhere, tomes rested on stands; books resided on shelves. Here and there were chairs, equipped with writing flats, with pens and inks and vellum sheets alongside.

This was Ordrune's laboratory, his alchemistry, his arcane athenaeum. This was his lair. This was his den. This was the heart of the Wizardholt.

And here in the very core stood Egil, shackled to the floor, his own heart beating as Ordrune slipped a dark glove on a long-fingered hand and from among the fiery coals of a brazier he extracted a searing pair of tongs shimmering yellow with heat.

Ordrune turned and faced Egil. "Your name . . . ?"

Egil paled, but said nought.

A smile played about the corners of Ordrune's bloodless lips. "Fool." With his free hand he took up an ampoule and released a drop of liquid onto the blazing pincers, then stepped toward the young man, the tongs sizzling, sputtering, tendrils of smoke rising up.

"What better lesson can you learn than the one I teach you today?"

Egil braced himself, ready to fight, for even though he was shackled to the floor he had the freedom of movement to the end of his chain.

And then the smoke from the sizzling tongs reached him, and his will to fight vanished.

Ordrune stepped before him, raising the burning pincers to Egil's face. But suddenly Ordrune's lashless eyes widened in delight, and a smile creased his hairless face. He lowered the tongs. "What better lesson? Oh, my. I do have a better one, indeed."

Guards marched Egil down and out from the tower and across the courtyard to the main building, where he was allowed to bathe and groom himself and given clean clothes. Then, shackled once more, he was escorted down and through a labyrinth of passageways to a chamber. Circular it was, similar in dimension to the room atop Ordrune's turret, and so he deemed he was in an underground hold directly below the tower. There he was again manacled to the floor, yet this time he was set at a table piled with sumptuous foods and breads, with wines and pure water to drink.

Although round like the laboratory atop the spire, this room was no alchemistry, but a chamber of horror instead, for it held manacled tables and hanging, man-sized iron cages and fetters dangling down on chains and chairs equipped with leather straps, and tables aclutter with pincers and knives and mauls and screws and nails. There were slender, round wooden poles embedded in the floor, their upright sharp points and shafts stained rust red, as of dried blood. Braziers of burning coals, metal boots, wheeled racks, iron slabs like massive leaves of a book, and other such hideous instruments set 'round the walls. A large vat filled with a drifting liquid stood off to one side, and across the room, from behind an iron door barred with three massive iron beams there came the sound of slow monstrous breathing and the stench of carrion.

All this did Egil take in as he drank water and ate great chunks of bread and meat. "When at war, my boy," had said his father, "eat your fill every chance you get, for you never know when the opportunity will come 'round again." And so in spite of the putrid malodor, Egil, clean-bathed and -clothed, stuffed food down his gullet as he waited alone in silence.

Ordrune came first and then they dragged in filthy, disheveled Klaen, and the young man's eyes widened at the sight of his well-groomed captain sitting at feast. They shackled the Fjordland raider to a dark, thick slant-board, and Ordrune turned to Egil. "Where shall we start first, Captain? The hands? Oh yes, let's do."

Ordrune sauntered to a table and took up a massive hammer, then stepped to Klaen's side and held the spike-faced maul up before the young man's gaze. "I use this . . . tool to make meat tender for my"—he glanced at the barred door—"pet." Klaen's eyes filled with terror and a moan escaped his lips, and he struggled against his bonds, to no avail.

Egil leapt to his feet and called out, "Egil! My name is Egil."

Ordrune looked back at Egil and shook his head and

smiled. "Too late, I'm afraid, Captain Egil." Then he turned and smashed the hammer down on Klaen's shackled hand, the iron maul splintering bones as blood flew wide. *"No!"* shouted Egil, but his cry was lost under Klaen's shrieks of agony, the screams slapping and echoing 'round the chamber. And from behind the iron door came a snarling wail, and the door thudded, the beams rattling, as something monstrous slammed against it from within.

Laughing, Ordrune moved to the other side of Klaen, and once more showed the heavy hammer to the shrieking man, the maul now stained with blood, bits of flesh clinging to the dull spikes. Klaen's screams rang out hoarsely and again he struggled, and Egil shouted *"No!"* but Ordrune merely smiled and shattered the other hand. As the iron door thudded and rattled, Klaen's shrieks climbed in pitch, and then stopped altogether. He had fainted, and only moans leaked from his lips.

"Fear not, Captain Egil," said Ordrune as he moved toward a table, "for *this*"—he took up an ampoule—"will revive him, and then we, you and I, shall start on his feet."

Egil wept and pled and lost all the food he had eaten, as Ordrune slowly destroyed Klaen, breaking bones with the iron meat-hammer, working inward from the extremities, the young man shrieking in agony, Ordrune's vials keeping him awake and aware. And all the while something behind the iron door roared and smashed at it from within, as if some enormous caged monster were being driven mad with blood lust.

And when Klaen finally was dead, his broken body was carried by lackeys from the room, and moments later there came the grisly sound of something eating something behind the barred iron door.

If the top of the tower was the vile heart of the holt then the bottom of the tower was its foul soul, for over the next forty days, Egil witnessed the destruction of his entire crew: Bram, Argi, Ragnar, the others, all the young men who had followed him. By fire and knife and caustic potion, by rending and crushing and slow bleeding, by evisceration and impalement and other penetrations they died. One by one. One each day. Always with Egil now forcibly bathed and groomed and dressed and sitting before an extravagant meal.

And though Egil begged and groveled and told everything he knew, and confessed to all his transgressions and peccadilloes and misdeeds and vices, and beseeched Ordrune to spare the crew and kill him instead, Ordrune merely laughed . . . and the laughter did not cease.

Finally there was only Egil left.

They stood once more in the top of the tower, did Egil and Ordrune: Egil again shackled to the floor, Ordrune smiling at him from across the width of the room—but strangely, Ordrune was now more youthful than when last he and Egil had met here.

Egil shifted, his chains rattling, and he growled, "What are you waiting for, Wizard? Why don't you just kill me and get it over with?"

"Oh no, Captain Egil, would I waste all I have striven to teach you? Instead I intend to set you free, now that you have learned. Was that not a fine game we played . . . our pleasure enhanced by the power we gained? But wait, what is this? I see you are disappointed. Perhaps you believe the better lesson I promised you, the better lesson I gave you, will fade, will be forgotten." Ordrune laughed and stroked his now-younger cheeks and hairless chin. "Fear not, Captain Egil, you will *never* forget for as long as I live"—again Ordrune laughed—"and Mages live forever."

"Not if I have a say in it," gritted Egil. "There will come a day when I'll see you in the black fathoms below."

"Well, my lad, you are welcome to try, can you find this place, this tower. Yet even though free, I think you will be incapable of coming again to my fortress. I will see to that."

Ordrune turned to the table beside him and took up a vial, then looking at Egil he said, "Resist not, Captain Egil, for you cannot prevail."

* * *

Egil found himself wandering along the shores of

Gelen. How he had gotten there, he did not know. There were gaps in his mind—thoughts, memories, experiences taken away by Ordrune. He did, however, remember setting forth from Mørkfjord in the *Sjøløper,* but not where he had sailed. He remembered each and every man of the crew he had named his Hawks and the gleams in their eyes as they had joined his venture, but he remembered no raids, no plunder, no booty, nothing to live up to the promise of riches and fame that had drawn the young men to him. And he remembered boarding a certain ship to capture its wealth, but neither its kind nor the waters wherein he and the Hawks had slipped alongside. He remembered the Wizardholt and all he had seen therein, but not its whereabouts. And he remembered Ordrune, vile Ordrune, and the crew the Wizard had slaughtered . . . and the manner of their deaths. Of this he could not forget, for Ordrune had cursed him, and each and every night, he relived the hideous slaughter of one of the men, a different man each night, and always he woke up screaming.

Ill dreams, indeed.

He finally took berth on a merchanter out of the port of Arbor in Gelen, and he worked his way from ship to ship until he came to Fjordland. And when he rowed into Mørkfjord on a midsummer's day, four years had elapsed since he and the forty Hawks had set sail for glory and gold.

Yet none came home but him.

CHAPTER 34

Arin reached up to gently brush away Egil's tears as his tale came to an end. But he turned his head aside and wiped the heel of his hand across his cheek.

Arin sighed but said nought.

"In Ryodo," said Aiko, setting aside her sword, "we would have mounted a voyage of retribution."

Huskily, Egil cleared his throat. "Just as would we."

Arin frowned. "But thy memories of where thou had sailed were gone."

Egil nodded.

"Your father knew where you were bound," declared Aiko.

"My father died of the fever but a scant week after we left."

Arin reached out. "I am sorry, Egil."

Egil took her hand. "So am I. . . . So am I."

"What of the map?" asked Aiko. "Do you yet have it?"

Egil shook his head.

"Then the sailor you bought it from, does he—"

"No," interjected Egil. "I spent time in Havnstad searching for him, with no success. Some there thought he had died. Others said he sailed away and was never seen again. Still others placed him in the deep forests inland."

They sat without speaking for long moments, the only sound that of someone in the yard below saddling a horse. Aiko stood and stepped to the window and observed the stable boy taking one of their mounts out for its daily round of exercise. As he rode away, she turned and said, "Mayhap the Mages in Black Mountain can restore your memory just as they did Dara Arin's."

Arin's eyes widened. "Aye. Either there or in Rwn."

Egil looked from one to the other, then said, "They would have to know how to lift a curse."

The following day, with Healer Thar present, Arin again removed Egil's bandages and, after examination, said, "The herbs have done their work. The wound is mending well. We can forgo the swathing."

"Shall I remove the gut?" asked Thar.

"Aye."

In a trice, all the fine stitches were nipped and extracted, Thar working his way down the ruddy scar running from forehead to cheek. When he was finished—"Where is my patch?" asked Egil, fumbling 'round on the bed.

"Here," said Arin, taking the crimson leather from a pocket, the tiny golden image of Adon's Hammer centered upon the eye piece.

Egil called for a mirror, and as Aiko held it steady, he tied the band 'round his head. He looked at his reflection and said, "Now I am truly Egil One-Eye."

The next day Arin pronounced Egil fit to begin walking, and on that same day Egil moved out of the Blackstein Lodge and into the sod-roofed, stone house he had inherited from his father. A sevenday passed, with Arin and Thar monitoring his progress and treating Egil's scar with herbal ointments, and Arin and Aiko walking with him as he regained his strength, each day the Ryodoan choosing more and more difficult paths as they trekked across the slopes.

During the seventh of these rambles, as they trudged up toward the crest of a tor overlooking the fjord, Arin said, "We must set out soon to find the mad monarch's rutting peacock."

On Arin's left, Egil looked down at her diminutive form—she but four feet eight and he at five feet ten. "Then the time has come for us to sail for Jute, aye? To the court of the mad queen?"

Arin smiled up at him. "Then thou dost plan on going with us?"

Egil glanced out at the deep, black fjord. "Is it not so that I am one-eye in dark water?"

"Forget not Alos."

In the lead, Aiko growled. "Alos is a runaway coward, Dara."

"Nevertheless, Aiko," said Arin, "we know not for certain who or what the rede refers to: it could be Egil or Alos, either or both . . . or neither."

Aiko sighed. "These are my thoughts, Dara: Egil is a warrior. He knows of a mad monarch. He fits the words of the rede. He is willing to go. All of these point to the fulfillment of the words of your vision. But Alos . . . he is a coward. He is a drunkard. He has fled in fear. He does not want to go."

Aiko fell to silence, but Arin replied, "Thou hast left one fact amiss, Aiko: Alos fits the words of the rede. And if we are to succeed, I would rather he join our quest until we are certain as to his role, if any, in finding the Dragonstone."

Again Aiko growled, muttering, *"Fuketsuna yodakari yopparai!"*

They walked a moment in silence, then Egil said, "There is another thing to consider."

Arin looked at Egil. "Another?"

Egil cleared his throat. "Actually, two things."

"And they are . . .?"

"First, I also know of Ordrune, and he was in Black Mountain when the Dragonstone first came. He left. The Dragonstone disappeared. Are these mere coincidences? I think not."

Arin turned up her hands. "Yet we know not that he took the green stone, that he has it."

Egil gritted his teeth. "He is vile, and if any would seek the owner of the stone, it is he."

"Hai!" barked Aiko, stopping, turning to face Arin. "This, Dara, is why we were to come to Mørkfjord. This is why Egil is the one-eye in dark water."

Arin stared at the Ryodoan. "Explain."

Aiko grinned at Egil. "He must be right: Ordrune *must* have the Dragonstone, the Jaded Soul. The Mage seeks to master the power of the stone, and when he has done so he will muster the warrior nation of Moko and conquer the world, as their prophecy ordains. But we strive to prevent such a calamity by following the words of your vision, the words of your rede. That is, after all, why we are in Mørkfjord. Why else would the rede lead us here if not to find Egil? I deem it is because Egil has been in Ordrune's strongholt and can lead us to the stone."

"But he knows not where that strongholt lies," protested Arin.

Aiko raised a finger. "Yes, Dara, but perhaps that is a task for one of the others of the rede."

Arin's eyes flew wide at Aiko's suggestion but narrowed again. "And if not . . . ?"

"Then again I say, there are always the Mages of Black Mountain; they recovered *your* lost memories, and perhaps can do the same for Egil."

Egil, who had remained silent, said, "But what if they cannot lift the curse Ordrune laid upon me?"

Arin shook her head, voiceless, but Aiko turned to Egil and said, "If not, they have a great map inscribed on a huge globe. By gleams of light and dark, it shows where each and every Mage dwells. Surely one of these glimmers is Ordrune."

Arin nodded. "Given what Egil has said, a dark glint I would deem."

"How many dark glints are there?" asked Egil.

Both Aiko and Arin shrugged, and Arin said, "An ample number. If we resort to this, it will be a long search against a formidable foe—they are Mages, after all, dark in their deeds and power."

"Then let us hope that your peacock or ferret or keeper of faith knows the way instead," said Egil.

"Mayhap Alos knows," said Arin.

Now it was Aiko's eyes that flew wide open.

They came to the crest of the tor overlooking the steep notch of the fjord, the deep black waters lying in the sun of the long summer day like a ribbon of obsidian, an ebon road 'round far bends to the distant unseen sea. A gentle breeze blew west to east, carrying the tang of salt on its wings, and the grass all around rippled like water. Aiko stepped down the hillside and knelt in the sward and plucked a pale yellow flower from among the green blades, but Arin and Egil stood on the crown, facing the breeze, surveying the whole of the world, the high blue sky above them bright and cloudless and pure . . . and time itself seemed to pause. Egil reached out and took Arin's hand, and she did not draw away, but stood with him side by side . . . wishing.

At last Arin took a deep breath and released it in a long sigh, then turned to Egil. "Would that this could last forever, but Fortune and Fate have decreed elsewhere."

"The quest," said Egil.

"Aye, Egil, the quest."

Arin faced west once again and they stood a moment more, sharing the comfort of one another, their thoughts running in parallel. Without turning, Arin said, "Thou didst say there were two reasons thee should join the hunt, yet thou named but the first. What is the second?"

Egil turned the Dylvana toward him and looked down at her, his blue gaze soft, gentle. "Just this, my *engel:* now that I have found you, quest or no, I would ask to ever stay at your side."

Momentarily, a range of emotions flickered across her face, as if warring with one another.

"Is something wrong?" asked Egil.

She looked at the ground. "Three things."

"And they are . . . ?"

Now Arin looked him directly in the eye. "First, thou art a raider."

"What does that have to do with my loving you?"

"Nought, Egil. But it does have to do with *my* love for *thee.*"

"I do not understand, Arin. We have always been raiders. It is an honorable profession among Fjordlanders."

"Dost thou not see? What thou and thy kind do is plunder that which others' labors have won. It is an evil thing."

"But we only raid our enemies."

"Is that what thou wert doing: raiding thine enemies when thou and thy Hawks sailed off to go where no Fjordsmen had been?"

Pain momentarily flashed in Egil's gaze, and he looked down at his feet. "Oh."

"Do not take me wrong, Egil, long apast when we were yet mad the Elven race did such things as raid merely for spoils. Yet there came a time when one of the very wisest of our leaders stood before his people and said, 'It is unjust to steal from one another, regardless of tradition and enmity. I shall plunder no more.'

"There was a great uproar among Elvenkind, and many protested, crying out, 'But they have done wrong by us. What of our own revenge?'

"And he replied, 'Raiding for vengeance is one thing; raiding for spoils another. If there is ever to be peace among Elvenkind, let it begin with me.'

"Oh, Egil, there is much more to this tale, and millennia passed ere the wisdom of his words was finally realized by all. And many believe it was because of him the madness finally passed away from my people—the evil withered on the vine—for he was the first, the very first who said, 'Let it begin with me.' "

"But you still seek vengeance."

"Aye, in a just cause. But even here, someday, perhaps, someone will say, 'Let it begin with me.' "

Silence fell between them, but at last Egil said, "I take it then, because of your beliefs, that you cannot live with a raider—one who plunders for spoils."

Arin nodded.

Egil sighed and looked away, his one-eyed gaze lingering long on Mørkfjord, but at last he said, "Then let it begin with me."

Arin smiled, yet doubt still lingered deep within her eyes, and Egil said, "That was but one of your reasons, my love, and you said there were three. What is the second?"

"Thou art human; I am Elf. I cannot bear thee any children."

Egil's eye widened.

"We are barren with one another—our two races cannot mix," added Arin.

"I do not understand," said Egil.

"Thou art from the Middle Plane, from Mithgar; I am from the High Plane, from Adonar. Elves can neither sire nor bear young on Mithgar; just as humans cannot sire nor bear young on Adonar. Some claim that the Fates have ruled it so. Others ascribe it to those who stand above Adon or Gyphon or aught others of the gods."

Egil shook his head. "Then it is true: there are those who rule even the gods?"

"Aye. And perhaps it is they who have decreed that human and Elf shall bear no young. Yet whether it is the gods, the Fates, a force of nature, or aught else, the fact remains that I can bear thee no child."

Egil frowned and fell into thought. Then he took a deep breath and said, "Often the men of my people fall in battle, leaving children behind. At times mothers fall ill and die. But these youngers do not grow up fatherless, motherless, for others take them in. They are loved no the less for being of other's blood. I was a foundling myself—my true parents unknown—but I was taken in and my new father and mother cherished me as if I were their own. They were barren with one another, yet our home was filled with love. We can do the same, Arin, should we find we want younglings underfoot."

Slowly Arin nodded, and Egil said, "That was two, my love. What is the third reason?"

Arin interlaced her fingers, gripping so tight that her knuckles paled to bone whiteness, and she stared down at the ground. "Thou art mortal; I am not."

Confusion filled Egil's face, but he reached out and covered her hands with his, finding her trembling. "Again I ask: what does that have to do with my loving you?"

"Just this: thou wilt grow old while I stay as I am, and when thou dost die as must all mortal things, it will shatter my heart."

"Were I one of your kind, could I not die?"

Arin nodded. "Aye, thou couldst be slain in battle or die in a number of other ways. Yet—"

"Then, love, let us savor the days we have and let tomorrow fend for itself."

Arin looked at the ground. "Egil, even should we both survive this quest, there is a chance that thou wilt come to resent what I am, as age grips thee but touches me not."

"Oh, my *engel,* how could you think I would ever resent you? You are my beloved."

Again, a range of emotions flickered across her face, warring with one another. And just as suddenly they disappeared, as if one or many had surrendered. With her heart in her eyes, Arin reached up and took his face in her hands and drew him down to her and gently kissed him on the lips, and Egil's own heart leapt within him, soaring into the high blue sky. And he scooped her up in his arms and spun about, laughing. And in that moment—

"*Sate!*" called Aiko, her arm outstretched, pointing.

With Arin yet in his arms, Egil turned to look. Down in the fjord, heaving into view 'round a turn in the distance came a ship.

"Is it a raider?" asked Arin.

Egil laughed. "No, my love; the lookouts sounded no horns of warning. Instead 'tis a Rianian carrack, a merchanter bearing wines and cheeses, salt and spices, trinkets and baubles, weapons and armor, and other trade goods. There will be a celebration in Mørkfjord tonight." He embraced her tightly and then set her to her feet and grinned and said, "It is an omen of our troth, decreed by those above the gods themselves."

Aiko came to the crest of the tor to stand beside them. And as they watched the craft slowly make its way along the dark waters of the fjord, Arin said, "Dost thou think we can take passage on such a ship unto Jute?"

Egil barked a laugh. "If so, it would be a long, slow ride. Better we ask Orri to take us there, when he returns."

"Nay, Egil," said Arin. "I would come unto Jute on a ship of peace rather than a raider's rig."

"The Jutlander queen's court is in Königinstadt, along the coast. We could slip ashore at night."

Again Arin shook her head. "Rather would I come announced unto this mad monarch than to scurry ashore in the dark, for I would enter her court invited, not in secret."

"But they say she's mad."

"Nevertheless, she is queen of a nation at peace with the High King. Hence, 'tis better we come in the open—and expected—than to be discovered skulking in the night."

Egil sighed and nodded. "As you wish, love. But tell me, my *engel,* how do you propose to garner an invitation?"

Arin turned to him and smiled and shrugged. "On such a ship as that one below, we will have time to think of aplan, neh?"

Egil laughed. "Aye. That we will. And though I would rather slip over the wall and snatch away the mad monarch's rutting peacock, there is much to say for your methods. Yet whatever plan we devise must succeed quickly, for I do not wish to spend a jot more time than necessary in any mad monarch's view. Hence, if it were up to me, I would simply grab the peacock and run—it is the raiders' way."

Arin laughed and then sobered. "One-eye in dark water. Mad monarch's rutting peacock. I do hope we follow the correct path."

Egil pointed to his crimson patch. "Love, you have me, and so that line of the rede is now fulfilled."

Arin sighed. "Mayhap, Egil, mayhap. Yet deep in my soul I feel Alos may have a part to play."

Aiko, who had remained silent, muttered something under her breath, then turned to Arin. "He is an old man. He is a drunkard. He is a coward. He would do nought but hinder us. Nevertheless, Dara Flameseer, would you have me find him and ask him again to join the quest? He will just run away screaming."

"What does thy tiger say?"

"On matters such as these, she is silent."

"I could talk to him," rumbled Egil.

Arin sighed. "We simply must find a way to convince him to come."

Egil puffed out air between his pursed lips and cast a glance at Aiko, then said, "Let us go down and see where next the carrack is bound. Perhaps indeed, it will bear us to Jute."

The two-masted ship was the *Gyllen Flyndre,* out of the port of Ander in northern Rian along the Boreal Sea. Her master was Captain Holdar. He had sailed along Fjordland, making port in town after town, where he had traded ship's goods for furs. Mørkfjord was the last Boreal Sea port he would call on, after which he was bound for the walled city of Chamer on the east coast of Gelen, where he would sell the furs for a handsome profit.

Holdar rubbed his ruddy jaw, then said, "I'll not stop in Jute, milady, but if you've a boat we'll lade her aboard— or tow her ahind—and set you free in the waters nigh."

Arin glanced at Egil. "Is there a small craft we can purchase?"

"I think I know of a ship," answered Egil. "One I can handle alone, though 'twould be better with a crew of two or three."

"Aiko and I can learn."

Aiko cocked an eyebrow, but Egil grinned and said, "Aye, that you can. But first let's see if she's still up for grabs for a coin or two." He stood and stepped to the bar.

Captain Holdar shook his head. "I'd not be going to Jute, Lady Arin, if I were you, and that's my sound advice. The queen, they say she's mad; just how, I don't know." He turned to Aiko. "But this I do know, yellow lady: if I were you, I'd steer clear of her court, for they say she likes to collect exotic things—birds, animals, creatures, whatever, people not the least—and I'll wager she's not seen the likes of you, what with your golden skin. Why, she's like to throw you into a cage, I wouldn't wonder. But, oi, I've no need to travel those ports, and of that I'm glad, yea, what with the furs along this coast and the good market in Gelen—and here's to Chamer hats and muffs and coats and such." Holdar hoisted his mug of ale, then took a great swallow.

A short while later Egil returned. "Tryg says Orri still owns the sloop he doesn't want, a small knockabout some thirty feet long—won it as a prize on a raid in Gothon."

Holdar hoisted his tankard again. "Then we'll tow her ahind, laddie buck, yea, for she's too long to lade . . . though I might say, a little sloop like that, she could be faster than my carrack. You might want to sail her instead, yes? . . . if your business in Jute be urgent, that is."

Egil shook his head. "I think not, Captain Holdar. The Boreal is no place for such a craft with an untrained crew. We'll take the *Flyndre* instead, and drop off nigh Jute."

* * *

Later that same day, Orri's wife, Astrid, bartered the sloop to Arin for her horses, glad to be rid of the craft. "All we did was keep it up. 'Twasn't useful in Orri's trade, him with his longship and all. The horses, now, we can use them to travel inland to see my kith, though Orri's likely to balk a bit at visiting those he'd rather not."

The sloop bore the name *Brise,* a Gothonian word none there knew the meaning of.

The long summer twilight fell, then darkness, and the citizenry of Mørkfjord continued its celebration of the arrival of the *Gyllen Flyndre,* while Arin and Egil held hands and were the recipients of many a stare. At long last, Egil retired to his stone cottage. Late in the night, Arin lifted his latch and slipped into his bed.

The next morning the new lovers awoke to find Aiko outside, resting on her tatami, her back against the door, her swords unsheathed and lying across her lap.

A week later the *Gyllen Flyndre* set sail towing the sloop behind, the small craft's canvas furled, her hatches battened tightly, her hold filled with stores.

Aboard the carrack, Arin, Egil, and Aiko leaned against the taffrail and looked down at her, the *Brise* bobbing aft on a long pair of ropes in the wake of the *Flyndre.*

Through the long notch of the fjord, the carrack made her way toward the sea, riding outward on the morning wind and tide. Finally they came to the open waves, the Boreal calm on a summer's morn, a splendid day for sailing, though with this ocean one could never tell, the Boreal perhaps the most fickle of waters in all the world.

Southwesterly they turned, a mile or so out from land, following along the coast, the braw wind bearing them at a goodly clip through the slow rolling swells.

Arin took a deep breath of the salt air, then said, "On our way at last, we three, toward the court of the mad queen. I only regret—"

The remainder of her words fell unspoken, for in that same moment hoarse raw screams erupted from the cabins below. In a flash, Aiko's swords were in her hands and she leapt down from the poop deck to the deck below, Egil on her heels, his Fjordlander axe at the ready, Arin coming last, her long-knife in its sheath.

And the screams crescendoed upward in pitch, upward in horror, as unremitting terror gripped a tortured soul.

CHAPTER 35

As sailors on deck turned toward the sound of the screams, Aiko flung open the door to the aft quarters. In the dimness at the far end of the hallway, she saw a shadowy form scramble down a rear ladder toward the holds below, taking the shrieks with it. To the right, one of the cabin doors swayed to and fro, the tiny quarters empty.

" 'Ware!" called Egil, but, gripping her swords, Aiko plunged after, the pommels of the weapons clattering on the rungs as she clambered down. Egil followed, with Arin close after.

They came into the crew's quarters, and men, startled, were looking in the direction the yowling form had fled. Their heads swiveled around as Aiko darted past, then Egil and Arin. "Oi, naow, what's all this—?" called out a crewman, but his words were left behind as down another ladder plunged the trio, chasing after the screamer.

Now they came into a darkened hold, and among the bales of furs they could hear a blubbering and hissing, a voice sissing out in a loud whisper, "The bilge. The bilge. They'll never look there. Never." Then—"Eee! Eee! Trolls! They're coming! They're coming! They're going to get me! Yaaaaa . . .!" and horrified shrieking filled the air once again.

Egil freed a hanging lantern from its short chain and used the striker to light it. Then holding it high in his left hand, his axe in his right, he followed Aiko toward the screams—which suddenly stopped, to be replaced by a sobbing and scrabbling sound.

They rounded a pile of bales to find a man on all fours scratching at the deck planking and sobbing and babbling to himself, "The bilge, the bilge, get into the bilge." He was a dirt-streaked, disheveled old man, who looked up at them with a blind white eye, his mouth stretched wide in fear, lips pulled back from brown-stained teeth.

It was Alos.

He shrieked and scrambled back from them, his arm outstretched to hold them at bay, all the while howling, "Trolls! Trolls! Eee . . .!"

As sailors swarmed down the ladder behind, Arin, her long-knife now in hand, snapped, "Aiko, what says thy tiger?"

Aiko shook her head. "Nothing," she growled. "Nothing at all." With a flip of her wrists, Aiko reversed her grips on the pommels and sheathed her swords, then stepped toward Alos.

The old man's eyes flew wide with terror. "Eeee—" he shrilled, then clapped both hands across his mouth to stifle his own screams, and squeaking and sissing he scuttled backward into the shadows and away, seeking refuge in the darkness among the bales.

"What d'ye think she be?"

"I dunno, Cap'n," replied thirty-year-old Alos, helmsman of the *Solstråle,* a merchant kravel out of the port of Havnstad in Thol. "Ne'er seen a thing like her."

Astern, a dark ship, long and slim and driven by both wind and oars, continued to draw closer, her black hull cleaving the waters and her dusky sails bellyed full.

"She looks to be a two master, Cap'n," added Alos, shading his eyes against the setting sun, bloodred on the horizon. "But her sails, wing-on-wing . . . huh, they both have the look of our mizzen."

Captain Borkson grunted and nodded. "Lateens, lad, both main and fore . . . like a ship o' th' southern seas. What a southern ship'd be doing in th' Boreal . . ."

Alos shook his head. "Southern may be her sails, Cap'n, but her oars, well now, I'd think they be northern—Fjordlander or Jute. D'ye reck' she's one o' them, fitted up with new riggin'?"

"Well, what e'er she be," said Jarl, the *Solstråle's* first bo's'n, "she be o'ertakin' us. A full eight candlemarks ago she stood on th' rim, and now she be halfway here. I make it she be runnin' near two knots faster than we."

"Aye, that she be," replied Borkson, "an' I nae like th' look o' her. Alos, fall off t' th' larboard, four points. We'll see if she j'st hap's t' be on th' same course or 'stead be tryin' t' o'erhaul us. Jarl, pipe th' riggin' t' make th' most o' th' wind."

"Aye aye, Cap'n," replied Alos, spinning the wheel as Jarl piped the signals to the crew.

The *Solstråle* heeled over as the ship swung to larboard, and the crew trimmed the sails to catch the wind now quartered off the port stern.

Moments later the black ship heeled over as well, her lateens now both set to starboard, her oars stroking the sea.

"Jarl, run up th' pennons askin' her t' identify hersel'."

Jarl piped the crew and signal flags were lofted. As the pennants ran skyward on the halyard, Alos said, "If she's a southerner, Cap'n, she might not know the Boreal codes."

Borkson did not reply . . . and neither did the black ship, and the wind in her sails and beat of her oars did not slacken.

"I think she still be o'erhaulin', Cap'n. Four miles astern, I gauge," said Jarl.

"Run up our own colors, Jarl," said Borkson.

As the sun set, again Jarl piped the crew, and the blue-and-yellow flag was lofted into the gathering twilight.

But still the black ship gave no indication of her identity, and her oars churned against the water.

"She be haulin' us in like a fish on a spindle, Cap'n, a fish t' be gaffed, I might add," said Jarl.

"Jarl, pipe th' officers t' th' poop, helmsmen, too."

Moments later, the bo's'ns and mates and helmsmen gathered 'round the captain. Hearing the signal as well, other members of the crew drifted up to the main deck, where seamen on duty pointed out the dark ship astern, her dusky sails silhouetted against the lavender sky.

After briefing the officers and helmsmen, Borkson said, "Here be my plan, gentlemen: we run on this course until full night falls, then we'll bring th' *Solstråle* hard astarboard to run a beam reach. In th' dark th' black one astern will nae be able t' see our extreme course change. Therc being no moon this darktide, we should gi'e her th' slip."

First Mate Sigurson glanced at the darkening sky, then raised his hand and, at a nod from the captain, said, "I judge it now be four candlemarks till full night. How close will she be when we make our turn?"

"I judge a mile, more or less," replied Borkson.

"Let us hope it be more than less," said Jarl, sotto voce, which brought chuckles to all lips.

Smiling and confident, Borkson said, "Spread th' word among th' crew, and ha'e them douse all light, then stand by until we're well away frae th' dark ship aft. And tell 'em t' be quiet as hold mice, for I'd nae ha'e rattle nor clack nor blather gi'e us away in th' dark."

Looking aft, Alos, his heart pounding, watched the dusky sails against the ever darkening twilight sky, the helmsman no longer able to see the black ship's hull against the waters of the Boreal Sea as she slowly drew closer. Some three candlemarks passed and stars glimmered erc he lost sight of her altogether, yet he could now hear the pulsing beat of a distant drum measuring out the strokes of her oars. Another candlemark passed and the drum grew louder, like the thud of an ominous heart, and lo! he espied luminous swirls in the water where the oars churned the brine.

"Stand ready," hissed the captain to bo's'n and helmsman, and as Jarl, unthinking, raised his pipe to his lips, Borkson said, "Nay, Jarl, I'll ha'e no pipes gi'e us away. Trim th' sails by word o' mouth, and in whispers at that."

Word was passed and the men stood by, and at last Captain Borkson gave the order "Hard over," and when the crew felt the ship begin to heel to the tiller, they haled the lines and swung the yards on the mizzen, main, and foremasts to bring the ship 'round twelve full points to set the wind direct on the starboard beam and make the most of it.

As the ship came to her new heading, Alos straightened the wheel and breathed a sigh of relief. But then, from aft, mingled with the drumbeat, he heard sinister laughter floating over the waves. Holding the wheel steady, Alos glanced rightward out over the sea toward the position of the dark pursuer, and of a sudden, a greenish glow enveloped the rigging of the black ship. Alos sucked air in through his teeth and gasped, "Adon!"

"Witchfire," sissed Sigurson, the first mate standing at hand. "Cap'n, she be burnin' with witchfire."

"Th' better for us t' see—" began Borkson, but then he broke off.

"Cap'n," hissed Alos, "she's turning on our—"

Suddenly, the *Solstråle*'s own rigging flashed into witchfire flames, the ethereal luminance writhing over masts and yards, halyards, lanyards, ratlines, and the like. A collective wail from the crew of the *Solstråle* moaned up to the sky, and men covered their eyes to be shut of the sight of the ghastly glow.

Harsh laughter sounded across the water, and the tempo of the drum increased, and the black ship, her oars churning, her rigging burning, haled closer with each stroke.

"Cap'n, what'll we do?" cried Alos, his voice tight with fear.

"Sigurson, break out th' weapons," snapped Captain Borkson, "arm th' men."

"But Captain," protested Sigurson, gesturing at the rigging above and then aft, "the witchfire, the black ship, she's got to have a Wizard aboard. How can we—?"

"I said, arm th' men," snarled Borkson. "She'll no take us wi'out a fight."

As the first mate scrambled down the ladder to obey, the captain turned and scanned the ship aft. "She'll be on us in a candlemark or two, lads. Be prepared t' swing her t' larboard or starboard, Alos. Jarl, ha'e th' men stand ready. We'll gi'e her a run for it."

"Aye, Cap'n," replied Jarl. Then, "Oh, Adon. Look. On th' poop of th' black ship."

Alos turned and looked as well, and his heart leapt into his throat and he groaned in fear, for there on the fantail of the ship stood a form flaming with witchfire, his dark robes burning blue-green. It looked to be a man . . . yet deep in his shuddering bones, Alos knew it had to be a

Mage. And the drum pounded and oars slashed down and through and up and back to its pulsing beat.

"Galley," hissed the captain. "I now remember. I ha'e heard o' these. Old ships, ancient ships, from realms far away—but I ne'er thought t' see one." He turned to Alos and Jarl. "We'll ha'e t' be nimble and stay off her bow, for 'tis told they bear rams."

"Rams?" Alos moaned.

"Aye, lad. Great underwater beaks. They'll hole our hull. Sink us down. We got t' stay clear."

His frightened face illumined by the witchfire in the rigging above, a sailor bearing blades came clattering up the ladder. "Y'r sword, sir." He handed the captain a saber, then falchions to Alos and Jarl.

His breath whistling in and out through clenched teeth, his heart hammering wildly, Alos took the falchion and slipped it through his belt.

Now the black ship, its rigging alight, was only three furlongs astern, drum pounding . . . then two furlongs, oars stroking . . . one furlong, laughter echoing across the waters . . . then directly astern.

"Oh, Adon, Cap'n," moaned Jarl, "they're Rutcha. Th' crew is Rutcha."

"And Drôkha," added the captain, grinding his teeth. " 'Tis a Foul Folk craft."

Black-fletched arrows whistled through the air, thunking into ship's wood or slashing through canvas sails, but one took Jarl through the neck, and he fell backward, dead before striking the deck.

Now the black galley pulled to the starboard, edging alongside. "Hard alarboard," shouted Borkson, snatching up Jarl's pipe and signaling the crew.

Gasping in fear, Alos spun the wheel leftward as the crew pulled the halyards 'round, and slowly the helm began to answer, but then the ship lost headway as the broad lateen sails of the galley sliced across the flow of air to the kravel.

"She's got our wind, Cap'n!" cried Alos. "The black ship has stolen our wind!"

"Bring her about!" shouted the captain, raising the bo's'n's pipe to his lips and sounding the signal, yet in that same moment—*thnk! chnk!*—grappling hooks thudded over the wales, and the black galley, her drum silent and her oars now shipped aboard, began to wrench the kravel to her side.

"Repel boarders!" shouted the captain, drawing his saber. But then, "Oh, Adon, Trolls."

In the light of the witchfire and clambering up to the main deck of the black galley from the rowing deck below came behemoth Trolls. The men of the *Solstråle* cried out in fear, some leaping overboard in their panic, while others fell to their knees. And on the stern of the dark ship, the Wizard, glowing with ghastly flames, laughed in malevolent glee.

As Trolls clambered across the wales from galley to kravel, Alos, shrieking, abandoned the wheel and sprang down from the poop deck and bolted through the aft cabin door. Howling in panic, he fled along the passageway and scrambled down the aft ladder and forward through the crew's quarters and down a second ladder and into the holds below. Sternward he ran, along the planked aisleway and among the piled barrels and crates and bales, Alos weeping and hissing, whining to himself, "Hide in the bilge. They'll never find you there. Hide in the bilge, the bilge."

Sissing, moaning, he started down through the stern trap to the bilge below, but the falchion in his belt snagged on the rim. As shrieking and bellowing and screams of terror came from above, Alos hurled the weapon away into the darkness, the blade tumbling and clattering along the plank aisle. And then he was down and through, slamming the trap behind.

On his belly, Alos slithered through putrid bilge water across ballast stones, groaning and crawling toward the bow, away from the trapdoor aft, his breath coming in harsh gasps, whines and grunts and moans leaking from his lips. At last he fetched up against a thwart and could crawl no farther.

Panting, hissing, lying in water sloshing over the round rocks, still he heard the sound of chaos adeck. Then footsteps clattered down from above as someone else fled into the hold. "Don'tcomehere, don'tcomehere, don'tcomehere," Alos gibbered and hissed through clenched teeth, trying to remain silent, emitting tiny squeaks instead. Then a ripping and rending of timber sounded, followed by a hideous roar, and a voice in the hold shrieked in terror, panicked footsteps running along the plank walkway. There came a massive thud, as if something had dropped into the hold from the deck above, followed by the sound of ponderous footfalls overtaking the ones fleeing.

"Ygahhh!" shrilled the man, and his footsteps ceased, then he howled and howled and howled, as if in the clutches of a monster who lifted him up.

The massive thumping treads came back along the walkway, bringing the screaming along with it. Yet, suddenly, there was a horrid roar and the snapping of metal. Then there sounded a hideous cracking of bones, and the screaming stopped, followed by a sodden thud as something fell to the planks. Now there was a heavy, deep grunting and moaning as the ponderous footsteps began again, but this time unevenly, as of a monster limping.

Blue-green light leaked down through a chink in the planking above Alos's head, and puffing and sissing, clenching his fists and teeth, trembling uncontrollably, Alos raised up and peered with one eye through the gap overhead, trying to see.

There in the dimness above, down the walkway a monstrous bulky form loomed darkly, approaching, faltering, as if lame, groaning with every other step as it hobbled toward the witchfire light shining through the rent-open hatchway to the deck above. Alos could see it was a Troll, and he started to scream, but he clamped both hands across his mouth, stifling the sound. And then the monster's injured foot—the right foot, the foot that had stepped on a thrown-away falchion that had somehow become wedged in a crack in the dark, the foot that had borne the whole of the Troll's weight on the sharp point of the blade—that foot came down directly above Alos's upturned face, and a dark ichor that burned like fire plopped into one of Alos's fright-wide eyes.

His hands still pressed across his mouth, Alos shrilled through his nose in agony, and he pulled his right hand away and frantically clawed at the eye. Yet the caustic burning drove deeply into the socket, into his skull. In unbearable anguish, Alos jerked down and away, rolling over and plunging his face into bilgewater. And as he shrieked, bilgewater bubbling, and raked underwater at his eye, the groaning Troll above, unheeding, clambered back to the deck.

Time passed, and more time, and at last the shrieking above ceased, though there were yet moanings and weepings, as of men captured by Trolls.

Below in the bilge, Alos trembled and waited in silence, his right eye yet in torment, though the water had washed some of the fire away, and again and again he submerged his face in bilgewater to try to relieve the burn.

Finally, feet clattered down the ladderway—not the ponderous treadings of Trolls but lighter steps, instead— and he could hear voices speaking in a tongue he did not understand. *Rutcha and Drôkha? Are they looking for me?* Again Alos clamped his hands across his mouth, sealing in his whimpers and whines, and he shrank back against the thwart, waiting for them to find him, waiting for his doom, wishing he had a weapon, wishing he now had his cast-off falchion, somewhere on the walkway above. *If I had my falchion and someone came after me, I could kill them in silence and be safe.* And he wept for his hurled-away blade. But the Foul Folk were not searching for Alos; they had come for the cargo instead. Grunting and swearing, they moved the barrels and crates toward the hatch, where Trolls lifted it to the deck above.

After a time, the Spawn left the hold behind, clambering up ladders and away. Alos could hear distant shouts and the beat of the drum, but these sounds, too, faded away, leaving silence after. Still Alos cowered in the bilge, trembling, weeping, moaning, his right eye filled with pain, and in the quiet the empty ship slowly rocked, swaying in the waves, the bilgewater sloshing to and fro across Alos.

But then he again heard the beat of a drum, drawing closer and closer still.

They're coming back to get me!

Alos whined and gibbered and wept into his hands.

Suddenly, with a horrendous crash, a great brass beak crashed through the side of the ship, timber splintering, water gushing inward after. Alos shrieked in fear, and tried to scramble hindward, but the thwart stopped him. Outside, the drum pounded and with a groaning and screeching the brass beak ponderously withdrew, the waters of the Boreal Sea thundering inward through the breech left behind.

Beneath the planking of the bottom deck Alos howled in terror, and choking, coughing, half strangling, he clawed his way across ballast rocks toward the distant stern, fighting through whelming torrents, attempting to reach the bilge trap. But the ship settled and Alos was plunged completely underwater, yet he clawed onward.

Again the brass ram crashed through the hull of the foundering *Solstråle* and judderingly withdrew, and more water thundered inward to flood the hold. The ship slowly canted sternward in prelude to its a final plunge downward.

Underwater, Alos finally reached the trap and was up and through, yet the hold was nearly full, but he swam straight up and into a trapped pocket of air. Coughing, gasping, he had only time for a breath or two before the pocket vanished under the rising brine. Now he swam toward where he thought the hatchway would be, and just as it seemed he could swim no more, he popped through. The canted decks were awash, the stern fully submerged, the *Solstråle* plunging fast. And as the ship went under, Alos was pulled down by the suck of the undertow. Down he was dragged and down, into the nightdark Boreal Sea, and though he tried to swim, he could not defeat the pull. And when the suck at last vanished, Alos drifted in the depths, spent, stunned, not knowing or caring which way the surface lay. But something slammed into him from below, and he was borne upward again. And tangled in wrack he came once more to the crest of the sea.

Overhead stars gleamed, remote and diamond cold, and of the black ship there was no sign.

* * *

Two days later a Fjordlander Dragonship fished Alos from the waters. They found him clinging to a shattered spar, nearly drowned and suffering from thirst, his right eye blind and burned and filmed over white. And he screamed when he saw the longship's oars and heard the stroke-drum sound. He gibbered for days, and spoke of a black ship, and shrieked in the night of Trolls. Yet all he would say when he seemed sane was that his ship had foundered.

They took him to Mørkfjord and set him aland.

He began drinking that day—"To forget," he said—and he stayed that way for thirty-three years.

Mewling and gibbering and hissing of Trolls, Alos crawled backward from Arin.

Sailors came up behind. One shoved to the fore, a sandy-haired man, the *Gyllen Flyndre*'s first mate. "What's all this houndin' one o' our passengers wi' swords and axes and knives, eh? We'll ha'e no murthers aboard this ship. Look at th' poor lubber; y' ha'e driven his wits away wi' fear."

Aiko growled and turned toward the mate, and he blenched but stood his ground.

Arin stepped between the two. " 'Tis not we who affright him so, but his own phantoms, deliriums."

"He's full of drink and seeing things," added Egil.

The sailors looked down at the cowering old man, and one of the men turned to the first mate and said, "Aye, Guntar, he was brought aboard unconscious drunk."

Arin turned to Aiko and Egil. "I don't understand why he's on the ship at all."

Aiko and Egil glanced at one another, as if sharing a secret, and Egil said, "After a week of searching, I finally found him last night . . . while you were packing provisions aboard the *Brise,* love. I knew there wouldn't be time to convince him to come with us, and so instead I took him to the Cove and bought him two flagons of Tryg's best brandy, and then I asked Olar and Yngli to lade him aboard the *Gyllen Flyndre* when he passed out."

Arin's eyes widened. "Dost thou mean thou spirited him here against his will?"

Aiko sighed. "Dara, you said that perhaps we needed him, that he might know the way to the holt of Ordrune."

Arin turned to Aiko. "Dost thou approve what Egil has done?"

Aiko lowered her head and peered at the deck. "Dara, I aided Egil, for I paid coin to Captain Holdar for Alos's passage to Jute."

Arin shook her head, and looked at Alos, the old man's mouth now stretched wide in a soundless scream as he clawed at invisible foe. Then she turned to the first mate and gestured at Alos. "Canst thou and some of thy men bear him to his cabin? I will fetch some balms to lay these phantoms to rest."

The mate nodded and signaled to two of the men, but it took six of them to carry the shrieking, wrenching, flailing, drunken old man to his tiny quarters.

CHAPTER 36

The sailors wrestled Alos into his bunk, the old man shrieking and flailing, and moments later Arin appeared, carrying a small satchel filled with packets of herbs and powders. She mixed a white medick in a cup of water, and as two of the men held the oldster down, Arin pinched his nose shut, and when Alos drew in a breath to scream, she poured the mixture down his throat. Hacking and coughing, Alos screeched, "Eeee, poison, poison," and then fell unconscious.

Arin nodded to the sailors. "Ye can leave, now. His phantoms are temporarily at bay." The men trooped out, and Arin began mixing another drink, this time crumbling a dried petal of a yellow flower into water and stirring, bits of the petal swirling 'round and 'round, changing the color of the liquid.

As the Dylvana treated Alos with her medicks and bathed the old man's brow, the *Gyllen Flyndre* fared southwesterly, riding upon the sapphire tides of the great Boreal Sea. Her sails were filled flush by favoring winds, and her hull *shssh*ed through the water, bearing her crew toward faraway Gelen, across the wide channel from Jute. It was in this channel, if all went right, where Arin and Egil and Aiko, and even perhaps Alos, would leave the ship to pursue their own destinies. But that would be three or four weeks in the future on a journey just begun . . . for the *Flyndre* was but a half-day out of Mørkfjord and sailing along the coast, the high cliffs passing a mile or so to larboard. She would keep to the seaboard lanes throughout the following days, for she was a coastal trader and seldom ventured far out upon the wide deep waters of the world; for the most, her captain and crew sailed within sight of land, especially when on the waters of the stormy Boreal Sea.

And while Arin ministered to Alos, Aiko and Egil spent time walking the deck, getting their sea legs under them, for it had been weeks since Egil had been upon a ship, and Aiko had only fared at sea a sparse number of times— when she crossed from Ryodo to the mainland, and a few trips to islands south. After a while Aiko stopped her pacing and sat in the sun and began treating her weapons and armor 'gainst the spray, oiling the steel and bronze and leather to ward off the brine. Egil, though, remained filled with a restless energy and he paced the length of the ship, striding back and forth, threading his way through sailors, asking any and all if they knew the way to the holt of Ordrune the Mage. Yet the men shook their heads, for none held the answer, and so Egil continued his prowling. He stopped now and again to watch the Rianians bring the carrack to a new tack, the helmsman haling the wheel hard over, the deck crew setting the yards such that the sails made the most of the wind. Too, he would stand long moments in the bow, as if willing his sight to fly o'er the darkling waves and spy out the distant goal, for he was now eager to be in Jutland, where there might be someone who could lead him to the lair of the sought-after Mage. At other times he would stand in the stern near the tiller, speaking quietly to Captain Holdar, master of the ship.

"Nay, Egil, I have not heard of this Mage you seek." Holdar stroked his ruddy jaw. Clean-shaven was the captain of the *Flyndre*, a short, stocky man in his mid-forties, dressed in dark blue jerkin and breeks, and he wore black boots and a black leather vest. His hair was close-cropped and ruddy red as well. His eyes were blue and set within the plump features of a well-fed merchant, though a hint of ruggedness lay deep in his gaze. "I've no business with Mages and such. Instead, I deal with trappers and traders, and the fur merchants of Gelen." Holdar paused as Aiko climbed up the ladder to the poop deck to join them. And after nodding to the yellow warrior, the captain turned to Egil and said, "Besides, laddie buck, what would I do with a Mage, eh? Ask him to charm the *Flyndre,* har?"

"Not this Mage, Captain. With him you'd be lucky to escape with your life."

"Oh? One of the black ones, aye?"

Glumly, Egil nodded

"Then it be just as well I don't know this, this—"

"Ordrune," supplied Egil.

"Aye, Ordrune. I'll give him wide berth, if you don't mind. But, hoy, why do you seek him, him a black one and all?"

"I have a score to settle with him," said Egil, his look grim.

Holdar's eyes widened, and he said, "Well now, my friend, him being a Mage, take care you don't bite off more than you can chew."

"I do not plan on going alone, Captain, unless there is no other choice. Instead, there are the bloodkith of forty Fjordsmen eager to take off his head."

Aiko pursed her lips and frowned . . . and then intoned, *"Take these with thee, no more, no less, else thee will fail . . ."*

Egil looked down at her.

She caught his gaze and said, "There is more at stake here than blood-vengeance, Egil One-Eye."

Egil sighed and nodded and gestured toward the quarters where Arin tended Alos, then said, "We know not whether Ordrune holds that which she seeks. Yet I will stay my revenge until her—until *our* quest is complete."

Aiko nodded, and in that same moment, Arin stepped forth from the cabins below. Egil and Aiko climbed down the ladder to the main deck and joined her.

"He has finally fallen into a natural sleep," said the Dylvana, glancing back at the aft cabin quarters. She reached out and took Egil's hand, as if seeking comfort, then said, "Whatever happened to him apast, it must have been terrible."

On the second day out from Mørkfjord, Alos stumbled from his cabin and to the main deck of the *Gyllen Flyndre*. Shielding his one good eye from the bright morning sun, he peered 'round the deck, stunned. "Eh, where in

Garlon's name am I?" he muttered, then shouted to any and all, "I asked, where in Garlon's name am I?"

Sailors turned and stared at this filthy oldster, his clothes stained and rumpled, one eye watery brown, the other blind and white, teeth missing here and there, the remainder coated with an ocherous film. Then the old man seemed to suddenly realize that he was on a ship, and he collapsed to the deck weeping.

The first mate shook his head and growled, "Jan, go get th' Elf. Her ward has got loose."

But it was the yellow woman who came to the deck. She tried to get the old man to his feet, but he was as slack as a sail in irons, and so she slung him over her shoulder and headed for the aft quarters, snarling at the cabin boy to fetch a tub and hot water and soap, as well as chewing sticks and mint leaves, if he had them.

For the next three or four candlemarks, there were howls and thumps and sloshings and cursings from behind the old man's locked cabin door.

"Surely there's something to drink aboard," whined Alos, slipping into his clean though wrinkled breeks, the clothes freshly scrubbed and sun-dried and faintly smelling of salt.

Aiko shook her head and held out to Alos another chewing stick.

"But my gums are sore from all this rubbing of teeth," wailed the oldster, fumbling with the tail of his shirt.

"They'll be even more painful if it is I who scrub at them again," she growled.

Reluctantly, Alos took the stick and gnawed on the end. "If I had a drink, this would be much easier."

Aiko cocked an eyebrow.

"All right, all right," mumbled the oldster, and he looked at the well-chewed end of the stick and, satisfied that it now was soft enough, he began brushing away at his brownish-green teeth.

For the next several days did the *Gyllen Flyndre* fare westerly, and under Aiko's watchful eye, Alos continued to scrub at his teeth and keep his clothes and body clean.

Yet the oldster took every chance he got to ask any and all of the sailors if there was aught to drink aboard. The answer from the crewmen was "Aye. The cap'n's got a keg or two o' brandy, but he keeps it locked up tight." Alos soon discovered that Captain Holdar's quarters were always locked as well. And some dastard had instructed the captain to withhold all liquors from the old man. Alos figured that he knew which one of his companions had done such a deed, yet he only glared at Aiko when her back was turned. And so, Alos, frustrated, spent the time moaning to himself and scratching his seemingly itching skin, and sniffing his apparently running nose—why he was being afflicted with such, he did not know. All he knew was that his whole body yearned and nought he did seemed to assuage the craving. Too, monstrous Trolls and Mages burning with witchfire stalked across his dreams and, like Egil, he woke up nightly screaming in terror, and but half awake, Alos blundered about his cabin, searching, though he could find no drink to soothe his tortured soul.

On the seventh day out, the *Gyllen Flyndre* swung southerly, still following along the coast, now sliding past two or three miles to the east.

And in early morn of the eighth day, the lookout atop the main mast called down, "Gronfangs, ho! Dragons' Roost ahead!"

On this day, Arin, Egil, and Aiko all stood on the upper deck larboard, near the stern, and Alos sat on a hatch cover nearby, his head in his hands.

Captain Holdar on the poop deck shaded his eyes, peering southerly. After a moment—"Ulf," he barked, "quarter to the steerboard. Agli, pipe the sails about."

The bo's'n trilled his pipe and called out orders, and the crew set to, haling the yards 'round and trimming the sails as Ulf spun the helm, and the ship angled out to sea.

Egil pointed toward the south, and low on the horizon Arin and Aiko could see what appeared to be great white talons clutching at the sky, marching out of the east and south and down to the water.

" 'Tis the Gronfangs." Egil's voice was grim. "They

reach down into the sea, passing from sight, plunging into the cold depths. Have you heard of them?"

Arin nodded but Aiko shook her head.

From behind, Alos looked up and said, "Some say the mountains stride 'neath the ocean on to the west, with islands standing where their peaks jut out of the water."

"Aye," answered Egil, turning to the oldster. "I've heard that, too. And the Seabanes fall where the mountains would be if they were to continue marching westward across the floor of the abyss. Tall stone crags, they are, and nothing lives thereon."

Aiko looked southward at the snowcapped peaks. "Why do we veer out to sea?"

" 'Tis the Seabanes we avoid," Captain Holdar called down from the poop. "Dangerous waters, cold and deadly they be, 'specially 'tween the Fang and the Banes, for there swirls the Great Maelstrom, a monstrous sucking hole in the ocean haunted by dreadful Krakens lurking within that twisting churn—" Captain Holdar broke off what he was saying and glanced up at the aft pennon. "The wind, she be shifting, Agli. Trim her up again. Hold our course to west-sou'west, Ulf."

Aiko turned to Egil. "What are these things he named Krakens?"

Egil took a deep breath. "I've never seen one myself, but they say Krakens are hideous monsters, with great ropy arms and clutching suckers, glaring eyes, and a terrible claw beak. They are supposed to be huge, big as a Dragon, it's told, with the strength to match."

"Dragons' mates, they say," added Alos from behind.

Egil called over his shoulder, "Dragons' mates, aye, Alos, that is the legend. 'Tis told among my folk that down through the ages, at rare times, Dragons gather on yon headland there." Egil stretched out his arm and pointed at a distant mount, just now discernible on the horizon. "There lies Dragons' Roost, last of the Gronfangs. Did not the Mages at Black Mountain speak of that place?"

Arin shook her head, but said, "Nevertheless, I have heard of it."

Aiko glanced at Arin. "What have you heard, Dara?"

"Rumors, in the main," replied Arin, taking Egil's hand. "But these are Egil's waters. Let him say what he knows, and if I have aught to add, I will do so."

Egil grinned and squeezed Arin's hand. "My knowledge is mostly sailors' yarns, too, but I'll tell you what they say." Egil looked at the distant headland. "Although it doesn't look it from here, Dragons' Roost is a mighty mountain, reaching up above the clouds, and its peak is forever covered with ice and snow, even in the heart of summer. Jagged it is, though near its base, its sides are sheer and fall plumb into the icy waters, a thousand feet or more. But above that fall and all the way to the ice-clad crest it is said that Dragons' lairs riddle the steeps— temporary dens when they forgather for the time of the mating. And on those cragged slopes there are many ledges where lie the lovelorn Wyrms, awaiting the call of their lovers from the sea. It is also said that from that aerie you can peer down into the Maelstrom itself, though no one I know has ever claimed that he stood there and looked. And anyone would be a fool to do so when the Drakes are about, for legends say that Dragons can somehow *sense* when strangers step into their domains.

"Be that as it may, the Drakes forgather, waiting, now and again raising their great brazen voices to bellow at the sky. And once in a great while, it seems, they do combat, one with another, though it is said that for the most part they *know* who is strongest and yield the higher places to them, the most powerful on the topmost ledge, and so on down to the least of them."

Arin nodded. "That agrees with what Arilla said when she told us the tale of the Dragons coming to Black Mountain."

Egil leaned forward against the top rail. "Aye, and at that time Black Kalgalath must have sat atop the highest perch."

"Indeed," agreed Arin, "though Daagor disputed his right to that place."

Captain Holdar, who had been listening, called down, "Ebonskaith, Skail, Redclaw, Sleeth, Silverscale: I would think they would all contest the topmost perch." Holdar's eyes widened. " 'Tis a good thing they themselves know who should sit above whom, else the whole w'rld would shake if they ever fought it out. But, ach, who knows the ways of Dragons? Not I."

They fell to silence, the quiet broken only by the hull *shssh*ing through the brine and the canvas and ropes creaking in the wind. Aiko peered long at the headland, and at last said, "Is that the whole of the tale?"

Egil put an arm about Arin. "There's not much more to the legends. The Drakes perch there night after night and bellow from dusk to dawn. And after many nights of this thunderous din, in the darktide, driven by the urge to mate or by lust or love—who knows?—one by one, Krakens come to the call, the greatest first, the least last, each burning with the green glowing daemonfire of the deeps, spinning in the vast roaring churn of the dreadful Maelstrom."

At the naming of daemonfire, Alos groaned and put his face in his hands, but neither Egil nor Arin nor Aiko noticed, for they were facing the opposite way.

Egil's voice dropped to a whisper. "And one by one the Drakes plunge into that fearsome spin, to be clutched in the grasping embrace of those hideous tentacles, each Dragon drawn under by a monstrous mate, lover and lover sucked into the whirling black abyss below, to spawn beyond the light of all knowledge.

"And later, somehow the Drakes return, bursting through the dark surface, struggling to wing up into the night air, and only the strongest survive."

Egil fell silent, but Captain Holdar added, "They say that the offspring of this mating be Sea Serpents, the long-wyrms of the ocean: those be the children of that vile spawning. I believe it, too! For I have seen a Sea-Drake, myself, not more than a day's sailing from here."

Arin looked up at the captain, her eyes wide. "Aye," he continued, "a long beastie 'twas, with a rippling crest all down its considerable length, snaking through the water. We ran, we did, and I'm not 'shamed to admit it."

"But then, Captain"—Aiko looked puzzled—"if nought but the serpents of the sea are the get of that breeding, whence come the Dragons themselves, or the Krakens, for that matter?"

Holdar shrugged and said, "All I know is it be said that

Drakes and Krakes both come from the sea." He held out a hand to Egil in a silent appeal, but Egil merely shrugged as well.

Aiko looked at Arin, and the Dylvana sighed. "Those who have spoken with the Children of the Sea say that—"

"Pardon, Dara," interjected Aiko, holding up a hand. "Children of the Sea?"

"Aye," replied Arin. "Children of the Sea: they are the Hidden Ones who live in the depths of the oceans of the world."

"Mermaids, y' mean?" asked Alos. "Mermaids and Mermen? People with fish tails 'stead of legs?"

Arin shrugged. "I think not, Alos, though I have never seen one."

"But I—" began Alos in protest, yet Aiko silenced him by holding a chewing stick out to the oldster. A look of dismay swept over the old man's features, but he reached out and took it.

As Alos began gnawing on the tip of the stub, Aiko turned to Arin. "I interrupted, Dara."

Arin smiled. "The Children of the Sea tell that after ages of swimming and feeding, the great serpents take themselves unto the unlit depths of a vast chasm located somewhere in the waters of the wide Sindhu Sea. There, three full leagues below the surface, in a lost abyss they settle upon dark ledges lining the chasm walls, where they exude an adherent and enwrap themselves into tight spheres. The adherent hardens and they are enshelled in a crystalline glaze to begin an extraordinary metamorphosis. After a time, when the change has occurred, the crystal shell is finally shattered, and just as some caterpillars emerge from their chrysalises as butterflies whilst others emerge as moths, well then too some serpents—the males, I would guess—come forth Dragons while others—the females—come forth Krakens. . . .

"Or so say the Children of the Sea."

"Well now," said Holdar, "be this tale true or false, fact or fable, rumor, speculation, or just plain opinion, I think something of the like must be. List: none has ever seen a small young Drake: all seem full grown from the first. And I don't think there has ever been found a clutch of

Dragon eggs aland: they seem to lay them not. And as far as I know, none has ever seen a female Dragon: they all be males.

"And as to the Krakens, well, I cannot say as to what they may be—male or female—but the sages tell that they be the Dragons' mates, and who be I to argue?"

Again a quietness fell upon them all as they stared over water at the far headland, dim in the distance. After a long while, Holdar broke the silence: "Ah me. Dragon, Kraken, Sea Serpent, I know not the which of it, but I do know that many a ship has been lost to *something* in those waters, be it Maelstrom or monster. Of those who have sailed in there, none has ever lived to tell of it."

Egil shook his head. "Captain, I think if a ship sailed 'tween Dragons' Roost and the Seabanes, 'twould be the Maelstrom that would drag her under, drowning all aboard, for none has ever escaped the suck of that hideous swirl."

Arin shuddered, and for some reason this talk of the Maelstrom brought to mind the whirling chaos of her vision, a maelstrom of its own, with dire events all spiraling about the jadelike green stone. *Will we all be dragged under by its hideous swirl?*

Driven by a following wind, the *Gyllen Flyndre* cut through the icy water, the white-capped Gronfang Mountains ashore sliding up over the horizon, soon followed by the craggy Seabane Islands asea, slipping leftward in the distance to be lost at last over the rim astern.

West now she fared for days, past the long shore of the Angle of Gron, a vile, baneful land, for therein dwell Foul Folk: Rutcha, Drôkha, Ogrus, Vulgs, Guula and Hèl-steeds, and other creatures dire, thralls of a Black Mage, or so it was said.

Past this dread realm *shssh*ed the *Gyllen Flyndre,* laden with sailors and a cargo of furs and bearing four passengers as well.

On they sailed across the waters of the Boreal Sea and the fickle weather thereupon, through sunny skies and moonlit nights, through rain and squalls and calms. At times the ship fell into irons, and rowers would debark in dinghies and tow the ship across glassy water in an attempt to find the wind. At other times the crew would need reef the *Flyndre*'s sails, as fierce wind and torrential rain unmercifully lashed the craft. Yet at other times, no matter its state, Captain Holdar pronounced the weather "bonnie" as long as the winds were favorable.

Up across the horizon came the headland where now the Rigga Mountains plunged into the Boreal Sea, where Gron ended and Rian began. Past Rian they sailed, then past the Jillian Tors, a far-flung set of craggy highlands wherein fierce clansmen dwell, noted for their endless feuds. On westerly sailed Captain Holdar and his crew, to fare along the shores of Thol.

Here, day after day Alos stood adeck and peered at forested land as it slid by, for Thol was once his home realm, but no more, indeed, no more.

They followed the long arc of the Tholian coast, gradually curving 'round from west to south, and somewhere along this route they crossed the uncertain boundary between the Northern and Boreal Seas. Now they fared toward the wide waters of the channel lying between Gelen to the west and Jute to the east.

Altogether it took twenty-eight days for the carrack to fare from Mørkfjord to the point in the channel where Arin and her companions would transfer from the *Gyllen Flyndre* to the *Brise* and set sail in the sloop on their own.

And when the *Flyndre* had come as close to Jute as she would, Captain Holdar ordered the ship to heave to, and he luffed up in the wind. Haling on the tow ropes, crewmen drew the sloop alongside, and Arin and Aiko climbed down the larboard ladderway and into the small craft.

Alos stood by, watching, the old man intending on staying with the *Flyndre* and sailing on to the walled port of Chamer. Yet seemed agitated, as if reluctant to part with those who had cared for him—Arin with her gentle ways, Egil with his friendship, even Aiko, though she was rough, making him bathe and all. However, he was sober for the first time in thirty-three years, and he did not like that at all, what with his dreams being filled with a witch-fire Mage and bloody monstrous Trolls.

Before clambering over the side, Egil turned to the old-ster and appealed one last time, "My friend, I would that you choose to go with us, for I need an experienced helmsman to aid me in sailing the *Brise,* and none else here among these sailors can go but you."

Alos turned away and stalked toward his cabin aft, and Egil, shaking his head and sighing, clambered down the ladderway to the waiting sloop below. He reached the deck and made his way aft to the tiller, then called up, "Prepare to cast off bow and stern."

Captain Holdar repeated the order to his crew up on the carrack.

"Cast off the stern," called Egil.

"Wait!" came a cry. Then Alos appeared above, his meager belongings bound in a bedroll. The old man peered down over the railing and declared, "I'll sail with you on your mad quest as far as Jutland, but no more, you hear me, no more."

Three days later on the evening tide the *Brise* sailed into the crowded Jutlander port of Königinstadt; ships rode at anchor throughout the bay and were tied up at dockside as well, a forest of masts jutting into the air like a barren thicket of trees. Among these ships wended the sloop, heading for the pier where flew the flag of the harbormaster, Alos at the helm, Egil and Arin handling the sheets, Aiko on the bow ready to cast a mooring rope to the hands lounging dockside.

And in the distance on a lofty hill beyond the sprawling city and above the bay, they could see a massive citadel, bright lanterns on the fortress walls, the windows of the castle within glowing yellow in the lavender twilight.

"There it is, love," said Egil to Arin, "the lair of the Queen of Jute, where we will find the mad monarch's rutting peacock . . . or so I sincerely hope."

CHAPTER 37

They paid the harbormaster a small docking fee and moved the *Brise* to the designated slip, where they packed a few of their goods and battened down the ship. Debarking, they trudged along a main thoroughfare up from the docks and into the city, passing among warehouses and fish markets and shops of crafters, many closed, though here and there workers yet toiled at tasks. They finally came in among taverns and stores and other businesses, all with dwellings above, and here the streets were awash with people, revelers and hawkers, with shops alit.

As they moved among the crowds, Aiko frowned. "Why do some wear iron collars?"

"They are thralls," replied Egil.

"Slaves?" asked Aiko.

Egil nodded. "Thralls, serfs, slaves: they go by many names. Their ancestors likely were defeated in battle and taken in bondage long past."

Arin shook her head. "Yet the defeat echoes down through the generations, for their children and children's children are slaves as well."

"There are serfs in Ryodo," said Aiko. "Yet they wear no iron about their necks."

Egil shrugged. "Most are born to the collar and will wear it throughout their life."

"Is there no way they can gain their liberty?"

"Once in a great while a thrall will win his freedom, through valor in battle or other high service to his master. Then, with grand ceremony, the iron is stricken and given to the man or woman as a symbol of their liberty. Yet for most, the only way to lose the collar is to lose one's head."

Arin sighed. "Long past, Elvenkind learned that slavery is a great evil, and one day mankind will come to know it as well."

Egil made a few inquiries, and finally the four took a large room in the Silver Helm, one of Königinstadt's numerous inns, modest by any measure, for they did not wish to call attention to themselves. Yet the mere fact that a *Dylvana* had come to the inn was enough to cause tongues to wag. Moreover, accompanying her was a *yellow* woman who seemed to be a *warrior,* no less, and wasn't that a wonder? And with these two came a pair of men—human males, that is, and not Elves: the younger of the two was a man with a red eye patch and a fresh scar down his forehead and cheek; the second was an oldster, another one-eyed man. And when these four strangers took to the same chamber and ordered hot baths, tongues wagged all the faster, for who knows *what* might go on behind their closed door?

Bathed and refreshed, they came down to the common room for a hot meal, and each had a mug of ale—all but Alos, that is, for although the oldster could eat whatever he wished, Aiko would not allow him even the tiniest sip of brew, no matter how pitifully he whined. And so the old man had to settle for honeyed, spiced tea to wash down his biscuits and mutton stew.

As they ate, all eyes followed their every move, patrons whispering among themselves in wild speculation:

Look at her, a tiny thing. An Elf she is, but taller I thought them.

Ja, a Dylvana she is one. The Lian it is who are tall.

The yellow one now, no Elf is she, but tell me, now, what land do you name her from?

Land I know not but a fighter she is, swords at her waist.

The young one—a fighter he is as well. See down his face the scar.

He could a duel have got it in.

Ja. Maybe a noble he is, a lady Elf he travels beside.

The yellow woman do not forget. The scar he bears she could have made, her blades carving his face.

Nie, I think not. A full head taller is he.

The old man and the younger, together they travel. Uncle and nephew they could be.

If so, in the family one-eyes run, har!

My tongue would I hold if I were you, and not the old man get angry—a curse he would lay upon you.

A Wizard he is, ja?

Nie, but a man with an evil eye . . . white and all does it glare.

The one with the red patch and scar a wide berth I would give. That axe at his waist your head he would lop.

On went the mumble and buzz concerning the foreigners, but then, mercifully, a bard stepped to the center of a meager stage and amid a scattering of applause, the patrons left off their speculations and turned his way. He raised up a small tambour and announced, " 'Gurd and the Monster Kram.' " A cheer greeted his words, followed by devout silence as he began intoning a sing-song chant to the beat of his tiny drum—a tale of a young warrior's hard-won victory over a terrible Drake.

Arin shook her head at the outrageous claims made by the words of the ode, and turning to Egil she asked, "Is this epic sung widely?"

Egil leaned forward and in a low voice replied, "Indeed it is, my love. Although most folks, including me, do not believe a Drake has ever been slain by the hand of a man, it does not in any way quench the wild popularity of the ode."

"Hmm," mused Arin, raising an eyebrow and tilting her head toward the bard. "Even though it is a saga treasured by those who hear it, I would suggest he not cant it to a Dragon."

Egil bellowed out a guffaw, then clamped his lips to stifle his laughter, though he snorted through his nose. A nearby patron glared at Egil, but then turned his rapt attention back to the bard. Smiling, Arin looked up at Egil and waggled a finger in admonishment, but then had to stifle her own laughter. It took some moments for them to gain control of themselves as the bard astage continued the epic to the beat of his small drum.

"I used to play one of those," said Alos, tapping his fingers in time.

"A tambour?" asked Aiko, her eyes wide, as if she never had considered Alos anything but a drunk.

"Yar, but where he uses his hands, I would use a cruik instead."

"Cruik?"

"A curved stick with a knob on the end to strike the drumhead. At least, that's what it's called in the Jillian Tors, where I first learned to play."

"Unh," grunted Aiko, noncommittally.

The bard finished his chant to enthusiastic applause, the patrons calling for more. "Mayhap he'll do 'Snorri Borri's Son and the Mystical Maid of the Maelstrom,' " said Egil.

Alos laughed and clapped his hands. "I know that one, Egil, m'lad, and a right bawdy tale it be."

Arin looked askance at Egil. He cleared his throat. "A sailor's song, love."

But the bard took up the "Lay of Jaangor," the horse made of black iron, and all joined in on the chorus, for this song was well-known too.

The third time the iron-collared serving maid brought three ales and a mug of honeyed, spiced tea to their table, Egil said, "You seem to have a good crowd tonight. Is it always this way?"

"Oh, no, sir. The festival it is."

"Festival?"

"Declared by Queen Gudrun all month to last. At a good time you have come."

"What does she celebrate?" asked Aiko.

The girl gasped as if taken aback, but they could not discern whether she was surprised by the question itself or by the fact that it had been asked by the yellow warrior woman. "Why she celebrates, milady, no one knows; as a complete surprise it came. Elwydd, enough it is that she does." With that, the serving girl scurried away.

Alos looked longingly at the mugs of ale and muttered when Aiko slid the tea his way, but what he said went unheard in the general babble.

* * *

They slept soundly that darktide, the only disturbances being 'round mid of night when Alos tried to slip past Aiko, the golden warrior meditating on her tatami before the latch-locked door. That and Egil's ill dreams.

The next day amid a scattering of visitors they walked up toward a citadel to have a look at the fortress. As they strolled through the city and toward the hill, they could see that bastion walls ran all the way 'round the crown of the tor, atop which stood an ornate castle of white stone, with turrets and towers jutting toward the sky, all set in manicured grounds. Topiary and hedges and gardens graced the enclosed estate, and here and there were scattered outbuildings, their purposes untold. All this they took in as they walked up the hill, though when they arrived at the base of the ramparts, all beyond was hidden.

The walls themselves were thirty feet high and made of granite blocks—huge, shaped, and grey. Crenellations capped the stonework, and warders bearing crossbows patrolled above. The main entrance was a wide archway with a twisting passage running under the barrier, and the leaves of the great iron outer gates stood open, the portal flanked by guards. Inside the tunnel a massive portcullis was grounded, and beyond the bars the corridor turned sharply, the route designed to slow invaders and prevent passage of great siege engines. No light shone through from beyond, and so they surmised that at the far end stood a pair of inner gates, closed. In the tunnel, machicolations gaped overhead—murder holes through which to rain destruction down upon an invading foe—and arrow slits lined the walls.

Both Egil and Aiko scrutinized these ramparts with a practiced eye, and Arin murmured, " 'Tis well warded."

Egil nodded. "Even so, love, at night a small band could slip over these walls undetected, given the spacing of the sentries."

"I would rather go in through the gate," she replied.

Alos blinked his good eye and nodded toward the portcullis. "Eh, the way is shut and it doesn't seem as if anyone's being admitted."

"It cannot always be closed," said Aiko, "for even a queen must eat."

"Stay here a moment," said Egil, "I'll see what I can learn."

They waited as Egil stepped up the roadway to one of the warders at the portcullis and engaged him in conversation. After a while, Egil turned and came back. "Only those with specific business are permitted in."

Alos frowned. "Specific business?"

"Aye," replied Egil. "Messengers, diplomats, invited guests, visiting nobles, queen's merchants, and the like."

"Oh my," said Arin, crestfallen. "And we have no recognized need."

Pondering, they turned and began the trek back toward the city.

"Perhaps we could pose as visiting nobles," said Alos, wiping his nose on a sodden handkerchief and then smiling a brown-stained, snag-toothed grin.

Aiko looked at the scraggly oldster and growled, but Arin said, "Nay, Alos. Too many townsfolk noted the manner of our arrival—coming as we did in a small sloop. Too, they know the quarters we took."

Alos shrugged. "So?"

Egil laughed. "What the Dara means, my friend, is that both our transport and lodging are well beneath the station of visiting royalty. Had we been of the nobility, we would have come in a great ship, been escorted by a retinue, and likely would have gone straight to the castle rather than taking quarters in a modest inn. But had we needed to stay atown, as nobles we would have selected the very best lodgings Königinstadt has to offer."

"Oh," said Alos. "Then what about merchants? Mayhap we can drive a wine wagon onto the grounds."

"Ha!" barked Aiko. "If you were put aboard a wine wagon, old man, the kegs would be empty ere we got to the gate."

Alos stuck out his chin. "Oh, you think so?"

Aiko looked at him and shook her head in resignation and said, *"Yopparai."*

"Tispe," snarled Alos.

Arin held up a hand. "Enough!" she commanded. "If we are to succeed, we need a way in. Preferably by invitation."

Alos glared at Aiko, then looked at Arin. "I say again, why not as merchants?"

Arin shook her head. "Not just any merchant can go in. Each must bear the seal of the queen. Besides, I do not think we can pose as merchants; we are too . . ."

"Too uncommon," supplied Egil. "Just look at us, Alos—an Elf, a golden warrior woman, a scar-faced one-eyed raider, and a—"

"A *yopparai*," interjected Aiko.

Egil shook his head. "No, Aiko. Not a *yopparai,* whatever that is"—he clapped a hand to Alos's shoulder—"but a worthy helmsman, instead."

Alos thrust out his chest and raised his chin and arched an eyebrow at Aiko . . . but said nothing as they came into the bustle of the city proper: hawkers, merchants, teamsters, patrons, street urchins and the like, all peddling wares, transporting goods, buying, selling, running errands.

Suddenly, Egil laughed and gestured at the hubbub and stir and ado. "I mean, even in disguise we couldn't pass ourselves off as common merchants. We look more like a strangely mixed band of traveling jongleurs. Nay, I say we go over the wall at night like the raiders we need to be."

Arin's eyes flew wide at Egil's words and she grasped his hand and said, "Thou hast hit upon it, *chier.*"

Egil grinned and clenched his fist. "Ah, over the wall at night, eh?"

"Nay," replied Arin. "Through the gate as a band of jongleurs."

"I'll play the tambour," said Alos.

By the time they found their vendors of choice, their plans were nearly set. In a music shop they purchased a tambour and cruik for Alos. Then at a clothier's, they selected tasteful but colorful cloth—all but Aiko, who merely chose a handful of bright ribands—and a bevy of tailors took the measure of Arin and Egil and Alos. Arin paid the proprietor a small gemstone, and he promised to deliver the outfits the very next morning.

"In a suitable trunk, if you please," said Egil.

"Oh, ja," answered the proprietor. "And deliver it where, shall I?"

"Why, the very best hostel in Königinstadt," replied Egil.

"Ja. The Queen's Crown."

"Indeed," replied Egil, glancing at the others.

Taking their leave of the Silver Helm, they moved all their goods to the Queen's Crown. And as Alos stood on the balcony and cruik-tapped his new arm-held drum, regaining his rhythm and skill, down below in the common room Egil approached the innkeeper and made him an offer.

The next night a colorfully dressed Dylvana sang Elven songs while Alos tapped the tambour, and the crowd sat rapt, weeping and laughing and joining in when asked. And they *ooh*ed and *aah*ed as a golden warrior took center stage, bright, flowing ribands tied 'round her arms and legs and waist and brow. And they gasped in awe as she spun and twirled and leapt, her ribands streaming, her gleaming swords flashing in a dazzling dance of death.

Swiftly the news spread 'cross Königinstadt: an Elven bard was singing at the Crown, and aren't Elves the best bards of all? And a yellow warrior-woman danced with swords, the steel and she but a blur, so quick was this golden maid.

Soon in the evenings there were no places left to sit in the common room of the Queen's Crown. And many who had thought to come early arrived only to discover the inn already filled. And so they stood 'round the walls and waited for the show and complained to any who would listen o'er the lack of seats, but when they left for home in the wee marks of the morn, they went away filled near to bursting with what they had seen and heard.

Too, the spectators were generous with their coin, yielding copper and silver and gold to the performers. Egil shared it out among them, holding back a goodly reserve which he stashed aboard the ship. Even so, there was enough surplus to purchase whatever anyone willed, all except Alos, for Aiko forbade him to buy drink. And so the old man hoarded his coins against the day he would at last be free.

There came a night when with deference and dread a richly dressed man was escorted to the center table at edge of the stage. And when he had seen what he had come to see, Egil was called to attend. When the man left Egil came to the others, an engraved blue card in hand. "We are," he announced, holding up the token, a broad smile on his face, "summoned to the castle by Queen Gudrun's lord chamberlain, who commands we perform for her."

CHAPTER 38

Just after dawn the next morn, Aiko was awakened by a tapping on the door. Sword in hand, she opened it to find two iron-collared footmen standing there, liveried in black and orange and gold. Their eyes widened at the sight of the yellow warrior, yet the elder of the two said, "Lady Aiko?" At her nod, he continued, his common tongue speech impeccable, "We have been sent by the lord chamberlain to fetch you and your companions to the queen's castle. At your convenience, milady, a carriage awaits below. We will stand by in the hall."

Aiko roused the others, and with Alos grumbling they performed their toilet and dressed and packed their goods. Aiko called in the footmen to bear their meager luggage as well as their costume trunk, and all proceeded downstairs. While the others stepped to the carriage, Egil went to settle with the innkeeper, who shook his head and refused to accept payment, declaring, "Nothing you owe me. The singing and sword dancing paid for all. Here to the Crown soon you will return, ja? Free room and board I will give, and handsomely will I pay, the profits even share."

Egil shrugged. "I know not when we may return, for the queen summons."

The innkeeper glanced at the carriage out front. "Ja, that I can see"—he drew in a sharp breath—"and answer you must if your necks you value. Hear me, now: your rooms for you I will save; in fact, the best will I hold that I have if come back you will do when done you are."

Egil smiled and nodded. "We'll think on it."

A landau had been sent by the chamberlain, and riding in style in the early morn, they were conveyed up the hill.

The way under the wall twisted and turned, and the coachman slowed the horses to a walk and maneuvered the carriage through, but as soon as they were clear of the barrier, he *chrk*ed the team to a lively step, and along the white pave they fared, hooves aclatter on stone. The way curved through ornate gardens, where topiary beasts stood tall and green and silent, flanking the pale granite road. And as they wended upward, from somewhere on the manicured grounds they heard a harsh call of some sort of creature—*Karawah, karawah, karawah!*—but whether beast or fowl or something altogether different, they knew it not.

At last the carriage drew up before the entrance, and one of the footmen sprang down and lowered the steps and opened the door while the other gathered up their goods. Egil stepped to the flagstone court and then handed Arin and Aiko down, and aided Alos to descend as well. They were met by a handful of servants, who were surprised at the lack of baggage. A steward bade them to follow, and led them through a grand foyer and into the hallways beyond, six thralls trailing after, bearing the small satchels and the costume trunk of the guests. They came to a chamber where sat a young man, peering at papers of state. He was but one of the chamberlain's many assistants, and he informed them they would be performing tomorrow night and directed the steward to show them to their quarters in the outer tower of the east wing.

They wended through passageways, bearing ever easterly, passing other servants and guests and members of the queen's staff. But as to which was which, they could not readily tell, though the steward bowed to several, and was bowed to by others as well.

One of these to whom the steward bowed was tall and black haired. Dressed in finery, he stood and watched as Arin and her comrades came toward him. His dark blue eyes widened at the sight of an Elf, and he sketched a bow. Then his eyes widened again as Aiko strode by, and once again he bowed. He merely nodded at Alos, but as Egil passed, the man's gaze narrowed upon seeing the Fjordlander's face and scar.

"Do I know you, sir?" he asked, holding out a hand to delay Egil.

"I think not," replied Egil, pausing. "I have not before come to these parts."

The man canted his head. "I am Baron Steiger of Duchy Rache. And you are . . .?"

Egil tilted his head in a like manner and said, "I am Egil . . . of here and there. If we had met, I would have remembered."

"Yet your face looks familiar," said the baron, "though it seems to me that perhaps I saw it in different circumstances altogether, just when or where I cannot recall. Yet give me time. I will recollect."

Egil smiled and said, "If you do, sir, then let me know. They say that each man has a double; perhaps you will lead me to mine." He glanced up the hall, where the others waited. "And now, sir, good morn to you." And he bowed and turned on his heel.

As Egil strode away and rejoined the others, Steiger stood stroking his chin. Just as the retinue began to move off, the baron's eyes widened, and he whirled and hurried away.

"What was that all about?" asked Alos.

"Someone who thought he knew me," replied Egil.

"Perhaps he does," said Aiko.

Egil shook his head. "If he does, then it was from elsewhere, for I've not been here before."

"Not to Jute?"

"No, no. Not to Königinstadt. I've been to Jute with Orri, but it was a goodly distance up the coast."

"Mayhap," said Arin, "it has something to do with the memories thou canst not recall."

Egil's eye flew wide. "You mean the memories Ordrune stole from me?"

"Mayhap."

Egil turned and looked back at the way they had come, but Baron Steiger was no longer there.

They were ensconced high up in the east tower, in a modest room with a windowed doorway leading to a balcony looking west. The room itself was furnished with a large, canopied four-poster with heavy drapes hanging down, a long leather couch, a small table and two chairs, a tall, wide cabinet which proved to be a wardrobe, and a chest of drawers. A small chamber, with a curtain for a door, adjoined the room, and it held a privy pot as well as a low chest of drawers containing towels and linens and on which sat a large pitcher of water and a wash basin and soap.

"There is a common bathing room 'round the hall," said the steward, stepping to the door. "The chamberboy will show you the way." He turned and called, "Dolph!"

A slight, black-haired lad popped into the chamber. He was perhaps eleven, and an iron collar graced his neck. He bowed to the four, his pale blue eyes widening at the sight of the Dylvana and the yellow Ryodoan. The steward arched a brow at the youth, then turned to Egil and said, "Dolph will see to your needs." He then bowed and withdrew.

When the steward was gone, Egil turned to Dolph. "We caught but a glimpse of the estate as we rode in from the city, lad. May we freely tour the grounds?"

"Ja, sir," replied the chamberboy. "At liberty to roam you are where you will . . . all but the queen's spire."

"Queen's spire?"

"Ja, there." The lad pointed out the window at the central tower. "Her private quarters those are. The balcony to her bedchamber from here you can see."

"Oh, which one?"

"That is the one at the top, sir."

Egil glanced up at the balcony, but it stood empty.

Aiko stepped over and looked as well, then she turned to Egil and shrugged.

"Is there aught else you need?" asked the youth.

"Chewing sticks and mint leaves," said Aiko, and Alos groaned in response.

As the boy turned to go, Egil said, "If we are not here when you return, we will be exploring the castle and grounds, should anyone ask."

"Ja, sir. On your way back if finding these quarters you have trouble, any servant just ask for the way; the green room of the east tower this is. To direct you they will be able."

"What's your name again, boy?" asked Alos.

"Dolph."

"Well, Dolph, we've not yet broken our fast. When and where do we eat?"

"Each tower a dining hall has down below—of course is best the east one. At dawn and mid of day and twilight meals are served, anytime you can eat though as guests. Here to your room food I can fetch, if rather you would. Of course, to the great hall you'll be going for the banquet tonight. A bell all will summon."

"And the great hall?"

"The central wing, sir, it is."

"Well and good, boy. Well and good."

Dolph looked from one to the other. "Breakfast to fetch would you like me?"

Aiko shook her head. "No. Just the chewing sticks and mint. We will find our own way to a meal."

As Dolph sped from the room on his errand, Egil said, "Let us break fast and then explore, gauge the defenses and the lay of the land and the plan of the buildings. We may need a quick way out, and depending upon what we find, we can set our strategy. Too, I would look for Baron Steiger; perhaps he remembers where we met. If not, even so, he may yield a clue as to my stolen memories."

After their morning meal, they strolled the grounds, passing among flower gardens and limpid pools containing what Alos called "calico fishies" but which Aiko named "koi." Aiko stood a moment at the edge of one of the pools; the brightly scaled fish swam to the surface as if they expected to be fed. "My father told me that in the pools of Lord Yodama there were many of these *uo*. They are highly prized in Ryodo." She stood a moment more, gazing down as if lost in thought. Then she spun on her heel and walked away, wiping her cheeks with the heels of her hands.

On they wended 'round the hill, and they came upon a hedge maze. Arin grabbed Egil by the hand and, laughing, pulled him into the labyrinth. They wandered through its convoluted corridors, lost, but finally found themselves at what they believed was the center, for there on a pedestal stood a white marble statue of a nude young woman, life-sized and lifelike in every detail. Affixed to the base was a golden plaque engraved *Die Königin Gudrun die Schöne*.

"Dost thou think it is our hostess?" asked Arin, eyeing the form critically.

"If it is," replied Egil, grinning, "modesty is not among her virtues."

Now Arin smiled and, standing on tiptoe, kissed Egil on the cheek. Then she took him by the hand and turned to go, just as Aiko and Alos came to the labyrinth center.

"Huah," exclaimed Alos, walking around the sculpture and viewing it from all sides.

Aiko, though, glanced at the plaque and asked, "What does it say?"

"Queen Gudrun the Comely," replied Alos.

"Ah so," mused Aiko. "If faithful in every detail, then perhaps we look upon the like of our mad monarch."

Alos, completing his circuit, asked, "Why do you suppose she has such a work sitting out where everyone can see?"

Aiko shrugged, but Egil said, "Perhaps this is why she is called 'mad.' "

"Mayhap so," said Arin. "It is a puzzle, nevertheless."

Egil nodded in agreement, then said, "Come. Let us go. There is much yet to see, and I would know the ground on which we stand. As I said before, there may come a time when we will need to know the best way to take flight."

"Or the best place to stand and fight," added Aiko.

"Aye," replied Egil, "or fight."

"Don't forget the rutting peacock," said Alos. "It is, after all, why we are here."

All three looked at Alos, as if surprised.

"Well I said I would go this far," snapped the oldster. "But no farther, d' y' hear? No farther."

Arin smiled. "Come. Let us leave."

They wandered through the labyrinth only to find themselves back at the statue. "Well, this *is* a puzzle, all right," declared Egil. "Easy to get in; hard to get out."

Again they turned to go, wending through the hedges, but found themselves at the statue once more.

"Y' know," grumped Alos, "a person could starve in here."

As they strode away from the statue, Egil said, "When next we find ourselves at the center, we should think on marking our way so we'll know where we've been."

Moments later they stood at the statue again.

Aiko rested her hands on the pommels of her swords. "I am of a mind to hack straight through."

Egil looked up at the form. "Perhaps this is why she's called mad—putting such a trap on her grounds, a trap that just anyone can wander into."

"Do you think it's cursed?" asked Alos.

Suddenly Aiko's eyes flew wide, and she turned to Arin. "Dara"—Aiko gestured at the statue— "could this be the cursed keeper of faith in the maze?"

Now Arin's eyes flew wide. "Oh, my."

Egil shook his head. "The Queen of Jute? Could she be both?"

Alos frowned. "Both?"

Egil held up two fingers. "The mad monarch *and* the cursed keeper of faith in the maze?"

"Oh," said Alos, enlightened.

All three looked at Arin, but she turned up her hands. "I do not know."

Egil sighed. "That's the trouble with redes and prophecies: they are riddles: a person never knows what in *Hèl* they mean until they come true. Why can't they simply be plain?"

He looked from one to another, yet none could answer his question, though Aiko said, "Who knows the ways of madmen and gods and prophecies?"

"Well, I think none of us will ever know even if we do escape from this maze," said Egil. "Regardless, let's get out."

Aiko nodded and started to draw her sword, but Arin gestured *No*. "I believe I can set us free from this trap, and then we shall deal with the question of the queen as the keeper of faith in a maze."

Arin turned and looked at the maze in her special way,

as if attempting to <see>. To her eyes it seemed to glow with a faint aura. Leading, she walked them through the maze and into the open. The way out was simple, straight-forward, and they could not understand how they had ever been befooled, though Alos said, "See, it *was* cursed . . . or magic."

Free from the hedge maze, they continued on 'round the grounds, encircling the castle proper, scanning walls and defenses, noting where stood doorways, eyeing places where they could conceal themselves if it came to such, noting as well the barricade encircling the hill, with its ramps and banquettes and gorges, and noting as well where men patrolled and where others stood sentry.

Directly behind the castle and a bit downslope they came upon a small granite courtyard enclosed by a low wall. The stone within was blackened, as if scorched repeatedly by fire. The way in was barred by a latched, low-set, wrought-iron gate. Scrollwork across the gate spelled out the word *"Geliebter."*

"What does it mean?" asked Aiko.

"Beloved," replied Alos. "Er, 'beloved man,' I think."

At a questioning glance from Arin, Egil said, "Funeral pyres."

Arin nodded, and they turned away.

They had circled perhaps three-quarters of the whole, when they came in among open-sided buildings set apart from the castle and housing caged animals on display.

"The mad queen's zoo," hissed Egil, so as not to be heard by nearby attendants.

They passed among confined snow jackals and cin-namon argali and mountain springers and black renders and other animals they could not name—all trapped in cages too small, where they paced or cowered or lay dull-eyed and inactive.

Now the four came in among the mews. Here they found raptors—trained hunting birds: grey falcons, red hawks, black kestrels, golden eagles. Among these raptors stepped an iron-collared attendant, removing the hoods from the perched birds and feeding them gobbets of raw meat.

"I say," called out Alos, "be these all of the birds?"

The thrall looked around and, spying them, removed his hat and said, *"Die allgemein Sprache kann ich nicht."*

"Ung," grunted Alos. "He doesn't speak common." The oldster then called out, *"Mehr Vogel? Wo?"*

The man's face lit up. "Ah." He gestured northward. *"Dort bei der Teich gibt es Geflügel."*

Alos smiled and sketched a bow and said, *"Wir danken Ihnen."* The man held his hat to his chest and bowed low. Alos then turned to the others. "He says there's more birds, fowl, that is, down by the pond."

They stepped from the mews and turned to the north and started down the slope. Just ahead and below they could see a small mere dug into the hillside, its far perimeter an earthen dam. As they approached, quacking ducks and gabbling geese paddled toward them, as if expecting a handout. But these common fowl were not what captured the gazes of the foursome. Instead it was a large iridescent bird with a crested head and brilliant blue-green plumage. When it saw them coming it spread wide its great tail coverts, and each of these long feathers was marked with an iridescent eyelike spot.

"Adon," breathed Arin, "it is beautiful."

"Is it our rutting peacock?" asked Alos, turning to Aiko.

"A peacock, yes," she replied. "Rutting, I cannot say, for I see no peahens nearby." Aiko gazed about, then gasped and stepped down to the edge of the mere, where she squatted and plucked out of the water a floating tail feather of the peacock. She glanced up at Arin and raised the plume, its eye-spot scintillant. "Dara, is this a one-eye in dark water as well?"

Arin sighed and shrugged, but Egil said, "Damnation. Are we to be plagued with symbols and portents, none of which we can be certain represents the truth?"

"Ha," barked Alos. "Now we have three different one-eyes in dark water: Egil, a feather, and me." He gestured over his shoulder. "And back there is a statue that might or might not represent a cursed keeper of faith in the maze. And here before us is what might be a mad monarch's rutting peacock, except there isn't a thing to rut, unless of course he rides the ducks and geese. What progress we are making, eh?"

Aiko shook her head and held up four fingers. "You left out one of the one-eyes, Alos: the honeyed Troll's eye we keep in a sack."

"Eep!" squeaked Alos, shuddering.

At this, the peacock craned its neck and emitted a raucous call: *Karawah, karawah, karawah!*

Egil looked at the bird and burst out laughing. When Arin's wide-eyed gaze fell upon him, Egil dropped to his knees and laughed all the harder, but managed to gasp out, "Adon, if we steal this thing, it'll give us away with its shrieks."

CHAPTER 39

With Egil on his knees, laughing, Arin said, "I do not plan on *stealing* it, *chier,* although we may take it with us. The queen shall have to consider it a loan for the greater good." This caused Egil to roar all the harder, and he pointed to Arin and then to the peacock. As if sensing an insult, the fowl craned its neck and bugled a *karawah, karawah, karawah!* Egil whooped and fell over backward and laughed up at the sky, and Aiko and Alos joined in, Aiko tittering behind her hand, Alos cackling in glee. Arin was caught up in the gaiety, her silver laughter blending in. And the bird strutted around and peered accusingly at them as they guffawed and tears ran down their faces. Finally they got control of themselves and, wiping their eyes, they left the offended peacock behind, though now and again one or another would break into laughter and the others would grin in return. Even so, they continued their exploration of the grounds, noting any detail they thought might be useful should it come to fight or flight. They walked along the banquette 'round the outer bulwark, peering over the edge now and again to spy out places where they might drop to the ground if they needed to flee across the wall. " 'Tis a thirty-foot fall, at best," said Egil. "I think we'll need a rope should we come this way."

Aiko looked at Alos. "Can you manage a rope?"

"Oh, I can slide down one," replied the oldster, then he looked at his hands, "but I'll need a pair of gloves. And climbing? Heh, I think I remember how; though strength plays a part, it's mostly technique, y' know."

"Umn," Egil grunted. "Let us hope it doesn't come to climbing or sliding at all"—he grinned at the other three—"especially with a squawking bird in hand."

Aiko smiled, then sobered and looked at Arin. "He does have a point, Dara: we wouldn't want the bird to sound an alarm. Does the rutting peacock need be alive? If not, we can simply wring its neck."

"We can knock it in the head and stuff it in the costume trunk," suggested Alos.

Arin made a negating gesture. "We will merely hood it; then it will make no sound at all."

Aiko glanced back at the distant mews. "Ah, like the raptors, yes?"

"Yes," replied Arin. "Now let us go onward. If we must flee, there may be an easier way out than rappelling down a wall."

They moved on 'round the banquette, as if out for a constitutional stroll, and when they came above the main entrance, they paused as if to rest. As they tarried, Egil talked casually with one of the guards, and discovered that the inner gate ordinarily was kept closed and the outer portcullis down, though during this time of celebration, queen's merchants and her guests came and went frequently, as well as those invited to perform.

Refreshed by their so-called rest, Egil and the others strolled onward, and when they were beyond earshot, Alos said, "Heh, this will be even easier than expected. I mean, we'll just come and go like the other entertainers. O' course, when we go, we'll have a hooded peacock hidden away, eh?"

Egil shook his head. "What you say is true on the surface, my friend, yet many a thing can go wrong 'tween now and then. We need at least one other plan in case this one goes ill." He turned to Arin. "I think I'll see if Dolph can get us a rope. If he asks, I'll say we need it for Aiko's sword dancing tomorrow night."

"Sword dancing!" exclaimed Aiko, her gaze growing hard. "Hear me: I demonstrate *kenmichi,* the way of the sword. It is not a dance . . . or if it is, it is a deadly one."

Egil grinned and bowed. "My error, Lady Aiko."

Mollified, Aiko canted her head, then said, "Alos needs gloves."

"And we need something to stuff a hooded peacock in," added Alos, "if we don't use the trunk, that is."

* * *

They located Dolph in their quarters and sent him to fetch a rope. When he had gone, Egil said, "Tomorrow, when he'll not think of it in connection with the rope, I'll ask Dolph to find us a sack." Egil glanced at Alos. "To carry the peacock in should we need go over the wall. And speaking of ropes and walls . . ." Egil rummaged about in his luggage and tossed a pair of gloves to Alos. The oldster tried them on and found they fit well enough.

Grinning his gap-toothed smile, Alos tucked the gloves away, then said, "What say we eat, eh?"

They took their midday meal in the dining hall of the east tower, and afterward explored the castle proper, all but the central spire. As they strolled about, they took special note of all points of egress in the event of a hasty exit. When they finally returned to their quarters, they found a length of rope lying on Lady Aiko's bed.

That evening, as Dolph had said there would be, they heard the ringing of a bell.

"We are summoned to the festivities," said Egil, slipping into a dark red jacket, accented in black, matching his accented breeks. His feet were shod in black boots, and 'round his waist was clasped a black belt with red buckle. He stuck his head out the door and called, "Dolph," and the chamberboy hurried inward. "We've not yet been to the central tower; will you guide us?"

"Ja, sir, I will." Dolph paused, then added, "But with you that axe you cannot take. Stahl only, the queen's champion, in her presence weapons to bear is permitted."

"But we're here to entertain the queen," said Egil, "tomorrow night, and it's part of my costume, lad, just as Lady Aiko's blades are part of her costume."

"Well, sir, into the great hall your axe you will be permitted tomorrow and Lady Aiko her swords. But for tonight only permitted small ornamental daggers are. Wear them all the lords do."

"Bah," growled Aiko. "In the hands of one who knows how to use it, a tiny dagger will kill as swiftly as a great sword."

Egil sighed and slipped his axe from his belt and laid it

on the table, signing for Aiko to do likewise. Muttering under her breath, she unbuckled her blades and laid them beside Egil's axe. But she did not remove the four shiruken hidden in a band at her waist.

"Do we look all right now, boy?" asked Alos, craning his neck in his ruffed collar. Alos was scrubbed and groomed and was dressed in green: pale green shirt with ruffles at the collar and wrist, emerald green jacket and breeks, black boots and belt. On his head he wore a dark green hat with a black plume.

Aiko, as usual, was dressed in her leathers, but she forwent her ribands, saying that she would wear them morrow night for her performance.

Dolph looked at them, but he seemed transfixed as his gaze alighted on Arin in her simple yet elegant satin gown of russet that fell straight to the floor from a tan bodice. Brown slippered feet peeked under the hem. Her chestnut hair was garlanded with intertwined beige ribbons, matching those crisscrossing the bodice. In a breathless voice, Dolph said, "More beautiful than you, milady, none will be," then immediately blushed and turned away.

Egil grinned and murmured to Alos, "Methinks he saw neither thee nor me nor Lady Aiko, but I suspect we are presentable."

When they came to the door of the great hall, Dolph, his wards safely delivered, sped away. Arin and her companions joined a slow-moving stream of nobles and diplomats and other guests pacing inward past a posted guard. Ahead, within the hall, a steward struck a great staff 'gainst the floor and called out the ranks and names of the guests as they made their entrances. Slowly the line advanced, and at last the four of them moved past the doors.

They came into a great long chamber, beringed by pillars against the wide-set walls. Spaced along the walls as well were huge hearths, all without fire, for it was early September and summer had not yet fled the land. The walls themselves were hung with tapestries, and staffs jutted out, from which depended the colorful flags of the different fiefdoms of Jutland arranged in descending order of rank—dukes' flags above those of counts,

counts' above earls, and so on, down through viscounts and barons—each flag bearing a coat of arms. Overhead, great wooden beams spanned from wall to wall, and dangling down from the timbers were chain-hung braces of lanterns; the chandeliers were lighted brightly, for only lavender twilight streamed in through high windows above. Three broad steps down from the wide entryway landing began a great center floor of smooth, polished stone, the whole ringed around by raised flooring where sat banquet tables. The amphitheater swept forward till it fetched up against four steps leading to a wide throne dais. Though the floor was awash with people, the throne itself was empty.

The hall was abuzz with conversation, and with Arin on one arm and Aiko on the other, and with Alos trailing after, Egil came to an aide standing beside the steward and whispered their names to the man. As other guests passed them by and were announced, the aide looked through a list and then said, "Ah yes. Here you are." He looked up at Egil. "You will be seated at Baron Stolz's table." He pointed to a table halfway along the left side of the chamber. "There, under the green flag with the white boar." At Egil's nod, the aide stepped to the steward, who struck the floor with his staff and then called out: "Milords and ladies and honored guests: the Dylvana Arin of Darda Erynian; Lady Aiko of Ryodo; Master Alos of Thol; and Master Egil One-Eye of Jord."

As they stepped forward down to the main floor, Arin glanced up at Egil and mouthed, [Jord?]

Egil leaned down and whispered, "Aye. Jute and Fjordland are ancient enemies, hence it would be folly to claim my true homeland when I stand in the court of the foe. And so I chose another. Jord and Fjordland are neighbors, and the Jordian accent is much like my own."

Now they moved down among the guests, and many eyes followed them, widening at the sight of the satin-gowned Dylvana and the leather-clad golden warrior at her side. As to Egil and Alos, the guests gave them little heed, their glances pausing only long enough to note Egil's scarlet eye patch and Alos's white eye, though some *did* make surreptitious signs of warding at the sight of the oldster's pale orb. Egil though scanned their faces closely, and he said to Arin, "Let us circle, love, for I would find Baron Steiger. Likely he'll be here, and perhaps by now has remembered where he and I met."

Slowly they wended among the throng, Alos and Aiko following. Searching carefully, they made one complete circuit about the floor, but of Baron Steiger there was no hint. "Shall we go 'round again?" asked Arin, yet in that moment there sounded a trumpet.

The steward hammered the floor three times and called out, "The queen approaches." Moving to places more or less in line with their respective feudal flags, people formed a long aisle down the center of the floor from the doors to the throne. With Arin and Egil leading, Alos and Aiko following, the four moved to a place along the aisle forward of Baron Stolz's flag. Moments later, the clarion flourished again, and the steward smote his staff against the floor three more times and called out, "My lords and ladies and honored guests, Queen Gudrun the Comely, monarch of all Jutland and of the Ryngar Isles, and her consort, Delon the Virile." Then steward and trumpeter stepped aside and bowed low.

In through the door swept a tall woman. She was dressed in a pale blue long-sleeved silken gown with a tight bodice and a skirt which flared out at the hips to fall widely to the floor. Yellow hair cascaded in curls down her back, and tight ringlets framed her powdered and rouged face. A golden tiara set with glittering jewels crowned her head. About her left wrist was clamped a silver bracelet from which a long silver chain linked her to the silver collar 'round the neck of the man following to her left and a step behind.

He was compact, no taller than she, perhaps five feet eight inches altogether. He had fair skin and pale blond hair and his age was perhaps thirty. He was dressed in dark purple, with bright lavender insets in the puffed shoulders and sleeves, and lavender ruffles at neck and wrist. His purple shoes and belt, with their lavender buckles, matched the rest of his garb, and he wore a wide-brimmed lavender hat adorned with three enormous purple plumes.

Gudrun paused, allowing any and all to admire her, and then permitted the consort to offer his hand as she descended the three steps to the amphitheater floor. Together they paced down the aisle, he once again a stride behind, and they smiled and nodded at the bowing and curtseying guests. When they came to Arin and Aiko, the queen paused and looked at them both, her pale blue eyes glittering. And no amount of powder and rouge could conceal the effects of the passage of the thirty years that had elapsed since the statue of her—the one in the hedge maze—had been crafted. She smiled at Arin, and the consort swept the plumed hat from his head and bowed low and smiled at Arin as well, though no hint of pleasure reached his eyes. Then they both moved on without saying a word.

The queen and her consort came to the dais and mounted up, she to sit on the throne, he to sit on the top step to her left. Her gaze swept across the crowd, and she raised a hand and said, "We are most pleased to have you join us in our celebration of new love." She beamed down at the consort, a man twenty years her junior, and he canted his head in obeisance. She batted her eyelashes and rattled the chain, the links of silver clinking softly.

Egil leaned over and whispered to Arin. "Adon! She treats him as if he were a pet dog."

Aiko, overhearing, shook her head. "Worse, for he is unmanned, as no pet dog would be."

Giggling, the queen stood and gestured left and right and commanded, "Let the celebration commence."

At these words, people began moving toward their assigned tables, Egil, Arin, Aiko, and Alos turning toward the one under the green flag sporting the white boar. As they took their places, the other guests at the table stared at the satin-gowned Dylvana and the leather-clad Ryodoan at hand. Egil introduced himself and the others, and received their names in return, though one of the seated ladies—the Baroness Stolz—gushed, "Oh, I've heard of you, Lady Arin. You are the Elven bard." She turned to Aiko. "And this must be the sword dancer."

Aiko growled under her breath, but held her peace.

At the baroness's side, a sour-faced man, Baron Stolz,

leaned over and whispered to her in a voice all could hear, "Hush, my dear. An Elf if she wasn't, the queen's guests at all they would not be. But common entertainers these are."

Again, Aiko growled under her breath. Egil, though, sketched a bow to the baron and said, "I daresay, dear baron, we are not in any way 'common,' as you will no doubt discover in the days to come."

The baron huffed but made no reply.

In through the doorway, to much applause, marched the entertainers: strong men, jugglers, prestidigitators, acrobats and tumblers, wrestlers and dancers and buffoons. They circled the floor to be seen, and then marched back out the door.

Inward came thralls bearing platters laden with food: fresh-baked loaves of bread, roast pig and lamb and beef, grilled fowl and broiled fish, and stewed vegetables such as beans and red cabbage and peas and parsnips, and great bowls filled with grapes and pears and peaches. More thralls entered, these conveying pitchers of foaming ale and mead and wine to the tables, and Alos looked longingly at each and every one that passed by him, though Aiko prevented him from snagging any.

The boards were set and groaned beneath the weight of the feast, and the guests filled their trenchers with food and their goblets with their choices of drink, all but Alos, for although he could choose whatever he wished from among the food, Aiko would allow him only water or tea, even though he gazed at the other libations and whined, "Just a taste. A little taste. What can it hurt, eh?"

But Aiko was adamant, and Alos growled, "I'll be glad when we've got what we've come for and all of you are on your way. Then I'll do as I please."

Aiko glared at him, and Alos ducked his head and snatched up a joint of beef. But 'ere he could take a bite, Arin reached out and stopped him, saying, "Wait," and gestured toward the throne.

On the dais, servants set a small table beside the queen. And they laded her trencher with the food of her choice. They also set a trencher down beside Consort Delon, and placed in it food at her direction. They poured wine into golden goblets, and set one of these by Delon as well. Satisfied, the queen raised her chalice and called out, "Let us begin."

A lord stepped forth onto the floor and raised his own goblet on high, proclaiming, "To the queen!"

To the queen! came the response.

The queen stood. "Nay. Not to me, but to love instead."

"Are they not the same?" called out the lord.

Baron Stolz hissed under his breath. "Bah! Toadying fool. Careful if he is not, next he will be."

"To the queen and love," called out the lord, raising his goblet on high.

To the queen and love! came the response, followed by a cheer.

And at a sign from the simpering queen, all dug into their food . . . except for Delon, who only seemed to pick at his meal.

In through the doorway came three buffoons in garish makeup: the first one stepped across the amphitheater as if walking on an invisible tightrope high above the floor, his arms outstretched, his entire body wobbling and jerking this way and that as if for balance; the second buffoon walked to one side, half crouching and looking upward, his hands held out as if to catch the first should he fall; the third buffoon was enwrapped in a cloak and he walked to the left and behind the first. Just as they reached the center of the floor, the cloaked buffoon drew a slapstick out from beneath his cape and with a loud *crack!* whacked the rope walker on the behind, who, with a descending scream, staggered and spun and lurched to one side as if falling, while the catcher, with his arms outstretched, ran wobbling to save him, and they crashed into one another and collapsed in a heap as the crowd whooped in laughter, the cloaked buffoon roaring and laughing and pointing at his handiwork. Then the three buffoons began chasing one another 'round and 'round in a tight circle, one whaling away with an inflated pig's bladder, one with a slapstick, and one merely whooping and howling and leaping each time he was whacked, his garish mouth gaping wide with his bawling. The guests roared at such farce, the queen herself pounding the arms of her throne and hooting with joy. But purple-plumed Consort Delon merely smiled.

Finally, in file, they ran from the great hall, howling and whacking and battering. Resounding applause followed them out, and they popped back in to bow to the acclaim, only to be whacked at one and the same time by a very long slapstick wielded by a fourth garish buffoon as they bent low—to the delight of the crowd.

Next came a man and a woman juggling flaming batons, and they whirled and danced and flung the blazing wands back and forth, several in the air simultaneously.

They were followed in turn by wrestlers and acrobats and a strong man and other entertainers. At last, long into the night, Queen Gudrun the Comely ordered a halt to the proceedings and announced, "The time has come to hear Delon sing."

As the table and remains of the meal were cleared away from the dais and a silver-stringed lute was brought to Delon, Baroness Stolz leaned across to an elderly lady and said, "I hear she found him in Thol while visiting the Tower of Gudwyn the Fair, an ancestor of hers, I believe."

"Oh no, my dear," responded the dowager, Lady Klatsch, "I believe he was taken in a raid in West Gelen."

"Hmph," harrumphed Baron Stolz. "Just a commoner he is told am I. To the castle he came two months past, advantage to take. Burned like the others he will be—serves him right—though longer than any of them he has lasted."

Delon removed his tri-plumed lavender hat and set it on the steps. Then he took up the lute and strummed it once, gauging its state of tune. Satisfied, he turned to the queen. "Have you a request, milady?"

She leaned forward and smiled coyly. " 'The Lovers.' "

Delon bowed. "As you will, my queen."

Once again he sat at her feet, then he began to sing, his voice gentle when the words were gentle, and sweet when they were sweet, strong and vibrant as called for, and whispery at need. The guests all sat silent, no coughs, no rustle of movement, no shuffling of feet, as his singing filled the hall. And the queen sat transfixed, her eyes drinking in the sight of him, her hands gripping the arms of the throne until her knuckles shone white, her breath coming in short gasps followed by prolonged sighs.

Arin leaned over and whispered to Egil, "If I knew not what my eyes saw, I would think him an Elf."

Egil whispered back: "If I knew not what my eyes saw, I would think her making love in bed."

Finally Delon's song came to an end, and applause erupted and there were many calls for more. But abruptly the queen stood, her eyes shining brightly. "It is late and we are weary. Come, Delon." And without another word, she swept down the steps of the dais and across the floor and out from the great hall, towing Delon on his silver chain after.

When Arin and the others returned to their room, they found that Dolph had turned down the beds and had opened the doors to the balcony, airing out the chamber. The September night was warm, and a half moon sank in the west, casting its light across the balustrade and into the room. Doffing their clothes, they prepared for sleep: Arin and Egil took to their bed, drawing the curtains closed; Aiko set her tatami mat to the floor and settled into cross-legged repose, her swords at hand, her back against the door; Alos glanced at her and, grumbling and huffing, lay down on his couch and pulled a thin cover over himself and fell instantly to sleep.

A quietness descended, the room silent but for the soft sonance of breathing. But then, drifting inward through the open balcony door, there came the distant sounds of someone, a female, in distress. Aiko's eyes flew open and she listened. . . . No, not distress, but rather the hoarse panting groans of a woman in the throes of passion, moans of pleasure climbing and building, ending at last with a climactic shriek. Aiko stood and stepped to the balcony and peered down into the courtyard below. She could see no one in the moonlight and shadows. As she turned to go back in, movement caught at the corner of her eye, and there on the central tower and above, on the balcony to the queen's bedchamber stood Delon. Even though he stood in gloom, Aiko knew it was he, for a silver collar girded his neck and a silver chain arced down and into the black of the room behind. He was leaning on his hands on the railing, and his head hung down as if he were fatigued. He was unclothed.

Aiko slid back into the shadows of her balcony. She stood and watched. Of a sudden, the chain jerked once, twice, thrice. Wearily, Delon turned and plodded back into the queen's bedroom.

Long moments later, gasps of pleasure began drifting down once again.

Muttering "Now I know what the mad monarch is mad for," Aiko walked back to her tatami and resumed her lotus repose as the groans built toward a climax.

After a while, the moans began again . . .

. . . and again . . .

. . . and again.

Finally, growling, "*Tenti!* Is she never sated?" Aiko closed the balcony door, shutting away the sounds of unhindered lust.

CHAPTER 40

In the candlemark before dawn, Egil began to moan in his sleep as another of his nightly ill dreams beset him; as if it were somehow contagious, Alos, too, began thrashing about . . . and *meep*ing. Aiko shook the oldster awake, and he raised up and looked about wildly, lost for a moment, but then with a groan he fell back onto the couch and pulled the cover over his head. In the canopied and curtained bed, Arin tried to awaken Egil, but could not until the flaying of Sturgi was complete. When sanity returned to Egil, he held onto Arin and wept and swore vengeance against Ordrune once the quest for the green stone was complete.

They settled back for what little remained of the night, yet when they finally awoke, the sun was well up in the sky.

Egil called for Dolph to help him prepare baths, and he and the lad filled tubs in the bathing cubicle and selected wood from the cord to build fires in the heating chambers underneath. As they were doing so, Egil said, "Dolph, we are going to need a rather large sack—something big enough to hold our rope and swords and drum and my axe and the other items we need for the act we are to put on for the queen. Do you think you can find us one."

"A grain sack, sir, would do, ja?" Dolph spread his arms wide, some three to four feet.

"Have you something a bit larger?"

Dolph managed to shrug as he poured another bucket of water into one of the tubs. "Know do I not, sir. Try will I."

Egil struck a spark and blew on the smoldering tinder to coax it into flame. He placed the shavings in the heating chamber and added small strips of kindling. As he watched the fire grow, he asked, "Dolph, do you know Baron Steiger?"

"So I think, sir. The tall one he is, ja?"

"Yes, and he has black hair and dark blue eyes."

"Seen him, sir, I believe I have."

Now Egil began adding heavier kindling to the fire, and he moved some of the burning brands to the grille under the second bathtub and added wood there as well, saying, "Dolph, I'd like to speak with Baron Steiger. Will you find where he's quartered?"

"Ja, sir, easy that will be. The chambermaids I will ask."

"Well and good, Dolph. Well and good."

When Aiko and Arin finished bathing, Egil and Alos took their turns, the old man yet swearing that too many baths would sicken a horse, much less a human being: "I mean, Hèl, boy, we could die of exposure."

By the time they were finished, Dolph had returned with an assortment of grain sacks, one burlap bag clearly large enough to hold the peacock, though the lad knew it not. Egil thanked him, and Arin smiled at the youth, and he blushed and rushed away with the surplus, stammering to Egil that he would locate Baron Steiger now.

They broke their fast in midmorn and then took to the grounds again to see what they might have overlooked. The skies had grown dark with a cloudy overcast. Arin held a hand in the air, feeling the drift of the onshore wind, then pronounced, "Ere this day is done, rain will come."

On they continued, committing the defenses of the citadel to memory. As they came into the eastern quadrant, someone hailed. It was Dolph, and they waited for him.

"Baron Steiger, sir, at the castle no longer he is." Dolph jerked his head toward the stables on the southeastern side of the grounds. "Yestermorn rode he away, tell me the livery boys do. Hard. Some mad errand he was on. A remount he took. And back he has not yet come."

"Hmm," mused Egil. "I wonder . . ." He glanced at

Arin and Aiko and Alos, but all three turned up their hands and shrugged.

"Mayhap he will return ere we depart," said Arin.

Egil took a deep breath and slowly let it out, then said, "One can only hope." He turned to Dolph. "Thanks, lad. Have the stableboys let you know when the baron comes back, and keep an eye out for him yourself. Then come find me."

"Sir, ja," said Dolph, and he sped away toward the stables.

Under lowering skies they continued strolling the grounds. At one point, they stopped in the mews and Alos paused in conversation with the Jutlander who tended the raptors. In due time, the man bobbed his head and walked with Alos to a shed and stepped inside. After a moment the man emerged and handed Alos something. With a *"Danke,"* Alos bowed to the man, who seemed surprised at the gesture but bowed in kind, and then Alos rejoined his companions. When they were away from the mews, "Think these'll fit the peacock?" he asked, showing them a shabby falconry hood and tattered jesses.

They strode on 'round the grounds, pausing at the kennels as if to admire the queen's hunting dogs, but in truth they had stopped there to make certain that the raptor attendant was not following.

Then, casually, they strolled to the pond and found the peacock nearby, and laughed when the iridescent fowl turned a suspicious eye their way, as if it were expecting ill-mannered gibes to fall to the ground from their lips. But Arin cooed softly to it and the bird drew near enough for her to gauge that the raptor hood would fit rather well.

Aiko walked under a nearby tree, a tall maple, its leaves rustling in the growing breeze, and she studied the ground below. Spying what she had come to find, she moved somewhat to the side and then gazed upward. "This tree is his nightly roost, for here are his droppings, and there above, some twenty feet up, is a suitable perch."

Egil glanced sidelong at the bird downslope and hissed, "Here we'll come skulking in the black of the night when the moon has set. One of us will climb in the dark and take the bird our prisoner, casting a hood over its head and tying it tight, then throwing the whole in a bag and lowering it to the others below."

Karawah, karawah, karawah!

"Fie, he has discovered our plot," Egil managed to gasp out between guffaws. "We are undone."

Laughing, the four conspirators continued uphill, where they took rest on one of the marble benches scattered here and there upon the grounds.

Aiko sighed, then said, "Dara, I still do not see how a peacock can aid us to discover the green stone."

Egil barked a laugh. "Perhaps he'll think it an egg and try to hatch it."

Arin smiled, then sobered. "Aiko, the ways of prophecies are mysterious. I, too, cannot see how a fowl can aid us. Yet I also do not see how *any* of us will fulfill the words of the rede. I merely know that we must go on . . . and trust to Adon that we will succeed."

In that moment, great drops of rain began spattering down, and the four made a run for the castle, Arin easily in the lead, Alos gasping and wheezing and bringing up the rear.

The guard at the door to the great hall stepped before Egil to bar the way. "Sorry, sir, but weapons into the presence of the queen you cannot bring."

Egil grinned and canted his head, then said, "Let me present Lady Arin the bard and Alos her drummer. And this is Lady Aiko the sword dancer, and I am Egil of Jord. We are entertainers and are to perform at the command of the queen, and these meager arms are but part of our costumes."

The warder opened his mouth to speak, but from behind came a commanding voice: "Let them pass. They are indeed mere entertainers."

They turned to see the lord chamberlain standing at hand. Egil flourished a bow, and the chamberlain nodded in return. The guard stepped back and clicked his heels together and stiffly canted his head, and the four moved into the great hall.

"Milords and ladies and honored guests: the Dylvana

Arin of Darda Erynian, Lady Aiko of Ryodo, Master Alos of Thol, and Master Egil One-Eye of Jord."

Again they moved past the steward and stepped down onto the amphitheater floor. This night Arin was dressed in her pale green gown, with matching ribbons laced in her chestnut hair. Alos was outfitted in his tan jacket and breeks and brown jerkin, and his dark brown boots and belt; he carried his tambour under one arm and his cruik was slipped through his belt. Egil wore black: shirt, jacket, breeks, boots, belt, soft beret—all jet; only his eye patch and axe were of a different color—the scarlet and gold leather band and the steel blade and dark oak helve enhancing his sinister air. Aiko was dressed in her leather armor, the hammered bronze platelets on her jacket dull in the lantern light. At her waist were girted her two swords, the four shiruken hidden. She wore a pair of daggers, one strapped to each thigh. Her helm was under her arm, now adorned with the peacock feather. Colorful long ribands were tied 'round her upper arms and forearms and wrists, and 'round her waist and thighs and just below the knees; and as she walked, they trailed and swirled. She looked every inch a golden warrior—danger afoot— yet with the grace of a dancer, and many a head turned her way.

Once again the four of them circled the floor, looking for Baron Steiger, yet with little hope, for Dolph had not brought word that the baron had returned. And with the rain pouring outside, it was likely that Steiger, even if he were on his way back, had taken refuge in some inn. Indeed, they did not find him among the milling guests.

Finally the trumpet flourished and the steward knelled the floor and announced the imminent arrival of the queen, and the guests formed an aisle. Again the clarion sounded, and the steward's words rang out and the queen and her consort entered.

This night she wore a peach-colored gown, and her golden hair was long and straight and fanned about her bare shoulders. Her tiara was gold and plain.

Following her on his silver chain came Delon, dressed in shimmering blues and greens, his sheening blue jacket long and tailed, with puffed sleeves inset with glittering green panels matching his green satin shirt. His pantaloons were blue-and-green striped, and he wore blue hosiery on one leg and green hosiery on the other. His shoes were sequined blue and green, and his hat iridescent blue, with a shimmering blue plume on one side and a shimmering green plume on the other.

The queen and her gaudy escort mounted the dais, she to sit on the throne, he to sit to one side at her feet, and she smiled down at him as if he were a prize stud on display, he to wanly smile back.

The entertainers paraded about the floor, this time Arin, Alos, Aiko, and Egil joining them, Aiko growling under her breath, yet she managed a smile of sorts—her teeth gritted in false exhibition. Afterward they rejoined Baron Stolz's table in time to hear him say, "Helga, see. *Told* you did I common entertainers they are."

Again this night, food was served, and, as before, the queen declared the celebration to be in honor of new love. And the festivity began.

Three garishly painted buffoons entered, arguing silently as they strolled across the amphitheater floor. Of a sudden, it seemed as if they collided with an invisible wall and crashed backward to the floor, to the amusement of the guests. Hands outstretched they felt their way along the invisible barrier; moments later it became clear that they were trapped in a large invisible box, for the unseen wall went 'round in a square, and they were enclosed inside. Two boosted the third upward, to see if he could climb over the wall, but his head crashed into an invisible ceiling, and all three crashed to the floor, while the guests and queen hooted in laughter and she pounded the arms of her throne. Now the three buffoons panicked and ran crashing into the unseen walls, falling and rising and running and crashing only to do it over again, and the queen's shrieks of laughter were lost in the howling roars of all, while Delon merely smiled. Then a fourth buffoon entered the banquet hall and stepped across the floor to the invisible chamber and took a great key from his pocket and unlocked an unseen door. He motioned to the others, and they came out one by one, only to be whacked with loud *crack*s by a slapstick wielded by their rescuer as he chased them out from the great hall, while the guests roared their approval and applauded. The four buffoons returned to take a bow, only to be whacked on the behind by a fifth buffoon as they bowed low.

When the applause and laughter died, a man with his hands in his pockets nonchalantly strolled in, followed by five small dogs dressed in gaily colored ruffed collars and walking upright on their hind legs. They leapt through hoops and climbed small ladders and retrieved juggled balls when the man dropped them . . . and other such tricks as well.

The performance of the man and his dogs was followed by a prestidigitator, and then three people who performed feats of balance.

Then it was time for Arin to sing. Dressed in black, his tawny hair shining like burnished brass, Egil stepped to the center of the floor and waited for all to grow quiet. Finally he turned and bowed to the queen. "Queen Gudrun the Comely"—he turned once again to the crowd—"and milords and ladies and honored guests, I present the lovely Dara Arin, Dylvana of Blackwood, of Darda Erynian. Accompanied by Alos of Thol, she will touch your hearts with song. Beware, for you will never be the same."

With Alos at hand, Arin, looking small and slight in her green gown, made her way to the raised floor to the right and below the queen's dais. Stepping forward to the edge of the amphitheater, Arin waited as slowly the mutter of conversation died, then in a clear voice announced, " 'The Shorn Bride.' "

A stir went through the crowd, for this was a tale of love bereft, and who knows how the queen might react? Quiet swiftly returned as Alos, standing behind and to Arin's right, began gently tapping cruik to drum.

Now Arin's voice softly filled the chamber, climbing in volume as she sang of Rald and Isalda: he was a young knight and she a maiden, and their love for one another was so deep as to be nearly beyond understanding. Their wedding was celebrated by the entire realm, for they were dearly loved by all. Yet on that very same day, news came of the slaughter of Rald's brother Gran, who had journeyed away on knight errantry to a far land. Rald swore vengeance, and after but a single night of sweet love, he set out to avenge his kith. Pining in her tower, the new bride Isalda waited for a year and a day, yet no word came of her husband. And so she set forth and journeyed after, disguised as a lad and posing as nought but a common goatherd. A year and a day of fruitless searching passed, but then in the hold of a renegade warlord she discovered Rald, locked and starving in a dungeon deep and dying from his terrible wounds. Oh, how she wept over his emaciated, torn body and strove desperately to save him, yet he died whispering his love for her. The dungeon warder, overhearing, took pity on her and allowed Isalda to bear Rald's wasted body away. She took him to a field at the edge of the forest, where she built a great funeral pyre. The warlord, spying the large heap of wood at the edge of the field, rode out to discover what was afoot, and Isalda slew him with a dagger to the heart. She cast his body to the foot of Rald, and then mounted atop the pyre and set all aflame and lay down beside her love. It is said to this day that when entwined curls of smoke coil up from a fire, they are the spirits of Isalda and Rald embracing in everlasting love.

When Arin's song came to an end, there was not a dry eye in the hall: Queen Gudrun sat on her throne for all to see and wept and gazed at Delon, choking back her sobs; and even though Delon was a bard who knew the song well, tears ran down his face; throughout the chamber there were sniffles and sobs and unrestrained weeping; even sour Baron Stolz broke down and cried. Behind Arin, Alos wept.

Arin turned to Alos and said, " 'The Ransomed Kiss.' "

Alos nodded and wiped his dripping nose on his sleeve, and then with a flourish he hammered a *rat-a-tat-tat* on the tambour. And as he rapped out a wild tattoo, Arin soared into an absurd ditty of a maid whose cow was stolen by the lad next door who held it as ransom for a kiss. The maiden refused at first, yet she needed the milk to feed her pigs, and so at last she agreed, but under her own terms: she would kiss him in the night in the dark in

her shut barn through a hole in a hanging blanket, for she
was shy and didn't want anyone to know, but only if he
brought the cow with him and only if he would put milk
on his lips so she could be sure it was her cow and not
some other. Too, he had to swear he'd not do this again.
The lad agreed for he dearly wanted that kiss. And so in
the night he led her cow into her barn and shut the door
after. In the pitch blackness she called to him, and fumbling about he discovered the hanging blanket and then
the hole therein. He turned and with one squirt from the
cow's teat, he got a handful of milk and smeared it on his
lips. And in the dark in her shut barn through a hole in a
hanging blanket, he received his kiss, a sloppy one with
the milk and all, and not what he imagined it would be.
But he left the cow behind and went back home, swearing
that he'd not ever do such again, and things returned to
normal. The lad always wondered thereafter, however,
why it was that one of her pigs seemed always to gaze at
him fondly.

Ta-tump!

Laughter rang out in the hall, and Arin and Alos bowed
to the giggling queen and her smiling consort, and then to
the crowd entire, and in spite of the calls for more they
made their way back to Baron Stolz's table, who, beam-
ing, leapt to his feet and bowed. "A drink, Lady Arin, this
calls for," declared the baron, and he handed her a goblet
filled with wine and steered her to his end of the table.
Lady Klatsch turned and offered Alos a goblet as well. He
glanced about, his eyes seeking Aiko, but she and Egil
had moved to the edge of the amphitheater in preparation
for Aiko's display, and Arin was distracted by the baron,
and so Alos eagerly reached out and took the chalice from
the dowager and gulped down the contents in one long
draught. He stood for a moment with his eyes closed as
the wine warmed his very blood. Then, smiling, he
reached for the pitcher to refill his emptied cup.

At last the applause died, and Egil once again stood in
the center of the amphitheater floor. Dressed in black and
looking every bit the sinister figure, he held his deadly
axe in his hands and slowly raised it above his head and
the hall grew quiet. "Dear Queen Gudrun"— again he

turned to the crowd—"and milords and ladies and honored guests"—he flourished his lethal weapon in a whirl and some ladies in the hall gasped—"I may seem Death's champion"—he grounded the steel head of his axe to the floor and leaned upon the oaken helve—"yet I am as nothing when compared to the exotic golden warrior of distant Ryodo, mysterious realm to the faraway east. I give you Lady Aiko"—Egil paused, one hand clutching his neck—"but I warn you: watch for your heads."

As Egil stepped from the amphitheater to stand below and to the right of the throne, Aiko moved to center floor. She bore her plumed helm under one arm, and her swords were sheathed in scabbards harnessed across her back. Upon reaching the midpoint, she paused, and then bowed deeply to the queen, followed by a bow to the guests left and right. She donned her strange helm, with the skirts of the cap flaring out to step down nearly to her shoulders and 'round the sides and behind. A nose guard projected down the front to join with the cheek guards. The peacock plume atop the cap arched over and back to lie at a shallow angle. If the guests had not seen her beforehand, they could not have said whether this warrior was male or female.

Aiko stood for long moments with her eyes closed and her arms extended out to her sides, her bright green and red and blue and orange and violet and yellow ribands hanging down and still. Then she whirled and spun, her ribands streaming, and suddenly her swords were in her hands, the steel flashing in the lantern light. And she danced, or drilled, depending on how one looked at it, twisting, turning, weaving, advancing, retreating, leaping and landing, forward, backward, side to side, the swords gyring and spiraling, her hands reversing their grips so that the blades lay along the length of her forearms, only to reverse again. She thrust ahead and thrust behind, and turned and kicked and thrust, and whirling she slashed the air, so swiftly the blades hummed. She ran up the floor and down the floor and 'cross the floor side to side, all the while hacking and slashing, spinning and cutting, her streaming ribands like streaks of rainbows trailing after, and the crowd *ooh*ed and *ahh*ed. And she whirled and

gyred, spinning faster and faster as she came up the floor
toward the dais, a blur of leather and bronze and steel and
color, until she was before the steps, and of a sudden she
stopped, facing the throne, her swords now sheathed—
just how or when she had done so, none could say. And
slowly, carefully, she removed her helm and bowed low
to the queen.

The hall erupted in roars of acclaim and thunderous
applause, and the queen herself pounded her trencher
table, setting crockery and knives and spoons aclatter.
And Delon in shimmering blue and green stood and
applauded, and he swept his iridescent plumed hat from
his head and bowed low. Seeing Delon's display, a flash
of rage crossed Gudrun's face, only to be replaced by a
smile that went no further than her mouth. She held up her
hands for quiet, and when it fell, "Most impressive," she
said, "but I wonder if it is as deadly as it seems."

Gudrun turned to her left and called out, "Stahl."

A tall man in black leathers with a saber girted at his
waist stood at a nearby table and bowed. "Milady?"

"Stahl, you are my champion. Can you best this yellow
warrior?"

The crowd drew in its collective breath and, from his
place to the right of the throne, Egil started forward, only
to be stopped by a glare and a raised hand from Aiko.

Stahl smiled and stepped to the amphitheater floor. He
was lithe and lean, perhaps thirty, and he towered over
Aiko by a head or more. "My queen, the true test of the
sword is in battle and blood . . . not in a dance."

Gudrun turned to Aiko. "What say you, sword dancer,
will you test your skills against my champion?"

Aiko glanced up at Stahl, now at hand, and said, "I do
not fight merely for show."

Stahl snorted in derision, but the queen raised an eyebrow. "Ah, then, golden warrior, you fight for principle or
prize?"

Aiko stared flatly at Gudrun. "Either or both."

"Then what will you have?"

Ignoring Egil's silent gesture of negation, Aiko asked,
"What do you offer?"

The queen gestured magnanimously. "If you win, take what you will."

Dissembling, Aiko looked about, her gaze passing over golden goblets and jewelry and other riches. "Would you give me a ring?"

Gudrun raised her hands so that her jeweled rings faced Aiko. "Any we wear."

Still disguising her true goal, Aiko then turned and gestured at a serving girl. "Would you give me a thrall?"

Gudrun smiled. "Any of our slaves."

Now Aiko drew nigh to that which she truly wanted and held out a hand toward the left-hand wall. "Would you give me an animal from your gardens, or perhaps a bird?"

Stahl growled, "She delays, my queen."

Agitated, Gudrun snapped, "If you win—ha!—we will give you all four: a ring, a thrall, an animal, and a bird. Do you accept?"

Aiko smiled slowly. "Oh, I will take but one and not all, if I but have your word that you will freely give me what I choose."

"You go too far, yellow woman, when you question our word. Yet we, Gudrun the Comely, Queen of the Jutes, do so swear."

Stahl turned to Aiko. "You have bargained for your reward should you win, yet it is a bargain made in vain, for I will be the victor. Regardless, there are two sides to any bargain, and so I ask: what will *you* give when you lose?"

Aiko looked up at him. "What would you have?"

Stahl turned to the queen. Gudrun shrugged noncommittally and said, "Ask what you will, my champion."

Stahl leered down at Aiko. "I ask that you spend the night pleasuring the royal guard."

The hall burst into laughter and there was a smattering of applause. But above it all there came a cry from Arin: "No, Aiko, pledge not."

Alos, goblet in his right hand, pitcher in his left, lurched to the edge of the amphitheater and called out in his native tongue: *"Nei! Nei løfte!"*

Egil, too, protested, shouting "No," but once again Aiko quelled him with a staying hand.

She turned to Stahl. "I do so swear."

Stahl grinned wolfishly and then turned to his table and called out, "Braun, my main gauche and helm!"

As a rotund man rushed out from the chamber, Aiko began removing her bright ribands. Egil stepped to Aiko's side and stood taking the ribands from her. As he reached out for the bright green one, he whispered, "Aiko, you don't have to do this. There are other ways to get what we came for."

Aiko looked at him and murmured back, "But this way we have it given to us freely."

"If you win, Aiko. Only if you win."

She glared at him, then her gaze softened. "Fear not, my friend, for I will not lose."

Finally the last of her ribands was loose, and Aiko took up her helm and removed the peacock feather and handed it to Egil, who slipped it through a band in his hat. She donned the helmet and drew her blades and stood and waited, her leathers dark, the small bronze plates sewn on her jacket dull in the lanternlight, her steel helm casting no glints, her swords now in hand. She looked every inch a grim warrior, and Stahl was taken somewhat aback, yet he was taller, heavier, and would outreach her by a foot or more.

The rotund man came scurrying back into the hall. He bore a main gauche and an open-faced helmet with chain-link hanging down 'round the back from side to side. Stahl donned his steel cap and handed Braun his belt with its scabbarded sword, then he drew the blades, the main gauche in his left hand, the saber in his right. Bearing the scabbards and belt, Braun scurried away.

Aiko faced him, her eyes shaded by her helm. "To first blood?" she asked.

Stahl nodded. "To first blood."

Together they walked to the very center of the amphitheater floor, Aiko seeming tiny beside his towering form. When they reached midfloor, Aiko called out to the assembly entire: "This will be no courtly mock battle with elaborate flourishes for show—but to first blood instead."

And Stahl called out: "But should someone suffer a fatal wound, well, can I help it if my skill is so great?" He bowed 'round to all as they cheered and called his name.

Alos, sitting on the edge of the amphitheater shouted out: *"Focka du!"* Then he raised his pitcher to his lips and guzzled from it.

Now Aiko and Stahl turned to face the queen and bowed.

"Let it begin," she cried.

The duelists faced one another and saluted with swords—Stahl's gaze arrogant, Aiko's impassive—then dropped into crouches, circling warily. Of a sudden in a whirl of steel, Aiko sprang forward, her blades but a blur—

—*cling-clang, shing-shang, cling-clang, shang-zs*—

—and after but eight quick strokes she disengaged and stepped back.

Frowning, Stahl looked at her—"First blood," she said—and then he felt the warm trickle running down his right cheek.

Unbelieving, he struck his right hand to his face and wiped. His fingers came away wetly scarlet. An incredulous gasp went up from the crowd, and Stahl, stunned, turned to his queen. "Milady, hers could not be but an accidental touch. I demand *true* satisfaction. Let not the whim of Fortune settle this match."

Aiko looked impassively at Gudrun. "Fortune goes to those who are most prepared."

The queen glared at Aiko and showed her teeth in a rictus grin. "To second blood," she hissed.

"Madam, I protest," called Egil.

But Aiko held up a hand to silence him and then turned to Stahl. "To second blood, Stahl. But be warned, if it's to third blood we must go, then it will be to the death."

Stahl clicked his heels together and bowed his head sharply in acceptance.

Once again they saluted with their steel, the look in the queen's champion's eyes now uncertain, wary, the look in Aiko's impassive. As before Stahl dropped into a crouch, but Aiko stood erect and waited, turning to face him as he circled. Then in a blur, steel skirling on steel, she attacked—

—shang-clang, shing-shang, chang-shang, clang-zs—

—and once again she disengaged and stepped back, calling out: "Second blood!"

The crowd groaned, for a trickle of blood now streamed down Stahl's left cheek.

Unbelieving, Stahl looked at the golden warrior and her blades, and opened his mouth to speak. But Egil had crossed the floor to come to Aiko's side, and he escorted her to stand before the queen. "Milady," he said, bowing, "Lady Aiko has proven her skill, not only by drawing first blood, but by drawing second blood as well. She bargained fairly for reward should she win, which as you can see she has done. Hence, let her choose her prize, then let us resume your celebration of love."

Queen Gudrun glared at her disgraced champion, then through gritted teeth hissed at Aiko. "Of the four that I offered, choose."

"Den flugl, den flugl!" cried Alos, waving his pitcher aloft, then whispering to one and all, "We want the rutting bird." And he gulped down another great swallow, red wine running across his cheeks to dribble onto the lapels of his tan jacket.

Aiko wiped the tips of her blades clean on one of the ribands Egil yet held, then sheathed her swords in the scabbards at her back. Then, with her hands on her hips and her feet apart in a balanced stance, she faced the queen.

Now Gudrun leaned forward on her throne and snapped, "Well, what will it be, yellow woman: ring, thrall, beast, or fowl?"

Silence fell as all waited to hear Aiko's choice, and somewhere in the distance above the susurration of rain a bugle sounded.

Aiko looked up at the angry queen and her gaudy escort, then she glanced at Egil with the iridescent peacock feather in his cap. Suddenly her eyes widened in revelation and she turned to the queen and smiled and pointed. "I'll have him."

She had singled out Delon the Bard.

CHAPTER 41

"*What?*" asked Egil, stunned.

Fire lighted Delon's eyes and he leapt to his feet.

"You cannot be serious!" exclaimed the queen.

"Oh, but I am, milady," answered Aiko. "It is Delon the Bard I want."

Wine sloshing in his hand-held pitcher, Alos staggered a few steps out onto the floor, shouting, "*Nei, nei, Aiko. Den flugl, den fockan flugl!*"

"You cannot have him," declared Gudrun.

Her gaze hard as flint, Aiko placed her left foot on the first step of the dais. "Would you go against the gods and break your word? The word of Gudrun the Comely? Pledged here before all your vassals? A thrall you promised, any of my choice, and the silver collar and chain marks Delon as such."

In the great hall the guests sat transfixed, silent but for a murmur here and there.

"You cannot have him, for he is to burn tomorrow and join my other beloveds."

Delon gasped in startlement.

A vision of pyre-blackened stone in an enclosure behind the castle flashed through Aiko's mind. Now she stepped her right foot to the second tread of the dais. Through gritted teeth she declared, "Then you will give him to me ere then."

"Bah!" shouted Gudrun. "I will give him to you afterward—his ashes, that is."

Now Aiko moved her left foot to the third tread.

"Stahl!" cried the queen.

But Egil stood with axe in hand between Gudrun and her champion, and Stahl raised his saber to guard. The guests drew in a collective breath, waiting.

In that moment the doors to the great hall boomed open, and inward, followed by the door warden, strode three mud-spattered men in dripping cloaks. They cast back their hoods, revealing the one on the left to be Baron Steiger; of the remaining two, the one on the right with a bugle depending by baldric from his shoulder was a young man who could have been Stahl's brother; the other was a bearded man in his forties, and Egil's eye widened in recognition and the scar on his forehead and cheek flared red. But ere he could say aught, Steiger pointed at Egil and shouted, "There he is, my Duke, the vile Fjordlander who slew your brother!"

Duke Rache drew his sword, as did the baron and the other man, and the duke called out, "Prepare to greet Hèl, Fjordlander."

"Kill them!" cried Gudrun, triumph in her eyes. "Kill them all!" Her finger stabbed out: "That man and his comrades: this yellow woman, the Elf there, and that old man!"

Before any could move, Aiko drew a sword, and with a single stroke, she clove through Gudrun's left wrist, the severed hand clanging to the dais as the silver bracelet struck stone then fell free from the stump. Gudrun shrieked in horror and pain, her eyes widened in shock as blood fountained from the cloven wrist, and Aiko hissed, "Be grateful it wasn't your head." As Gudrun's eyes rolled up and she fainted, the golden warrior turned, and in the same movement sent a shiruken whispering through the air to take Baron Steiger in the throat, and he fell to the floor gurgling.

A second shiruken *thunk*ed into the back of the neck of the door warden, who had turned and was running for the exit, and he stumbled and fell, his spine severed, the man dead before striking the floor.

Guests screamed in fear and scrambled back against the walls . . . all but Arin, who reached beneath her gown and drew her long-knife from the scabbard strapped 'tween ankle and knee. She moved to stand in the main doorway, her blade gleaming in the lanternlight. The guests, many armed with nought but ornamental daggers, did not try her skill.

"Get her," cried Duke Rache, pointing at Aiko. "The Fjordlander is mine and mine alone!" and with a snarl he attacked. Stahl and the other man charged toward Aiko, and she whipped her second sword free and stood on the dais waiting. Delon dashed left and down, the silver chain and bracelet ringing upon the stone.

Rache's sword clanged against the Fjordlander's axe, driving Egil back and away, so great was the duke's fury. But then Rache's blade met swinging axehead and shattered at the hilt. Momentarily, Rache looked at the bladeless grip in his hand, then flung the hilt clanging away, and shouting in rage, his arms outstretched, his hands like claws, Rache leaped at Egil, and was slain by a blow to the skull. Without giving the duke a second look, Egil turned and ran toward the dais to aid Aiko.

Stahl sprang up the steps and closed with the golden warrior—*shing-shang*—to be skewered. "Third blood," growled Aiko, jerking her sword free from Stahl's toppling corpse in time to meet the next foe.

This man moved upward warily, his rapier held across his body. But then from behind a silver chain whipped 'round his neck, and he was jerked from his feet and fell backward down the steps, his head striking granite as he tumbled, and when he came to the bottom, he moved no more. As Delon untangled the chain, he looked up at Aiko. "Time to go, I believe."

In a hall filled with weeping women and quailing men, Aiko glanced at unconscious Gudrun, the queen's wrist yet pumping blood. Aiko turned to the cowering guests and called out, "I will take my prize, now, and leave you with that which you have earned." Then the golden warrior moved down the steps.

When she reached the bottom, Egil said, "We are in the stronghold of the foe and must needs go over the wall, yet our rope is in our room. Too, we have to get the rutting peacock."

Aiko shook her head and jerked her chin toward Delon in his gaudy, iridescent apparel. "Look at him closely, Egil. What else could he be but our rutting peacock?"

Delon glanced from one to the other, then in a low voice said, "I can get us out."

Egil leaned forward. "How?"

Delon gestured at the fallen foe, then began stuffing the loose end of the silver chain down the front of his shirt. "The same way they got in, if their horses are yet out front. I know the signals. By Adon, I've heard them enough. Get Duke Rache's cloak; Steiger's, too."

Delon bent down and began stripping the wet cloak from the duke's dead champion, taking the bugle as well. He buckled on the fallen man's sword, then he donned the garb, slipping the bugle's baldric across his shoulders.

Aiko retrieved her shiruken from the baron's throat, and she took his cloak and sword and belted scabbard too. She stepped to the fallen warder and retrieved her second shiruken, then moved to the door and handed the baron's gear to the Dylvana and bade her to put them on ". . . and hurry, my tiger whispers of danger."

Egil, now cloaked, cast his hood over his head and said, "Ready?" Then he turned and looked, his gaze searching. "Where's Alos?"

Among the bodies on the floor lay the old man. Egil stepped to him and knelt.

"Is he dead?" asked Delon.

"Damn, damn, damn!" hissed Egil. "Dead drunk." Then he hoisted Alos across his shoulders, surprised at how light the oldster was. "Come on, let's go."

As they moved through the doorway, Aiko stopped and turned to the quivering guests, crimson blood yet dripping from her blades to the floor. "I will not be riding with my mistress to escape. Instead, I will be standing just beyond the door. If any come through before the bugle sounds, I will slay whoever is the fool. Which of you will be the first to die?"

Without waiting for an answer, Aiko spun on her heel and stepped outward, closing the doors behind.

Swiftly she caught up with the others, wiping her swords on her cloak as she ran.

They strode through the halls, stopped by none, and out front in the rain they found the horses, six altogether and saddled, for the baron and duke and his champion each had a remount. Even so, the steeds were yet blowing, for they had been ridden hard. Egil handed Alos to Delon and mounted, then took the old man back, Delon flopping Alos bellydown across the saddle in front of Egil.

"Hurry," hissed Aiko, ahorse, her weapons now sheathed at her back. "My tiger growls of danger."

Arin hiked up her gown and mounted.

Delon cut loose the remount from behind Egil and sprang to the saddle, and all four spurred their horses away, two remounts following, towed behind Arin and Aiko.

Ignoring the curved stone road and praying that the horses would keep their feet, they galloped crossland down the hill through the rain-dark night, riding as if all the hounds of the Dark One were on their track. From behind, shouts of alarm sounded, for some of the guests had braved the door.

Now Delon raised the bugle to his lips and sounded an urgent call: *ta-ra, ta-ra, ta-ra, ta-ta-ta-rah!*

Ahead, by lanterns within the passageway, they could see the inner gates swinging open.

Ta-ra, ta-ra, ta-ta-ta-rah! Delon sounded again.

Clots of earth were lofted by flying hooves, and toward the open gate they hurtled. But as they came to the portal, a bugle from the castle rang out an alarm.

Into the twisting passageway they hammered, haling back on reins to slow the steeds. Hooves aclatter, through the stone way they fared as swiftly as the horses could move and still remain afoot. Above they could hear cries of alarm sounding down through the murder holes. And then they turned the last corner and the raised portcullis was ahead of them, but it had started downward. Egil shouted and spurred his horse forward, and the others galloped after, all ducking low, while downward thundered the deadly teeth of the massive grille. Outward dashed the horses, all winning free but one, and that the remount trailing after Arin; the animal screamed as it was skewered by tons of steel, a scream that abruptly chopped shut. Arin's horse jerked when it came to the end of the tether, but the long lead snapped and she raced onward.

A smattering of arrows hissed through the rain after them as they pounded away, but no one was struck by the shafts.

Down from the citadel they galloped, down from the

fortress and through the town along the rain-slick streets, a few pedestrians cursing at them as they hammered past. To the docks they ran, where Egil in the lead reined to a halt, just as Alos vomited down into Egil's right boot.

Dismounting and slapping the horses on the rumps, and with Delon carrying the old man, clumps of vomit yet sliding down his chin, they scurried to the sloop as the animals clattered off into the night.

Swiftly Egil and Arin raised the mainsail and jib, and Aiko cast off, she and Delon shoving the craft out from the slip and leaping aboard. Tacking against the storm-driven onshore wind, Egil slowly maneuvered the sloop out and away from the docks and into the harbor. And as sheets of rain pelted them, they hove through chop and out toward the raging waters of the Weston Ocean, while behind and silhouetted against the lights of Königinstadt, they could see mounted soldiers thundering through the streets of the city.

CHAPTER 42

Through the black of night and blowing winds and pelting rain, the sloop *Brise* struggled out from the mouth of the harbor and into the cold fury of the Weston Ocean, where storm-driven waves crashed over the wales and rolled the small craft side to side, threatening to swamp her.

"Quarter her up against the wind," cried Egil, and Arin angled the tiller, while Egil shifted the boom of the mainsail about and Aiko hauled the sheets of the jib.

Into the waves plowed the bow of the *Brise,* the little ship riding up the oncoming slopes and crashing through the caps to slam down onto the backslants of the waves as the crests thundered by. Time and again she did such, wind-driven rain and spume and hurtling water hurling across the deck to drench them all.

"We've got to get into our foul-weather gear before this water sucks away all our heat," called Egil. "Aiko, go now."

Aiko slid open the watertight door, and silhouetted by swaying light from within, she disappeared into the cabin, to emerge long moments later dressed in sealskins and an oiled cloak.

"You go next, Egil," called Arin in her gown, the drenched silk plastered against her body. "My people are less affected by heat and cold."

Now Egil slid open the door and popped into the cabin. A wildly swinging storm lantern lit the interior, casting gyrating shadows within. Alos, passed out, lay on one of the bunks, Delon, tightly gripping a stanchion, sat on another, the bard pale, sickly, with a bucket trapped between his feet. As the craft pitched up and over a wave and boomed down, in the stark lanternlight Delon gauntly looked at Egil. "Never could stand boats." He leaned over and tried to retch into his bucket. Only a thin stream of greenish fluid rewarded his gagging efforts. "Nothing left," he groaned, collapsing back against a bulkhead. "Adon, but I am worthless."

Egil did not respond, but shucked his water-logged boots, withdrawing a vomit-lathered foot from the right one. When Delon saw this, again he retched, to no avail. Swiftly Egil doffed the rest of his clothes and pulled on his sealskins and threw an oiled cloak across his shoulders. Finally he turned to Delon and gestured at Alos. "If we go down, get the old man out." Without waiting for a reply, he turned and slid open the door.

All night they battled the wind and waves and rain, and as dawn drew nigh, the rain passed, and slowly the wind fell. Last to settle was the ocean, but ere the noontide the skies cleared and the whitecaps vanished, leaving behind high-rolling billows beneath a September sun.

Now Egil swung the craft to a southerly course, the wind abeam, and he and Aiko raised the top- and stay- and foresails. With all canvas gathering air, down the wide channel between Jute and Gelen they fared.

Delon, wan and weak and trembling and holding onto whatever he could, made his way out from the cabin and onto the deck and plopped down on a side bench in the cockpit. The bard was yet dressed in his gaudy silks, now rumpled and stained, though no longer wet. A polished obsidian stone on a golden chain dangled down from below the silver collar 'round his neck. Aiko took one look at his pallid face and said, "Fear not, Delon, the nausea will pass eventually."

"Adon," groaned Delon, gripping the bench, his knuckles white, "let us hope it is sooner than later. I've lost everything there is to lose. My stomach itself is next."

Egil smiled grimly. "There're clothes in the lockers below. Some of mine will do, though they may be a bit overlarge on you."

"Alos's would fit better," said Aiko, "though he has but few."

Delon looked about. "Where are we? I see only rolling waves."

"Somewhere 'tween Gelen and Jute," answered Egil.

"Whence bound?" asked Delon.

"Pendwyr," said Egil.

Now Delon looked at Aiko. "Why did you free me? Oh, not that I am complaining, mind you, for I was headed for that madwoman's pyre. But still, why did you free me?"

Aiko smiled and reached out and plucked at his iridescent garb. "Because you are the rutting peacock, Delon, and we need you on our quest."

Delon raised an eyebrow. "Peacock? Quest?"

Before Aiko could respond, from the cabin there came a howl and a string of oaths. Cursing, Alos appeared in the opening to the ship's quarters and clambered onto the deck. Holding his aching head, he looked about and confirmed his suspicions, then demanded, "What is the meaning of this? I told you I wasn't going any farther than Jute, but like the skulking press-gang you are, you have thrown me onto the ship and dragged me out to sea again . . . against my will, I might add."

Aiko snorted, but Arin said, "We couldn't leave thee behind, Alos. Thou wert one of our party and would have been slain, mayhap tortured—the queen would have so commanded."

"If she survived," added Aiko. "If no one aided her, she might be dead from loss of blood."

"Even so," said Arin, "Alos would have paid with his life had we left him behind. The chamberlain and others would have seen to it."

Delon nodded. "Even though she was mad, regicide is a crime no realm will allow to go unpunished . . . though in many a case it should be encouraged and rewarded instead."

Alos, squinting against the sun, looked puzzled. "What happened to the queen?"

Delon stared at the old man. "You don't know?"

Alos shook his head, then winced from the movement. "I, ah . . ."

"You got drunk and passed out," said Aiko, accusingly.

Alos glared at her. "So *that's* when you dragged me to the ship against my will, eh?"

Aiko turned away in disgust.

"Ha, I thought so," accused the oldster, his white eye glaring.

" 'Twas for thine own good, Alos," protested Arin.

The old man looked at the Dylvana, then at Egil, who nodded and said, " 'Tis true, helmsman."

Barely mollified, Alos grunted, then turned to Delon. "What's this about the queen? Why would she have had me killed?"

"Well," said Delon, grinning, hauling the silver chain and cuff out from his shirt, the links still affixed to the argent collar 'round his neck, "Lady Aiko cut off her hand and set me free."

"*Møkk!*" spat Alos. "I know these Jutes. They'll pursue us to the ends of the world."

"Especially if the queen lives," agreed Delon. "She'll not rest till we are dead . . . and the bloodier, more painful the means, the better she'll like it."

"*Hng,*" grunted Egil. "It's not as if we can simply disappear into the crowd. I mean, look at us: a Dylvana, a yellow woman, and two one-eyed men."

"And a rutting peacock," added Delon, "whatever that is."

"Maybe they'll not know we are at sea," said Aiko.

Egil shook his head. "As soon as they speak to the harbormaster, they'll know."

Aiko nodded glumly, then said, "That means they'll send out ships to run us down."

"Not just any ships," replied Egil, "but Dragonboats swift."

"Mayhap they'll head north, *chier,*" said Arin. "Toward Fjordland, for they know that is thy home."

"Likely," replied Egil. "Yet they'll scour southward, too. And west. I think it best if we stand well out to sea and hope they believe we flee along the coast, sailing at night and holing up in coves by day to avoid detection."

Aiko looked at Egil and said, "If on the other hand they deduce that strategy, then we are at risk should they run us down at sea. They will be many to our few, and we will not be able to outrun them."

Egil canted his head. "Aye, Aiko. Yet we have the vast sea to shelter us. It will be like searching for a grain of wheat in a field of chaff."

Arin nodded. "I agree. Had they known our destination, then the odds would be much shorter. Yet they do not, and so, indeed, we will be hidden in the brine, our ship steered by good helmsman Alos."

"Perhaps they'll think we've sunk," said Delon, "drawn down by last night's storm."

Egil looked at him and shrugged. "They'll search regardless."

For a moment none said aught, then Delon cleared his throat. "And we go to Pellar, you say?'

"Aye, to Pendwyr," replied Egil.

"But no farther, y' hear," declared Alos, tasting his tongue against the roof of his mouth. "I'll go with you that far, but then we part company." Grumbling, Alos moved to the tiller and plopped down across from Arin. Shielding his eye and glaring up at the sails, he said, "You've not quite caught the wind, Dara." He turned to Egil. "And the sails need trimming. Here, let me take the helm and we'll get there all the faster and then I'll be quit of this insanity. You can then chase the green stone on your own. I'll no longer be part of this mad mission."

Delon's gaze shifted to Aiko. "Green stone? Hmm. Ever since I was a lad in Gûnar, I've wanted to be part of a grand adventure. You'll have to tell me of this quest of yours."

Aiko shook her head. "It is Dara Arin's vision we follow, not mine."

Delon turned to the Dylvana. "Tell me what you seek. Tell me, too, why Lady Aiko calls me a rutting peacock, though I think I know the answer. And isn't there some way we can get this blasted collar off my neck?"

"Ah, so that's it," said Delon in the late afternoon sun, the bard feeling much better now that his nausea had passed. "Well then, count me in. I can make a sweeping saga of it whether or no we succeed."

"Hold still," snapped Aiko, pressing and rocking the keen edge of her blade of steel against the remaining fastener of the silver collar. "I'm nearly through."

tk

The blade clove through the last of the soft silver rivet and the collar fell free.

Delon took a deep breath and slowly let it out, then rubbed his neck all 'round and stretched it side to side. "Adon, but it's good to be shed of that thing at last, and I thank you, Lady Aiko." Laughing, he took up the collar and chain and bracelet and weighed them in his hands. "Paltry wages for what I was put through."

Egil looked across at him. "Which was . . .?"

Delon glanced at Arin and Aiko, then said, "It was mine to keep her, um, satisfied." He shook his head. "She was too much even for me."

"Hah!" barked Alos. "Then how *did* you keep her content?"

Delon tilted his head and smiled wanly. "There is more than one way to pleasure a woman."

Alos cackled aloud, then sobered and turned to Aiko. "I hope you haven't made a mistake. I mean, we left the real peacock behind, and I don't want to go back after him. And as to the rutting: he's probably back there doing the ducks even as we speak."

"Nay, Alos," replied Aiko. "Fowl seem destined to remain true to their kind."

"Then how did you know Delon, here, was the rutting peacock?"

Delon looked at her, smiling slightly, awaiting her answer.

Aiko shrugged. "The balcony was open to the queen's bedroom, and she wasn't silent in her copious and repeated indulgence. As to the peacock—"

"As to the peacock," interjected Delon, holding out his arms wide and peering down at his clothes, "look at me. What else could I be but Gudrun's peacock? As if I were one of her creatures on display, she garbed me in apparel so gaudy it's a wonder no one went blind." Delon nodded to Aiko. "Indeed, Lady Aiko, I *am* the mad monarch's rutting peacock—just one of hundreds, I understand—yet I am most grateful you set me free ere I met their fate."

"How did you, um"—Alos grinned his gap-toothed smile—"come to serve her?"

Delon laughed and said, "I like this dirty old man." Then his expression grew solemn. "As to how I came to serve her, well, I walked into it with my eyes wide open. . . ."

Delon whistled as he disembarked from the Gelender ship making port in Königinstadt. If the rumors were true then he would soon be living in endless luxury as the queen's favorite lover, of that he had no doubt. He would first make love to her with his eyes and his voice—

Delon fingered the amulet at his neck, given over to him by his father, Elon, who had gotten it from his own father, Galon, and so on back into the mists of time. Where the amulet had come from originally, none now living really knew, though 'twas said that long past it was a gift from the Mage Kaldor for a service well performed. In any event it seemed to have the power to enhance the voice, and when coupled with bardish training, it made one sing like the Elves.

—and when she had accepted him, he would make love with his hands and lips and whispered endearments and his entire body. That he could pleasure her, Delon was certain, for he had spent much of the last fifteen years in the company of women, primarily in their beds, and he had yet to meet a woman he could not satisfy. And the rewards had been substantial: the best of foods and wines and added delectations of taste and olfaction, rich clothing, engaging books, small treasures and trinkets rare, and other delights throughout every day—oh, not necessarily physical pleasures, though they were considerable, but pleasures of the mind and spirit and heart and soul as well. And travel and adventure: these too were his to choose, though as of yet he had avoided anything strenuous, for he loved luxury too well. Certainly, there were times when he had to flee the comfort of a woman—when her father or brother or husband or betrothed came unexpectedly to her chamber—and there were times when he had to fight his way clear, for he was skilled in the use of a rapier, though mostly he talked his way free. But on the whole he strayed from one place of comfort to another when his appetite for a particular locale or abode or woman waned. And from mansion to manor to estate to chateau to villa he drifted, seeking pleasure, seeking . . . he knew not what else.

Yet he had heard of the Jutlander queen who seemed to be searching for a lover. And since he had never bedded a queen before, much less one as rich as she, he thought to try his hand at this game as well. Oh certainly there were whispered rumors of lovers apast, as well as rumors of her strange penchants—unbelievable tales concerning dogs and horses and other beasts—yet he himself had had lovers aplenty, and his own inclinations were sometimes exceptional, and the tales cuckolded lovers spread concerning him were just as palpably false.

And so he came to Königinstadt with but a simple plan: to make love to the queen. Little did he know what he bargained for.

It took less than a week for him to be invited to sing before the queen, and less than a candlemark afterward she took him to her bed.

Completely exhausted by her recurrent demands, he slept as would the dead, and when he awoke he had a silver collar 'round his neck and a silver chain linked to the bracelet she wore.

Then, one night in the afterglow of lovemaking, in a whispered lover's confidence, he discovered why she was called mad: she tenderly told him that her previous hundreds of paramours had been sacrificed one after another when they had ceased to satisfy. She had personally burned each one alive amid a glorious show of grief, Gudrun weeping and calling out her father's name over and again as each of her fancy men screamed in agony while flesh was seared from bones and life was burnt away.

Yet at last she believed she had found her eternal lover, for surely Delon could and would see to her every carnal need.

Delon was horrified, and he nearly failed her at that

moment, but he knew of more than one way to pleasure a woman, to the queen's delight.

As to Delon, his every need, his every want was catered to. Except for giving him his liberty, he could not have asked for more—food, wine, clothing, luxury, everything he desired. Yet he would have given it all simply to be free.

And he knew not how long he could continue to pleasure her to her satisfaction, how long he would continue to live.

". . . then you four came and saved me." Delon fell silent, his tale told, what there was of it.

Aiko growled, "Why didn't you simply kill her and escape?"

Delon shook his head. "I don't know. It seemed to me that I was powerless to do anything. I was simply her thrall."

Arin frowned, then she looked at the chain and neckband dangling from Delon's hands. She canted her head and attempted to <see>. To her eyes a faint aura seemed to flicker upon the silver. "Hmm. I think there is a charm on thy neckband and chain and bracelet, Delon." She looked at the bard. "A charm, too, on the amulet thou dost wear."

Delon touched the polished obsidian stone on its slender golden chain. "This one I'll keep. But the other . . .?"

"Destroy it," said Aiko.

Egil objected. "Nay. If it compels docility, we may ultimately have a use for it on our quest."

Arin looked from one to the other but said nought.

Southerly they fared, angling slightly eastward, aiming for the Straits of Kistan. For twelve days they plied the ocean, moving into warmer waters. At times the wind was with them; at other times they had to tack into the breeze; at times it failed altogether for short periods. And it rained again on two of the days—stiff gusts blowing sweeping brooms of falling water across the rolling surface of the sea. And during this time they saw no evidence of Jutlander ships, though they did pass a Gelender ketch heading northward toward home, and a Gothonian packet bearing westerly; neither ship came close enough to hail. Twelve days along this course they fared, and on the twelfth day a waning half moon fled before the sun across the sky. Night fell, and when mid of night came, in the confined space of the decking, Arin chanted and stepped out of the ancient Dylvana rite celebrating the autumnal equinox, Aiko matched her every move, Egil and Delon mirroring, and even Alos followed part of the way.

On the eve of the sixteenth day, they sighted the Straits of Kistan and maneuvered the *Brise* northeasterly, toward the shallow waters along the coast of Vancha. They hoped to hug the shoreline and escape the notice of the Rovers of Kistan, whether or not these pirates yet blocked the way. For if the Rovers still picketed the opening into the Avagon Sea, then a small sloop following the shoreline might slip past them unnoticed. But even if the Rovers' blockade was broken, still the picaroons plied the straits, boarding ships, pillaging, raping, murdering, then hieing back to the safe havens of the jungle island of Kistan.

And so, through the gap and into the sapphirine waters of the Avagon Sea they fared, sailing the shallows of Vancha. Five days passed, and they saw none of the crimson lateen sails of the swift dhows of the Kistanian Rovers.

On the thirtieth day of September, in the noontide, they made port in Castilla on the southern flank of Vancha. As they sailed in among the ships anchored in the sheltered bay, they passed an Arbalinian craft, her hull blackened by the scars of fire, one of her masts broken, a hole in her hull near the waterline. Aboard this vessel, men labored to repair the damage and refit the ship. Some of these men were swathed in bandages.

"What ho?" cried Delon through cupped hands.

"Rovers" came the terse reply.

Delon turned. "It's a wonder they survived."

"No," replied Egil. "The Rovers pillage and rape, and slay most of those who resist. Sometimes they take captives for ransom; sometimes they take the ships for ransom, too; sometimes they sink them out of spite; but on the whole they set badly damaged crafts free."

"Oh?"

"Aye, so that they can be refitted and raided again."

"Damn Rovers," spat Alos, glancing back at the damaged ship now aft.

Egil stared aft as well and nodded in agreement. "Damned Rovers," he echoed.

Arin fixed Egil with her hazel gaze. "Why dost thou curse them, *chier*?. Is that not what Fjordlander raiders also do: pillage the property of others; mayhap rape the women of the conquered; slay most of those who resist; take captives for ransom; take property for ransom, too; at times destroy things out of spite; but on the whole leave enough behind so that in subsequent years, other raids can be just as successful?"

Egil looked at her, his one blue eye glittering. "Aye, love. I have done all those things you name, and perhaps others as well. But as I pledged on the heights of the fjord where I was born: I shall raid no more. Let it begin with me, I said, and so did I mean."

Arin reached out and took his hand in hers and pulled him down beside her and kissed him. Egil smiled and stroked her hair and said, "But of course, that doesn't mean I won't steal a peacock now and again."

Arin laughed. "Borrow, *chier,* borrow."

Two days later, with the ship resupplied and with both Delon and Alos outfitted in clothing suitable for the sea—except for Delon's iridescent belt with its large, ornate buckle, which the bard wore as a gaudy reminder of an ambition not well conceived—they set sail on the final leg to the city of Pendwyr, the *Brise* yet hugging the coastal waters of Vancha, for although the High King's fleet had broken the blockade, Rovers yet plundered some ships plying the straits. In less than a sevenday they were well clear of the northern Straits of Kistan, and they set out on a northeasterly course, now faring across the indigo depths of the Avagon Sea. The wind held, though it rained now and then. Yet onward they sailed, the realms of Hoven and then Jugo unseen beyond the northern horizon.

Three weeks into October they fared through waters muddied by the vast outflow of the mighty River Argon and by sundown they came upon the coast of Pellar. In the late candlemarks of the third day after, under starlit skies they sailed into Hile Bay, the harbor ringed 'round by sheer cliffs, towering upward a hundred feet. As they fared toward the anchorage, on the high precipice above twinkled the lights of a city, its buildings ranging along the lengthy, steep-sided headland sheltering the bay.

They had come to Pendwyr at last, the place where they hoped to find a ferret in a High King's cage.

CHAPTER 43

After securing the *Brise* in a slip assigned by the harbormaster, Arin and her companions made their way up the steep cliff-side road to the headland above, Alos wheezing and complaining all the way, the old man stopping at intervals to rest and catch his wind.

"I should have stayed at one of the dockside inns," Alos declared.

"Ha!" barked Aiko. "At a dockside tavern, you mean."

Alos stuck out his chin. "Inn. Tavern. What do you care? You've no claim on me. When you get what you've come for and are on your way to who knows where, I'll not be with you. I'm free at last and no longer part of this madness, dragging me over the oceans of the world and stealing peacocks and chopping off parts of queens. You've no claim, y' hear?"

Aiko growled, but Arin sighed, and the old man would not meet her eyes. Delon hefted the oldster's gear, and Egil said, "Let's go."

They came in among buildings of stone and tile and brick; the only wood in sight was that of brightly painted doors. They made their way into the city and, after asking about, procured rooms in the Blue Moon, an inn overlooking the bay below.

Following hot baths and a hot meal they took to their beds, and when morning came Alos was gone.

"Gone?" asked Egil. "Gone where?"

Delon shrugged and gestured out beyond the windows of the common room, where an early morning fog curled up across the headland and through the streets of Pendwyr. "I don't know. His bed had been slept in, but when I awoke he wasn't there. His goods are gone as well."

Egil gazed at Aiko, but the yellow warrior merely stared back, her face impassive. Then he turned to Arin. "Fear not, love, we can always find him and cast him aboard the ship."

Arin looked away from the fire in the nearby hearth, the blaze driving the damp chill away from the room. "Nay, *chier,* let be." She glanced at Delon, then back to Egil. "To do such to Alos would be no better than clamping an iron collar 'round his neck."

Egil took a deep breath then let it out. "As you will, love. As you will."

A serving girl came to the table bearing a great platter heaped with eggs and rashers of bacon and biscuits and honey and a pot of freshly brewed tea. Delon took it upon himself to serve them all, shoveling food onto each of their trenchers and filling their mugs with hot drink.

As they dug in, Egil peered 'round the table. "I suppose our next move is to go to the caer and look for the High King's cage, eh?"

Delon set his mug aside. "Perhaps it isn't at the caer at all. Perhaps there's a garden of beasts elsewhere."

"It may be that King Bleys doesn't keep ferrets at all," said Aiko.

Delon cocked an eyebrow.

Aiko shrugged. "Perhaps the ferret in the High King's cage is a person, just as you were a mad monarch's rutting peacock."

"If I am indeed the peacock of the rede and it's not that preening bird in her garden," said Delon.

"Hmm," mused Egil. "Regardless as to whether or no you are the peacock—though I think in fact you are— still Aiko may be right: the ferret could be a person, too. If so, then the High King's cage could be the caer itself or a dungeon within the caer or—"

"Or the city jail," interjected Delon.

"Could be a brig on a ship," added Egil.

"My songs would have it be a remote tower . . . with a princess locked away in a chamber at the top." Delon grinned.

Egil looked at Delon. "Does the caer have a tower?"

Delon shrugged. "Perhaps. Perhaps not. Tower or dungeon: I don't know. I've not been here before."

Egil turned to Arin. The Dylvana had stopped eating and was again staring fixedly into the fire. "Are you well, love?" he asked.

Arin looked at him and sighed. "Nought. I can see nought in the flames. I have had no visions since the one concerning the green stone. Could I but <see>, mayhap we would have some guidance, some hint of what to do. Yet I think the fires will be empty until this quest has run its course."

Egil reached out and laid his hand atop hers.

"Wild magic," said Arin. "That's what Dalavar called it: wild magic. It comes at its own beck, and I can do nought to make it occur." She sighed and stroked his fingers, then freed her hand and took up her knife and began cutting a strip of bacon.

"Well," said Egil, "I say we need visit the caer and see what there is to see concerning the High King's cage, and discover what we can about the ferret, whoever or whatever it may be."

"The jail, too," added Delon. He scooped up a spoonful of egg and biscuit and stuffed it all into his mouth and chewed thoughtfully. Finally he took a great gulp of hot tea and said, "If the High King has a ship of his own, we ought to see if anyone is in the brig."

Arin set aside her knife. "It is so frustrating: all is clouded in mystery. We know not if the ferret in the High King's cage is even in Pendwyr. Yet, there is this: if Aiko is the cat who fell from grace, and if Egil is the one-eye in dark water— recall, we have four one-eyes to select from, three with Alos gone—and if Delon is the mad monarch's rutting peacock rather than the bird we left behind, then we are stumbling along the correct path regardless of being blind. And so, we must search Pendwyr for the ferret. Whether or no we truly find what we seek is left up to Fortune's whims—and may She turn Her smiling face our way. Even so, even if we leave here with the ferret, then we must seek the cursed keeper of faith in the maze, and we have no inkling as to where to look for whoever or whatever that might be. More than that I cannot say."

Aiko reached for a biscuit. "Forget not the statue in the hedge, Dara; the keeper of faith in the maze might yet turn out to be the one-handed queen."

Delon laughed, then sobered as his eyes flew wide. "Say, we're not going to go back for her, are we?"

"If we do," replied Aiko, slicing the biscuit with her trencher knife, "then perhaps I'll bring her along as the queen with no head."

Arin held a hand palm out. "If she *is* the keeper of faith, then I would think we need her alive to complete the quest."

The corners of Aiko's mouth turned down. "Then when this quest is over . . ." She drew a finger across her throat. As if contemplating Gudrun's demise, Aiko smiled and calmly spooned honey over the cut biscuit halves.

Arin shook her head. "'Tis the ferret we are after at the moment and not the keeper of faith."

Egil said, "Surely the ferret is here in Pellar and not elsewhere. I mean, where else would Bleys keep a cage?"

All eyes turned to Delon, and he shrugged. "I hear he has a fortress in Rian. Challerain Keep, I believe."

Aiko groaned, then asked, "Where is this Challerain Keep?"

Delon shrugged. "I've not been there."

"Rian itself lies along the Boreal Sea," said Egil. "As to the keep, it must be inland, for it's not along the coast. In any event, it's far north from here."

"Would we had known when we were sailing that ocean," said Aiko. "It might have saved us a trip."

They ate in silence for a while, and then Egil said, "Look, ere we go haring off to Challerain, let us first search this city. Perhaps, as Arin says, Fortune will turn Her smiling face our way."

Arin looked up from her trencher. "We can only hope."

As they stepped through the doorway of the Blue Moon and into the cobbled street, Egil said, "Well, I talked to the innkeeper, and the only High King's cages he knew of were the kennels where Bleys keeps his hounds and the mews where he keeps his hunting birds. The caer has no dungeons, as far as he knows, but there is a city jail—at the moment filled with cutpurses and thieves and captured Rovers awaiting execution. It seems that when the High King's fleet broke the blockade, he brought back Rover captains to make examples of. They're to be hanged at sundown."

"Huah," grunted Delon. "Hangings will not stop the Rovers. They come from a nation of pirates: Kistan—its myriad jungle coves providing shelter for the picaroons."

"Ah, well, that's neither here nor there," said Egil. "Our concern is altogether different." He turned to Arin. "Shall we?"

They set out for the caer.

As the fog burned away with the coming of the morning sun, they passed through a city made primarily of stone and brick and tile, and of stucco and clay, the buildings for the most part joined to one another, though here and there were stand-alone structures. Narrow streets and alleyways twisted this way and that, the cobblestones of variegated color. Shops occupied many first floors, with dwellings above. Glass windows displayed merchandise, the handiwork of crafters and artisans: milliners, copper smiths, potters, jewelers, weavers, tanners, cobblers, coopers, clothiers, tailors, seamstresses, furniture makers, and the like.

Delon paused at the window of one of the stores. "I need outfit myself with a good set of leathers. Likely I'll need such ere this venture is done."

Aiko cast an askance eye his way. "Will you insist they match your belt? If so, I have a feather for your hat." Delon grinned as Aiko giggled behind her hand, while Egil guffawed aloud. Arin merely smiled, then tugged Egil onward, the other two following.

Pedestrian traffic was light, and heavy, horse-drawn wagons trundled through the streets. At one point, Arin and her companions had to pause while a water wagon maneuvered 'round a twisting turn. As they moved onward, water wagons in the early morn became a common sight, for Pendwyr was a city without wells, and water was hauled in from the shafts and springs down on the plains of Pellar.

Not that the city was without its own water, for nearly all of the buildings in the city itself had tile roofs, and they were fitted with gutters and channels cunningly wrought to guide rainwater into cisterns for storing. This supply was augmented by the water from the plains.

That a city had been raised on land with no water was an accident of history, for Pendwyr had grown a building at a time as merchants and craftsmen had settled on the headland to be near the fortress. The bastion itself was where the High King had quartered after the city of Gleeds near the mouth of the Argon had been burnt to the ground, an event precipitated long past by the Chabbains from across the sea.

Yet situated where it was, rain came often to Pendwyr, and seldom had the city needed to rely wholly upon water from the plains.

Neither Arin nor Egil nor Delon nor Aiko commented upon this history of Pendwyr, for they did not know how the city had come to be. Instead they strolled along without speaking for the most part, eyeing the richness all 'round.

Past shops and stores, past restaurants and cafés and tea shops, past inns and taverns, past large dwellings and small squares, past greengrocers and chirurgeons and herbalists they strolled. And they crossed through several open market squares, with fish and fowl and meats, with vegetables and fruits and grain, with woven goods and flowers and the like. But Arin and her companions did not stop to finger the wares, though Egil commented that here was the place to come to resupply the ship.

Onward they walked, to pass through a gateway in a high stone wall which ran the width of the narrow peninsula. Beyond the wall the character of the buildings changed, for here were located a great courthouse, a tax hall, a large building housing the city guard with a jail above, a firehouse, a library, a census building, a hall of records, a cluster of university buildings, and other such—here was the face of government, the agencies and offices of the realm. As they passed through this section of Pendwyr, they heard a loud *thnk!,* and down a side street and in a large, open city square behind a low wall they could see a gallows of many ropes being tested. And even though it was early in the day, street peddlers were arranging their carts in the square, maneuvering into the best positions to sell their wares at the public spectacle.

Arin sighed. "Humans: they make a carnival of death."

Egil looked at her. "Perhaps, love, it will give others pause. They will think twice ere committing a like crime."

Arin shook her head. "As Delon said, such spectacle will not stop the Rovers."

Egil shrugged, and they walked onward.

Ahead, stood Caer Pendwyr itself, the citadel tall with castellated walls all 'round and towers at each corner, enclosing the castle of the High King. As they neared the caer, of a sudden they realized that it sat on a free-standing spire of stone towering up from the Avagon Sea below. The fortified pinnacle was connected to the headland by a pivot bridge, a span which could be swiveled aside by a crew in the castle to sever the fortress from the headland.

A line of petitioners stood outside a low building away from the bridge. After an enquiry or two, Arin and her companions took their place at the end of the line. People turned and gaped at them, for seldom had any seen a Dylvana, and none had ever seen a yellow warrior woman. At the distant door, a warder stepped inside as a whispered mutter made its way up the line. Moments later a soldier dressed in the red and gold of the High King's guard emerged with the warder, who pointed at the foursome. The warder took his place at the door again, but the kings-guard marched toward the four.

Aiko shifted into a balanced stance as if readying for battle, though she left her swords scabbarded at her back.

"Do you think they know about Gudrun and are coming to arrest us?" whispered Delon.

Egil shrugged. "Not likely," he responded, yet his hand fell to the axe slipped through his belt.

The kingsguard stepped before them and bowed. "Milady," he said to Arin, "bring you word of the King?"

"Nay, I do not," replied Arin. "I am here to see him instead." As a look of disappointment flickered across the kingsguard's face, Arin added, "I take it by thy question that King Bleys is not in Caer Pendwyr."

"He is not, milady," replied the guard, his gaze flitting to Aiko and back. "Lord Revor presides."

"We have traveled far to see the High King," said Arin, "but if he is not here, then we would seek audience with his steward instead. Our mission is pressing."

The kingsguard shook his head. "I am most sorry, milady, but the lord steward is seeing no one today. He prepares for an urgent journey."

Arin drew herself up to her full four feet eight. "Tell him that a representative of Coron Remar of Darda Erynian is here seeking aid."

The kingsguard swept his hat low in an elaborate bow. "Wait here, milady. I will see what I can do."

They returned to the caer for the afternoon appointment that the kingsguard had arranged. Within a candlemark, a warder escorted them across the bridge and into the walled castle. They passed among corridors and at last emerged through a postern to find themselves crossing a rear courtyard toward a short suspension bridge a hundred or so feet above the rolling sea. The bridge itself spanned from the castle to another sheer-sided pinnacle on which were low stone buildings—lodgings, said their escort, for the King's closest advisors.

"When I was a lad in Gûnar," said Delon, peering down at the sheer stone as they crossed the swaying bridge, "my father and I oft climbed rock faces such as this. Those days in the Gûnarring are long past."

Looking ahead, they could see a third pinnacle beyond, and another suspension bridge spanning the gulf between this one and that. On the far pinnacle stood the High King's private residence; they did not cross over to the King's spire, but instead were taken to a stone dwelling at hand, where they waited in a foyer for another candlemark or so. Finally, a slight, balding man stepped through a doorway and bowed to Arin. "Milady, I am the Lord Steward Revor," he announced, "and I understand you have urgent business."

"So, milord," said Egil, "King Bleys is not even in Pellar at the moment."

Revor shook his head as he hastily examined papers, stuffing a few into saddlebags and placing others back among the piles upon the desk he stood behind; as he had told them, he would be shortly sailing northward across the bay to deal with a matter of high justice concerning the garrison in the Fian Dunes, but he could spare them a moment. "No. Bleys is to the north. No sooner had he come back from breaking the Rovers' blockade, than word came of the Lian campaign against the *Rûpt*—"

"Campaign?" burst out Arin. "What campaign?"

Revor looked across at her. "It seems that some of the great trees of the Larkenwald were cut down by the Foul Folk, and the Lian took up arms against the tribe of *Spaunen* that did it." Revor glanced at Arin. "From the message that came, Elven vengeance was swift, milady, utterly without mercy, as it should have been. Chilling examples were made of the axe wielders, and their remains are even now being displayed to the *Spaunen* kindred in their mountain haunts. At times battle ensues, and the Lian hew down those *Rûpt* who take up arms. That is where High King Bleys is: he rides with the Lian."

"What does the felling of trees have to do with Bleys?" asked Delon.

"Why, eldwood trees are protected by edict of the High King," replied Revor, returning to his task. "Too, King Bleys is not one to stand idly by when there are arms to wield." The steward gestured at the piles of paper and scrolls yet awaiting his scrutiny. "He'd rather leave the administration of the realm to others. In any event, as soon as he returned from breaking the Rovers' blockade, he and Phais and a small warband rode off to join the Lian on their ride through the Grimwall."

"Phais?" asked Egil.

"She is the High King's advisor," replied Revor. "A Lian herself, she was outraged when the word first came." Revor paused in his scrutiny. "Huh, last October it was, a year past. But then Bleys was readying the fleet to sail against the Rovers, and although he gave Phais permission to ride to the Larkenwald, she stayed by him. Now he fares at her side. They rode to join the Lian in late July—three months past."

"Milord, how goes this war?" asked Delon.

The steward shrugged. "Other than the original message, we've no word." Revor stuffed a last paper into his saddlebag and buckled it shut.

He looked across at them. "But here, you did not come to speak of war; it was to see the High King instead." Now he gazed directly at Arin. "You seek aid, Dara Arin of Darda Erynian, the Blackwood, representative of Coron Remar. How may I help you?"

Arin glanced at Egil, then said, "We've come looking for a ferret in the High King's cage."

Revor's eyes widened and he sat down. "And this is your urgent business?" His tone was sharp.

"Aye, 'tis the rede of a prophecy we follow . . . one thy High King should now know about, given that he has met up with any who rode with me to Black Mountain."

"Prophecy?" Revor took a deep breath and blew it out. "Milady, the High King keeps no ferrets."

"Are there any in Pendwyr?" asked Delon.

The steward shook his head. "None I know of. I am afraid that if your mission calls for the finding of a High King's ferret, you are to be disappointed."

Aiko spoke for the first time. "Has the High King any cages?"

"He kennels dogs," replied Revor, cocking his head at her unfamiliar accent. "Falcons and the like."

"May we examine them?"

Revor blew out his breath again. "I'll arrange for someone to escort you, though you'll find no weasels, stoats, ferrets, mousehounds, or other such within."

"Does Bleys keep cages elsewhere?" asked Egil.

Revor shrugged. "Perhaps some at Challerain Keep, though I would be most surprised if any contained ferrets."

The steward looked from one to another. "Is there aught else you would ask of me?" None replied, and Revor stood and threw on a cloak and hat, and took up his saddlebags. "There is a tale here for the telling and would that I could hear the whole of it, but I, too, have urgent business."

As the steward led them toward the door, Delon said, "There is one other thing you could do for us, milord."

Revor looked at him and cocked an eyebrow.

Delon said, "You could give us permission to speak to the prisoners in the jail."

"Huah," grunted the steward. "But for a few drunkards, the rest are to be hanged at sundown."

Delon shrugged. "Nevertheless . . ."

Revor snorted and then his eyes widened. "Oh. I see. It is the High King's cage. Certainly."

Then Lord Revor frowned, as if chasing an elusive thought. But ere he could catch it, a page stepped through the doorway. "Milord, I am to tell you your ship awaits."

Revor waved him away. "Yes, yes, lad. I'll be right there."

"Speaking of ships, milord," added Delon, as they moved outside the lord steward's quarters, "we'd like permission to speak to any prisoners in brigs as well."

The steward shook his head. "The brigs are empty, lad; all are in gaol. Regardless, I'll get you a pass to the prison." Revor called a kingsguard to him and gave him instructions, then bade good-bye to his guests and, shouldering his saddlebags, strode away toward the bridge to the caer.

"Well, Lord Revor was right about one thing," said Delon, "there are no ferrets in any of these cages."

They stood in the High King's mews, the birds unhooded, their jesses free, their eyes glaring.

"Ha!" barked their escort. "A ferret wouldn't stand a chance with these beauties. Look at those claws, those beaks: what ferret could withstand such?" He jerked a thumb over his shoulder, back toward the kennels where the dogs yet stirred and yipped at these strangers who had passed by. "Nor would a weasel or such last long with the hounds," added the kingsguard.

"All right, then," said Egil, "take us to the prison where languish the Rover captains."

The guard looked at the sun, a handspan above the horizon. "Not for long," he said. "In a candlemark or so they'll be languishing at the ends of ropes."

Out from the mews they stepped and past the stables. They walked across the central thoroughfare and toward the jail. Down the side street where stood the gallows there came the hullaboo of a crowd. Arin shivered in revulsion. "Mankind and his spectacle of death," she muttered.

Egil took her hand as they strode toward the lockup. "Can you say Elves are any different?"

She looked up at him, a question in her eyes.

"I mean, love, the Lian are even now displaying the remains of slaughtered Foul Folk to their kindred. If that is not a spectacle, I know not what is meant by the term."

"But they slaughtered trees," said Arin.

"And these pirates slaughtered people," rejoined Egil.

For a moment they walked onward in silence, then Arin said, "Thou art right, Egil. The felling of people is of more concern than the felling of trees. Yet heed, the crowd down by the gallows has come to be entertained, whereas the warband of Lian seek only vengeance pure, and they seek only to prevent such from occurring again. They feel no joy in what they do; only justice."

Now Egil fell silent, and as lamplighters moved along the street preparing for the oncoming dusk by igniting the oil lanthorns atop lampposts, at last Arin and her companions came unto the jail.

Upon orders from the desk warden, they laid their weapons aside. A guard searched them all and found Aiko's shiruken; in spite of her low growls, he set them in the vestibule as well. "Care for them as if they were your children," she said, "for if they are not here when we return, you shall father no offspring in the future."

A jailor led them up a stone stairwell and in among enshadowed holding cages, dark with the coming of eve.

Through the barred windows the crowd waiting in the street below could be heard: hawkers selling their wares, children shouting and screaming in play, strident voices calling for the show to begin, a low mumble and mutter of people pressed together. Some prisoners peered out through windows at the gallows below, while others sat upon the floor and wept.

"These are them what are to be hanged," said their jailor escort, gesturing at the cells to the right. "Pirates and cutpurses and such. Them others over on this side are drunks and debtors. Hang them too, says I. It'll clear the city of such." Then he turned to Arin. "Mind you now, you got to hurry. The rope dancing is about to begin, and me, I want a fair seat for the show. In fact, I'll go get Rob to save me one. Take care now not to get too close to the bars and I'll be back before you know I was gone." With that he turned and hurried away.

Aiko prowled down the side holding the drunkards and debtors, her gaze searching the cells.

Of a sudden, Delon called out "Ferret!" his voice ringing throughout the pens.

There was no answer.

Slowly, Arin and Egil moved along the right-hand cages, peering within. Some of the prisoners were dark skinned; these were obviously the Kistanians—the captured Rover captains. Others were pale and trembling—"Cutpurses and thieves, most likely," said Egil. Feral eyes turned their way and some prisoners spat curses at them in an unfamiliar tongue. Some captives turned their backs upon these gawking visitors, while others reached out through the bars, beseeching, pleading for the Dylvana to save them, tears running down their faces.

"Adon, deliver me from such a place," muttered Delon, and he strode on ahead.

A fair-skinned youth with dark brown, shoulder-length hair moved forward through the shadows to fetch up against the bars of a cell. As Delon stepped past, the youth reached out and caught at Delon's sleeve. "Good sir, you called for Ferret?"

Delon drew back, away from the clutching fingers. "I did."

The youth, alone in the cell, said in a low voice, "I am she, unjustly imprisoned."

Delon's eyes flew wide and he looked closely. "By Adon," he gasped, "you *are* a female!"

She held her arms wide and pirouetted. Dressed in lad's clothing, she stood a slender five feet three or four. Her enshadowed eyes were dark brown, matching her hair. She could be no older than twenty-one or -two.

"And you are named Ferret?" asked Delon.

She turned up a hand. "Yes." She gazed up at him, her eyes wide and filled with as much maidenly virtue as she could muster. "Surely, sir, you can see that I am innocent."

Delon looked rightward. "Dara!" he called. When Arin turned, Delon said, "This lady names herself Ferret."

Arin quickly stepped to the cell. "Is this true? Thou art Ferret?"

"That's what I am called, milady," answered the girl-woman, "though my true name is Ferai. 'Tis Gothonian, as was my dear father, rest his soul."

"Ferret, Ferai, regardless," said Arin, "we must get thee free of this place."

Ferai's eyes lighted at these words, but no sooner were they said than the jailor came rushing back. "Time's up. I've got my seat, and they're ready to start the hangings. You'll have to leave."

"Wait," demanded Arin. "You must set this one free."

The warder stepped back, as if startled. "Her? Why, she's one of the worst. Queen of All Thieves, that one. No, milady, she'll dangle among the first, she will."

"But I am innocent," declared Ferret, attempting to summon up a tear but failing.

"Ha!" barked the jailor. "Guilty as sin."

"Chien haleine bâtard!" snarled Ferret.

"Guilt or innocence is not at issue here," declared Arin. "Our mission is vital and she must go with us. Set her free."

The jailor shook his head. "I'll do no such, milady. She's to hang, and that's a fact."

"This cannot be," protested Arin. "Take me to the chief warden."

"It won't do you no good," said the jailor. "He's got his orders, too."

"Even so," said Egil, "we would talk to him."

"Aiko," called Arin. The yellow warrior had reached the end of the cells on the left. "Hurry. We must see the one in charge."

Aiko swiftly came to Arin's side, and with the warder leading in righteous indignation, they moved back down the corridor.

As Delon started to follow, Ferret plucked at his sleeve again. "Give me your belt."

"What?" He looked down at the gaudy leather.

"Don't question," she hissed. "Just give it to me."

As Delon slipped the iridescent belt with its ornate buckle from about his waist, she said, "Where shall I meet you?"

"Meet us?"

"Yes, you fool. Where?"

"Um, we are staying at the Blue Moon, but we have a ship at the docks: slip thirty-four; the *Brise*."

She snaked the ornate belt through the bars. "The ship it is. Go now, before he turns."

Delon hurried to catch the others.

After they retrieved their weapons, the warder escorted them to an office on the first floor. A tall, lean man in his early forties was putting on his hat as the Dylvana entered. He cocked an eye toward the warder.

"They insisted on seeing you, sir," the jailor huffed. "Wouldn't take my word, oh, no." Nose in the air, he marched away.

"What do you want?" demanded the chief warden, gazing out the window where the sun lipped the rim of the world. "I am in a hurry."

"There is a prisoner we need," replied Arin. "One who must be set free."

The chief settled a cloak about his shoulders. From the corridor there came the tramp of feet. "If it's a drunk or a debtor, simply pay at the desk," he snapped.

"Nay, chief warden, 'tis one about to hang," replied Arin.

A jailor stood in the doorway. Arrayed in the hallway behind was a troop of men—swords at their sides, manacles in hand. "We are ready, sir."

The warden nodded and tossed him a ring of keys. "Go on up, sergeant. Take those in the first cell. I'll be there in a moment."

The jailor saluted and turned and called out a command, and the troop tramped away, heading for the stairs.

The warden took up a sheaf of papers. "I'm sorry, but you are too late. I have these warrants to execute. No prisoner to be hanged will be set free."

Aiko growled, and touched the wide leather sash at her waist, the belt holding the hidden shiruken, but Arin stopped her with a glance. The Dylvana turned. "I represent Coron Remar of Darda Erynian, chief warden, and am here at the behest of the Lord Steward Revor. He will tell thee that what I request is to be honored."

"Have you proof of this?" asked the man.

"Nay, yet I can get it."

"Then do so," he replied, stepping toward the doorway. "Until I see such, though, the hangings will go on as scheduled."

"But the steward has set sail, chief warden," protested Arin. "I cannot—"

From the hall came shouts of alarm and the clash and clang of weaponry. Bloodcurdling shrieks and howls of battle rang throughout the building. Horns sounded above the furor, and swarthy men armed with swords and manacle chains clattered down the stairs.

"Escape!" shouted the warden, but whether his was a command to flee or a statement of fact was uncertain. Regardless, he drew a weapon and charged into the fray, his steel riving.

Aiko's own swords were in her hands, and Egil held his axe. Drawing his rapier, Delon looked to Arin. "Now is our chance to save Ferret," he called above the clangor of battle.

Gripping her long-knife, Arin nodded sharply, and Aiko led the way. The battle had spilled into the streets, and the way to the stairwell was empty of combat, though bodies lay here and there—some were Rovers, others warders; some yet alive, others thoroughly dead.

Up the stone stairs Delon dashed, following Aiko's lead, the bard shouting "Ferret! Ferret!" Arin and Egil came after.

When they got to the upper floor, they found men dead and dying; and even though one of the slain jailors—the sergeant—yet held the ring of keys, all the cell doors stood unlocked and open, the cages empty, even the drunks and debtors were gone.

From all appearances, the troop had been ambushed and their swords and chains taken by the escaping prisoners.

As to Ferret, she was nowhere to be found.

Arin and her companions looked at one another in bewilderment, and through the windows came shouts of alarm and calls to arms and cries of frightened women and children.

"The ship," said Delon, "the *Brise*. Ferret said she'd meet us there."

"What?" asked Egil in surprise.

"She said she'd meet us there," repeated Delon. "I'll explain later."

"Let us go," said Aiko. "My tiger whispers of peril."

"But the wounded . . ." protested Arin.

"Surely someone is even now fetching healers," said Egil. "Besides, the chief warden is likely to blame the escape on us."

"Indeed," said Delon. "And he'd likely be right."

Aiko shot him a glance, then said again and more strongly, "Let us go. Now."

Back down the stairs and out they ran, emerging into a madhouse of clamor and chaos, with shouting men, like hounds in pursuit, running this way and that, Rovers fleeing before them.

"Quick," hissed Egil, "to the Blue Moon to get our things, then to the ship."

They scurried through the streets, making their way along the headland toward their quarters. As they ran, of a sudden Egil stopped. "Adon," he said, and pointed through the twilight.

Down in the bay and at anchor stood a Dragonship, and from its mast flew a striped flag: black and orange and gold.

" 'Tis a Jutlander ship," said Egil. "Come searching for us, I deem."

"Ar, your friend came looking," said the innkeeper. "Not a candlemark past."

"Friend?" asked Delon, the bard alone, for the others would be more readily recognized by anyone watching.

"Spoke with an accent, he did," added the innkeeper.

"Was he old, one of his eyes white?"

"Nar. This was a young man with yellow hair. Dressed in black, he was, though his hat was orange and gold. He said, real snootylike, I wasn't to tell you. Said he and his friends wanted to spring a surprise. Ordered me to keep my trap shut, he did. But I thought you should know; besides, I never did like taking orders from strangers."

"Well, if he comes back," said Delon, sliding the 'keep a gold coin, "tell him we dine at the caer. Have him and the others wait in our chambers. We will be late returning."

Delon turned and, pulling his hat low, stepped back to the street. He walked a few paces along the lantern-lit thoroughfare, then ducked into a dark alleyway. "You were right, Egil," he hissed to the three waiting there. "The Jutlanders are looking for us."

"Rauk!" said Egil, turning to Arin. "Then they must know about the *Brise*."

"How so?" asked Delon.

"They would have learned the name of our craft from the harbormaster in Königinstadt," said Arin.

"And they would have asked the harbormaster here if we had docked," added Egil.

Aiko growled. "Then our ship will be under their eye. Perhaps they even lay an ambush for us, and this is what my tiger whispers of."

"Oh Hèl!" hissed Delon. "Ferret's going there."

"Oh, my," exclaimed Arin. "There is something else."

"What is it, love?" asked Egil, his gaze sweeping the street but seeing nothing of alarm.

"Alos. If they find him, they will slay him."

"Damn!" spat Egil. "And it's not like he can hide—an old, one-eyed man."

"We must find him," declared Arin. "Take him to safety."

Aiko grunted. "He is, or was, at a dockside tavern: the Foaming Prow."

Egil turned to her. "You know where he is?"

"I followed him last night when he slipped away."

"Well, let's stir our stumps," said Delon. "The Jutlanders will be back soon, and I'd rather not be the guest of Gudrun again."

Abandoning their meager goods, they slipped away from the Blue Moon and headed for the docks. Full night had fallen by the time they came to the road to the wharves below, and only a handful of lanterns were lit down on the docks. Against the dim yellow light, they scanned the way for Jutlanders coming upward, but none were seen. They scurried down to the piers, and keeping to the darkest shadows, they headed toward the taverns. Soon they reached the Foaming Prow, a ramshackle grogshop much like the Cove in Mørkfjord.

Once again, since he was the least recognizable—being neither an Elf nor yellow nor having one eye—they sent Delon in to investigate. Pulling his hat down to shadow his face, Delon entered the tavern, while Aiko, Arin, and Egil, weapons ready, waited in the darkness outside.

Moments later Delon emerged, with Alos draped over his shoulder, the old man dead drunk and passed out.

Now they made their way back in the direction of the sloop, this time with Arin and Aiko to the fore, the Dylvana's keener eyesight probing the darkness ahead, the Ryodoan at her side, a sword in each hand.

"The peril grows," hissed Aiko.

They stashed Alos behind a great number of bales of flax waiting to be laded aboard a ship. Then they crept onward through the darkness, using shadows and kegs and crates and bales to conceal their progress.

Of a sudden, Arin stopped, Aiko with her. The Dylvana turned and pulled Egil and Delon close. "There," she breathed. "In the darkness nigh the slip. Jutlanders. Seven—no, eight altogether."

"Splendid," hissed Delon, peering in the direction Arin

pointed. "That's but two apiece. Yet I see nothing but darkness where you say they are."

"Elven eyes see well at night," murmured Arin, "by lantern or starlight alone, even in shadows."

Egil touched Delon on the shoulder. "Neither you nor I can see them, yet recall: the Jutes wear black."

Delon nodded, still unable to make out the foe. "What now?"

Aiko looked at the bard and Egil. "Let us turn the tables."

"How so?" asked Egil.

"Waylay those who think to waylay us," she replied. "Lead them into a trap of our own devising."

"Is there no other way?" asked Arin.

"Perhaps a thousand, love," said Egil, "yet we must act now ere Ferret comes."

"She may already be here and their prisoner," sissed Delon.

Aiko said flatly, "They are skulkers, set to kill us. Your mercy is misplaced, Dara."

Egil scanned the docks. "I can decoy them. Get them to run past here, where you could take them from behind— that would cut down the odds quickly."

Aiko nodded in agreement and hissed, "*Subarashii!* Remember: take them from behind!" and before any could move she sheathed her blades and stepped out into the light of a distant lantern, and, singing a Ryodoan song, she swaggered down the dock toward the waiting ambush.

"*Rauk!*" spat Egil, but then turned to the others. "Make ready."

They watched as Aiko sang her way toward the *Brise*.

"What if they have bows?" sissed Delon.

"They don't," said Arin.

As Aiko neared the sloop, armed men in black moved out into the dim light. "*Aufhalten!*" rang out a command.

Aiko looked up as if surprised. "Oh!" she squeaked, quailing back.

The Jutlanders moved toward her, and shrieking, Aiko turned and ran back the way she had come.

One of the men shouted, "*Ergreifen Sie sie!*" and they

thundered after her, their longer legs eating up the distance between.

Up the docks she came, the men gaining, and in the darkness Egil's knuckles were white upon the helve of his axe, as were Arin's on her long-knife and Delon's on his rapier.

Aiko ran some yards past their position, then whirled, drawing her swords. Now she shouted, *"Kuru! Ajiwau hajgane!"*

The pursuing Jutes skidded to a halt, for suddenly the victim had grown fangs.

"Vorsicht!" warned one of the men, and just as they began to spread wide to take this yellow woman from all sides, from behind the trio struck: Egil's axe hewing down a man with a single blow; Arin's long-knife sliding under a shoulderblade to pierce through another's heart; Delon's rapier thrusting into a third Jutlander only to become lodged against bone. Men in black whirled, facing these new opponents, and one raised a horn to his lips to sound a call. But ere the trumpet belled a single note, from the blackness there flashed a dagger tumbling through the air, and the blade sprang full-blown in the man's throat, and dropping his horn and clutching his neck the Jutlander fell gurgling. In the fore, Aiko slew one man and then another, while Delon's blade was wrenched from his hand as the man he had killed fell to the pier, taking the lodged rapier down with him. Delon looked up to see a Jutlander blade swinging at his head, and he sprang aside as another dagger flashed out of the dark to pierce his attacker's breast. The man staggered backward and fell over a slain comrade and did not rise again. Egil's axe took down the last Jute.

They looked at one another panting, and a figure stepped out of the darkness.

"Where have you been?" she demanded, a brace of throwing daggers in hand.

It was Ferret.

"Ferret!" exclaimed Delon.

She ignored his greeting. "The kingsguard will be down here soon, looking for escaped Rovers, any that got away, that is, for they're likely to try to steal a ship."

In the lanternlight they could see bandoliers of daggers crisscrossing her chest. She stepped to two of the slain Jutes and retrieved her knives, cleaning the blades on the dead men's cloaks. "These bastards were waiting. I thought them kingsmen. I didn't know they would attack you. Fortunate I stopped to get some of my things, eh?"

"Come," said Arin. "Ferai is right: kingsmen will soon be here to stop pirates from stealing ships, to say nought of other Jutlanders searching for us. We must flee."

"What about these bodies?" asked Delon.

"Let be," answered Egil. "We will be gone in less time than it would take to hide them."

"I will get Alos while you ready the ship," said Aiko, and she started back toward the bales of flax.

"Alos? Who is Alos?" asked Ferret, stepping into the shadows to emerge with a small satchel.

"He's one of the one-eyes in dark water," replied Delon without elaborating. "Now come on, let's get out of here before the warders or more Jutlanders arrive."

As they hurried toward the ship, from a pocket she fished out his belt and handed it to Delon. "Thanks. The buckle tongue makes a suitable lockpick for cell doors."

Delon laughed and took the belt and fastened it about his waist.

Now they came to the *Brise*. As Arin and Egil began raising the sails, Delon said, "Help me with these lines, Ferret."

"These Jutlanders: they were the men in black?"

"Aye. Men in black, with orange and gold hats on their heads. They're after us."

"Hmm, Jutlanders after you, kingsguards after me. I'd say it's time to fly."

"Sooner than you think, lass," said Egil. "When it occurs to the Jutes to come and see about the ambush, we need be long gone. Their Dragonship is faster than our sloop."

"Hsst!" hissed Arin, "someone nears."

They peered through the shadows along the docks. A figure came carrying a burden.

It was Aiko, and draped over her shoulder was Alos, the old man dead to the world. Bearing him like a sack of grain, she clambered over the wale and headed for the cabin as Delon and Ferret shoved the sloop out from the slip, vaulting on board as they did so.

And with all now aboard they sailed away into the sea underneath the glimmering stars.

CHAPTER 44

When the bark *Red Hind* had just passed the midpoint of her journey across Hile Bay—the ship being some ten nautical leagues out from Pendwyr, with nine leagues yet to go—Lord Steward Revor startled awake from a sound sleep in the dead of night.

The elusive thought had been captured at last.

He fumbled about on his bunkside table to find the lanthorn striker. Moments later yellow lamplight filled the tiny cabin.

He dragged the saddlebags from under his bunk, and he searched among the documents. At last he found the list he was looking for, and there on the slate of names of those to be executed was the one that gave him pause: Ferai.

Can this be the ferret Dara Arin is looking for?

He gazed out the porthole. Black night slid by.

Not likely, for Ferai is a thief, and what would a Dylvana want with a thief? Still, there is a slim chance.

Lord Revor sighed and looked at the list again.

In any event, it is long past sundown and entirely too late. She is dead by now. Still, if I hadn't been so pressed . . .

Lord Revor slipped the papers back into his saddlebags and slid them beneath the bed. Then he blew out the lanthorn.

He sat on the edge of the bunk in the dark for a while, then finally he lay back down.

Sleep was a long time coming.

CHAPTER 45

Just ere dawn, riding an all but spent horse with an exhausted remount trailing after, the kingsman galloped into the streets of Pendwyr. Past the Blue Moon he hammered, where in a suite of rooms a group of Jutlanders waited impatiently for the mutilators and slayers to return. The rider did not know that men in black and gold and orange lay in ambush within. Nor did he know of the kingsguards who even now were patrolling the docks and searching for more pirates, brethren of those who had evidently slain a group of honest Jutlanders and had stolen a ship—the sloop *Brise,* according to the harbormaster—for who else would have done such a dastardly deed as to slaughter these innocent visitors and just leave their corpses lying about for the wharf rats to gnaw upon. The critical thing the rider knew was that he bore a message from High King Bleys to be delivered into the hands of the lord steward at the caer. He had traveled some twelve hundred miles in twenty-six days, a remarkable journey all told, though he would have arrived sooner had he not lost one of his remounts, and had he not been delayed by illness. Nevertheless, he at last had come to Pendwyr, and now the caer was in sight.

Finally he reached the span across to the castle spire, where he was challenged by bridge warders. Quickly they passed him through.

Lord Otkins, first understeward, was roused from his bed. He was out of sorts, having had but little sleep this nighttide—pirates had escaped, men had been slain, some had been sorely wounded; thieves and cutpurses had fled in the dusk; even the debtors and drunkards were gone. Many escapees were yet at large, though some had been recaptured and others lay dead. And when his man had awakened him, Lord Otkins thought he brought news of the miscreants. But no, instead it was a missive, one from Bleys himself.

Lord Otkins took the folded vellum and broke the seal and read the message within:

Revor
We are with Coron Aldor's warband in the Grimwall near Drimmen-deeve. Vanidar, a Lian, brought word of Dara Arin, a Dylvana, who may or may not come to Pendwyr. If she does, she may be accompanied by several others, in particular by Aiko, a yellow warrior woman. Give the Dara aid; let her have whatever she wants, for the mission she follows is vital. Too, tell Dara Arin that I keep no ferrets whatsoever, much less in cages.

~ Bleys

A second sigil from the High King's ring was impressed in red sealing wax below Bleys' signature.

Huah. Well and good. I will keep an eye out for this Dylvana. What is it, I wonder, she wants? And what's all this about ferrets? Bloody odd, that.

Mumbling to himself, Lord Otkins lay back in his bed and pulled the covers up to his chin. He would issue orders later in the day to watch for this Elf. But right now there were more important things to worry about: Blood and guts, man, there had been a prison break!

CHAPTER 46

"I think they'll fare along the coast when they discover we are gone," said Egil, eyeing the set of the *Brise*'s sails by the light of the stars above.

"Which way: east or west?" asked Delon.

"East, I think," replied Egil. "That was the direction we sailed to reach Pendwyr, and I think they will assume we will continue that way, fleeing before them."

"Perhaps they'll believe we've doubled back to elude them, and head west instead," said Aiko, now adeck with all the others, all, that is, but Alos, who lay unconscious below.

At the tiller, Arin said, "Speculating on which direction the Jutlanders might take is not as vital as deciding which way *we* should sail. And until we can choose a destination, let us continue south into the open sea."

"What lies directly south?" asked Egil. "Islands? A port? What?"

"Hm. Sabra, I think," said Delon. "All the way across the Avagon—two thousand miles or so. Why do you ask?"

"The Jutes might think we sail for a major city, and if Sabra is one, I think we ought to veer east of due south, or west." Egil turned to Arin. "Regardless, love, your plan is sound. Sail into the open ocean where they are less likely to search. And even if they do search, from what Delon says, the Avagon is a wide, wide sea."

"But wait a moment," said Ferret, biting into a ration of waybread as she sat cross-legged on the cabin housing. "Why *don't* we simply head for a rich city? There's hundreds to choose from, and the likelihood of anyone finding us is slim at best. Besides, what better thing is there to do?"

"Better thing?" asked Arin, glancing at the sky, as if choosing a star to guide upon. "Mayhap nought. Yet it is not a so-called better thing we search for, but something needful instead." Arin turned to the girl. "Ferai, we are on a mission, and have yet one other some*one* or some*thing* to find ere we can seek out the green stone—wherever *it* may be."

Ferret looked up from her waybread. "A mission? Now wait a moment . . . although you got me out of a tight spot back there, I'm not at all certain that I want to go on some mission. Of course, I might be persuaded if . . . —Just where *is* this one other someone or something? And what's this about a green stone?" She turned her gaze toward Arin, Ferai's features studiously ingenuous, and she casually asked, "Is it a treasure?"

Arin smiled. "As to the location of what we next seek, I don't know. Just as I do not know where the green stone lies."

"But you have a treasure map, eh?"

"We have a rede."

"Rede?"

"Aye. A riddle."

"You mean you travel over the world following a riddle, searching for somethings and someones and a green stone?"

"Exactly so."

Ferret fell into thought, then said, "This riddle—it's solved, right?"

Arin shrugged. "We have only guesses as to its meanings, but whether they are right or wrong, we know not."

Ferret threw up her hands and demanded, "Then how do you expect to find this someone or something?"

Delon reached across and patted Ferret on the knee. "I was hoping that you could tell us where next to go, luv."

Ferret's eyes flew wide. "Me? Why, I don't even know why you, um, helped me in the first place"—she stroked her throat with the fingers of one hand—"though I am quite pleased that you did. What do you mean that I am to tell you where next to go?"

"Yes, Delon," said Egil, "just what *do* you mean? I, too, would like to know."

"Well," said Delon, looking at Arin, "correct me if I'm wrong, but it seems to me that each new step of your quest—of *our* quest—depends, or at least *has* depended, upon the last step taken." Delon held up a hand to stop the burgeoning questions. "Hear me out:

"Several steps led you to Black Mountain, Dara, where you found Aiko, a cat who fell from grace. And she in turn was the one who suggested that dark water might be the name of a place, and that led you to Mørkfjord, where you found two one-eyes: Egil and Alos. It was Egil then who told you that the only mad monarch he knew of was the queen of Jute, and that led you to me, a rutting peacock. In my turn, in Pendwyr I suggested that the High King's cage might be the jail, and when we were inside I called out 'ferret,' and that led us to her." Delon now turned to Ferret. "And so, luv, if the chain holds true, you will help us solve the next step and tell us where we can find the maze."

"Maze?" asked Ferret.

Egil cleared his throat. "That I am the one-eye in dark water, I have no doubt. Yet is it not possible that all the others were chosen simply because they seemed to fit the words of the rede? For instance, there was a true peacock in the queen's gardens, though we, er, though Aiko chose you instead, even though at the time I thought it was the preening bird we were after. Could it be that no matter where we go we will find someone or something to fit what we seek?"

Aiko shook her head and growled, "I *am* the cat who fell from grace, and we have seen no other. You question my choice of rutting peacocks, yet you, Egil, are but one of four one-eyes. Even so, you claim to be certain that you are the one-eye of the rede."

"By Hèl, I *am* the one-eye," declared Egil. "It's the rest of you that I—"

"There can be no other ferret," protested Delon, stabbing a finger toward Ferai. "And what else could I be but the—"

"Silence!" snapped Arin, slapping a hand to the bench. In surprise, all eyes turned to the Dylvana. Now that she had their attention, she said, "It will do no good for us to squabble among ourselves. Mayhap Egil is right: mayhap no matter where I go, where *we* go, we will find that which we search for, whether or no it is the true thing wc seek.

"Yet there is truth in that which Delon has said: each new step depends on the one just taken. And in this instance, it was the finding of the ferret in the High King's cage that should lead us to the cursed keeper of faith in the maze."

All eyes turned to Ferai. She threw up her hands in frustration and exclaimed, "I don't even know what the Hèl all of you are talking about!"

Even as they looked at her, there came a howl from below decks.

Alos was awake.

"Damned press-gang, that's what you all are!" shouted the oldster as he lurched back and forth across the deck, shaking an accusing finger in each of their faces, including Ferret's, even though Alos paused in puzzlement for a moment as he looked at her, wondering who she was, but deciding she was guilty in any event.

"But Alos," protested Delon, "they would have killed you."

Alos swung about, lurching sideways a bit as he tried to focus upon the bard. "Wcll maybe I'd rather be dead!" he bellowed, his white eye glaring. "You never stopped to think of that, did you? Oh, no, it's not what he might want, is it now? Instead you just grabbed him and threw him aboard the ship, regardless." He lurched forward and leaned a hand on the cabin bulkhead, breathing ale-laden fumes into Delon's face. "Uh, jst, jst, just who is it that was going to kill who, eh? Who is it y'r goin' t' kill? Who are we after?"

Bcfore Delon could answer, the old man's watery blue eye rolled up and he collapsed forward into Delon's arms.

"Still drunk," muttered Delon. He hoisted Alos across a shoulder and headed below deck.

"Watch out for your boots," said Egil.

Ferret had observed Alos's tirade with a detached air of amusement. But when Delon came back adeck after safely ensconcing the oldster in a bunk below, she turned to Arin. "Tell me, now, what's all this about a mission, a rede, someone or something you need to find, and a green stone?"

Arin gave the tiller over to Egil. "It's a long tale, Ferai, yet let me begin. . . ."

The east held the glimmerings of a false dawn when Arin finished her tale, though a waning quarter moon rode high in the sky and stars yet glittered above. Alos was still asleep below, as were now Delon and Aiko. Egil yet manned the helm, and the sloop continued southward into the open Avagon Sea, the ship now some twenty or so nautical leagues south of Pendwyr, some seventy miles all told.

Ferret took a deep breath. "A cat, a one-eye, a rutting peacock, a ferret: all these you have found. And now you need to locate a cursed keeper of faith in a maze?"

Arin nodded.

Ferret tilted her head sideways, peering through the starlight. "And you expect me to know of him?"

Arin shrugged. "I can only hope, Ferai."

"This Dragonstone—pale green and translucent and the size of a melon: very fine jade, I would say, judging from your description. It must be worth a fortune, even if broken up . . . though as a whole piece, it would be price-less." She looked at Arin. "The Mages—they would pay handsomely to get it back, eh?"

Arin shook her head. "Ferai, we are not in it for reward, but to keep its terrible doom from falling."

Ferret held out a calming hand. "Oh, yes. That, too. But should someone with a fortune decide to share it with the finder of the green stone, who could refuse?"

Arin looked at Egil, an unvoiced question in her eyes, but he merely smiled and shrugged.

Ferret yawned and stretched. "Ah, me, but I am weary. I've had little sleep in the last few days, as you can under-stand. Is there a bunk for me below?"

Egil nodded. "The *Brise* sleeps four. We take turns: some rest while others crew the ship. You rest. We'll awaken you when it's your duty."

"But I don't know how to sail," said Ferai.

"Fear not. You'll learn, just as did Arin and Aiko and Delon—trained sailors all, now."

"Well, I can't say that sailing the *Breeze* is my heart's desire, but if I must . . ."

"What did you call her?"

"Who?"

"The ship."

"Oh, that. I called her the *Breeze:* that's what *Brise* means—it's a Gothonian word."

"Ah," said Egil. "We didn't know."

Ferret frowned. "The ship *is* Dara Arin's, isn't it?"

Egil laughed. "Aye, that she is. And a good one, too. Good enough to take us around the world."

"Hmm," grunted Ferret. "I hope we don't have to go that far to get this green stone we're after."

"Then thou wilt go with us?" asked Arin.

Ferret nodded. "For such an object? One that Dragons fear . . . or worship? Indeed, I will go with you. Recall, the rede says that you will fail without me. Besides, I owe you that much for . . . um"—she jerked a thumb in the direction of Pendwyr—"back there."

Squinting against the sun and cursing, Alos emerged from the cabin. Delon sat at the helm; Aiko was adeck to handle the sails.

"You!" shouted Alos, the old man pointing an accusing finger at Aiko. "You did this to me again!"

Aiko looked at the oldster impassively, saying nothing.

"I told you I was done with you, done with you all, but oh no, you spirited me away instead."

"Sorry, Alos," said Delon, "but they would have killed you. Aiko saved you from certain death."

"Who?" demanded Alos. "Who would have killed me?"

"The Jutes, old man," replied the bard. "Don't you remember? We talked a bit about this last night."

"Ha! A likely story," barked Alos.

"Truly, Alos, the Jutes sailed into Pendwyr the day after we arrived. They discovered our lodgings at the Blue Moon and were down at the wharves as well. It's a good thing they hadn't gotten around to searching the dockside taverns, else you'd be dead. You can't very well go unnoticed, what with your white eye. Aiko saved you."

Alos glanced over at Aiko. "Is this true?"

She looked long at him, as if considering whether to deign to answer, but at last she nodded *Yes.*

"They set an ambush for us," added Delon, "eight of them. They're all dead. But there's thirty, forty more yet in Pendwyr I think, given the size of their ship."

"Huah," grunted Alos, then sat down heavily. "Well I, um, I suppose I should thank you both for saving me from the Jutes. But Adon's balls, don't you see, I'm back in the madness of this venture, and I don't like that one bit." He looked across at Aiko. "You should have left me in Mørkfjord. I was happy there."

Aiko shrugged, but Delon said, "Were you really? It seems to me that the only times I saw joy in your face were when you were here at the helm."

Alos canted his head and shrugged.

"And when you played the tambour," added Aiko.

He looked at her, startled surprise in his eye. "Huh, I didn't think you cared."

Aiko turned her face away from him and looked out at the sea.

Delon leaned forward and sotto voce whispered to the oldster, "She saved your life, Alos."

Alos looked long at Aiko, her face away from him, then he swallowed and glanced at the set of the sails and the angle of the wind pennon and said in a gruff voice, "Here. You've got it all wrong. Give me the helm, and trim up the tops and stays. And tell me, what be our course?"

CHAPTER 47

ourse?" Arin glanced at Ferret then faced Alos again. "South-southeast, until we can decide upon a destination . . . or until Ferai gives us one."

Ferret pointed a finger at her own chest. "Me? I should choose? Ah, wait, I see: we're looking for the cursed keeper, right?"

Arin nodded.

Ferret turned up her hands. "Well I don't care what Delon says about me being the one to lead us there, I simply don't know of *any* cursed keeper." She swept wide gestures leftward and rightward. "*Peste et mort!* he could be anywhere, including up in the clouds above or down in the depths below . . . or even on another Plane."

Aiko looked up from oiling one of her swords. "I yet say the cursed keeper could be in Gudrun's hedge maze."

Delon vehemently shook his head. "No, no, Aiko. Although she was indeed cursed, she is no keeper of faith."

"Well we can't just keep on sailing sou'sou'easterly," declared Alos. "I mean, we'll eventually run out of sea— unless you expect me to sail 'cross the barrens of Chabba as well."

Delon looked out across the slow-rolling ocean waves. "Where are we?"

Arin glanced at the sun. "Some thirty-five leagues south of Pendwyr."

None questioned her word, for all understood Elves simply *knew* at all times where should stand the sun, moon, stars, and the five wanderers. And given that power, Elves need only glance at the angle of any of those to gauge where on Mithgar they stood. Hence, if the Dara said that they were some thirty-five leagues south of Pendwyr, then without a doubt, that's precisely where they were.

"Look," said Delon, "there's got to be a way to cipher out where we should go." He looked at Arin. "I mean, Dara, you would not have spoken a rede if there weren't a means to fulfill it . . . hence there must be a way to know our next destination."

Arin shrugged, and said, "Mayhap Egil is right after all: mayhap no matter where we fare, we will discover something we deem meets the words of the rede."

"I don't believe that," objected Delon. He turned to Ferret. "I believe instead that you hold the answer, luv."

Ferret took in a deep breath and then noisily blew it back out and shrugged.

"She doesn't know where we should go," grumped Alos.

"Ah, but I believe she does," replied Delon. "She just doesn't know she knows it."

"Well if I know this thing, but just don't know that I know it," said Ferret, "isn't that the same as not knowing it in the first place?"

"Ha!" barked Alos. "She's got you there."

"Not at all, Alos," said Delon. "We simply need a way to reveal it."

"As my rede was revealed," said Arin. "Yet in my case I had vague notions that my vision held more than I could recall, though what it was remained concealed until Lysanne unveiled it."

Aiko shook her head. "She was Mage trained, Dara, and we have no Mage here."

"Then how are we going to discover this knowledge you say I have?" said Ferret.

All eyes turned to Delon. He shrugged, then said, "Perhaps we can jog your memory."

"How?"

"Well, for instance, luv, tell us something of yourself."

"Like what?"

"Oh, say, tell us of your mother."

"My mother is dead."

"Then your father."

"He's dead, too."

Delon reached out and took her head. "Then tell us of your life."

"There's not that much to tell. I spent a rather uneventful childhood, and then came to Pendwyr."

Delon dropped her hand in exasperation. "Then tell us how you came to be in prison and about to be hanged."

"I was innocent!" declared Ferret.

"Ha!" barked Delon. "They called you Queen of All Thieves."

"Leave me alone," Ferret cried out, and, turning away, she scrambled toward the bow of the ship.

Delon started to follow, but Arin plucked at his sleeve and shook her head. "Let be, Delon. I sense old wounds lying deep. She will talk to us at her need, not ours."

Delon looked toward the place Ferret had gotten to. Then he glanced at Arin and nodded and settled back. And on the pitching bow of the *Brise*, Ferret watched the waves roll by. . . .

When Ferai was six, her mother and father began training her for the act—Janine teaching her the trapeze and acrobatics and how to walk the rope, Ardure showing her the tricks of locks and knots and contortions and such—for Janine was an amazing acrobat and Ardure could escape from anything, or so the broadsheets and criers claimed. Oh, not that they had always been so, for when they first were married, he was a locksmith, and she his lissome young bride. A year passed and a babe was born; Ferai they named her, and she was well loved, and they sang to her every night and told her marvelous tales. Yet she was another mouth to feed and times were hard and business bad, and so they took to the road. By happenstance they came across a young man in need of a worthy locksmith; he was Lemond, new owner of a traveling circus. It seemed his father had died of a sudden and painful stomach ailment without revealing to his estranged son where he kept the keys to the weighty iron money box. And though Lemond had virtually dismantled the entire circus, no keys were to be found. Ardure solved his problem in a trice, and Lemond offered him a position in *Le Cirque de Merveille*—that of an escape artist, could he master the tricks.

Ardure accepted, for this was steady work, and he and Janine and little Ferai traveled throughout Mithgar. When Ferai was but three, lithe Janine began taking lessons from the acrobat Arielle, then Janine, too, joined the show.

Lemond was a heavy drinker with an eye for the women, and often the circus would hastily pull up stakes and leave town ere the scheduled run was complete—all because of Lemond's drinking and whoring, said some. And Lemond spent long candlemarks watching Janine practice—gauging her talent, he said, though others thought differently. But nothing came of Lemond's interest, for Ardure was never far away, and neither was wee Ferai.

As to Ferai's own lessons, they went swiftly enough, and soon she was astage with her sire or dam, where she became a darling of the patrons though she was not quite seven. Throughout the next few years not only did Ardure and Janine teach Ferai the tricks of the trade, but they taught her to read and write as well—skills uncommon among many of her professional colleagues. Even so, they, too, took her to their bosoms and showed her many things—including the riding of animals and the throwing of knives and even the art of buffoonery, consisting of garish makeup and baggy clothes and acting the fool in the main. And then there was the old fortune-teller, Nom, examining palms and gazing into crystals and casting her bones and reading her special deck of cards. For the most part she taught Ferai how to dupe customers, to beguile and mislead them altogether and send them away feeling as if someone had seen their life's secrets and had given sound advice.

And her parents continued to sing to her every night as they tucked her in bed.

But then, when she was but twelve, a terrible thing occurred: in a tragic fire of unknown origin, Ferai's parents died. Why they had not simply escaped will perhaps never be known; for some unknown reason it was as if they were unable to grab Ferai and flee. Miraculously, it seems, Lemond was passing by and managed to rescue the child. And comforting her, he took her to his wagon.

It is not told what happened that night, but the next morning Lemond was found slain in his very own bed, a dagger through his heart. And in the other bed, where Ferai had slept, there was blood as well, in the center of the sheet. Some said 'twas virgin's blood and decided that she had been raped and borne off by the fiend that had slain Lemond, while others claimed that Ferai, too, had been murdered and it was her corpse that had been carried away. But raped or murdered, the twelve-year-old was nowhere to be found.

She made her way to Pellar and lived as a street urchin in the city of Pendwyr, cadging for food or coin. That she did not practice her trade is understandable, for she believed, unlikely as it might seem, that news of a child performing feats of escape and acrobatics might perk up the ears of the authorities and she would be arrested for a killing that occurred in a nearby land. After all, in Pendwyr, the capital of the realm, news often came from lands both near and far, as did notices of murders and rewards.

Through another street urchin, a lad she liked, she fell in among a band of thieves, and soon her skills proved invaluable, for locks did not stop her, nor did gates nor walls nor dogs nor the city watch nor private guards . . . she never failed to find a way to get 'round each and every one.

And they taught her the art of picking a pocket and of cutting loose a purse without the victim discovering it until it was too late, and she quickly acquired the skill. Too, they showed her how to swindle a gull by first winning his or her confidence and then duping them in the end. In this, too, Ferai was a fast learner, for it was little different from what Old Nom had taught her in days past, though here the risk was much, much greater, yet so were the rewards.

It was this band of thieves that took to calling her Ferret, for as one said, "We're simply undoing what that awful Gothonian accent has done to your name." And in spite of the fact that she protested, saying that the word for ferret in Gothonian was *furet,* still she had to agree that in her native tongue it sounded quite a bit like Ferai, and so the name stuck.

She stayed with this band for four years, but in the end she tired of the incessant bickering and squabbling among them and so struck out on her own.

Some of her thefts were spectacular, for they involved silently crossing on a slender rope from one building to another above a patrolling watch, or slipping through a ring of alert guardians, or opening an unopenable lock, and other such sensational feats.

For nearly ten years she lived by her wits in Pendwyr, and the killing of that pig Lemond faded into the past. But her parents were in her thoughts each and every day, and she often wept for the remembrance of them, in particular when anyone sang.

Aye, she lived by her wits for nearly ten years—much of that in relative comfort—ere the city watch came for her, and that just three weeks past. They burst through her door and into her room and arrested her before she could escape, and they discovered under her mattress a single golden earring. How it had gotten there, Ferret did not know, but it proved to be one of many items taken in a theft. As to why the watchmen had come for her, it seems that someone had named her the miscreant in a case where Lady Brum had been wounded when she had come across a thief burgling her house in the night.

It was later rumored that an old compatriot of hers from her erstwhile days had collected the reward for her capture.

In spite of her protests of innocence, she was quickly convicted and sentenced to death for stealing a Lady's jewels and attempting to murder her.

They threw her in a cell next to those housing the Rover captains, though some called for her to be thrown in with the pirates instead: they'd visit a right proper punishment on her before she went to the gallows, wouldn't they now?

She languished in her cell awaiting death. And the warders were careful to keep anything from her which might be used as a pick, for whoever had turned her in had reported that she was a wonder with locks. As proof, the city watch noted that the complex lock on Lady Brum's jewel box had been opened without the thief leaving a single mark; either that or the jewel box had inadvertently been left open, which Lady Brum angrily denied.

And so, Ferret was trapped in a cell with no way to open the door.

The day of the hanging finally arrived. . . .

And then Arin and Egil and Aiko and Delon the bard had come along. . . .

And now Ferret sat on the bow of the *Brise* and watched the waves go by. And Delon at the stern lifted his Elven-sweet voice in song.

Ferai began to cry.

CHAPTER 48

"Why do you weep, luv?" Delon sat at the bow and held Ferai's hand.

"Because you sang."

"Am I that bad?"

She cast him a glimmer of a smile and wiped her cheeks with the fingers of her free hand. "No, Delon. You sing beautifully. It's just that . . ."

Her speech faltered, but Delon remained silent. After a moment she said, "It's just that I was remembering."

Fresh tears welled and ran down her cheeks. Gently Delon pulled her to him. "Cry all you need, luv." And he cradled her against his shoulder as she wept.

And the *Brise* cut through the translucent waves of the deep blue indigo sea.

A long while later, Ferret said, "Would you sing more another time?"

Delon looked down at her. "For you, luv, indeed."

Onward sailed the *Brise,* Delon yet holding Ferai next to him. In the distance, skimming low over the waves, glided a white bird with long, long wings. Delon pointed it out to Ferai.

"What is it?" she asked.

"An albatross, I think. They say it spends its entire life on the wing."

Ferret sighed. "As sometimes I think do I."

Delon looked again at her. "Me, too, luv. Me, too."

They watched the bird for a while, until they could see it no more down among the waves, and Ferret said, "Do you really think I know something that will tell us where to go?"

Delon shrugged. "It's been that way so far: each new person the key to finding the next. All but Alos, that is, though Arin thinks he yet may have a part to play.

"And as for you, luv, I truly do believe you hold a key as well. As to what it might be, I cannot say. Perhaps something from your past: something your father or mother said; a picture you saw; a rumor you heard; a song, a story, a poem, a saying; or something altogether different."

"From what you say, Delon, it could be anything," protested Ferret.

"No, luv, it can only be one thing: a keeper of faith in a maze."

"But I don't know any keepers of faith."

"Well, then, perhaps you know of a maze."

They continued sailing south-southeastward and two more days passed, days and nights filled with discussions and debates as to where they should go next:

Aiko argued that they should go back to Jute and take Gudrun captive, for she had the only cursed maze that they knew of. And when someone pointed out that the rede called for a keeper who was cursed and not the maze, Aiko replied that given her appetites, surely Gudrun was cursed as well.

Delon recommended that they head for Black Mountain, so that Lysanne could work her magic on Ferret.

Egil suggested that since they were in the *Brise,* they could sail to Rwn and do the very same thing: have one of the Mages there reveal whatever knowledge might be hidden deep within Ferai's mind. Too, they could perhaps lift his own curse—for his nightly ill dreams continued unabated—and perhaps the Mages could recover his lost memories as well.

Ferret herself objected to anyone, much less a Mage, rummaging about in her thoughts, her memories, her very essence.

Alos argued that wherever they went, he was quitting this mad quest.

Arin calmly listened to all, weighing the choices before them.

During this time the only thing they settled was the makeup and shifts of the crews: Egil, Arin, and Aiko sailed the *Brise* throughout the night; Alos, Delon, and Ferret handled her by day. Of course there was a goodly overlap from midafternoon till mideve, and this was when the debate as to what to do and where to go became most heated.

But during the quieter moments, Ferai racked her memories for some clue that Delon was certain she knew. Many of her memories were painful, others sad, but she was surprised to find that many brought joy to mind—especially those of her dam and sire singing and telling her tales.

These songs and stories she tried to remember in their fullness, for Delon had mentioned that perhaps something of the sort was where a hidden memory lay. But try as she would, nothing came to mind, and she was convinced she'd have more success at finding a rainbow's gold.

It was in the depths of the second of these nights that she awoke with a start. "Delon," she hissed, swinging her feet over the edge of the bunk. She reached across the tiny cabin and shook him by the shoulder. "Delon."

He came groggily awake. "Unh?"

"Wake up. I just remembered."

Delon sat up, rubbing his fists into his eyes. "Umh," he yawned. "Remembered what?"

"Something Old Nom used."

"Old Nom?"

"She was a fortune teller."

"And she used . . .?"

"In her readings she had a card she called the Door to the Temple of the Labyrinth."

"Temple of the Labyrinth?"

"Yes. Its door."

"This temple, this door: what else do you know of it?"

Ferai paused a moment, then said, "Old Nom told me that if you are ever dealt this card it means a dangerous and confusing passage in your life, but that if you can reach the door, you will reach safety. When the card is dealt out upright, it means that you will likely succeed; inverted means you will most likely fail."

"Huah," grunted Delon. "Do you know aught else about this temple?"

Ferret shook her head. "No, though as to the card, I can draw its picture, even the words above the door. Adon knows, I saw it enough when she taught me the trade."

Delon took up a striker and lit a lantern. "Do so, luv. This sounds promising."

"Do you really think so?" Ferai reached for the ship's log as well as for quill and inkpot.

"Indeed."

Alos groaned and turned over and glared at them. "I'm trying to sleep here."

"Ferret may have a clue as to where we should be bound," said Delon as he watched her carefully sketch an elaborate doorway.

Alos sat up and rubbed his face and scratched his belly and then watched as well.

Studiously she drew symbols upon the vellum. Then she sketched what seemed to be an entryway into a building. Finally she turned the logbook so that all could see and said, "This is what was on the card: a door carved in a wall of stone. Above the door were these symbols, words, I think, engraved in the lintel, in a language I do not know.

"Can any read this?"

מדרש המבוך

Delon leaned over and peered at the lettering, then said, "I can't read it, but it looks like Hurnian characters to me . . . or Sarainese."

In that moment the door to the cabin slid open and Egil stuck his head in. "Is something amiss?" Delon turned and smiled. "No, no, Egil. Ferret has remembered something. Come look at this. —No wait. We'll bring it adeck so that all can see."

Arin looked up from the sketch and asked Ferret, "Dost thou know of a doorway of this likeness?"

"Only on Nom's card."

Arin turned to the others. "Do any of ye know aught of such?"

Each peered closely at the drawing, each shrugging *No.*

Now Arin gazed at Delon. "Thou sayest these letters are Hurnian?"

"Or Sarainese. They're much alike, but I am no linguist . . . or calligrapher, for that matter. It's just that I've seen writing like this in my travels."

"And thou hast seen no such door?"

Delon shook his head. "I've never been in Sarain, and I saw no such door in Hurn. But it is a wide land and I was only in the city of Chara, along the coast. . . . I was stranded there for a couple of months three years back. I'd not care to go there again, for not only does a particular lonely woman seek my heart, so does her angry husband."

"Where is this land?" asked Aiko.

"East. On the Avagon. Past the Islands of Stone," Delon replied.

"And Sarain?"

"South of there, I think."

Alos cleared his throat. "Aye, Sarain is south of Hurn, and full of warring tribes fighting over water and land and theology, or so my old captain used to say."

They fell silent for a moment, and finally Delon said, "Listen, whether it is in Hurn or Sarain, what more promising place than in something called the Temple of the Labyrinth are we likely to find a cursed keeper of faith in a maze, eh?"

"Yes," said Aiko, "but if these lands of Hurn and Sarain are wide, we may be a long while searching."

Egil nodded, then said, "If we could only read the inscription, perhaps it would let us at least narrow our choices down from two to one."

Arin turned again to Ferai. "Is there aught else thou knowest of this place, or even of Nom's card?"

Ferret closed her eyes, trying to remember. At last, without opening her eyes, she said, "The stone is red."

Arin looked at Delon. "Does either Hurn or Sarain have red stone?"

"I don't know about Sarain, but it seems to me that the

coastal areas of Hurn were mostly yellow and tan and grey, though the stone might be red inland."

They turned to Alos. He shrugged.

Arin glanced at each of them. "Is there aught else any would add?"

"Just that we should decide," said Egil.

Arin lowered her head for a moment, considering. Then she looked up and said, "This then is what I propose: that first we go to Sarain and find a city along the coast. There we shall seek out one who can read and ask him to decipher this. If it is not Sarainese, then we shall fare to Hurn and do the same. Then we shall choose our course from there."

Again her gaze swept across them all. "Agreed?"

One by one they nodded, and then Egil said, "Not that I differ, my love, but what made you pick Sarain?"

"What Alos said, *chier*."

"Me?" barked Alos, surprised.

"Aye. Thou and Ferai. Where there is theology, oft there are temples. And thou didst say the Sarainese tribes fight over theology, among other things, and where there is religious warfare, a sect will at times conceal itself. And remember what Ferai didst say: if the card is dealt to thee it indicates a dangerous and confusing passage in thy life, but that if thou canst but reach the door, thou wilt then reach safety. Mayhap the dangerous and confusing passage is one through a maze, and given its name, mayhap the temple itself is concealed in a labyrinth."

Ferret took a deep breath and slowly let it out. Delon turned to her. "What is it, luv?"

She looked at him and shook her head. "I can't shake the feeling that we will actually be living inside of Old Nom's card."

Delon raised an eyebrow. "And . . . ?"

"And, Delon, I can't help but wonder whether the card is upright or inverted."

CHAPTER 49

Alos swung the *Brise* southeastward, quartering the prevailing winds off the starboard stern, saying, "Sarain: it's across the Avagon, 'tween Chabba and Hurn. Just keep her headed southeasterly and we'll strike land sooner or later." And then he headed back to bed, under his breath grumbling, "The next bedamned seaport we come to, someone needs to get some bedamned charts so that someone can properly navigate and reckon, for who knows how far the bedamned coast of Sarain is and who knows where along the bedamned shores we'll make landfall and . . ."

The next days saw the ship heading southeasterly, at times running before a spanking breeze, at other times drifting slowly, nearly becalmed. And though the air was at times capricious, for the most part the weather held fair, but for a running three days of rain.

Yet in spite of the wind or its lack, in spite of the rain or not, now and again throughout the day Delon would sing to Ferai, and she would listen raptly, while in the stern Alos would smile and tap out a rhythmic beat.

And all along the course, especially at the change of shifts, in the twilight Arin and the others continued to debate the merits of following after a fortune-teller's card, debating as well what they might find at journey's end:

"Perhaps the labyrinth is inside the temple," suggested Egil, "rather than without. Perhaps that's where the confusing journey Old Nom spoke of is, perhaps that's where it both begins *and* ends."

Aiko blew out a long puff of air, and at a cocked eyebrow from Arin, the Ryodoan said, "Perhaps the confusing maze is in the very religion itself, and one must escape it altogether to be free."

"You mean leave the temple?" asked Ferret.

Aiko shook her head. "No, Ferai. I mean leave the religion itself behind."

"Oh."

They drifted slowly long moments more, the wind but a waft of air, the ship nearly in irons. Finally Ferret said, "I'm not a very religious person. It seems rather foolish to me."

"Huah," grunted Delon. "You do not believe in Adon or Elwydd at all?"

"Or Garlon?" added Alos.

"Oh, I suppose I do," Ferret replied, "if only to call upon them in oaths now and then. It's just that in my life they seem to hold no sway." She turned to Arin. "What about you, Dara? Do you worship Adon or Elwydd? Pray to them? Make offerings? Do you think that following a particular religion, that believing in a god or gods makes you a better person?"

Arin smiled. "Nay, Ferai, I do not. Adon Himself says that deeds, not faith, mark the goodness of a person."

"You've spoken to Adon?" asked Delon. "Seen Him?"

"Nay, I have not," replied Arin. "But there are those who indeed have."

Delon blew out a breath. "Adon. The God Himself."

Arin shook her head. "He does not claim to be so. He says that the true gods are far above Himself, Elwydd, Gyphon, Garlon, and the others."

"Even the gods are ruled by the Fates," intoned Egil. "Or so my people say."

Ferret turned to Egil. "Then those above Adon and the others, those are the Fates?"

Egil turned up the palms of his hands. "You'll have to ask someone other than me, lass, for I don't know."

They drifted onward, and then Delon said, "What do you suppose the cursed keeper of faith in the maze thinks of religion and gods? And why do you think he's cursed?"

Some seventeen days after they had fled the city of Pendwyr, they sighted a coast ahead. The setting sun lent an orange cast to the land, but along the stretch the stone itself was dun colored, and not the red expected.

Ferret groaned. "Oh, no. The door on Old Nom's card is in rock the color of blood."

"Perhaps this is not Sarain," said Delon.

"Even if it is, Delon, mayhap it is as thou hast suggested," said Arin. "Mayhap the red stone is inland."

"The thing to do," said Egil, "is to find a port city and see where we are. Whether or not this is Sarain, let us find a scholar to translate the runes on Ferret's drawing. If the scholar can read them, then we might know, or perhaps he can advise us, where we need next go."

Arin nodded, then turned to Alos. "Canst thou find us a port city?"

Alos snorted. "Not immediately. But perhaps she can." The oldster pointed southward along the shore. There in the near distance fared a small dhow, her sails blooming orange in the light of the setting sun.

They swung the ship to starboard and closed with the dhow, though it was deep twilight ere they overtook the craft. It was a fishing boat crewed by three, and they cast down their knives and threw up their hands in surrender.

"Heh," cackled Alos. "They think we are pirates."

Arin showed the crew her own empty hands, attempting to convince them that they had little to fear. Then she and the others tried all the languages they knew—and between them, Ferret and Delon proved to know many—to no success. Finally Alos snapped, "Here, let me," and called out, "Sarain?"

The fishermen nodded and bowed, and gestured toward the coast.

Then Alos called out, "Chabba?"

And the crew of the dhow pointed to the south.

"Well and good," cried Alos, and saluted.

Then the oldster sat back down at the helm. "South we go. The port city of Aban is on the border."

As they swung away from the dhow amid gestures and calls of farewell, Aiko turned to Alos and said, "That was clever of you, *ningen toshi totta*."

Alos looked at her, then growled, "I'm a drunkard, not stupid."

* * *

Two days later in early morn they came to the gape of a great bay, its waters faintly colored by the outflow of the distant River Ennîl, according to Alos, the border between Chabba and Sarain. Into the sound they fared, sailing easterly most of the day, the waters darkening with each nautical league as they came closer to the estuarial flow. Just after dawn they sighted the wide mouth of the river and up the slow-moving stream they sailed, its waters muddy with orange-laden silt. Some ten miles inland they arrived at last at the port city of Aban, with its docks to the left and right. They chose the piers larboard, for those were the ones in Sarain.

A hot golden sun rose through the midmorn as Arin and her companions trudged uphill along the narrow, twisting streets of Aban, the ways crowded with horses and camels and people moving to and fro. The men for the most part were black haired and brown skinned and swathed in robes, though some wore other garb—especially those men who rode horses, with their lavish cloaks and capacious shirts and wide-legged pantaloons, the latter tied tightly at the ankle on the outside of the boot. Bright turbans adorned the men's heads, that or red fezzes with black tassels hanging down.

Women were there, too, or so the comrades surmised, for the females were covered from head to toe with voluminous robes and only their eyes and hands could be seen. Some of these moved through the streets without speaking in groups of three or more, while others rode singly in enclosed litters, borne by burly men.

"You were right, Delon," said Ferret, pointing to signs above shops and inns as she and the others walked along the streets of Aban. "The writing, the letters: some of them look to be the same as the symbols in the inscription on Old Nom's card."

"Don't jump to conclusions, luv," replied Delon. "The lettering in Hurn is nearly identical. I think we'll have to wait until we can find someone who can read what you've written."

"When we find the Golden Crescent," said Egil, "we'll

ask the innkeeper to translate it for us. That should prove quickly enough whether it's Sarainese or not."

"If it's not Sarainese," wheezed Alos, panting with the effort of walking uphill, perspiration runnelling down his face, "then as Dara Arin said, we'll sail on to Hurn, eh?"

"As soon as we've restocked the ship," said Egil. "You and I will see to it when we've settled in."

Alos nodded. "And we'll get some charts, too, right? At least of the Avagon."

Aiko looked at the oldster. "I thought you were quit of us, Alos."

Alos glared at the Ryodoan, but then his gaze softened. "There's no taverns in Aban. Damnfool religions and their damnfool beliefs."

"Ah," said Aiko, and then fell silent.

Following the harbormaster's directions, along the ways they fared, and often street urchins or mendicants or merchants would approach them to plead for alms or to sell various wares. But one look at Aiko with her yellow skin, or at Arin with her pointed ears, or at both with their tilted eyes, and the beggars and haranguers would back away, muttering and making signs.

Soon they reached their destination, a gilded crescent on a sign outside announcing the name of the hostel. The innkeeper nervously assigned them rooms, apprehensive at these women in the group—two exotics and another, all of them wearing men's clothes and none having the decency to cover her face. Infidels all.

"Here," said Ferret, pulling out her sketch of Nom's card, the page cut free from the logbook. "I have something to show you."

But before she could unfold it, Aiko reached out and stayed her hand. "No, Ferai," said Ryodoan. "Not here. Not now. Not him."

"Wha—?"

"My tiger says no."

"Tiger? Oh."

Ferret refolded the parchment and tucked it away.

"Where did you get this," hissed the *'âlim*. The scholar quickly folded the vellum shut and slid it back across the

table while looking 'round the interior of the great library
to see if any nearby students had seen the sketch.

Ferai stood before him, flanked by Arin and Aiko, the
Ryodoan's swords sheathed. At the entry stood Delon. Of
Egil and Alos there was no sign.

Ferai took up the parchment and glanced about also.
Scattered at tables here and there, young men ducked
their heads, embarrassed at being caught staring at
exposed female faces, faces out in the open for any and all
to see. Foreigners, they were—foreigners and infidels—
and even though Aban was a port city, seldom did naked-
faced outland females venture within; when they did, it
seems the whole city would stir with the news. But these
were not merely naked-faced females, oh, no, for two of
them were pale skinned, and one was yellow! And two
had tilted eyes, while one had pointed ears. They were
northerners, outlanders, Elves, djinn, peries, succubi,
houris, demons, angels, seraphim, cherubim, or any
number of other such beings, depending upon one's theology, or teachings, or upon experience itself.

"It was a drawing on a card," said Ferret.

"I would not go waving it about, if I were you," murmured the wisp of a man, his nut brown features taut with
alarm.

"Why?" asked Ferai, lowering her own voice.

"Because it is proscribed."

"Proscribed?"

"Shhh," shushed the scholar, looking about. Then he
whispered, "It represents a forbidden religion."

Ferret whispered back: "Forbidden? Why?"

"Because it is associated with demons."

Arin cleared her throat. The man flinched, and he did
not look directly at her, she of the slanted eyes and tipped
ears. The Dylvana murmured, "Tell me, scholar, what
says the inscription?"

"Come, let us go to a place where we may talk freely,"
sissed the *'âlim.*

He led them through the stacks, pausing long enough to
select a particular roll from among many, each ensconced
in its own pigeon hole. Then, motioning them to follow,
he stepped to a small chamber, brushing in past a hanging

bead curtain. Delon, following, at a word from Ferai, stood ward at the chamber entry.

Inside the room stood a table equipped with inkpots and quills, and with several chairs ranged 'round. The man gestured for them to sit, and as they did so, he asked, "Who are you, and why have you come to me?"

Aiko and Ferret looked to Arin, and she said, "We came to these archives seeking aid, seeking knowledge."

The man snorted. "There are any number of scholars herein. Why me?"

Arin glanced at Aiko, and the Ryodoan said, "I chose you, sage, for you are safe."

"Safe?"

"So I was told," answered Aiko, touching her chest.

"Who sent you?"

"None," replied Arin. "We came on our own."

For the first time, the *'âlim* looked her squarely in the face, as if seeking a sign that she spoke truly. Arin gazed back at him, and he lowered his eyes.

"This knowledge you seek, why do you want it?"

Now Arin hesitated, but Aiko nodded, and the Dylvana said, "We follow a rede in the hopes of diverting disaster."

The scholar nodded, then asked, "And what does the sketch have to do with the rede?"

Again Arin glanced at Aiko, and again the golden warrior nodded. Arin sighed, then said, "We are not certain, yet it may be a vital link to something we seek."

Silence fell within the chamber, the sage considering what he had heard. Finally, as if he had made up his mind, he said, "You were fortunate to have chosen to come to me, for I am one of the few who will not report you and the knowledge you seek to the *imâmîn* of the Fists of Rakka."

"Fists of Rakka?"

"An arm of the ascendant religion in Aban. They believe they know the one true way."

Ferret raised her eyebrows. "The one true way?"

The sage glanced at the doorway and then intoned, "There is no God but Rakka. Fear Him and obey Him, for

He is the Lord of all." The scholar sighed. "It is but one of many 'one true ways.' "

Aiko grunted, then asked, "What has this to do with our mission?"

"Just that the thing you seek is but another 'one true way,' though this one has been driven into hiding."

Ferai unfolded the sketch and slid it across the table to him. "These symbols, are they Sarainese or Hurnian?"

"Hurnian?" The sage took up the paper. "Ah, yes, I see; to the untutored eye they are much the same. No, no, the inscription above the door, it is written in Sarainese and it names a place: Mikdash Hamavokh—the Temple of the Labyrinth." He slid the sketch back to Ferai.

Arin leaned forward. "And this temple, what dost thou know of it?"

"Just that it is said that decades past the *niswân imâmîn min Ilsitt* took refuge there from persecution."

"Nis-nis—" Ferret paused and shook her head. "What did you just say?"

"Niswân imâmîn min Ilsitt," replied the sage. "It means the women priests of Ilsitt."

"Ilsitt?"

"She is a goddess and goes by many names: Ilsitt, Shai-lene, Elwydd—"

"Elwydd!" exclaimed Arin.

The sage nodded.

"Is she also named Megami?" asked Aiko.

The sage shrugged. "Perhaps. Though I've not heard that name before."

"What about this god Rakka?" growled Ferai. "Does he go by many names as well?"

"Indeed," replied the scholar. "Rakka, Huzar—"

"Gyphon?" interjected Arin.

Without looking at her, the sage nodded.

Arin exhaled a long sigh, then said, "This Temple of the Labyrinth . . . how do we find it?"

The scholar took up the large vellum scroll and rolled it open upon the table and sat inkpots at each corner to hold it flat. It was a map. He stabbed a finger down to the parchment. "Here is Aban, and here"—he slid his finger in a straight line across the map—"to the east lies this maze, and somewhere within is the temple."

"Maze?" Ferret frowned. "But this section of the map is blank."

"Not quite," said the sage, pointing to a faint irregular boundary. "This is its extent."

Inscribed within the faded tracery were added Sarainese symbols:

"What do these mean?" asked Ferret, pointing to the ornate characters.

"Um, *Mevokh Hashed*—the Demon's Maze."

"Demon?"

"A number of years past, it is said that the labyrinth became haunted by a demon. Sent there by Rakka to punish the unbelievers, or so claim the Fists of Rakka."

Ferret looked at Arin. The Dylvana merely turned up her hands. Then Arin said, "This maze, this labyrinth, what is it?"

"A great area of entangled canyons," replied the scholar. "Cut by rivers long past, say some; land fractured by wrathful gods shaking the world, say others; a realm broken by great stones from the sky, claim others still. As to which of these are true, or if it is something else altogether, I cannot say."

Arin nodded. "These canyons, this labyrinth, how extensive are they?"

"Your measure is the mile?"

"That or the league, three miles to each."

The sage consulted a scale on the map, then took the measure of the blank area within the irregular bound. "I make it some hundred or so miles east and west, and"—he took another measure—"nearly half again as much north and south—one hundred fifty miles in all."

"And this temple, where does it lie?"

The sage shrugged. "It is hidden."

Arin blew out her breath and then, judging by the width across the faded bounds and then measuring how far to the east of Aban the blank area lay, Arin said, "Some thirty-five leagues to the marge. Is the route to the labyrinth direct?"

The sage nodded. "Yes. But I would not advise—"

Ferret blurted, "But Dara, that's a vast area to search. A hundred and fifty miles by a hundred. That makes it, um, let me see . . . um—"

"Fifteen thousand square miles," supplied the sage, "or thereabout."

"Elwydd's grace!" declared Ferret, which brought a start from the scholar, and he glanced at her and then away. But she did not notice the effect her oath had had upon the sage, and she turned to Arin and said, "I cannot even imagine what fifteen thousand square miles is, much less how long it would take to search it out, given that it *is* a maze. We'll be a lifetime at it!"

Aiko shook her head. "Dara Arin has a way with mazes."

"Mayhap," murmured Arin. "Mayhap not."

"As I started to say," interjected the sage, "I would advise against going to the maze. It is a horrid place. Nothing but fractured stone. And barren. No plants. No water. No wildlife."

Aiko stared impassively at the scholar, then asked, "If that is true, then how do these priestesses of Ilsitt survive?"

The sage looked toward the beaded curtain, then leaned forward and whispered, "It is said that Ilsitt yet has believers within Sarain. Perhaps they bear supplies to the maze, perhaps to the temple itself."

"Then there may be a trail, Dara," said Aiko.

"You are bound to do this thing?" asked the sage.

"Aye," replied Arin.

The *'âlim* sat long moments in silence, looking at the map and then at the sketch before Ferret. Finally he said, "Then here is an entry." He tapped at a place on the map along the faded boundary. "The Island in the Sky. It is the point of a plateau projecting into the maze."

"But that's somewhat north; aren't there any places closer where we may enter?" asked Ferret.

"Indeed there are," said the sage, "but I would think this a better place."

Arin looked steadily at the scholar, but he would not meet her gaze. The Dylvana then glanced at Aiko, and the Ryodoan canted her head and shrugged.

Arin sighed, then said, "Well and good, sage. Is there aught else thou wouldst advise?"

"Three things." He turned and addressed Ferai. "Call not upon Ilsitt by any of her names, be they Elwydd, Shailene, Megami, or aught else, for unfriendly ears may overhear. In fact, I would not call upon *any* gods if I were you, any of you." He paused and glanced at each of them, and added, "Too, veil your faces ere you leave this city, else someone inland less liberal than I may haul you before an *imâm* and demand that you be stoned as harlots."

Aiko growled and narrowed her eyes, but Arin nodded. "And the third thing . . .?"

For only the second time the scholar looked directly at her, and in this instance held her gaze as he said, "Not all paths are what they seem. Search well; choose wisely." Then he looked away.

Arin waited, but he said nothing more, and finally she turned to Ferret. "Wouldst thou, Ferai, trace the significant part of the map onto our own vellum? Show Aban and this 'Island in the Sky' and the route 'tween, as well as direction and scale. Sketch, too, the bounds of the labyrinth so that we may know where they lie."

Ferret glanced at the scholar, and he passed her an inkpot and quill.

"Inland?" moaned Alos. "Not by boat? Not by the *Brise*?"

Arin nodded.

"But we just got her restocked and all," whined the oldster, appealing to Egil.

The younger man shrugged and studied the map. "The *Brise*'ll wait for us at the docks, Alos."

"But how are we going to get there?" whined the oldster. Then he straightened up and stuck out his jaw. "I'm not walking, I'll have you know."

Aiko fixed Alos with an exasperated stare, but Arin said, "Given what we heard about the bleakness of the land, I deem we need camels for the journey."

"Camels!" moaned Alos. "Great, tall camels? I was thinking more along the lines of a low ass."

"Indeed," said Aiko, dryly, and Ferret broke out in loud guffaws.

Three days later in the dawn they set forth upon camels, the beasts eructing belligerent *hronks,* complaining and grumbling as the riders prodded them forward across the sunbaked land and away from the river greenery. Alos, too, moaned and whined and fussed, almost as loudly as the beast he rode. Arin, Aiko, and Ferai wore silken scarves across their faces, heeding the sage's advice, although Aiko was furious at having to do so because of the reason stated—that she might be taken as a harlot by stupid hidebound men. But Delon told her to think of it as a disguise, and she remembered former days ere she fell from grace, days when she had ridden into combat with her face masked. These thoughts mollified her somewhat . . . though not entirely.

Riding six camels and towing six—animals protesting, Alos complaining, and Aiko grinding her teeth, and Delon singing a gay song of the road—out away from Aban they fared, heading easterly into the sunrise, aiming for a place the sage had named "the Island in the Sky."

"My god," hissed Delon, "but it looks like a vision of Hèl!"

In the setting sun, they stood upon an outjutting point of a high plateau, its face falling sheer a thousand feet or more down into an endless tangle of high-walled canyons, fissures beyond count twisting and turning this way and that through bloodred stone for as far as the eye could see. Whether cut by ancient rivers, or torn asunder by wrenching land, or cracked apart by rocks falling from beyond the sky, none could say, yet it was a riven land, a fractured land, a land ripped, split, ruptured, with huge, deep, tortuous, jagged chasms zigzagging, crisscrossing, dead-ending, curling, twisting back on themselves, the great entanglement shattering out to the horizon and beyond—fifteen thousand square miles in all.

Aiko stared long down into the fractured land, her left hand pressed tightly against her chest, there where a hidden tiger glared, and at last she said, "In there lies death."

And from far dark shadows of the canyonland maze, faintly echoing and slapping across the bloodred stone, there sounded a distant ghastly howl, as if some dreadful and deadly *thing* prowled deep in the labyrinth afar.

CHAPTER 50

"G arlon!" Alos flinched back, preparing to flee.

And Ferret clutched at Delon's arm as the distant echoes of the far-off wraul faded to silence. "The *'âlim,*" she breathed, "he said the maze was demon haunted."

"Let's go," whined Alos, "back to Aban."

"Nay, Alos," said Arin. "Our way lies yon." She pointed into the maze.

"But you heard Ferret," cried Alos. "It's demon haunted."

"That could be but a falsehood planted by the Fists of Rakka," said Arin. "Even so, something within the maze howls. Aiko, what says thy tiger?"

"She growls of death, Dara," replied the Ryodoan. "Whatever is in there, it is fatal."

One arm now around Ferret, Delon nodded. "I for one believe it. And as to what it might be, a Hèl-spawned demon is as good a guess as any." With his free hand he gestured at the ruptured land, crimson in the setting sun. "What else could that be but a demon-laden, blood-drenched Hèl?"

"Your vision of Hèl is different from mine," said Egil. "But, Hèl or not, demon or not, something is down there tonight."

"See!" declared Alos. "We're all agreed. Let's turn back."

Arin merely shook her head.

Egil glanced at the oncoming twilight. "Well, whatever it might be, I'd rather not meet it in the dark. I say we camp here on the plateau for now and follow the way down into the maze in the morning, seek the temple in the light of day."

Alos groaned. "What makes you think this is the way to the temple?"

"If it were not," said Egil, "the *'âlim* would not have sent us here."

His hands flapping all 'round as if searching for a drink, Alos quavered, "Maybe he was lying. Maybe this isn't the way at all."

"Nay, Alos. We must have faith in what he said."

"Ha! And just why do you think we can trust him?"

Egil canted his head toward Aiko. "A tiger told us so." The Fjordlander then turned away from the brink and started back toward the kneeling camels.

"But that same tiger told us that death waits down there," Alos called out to the others as they followed Egil back. Then the old man glanced at the crimson labyrinth behind—"Eep!"—and hastily scuttled after them.

They made a tiny charcoal fire on the barren stone and heated water for tea. And as they waited for it to come to a boil, Delon turned to Egil and said, "So your vision of Hèl is different from mine."

Egil nodded. "Yes. My Hèl is frigid, bleak, ice-laden. It is dark and freezing cold, with no protection from the bitter winds, no shelter of any kind. There is no heat to be had; no comfort of a fire. Souls abandoned there are doomed to endless wandering across the frozen 'scape, with bottomless crevasses and mountains of ice barring the way."

Alos held his trembling hands out toward the tiny charcoal glow. "No heat to be had, eh? Rather like this camp, I would say."

Egil smiled. "Much worse, Alos. Much worse." The Fjordlander then shrugged. "If there is a Hèl, that is." Egil turned to Delon. "I take it your Hèl looks somewhat like the labyrinth."

Delon nodded. "As you say, if there is a Hèl. I've always believed Hèl is rocks, schist, boulders, endless canyons shattered through stone. No water. No plants. No animals. Just hard, hard rock . . . nothing soft . . . no place to lie down and sleep. And like your Hèl, it is dark, and souls are fated to wander forever looking for a place to rest, a place of comfort, but not finding any."

Ferret shook her head. "Hèl is a place of endless howling winds, the dark air filled with hurtling, slashing sand. The land is covered everywhere with stabbing thorns dealing piercing wounds that never heal."

Ferret turned to Alos. The old man seemed to shrink within himself. "To my way of thinking, Hèl is black, no light whatsoever, and filled with pits, chasms, and things hunting." Alos shuddered, then added, "Maybe things like whatever howled."

All eyes turned to Aiko. "I do not believe there is a Hèl, nor a Paradise for that matter." She gestured about. "There is only this and nothing more. Dead is dead, with nothing after."

Alos glanced up at her. "Then how do you explain ghosts?"

Aiko turned her impassive gaze toward the oldster. "I do not believe in spirits."

Alos stabbed a quivering finger in the direction of the labyrinth. "Then how do you explain whatever it is we heard howl?"

"If it is an *akuma*—a demon—then it is no ghost, but something very much alive." Aiko touched the hilts of her swords. "And things alive can be killed."

Silence fell among them awhile. Finally Delon turned to Arin. "And what do you believe, Dara? About Hèl, that is."

Arin looked over at the bard. "If there is a Hèl, then I would think it a great emptiness, a void, an abyss, with absolutely nothing therein, no light, no dark, no substance, no force, absolutely nothing whatsoever. And there is no one in this emptiness, this void, but thine own self. Canst thou think of a punishment worse?" She looked 'round the circle, but no one had a response.

And then the water began to boil above the charcoal fire, and soon talk turned to other matters as they drank hot tea and ate a cold meal on the edge of an endless maze.

As they had done all along on the trail, each took a turn at ward. And in the dead of night during Delon's watch there echoed from the bowels of the labyrinth afar another ghastly howl, one which startled all the sleepers awake, and they were long in regaining slumber.

Arin stood the final watch, and she soothed Egil when he was visited by his nightly ill dream, this one of Lutor being slowly pulled apart.

Dawn lay on the horizon when the Dylvana lit another charcoal fire and set a kettle for tea; when the water came to a boil, she wakened the sleepers. As the others relieved themselves and readied for the day, the Dylvana walked to the perimeter of the precipice and looked at the pathway down. She stood a moment on the lip and sipped tea and chewed on a bit of waybread. And then she attempted to <see> in her special way. To her right something faintly glowed among a cluster of jagged boulders. Keeping an eye on the nebulous tracery, she stepped along the rim to the pile, and there between two of the huge rocks, hidden in a manner she could not fathom, she found another path leading to the verge and downward.

Her thoughts echoed the *'âlim*'s warning in the archive: *"Not all paths are what they seem. Search well; choose wisely."* Arin took a sip of her tea and looked back at the other path and then again at this new one. *Which, I wonder, is the true way to follow?*

Arin extended her exploration a goodly distance in both directions along the perimeter, but no other paths did she find.

"Two paths?" Egil looked at her in consternation. "Where is the second?"

"Beyond those jagged boulders," replied Arin.

Ferret gazed toward the cluster then leftward to the way they had seen last night. "Which one should we follow?"

"The one at the rocks, I should think," said Arin.

"Oh?" said Alos.

Aiko glanced at Arin and nodded in agreement. "The path at the boulders is hidden, as is the temple."

"Exactly so," said Arin. "Too, this new path may have a charm upon it."

Delon touched the amulet at his neck. "Let us go see."

* * *

"If it has a charm upon it," said Delon, looking at the narrow trail, "it's not one of invisibility."

"Perhaps it's a ward of some kind," said Ferret, standing at Delon's side. "Perhaps one that is not meant for us, but for foes of the temple instead—the Fists of Rakka, for one."

"You mean it hides the path from them and only them, or perhaps turns them aside?"

Ferret looked at Delon and nodded. "Aye. That or the like . . . if charms can do such things."

All eyes turned to Arin, but she shrugged. "Were I a Mage, mayhap I could say yea or nay."

"This is what the '*âlim* meant," said Aiko, gesturing leftward at the other way, "when he said that not all paths are what they seem. He was warning us away from the obvious."

"That is my belief as well," said Arin.

Alos cocked a skeptical eyebrow but remained silent.

Egil looked at the others and then at the sun, now poised on the rim of the world. "Let's not waste the daylight."

As they returned to the camels, Arin said, "I shall lead the descent."

Both Egil and Aiko protested, especially the Ryodoan, saying that if danger came, a warrior should take the brunt.

But Arin was adamant. "This path has a charm upon it, one we do not know, and among this band only I can <see>. And should it change in any manner, 'tis I who can best decide what it portends."

"But, love—" Egil began, yet, with an upflung hand, Arin stopped his words.

"Once we are down within the labyrinth, where I ween the way is wider, then Aiko or thou canst lead. But as we descend along the charmed way, 'tis mine to do."

Egil glanced at Aiko, and she blew out a long breath, then stiffly said, "As you will, Dara. As you will."

Swiftly they laded the camels, and amid *hronk*s of protest mounted up and got all the animals to their feet. Each towing a beast, they moved toward the precipice,

Arin in the lead, Aiko immediately after, then Egil, Alos, and Ferret, with Delon bringing up the rear. They paused on the verge and looked out over the endless canyons plunging deep into the crimson stone.

Delon sighed and said, "Of all our philosophies, why is it only I who believe we are about to step into Hèl?"

In the lead, Arin urged her camel forward and started down within.

CHAPTER 51

As the waning half moon above fled before the on-coming sun, down the path Arin and her comrades edged, stone rising sheer on the right and falling sheer on the left, the way narrow and steep. Alos took one look down leftward at the precipitous drop, and, moaning, quickly turned his face to the stone on the right and closed his eyes tightly, whimpers leaking from his lips, the old man praying for Garlon to guide his camel true.

Egil, too, was somewhat daunted by the height, for, like Alos, he was a man of the sea and no climber of stone. And though he was raised on a steep-sided fjord, it was nothing like this. So he gritted his teeth and for the most stared straight ahead and trusted to the camel's sure feet.

Aiko, however, was unfazed by the drop, for her training in Ryodo had included many a vertical climb. But even though the fall held no fear for her, still Aiko was distressed, for her tiger was greatly unsettled and Dara Arin rode ahead; if danger came upon them, she and not Aiko would meet it first.

In the lead, the drop into the depths held no meaning for Arin, only the faint ribbon ahead, for she concentrated fully on the pathway downward in her attempt to <see>.

Near the rear of the procession, Ferret leaned over and looked at the ruddy stone falling sheer below. Then she glanced back at Delon to see him staring downward, too. "Are you not afraid?" she called. "It's quite high, you know."

Delon smiled. "No, luv. In my youth in the Gûnarring, my father and I often scaled such steeps, though not in a bloody red Hèl like this. —But I say, what about you?"

"I walked the rope before I was nine," she replied, "and

flew the trapeze as well. Heights are to be respected, not feared."

"Aren't you afraid your camel will bolt?"

At Delon's question, Alos moaned and clapped his hands over his ears.

"Animals have more sense than to do such," replied Ferret. "At least in the *cirque* it was so."

"*Cirque?* You were in a *cirque,* luv? You'll have to tell me of it."

Ferret took a deep breath and then let it out. Except for the story about Old Nom, Ferai had told none of the others aught of her past, not even Delon. She looked down into the depths below and then back at the bard to find him yet looking at her, awaiting a reply. "Someday, perhaps," she called out to him, then turned and faced front once more. *Someday, perhaps, someday.*

Down they went and down, twisting and turning into the depths of bloodred rock, the angled way sometimes shallow, sometimes steep, but always narrow and ever clinging to vertical ripples frozen forever on the face of perpendicular stone. Along this slant they rode for nearly six miles, the path arcing 'round meandering curves and angling past sharp bends, until at last they came to the enshadowed floor of the jagged canyon below, where crimson walls rose some fifteen hundred feet straight up to a ragged slash of sky. Here in the depths they could no longer see where they had begun high on the rim above, for it was lost beyond uncounted crooks and twists and turns in the pathway behind.

Though fairly level, the canyon floor was no more than ten paces wide, with schist and scree and shattered rock strewn throughout and piles of rubble ramping up against the vertical walls. All was barren stone—no soil, no plants, no life whatsoever could be seen—and a raw drift of air whispered through the chasm, like voices murmuring on the very edge of perception. And here the world was scarlet-drenched, as if the very rock itself had been drowned in blood. Even the shadows seemed to take on a crimson hue.

"Adon," breathed Delon, "but it *is* a vision of Hèl."

Two paths stood before them, twisting away left and right.

"Which way?" asked Aiko, looking to Arin, as did they all.

The Dylvana stared at the canyon floor. "The rightward path has a faint glow."

Aiko touched her chest. "Peril lies that way as well, Dara."

Arin shrugged "Nevertheless—"

"Perhaps we ought to turn back," interjected Alos.

Arin looked at the old man. "Nay, Alos. Herein we should find the cursed keeper of faith in the maze."

"But we don't even know if this is the right maze," quavered the oldster.

Egil canted his head. "Come, helmsman, of the two we've encountered this seems the best bet."

Alos glanced at Aiko only to meet an impassive gaze. He lowered his eye and nodded.

Rightward they turned, now Aiko and Egil able to ride alongside Arin: Aiko to the left; Egil to the right. Following behind came the three pack camels on their tethers, and then after came Alos, Delon, and Ferret, each of the trio also towing a camel.

"Which way is north?" asked Ferret. "We've twisted and turned so much that I'm all at sea. And down here I can't even tell."

Alos grunted and pointed to the fore and left even as Delon pointed back and to the right. Delon shook his head and burst out in laughter, but Alos growled and said, "Look, I'm a helmsman so I ought to know which way north lies."

But Delon pointed to the red canyon walls high above. "See the angle of the sun? Well, not the sun itself, but the shadows, instead. It's yet early morn, and so they fall from east to west. And given their slant, that puts north off to our right. We are headed southwesterly."

As his camel plodded forward, Alos looked long at the rim above, then shook his head in resignation.

"Don't feel bad, old man," said Delon. "I was raised in the mountains, while you were raised at sea. And when we are on the waters again, 'tis you will know and I who will not."

They held this direction for less than a furlong as the canyon bent back on itself. Twisting and turning, within a mile they came to a junction, where three slots lay before them. Again Arin chose the right-hand way, and zigging and zagging, veering and wrenching, through the labyrinth they fared, at times the way wide, at other times narrow where they could go but single file—and through these slots Aiko took the lead with Egil next after. And time after time they came to junctions: two-way, three-way, four-way splits, some narrow, some wide, some but cracks, some paths smooth, others rough, some choked with shattered debris. At these breaches, Arin would gaze at the choices before her and spy out the glimmering way, and onward they would fare.

Midmorning came and then midday, the sun directly overhead, pressing back the crimson shadows, replacing them with a bright red glare. Yet they paused not for a midday meal but ate as they moved ahead, for they did not want to camp in these canyons at night, hoping to reach the temple instead—wherever it might lie. At times they rode, at other times walked, giving the camels some respite, but always they pushed forward.

"I don't think we're on the right road at all," puffed Alos, during one of these strolls. "We'd better turn back, get out from these blasted canyons with their pressing walls."

"Why's that, old man?" asked Delon.

Alos fixed his white eye on the bard. "Surely we'd've reached it by now if this were the way. I think we've taken a wrong turn somewhere. Either that, or the temple isn't even in this place at all."

Ferret shook her head. "Look about you, Alos. The stone is crimson, as shown on Old Nom's card. And the 'âlim said this is where we'd find it. As to the wrong turn, have faith in Dara Arin. Think on this, too: it is a great treasure we are after: a pure, translucent pale jade egg . . . the size of a melon. Surely we can sell it for an enormous sum, even if we have to carve it up. There's a buyer out there somewhere: a Dragon, a Mage, a collector, someone who will make all this worthwhile. We'll be set for life. No more hunger, no more wanting, no more having to—" Ferret glanced at Delon and abruptly stopped talking.

They walked in silence for a while, and at last Delon said, "Luv, as much as I cherish the good life—fine wines, delectable foods, pleasures for all the senses—we aren't after this thing for reward. It isn't a treasure we seek. Instead it's a token of power whose doom we hope to entirely set aside."

Ferret looked over at him, but what she was thinking did not appear in her eyes.

Ahead, Arin called for them to mount up again, and onward they rode through chasms of bloodred stone.

The midday sun passed beyond the rims above, though now and then as the canyons twisted and turned they could see it in the west. Midafternoon came, and then late day, and all about them scarlet shadows mustered once more as the angle of light shifted with the sinking of the sun. Finally there was a short twilight down in the canyons below and darkness fell in the land of red stone, and still there was no sign of a temple.

A narrow slash of glimmering stars emerged overhead with the onset of night, and Arin reined her camel to a halt, the others stopping as well. The Dylvana turned in her saddle and said to all: "The time has come for us to decide: shall we push on, or instead make camp? Have ye any preference?"

Egil said, "I think we need rest the camels. They've had little ease all day, nor aught to eat or drink since yester."

Aiko reached down and tapped her mount on its ribs. "Fear not for the camels, Egil One-Eye, for they can go long without either food or drink." She gestured ahead along the canyon. "Fear instead for us; with every step forward our danger has grown."

In the glint of starlight, Arin nodded, but Egil raised an eyebrow. "Your tiger?"

Aiko inclined her head.

"I think we should go back," said Alos. "This 'âlim of yours has led us into a trap."

Aiko grunted yet did not gainsay his words, but Arin

said, "I think not, Alos, for Aiko's tiger found no untoward peril in him."

"That's because the peril's out here," retorted Alos.

"That I do not deny," said Arin.

"Why don't we just set up camp in a place we can easily defend?" suggested Ferret, touching the bandoliers of daggers crisscrossing her breast.

From the bowels of the labyrinth there came a long, ghastly howl, the echoes slapping back and forth across the canyon walls.

The camels flinched at this sound, yet held their ground for it was distant still. But Alos groaned and cowered down in his saddle.

"Adon, but that was much louder than before," said Delon.

"We are closer to whatever it is," said Arin.

"We are closer to peril," said Aiko.

"Since it seems to come out only at night, I think Ferret has the right idea," said Egil. "We should make camp in an easily defended place."

"There is that narrow canyon a furlong or so back," suggested Arin.

They set up camp in a box canyon, more of a fissure than aught else, for it extended into the crimson rock less than a hundred feet.

"This is good," said Egil, surveying the site.

"Good?" muttered Alos. "This stone crack?"

"Aye," replied the Fjordlander. "They can only come at us from one direction."

"They?" quavered Alos.

"They. The foe. Whether one or many," replied Egil.

"Like the thing that howls," added Ferret.

"*Eep!*" squealed Alos, and he huddled down against the stone wall behind.

That night they stood ward in overlapping shifts: Aiko and Alos, Alos and Delon, Delon and Ferret, Ferret and Egil, Egil and Arin, Arin and Aiko. Again there came in the middle of the night another prolonged howl, seeming louder than before, jerking sleepers awake, weapons springing to hand, yet nought came at them from the darkness.

With a half moon above, just ere dawn Egil moaned and thrashed in his sleep, visited by a hideous dream.

They broke camp as the slash of sky lightened, and soon were on the trail again, the camels grunting in sullen ire, angered at having had nothing to eat but a meager amount of grain and nothing to drink at all, angered as well at having to bear riders and cargo, or so it seemed.

Once more the dark shadows turned scarlet as the day seeped down into the land of red stone. The trail twisted and wrenched through the labyrinthine maze, passages shattering off in directions without number, leftward, rightward, veering hindward as well. Choice after choice Arin made as the rarely glimpsed sun angled up in the sky, seen only when the chasms skewed easterly.

"Garlon, but I'd swear we're going in circles," grumped Alos. "That, or we're lost altogether."

"What makes you say that?" asked Ferret.

"This canyon, that rock, I vow we've passed it a thousand times."

"A thousand times?"

Alos growled. "Well, more than once, that's for certain."

Ferret shook her head. "I don't think so, Alos. I believe with all this red rock, everything looks the same."

Delon grunted in agreement. "Even the red is beginning to look normal to my eyes. —I wonder if it's possible to become used to Hêl."

Midday came and went, and still they pressed onward, riding and walking, peril growing with each stride, Aiko now insisting on taking the lead every step of the way, though she paused at the junctions for Arin to make a choice.

Midafternoon came and then eve drew nigh, the crimson shadows mustering again deep in the chasms below.

Alos groaned. "Another night in this blasted maze, with night after night to come. Lost in your Hêl, Delon. Trapped forever. We'll never find our way back out."

Before Delon could reply, Aiko rounded a turn and there before her in solid rock stood the opening of an arched tunnel, low and narrow and black. *"Yojin suru!"* she called. "Beware."

"This is carved, not natural," said Egil. "See: hammered drill rods and mattocks shaped this way."

As Aiko looked up at the steep canyon walls, a canyon dead-ended but for the tunnel, Arin said, "The trail goes in."

Egil glanced from one to the other. "Then so do we."

"Can the camels squeeze through?" asked Ferret. "I mean, it's like an eye of a needle."

Delon looked at the camels and then at the opening before them. "I think so. But we'll have to lead them."

"Not yet," said Egil.

Aiko, her swords in hand, nodded and said, "Egil is right. I would not want to be trapped in there with camels blocking the retreat. I will go afoot and see where this leads."

"Not alone," said Egil. "I will go with you."

"As will I," said Delon.

"Me, too," added Ferret.

"I'll guard the camels," said Alos, drawing back from the dark entrance. "But not by myself."

Arin looked from one to the other, and then sighed. "I will stay with thee, Alos."

Egil turned to the Dylvana and embraced her and said, "Be ready to flee." Then he kissed her and stepped away and hefted his axe.

Delon lit a small oil lantern, and weapons at the ready, they entered the dim opening.

The tunnel floor was level, and within ten strides the corridor turned sharply to the left. "It reminds me of the way beneath Gudrun's fortress walls," whispered Egil.

"Just so," said Aiko. "Carved to keep siege engines at bay."

"There are no murder holes," hissed Delon.

"Not in this stretch, at least," replied Egil.

Again the corridor turned sharply, this time to the right,

and ahead they could see a portcullis down and a glimmer of the dying day beyond.

"Put out the light," sissed Aiko. As Delon quenched the lantern, Aiko added, "Go softly. The peril lies just beyond the gate."

Cautiously they approached the heavy grille, and in the dim light, just as they reached the bars a voice called out, *"Mîn int?"*

Startled, they flattened themselves against the walls in the narrow way. And again the voice called out, *"Mîn int?"*

It came from above.

Egil looked up, but saw nought. He took a deep breath. "We are friends."

There was a slight pause, and then: "Friends?" replied the voice, a woman's, accented as was the *'âlim*'s. "Yet you come with weapons in hand?"

Egil glanced at Aiko. "We sensed peril."

"Ah. Many things are perilous. What do you seek?"

Again Egil looked at Aiko, and then at Ferret and Delon. At a nod from each he replied, "We come in urgency and seek a keeper of faith in the Temple of the Labyrinth."

Long moments passed, but finally, with a clanking and grinding of gears and the clack of a ratchet, the heavy portcullis screeched upward in its tracks. It stopped at the halfway point.

"Enter," called the voice.

Egil started to stoop under, but Aiko stopped him. He turned to her and said, "If the temple is here, we must take risks."

She looked at him, her gaze impassive, and then nodded.

Together they ducked under the teeth of the grille, Delon and Ferret following.

They came into a vast opening, a sheer-walled circular basin nearly two full miles across, hemmed in all 'round by vertical red stone reaching up to the evening sky above.

"Stand!" came a command from behind.

They stopped and slowly turned.

Behind a low castellated parapet upon a wall above the portcullis stood perhaps fifty dark-haired women of varying ages, all dressed in red robes matching the stone and armed with bows drawn to the full, nocked arrows aimed at the foursome's breasts. Among them and in the center, at a notch in the wall where leaned a ladder, stood a tall man dressed in a red robe as well. Looking to be in his early thirties, he was some six feet four and weighed perhaps two hundred twenty lithe pounds. His hair was a sunbleached auburn, his skin desert tanned, and his eyes were ice-blue. His hands rested upon the hilts of a great two-handed sword, its point grounded on the banquette above.

Aiko looked at him, puzzlement in her eyes, and she sheathed her swords and said to Egil, "I do not understand. He is not the peril, yet the peril is within him."

CHAPTER 52

"Y ou say you come seeking a keeper of faith," called
down one of the women, an elder, standing to the left
of the man. She wore no veil, nor did any of the women.
"We are all keepers of faith herein."

Egil slipped his axe into his belt and motioned Delon
and Ferret to sheathe their weapons. As they did so, the
woman called out in a low voice, *"Wakaf lataht'."* The
women released the tension on their bows and lowered
the weapons.

Empty-handed, Egil said, "We have come far and have
a tale to tell."

"Before you begin, do you wish me to send someone to
bring in your last two companions along with your
camels?" she asked as she signaled to the man to descend.
Shouldering his great sword, he started downward, the
woman following.

Egil glanced at Aiko. Keeping a wary eye toward the
big man descending, the Ryodoan nodded and said,
"Unless provoked, there is no peril in these women. But
as to the man, I cannot say. Even so, Dara Arin should be
safe."

By this time, the man and woman had reached the base
of the ladder, and now many of the other women started
down, though some stayed on the banquette.

The woman turned to Egil. "Well?"

"Indeed, Lady, send someone to fetch our companions,
for 'tis the Dylvana who should speak of our mission."

"Dylvana? An Elf?"

At Egil's nod, the woman turned and commanded,
"Maftûh ilbauwâbi!" As the portcullis began clanking the
rest of the way upward, she motioned to a young woman

and said, *"Kawâm, Jasmine, jâb iljauz khârij."* The acolyte bowed to the elder and spun on her heel and hastened
toward the rising bars and the passageway beyond.
"Kânmâ fiz 'ân!" the older woman called out after her,
then she turned to the foursome. "I told her to be not
afraid, for she may think the Dylvana a djinn."

As the elder woman gave her attention to the foursome,
Ferret asked, "Are all of you priestesses of Ilsitt?"

At the naming of Ilsitt, on each hand the woman ritual-
istically touched forefinger to thumb to make small
circles, as did all the women within earshot, as well as the
sword-bearing man. "Indeed we are. All but Burel, here."
She turned a hand toward the big man. "Though he is a
keeper of faith as well."

Delon stepped forward. "We are forgetting our man-
ners. My Lady, may I present Lady Ferai of Gothon, Lady
Aiko of Ryodo, Master Egil of Fjordland, and I am Delon
of Gûnar."

As they were introduced, Aiko and Ferret pulled down
the scarves veiling their faces. The priestess inclined her
head to each, her eyes showing some surprise at Aiko's
golden hue and tilted eyes.

"I am—" She turned to the man and spoke rapidly in
Sarainese.

"Abbess," he replied.

"I am Abbess Mayam, and this is Burel, who has no
title, though his father was known as, um"—again she
turned to Burel—*"yâ sîdi? Yâ sîdi Ulry?"*

"Sir," rumbled Burel, leaning on his sword. "He was
Sir Ulry, of Gelen."

Behind them they could hear camels complaining at
being coerced through the tunnel. Shortly Jasmine appeared, hauling a string of four of the recalcitrant beasts
behind, followed by Arin tugging four more, and then
came Alos after, four grumbling camels in his wake, the
old man complaining as well. As the last camel emerged,
the portcullis was lowered in its track to bottom out in
socket holes in the stone.

Arin and Alos were introduced to Mayam and Burel,
the abbess clearly dazzled by the diminutive Dylvana,
though she tried to conceal her fascination.

"You must be hungry," said Mayam. "Come let us go to a place where, after vespers, we can sup and talk, and you can tell me why you have journeyed here."

At a nod from Arin, the abbess turned to the waiting women and spoke in Sarainese, and acolytes came forward to take the camels away. Then the abbess and Burel led Arin and her companions angling across the great, sheer-walled basin as twilight began to fall. And nearly all the women followed.

Ahead, they could see a great portico, with columns carved into the vertical face of the looming wall. Soon it was clear that this was their destination. As they drew closer it also became clear that this was not a full portico, but instead was sculpted in high relief. Two acolytes bearing tiny oil lamps emerged from the central opening, a doorway into the stone, and they set the lights upon free-standing pedestals, then went back inside.

Toward this light Mayam led them, until Arin and her companions were close enough to see carved in the red stone lintel above the doorway the words:

מבוכ השׁד

"Ah, luv!" cried Delon, grabbing Ferret about the waist. "You were right!"

And he took her up and spun 'round and 'round and kissed her soundly on the lips.

Of a sudden he stopped turning and set her down, puzzlement in his eyes. And then he kissed her again, this time gently and long. Surprised, at first she stood rigid, then less so, then melted into his embrace and clasped him tightly. Finally, lingeringly, he released her, and held her at arm's length and looked at her in wonderment, just as she looked stunned at him.

And in that moment there came a horrid, prolonged howl, as if some hideous creature were loose within the bounds of the great basin.

Alos screamed and bolted for the doorway, and Aiko's swords flashed into her hands. Egil drew his axe from his

belt and turned this way and that, seeking the direction of
the yowl but failing as echoes slapped and reverberated
among the high rock faces. Delon gripped his rapier, and
a dagger was in each of Ferret's hands. Arin held her
long-knife, her eyes searching for foe.

"Oh, my," declared Mayam, as the drawn-out juddering
cry diminished, the echoes dying as well, "I should have
warned you."

"Warned us?" hissed Aiko, yet searching for foe.

"Put away your weapons. There is nothing to fear. It is
just our demon."

Arin looked at the abbess, the Dylvana's eyes wide.
"Your demon?"

"Indeed. Though its roots are true, the demon itself
is entirely false. Its terrible roar nothing but a many-
chambered horn blown by great bellows driven by a
rather large weight raised by a windlass and dropped.
Twice a day we sound it: at eventide and in the mid of
night." The abbess glanced at Arin and winked. "It keeps
the zealots of Rakka out of the maze altogether . . . as
well as others."

Arin sighed and sheathed her weapon, as did the rest.
Then the Dylvana said, "Would that we had known the
peril was false."

Aiko shook her head and tapped her chest. "The peril is
not false, Dara."

The abbess looked at the Ryodoan and said, "Indeed, I
do agree. Yet it cannot enter here."

They followed Mayam through the doorway and into
the temple, Burel coming last. They passed through an
entrance hall—a narthex—and stepped into a large oval
nave, a high-vaulted ceiling above the chamber of worship, a polished floor below, the place aglow with the soft
yellow light of sconced candles ringing 'round. Benches
sat against the smooth curve of wall, arcing to left and
right. At the far end they could see a high altar, a circle of
life carved upon its outward face—the symbol of Ilsitt, of
Elwydd in her many names. In the center of the floor
another circle of life was inset into the stone. Mayam
paused at the entrance and bowed in obeisance, her fore-

fingers touching her thumbs to make small circles. Beyond the altar, two acolytes knelt at each side, their voices low, pleading. Mayam started across the space, stepping wide of the circle of life embedded in the polished stone, as did those who followed her. As they approached the altar, they could hear someone hissing and babbling: it was Alos, huddled down against the floor behind, gibbering of demons and monsters and Trolls, while the acolytes speaking in Sarainese tried in vain to soothe him

"Well, someone should have told us it was nothing but a horn," snapped Alos, glaring 'round the great stone table. "Scaring people half to death like that, springing such a thing upon them unannounced."

They waited in an alcove somewhere beyond the sacristy behind the altar and nave. Egil and Arin sat side by side, his fingers interlaced with hers, both gazing about, surveying the room, though there was little to see. Aiko sat opposite Alos, staring impassively at the oldster, her disgust lying just below the surface of her gaze.

Ferai and Delon also sat on opposite sides of the table from one another, their eyes would meet and then glance away, avoiding contact, as if frightened by what a kiss had revealed.

And drifting through the stone passageways, they could hear the evensong carols as the followers of Ilsitt celebrated their faith.

Egil smiled and looked at Alos and shook his head. "It was a startlement, indeed, Alos, coming unexpected as it did."

"Unexpected?" said Burel, entering. From the nave the sound of singing went on.

"The demon horn," replied Egil.

"Oh, that. As Mayam said, it keeps the Fists of Rakka at bay." He stepped from the chamber into a side room, and they could hear a dipping and pouring of water, and the clang of a kettle on a grate. Above these sounds he called out, "But horn or no, it did not stop you from coming." Shortly he returned, bearing a tray of cups, only to disappear again.

"How did you create such a device?" asked Delon, raising his voice.

"We didn't," Burel called back. "The abbess tells me it was here when the Order of Ilsitt first came. When they discovered what it did, they put it to use at need."

Delon looked at the others 'round the table and raised his hands in question. Arin murmured, "No doubt the abbess or someone will tell us how this came to be."

Still the evensong caroling came drifting inward, and now Burel began to sing in underharmony, his voice a deep baritone.

When the song came to an end, silence fell. The ceremony ended. Burel stepped back into the chamber, this time bearing a second tray on which rode a steaming pot of tea and a jar of honey. He set the tray down and began filling cups and passing them around the table. As he passed a cup to Alos, he said, "I am sorry the demon horn frightened you, but it is our—how shall I say?—our unrevealed weapon. We carefully foster the rumors of a demon-haunted maze, and the horn gives credence to the tales."

"Well," grumped Alos, "you should have found a way to tell us."

Burel shook his head. "We did not know you were coming until our lookouts spotted you afar. Even then we knew not who you were—still do not, for that matter. Ordinarily, the only ones who know the truth, as well as the way, are our supporters outside."

"Supporters?" asked Ferret.

"Followers of Ilsitt, luv," said Delon, "or so I surmise."

At mention of Ilsitt, Burel's fingers formed the ritualistic circles. "Yes, worshippers of the Lady."

"Elwydd," murmured Arin.

Wide-eyed, Burel looked at the Dylvana. "Indeed, though it has been long since I've heard that name, and then only because it was the name given Her by my father, or so I was told."

The big man passed the honey 'round the table to sweeten the tea. Each took a small portion of this rare treat, except Alos, who glopped in three spoonfuls.

"You say your lookouts spotted us from afar," said

Egil, "yet in this maze with all its twists and turns, how is that possible?"

Burel jabbed a thumb toward the ceiling. "From the rim above, there are places where sections of the trail can be seen, especially in the last few miles."

"Ah," said Egil, taking up his cup.

As they settled back to sip the brew, Burel said, "I meant to ask, did you erase all sign of your passage through the maze? It would not do if the Fists of Rakka or others of like mind could follow the path."

"We set no fires, pitched no tents," said Egil. "And camels' feet are soft on the land, and they left no track on the stone. I think we left no traces."

"Did you clean the way of your camel dung? Or that of your own? Bring it with you?"

Wordlessly, Egil shook his head.

"Then you must do so on your way out," said Burel. "That which now lies along the way as well as any new-made."

Egil glanced about at all the others and then nodded.

They drank tea in rebuked silence, none saying aught.

Moments later, however, Mayam strode into the chamber, the abbess bearing a tray of breads and a steaming tureen of soup, spoons and bowls on the tray as well.

Soon all were served and as they ate, Mayam said, "Vespers tonight were particularly suffused with joy. Visitors to this temple always create such a stir, though they are usually adherents and not strangers such as you."

"This temple," said Delon, "it has always nurtured your faith?"

Mayam canted her head. "It was created in a time no one remembers and crafted by unknown hands for purposes unrevealed. Centuries agone, some adherents of my order discovered it. It had been long abandoned. Yet the symbols of the Lady were in the floor of the nave as well as on the high altar when we found it.

"At the time of the bloodletting, we retreated here."

Aiko frowned. "Time of the bloodletting?"

"Slaughter of the worshippers of Ilsitt," Burel growled.

Aiko's eyes narrowed, but she said no more.

"You say that there are yet adherents who live outside the maze?" asked Ferret.

Mayam smiled. "Indeed. Without them, we would be hard-pressed to live here. They bring us supplies to help see us through. Our gardens can only provide so much."

"Gardens?" said Ferret. "But what do you do for water?"

"Ah, that." Mayam smiled. "There is a lake hidden in the stone, or so we deem, for our wells never run dry."

"Ah, I see."

They ate in silence for long moments, and then Delon said, "Except for you, Burel, I've seen no other men. Are they—?"

"I am alone," said Burel.

Delon smiled. "With all these women. . . ."

Burel shrugged.

"Ordinarily," said Mayam, "there would be no men whatsoever. But Burel is a special child. Raised here in the sanctuary of the labyrinth."

"But surely, Burel, you have been elsewhere," said Ferret. "To the city of Aban, or the like."

Burel shook his head. "I have never been beyond the iron of the portcullis."

Egil glanced from Burel to the abbess and back. "There is a tale here for the telling."

"Indeed," replied Mayam. "Yet although it is Burel's tale, I think I must do some of the telling, for I was a witness, whereas he was not yet born. But it will wait until after your own tale is told. How did you learn of the trail through the labyrinth? And what is it that brings you here?"

Arin sighed. "It is a long twisting path we have followed, and not just the one through the Demon's Maze. Let me begin at the beginning, at a campfire in Darda Erynian when I first beheld the green stone."

"Green stone!" exclaimed Burel. A look of surprise passed between Mayam and him.

"Know you of this thing?" asked Arin.

Mayam turned up a hand. "Perhaps we do. Tell your tale and we shall see."

* * *

It was near mid of night when Arin finished her accounting of all that had befallen, starting with her vision in Darda Erynian, and ending with the journey through the labyrinth.

Mayam sat in silence for a while. Then she looked at Alos asleep, the oldster's head cradled in his arms on the table, his snores sounding softly in the alcove. "It is late," said the abbess, "and you have journeyed far. Tomorrow will be soon enough for us to tell you what we know. Yet this I will say: Burel would seem to be the one you seek— the cursed keeper of faith in the maze. And the green stone of your vision is the cause of his bane."

CHAPTER 53

In spite of her late bedtime, Aiko arose just ere the first light of day. She donned her leathers and boots and helm, and took up her swords and shiruken and stepped from the acolyte cell assigned to her last night by the abbess. Like the small chamber and all else in this place, the hallway beyond was cut through red rock, and she turned leftward for the archway leading outside. Emerging into the great basin, she made her way toward a place where the light would fall whenever the sun cleared the eastern rim, for she would have its golden rays discover her drilling in the way of the sword. But she found she was not alone in her desire, for Burel was already there, dressed in a metal breastplate and helm and breeks and boots, his great sword cutting the cool shadowed air of the dawn.

Aiko stood in the semidarkness and watched awhile as the big man, light on his feet, danced and whirled and thrust at imaginary foe or cut in great rounding sweeps, wielding his weapon as if he had been born to the steel. Even so, Aiko frowned at his exercise, for it spoke of ignorance of battle. He seemed adept at handling the blade, but not in the ways of war.

So as not to take him unawares, Aiko began whistling a tune as she strode out across the flat toward him, and Burel stopped his spinning and stood awaiting her.

As she came before him she said, "I thought that only I would be up early to drill at *kinmichi,* yet I find you already at practice."

"*Kinmichi?*"

"The way of the sword."

"Oh."

Aiko stretched and turned and moved her head from side to side while Burel watched. "It would not do to pull a muscle or have a cramp in mere practice," she said. "In war, one does not always have the luxury of loosening up, but drill is an altogether different matter."

Burel grunted noncommittally, though he watched carefully, as if noting each and every detail.

Finally, Aiko stood still, her eyes closed, her breathing deep and regular. "I am now visualizing the drill," she murmured, as if speaking any louder would break her concentration.

Burel nodded, but remained silent.

Then Aiko exploded into action, her swords appearing in her hands as if they had somehow been there all the while. And she spun and whirled, her blades humming through the air, cutting high and slicing low, thrusting and backing and cross-blade blocking, driving forward in running flèches, battering, parrying, retreating, crouching, leaping, striking, ducking, dropping to her knees and all the while her steel singing hissing songs of death— swords, daggers, shiruken, appearing, disappearing, lethal weapons always in hand . . .

Whuff! The air exploded from Burel's lungs with the wonder of it all, and he watched in awe as she gyred and fled and charged and stood, her blades but a blur.

At last she stopped, her steel once again tucked away.

Burel drew a deep, shuddering breath. "That was magnificent," he said. Then he looked at his great sword. "I could never do such."

Aiko nodded. "Your weapon is meant for battle against heavily armored foe and generally in single combat."

Burel nodded. "Have you experience with such weapons?"

Aiko turned up a hand. "They were part of my training."

Burel frowned. "Even though I can easily handle my father's sword, I have had no mentor to tell me whether what I do is right or wrong. —Will you teach me what you know?"

Aiko smiled. "I will do more than that, Burel. I will teach you other weapons as well."

"I already know the bow," said Burel. "The women here have taught me, albeit my skill can be honed. And though I would gladly learn other weapons, I need especially to learn this sword, for I have a task to do."

"But a quick foeman can defeat such a sword."

"Surely," said Burel, nodding. "By arrow cast or thrown dagger, by sling or dart or perhaps even by one of those star-blades you bear."

"Yes, Burel. A missile weapon will indeed do in a swordsman, if the missileer gets the chance and has the skill. But I am speaking of single combat with hand-held blades, neither foe casting. More often than not, quickness and craft will defeat your blade."

"Oh?"

"Let me show you. —Take up the sword."

Aiko drew one of her daggers as Burel hefted his blade.

"Swing at me," said Aiko.

"What?"

"Swing at me," she repeated. "Cleave me in two."

"Lady, I will not."

"If you expect to learn, if you want me to be your mentor, you must do as I say. Now swing at me and fear not, for I will evade."

Gritting his teeth, Burel took a half-hearted cut through the air.

Aiko easily stepped away. Shaking her head, she sheathed her dagger. "You do not want to learn." She started to turn away.

"But I do want to learn," said Burel through gritted teeth. "I just don't wish to kill my teacher."

Aiko faced him and captured his gaze with her own. "Then you must trust me." Again she drew her dagger.

Taking a deep breath, Burel stood long moments staring at her. Then he hefted his sword, and this time the blade hummed as it cut through the air and past Aiko, and viper quick she stepped in and tapped his neck with the flat of her steel as the two-handed blade carried onward.

"Dead man," she said, resheathing her dagger. And in that moment the sun burst over the lip of the scarlet basin, shedding its golden light down and in.

* * *

On the bed pad in their acolyte cell, alone for the first time in weeks, Arin and Egil, lost in one another, made gentle love again.

In an adjacent cell, Ferret sat with her back to the wall, her head in her hands, wondering at this inchoate feeling deep inside her, wondering what to do.

In his own cell, Delon fingered his amulet in reverie. *Ah, Ferai, my sweet Ferai, I've sung about* amour *all my life, yet I've never known its touch. Is this what it's like? Am I truly in love?*

On his pad in yet another acolyte cell, Alos snored away, the oldster weary from the long trip. Too, he was weary from being startled awake in the mid of night by the howl of the demon horn, and, shrieking, had started to scramble beneath his bedding ere he remembered that it was but a bellows-driven chambered contraption. The oldster had shouted into the hallway about not being able to get any sleep and how could they do such a thing to their guests? But moments later he was snoring again.

In the nave, priestesses of Ilsitt gathered together 'round the circle set in the floor to sing sunrise matins, their sweet songs drifting throughout the corridors and chambers of the convent and across the red basin as well, as the women sang praises to Ilsitt, to Elwydd, to Shailene, to Megami, to the Lady, whatever her name. And they pled for good harvest, for contentment, for peace.

And out on the scarlet flat, Aiko slow-stepped Burel through a deadly dance of the sword.

It was nearly midmorn when they gathered together to break their fast. "Abbess Mayam is in the far field, but she said she would join you at the noon meal," said Jasmine as she served tea and spooned a small portion of oatmeal into bowls to stave off their hunger till then.

Side by side, Egil and Arin eagerly dug into their porridge, as if they relished the day. Alos, though, seemed yet weary, and he stirred the contents of his bowl as if too exhausted to eat, though he drank his tea well enough. Delon took seat next to Ferret, the bard smiling somewhat shyly, which she returned in like kind. Burel and Aiko, their hair plastered down with sweat, commandeered one end of the table, the two yet in deep discussion about the particular ways of fending as well as means of getting through, their tea and oatmeal ignored. Finally, Aiko looked across at him and said, "Eat up, and when we are done, I will show you just what I mean." Burel, eager to learn, spooned in great mouthfuls of the boiled meal, for the sooner finished, the sooner he and Aiko could resume. But Aiko ate slowly and carefully, as if the rite of taking in food was as important as aught else.

Looking at her porridge in dismay, Ferret said, "Well, Dara, if Burel, here, turns out to be the cursed keeper of faith in the maze, then it's time to go after the treasure."

Burel, his full spoon halfway to his mouth, paused and looked at her. "Treasure?"

"The green stone."

"Ah."

"It should be worth a fortune, you know. —To the right buyer, that is."

Arin said, "Ferai, I think it no treasure, but a thing we must give over to the Mages—in Black Mountain or in the college at Rwn."

Without replying, Ferret returned to her oatmeal, but Burel said, "What is it again that the rede named it?"

Arin sighed. "The Jaded Soul."

Delon began tapping the table with his spoon, and as he did so he chanted:

> *"The Cat Who Fell from Grace;*
> *One-Eye in Dark Water;*
> *Mad Monarch's Rutting Peacock;*
> *The Ferret in the High King's Cage;*
> *Cursed Keeper of Faith in the Maze:*
> *Take these with thee,*
> *No more,*
> *No less,*
> *Else thou wilt fail*
> *To find the Jaded Soul."*

Burel nodded, then leaned back. "And what do you think the rede means when it calls the green stone a 'Jaded Soul'?"

Arin shrugged, but Alos said, "Huah, Burel, I would have thought you'd know."

"Me?"

"Yes. I mean, given that you're here in the temple and all, you should know about souls."

Burel smiled and shrugged.

Aiko said, "If some of the priests of Ryodo are to be believed, perhaps it is a soul in waiting. They hold that the souls of the departed are reborn right here in this world."

Ferret looked at the Ryodoan. "Reborn?"

"Not that I deem it to be true," said Aiko.

"Say on," urged Burel.

Aiko sighed. "They believe every living thing has a soul, be it a lowly worm or a butterfly or a fish, an eagle, or person, or—"

"What about plants?" asked Ferret.

Aiko shook her head. "I think not."

Egil glanced at Arin. "Not even the eldwood trees?"

Aiko shrugged. "I cannot say. It is not my credo and so I have not studied it closely."

Burel leaned forward in his chair. "Go on, Lady Aiko. I would hear what you *do* have to say. What happens to these souls?"

Aiko graced him with one of her rare smiles. "A given soul, let us say, your soul—with each death and rebirth— will progress into higher and higher forms, until it reaches personhood. Then, no matter how mean your status, if you live an honorable life, you will come back in a higher state. But if you live in dishonor, your status will be lower upon rebirth. Why, given enough dishonor you may even come back as a worm . . . or worse."

"Oh, my," sissed Delon. "I'd better watch out."

But Burel looked at Aiko intently. "What if a person, what if *I* live in great honor upon each rebirth and never fall back?"

"Then you will ultimately be raised to Paradise. I am told it is the last elevation, that the cycle is complete.

They say this is the true purpose in life: to learn, to grow, to evolve throughout the cycle of many lifetimes to ultimately attain Paradise."

"And many believe this?"

She nodded. "In Ryodo, yes. As for me, I do not believe in souls and an afterlife."

They ate in silence for a while, and then Delon said, "Tell me, Aiko, if dead is dead and there is nothing after, then what does it matter what we do in this life. Why not just grab all we can get no matter what it does to others? I mean, if nothing comes after we die—no rewards, no punishments, no rebirths into higher or lower states—then why not simply do as we will?"

Ferret looked at Delon. "You mean . . . ?"

"I mean rape, steal, rob, take what we want. It doesn't matter in the long run."

Ferret looked away, as if unable to meet his gaze, but Aiko said, "There is no honor in what you suggest."

"I realize that," replied Delon, "but so what? I mean, why not be dishonorable? Seize whatever we covet? Do as we will? If dead is dead, then in the long run it won't matter."

"Aye, in the long run it may not," said Aiko. "But in the short run it does. Honorable people may at times fear the acts of the dishonorable. Dishonorable people not only fear the acts of their own kind, but they also fear just retribution. If we all lived in dishonor, then we would all live in fear. But if all would live in honor and respect one another then all could live together in comfort, free from fear."

Delon raised a finger. "Isn't that true for the most part? I mean, we all live fairly free from fear and in reasonable comfort under the justice of the king."

"Ha!" barked Ferret. "I have no love for the king's justice."

Delon looked at her.

"I was innocent," she declared.

"Mistakes are made, luv. What I meant to say is that for the most part is it not so that people live free from fear and in comfort under the rule of kings?"

Arin set down her cup and said, "No, Delon, it is not

so: remember Gudrun: was her justice free from fear? Did all live in reasonable comfort? If so, what of the thralls? Recall, she sanctions slavery, as do many monarchs. Indeed, I am afraid that much injustice exists in the world, kings or no. Yet that does not excuse acts of wanton selfishness. Aiko is right: we could all live in comfort and free from fear if all peoples would respect the rights of individuals, not only in the short run but in the long run as well."

"The long run?"

"Indeed, Delon. Recall, I am a Dylvana—an Elf—and age has no hold o'er me and my kind. Barring death by accident, war, disease, poison, malice, or ill fortune, eternity lies before us. And so, no matter how many seasons pass, we will always be at the beginning of our lives. Hence, looking at things in the long run is our natural bent."

"Oh, my," exclaimed Burel.

All eyes turned to him.

He shrugged. "It's just that I was thinking, if what Aiko told us of souls and rebirth is true, and if Elves live forever—barring accidents, or death from disease, or poison, or combat and such—then death and rebirth is beyond your grasp. How will you ever reach Paradise?"

Arin smiled. "Indeed, Burel, if it is true what the Ryodoan priests claim, then Elvenkind will simply have to evolve into higher states without the benefit of death."

Egil took Arin by the hand and kissed her fingers. "The evolution has already begun, love."

"Indeed it has, but how did you know?"

"It was you, love, who spoke of one who began lifting Elvenkind out of madness simply by saying, 'Let it begin with me.' "

Now Arin raised his hand to her lips and returned the kiss.

Delon sighed and looked at Aiko. "Perhaps these countrymen of yours are right, Aiko; perhaps how we live our current life will affect in what form we are reborn. If so, then I've a lot to do ere I go to my grave. —Oh, not that I've done anything truly bad, but neither have I done anything truly good."

Delon looked across at Ferret and smiled, but she did not meet his gaze.

After breakfast, while Burel and Aiko returned to their swordplay, Jasmine took the rest on a tour of the sheer-walled basin, where most of the land which wasn't rock was given over to fields and gardens—over to the growing of crops—the soil irrigated by sweet well water and enriched by worked-in dung.

"So this is why you wanted our camel droppings," said Alos. "Manure for your soil."

"Oh, did they tell you that?" asked Jasmine. "Regardless, it is true, though most of the dung we provide ourselves."

"My, my," said Delon. "Food grown in priestess droppings. Skat of the gods, I would say."

Ferret shot him a look of disgust, but smiled behind her hand.

"What do you do for meat?" asked Egil.

"We rarely have it," said Jasmine. "Over there is a pen containing fowl, mostly for their eggs, but occasionally for their meat. Wheels of cheese are more to our taste, brought in by the adherents from outside."

"I don't think I could live this way," hissed Delon to Ferret as they followed Jasmine toward the living quarters carved in the walls of stone. "I mean, I need a good roast joint now and again—a haunch of venison or beef—and a jack of rich foaming ale. And sweetmeats, oh, my, yes, sweetmeats especially. And gravies, we can't leave out the gravies. Breads, oh, yes. And . . ."

With Delon waxing rhapsodic about delectable foods, they walked through sparse chambers and brief corridors carved in the red rock.

"I wonder if the Drimma made this?" said Arin, as Jasmine led her and her companions sidling past cooks and helpers through a kitchen of red stone as they prepared the noon board, the largest meal of the day.

Jasmine cocked her head to one side. "Drimma?"

"Dwarves," replied the Dara.

"I think not," said Egil. "It seems sized to fit humans, not Dwarves."

"Perhaps they fashioned it to order," said Alos. "Hired by someone long past."

Jasmine shrugged and led them onward through chambers carved by unknown hands in the scarlet stone.

"Who set the charm upon the way?"

Mayam looked at Arin, puzzlement in her eyes. "Charm?"

Arin nodded. "At the Island in the Sky the start of the pathway leading here is hidden by a charm. Too, the path itself seems enspelled; with my <sight> I could dimly make it out."

Mayam laid down her knife and spoon. "I did not know."

Egil glanced up from his food. "If you did not know, then how is it that the Order of Ilsitt found the temple in the first place?"

The abbess turned up her hands. "Again, I do not know. Some say those fleeing were guided by the Lady Herself." Mayam tapped forefingers to thumbs, as did Burel.

"Then how does anyone else find this place?" asked Ferret. "Those who bring you supplies, for instance."

Mayam glanced at Burel, then said, "They follow the secret signs."

Now Arin looked at the abbess in puzzlement. "Secret signs?"

"Yes. Marking the way here."

"We did not see them," said Arin.

"It seems we have both learned something today," replied Mayam.

They ate in silence for long moments. But then Aiko, freshly bathed after her sword drill, said, "It is well and good to speak of these things, but we came here to find a cursed keeper of faith in a maze. If Burel is indeed such, then I would hear why you believe it to be true."

Mayam turned to Burel. The big man, also freshly bathed, swabbed a chunk of bread 'round his trencher and popped it into his mouth. He chewed a moment and then swallowed. As an acolyte replenished his cup of tea, he said, "This is the tale my mother told:

"My father was a knight in the service of the High

King. As always, the realm was beset by trouble and my father had much to do. Yet in the summer season of IE9216, some thirty-seven years past, it seemed those troubles increased tenfold. Many were sent out to discover why, my father among them. Alone and in secret he went to the Isle of Kistan, his skin stained with oil of walnut—"

"What about his eyes?" asked Egil.

"His eyes?"

"Were they blue like yours? Ice-blue?"

Burel turned to Mayam. She nodded and said, "As I recall, they were indeed blue."

"Then didn't it look somewhat suspicious that someone claiming to be a Kistanian had eyes of blue?"

Delon shook his head. "No, Egil. The Rovers often take captives, women among them, whom they rape and who bear their children. Among these half-breeds, there are many Kistanians with light skin or blue eyes or both."

"Half-breed," murmured Arin. "That seems an ugly term."

"Indeed," said Burel, glowering at Delon. "I am, as you say, a half-breed myself: my dam, Eruth, was Sarainese; my sire, Sir Ulry, a Gelender."

"I meant no offense," said Delon. "I merely wished to explain that your father would easily pass as a Kistanian, regardless of his eye color."

Ferret said, "That may be true, Delon, yet in Pendwyr the Rovers in the cells next to mine were all dark eyed."

Mayam rapped the table. "It is of no moment to Burel's tale." She turned to the big man. "Please go on."

"Some two years after reaching Kistan, by happenstance my father became a crewman on a powerful Wizard's ship. The ship came to Aban, where the Mage hurried ashore to confer with the high priest of the Fists of Rakka.

"While they were in conference, my father discovered in the Wizard's quarters a chest containing scrolls. Ordinarily this chest was locked, but on this day it had been left unlatched, overlooked by the Mage in his haste. From those scrolls my sire could read he discovered why the Rovers were raiding more frequently: it was to finance a campaign of terror that was to come. Among these scrolls, however, there was one which told of the secreting away of a powerful talisman—a jadelike green stone hidden in a chest of silver. But before my father could read more than a line or two, the Mage returned and my father just barely escaped detection. Even so, he had learned enough to tell the High King what was afoot, and that eve, bearing only his sword and helm and breastplate, he slipped over the side and fled.

"But apparently the Mage discovered that he had left the chest open, and through castings, or charms, or other such arcane art—who knows the ways of Mages?—he determined that my sire had delved within. Enraged, the Mage sent some of the crew to capture my sire.

"Somehow my father learned they were after him and he sought out the aid of those opposed to the Fists of Rakka. Yet the hounds were upon him and, guided by my mother, he fled across the land to ultimately come to here, for she was an adherent of Ilsitt and she knew the way.

"But when the crew returned to the Mage and told of their failure, for they had lost his track in the Demon's Maze, the Mage summoned a true demon and set it in pursuit, or so we believe.

"And that demon came to the gate and challenged my sire, bellowing that he would die for knowing of the green stone.

"By this time, my mother was pregnant with me, and my sire took up his sword and armor and helm and went forth to slay the demon."

Burel turned to Mayam. "Here I believe that you should continue, for 'twas here you became a witness."

Mayam cleared her throat. "Three days the monster bellowed, three days of incessant haranguing, the creature calling out that he would not leave until the blood of Ulry stained the crimson walls. Eruth begged *Yâ sîdi* Ulry not to go forth, for they were safe here upon holy ground where demons fear to tread. Yet *Yâ sîdi* Ulry was adamant, saying that he would have no demon after his blood or after the blood of his child, for so he deemed was the command the Wizard had given the demon. And on the fourth day *Yâ sîdi* Ulry donned his breastplate and helm and took up his great sword and went out when the sun stood on high.

"At that time I was but an acolyte, and it was my duty to stand watch atop the entry bluff that fateful day some thirty-five years past. Although I was nearly two hundred fathoms above, I could see the events quite plainly:

"*Yâ sîdi* Ulry emerged with his great sword, to face that black monster waiting there in the canyon below. The creature had a sword of its own, a black thing to match its own blackness. And they came together with a great shouting rush. *Yâ sîdi* Ulry fought mightily, yet it seems no matter what he did the demon was immune from harm. And it laughed and toyed with him for what seemed an eternity, but at last it slew him, beheaded him with a single, wide-sweeping stroke.

"And then it strutted back and forth before the entry tunnel and raised up *Yâ sîdi* Ulry's head by the hair and bellowed of its victory and called for Eruth to come forth and be slain as well. But she did not answer his challenge, and two days later it vanished sometime in the night. Just exactly when it had gone, or where or how or why, we did not know. It simply no longer stood outside and called for Eruth to come forth.

"It was then and only then that we ventured out through the gateway to claim *Yâ sîdi* Ulry's remains, and we wept for him and laid him in his cairn. I think Eruth wished to die right then and there, but she knew she had to live for *Yâ sîdi* Ulry's child. And so, in the event that it would be a male child, she stored away *Yâ sîdi* Ulry's sword and helm and armor, and then covered her beloved with a mound of stones.

"Seven months later, Burel was born. Shortly after, the next supply train arrived bearing word that the plans of the Fists of Rakka had been thwarted by the High King, and so the information we had seemed useless."

"Useless?" said Egil. "But what about the green stone? Not only was it the cause of Sir Ulry's death, it is central to our quest."

Mayam shook her head. "For all we knew it was merely a Wizard's talisman, and all Mages have talismans which they jealously guard. And even though the Wizard sent a demon after *Yâ sîdi* Ulry simply for knowing of the stone's existence, we knew not its import until we heard Dara Arin's tale."

Aiko raised an eyebrow. "The odds grow steeper the farther we go, for now to find the green stone we must read a Wizard's jealously guarded scroll, and Wizards wield deadly power."

"Now wait just a moment," objected Alos. "Before anyone goes haring off after some Wizard's scroll"—he glanced at Burel—"I'd like to know how this man's story makes him the cursed keeper of faith in the maze."

"There is peril linked to him," said Aiko, touching her chest where a tiger lay. "It has beaten at me constantly, ever since we reached the maze."

"The peril—the curse—is tied to the blood of my sire," said Burel, "or so my mother held. Blood, I might add, which runs through my veins.

"My mother believed that somewhere in this world a demon waits for me, the very same demon which slew my father. She told me I should never leave these holy grounds. Yet I have always known there would come a time when I would need to go, not only to face the demon but also to face the Wizard who bound it to this task." Burel now turned to Arin. "I am the cursed keeper of faith in the maze."

Arin glanced at Aiko, who nodded. The Dylvana took a deep breath and said, "I do so accept thee, Burel." Arin then looked at Mayam. "Tell me, Abbess, dost thou know the name of this Mage who holds the scrolls of the stone?"

Mayam glanced at Burel then said, "Indeed, we do. His name is Ordrune."

CHAPTER 54

"O rdrune!" Egil slammed the flat of his hand down to the stone table.

Startled, Mayam said, "Yes, *Yâ sîdi* Ulry so named him."

Egil turned to Arin. "*This* is why I am the one-eye in dark water, love, for I know the layout of Ordrune's lair." Unbidden, Egil's mind flashed back to that terrible time:

Egil was shackled to a ring in the floor and he and the Mage faced one another—one silent, the other sneering.

"I am Ordrune, Captain. And your name . . . ?"

Egil said nought.

"Your silence is of no moment," said Ordrune. "I will have your name shortly. You will be eager to speak." The Mage turned aside and made his way across the room.

The chamber itself was completely circular, perhaps thirty feet in diameter. Here and there stood tables laden with arcane devices: astrolabes and geared bronze wheels and alembics and clay vessels, mortars and pestles, clear glass jars filled with yellow and red and blue and green granules, braziers glowing red . . . with tools inserted among the ruddy coals. Small ingots of metal lay scattered here and there: red copper, yellow brass, white tin, gleaming gold, argent silver, and more. And 'round the walls there were casks and trunks and cabinets of drawers and a great, ironbound, triple-locked chest, and desks with pigeon holes above, jammed with scrolls and parchments and papers. And four tall windows equipped with drapes were set in the stone at the cardinal points. Elsewhere, tomes rested on stands; books resided on shelves. Here and there were chairs, equipped with writing flats, with pens and inks and vellum sheets alongside.

This was Ordrune's laboratory, his alchemistry, his arcane athenaeum. This was his lair. This was his den. This was the heart of the Wizardholt.

Egil clenched his fist and shook his head to clear it of these memories, all but one. "I think I have even seen the chest wherein the scroll is kept." Egil turned to Burel. "It is large—" Egil held his hands wide apart—"and bound with iron, and three heavy locks hold shut its hasps."

Burel turned up a hand. "Perhaps. But my mother never described it other than as a chest my sire discovered unlatched one fateful day."

Egil made a negating gesture. "Regardless, Burel, it is to Ordrune's strongholt we need go to find the way to the green stone as well as take our vengeance upon the Mage."

Burel clenched a fist and nodded, but Arin said, "Nay, Egil, vengeance must wait, for the finding of the stone takes precedence o'er all."

"But he is responsible for the death of my father," objected Burel.

"And the torturous slaughter of forty good men," added Egil.

Arin shook her head. "Nevertheless, ye two, stopping the slaughter of a world is of more import than exacting retribution against a single evildoer. Our need is to gain the scroll, and then the green stone. And to that end thy vengeance must wait."

Alos shuddered and said, "This is insane. We cannot hope to steal from a Mage. He will send a demon after each of us, just as he did against Burel's father. Count me out. I'll not take part in such madness."

Aiko stared impassively at the oldster. "As I said before, Alos, whatever lives can be slain."

Alos shook his head. "Maybe so. But we don't even know where the Mage's tower is. And Kistan is an enormous isle—eight, nine hundred miles across in any direction you'd care to go, and all of it jungle. And it's filled with pirates. We'll be forever—*you'll* be forever finding the Wizard's stronghold if the Rovers don't kill you first. Besides, his chest is locked, probably warded with magic, too."

Ferret said, "As to the locks, I have yet to see one I could not open."

Delon looked at her in surprise.

"My father was a locksmith," she said by way of explanation. "And an escape artist in the *cirque,* as was I."

"Ah, then perhaps that's why you are needed on this venture, luv," said Delon. "To open the Mage's locked chest when Egil One-Eye leads us to it."

Egil shook his head. "Even though I can lead you to the chest, I cannot lead us to the tower, for I know not where it lies. And Alos is right: Kistan is a great isle, as the charts we bought in Aban show." Egil glanced at Burel. "Did your father say where Ordrune's strongholt lies?"

Burel grunted. "All I know is the name of the place where my sire signed on to Ordrune's ship in Kistan, though whether or no it's where lies the Wizard's stronghold, I cannot say. But the ship sailed out from Yilan Koy, or so my mother said."

"Yilan Koy?" asked Delon. "Is that a town?"

Burel shrugged. "My mother did not know."

Egil sighed. "Well, at least it's a place to start."

"Fools," hissed Alos. "You are all harebrained fools."

After the sounding of the demon horn at dusk, both Arin and Delon sang at the evensong service, Arin's hymn a paean to Elwydd, Delon's an invocation to Elwydd's father, Adon, asking that He protect this refuge from all harm.

Later that night from the open red stone of the basin there echoed the skirl and clang of steel upon steel as by lanternlight Aiko drilled Burel at blades.

Over the next two days, Arin and her companions prepared for the return to the port of Aban. In a storeroom, Mayam found the saddle from the camel that had borne *Yâ sîdi* Ulry to the Temple of the Labyrinth so long ago, and she gave it over to Arin, who fitted it to one of the camels for Burel to use. And when he wasn't training with Aiko, Burel prepared as well, for so the rede required: *Take these with thee, no more, no less . . .*

Too, Burel needed time to say his good-byes, for not all

the acolytes of Ilsitt had sworn vows of celibacy, and they spent the nights visiting him one last time.

During these same two days, Delon and Ferai took long walks together around the steep-walled basin, talking, laughing, singing, sharing: Ferai told him of her early life, up to the time of her rape, but no more; and Delon spoke of his own childhood, living in the fringes of the Alnawood at the wall of the Gûnarring. And these two often met Egil and Arin coming the other way, the Dylvana and Fjordlander laughing and sharing as well.

Alos discovered that the women of Ilsitt had a small store of medicinal brandy, and he wheedled and begged until they gave him a tot just to shut him up. But that was all, no matter his appeals, and he was left with but an empty glass and a terrible thirst.

On the morning of the twenty-seventh of November, seven of the grumbling camels were saddled for riders, while the remaining five were laden with supplies for the trip.

Arin and her companions bade farewell to the followers of Ilsitt, and the women wept to see Burel go, for he had been among them all his life and many now looked upon him as a brother or son, while to others he had been a lover ere they had taken their final priestess vows, while to a few he was their lover still. And these latter acolytes stopped him for one last kiss, and then fell into one another's arms, sobbing, as in breastplate and helm and with his sword on his shoulder he led the procession to the dark way beyond the portcullis.

Into the corridor under the towering canyon wall they went, Burel pulling his mount, a second camel in tow, Aiko coming after, the Ryodoan leading two camels as well, then Alos with two, and then Ferret with one followed by Delon with two, and Egil drawing two behind him, Arin trailing with her animal last.

Into the narrow way they went, the camels *hronk*ing in dismay at the tight confines, being drawn through an eye of a needle, or so Ferret had said. In the lead, Burel came to the sharp turn leftward, and then the rightward turn,

Aiko coming slowly after, following his ill-tempered beasts, dragging her own surly animals behind.

And as Burel stepped out into the canyon beyond, Aiko shouted, "Ware!" for the unremitting peril her tiger had sensed since reaching the maze suddenly exploded.

And a stride or two past where stood Burel, the demon stepped out from the face of solid crimson stone and hissed at the man, "At last. By the blood of your father, I knew you would come forth some day." And as if flexing long dormant muscles, with a ripping upward slash of its great, jagged, obsidian sword, the demon clove through the camel's neck, the sundered head flying up and away as the corpse of the beast collapsed in the entry, blood gushing from the cloven stump.

In the tunnel, camels bellowed in fear, their cries of panic blaring as they wrenched and jerked back and away from the reek of blood and the stench of the demon, their feet drumming in terror as they lashed and thudded side to side and tried to turn and flee in the restricted confines of the narrow passage, heedless of the people trapped within.

And outside, Burel hefted his great sword and faced the monstrous foe, the angular creature some eight feet tall and shiny black, its entire being covered with a hard bony layer—smooth, chitinous panes. It was cloven hoofed, and where a knee should be was a joint bending backwards at an angle, and somewhat above that one bent another, this joint flexing forward. Narrow shoulders topped a plated torso. and its head was elongated with fang-filled jaws protruding forward, and its eyes were glaring and wide-set. Angular arms dangled down, ending in long bony grasping fingers, and it clutched a great, jagged, ebon sword half again as long as the one in Burel's hands.

Oblivious of the pandemonium in the tunnel behind—camels bellowing in a frenzy of fear and kicking out, thrashing hindwards, trying to escape—Burel sprang toward the black apparition and cried, "Ilsitt, aid me!" and lashed out with his father's steel, only to have the creature's obsidian blade fling him backward with stunning force, the man stumbling on the crimson stone.

As the demon stalked forward on its ill-jointed legs,

Burel recovered his footing, and planting himself squarely he swung his two-handed sword in a mighty, sweeping
blow. With a loud *chank!*—like steel crashing on stone—
it slammed into the jagged blade to be stopped cold.

Again Burel swung and again the demon blocked the
blow. And again and again.

Then with shocking power, the demon lashed out with
its black blade to send Burel's sword flying from his
hands. And ere the man could move, the creature smashed
him hindwards with a backhanded blow, knocking him
into the crimson wall, and Burel fell sprawling and senseless to the stone.

In the tunnel, Aiko was battered backwards by Burel's
pack animal, the camel lunging against the rope fastened
to the ring in its nose and tethering it to the slain beast
lying in the exit ahead, an exit beyond which some creature of horror stood. All the other companions, too, were
hammered against the walls by the bellowing beasts,
and they lost control of the animals, and could only throw
their arms over their heads for protection and try to keep
their feet so as not to be trampled. Alos shrieked in fear,
Ferret screaming as well, their cries lost in the uproar.
And none knew the cause of this pandemonium, only that
the beasts were frenzied and trying to escape something
somewhere. And even though Aiko cried out "Burel,
Burel, deadly peril!" her voice was heard by none.

Yet Aiko, as quick as she was, abandoned her camels
and dodged this way and that, and ducked down to
scramble under and past the panicked pack animal ahead.

Springing forward, her swords now in hand, she
scrambled over the slain creature blocking the exit.

Above Burel, the demon laughed and raised its sword
to deliver the final blow, the one that would at last set the
summoned fiend free from the Wizard's binding command. Yet the creature waited and waited, waited until
Burel opened his eyes, the man yet dazed but looking
up at the apparition. Then, down flashed the obsidian
blade . . . only to meet Ryodoan steel.

Aiko had come at last.

*   *   *

Arin managed to drive her bellowing camel backwards under the portcullis and into the sanctuary. Abandoning the fleeing beast and calling to the gathered priestesses for help, she dashed into the uproar of the narrow tunnel once more, several of the women on her heels. With Egil shoving his panicked lead camel hindwards, and Arin and the women hauling at the frightened, thrashing rear beast from behind, they managed to back two more of the terrified animals out from the passageway, the creatures bolting across the ruddy stone as soon as they were free.

Now Egil and Arin and two of the women ran again into the tunnel to aid Delon in backing his flailing camels out.

Shang! Aiko could not stop the powerful demon's downward blow, could only deflect it instead, the obsidian blade shocking into her steel with numbing force and sliding along her sword to *Chank!* into crimson stone next to Burel's head. Even as the black edge shattered red rock, with a backhanded sweep Aiko lashed her second sword up and at the creature's neck. But, lo! the demon smashed her cut out and away with an upward bash of its angular arm, her blade sliding along the bony chitin like steel sliding along armor.

Yet Aiko lashed her right-hand weapon up in a slashing cut, only to find the demon's black blade blocking the way.

Aiko sprang leftward, along the demon's flank, but stunningly quick the creature whipped about, its sword seeking her. She managed to deflect the blow even as she dodged back.

In a blur of steel, Aiko attacked, yet the creature fended the blows of both of her blades with its single dark sword. Again Aiko sprang back, her breath now coming in harsh gasps.

Momentarily they paused, and as if considering which of these humans to slay first, the creature glanced at Burel, the man yet stunned and ineffectually scrabbling at the ground in an attempt to rise but falling back, unable to gain his feet. Then the demon turned its elongated head toward Aiko, its fangs dripping with a viscous saliva, its wide-set eyes glaring.

"Bakamono!" it hissed in Aiko's native tongue, and then the eight-foot-tall angular monster wrenched its great, jagged, ebon sword up and stalked toward her on its backward-bending, cloven-hoofed legs.

Delon's bellowing camels had been set free of the tunnel, and now he and Egil and Arin went after Ferret's, but as they entered the narrow way, her terrified beast came backing toward them, Ferai's training in the *cirque* enough for her to manage the beast. Even as this animal was loosed to flee across the scarlet basin, Ferret turned and ran back toward the tunnel, crying, "Alos may be down and like to get trampled to death."

Shing-shang, cling-clang, chang-shang . . . The steel of Aiko's blades skirled and rang against the demon's sword, as she attacked and retreated, parried and riposted, blocked and counterstruck, but the demon's power and quickness drove her back and back, and it was all she could do to fend the creature off. Never had she faced such a foe, for it was strong beyond measure and blur-ringly fast, its blows stunning, its guard impenetrable. And it beat aside her own two blades as if they were chaff, trivial, worthless. Her shiruken were gone, lying somewhere on the bloodred stone, batted from the air by the dark sword. And now—*ching-shang-clang-ching*—the monster drove her against the towering crimson wall of the narrow canyon.

Shing . . . ! The sword from Aiko's left hand flew spinning through the air to strike vermilion stone somewhere in the distance.

Shkk . . . ! The ebon blade sliced down and across through leather and bronze, and Aiko's scarlet blood welled from the diagonal cut high athwart her chest.

Ching-chang-shing-shang . . . Now she fended with but one blade, the demon's ebony sword and her own steel but a blur as she fought fiercely against a monster she could not defeat.

Cling . . . ! Now her sole remaining sword tumbled

through the air, spinning as it arced up and over and down to land with a clatter on the crimson rock.

Desperately, Aiko lunged for the dagger in her boot, but the demon smashed her back with its fist, and she crashed down to the red rock. Now the monster bent over and with its long, bony, grasping fingers clutched her bronze-plated jacket and snatched her up from the scarlet stone, preparing to behead her. But Aiko's leather armor ripped open along the diagonal cut, and she fell back, the crimson tiger between her breasts exposed.

The demon jerked back, its eyes wide at the arcane sigil revealed, and from nowhere, somewhere, everywhere there exploded an enraged chuff—RRUH!—as if coughed from the throat of a wild savage beast, and in that moment, with a strength she alone did not possess, Aiko twisted the creature's own jagged ebon sword in its grasp and slammed the blade up and into the monster's gut, the demon still gripping the hilt.

Phoom! Furious flames burst forth from the demon's torso, and the creature shrilled in agony and reared up and back and ineffectually tried to draw the flaring black blade from its bony carapace, but in that moment from behind—*Shkkk!*—Burel's two-handed sword sheared off the demon's head, and the burning, decapitated monster toppled over sideways, dead even as it struck the ground.

Dropping his great blade, Burel snatched bleeding Aiko up from the crimson stone, and in spite of her protests— "My swords. Get my swords"—he headed for the tunnel and the aid of the healers beyond. Just as he reached the opening, Egil One-Eye emerged, the Fjordlander clambering over the dead camel to do so.

"Wha—?" Egil started to say, but in that very instant there came a whelming blast, the shock hurling Burel and Aiko into Egil, slamming all three to the blood-slathered stone.

CHAPTER 55

In a far-off tower on the Isle of Kistan the aethyr within the sanctum rang with an unheard note. The Black Mage therein raised up his gaze from an arcane tome and cocked his head as if listening.

Ah, the demon Ubrux is no longer on this Plane, which means the geas is achieved.

Laughing to himself, Ordrune bent his will once more upon the cryptic tome.

CHAPTER 56

His ears yet ringing from the blast, Burel gained his feet and once again lifted Aiko into his cradling arms, freeing Egil to stand. As the Fjordlander scrambled up, Delon came through the tunnel, Ferret and Mayam on his heels.

"What made that bloody din?" asked Delon, clambering over the corpse of the camel, his gaze sweeping the scene of carnage. "And what in blazes happened here?"

"She is wounded," rumbled Burel.

"Here, let me see," said Mayam, now outside as well.

As the abbess lifted the slashed leathers to examine the wound, Aiko, bleeding from the gash across her chest, struggled to get down from Burel's embrace, her effort weak and ill-directed. "My swords. Get my swords."

"Where?" asked Ferret.

"Back there," said Burel, pointing with his chin.

"Let them care for you, Aiko," said Ferret, glancing down the crimson canyon, where scattered black bits of something burned. "I'll retrieve your swords."

"Shiruken," said Aiko, then she lost consciousness.

Frowning, Mayam looked up from Aiko to Burel. "I do not understand. Her wound does not look severe, yet— We've got to get her back inside, where we can tend to her. It may be poison." The abbess turned to Egil and Delon. "You men, and you, Burel, pass her across that dead animal."

Egil and Delon scrambled back across the carcass, Egil stopping halfway, Delon going completely across. Then Burel gave over the Ryodoan to Egil, the Fjordlander reaching out to receive her, and Egil in turn passed her to Delon. Burel clambered across the slain beast to take her in his arms once again, and bearing the unconscious warrior, the big man headed toward the basin beyond, Delon and Mayam at his side.

Behind, Egil and Ferret walked warily out into the canyon, Egil now with his axe in hand, Ferret gripping daggers. Parts of some black creature were scattered across the crimson stone, here and there dark pieces afire, others lying about in the scarlet shadows like shattered bits of obsidian.

"Adon," breathed Ferret, her eyes wide. She looked down at an elongated, fanged, chitinous head severed from a monster, vile eyes filming over even as she watched. "What *was* this thing?"

Egil squatted and looked closely. Finally he drew in a deep breath and said, "Methinks we look upon the demon that slew Burel's sire . . . or rather what remains of it."

Ferret glanced at Egil. "Elwydd! Are we going to have to fight one of these things every time Burel steps through the gate?"

Egil stood. "Adon's balls, I hope not."

Together, they moved on down the canyon, Ferret taking up one of Aiko's swords and four of her shiruken, Egil hefting up Burel's two-handed sword. As Ferret knelt to retrieve Aiko's last sword she said, "Lord Adon, Egil, look at this hand."

The Fjordlander stepped to her side. One of the demon's long-fingered, bony hands and part of its black-carapaced arm lay on the red stone. "How big was this thing?" asked Ferret, looking at the length of the grasp, fully three times her own.

Egil squatted at her side and slowly shook his head. "I cannot say, though given a right hand like that, it must have towered."

"Look here," said Ferret, pointing at the wrist. Four deep gouges were rent entirely through the chitin, and a black ichor oozed out. "It looks as if some roaring wild beast has clawed the demon's arm."

"Well, it's not poisoned," said Mayam, sponging away the seeping blood, "or at least I think not."

"Then why is she senseless?" rumbled Burel, the big man sitting at Aiko's bedside and holding her hand in his.

"By the grace of Ilsitt, I would say that she is merely spent."

Delon looked down at the oblivious Ryodoan. "Spent?"

"It's as if she has performed some feat of labor beyond her means."

Burel grunted, then said, "She ran the demon through with its own sword, yet that creature was strong beyond belief." He looked down at the unconscious Ryodoan. "I did not think one so small could have such power."

Mayam nodded. "Perhaps that is what drained her so."

The abbess turned to Arin, the Dylvana cinching the last of the bindings on Alos's ribs, the old man groaning and cursing stupid camels, his voice feeble as the sleeping draught took hold. As Alos's words fell to mumbles, Mayam said, "Dara, would you examine Lady Aiko?"

Arin stepped away from Alos and to Mayam's side, leaving the old man slipping into snores. With the abbess sopping up oozing blood, the Dylvana examined the long, diagonal wound. Arin then pressed her cheek to Aiko's forehead. "I sense no fever." She straightened. "Is this the only wound she took?"

"Aye."

Arin frowned and shook her head. "This will need sewing. Hast thou gut?"

Mayam motioned to one of the acolytes, and she handed a curved needle threaded with fine gut to the Dylvana. Arin eyed the needle and thread in the lantern light. "Has the wound bled sufficiently clean?"

"A candlemark, at least," replied Mayam.

"Then let us begin."

Carefully, with fine stitching, Arin closed the wound, Burel looking on and grimacing each time the needle went in and the gut was pulled through, yet he held onto Aiko's hand, his grip gentle, steady.

Egil and Ferret came into the infirmary, Ferret with Aiko's blades, Egil with Burel's. They stood beside Delon and watched as Arin closed the long cut. At last the Dylvana said, "There. 'Tis done." She turned to Mayam.

"Hast thou a poultice we can apply? Gwynthyme? Eretha? Or other such?"

"Poultice?"

Arin nodded. "She has no fever and her color is good, and so I, too, deem the weapon bore no poison, yet a poultice against such cannot harm."

Mayam nodded, and she opened a chest nearby, fetching herbs from within. "This I would use," she said, displaying a handful of yellow mint leaves.

"Gwynthyme," said Arin, approving.

"Malak waraka," said Mayam.

They prepared a poultice of gwynthyme leaves—the minty fragrance heartening—and applied the warm, wet pulp to a cloth and bound it to Aiko's wound with strips of clean linen. At last Arin stepped back and viewed her handiwork. Nodding to herself, she said, "Now we must let the tiger sleep."

With Alos drugged and Aiko unconscious, the others quietly moved out from the infirmary, all but Burel, who stayed behind holding Aiko's hand.

In the late morn, with Egil, Arin, Delon, and Ferret standing ward, the priestesses harvested the slain camel at the tunnel entrance, and the meat and hide and guts were all carried back inside, where the whole of it would be put to use: some meat to be cooked; some to be pulled into jerky and set out to dry; the viscera to be used to make spiced sausage and cooked as well; the hide to be scraped and salted and stretched in a curing frame; and the inedible and otherwise unusable parts to be tilled into the fields.

Yet although they were guarded, nothing came to disturb the women's bloody work.

Just before dawn Aiko awakened to find Burel asleep in a chair at hand with his head cradled in his arms on the bed at her side. And as she stirred he came awake. He looked up at her and sighed in deep relief. Then noting where he was, he jerked erect. "I beg your pardon, Lady Aiko, but I did not mean to presume."

She smiled at him, then suddenly sobered and bolted upright, the sheet falling away revealing poultice bandages high across her chest and a glaring red tiger between her firm breasts. "The demon!"

"Slain," interjected Burel, looking away as she recovered her modesty. "You impaled it on its own sword. And though I took off its head, I deem it was already as good as dead."

Wincing slightly with pain, Aiko leaned back and looked about, the Ryodoan noting Alos snoring away in a bed across the room. "Where are we?"

"In the abbey, in the infirmary."

"And my swords?"

"At hand," he replied, nodding toward a table where rested her blades and shiruken. "Ferai retrieved them."

"And your blade . . . ?"

"Egil."

"What of the demon's dark weapon?"

"They say there is no sign of it."

Aiko glanced over at the old man. "And Alos . . . ?"

"Battered and bruised, and some broken ribs. He was stepped on by a camel wild to escape the demon's stench."

Suddenly Aiko's dark, tilted eyes widened.

"Milady?" Burel inquired, frowning.

She looked at him and reached out to touch his hand. "The peril, Burel: it is gone."

"Gone?"

"Entirely." She grinned and withdrew her touch. "I think you are no longer cursed."

Something unspoken hammered at his lips, but all he said was, "Thanks to you, Lady Aiko."

They sat in silence for a moment, then Burel said, "Are you hungry?"

"Immensely."

Burel shot to his feet. "I'll be right back with your breakfast."

As he rushed away she smiled and slid down under the covers; for the first time in her life she was ready to be cared for by a man.

* * *

"But I don't know how I did it," said Aiko, shaking her head in puzzlement. "There was a moment when everything went red, and next I knew Burel was carrying me."

They sat outside in the afternoon sun—Arin, Egil, Ferret, Delon, Aiko, and Burel. Alos was yet abed in the infirmary, demanding the acolytes serve him a tot of medicinal brandy to soothe his battered frame, or so he claimed, though nought was given him.

Aiko looked from one to another, her brow furrowed in perplexity.

"Was there nought more?" asked Arin.

Burel cleared his throat. "There was a loud sound, a strange sound, short and sharp and savage, something between a cough and a roar."

"Can you imitate it?" asked Delon, his bardic curiosity aroused.

Burel frowned and closed his eyes, remembering, and then he barked: *"Gruh!"*

Aiko looked at him, her eyes wide, but it was Ferret who said, "Did it sound rather like: *Rruh!*"

"Yes. That is more like it, but louder, much louder," replied Burel.

Ferret looked at Aiko, her gaze centered on the Ryodoan's chest, as if trying to see through her silken shirt; then Ferret turned back to Burel. "That is the chuff of an enraged tiger."

Now all eyes turned to Aiko, but she was as bewildered as any.

Egil asked, "How know you this, Ferai?"

"We had tigers in the *cirque*." Ferret looked toward the gate beyond which the remains of the demon lay, her thoughts on the furrowed right arm she and Egil had seen, an arm perhaps clawed by a savage beast, perhaps rent by the talons of a tiger when it aided Aiko to turn the sword backward and shove it into the demon's own gut. Ferret looked at the tiny Ryodoan and then shook her head to clear it of these vagaries.

Late that afternoon, armed and armored, Arin, Egil, Ferret, Delon, and Burel stepped under the portcullis and made their way through the tunnel.

As they came to the dark ruddy stain where the camel's blood had pooled on the crimson stone, Egil held up his hand, stopping all. Yet it was not blood from a camel that the five had come seeking, but a demon instead. For although Aiko sensed no peril in Burel or the surround, still they would put it to the test. Egil turned to the big man. "Remember, if a demon appears, step back inside."

Burel grunted and moved past Egil to stand just inside the opening, his two-handed sword gripped tightly. Then, weapon raised, he stepped forth from the holy ground to see whether or no another demon would appear.

None did.

Burel retrieved the demon's severed head, declaring, "In the name of my father, this I must destroy." But as he stepped back into the tunnel, lo! the head crumbled to dust and fell to the stone, where it burst into furious flames. Burel sprang aside, and the others stepped back from the raging fire, the heat intense.

"Huah!" grunted Egil. "Now we know why it didn't come in after you or your mother."

They turned to go back to the cloister, only to find Aiko standing behind, her swords glittering in the crimson dark.

"My Lady," protested Burel. "You should not be—"

"Oh, but I should," she replied.

They spent another fortnight at the abbey, Aiko's wound healing rapidly under the ministrations of Arin, though the Dylvana declared that it had less to do with her own skill and more to do with Aiko's splendid vitality, as well as the aid of the gwynthyme. Even so, the Dylvana bade Aiko to do no strenuous exercise, and so the golden warrior forwent her daily drills, though she did school Burel morning and night.

During this same fortnight, Alos, too, was treated with the golden mint, this in the form of a tea, which he grudgingly took, complaining that any fool knew a jot of brandy would make the tisane a much better medick. And even though bones knit slowly in the elderly, at the end of two weeks he was declared fit to travel, as long as he did not overexert himself and put pressure on his ribs.

* * *

Just after dawn on December 12, 1E9253, five hundred thirty-three days after Arin had had her vision, again the seven set out from the Cloister of Ilsitt, and once more women wept to see all of them go, but especially at Burel's leaving, for when he was gone, it truly would become a nunnery where no man trod, an unwelcome state for several within. Even so, these last two weeks, Burel had not pleasured any of those who had yet to speak their abstemious vows.

The demon, said some, *took his desire away.*

But others looked at the regard he paid to the yellow warrior and nodded to one another knowingly.

And amid tears and kisses and anguished good-byes, through the tunnel they fared—Aiko in the lead, her armor repaired, Burel following after, then Egil, Delon, Ferret, and Arin.

Once they were clear of the tunnel—and nothing untoward had occurred—then led by acolytes the camels came next: seven saddled for riding, four bearing supplies. As if remembering past terror, the animals balked at entering the confining way again, yet the handlers were adamant, and grumbling and protesting, the beasts finally went through the narrow passage.

When those also reached the far side—again with nothing of note coming to pass—then and only then did Alos venture into the dark strait, Mayam at his side, the old man moaning about his cracked ribs, though the abbess knew his words were impelled by fright. At the distant end, he peered out cautiously, trembling, and finally stepped forth, ready to bolt inward at the slightest need. But nothing appeared and so, grudgingly, Alos trudged to his camel.

Mayam stepped to each of them and murmured, "May Ilsitt favor you with her protecting hand."

She embraced Burel and kissed him one last time, then stepped back as they mounted, the camels *hronk*ing and grumbling as they stood, their long legs awkwardly levering them and their burdens upward.

When they were erect and ready to go, Mayam called

out, "Each and every one of you are welcome to return as you will. Fare you well."

And amid growls of camels and cries of good-bye, the small caravan set off down the deep slot in the towering crimson stone.

CHAPTER 57

As they set about cleaning up the camel dung, Burel said, "I have always known that the demon and I would meet someday, for it was written. What I did not know is that Lady Aiko would be there as well." The big man smiled over at the Ryodoan, receiving a smile in return.

Ferret cocked an eyebrow. "It was *written*?"

Basking in Aiko's grin, Burel swung his gaze to Ferret and nodded.

"What do you mean, 'it was written'?"

"Something my mother told me before she died," replied Burel.

"Oh," said Aiko, her voice all but unheard, her smile fading.

"What is it, my Lady?" asked Burel, turning his attention again to her.

Aiko sighed. "I was hoping your mother yet lived."

"No. She died of fever when I was but ten or so."

Aiko looked down at the red stone. "My own died giving birth to me."

Burel dropped the bag he was carrying and stepped to the Ryodoan and embraced her. "I at least have my memories," he rumbled, "whereas you have none."

His arms around her, Aiko looked up at Burel as if studying his face. At long last she said, "I've never told anyone this, Burel: I never knew my mother, but even so, I miss her."

He looked at her and wanly smiled. "As do I, Aiko. As do I."

Aiko's heart suddenly leapt, for it was the first time he had addressed her in the familiar.

"My mother is dead, too," said Ferret. "And my father. Murdered both."

She gazed back at the campsite where the others readied for the day's travel. "I wonder if any of us have parents alive."

They walked and rode all that day, pausing to take up old camel droppings they had left behind on the way in, as well as taking up any new; too, they cleaned up their own excrement old and new as well, leaving nothing behind to point to the temple in the maze. At sunset as they made camp they heard the demon horn howl, and Alos jumped and spat oaths. It sounded at midnight as well, startling the old man awake once more. "I've heard that cursed thing twice a night for the last, um, twenty, thirty days. Is it to plague me the rest of my life?" In spite of his ire, he fell instantly asleep again.

As they fared for the second day through the twisting rock canyons carved deep in the scarlet maze, the talk did turn to parents, and only Arin of them all had a dam and sire who yet lived, though not upon Mithgar but Adonar instead. All the others had died of illness or in battle or of natural causes, or had been murdered, or, in the case of Aiko, her father had died broken and disgraced, denied even the honor of committing *seppuku* when his daughter had been unmasked.

Upon learning this, when next they led the camels, Burel slipped an arm about Aiko and they walked along in silence.

"Well then," said Delon, after a while, striding alongside Ferai, "we'll just have to become our own family, though I'll consider you, my sweet, as but a remote tenth cousin."

Ferret looked up at him. "Tenth cousin? But why?"

"I would not have you be close kin, for then I couldn't do this." And he paused and took her face in his hands and kissed her long and gently.

Their camels, disturbed at being stopped, emitted loud *hronk*s.

Alos, following, broke out in a cackle.

Ferai, her heart pounding, her face reddening, drew

back from the bard. But he threw his arms wide and broke out in song.

Together they tugged on their camels, the beasts growling in dismay for now, of all things, they were being asked to move again, when they had just barely gotten stopped.

And down the canyon they continued, Delon singing a heartfelt refrain shared by two other men deeply enamored, each of them oblivious to the fears of those they loved: Dara Arin, who dreaded what the oncoming decades would do to her mortal lover and how he might react; fierce Aiko, who could but barely acknowledge that she had room for love in her warrior heart; and untrusting Ferai, who'd been raped as a child.

That night, as a distant demon howl echoed through the scarlet maze, they made camp on the Island in the Sky. While they waited for the water to boil above the charcoal fire, Ferret glanced across at Burel and said, "Tell me more about these things which you say are, um, *written*. Just exactly what do you mean by that?"

Burel did not look up from the fire. "I will ask you this, Ferai: do you believe that you can choose your paths in life?"

Ferret poked her riding stick at the charcoal, nudging a lump to where it would catch fire. "Yes, Burel, I am totally free to do anything I so choose."

Burel shifted his ice-blue eyes away from the glow and toward her. She shivered as if from a sudden chill, but she did not look away. For a moment his gaze held hers, then he looked to the eastern night sky and pointed at the full moon shining aglance o'er the crimson maze. "If you so desired, could you step to the moon?"

Her own gaze followed his, and for a long while she did not answer. But at last she said, "Perhaps. But it would take long training in the ways of Magekind." She glanced at Burel's sword, then added, "Or in the ways of Dwarven crafting to make a ship that can sail the skies above."

Burel grunted, then said, "But you cannot step there now merely by wishing it so."

Ferret grinned and shook her head. "Alas, I cannot."

"Then there are limits to your totally free choices, eh? You cannot step to the moon, cannot fly, cannot change into a fish, cannot do countless things. They are beyond your means. That is, merely oft what you may desire is not a choice at all."

"True, Burel. Nevertheless, my will *is* entirely free. Of all those things within my power, I can pick and choose which to do."

The big man shook his head. "I think not, Ferai. I think all is predestined, and this notion of free choice, of free will, is but an illusion."

"How so?"

Burel took up a pebble. "Consider this stone. If I were to place it so that it would roll down a slope and strike another stone of like size lying on the surface, would it not cause that second stone to roll downslope as well?"

Ferret nodded but remained silent.

Burel continued. "And if I knew precisely where the first stone would strike the second, would I then not know exactly how both stones would react, the angle and speed at which the first would bound, as well as the direction and pace of the second?"

Again Ferret nodded.

"Then consider this: if those above Elwydd and Adon created all, and know all, and set all in motion, would they not know, *know,* our destinies? Are we not merely like pebbles impelled by the many collisions in our lives? Collisions which the highest of all already know the outcomes, and the outcomes of those outcomes, and so on forever?

"You may believe you have choices, Ferai, yet the collisions in your life are already set and your path is immutably determined . . . just as is mine, just as is all that was, that is, and that will ever be. We are merely moving through an endless story already told."

"Ha!" crowed Ferret. "If it is an endless story, then how can it already be told?"

Burel merely shrugged.

Ferret shook her head. "If you think the path is already set, then why strive to do anything, why make any choices whatsoever?"

"Because it is written that we shall do so, written that we shall strive and make choices though, like the pebbles, we merely rattle down the preordained way."

"Bah!" growled Ferret, then she turned to Arin. "What say you to this mad man, Dara?"

Arin smiled. "My view is different."

"How so?"

The Dylvana scratched a line in the rocky soil. "All lives are made up of choices. Should we choose this way, then here we shall go." Her line in the grit jagged left. "But should we choose elsewise"—she moved her stick back up the scrape and jinked it to the right—"we go this way instead. Life itself consists of branching pathways, turning left and right and running straight, or swerving at any number of angles, some paths more likely than others, though any path may be taken. And each choice we make leads to still more branches ahead.

"When we live a simple life, perhaps isolated and full of routine, then the impinging events and choices are few. But as our lives cross with those of others—family, friends, strangers, foe—their choices at times affect what we do, as our choices at times affect them. And the more people we encounter, the more our paths cross and criss-cross and cross again. The more people and events, the more branches, the more confusing the tangle . . . so many choices and interlinked branches as to represent chaos itself.

"However, because as Burel says, most people cannot choose to step to the moon or burst into flame or lift a mountain or become a god . . . or a countless number of things entirely beyond their power, then this endless tangle of branches is indeed bounded by practicality—a bounded chaos, if thou wilt.

"Looking into the past, though, we see the tangle resolved into sets of choices made, chaotic no more but fixed instead—much as Burel would have it. But looking into the future is like looking into an endless snarl of choices, like looking into chaos itself all knotted and meshed and entangled, as you, Ferret, believe.

"There are, however, past and present and future events which stand out above the confusion and chaos, with virtually all paths leading from them or to them in due time, almost regardless of what choices are made."

"Like wyrds?" asked Egil.

Arin nodded. "Thou couldst think of it that way: wyrds for individuals, couples, families, clans, communities, nations, the world. These are the ways of prophecy . . . ways leading toward signal events."

"And this is what you deem the green stone to be, eh? A wyrd for the world?"

"Yes, Egil, I do."

Delon shook his head. "But Dara, first you tell us we have choices, and then you tell us that all paths lead to signal events. If all paths lead to such an event, then what we try to do is hopeless."

"I did not say *all* paths lead that way—"

"She said *virtually* all paths," interjected Ferret.

"Bah," snorted Alos. "Immutable destiny. Choices. Wyrds. It's all nonsense. It's the fickle gods who reach down and meddle with our so-called destinies, shoving us this way and that, visiting calamity upon us when we least expect it."

"No, Alos," protested Delon. "Although the gods may meddle, I think our destinies are written in the stars." He looked around for agreement, but found none. "Even so, there are choices to make, for it is said that the stars impel but do not compel, though one should heed their urgings."

Burel turned to the Ryodoan. "I would hear what you think, Aiko."

She looked up from the glowing coals, her eyes dark and unreadable. "Whatever comes, we must endure." Aiko fell silent and said no more.

Ferret said, "Well I think Dara Arin is right: all before us is chaos and we have free choices to do that which is within our power."

"The chaos is but an illusion," said Burel. "In truth the paths we take are already set before us, and nought we do will alter our steps along the way."

"Ha!" barked Ferret. "Not mine, Burel. I will not march lockstep on a path not of my choosing." She leaped up and with consummate ease twirled in pirouette then executed a backflip.

Delon clapped his hands together in pleasure and shouted, "Bravo, luv!"

Breathless and laughing, Ferret sat down again. "There, Burel, was that foreordained?"

Burel merely nodded.

Ferret snorted.

"Perhaps, Ferai," said Burel, "you are along to make us believe that we indeed have free will."

"And perhaps, Burel, you are along to make us believe we do not."

"Here, let me show you. See, the arm moves in an arc, and a curved blade matching that arc will sustain contact throughout a long slashing cut, whereas to do so with a straight blade requires you to alter the stroke as you cut, and here the edge may either lodge or lose contact altogether."

"But, Aiko, such a curve in a blade would hamper a clean thrust."

"Yes, Burel, it would. The straight blade is best for thrusting, piercing; the curved for slashing, cutting."

"My sword will cleave anything."

"Indeed it will, though to do so it carries great weight, and given a chance a quick foe can defeat it."

Burel touched his neck. "I remember."

In the light of the rising sun Aiko drew one of her swords. "My blades have a delicate curve, not too much to hamper thrusts, but enough to aid a slashing cut." Aiko momentarily paused, as if considering, then she handed the weapon to Burel. He received it as if it were a fragile treasure.

"Aiko!" called Arin.

The Ryodoan turned. "Yes, Dara."

"Let me examine thy wound."

Aiko sighed and, casting a glance at her sword in Burel's hand, she reluctantly trudged toward the Dylvana, the Ryodoan unfastening her leather jacket.

After moments: "Hmm. I do believe we can remove thy stitches ere we set out today."

"What of *kinmichi*?"

Arin nodded. "Thou canst begin again . . . slowly at first."

"*Hai!*"

As the camels headed westerly, Ferret reined back to ride alongside Arin. Both of their faces were now covered with silken scarves, for they now rode across a land where hidebound fools held sway. "Dara, I would speak to you in private."

Arin glanced at Egil. He shrugged and tapped his camel with his riding stick, calling out, "Hut, hut," and moved ahead to join Burel and Alos, while Delon to the fore rode alone in the lead.

As Egil looked back, masked Aiko rode up to join Arin and Ferret, and she was not turned away. "Hmm," said the Fjordlander, "what is it they share?"

Burel looked about. "The women of Ilsitt were always talking together—especially when their blood came upon them . . . or not—and often when I came near they would stop."

Egil sighed. "Women's secrets, I suppose."

"Heh," barked Alos. "Females. A bunch of cackling hens, if you ask me."

"Have you been around many females, Alos?" asked Burel.

The old man looked at the big man, Alos's white eye glaring. "Me? Of course not. I've other interests."

Now Burel looked at Egil. The Fjordlander shrugged and replied, "Some. Though I think when it comes to these matters, Delon has the most experience of us all."

"Let's go see," rumbled Burel. "I have a question to ask."

Together, Burel and Egil urged their camels ahead, but Alos did not ride forward with them.

"How will I know I am in love, Dara?"

The Dylvana looked at Ferret and smiled. "Thou shalt know, for every idle thought thou hast will be filled with pleasant visions of him. Thou wilt admire his strengths, see his goodness, but not be blind to his failings. And thou wilt desire intimacy—"

"Intimacy?"

"Not merely lust, Ferai, but a sharing of feelings, of heart and mind and soul as well as a physical sharing."

Aiko let out a long sighing breath. "What you name physical sharing, Dara, seems like surrender to me."

Arin looked at Aiko in surprise.

"Surrender?"

"Yes, Burel, it *is* somewhat like surrender. You are, um, invading her being."

Burel sighed. "I don't believe that Lady Aiko has ever surrendered to anything in her life. She is a warrior beyond compare."

Delon nodded, then said, "But she is also a woman and you are a man. You must woo her, and if she desires you, she will make it known."

Burel blew out a breath. "I have no experience in wooing. The women of Ilsitt came to me, rather than I seeking them out."

Delon laughed. "It must have seemed as if you had found Paradise, eh?"

"They seemed to enjoy it, as did I, physically. But something was ever missing," replied Burel. "There always seemed to be a fulfillment lacking, as if there were no true sharing."

"A sharing?"

"Yes, Aiko, a sharing." Arin glanced far ahead to where Egil rode. "When I am with Egil I do not feel as if I 'surrender,' but as if I share instead. Each of us cares for the other's need—physically, mentally, emotionally, spiritually—and we are both fulfilled." Arin rode a moment in silence, then said, "Do not take me wrong: one need not be in love to crave a physical sharing—honest lust will drive one to the heights of desire, and slaking that desire most wonderful. But without love there is no lasting contentment . . . pleasure, yes; tranquility, no. Lust without love is that way: full of fire and passion, but empty of serenity when quenched."

Ferret shook her head. "As to the physical part, in my long experience there was no pleasure, no caring involved

. . . only force and brutality, only violence." She gritted her teeth in memory.

Arin looked at her in dismay. "A man did this to you?" Ferret nodded.

"Does he yet live?" growled Aiko.

"No," replied Ferret, her voice grim.

"For the first time in my life," said Delon, sighing, "I believe I am truly in love. Yet Ferai seems to withdraw whenever we begin to get close."

"Adon," said Egil, "that's not the case between Arin and me."

Burel looked at Delon. "Perhaps it is something in Ferret's past which pushes her away."

Arin sighed. "Ferai, thou must try to accept the past for what it truly was: the man who forced thee was an uncaring, savage animal interested only in its own immediate gratification. There was no love involved, not even sharing. There are many like him in the world. Yet, there are uncounted more who are gentle and caring. Egil is one such. So, too, I deem, are Burel and Delon.

"And thou, Aiko, thou shouldst set aside this notion of surrender. When thou dost finally take a man into thine embrace or unto thy bed, it will be thou who wilt choose, thou who wilt say yea or nay, and should he be an uncaring beast—"

"He will not survive," growled Aiko.

Arin smiled. "Ah, yes. But should he be gentle and loving and caring, then it will be no surrender but a glorious alliance instead."

"I think Burel is right, Delon," said Egil. "Something untoward may have happened to Ferret in the past. Yet any fool can see she cherishes you . . . or at least *this* fool can see such. You must be nothing but gentle with her, and perhaps her inclination to withdraw will fade.

"And you, Burel. Aiko is indeed a warrior without peer. You must treat her as no less. But as Delon says, she is also a woman. If you love her and she loves you, there will come a time when you two will become lifemates, soulmates, as have Arin and I, and that void you've felt with other women will be filled at last."

"No invasion? No surrender?"

Arin shook her head, *No*.

"Hmm." Aiko looked speculatively ahead at the men faring westward on their camels. Then she sighed, and as if reluctant to admit any kind of weakness, she said, "I have absolutely no experience in this at all, Dara."

"None of us do at first, Aiko," replied Arin. "I will help thee all I can."

"And my experience is all bad," said Ferret. "Too, I am frightened."

"Oh, my child, thou must set aside thy fear. It will not be easy, for given thine experience thou wilt need the most courage and trust of all, yet thou couldst not have survived on thine own if thou didst not possess grit. As to the trust, that can only come with time and gentle touch, yet it will not come at all if thou dost take no risk."

And so they fared westerly, three males in the lead in deep conversation, three females trailing a distance after in gentle dialogue as well, and in between rode an old man who snorted, "Lovers and would-be lovers, bah!"

They came into Aban on the seventeenth of December, just after the setting of the sun. Once again they made their way to the Golden Crescent inn. And on this night as Egil and Arin arranged for a room of their own, Aiko stepped to Burel and, looking him in the eye, said through her silken veil, "Will you share my room?"

As Burel stammered out his reply, Delon caught Ferai's gaze with his, and she looked long at him, but in the end she said, "I will sleep alone."

Egil made arrangements through the innkeeper to sell the camels back to the stable from which they had come, and then, as Arin arranged for hot baths for all, he and Alos made their way down to the docks to see to the state of the *Brise*.

* * *

"We couldn't find any Yilan Koy on any chart that Alos and I bought," said Egil, freshly scrubbed and seated at supper, the first hot meal any of them had had since setting out from the Temple of the Labyrinth six days past. He turned to Burel. "It *was* Yilan Koy, right?"

Burel nipped another mouthful of shish kebab from his skewer. He chewed slowly, thoroughly, and finally swallowed and then said, "That's what my mother said. My father sailed from Yilan Koy somewhere along the coast of Kistan."

"This would go well with ale," said Alos as he plucked up a gobbet of lamb that had fallen onto his plate. Like all the others, the old man was clean again. It hadn't even required any urgings from Aiko for him to take his bath, for as he had said, he "needed to get the red out."

As Arin reached for the steaming rice, she said, "Perhaps it is shown on thy charts by another name."

"True," replied Egil. "Yilan Koy sounds like no common name I ever heard. And the charts we purchased are written in the common tongue."

"Damned hard to find, too," grunted Alos. "We had to pay a pretty penny to get ones we could read."

She turned to Ferret. "Mayhap our scholar at the archives can translate for us."

Ferret nodded but did not speak, seemingly occupied by her food instead, though she consumed little.

That night, Ferret watched as Arin and Egil retired to one room, and as Aiko and Burel stepped into another. Delon stood across the hall and softly said, "Goodnight, luv," then he entered the room where Alos was, leaving Ferret in the corridor alone. She sighed and stepped into her chamber and softly closed the door behind.

Removing her veil and bandoliers, she fell backward onto the bed and stared up at the stucco ceiling, with its stipples and dimples and rough texture holding all patterns and none. Finally she roused and doffed her boots and leathers, and poured clear water from the pitcher into the basin at hand and washed her face.

Toweling off, she blew out the lantern and fell once more to the bed.

As she lay and stared into the darkness above, through her window she could hear noises from the city outside: people passing to and fro, the occasional sound of an ired camel, horses' hooves now and again, muted conversation and laughter.

Unbidden, images of Delon came into her mind, echoes of words said, visions of him riding and walking and sitting and singing, fragments of melodies . . . words from Arin: *When thou dost finally take a man into thine embrace or unto thy bed, it will be thou who will choose, thou who wilt say yea or nay . . . no invasion . . . thou wilt need the most courage and trust . . . it will not come at all if thou dost take no risk . . . Ferai, thou must try to accept the past for what it truly was . . . for what it truly was . . . set aside thy fear . . . it will be thou who wilt choose . . . it will not come at all if thou dost take no risk . . . risk . . . risk . . .*

The pale yellow light of a rising gibbous moon came creeping in through her window, and in the soft radiance again she got up and washed her face in cool water, and then lay down once more.

Still, images of Delon came unbidden to her mind, and she lay in her bed, her lips afire from the memory of his kiss, her loins and breasts burning, her entire body aflame . . .

. . . *risk* . . .

It was near mid of night when she at last arose and padded across the hall to tap on Delon and Alos's door.

The next morning, when Alos awoke he found he was in the room alone.

CHAPTER 58

Delon stood on Ferai's balcony, singing bliss to the world at large, and people in the street below paused in wonder at the lyrical joy in his voice, though they understood not a word. And in the chamber behind him, soundly asleep with a smile on her face, lay the subject of his rhapsody.

And across the hall and down, Arin and Egil lay together and held hands and listened to the paean and smiled, for although they knew not for certain the cause of such gladness, they could not help but suspect.

And beyond their own balcony and down in the enclosed courtyard below, steel skirled on steel as two warriors practiced stroke and counterstroke, while shocked servants and guests stared in disbelief, for although one was a man good and proper, the other was of all things a female, and surely this bordered on blasphemy, or so the Fists of Rakka would say. But none suggested this to the woman, for she was entirely too formidable, and a person would have to be a camel-brained fool to even dare whisper to her such words.

And above them and alone in his bed, a one-eyed old man fell back to sleep while songs of love and steel sang all 'round.

Later that morning, Arin, Aiko, Ferret, Delon, and Burel made their way to the archive. When they arrived, once again Delon took station at the entrance, while the others went all the way in. As they approached the central desk, the scholar looked up and smiled, and then his eyes widened. "Burel," he breathed. The 'âlim leaped up from his station and rushed to Burel and embraced him and kissed him on the cheeks, a string of Sarainese tumbling from his lips.

Burel smiled and hugged the man and kissed him in return and murmured, "*Khûri* Ustâz."

Aiko's tilted eyes widened. "You know this man, *saia no hito?*"

Burel nodded, saying, "He is"—Burel glanced about to see if any of the patrons were listening; none were, yet Burel lowered his voice—"another keeper of faith." He turned to the scholar. "*Khûri* Ustâz, let us go where we can speak."

The *'âlim* nodded and, motioning to Delon, led them back to the same chamber he had previously used. Once again Delon took station at the beaded curtain.

Inside, Burel said, "*Khûri* Ustâz, I would have you meet my companions: Dara Arin of Darda Erynian, Lady Ferai of Gothon, and at the door stands Bard Delon of Gûnar. And lastly, let me present my *kalb w nafs,* Lady Aiko." Burel turned to his companions. "My friends, this is *Khûri* Ustâz, a priest of Ilsitt."

As the *'âlim* acknowledged the introductions, he said, "I have met all these before, Burel, though I did not know their names."

As he came to Ferret, she said, "No wonder you knew how to tell us where to find the temple, though your instructions weren't very clear."

The priest-scholar smiled and shrugged. "You could have been agents from the Fists of Rakka, though I am glad you are not."

Then he turned to Aiko and looked long at her and finally said, "So you are Burel's *kalb w nafs.*" It was a statement and not a question. Then without warning, he stepped forward and embraced her.

Perplexed and wary and merely tolerating the *'âlim's* embrace, Aiko looked up at the grinning Burel. "What have you told him?"

"That you are my heart and soul."

The scholar stepped back and nodded. "*Kalb w nafs:* heart and soul." Then he turned to Burel. "My boy, I never thought to see you beyond the compound's walls. You must tell me what brings you here."

* * *

"Yilan Koy," said Arin. "They are Kistanian words meaning 'Serpent Cove,' or so said the scholar-priest."

"Serpent Cove, Serpent Cove," mumbled Egil, scanning the charts he'd brought from the *Brise*.

"Here," said Alos, jabbing a forefinger down to one of the parchments.

Egil rotated the chart 'round to the place where Alos had pointed. The map showed an inlet, long and narrow and sinuous. "Hmm. Yes. Shaped like a snake." Then he looked up at the oldster. "That was quick."

"When I heard the common name, I knew where it was," growled Alos, "for I've been there. And let me tell you, it's no place for an honest man."

Egil's eye widened. "You've been to *Yilan Koy*?"

Alos nodded. "The cove as well as the town in the viper's throat . . . if there's ever been a worse den of thieves, I've yet to see it." Then he glared with his white eye at Egil and Arin. "I swore when I was there if I ever escaped that pit I'd never go back."

"What wast thou—?"

"Delivering a shipload of pomegranates," snapped Alos, before Arin could finish her question. "Cap'n Borkson took on that damnfool cargo in Chabba because no Hyrinian dhows were in port at the time, and because no others would haul it. 'They gave us a pilot and triple fees,' the cap'n crowed . . . the more fool he. We barely made it out of there with our hides."

"Why so?" asked Ferret.

"Because once we'd been there, that meant we knew the way in."

Burel looked down at the chart. "The way in?"

"Why d'y' think it's called Serpent Cove?" Before Burel could respond, Alos pointed his finger to the mouth of the inlet and answered his own question: "Not only does it look like a snake on the chart, but there's rocks like serpent's fangs barring the way. This whole coastline's that way—for league upon league in either direction there's jagged stones to hole any hull that comes near. And as to the rocks, the fangs 'cross the inlet, tricky they are, and not just anyone can sail past 'em. I'd say there are no more dangerous shoals lying in any of the waters throughout the whole wide world."

Delon looked at the long narrow cove on the map. "Hmm. They don't show up here."

Alos snorted. "Any chartmaker that'd scribe it so would have his throat cut."

Now Egil's one good eye fixed Alos's. "But you know the way in."

"Of course I do; I'm a helmsman, ain't I? —Now wait a moment here. I said I'd never return, and I meant it!"

They reasoned with Alos the rest of the day, but the old man was adamant: he would not go back to the cove, and that was final.

As eve drew upon the land, Burel and Aiko retired to the courtyard, where again they drilled at swords, the big man now using a long, curved blade Aiko had selected for him that very morning from an obsequious arms merchant nearby. The kowtowing dealer had called it a *sayf*, but Aiko named it saber. It was rather broad bladed and had an ivory hilt with a hooked silver pommel that partially curved around the back of the hand. When sheathed, the weapon was meant to be carried in front, slung by a strap from two rings on a broad band high around the neck of the black scabbard, yet Aiko arranged for a belt which could be fixed across the back or secured around the waist. "But this is a weapon meant to be used from camel-back," had protested the merchant, adding an "if you please." But Aiko had replied, "Where we go there will be no camels."

And now in the courtyard she and Burel stepped through stroke and counterstroke, while dark-eyed men stood in the shadows and glared at the unveiled yellow woman and her red-headed outlander man, the cloaks of these disapproving observers bearing the sigil of a clenched fist.

The nighttide swept over the land, and Egil and Arin bade all good night and, holding hands, headed upstairs for their bed. Somewhere above, water splashed in the bathing chamber and a big man laughed and a female voice called out, *"Bukotsomono!"* but laughed as well. In the lanternlight of the veranda, Ferret, uncertain, glanced at Delon, and he smiled and gently took her hand and kissed her fingers and whispered, "I love you, my sweet Ferai." Tears trembling on her lashes, she clasped him to her.

Dawn came to Aban, and once again Alos awakened to the sound of singing and the skirl of steel on steel. Groaning, he rose from his bed and stumbled to his balcony. Below, Aiko and Burel were practicing, and even more dark-eyed strangers watched the drill, stirring and muttering among themselves.

"Hoy!" yelled Alos. "We're trying to sleep up here." Not waiting to see what his shout accomplished, the old man lurched back to his bed and fell asleep once more.

After another day of fruitless discussion, at last Egil sighed and looked across at Arin. "I suppose we'll just have to attempt it on our own, Dara. I mean, Alos is determined he's not going back." Egil turned to the oldster. "You'll have to tell us all you know about the town and the cove, especially about the way to get past the Serpent's Fangs."

The seven sat in long shadows at evening meal on the veranda, the last of the sun nearly sunk, the western sky orange, the eastern deep violet.

"Can't we make anchor elsewhere and go in overland?" asked Delon.

"That's a damnfool suggestion," barked Alos.

Ferret reached out and took Delon's hand and glared at the oldster.

But Alos ignored her and stabbed a finger at the bard. "Didn't you listen when I said the whole coast is fanged in that region? For decades of miles upshore and down it'll pierce any hull, sink any ship whose captain is fool enough to sail nigh."

Arin also reached out and took a hand—Alos's. "We cannot and will not force thee to guide us safely past the shoals. Yet heed, I deem that this is why thou art a one-eye in dark water, for this is thy hidden purpose in the rede. And without thee, we shall fail."

Alos looked down at the small hand gripping his, and then at the Dylvana. With his chin atremble he opened his mouth to say something, but at that very moment, *Khûri* Ustâz strode quickly onto the porch and, staying in the shadows and glancing left and right, hissed, "Burel!"

Burel looked up, but before he could say aught, Ustâz said, "The Fists of Rakka, they're coming to get you and your *kalb w nafs,* Lady Aiko. Blasphemers, they name you both. They come to punish you, to batter you to death in the public square."

Aiko growled and leapt to her feet. "If they want a fight, they'll get it," she sissed through gritted teeth, then turned to Burel and snapped, "Swords," and started for her room, all others springing to their feet to follow, all but Arin and Alos, the Dylvana standing and calling out "Wait!" while the old man shrank down in his seat.

They turned and looked at Arin. She pointed at Burel and declared, "We have what we came for—the cursed keeper of faith in the maze. The Fists of Rakka can wait."

Now Arin turned to the *'âlim.* "How soon will they be here?"

"A candlemark. Two at most," he replied.

"Then I say we get to the ship and leave."

Aiko growled in protest, but Burel said, "She is right— the green stone comes before all." He stepped to *Khûri* Ustâz and embraced him. "Thank you for warning us. Now you must go, else they will find you here."

As Burel stepped back from the *'âlim,* Egil looked at Alos still cowering in his chair and asked, "What about you, Alos?"

Before the old man could reply, Ustâz said, "The Fists will kill anyone left behind."

"Eep!" squealed Alos, and jumped to his feet. Then he whined at Aiko, "This is all your fault! Dragging me off on a damnfool—"

"Aru shizukana!" Aiko spat, and spun on her heel and headed for her room.

* * *

They collected their weapons and clothing, and Egil settled the innkeeper's bill. Then, with Aiko and Burel bringing up the rear, and with Alos squeaking in fear in the lead, they hied along the streets in the dusk, pressing through the throngs for the docks, Alos's trembling voice crying out, "Make way! Make way!" At last they came down to the river proper, its yellow-orange waters black in the oncoming night. Reaching the wharves where the *Brise* was moored, Alos scrambled over the wales to the tiller, all the while hissing, "Hurry, hurry,"as the others clambered aboard. Egil and Delon began raising the sails, while Aiko and Ferret cast off. Even as they pushed away to be carried downcurrent, in the yellow light of street lanterns men in dark robes could be seen striding through the crowd, the masses parting before them as they marched toward the jetties. Yet the sloop was well away ere the Fists of Rakka reached the abandoned slip. Finding it empty, they milled about in thwarted frustration, tulwars and scimitars slashing the remnants of the twilight air while the men called down curses upon the blasphemers and all their ilk. And even innocent believers drew back into the darkness and out of sight of these tyrannical followers of yet another intolerant one true way.

Tacking by the light of the glimmering stars, in twelve candlemarks they reached the wide lower part of the River Ennîl. The tide began to flow against them as they tacked and hauled through the estuarial waters, and it took awhile ere they crossed the marge into the bay. Behind them a waning half moon slid above the horizon, adding its light to the gleam of the stars.

Finally the sloop reached deeper waters, where it could make good headway, and Alos brought the *Brise* around from her northwesterly heading to beat into the eye of the wind, her overall course now westerly.

After a while, Arin said, "Where shall we drop thee off, Alos?"

The oldster looked long at her, sighing and shaking his head. At last he said, "Not anywhere in these waters, but somewhere else instead. Somewhere after you've escaped Kistan."

"Escaped Kis—?"

"I'm a bedamned fool for pledging this, but I'll sail you past the shoals at Serpent Cove." He raised a trembling hand to his forehead to wipe away sudden sweat, and his voice quavered as he added, "I'll take you there and get you back out."

"You mean you'll go with us?" blurted Delon.

"Masani?" Aiko's eyes flew wide.

The oldster stuck out his chin and glared at the Ryo-doan. "I said I would, didn't I?" Even so, he was gasping as if he couldn't get enough to breathe.

"But I won't go ashore to fight no Mage. And if you get caught, I'll not stay around. But if we sail out of there together, you can drop me off at the first friendly port, for then I'll be quit of this damnfool venture, you hear?"

"Well and good," cried Egil. "Let's give him a cheer."

And as Delon and Ferret and Burel and Egil and even Aiko sounded three *hip, hip, hurrah*s, Arin reached over and took the frightened old man's hand and simply said, "I thank thee."

Still trembling, Alos leaned back against the stern thwart. As if suddenly aware that all eyes were still upon him, he glared at the sails and snapped, "What are you, a bunch of lubbers? Look at those sails and the lubberly sheets. Trim up, you hear me, trim up."

Delon began singing as he and Egil adjusted the sails and cleated the sheets, and Ferret and Aiko coiled the spare, Burel lending a hand. But Arin slid over to the old-ster and pointed to a guiding star as she put an arm about his yet quaking shoulders.

And thus did *Brise* sail away from Sarain by the light of a silver half moon.

CHAPTER 59

Through deep waters indigo blue fared the *Brise* on her southwesterly course, the little ship tacking on long, long beats against the winds blowing west to east across the wide Avagon Sea. As before, the companions took turns sailing the ship, with Delon and Ferret and Alos crewing from dawn till dusk, while Burel joined with Aiko and Arin and Egil to sail the seas at night. A crew at a time, they also took turns sleeping in the cabin below, there being but four bunks in all. Still, there was considerable overlap between one crew coming on watch and the other crew taking leave, and during these times— unless it was raining—by unspoken consent the cabin was ceded for lovers' trysts, while those left on deck relaxed.

At the mid of night of the winter solstice, in the restricted confines of the sloop, Arin began chanting and stepping out the Elven rite hallowing the turn of the sun, with Delon and Egil guiding Burel through the steps, while Arin and Aiko guided Ferai. They were lost in the ritual and in Arin's chant when the silver half moon arose and cast its argent light aglance across the celebrants.

Below in the cabin Alos was awakened by the canticle and the pace of gliding steps. He listened for a while, but the rhythmic cadence soon lulled him back to sleep.

Six days later in early morn they sighted the Island of Gjeen, and for the next three days they rounded its southern flank. As the island disappeared over the horizon astern, Egil looked up from the charts. "Sabra," he proclaimed. "We'll head for Sabra to reprovision."

Delon glanced at the map. "The city at the edge of the Karoo?"

Egil nodded.

"Hmm, wasn't that one of the places where the Jutlanders might go to look for us?"

Egil grunted. "Aye. But that was two months back. I think that they would have come and gone by now."

"Jutlanders?" asked Burel, frowning. Then he looked at Aiko and his face brightened. "Ah, Queen Gudrun's hounds, eh?"

Aiko nodded, her gaze impassive, but she said nought.

Alos sighed. "I wouldn't want to meet up with them again."

Delon laughed. "Alos, old man, you were passed-out drunk both times."

Alos bristled. "Nevertheless!"

Egil held up a hand. "Look, we'll sail into the mouth of the port, and if we see a Dragonship we'll sail right back out. I think we've enough water to get us to Khalísh."

"Khalísh?" Delon leaned over and gazed again at the chart.

"Here, in Hyree," said Egil, pointing.

"Oh. Hyree. I'd rather not, if we have a choice, for they're almost as bad as the Kistanians."

At high noon on the sixth day of January they sailed into the harbor at Sabra, the curve of the city before them baking in the sun.

They discovered from the harbormaster that not only was there no Dragonship in port, none had been seen for a number of years, and that one but briefly.

With Aiko and Arin and Ferai's faces covered in veils, they pressed through the throngs and took rooms at the Crescent and Star, a modest inn on the slopes above the bay. From their balconies and to the south, and far beyond the city walls, they could see the great arc of the erg, the sands of the mighty Karoo shimmering in the heat. Yet this vast desert was not on their minds, but a serpentine cove instead.

* * *

"All right," said Alos, pointing at the sketch he had drawn. "Here's the fangs. See these three? They're the guide-rocks. We zigzag through all the other fangs this way"—on the parchment his finger scritched south-southwest, then jinked north-northwest, then scraped southwest—"we pass the first guide-rock close to larboard while running toward the second, jibing 'round the second one starboard tight, then running straight for the third one, taking it close to larboard, and then swing true southwest and into the throat of the snake."

"How do we single out the three guide-rocks?" asked Egil.

"The first two are taller than the other fangs"—Alos pointed—"the first tall one is somewhere out here on the edge, while the second is down 'round here among the other rocks. The third one, about here, is, um, marbled with white veins." He looked up at Egil. "See, it's simple, once you know."

Aiko, not taking her eyes from the map, asked, "Where is the town?"

"Just beyond the first bend. Out of sight."

Now the Ryodoan glanced up, first at Egil and then to Alos. "And Ordrune's tower?"

"I didn't see no tower," said Alos, scratching among the long hairs of his scraggly white beard. "Just the town, though the cove itself slithers way beyond—deep into the jungle for miles. We didn't go past the town."

"And the entrance to the cove," asked Burel, "is it warded?"

"They keep a daywatch," said Alos. "Sounded the alarm when we escaped. But as to a nightwatch, I don't know. There was some talk that the Rovers scavenge ships that founder on the rocks, and that's why they keep a watch on the entrance. As to the truth of it, I cannot say."

"I would think they keep a watch to warn of the King's fleet, and they hide the town for the very same reason," said Aiko.

"When is the best time to take the *Brise* in?" asked Egil.

"High noon, so I can see how to maneuver," replied Alos.

"No, Alos," said Aiko. "In the dark of night to avoid the watch."

"But I won't be able to see," snapped the oldster.

"How about dusk instead?" asked Ferret. "No, wait. If we can see to sail in, then the warders can see us, as well."

"Indeed," said Arin, "and unless we have a ruse we can successfully carry out, we must slip in unseen."

"We won't make it past those fangs if I'm blind," said Alos.

"I will be thine eyes, Alos," said Arin. "I see quite well by starlight alone."

"What about a ruse?" asked Delon. "Any ideas?"

"Does anyone speak Kistanian?" asked Ferret.

All shook their heads, *No*.

"Then a ruse is not likely to succeed. Besides, an Elf, a Ryodoan, and five white northerners do not look at all like Kistanians."

"I could stain myself as did my father," said Burel, "but I cannot speak the tongue." He frowned, then said, "Perhaps I could go in as a deaf mute."

"But we couldn't all stain our skins and pretend to be deaf mutes," said Ferret. "I mean, it would be beyond credibility."

Silence fell, and after a moment, "How about Hyranian? Anyone speak it?" asked Delon. "They're allies, I hear."

Again all shook their heads.

"Then for the moment I would think a ruse is out," said Delon. He turned to Alos. "And you say that the shore is fanged like this for miles?"

"Fifty, sixty, eighty miles in either direction," replied the oldster.

Aiko looked across at Egil. "For the moment, let us presuppose that we have won past the fangs. If so, then I would think we next find the tower."

Egil nodded. "And reach the chamber atop and get the scroll. That will not be easy, for the walls are well warded." Egil turned the parchment over and sketched as much as he knew of the layout of Ordrune's fortress.

As he drew, Ferret asked, "What if we don't find the tower? It might not be in Serpent Cove, you know."

Before Egil could answer, Aiko said, "Then one by one

we take prisoners from the town until we discover someone who knows its whereabouts."

"But, Aiko," protested Arin, "we may collect many prisoners ere we find one who knows. What will we do with the captives till then?"

Aiko looked impassively at Arin, and finally said, "We cannot leave anyone alive who might warn the Mage."

"But that would be cold-blooded murder of innocents," said Arin.

"Pah!" snorted Alos. "There are no innocent Kistanians."

Arin looked at Alos and shook her head in rue. "In that, my friend, thou art mistaken. All races, no matter how corrupt, have innocents among them."

Again Alos snorted, then asked, "Even the Foul Folk?"

Arin's eyes widened in sudden shock, and she did not know how to respond.

Egil, finishing his sketch, said, "Let us just hope the need to take prisoners doesn't come." He slid the draft to table center, saying, "Much will depend upon what we find when we get there, yet this is what I know about Ordrune's stronghold."

Delon studied the drawing, then tapped his finger on the parchment. "Are there any windows atop this tower?"

"Four. Unbarred," said Egil. "One aligned with each of the cardinals."

"Well then, look at this," said Delon, pointing. "The tower is at a corner in the fortress walls. The banquette doesn't seem to go around the outer curve, but only about the inner instead. If that's true, then perhaps we can scale undetected this outer wall and go in through a window, if they are large enough, that is."

"Though it might be a squeeze for Burel," said Egil, "I think we can all get through."

"Not me," said Alos. "I told you I ain't going to fight no Mage. I'll just wait on the boat. There'll be plenty of places to conceal the *Brise* . . . it is a jungle, you know— the whole island—with streams pouring into the cove. We'll just find one of them and slip the *Brise* into hiding."

Egil grunted an assent, then he looked 'round the table. "Who here has experience in scaling tower walls?"

Delon said, "It should be no different from rock climbing, and I for one have clambered many a sheer rock."

Aiko's gaze was impassive as she said, "I have scaled tower walls in war."

Burel looked at her in surprise, then said, "In the basin of the temple, I often climbed the face of the cliffs."

"I've not climbed rocks in particular," said Ferret, "but I've scaled many a sheer building. Climbing a tower should not be that different in kind. Yet if it is, then if someone will set a rope, I'll be up in a flash."

"As will I," said Arin.

Delon turned to Ferret. "You've climbed buildings? Part of your *cirque* training?"

Ferret looked at him, something unreadable in her eyes, but she remained silent.

"All right," said Egil, "then here is but one plan of many: some will climb ahead and set ropes for the rest of us to swarm up. When we get ready to enter the chamber, those who fight best will go first: Aiko, me, Burel, Delon. Should Ordrune or some of his lackeys be inside, we kill them. When it is safe, Ferret will open the chest and Arin will find the scroll; the rest of us will stand ward."

"Then we get the Hèl out, eh?" asked Delon.

"Back the way we came," said Egil, nodding. He looked 'round the table and received like nods from all.

"Well and good," said Aiko. "Now let us conceive another plan. One, say, where we go over the wall instead of climbing the tower. . . ."

For the next two days they fumed and fretted about how to get into the cove unseen, alternatives as to how to covertly and overtly assault the tower, what to do should the tower not be found, what to do should the scroll not be found, what to do with any prisoners they might take, how to get back out of the tower and cove, and what to do if detected during the execution of any of their plans.

During those same two days, Egil and Alos reprovisioned the *Brise* with food and water. In addition, they purchased whatever gear they deemed was needed to carry out any one of their many alternative plans to obtain the scroll: climbing gear, ropes, additional weaponry, lanterns, oil, and so on. Ferret made rounds of several locksmiths and tinkers and jewelers and even a black-smith or two, and added to her already extensive set of fine lockpicking tools. Aiko and Burel continued to prac-tice at blades, though they rented camels and rode away to the headland to do so beyond sight and sound of any would-be observers. Arin visited herbalists and heal-ers and acquired tisanes and poultices and herbs and roots and other such, should a range of healing be necessary. And on the third night in port Alos slipped away to a wine merchant; just after dawn, as Aiko hefted him over her shoulder and took him aboard the *Brise* and below, Egil said, "Seems as if the only time he'll get on a ship is when he's dead drunk or running in fear."

Some nine days after the turn of the year, the day they sailed from Sabra, the winter rains began sweeping across the Avagon Sea, like long grey brooms driving white-capped waves over the darkling deeps, with blowing, scudding foam flying in the wind before them. But in between the frequent storms the sun shone down upon the little sloop, her prow shouldering into the rolling brine as she beat toward a far distant isle, bearing her rede-driven crew closer to fateful but unknown ends.

Yet the Isle of Kistan was many days away, and the sloop a confining rig, and because there was little room to do aught else, they spoke of many things. . . .

"Look, Burel," said Delon, at the change of shift, "I asked this of the others, back when we had not yet come to the Temple of the Labyrinth. Then we were talk-ing about whether or no there is an afterlife, but it seems just as valid to ask it of you against the light of your philosophy."

Burel at the tiller looked through the twilight and across at the bard. "Say on."

"Well, it's just this: what good does it do to try to be fair and just if our paths are already fixed? And if paths are immutable, determined, then nothing we do will change things one whit: evil will be evil, good will be good, and nought anyone does will move us away from our preordained track. And if, for example, I must be good to obtain the reward of a pleasant afterlife, but if my predetermined path is to be evil, well then, how can I possibly be held accountable for the evil I will have done?" Delon flung his arms wide, taking in all that could be seen. "I mean, isn't it the fault of those who set the planes in motion? Aren't they the ones to be held accountable since they determined my path at the moment of creation? And another thing: why are we even here if everything is already determined? Why play out a story which, as you say, is one completely told?"

Burel shrugged. "I know not the minds of those who let slip the leash of existence, but if they are indeed all powerful, all knowing, then how can they not know down to the finest detail how each of us will react as we are acted upon and as we act upon one another? If they are all knowing, then they *must* apprehend the outcomes of each and every last thing."

"Perhaps," said Delon, "they deliberately created something with ambiguity in its nature. Perhaps it is as Ferret says, and they gave us free will. If so, then they may not know that which is to come."

Burel shrugged. "You may be right, my friend, but then again you may be wrong. Yet right or wrong, I know not how to answer your questions with any certainty."

Delon stroked his jaw. "I understand, Burel. But listen, if everything is already determined, if the story is completely told, I can't think of a *single* good reason as to why we are even here. Can you?"

Burel laughed.

"What's so amusing?" asked Delon, smiling.

"Ah, my friend, you have just asked me: what is the purpose of life?"

Delon sighed and shook his head. "I did, didn't I?" He looked out to sea with its sapphirine waves rolling from rim to rim. But then he turned back to Burel and said, "Still, Burel, given your philosophy, can you think of even a single reason, good or no, as to why we are here?"

Burel frowned in thought for a moment, but finally said, "Perhaps there is a clue in what Lady Aiko related as a Ryodoan belief: perhaps we are born and born again, living many lives before we reach Paradise, or reach the next world, or move on to whatever awaits, indeed if there is anything awaiting us at all. If it is true that our souls migrate from one life to the next, then it may be that all is predetermined so that each of us will learn by experience *exactly* what it is to be good *and* to be evil *and* to be a mixture of each, what it is to be hated and loved and ignored, to be a thief and a murderer and a rapist and a priest and a devout worshipper and an unbeliever and any other thing you can name, including worms and gnats and snakes and all other things which swim and slither and crawl and walk and fly. And perhaps when we have learned all—all sides of what it is that we can do and be— perhaps then and only then are we permitted to leave this world and progress to the next, be it Paradise or no. For then and only then may we have lived enough and know enough to measure up to this new place in which we will then find ourselves."

"Good grief, Burel, that would mean we'd need live countless lives throughout an eternity!"

"Don't take me wrong, Delon: I'm not saying that I *know* this to be true. I am also not saying that one should countenance evil, or believe in the migration of the soul, or in Paradise, or in anything else whatsoever. I am merely saying that I do not *know* aught for certain, yet I have faith: faith in the goodness of Ilsitt; faith that those above the gods are all knowing and, hence, they know all outcomes, then and now and forever; faith that what we do is preordained; and lastly, faith that one day I *will* know."

Delon took a deep breath and slowly let it out. Finally he said, "Burel, you are indeed a keeper of faith."

Burel glanced forward to where Aiko stood in the bow, then turned to Delon once again. "There is, of course, one thing I *do* know for certain."

Delon cocked his head. "And that is . . . ?"

"I do love Lady Aiko."

Delon laughed and lifted his voice in a brief but glorious song of adoration unbound.

When quiet fell again, Egil looked at Burel and said, "I once would have claimed that the purpose of life is to live bravely, but experience has taught me that living bravely is not enough. Besides, living bravely is not a purpose at all, but merely a manner of thinking and behaving, a manner in which one gains approval from one's love and family and clan . . . and perhaps from the gods themselves. Perhaps our only purpose in life is to gain the approval of the gods."

"I would not go too far down that path, Egil," said Burel.

"And why is that?"

"Let me give you an example: the Fists of Rakka say that the purpose in life is to fear Rakka, to worship Him, to obey Him. They claim there is no God but Rakka, and we are here to glorify Him."

Egil shook his head. "I could not glorify a god who rules through fear."

Burel nodded. "Neither could I, yet this is an example of how one goes about gaining the approval of a given god."

"Ah, Burel, I see."

Aiko made her way back from the bow and sat down beside Burel. He took her hand. "Tell me, Aiko, what is the purpose of life?"

She looked at him and finally said, "The first rule of life is to live."

"Nothing more?"

"Nothing more."

Alos snorted. "If you ask me, the only reason we are here is so the gods can have someone to meddle with for entertainment."

Delon laughed. "I think you have it, old man. If indeed the gods—or those above the gods—are responsible for life, they did it to be entertained. And that is our purpose: to put on a show."

Burel looked at Ferret, but she merely shrugged, and so his gaze moved on to Arin.

The Dylvana cleared her throat. "We can't know what the prime movers had in mind when they set all in motion. Perhaps each of us is but an insignificant link in a long chain which arose from a lowly beginning and is meant to span to some exalted end. Just where that chain began, I cannot say; nor can I say where it now stands nor where it will ultimately end, if indeed it will end at all; for I know not the minds of those who forged the very first link. Yet each of us is but a link from the past to the future, and none I know of can say what the chain overall is meant to do. In this, I believe Ferai has the right answer."

Delon turned to Ferret, his eyes wide. "What did you say, luv?"

"I didn't say anything," Ferret answered. "I merely shrugged my shoulders, for when it comes to the purpose of life, I simply do not know."

"Exactly so," said Arin. "Exactly so."

"According to the charts," said Egil, "we're verging into Rover waters. Keep a sharp eye, and if you spy a sail—"

"A maroon sail," blurted Alos, his voice high and tense.

"Ah, yes, a maroon sail, well then, call all hands and make ready to drop our own canvas."

"Drop our own canvas?" asked Ferret. "But why?"

"So we'll be harder to spot," replied Egil. "Our hull rides low in the water, and a bare stick—a bare mast, that is—will be difficult for them to see. But should they spot it regardless, well then, with all hands haling, we can be up and running within twenty beats of a heart."

"Can we outrun a Rover?" asked Delon.

Egil turned up a hand and looked to Alos. Drops of perspiration clung to the oldster's upper lip and he snapped, "Adon's balls, how should I know?"

Egil swung back to Delon. "Perhaps they'll not bother to come after us when they see we're but an insignificant sloop and not a fat mercantile ship instead."

Aiko growled and gestured to Burel and Arin, saying, "Should any draw near they'll first have to deal with our arrows, and I've seen Dara Arin's skill, and I know my own and Burel's. And should that fail to stop them, then they'll have to answer to the edge of our steel when we board them."

"When *we* board *them*?" asked Delon, then laughed.

He was joined by the others, all but Alos, who sat at the

tiller heaving and puffing, his breath coming in tremulous gasps.

For twenty days and twenty nights, through fair weather and foul, the *Brise* had cut through the Avagon Sea, beating a zigzag away from Sabra to run a westerly course. And in all that time they had seen but one other ship and absolutely no land whatsoever, not even a tiny isle. But just at dusk on the twentieth day, with the seas yet running high from the blow of the day before, below the thin crescent of a new moon standing on the far western rim, like ebony clouds of a gathering storm lying low in the distance ahead, they saw land at last, seemingly black in the onrushing night.

"There it is," said Egil, "the Island of Kistan."

CHAPTER 60

Arin glanced at the crescent moon, new and vanishingly thin, the slender arc now sliding downward beyond the dark silhouette of Kistan. "Alos, I have decided: we must make the run at night. Art thou up to it?"

Alos's jaw dropped. "Are you mad?"

Aiko leaned forward in the dusk to come nearly nose to nose with the oldster, the Ryodoan's dark eyes glittering. "Answer the question," she hissed through gritted teeth.

"It'll be night, Dara. Black as pitch. There'll not even be moonlight by the time we get there."

"Indeed, it will be dark, Alos," agreed Arin, "yet what better time to slip in unnoticed?"

"Look, I told you before, I can't pilot the *Brise* through the fangs if I can't see. No one can."

"And as I said before, Alos, there will be starlight, in which I see quite well. I will be thine eyes."

The old man puffed and wheezed, and finally said, "There's a good chance we'll all get killed."

"Regardless, Alos, canst thou pilot if I guide?"

"Those rocks are like fangs!" he sissed.

Egil spoke up. "We'll use an old Fjordlander trick when raiding in unknown waters: go in when the tide is high to better the chances that there will be more water 'tween lurking shoals and hull."

"When is high tide, I wonder?" asked Delon, glancing at the disappearing crescent of the moon, then across at Arin. She in turn looked to Alos.

"With a moon like that, it'll be 'round mid of night," groaned the oldster, "but even so, it would be a damnfool thing to try to sail the fangs in the depths of the dark."

"Wouldst thou rather sail in under the eyes of the Rovers?"

"Madness. Madness. It's all madness," moaned Alos.

"Nevertheless . . ."

"All right. All right," the oldster whined. "We'll make the attempt at high tide. But when we get killed, don't come running to me for forgiveness."

Delon burst out in laughter.

With the seas yet running high from the storm of the day before, onward they sailed toward the isle, the offshore wind now blowing directly from the land with the coming of the dark. As the stars wheeled through the sky, the night inched forward by six candlemarks, and they came to where Arin could hear the roll of distant surf crashing against jagged rocks. Still they tacked onward, and soon all could hear the surge and swash of billows dashing against uncounted teeth of stone and purling back through, leaving behind a faint swirl of luminous wake. On they sailed and on, drawing nearer to the thunder of surf whelming on unyielding rock. Egil scanned his charts and conferred with Arin, who gazed at the stars above. Finally he said, "If these charts be right, Alos, then we've struck land north of the cove. Bear south a league or so."

"Prepare to come about," called the oldster to his seasoned crew, and Delon, Aiko, Ferret, and Burel all laid hands upon the sheets, ready to uncleat the lines at Alos's command and pay out or take up as needed. "Coming about," called Alos, and he shoved the tiller hard over, his crew on the starboard loosing sheets while those on the larboard took up. And the *Brise* swung her bow through the eye of the wind, her momentum carrying her past the luff, her sails bellying full and snapping taut as she came onto the new heading and bore south on a starboard beam reach, running parallel to the glimmering coastal waters thundering upon the shoals.

As she fared this direction, Egil bade the crew to lower all sails but the main and jib, for maneuvering through the Serpent's Fangs at night would be a dangerous task, requiring swift response on behalf of all, and this meant running without four of the canvases: the jib top, the fore stay, the square, and the gaff top. Yet though they fared on but two of her sails, still the *Brise* ran fleet, for the off-shore wind blew braw and filled the canvas fair.

South they scudded along the shore for a full league and a half, and then Arin pointed to the fore and right and said, "There is the mouth of a cove."

None other aboard could see aught but the faint glimmer of the pounding surf and the dark silhouette of the isle looming nigh.

"Sail on past," Egil commanded Alos. " 'Tis a goodly while ere midnight, ere the tide is caught high 'tween flow and ebb, and Arin will see if this is Serpent Cove and if the guide-rocks yet stand."

"Bear starboard somewhat," said Arin, and Alos, shivering, edged the tiller over until she called "Enough."

Now the *Brise* skimmed alongside the rocks, the fangs some tens of yards away, great surges lifting the ship, surf booming against the rocks, as across the width of the cove fared the sloop, with Arin leaning out over the starboard rail and peering ahead.

"Aye, there's one of the tall ones," said Arin, "and across another, and . . . finally the third." She turned to Egil as the ship clove onward. "This is indeed Serpent Cove."

Egil shook his head in wonder, for all he could see were shapes black on black in the upflung water, shapes he surmised were rocks.

"Turn to the larboard," said Egil, "and run her out to sea and back up the coast. We'll come again when the tide is slack, but this time we'll take her through."

"But the surf, Egil, the surf," wailed Alos. "It's too high and hammering against the rocks. We'll never get past them all."

"The seas are still running with yesterday's blow, yet we've no choice," said Egil. "We cannot remain standing offshore until they settle down, for Fortune alone has kept us from being spotted; we cannot count on Her keeping Her smiling face turned our way. Nay, Alos, to delay risks all, and I would not have us taken by the Rovers while we wait for the waters to run calm. —Now run her back north and fare in an oval till it's time to take her through."

Moaning and trembling, Alos called for the crew to

make ready to come about, and then he and the others swung the ship away from the rocks. When they were well out, he made another turn to the north, chill sweat adrip from his brow.

"You have the eyes of a cat, love; either that or the gaze of an owl."

Arin smiled at Egil, then clasped his hand and leaned her head on his chest. Yet she said nought.

"I need a drink," said Alos. "Medicinal brandy will do. And don't tell me you have none, for I saw what you put in that locked chest of herbs."

"Nay, Alos," replied Arin, without lifting her head. "We need thee steady and sober to get us through."

"But that's just it, Dara, I ain't steady. Instead I'm shaking like a leaf. Surely one little tot would settle me right down, don't you know?"

Aiko growled and moved away from Burel to sit next to the oldster. Then she whispered something in his ear. "Eep!" squeaked Alos and clutched his crotch and flinched aside.

As Aiko returned to Burel's side, Arin loosed Egil and moved to Alos and put her arm about his quaking shoulders and began to hum a crib song she'd heard a human mother sing long past. In the starlight she did not miss the doleful look that stole over Alos's visage and crept into his good eye, a look which only she could see. Finally she whispered, "Fear not, Alos, together we shall succeed."

"Stand ready on the jib; stand ready on the main," shrilled Alos above the roar of the surf.

"Starboard a bit, Alos," cried Arin, leaning out over the larboard rail and peering ahead into the spray. "That's good. That's good. True her up now."

The *Brise* cut a foaming white wake in the water, the churning trail faintly luminous as the sloop ran at an angle toward the jagged Serpent's Fangs, waves booming into the stone though the tide stood between turns. And the glittering stars, cold and silent, looked down on the desperate run, for speed was needed to keep the surf from carrying the ship and all her crew onto the deadly rocks.

Now the ship fled in among the fangs, the first guide-rock nearly grazing the larboard hull as Arin quickly moved to the starboard to sight on the guide-rock ahead. Billows crashed in against the stones, upflung water hurtling over the *Brise* and down upon all, drenching ship and sails and crew. Swiftly Arin swiped at her eyes and stared steadily at a rock taller than the others, the salt stinging and filling her gaze with tears, tears which she blinked away.

"Larboard, ease larboard, Alos!" she called. "Now steady as she goes!"

"Stand by to come about," screeched Alos, his frightened voice all but a squeak.

And the ship sped through the roaring blackness, death to the left and right, her bow crashing, waves smashing, spume flying, water drenching all.

"Now, Alos! Now!" shouted Arin.

"Now," shrieked Alos, haling hard on the tiller, "bring her about!"

Zzzzzz . . . Loose ropes buzzed against cleats as strong hands haled hard against the lines. 'Round came the bow of the *Brise,* a tall rock to the starboard looming but an arm's span away.

As the ship heeled over, *Whoom!* a great wave crashed into stone, the curl smashing down to the decks as Arin shifted toward the larboard rail. She lost her footing in the thundering wash and hurtled hard into the coaming. Floundering a moment, at last she reached up to grip the larboard side rail, and groggily she struggled to her feet. Shaking her head to clear it, she leaned out and peered to the fore, as spume and spray and roaring water crashed down on the *Brise.*

"Alos! To starboard!" she screamed. "Starboard now!"

Even as the oldster hauled the tiller hard over, a great darkness loomed on the left and—*gwrrrwwwkkk* . . .—the hull ground against stone, the speeding ship shuddering as the rock juddered along its side; but a surge in the water lifted the *Brise* banging and thudding up and away, and suddenly they were clear of the fang and racing toward disaster beyond.

"Starboard, starboard," cried Arin above the roar of the

hammering waves. Again Alos hauled on the tiller, and the *Brise* responded, and moments later Arin called out, "Now swing larboard a point and square her up and stand ready."

As the ship flew along its new course through fangs and thunder and spray, Alos tried to cry out, but all he emitted was a thin squeak, and so Egil shouted to the crew, "Stand ready to come about to larboard, ten points on my command!"

Whoom! Waves thundered into rock, water leaping to pour over all, and yet Arin cleared her vision and cried, "Stand by! . . . Stand by! . . . Stand by! . . . Now! Now, Alos, now!"

"Now!" shouted Egil. "Come about, now!"

Zzzzzz . . . Again wet rope buzzed against cleats as the *Brise* swung leftward 'round a great striated stone to veer sharply larboard, from north-northwest by the compass toward a southwestern run, Alos hauling the tiller hard over to make the sharp-angled turn, the jib and main luffing as the bow swung through the eye of the offshore wind; then the canvas snapped taut once more as it filled with the sharp-driving air and the sloop put her shoulder to the sea and ran through a tangle of deadly rocks for the cove beyond.

"True southwest," called Arin. "Steady as she goes."

Past her fangs, past her rocks, past her booming surf, into the throat of the serpent they sailed, the *Brise* battered but running true. And as they came into clear water at last, pressed beyond his meager limits, Alos fainted dead away.

CHAPTER 61

As Aiko carried unconscious Alos to a bunk below, Egil took the helm. "Keep a sharp lookout, there's a Rover town somewhere ahead, and perhaps a Wizard's tower. Arin, love, I'll especially need your eye."

Into the narrow cove they fared, the inlet but a mile or so wide, and they tacked southeasterly along its length for a league or so before the snake began to bend, swinging sinuously to the right. To either hand stood jungle shores, trees thick and tall, vines dangling down, fronds and undergrowth choking the way below, or so Arin said, for in the starlight only she could make out the lay of the entangled surround.

As they came 'round the turn, Arin hissed, "Fare to the larboard, *chier,* I see lights ahead. Lanterns." But Egil had already pushed the tiller over, for he had espied them as well. "Trim up," he called to his crew, keeping his voice low.

They swung to the larboard and more lights came into view, the distant yellow glow of lanterns scattered here and there, some shining through windows, others aswing in the breeze.

" 'Tis a fair-sized town," said Arin, "tucked in the curve of the land. Ships lie at anchor or moor at piers along the starboard shore."

As they drew closer, Egil said, "It's after the turn of the night. I ween for most part the town lies asleep as do the ships' crews. But even so there'll be watches aboard as well as patrolling the streets. Take care and keep talk low, for well does sound carry over water. We'll slip past along the larboard shore."

"I'll ply a plumb line," said Aiko. "It wouldn't do to run aground on their very doorstep."

Egil grunted his assent. "Signal only if the depth is less than two fathoms."

Aiko moved forward, pausing at a midship deck locker to dredge up a sounding line, then she stepped to the bow and began casting the bob.

Egil changed course again, for now the headwind was blowing directly down the channel and he had no choice but to tack. Still he clung to the larboard shore, hauling into the wind, beating forward in short tacks, changing direction often to remain as far away as practical from the town on the starboard shore.

Steadily they drew nigh the town, and now they could hear a man singing somewhere, while elsewhere a woman shrieked in a rage cut short. A dog barked, and then another, to lapse into yips then silence as a gruff voice shouted imprecations in an unknown tongue— Kistanian, they presumed.

Keeping to the darkness cloaking the larboard shore, they tacked opposite buildings and ships across the channel on the southeastern end of town, and from the stern of one of the dhows there came a muted giggle and the slap of a hand on broad flesh.

Once again Egil turned on a new tack, the only sounds issuing from the sloop were that of rope gently creaking and the soft plash of Aiko's leaden bob. And still the Ryodoan had made no signal, the water being more than two fathoms deep where they fared.

Again, somewhere, a dog began barking in the stillness, this one to keep up its clamor, but whether it was sounding a warning or after a rat or some such, none aboard the *Brise* could say, and none ashore seemed to care.

Finally they slipped past the northerly end of town— with its buildings ramshackle, and its weatherworn ships anchored sparsely or beached, fishing vessels mostly, or so did Arin describe.

And tacking and beating on close hauls, soon they were beyond another turn of the snake, the *Brise* now out of sight of the town and running in midchannel once more.

Dawn found them yet faring more or less westerly within the long, long cove, some fifteen miles past the

Rover town in all. And still Arin had seen no Wizard's tower ensconced on the jungle slopes. Nor had she seen signs of any other dwellings along the tropical shores: no beached boats, no piers, no pathways, no buildings or huts, not even a lean-to. All seemed abandoned, or as if it had never been inhabited in the first place. Yet clear-water streams tumbled down from the slopes and into the brackish inlet; fish could be seen in the channel; trees bearing fruit stood along the shore; and as the day came unto the land, monkeys began chattering in the high canopy and iridescent birds sang and flitted through the air, these dawnlight movements and sounds adding to the incessant whirl and whine of midges and gnats teeming 'round, the swarm now joined by tiny, blood-hungry black flies, all held at bay by the pungent liquid Arin had smeared on the flesh of the crew.

"Well," said Delon, as he scanned the shores nearby and found no sign of habitation, "it seems as if there isn't anything worth coming here for, else we'd've seen signs of living."

At his side, Aiko said, "Either that, or something dreadful lies ahead."

Burel looked up from the blade he was oiling. "Your tiger?"

Aiko nodded and said, "She begins to whisper of peril."

Burel grunted and took stone to the curved edge of his saber once more.

Egil at the tiller said, "I think we need lay anchor here and take ease. It's been nearly the full day 'round for some, and a half day 'round for the rest. Still, someone should stand watch while the others sleep. Delon, Ferret, you've been up longest; take to the bed now." Egil turned to Arin. "And you, love, to bed as well, for you've been on watch all night. Burel and Aiko and I will moor the ship, then I'll stand first ward. When I need to take my own rest, I'll awaken someone to spell me."

"Alos," declared Aiko. "By midmorn he'll have slept long enough."

When midmorn came, the heat was oppressive, the air muggy and completely still, and but for the whine of an insect or two, a vast silence fell over the jungle, as if life itself refused to move in the stifling atmosphere.

Alos was bathed in dripping sweat, his sparse fringe of hair plastered against his neck, his clothing drenched, great droplets of perspiration runnelling down his face and body and limbs, all of it refusing to evaporate in the sultry air. And although the oldster drank copious quantities of water, still he could not seem to get enough. And every now and again he dangled his shirt over the side to dip it down into the cove, drawing the cloth up sopping wet to wash over his face and arms and chest.

The comrades were scattered all over the decking, for it was too sweltering to sleep below, and even though they lay in shade in the open air, still they found little rest.

Somewhat past the noontide, Egil began to moan in his sleep, and Arin awakened to hold him while another ill dream tormented his soul.

Weary and haggard, they got underway in early afternoon, the *Brise* now moving slowly in the light air wafting inland up the cove, the breeze providing little relief from the stultifying heat.

Still they journeyed onward, the ship's sails set wing on wing in the light wind. Another league they went and another beyond that, the breeze seeming to freshen the deeper into the cove they fared.

The land about them began to rise, and here and there they started seeing runs of sheer stone. And still they sailed forward, while the sun slid down the sky, a thin crescent moon chasing after.

And all the while Aiko's tiger growled of nearing peril.

And as the sun lipped the horizon, they rounded a final turn, and in the distance dead ahead to the south they could see the root of the snake hemmed in by soaring stone. But it was not the sheer-sided bluffs at the end of Serpent Cove which drew their full attention, nor was it the dhow moored at a dock below; instead it was the fortress atop, the setting sun highlighting a tower in one corner and standing above the walls.

And even as they heeled the ship sharply full about and

reversed course to slide back out of sight, Egil at the tiller ground his teeth and hissed, "At last I've found you, you bastard," for he was certain they had finally located the tower of the Wizard Ordrune.

CHAPTER 62

In the twilight they slipped the *Brise* into hiding in a cut along the southern shore. And as they assembled and packed the gear they planned to use to gain the top of the tower, Alos looked on in desperation and groaned, "This is madness, I say, madness. Assaulting a Wizard's tower. Sheer madness."

"We know what you think of it, Alos, old man," said Delon, as he arranged a climbing harness in his pack. "Nevertheless, it's what we must do. And you're welcome to come along."

"Me? Come along? I'm not foolish enough to go anywhere near. I'm staying here with the ship."

"*Okubyomono,*" hissed Aiko, binding a rope into a hank.

Paying her no heed, Alos said, "When you all get caught, don't think I'm coming to fetch you. No sir. Come first light and I'm hauling anchor."

Arin paused in her preparations and stepped to the oldster and took him by the hand. "Alos, first light may be too soon, depending on what we find. I would have thee wait through two full nights ere taking leave."

Alos puffed and heaved and would not look her in the eye, yet she gently grasped his trembling chin and turned his face her way. A tear trickled down the oldster's cheek, and finally he nodded sharply once.

"Well and good, Alos. Well and good." Arin stepped away and strung her bow.

Soon all was set, and they unshipped the small dinghy from atop the cabin and lowered it into the water. Aiko and Burel hefted their backpacks and took up their weapons and clambered over the side and into the boat, and Egil ferried them to the shore yards away. On the next trip he tethered a rope to the small craft so that Alos could haul it back to the sloop, then he rowed the rest across.

All now ashore, Egil adjusted the straps on his own backpack, then turned to the others. "Ready?"

Ready.

"Then let's go."

As they turned to enter the jungle, Alos called out one last time, "If you get caught, I'll not lift a hand to save you. Not lift a hand, you hear?"

Into the undergrowth they disappeared: Arin leading the way, Aiko immediately after, with Burel, Delon, and Ferret following, Egil in line coming last.

Darkness engulfed them, for the sun had set and the moon with it as the eventide had swallowed the land. Above the canopy, stars now glittered brightly in the night sky, though only a faint glimmer of their light filtered down through the interlace to reach into the jungle below. Even though Ferret carried a hooded lantern, its light gleaming out through a slender crack, except for Arin with her Dylvana eyes, to the companions all was dark shapes looming at hand, black on black in blackness, and only by following closely did they not lose one another or the way ahead. And they did not wish to risk detection by opening the lantern hood wider to see through the ebony murk. In this utter gloom they could hear stirrings and swashings, and something scurried away through the thick leaf mold, and something else crashed through the brush, and they drew weapons and faced outward, seeing nothing, yet nothing came upon them. Through ferns and fronds they pressed, past dangling vines and small clinging plants and over great fallen trees, the trunks covered with moss and mold and wet toadstools and other soft, pliable growths.

Slowly the land rose, and upward they fared, and as they gained in altitude the darkness became less black, for the soil turned rocky and the jungle thinned. Finally they came into the open along a high rocky bluff, and down below lay Serpent Cove, what there was left of it.

Ferret slammed the lantern shutter down tight, for in the near distance stood the fortress, no more than a mile away, its stone walls flickering with yellow torchlight, its tower looming up in the darkness. Great iron gates stood in the center of the north-facing bastion wall, a barbican atop looking down into the cove below. A roadway issued out from the gates to run alongside the fortress and then, in a series of switchbacks, twist down to the pier below, where the dhow was moored.

Arin and her companions stood on the east bluff of Serpent Cove; the tower stood at the northwest corner of the bastion. After a moment Egil said, "There's no moon to reveal us, and only starlight above. We should be able to follow this bluff a good way, then work our way 'round sides and back, to seek advantage in what we might find, and if nothing better, continue on 'round to come straight at the tower and up its side as planned."

As they drew closer they could see warders posted atop the ramparts. And closer still they heard a clatter of gears, as of a portcullis being raised. The iron gates swung open, and a torch-bearing troop marched out and down the switchbacks toward the dhow as the portcullis behind clattered again.

"They look like Foul Folk," said Arin. "*Loka*, I ween."

"What would Drôkha be doing here?" asked Delon.

"It is said that Black Mages draw the Foul Folk to them," replied Arin.

"And Ordrune is indeed a Black Mage," growled Egil.

"If what you say is true, Dara," said Delon, "then perhaps Trolls and Ghûls and Hèlsteeds and other such reside in Ordrune's tower. If so, then our task may be doubly hard."

Aiko touched her chest—there where a red tiger lay—but the golden warrior said nought.

Finally they faded into the fringes of the jungle and began slowly working their way 'round the fortress, pausing now and then to slip forward and see if there was aught to give advantage in going over the parapets rather than climbing up the outside of the tower.

The walls themselves stood some thirty feet high, and a wide strip of land had been cleared of growth about the bastion, the land laid bare to give archers above clear arrowcasts at any attacking foe, laid bare as well so that enemies could not easily come upon the fortress unseen. Even so, the companions had come prepared, for at Ferret's suggestion in Sabra, they had purchased reversible cloaks in the event they might prove useful, cloaks which would blend into the terrain—greyish brown on one side, grey-green on the other—cloaks that were now rolled and lashed to their packs. And as they examined the open strip and the bulwarks beyond, she whispered that they could cover themselves and crawl forward undetected across the bare land, or so she believed.

And the stars wheeled silently above as the comrades watched swart guards pace atop stone walls.

Finding nought to change their plans, back the companions faded into the jungle to creep 'round to the south, and then once again move forward to examine the back wall. Long they looked as the night deepened, and just as they had found on the eastern bulwark, there seemed no advantage here either, nothing to change their plan to climb the tower.

Once again they faded back. Slowly they worked around to the west as stars wheeled above. When they moved forward to the edge of the bush and examined the western ramparts, still climbing the tower seemed best.

Now they passed through the undergrowth and vines and trees to come opposite the northwest corner, to come opposite the high stone tower, wavering torchlight illuminating its inner side.

Delon murmured, "It seems your drawing was right, Egil: there appears to be no banquette around the outer wall of the tower."

"There are arrow slits, though," said Arin. "And if warded on the inside—"

"Fear not," said Delon. "From what I have seen, the walls and tower are large blocks piled atop one another, some mortared, others not. I believe there's enough crevices and handholds so that we can all free-climb the stone. We'll not need to drive a single rock-nail; our ascent will be silent."

Arin glanced at the sky. "It is nearing mid of night."

"Then let's go," said Egil, untying his cloak from his pack. He looked at Ferret in the starlight. "Dun side out?"

"Indeed," she replied.

Slowly, carefully, a yard at a time, on their stomachs they inched across the open terrain, listening for sounds of alarm while watching the movement upon the walls to see if there were any change. Now they came into the shadow of the tower, and all seemed at ease, yet of a sudden there was a flurry atop the ramparts and a great shouting erupted.

Ferret called out quietly, "Steady. Don't move. It may not be us."

With a grinding clatter, the portcullis was raised.

"Be ready to flee," sissed Egil. "They are too many to fight. We must at all odds avoid capture by that monster inside."

Aiko growled, but said nought.

Now several Drôkha marched out to peer over the precipice and down into the cove.

Horrified screams came wailing from below, shrieking up and over the rim, followed by keening and blubbering and then more terrified shrieks. And a troop of Foul Folk came trampling up the final switchback and onto the verge above. And stumbling among them and jerked along, shackled and screaming and pleading, floundered a weeping one-eyed old man.

Alos.

CHAPTER 63

As the Drôkken band dragged screaming Alos into the fortress and the portcullis clattered down, Egil declared, "We must rescue him."

Aiko, nearby, in a toneless voice said, "If we attempt to do so it will jeopardize the mission."

Egil turned his head toward her and replied, "If we do not, he will die horribly."

Ferret hissed, "But this is the man who said if we were captured he would not lift a finger to help us."

Egil now faced her. "He was not put to the test."

Aiko said, "If he had been, he would have failed."

"Would you have us fail, Aiko?" asked Egil. "For it is we who are now being put to the test."

Aiko looked at Egil impassively and said, "Do you ask that we balance the life of a single man against all those to be lost should this mission fail?"

Delon hissed, "Regardless as to whether we weigh the needs of one against many, we must go forward now while the guards are occupied with the spectacle of a shrieking old man in chains." Delon began crawling forward, toward the base of the tower, depending on the concealment of his cloak as well as the distraction of Alos's capture to see him safely to his goal.

The others followed after . . .

. . . and in a trice they had reached the spire.

Still the old man's screams drifted on the air, but suddenly they were chopped off, as if a door had closed.

Delon stood in the darkness below the tower and examined the stone. Beside him Ferret ran her hands across the blocks and said, "Rather effortless, I would think."

Delon nodded, then turned to the rest. "The blocks are

large and rough and the mortar sparse. We should all be able to free-climb, though I will snap a short line from me to Dara Arin, while Burel does the same with Egil."

"But Burel and I must both be unfettered in case there is a need to fight," protested Egil, examining the stone. "In spite of my inexperience, I think I can manage this."

Delon looked at the Fjordlander, then said, "Burel, stay near him in the event he needs aid."

Aiko said, "I will lead."

They shed all unnecessary equipment, and even though they planned on using no climbing gear, still they donned the harnesses and attached ropes and lanterns and hammers along with rock-nails and snap-rings, for as Delon said, "We simply don't know what might lie above."

Aiko and Burel rearranged the straps and buckles of their sword belts to sling the weapons across their backs. Arin slipped her bow and quiver across her shoulders, and then Delon snapped a rope between himself and the Dara.

Finally all was ready, and with Aiko in the lead and Egil immediately after, up the fortress wall they clambered, the Ryodoan whispering instructions to guide his hands and feet. To Egil's left and slightly below climbed Burel. Delon followed with Arin trailing after, Ferret at her side.

Up they scaled, up the rough stone, some blocks with knobs and sharp projections on cragged faces, others smooth as if worked. But in the main it was cracks and crevices between the blocks they used to ascend, toeholds and footholds, fingerholds and handholds. And neither Arin nor Egil, with their lack of experience, found the going difficult, though at times the diminutive Dylvana had to stretch to grasp the next purchase.

Up the outer wall they climbed, in the darkest shadow, for torches atop the fortress walls yet illuminated the night. Now they mounted past the level of the parapets, depending on the girth of the spire to shield them from the warders on patrol. Up past dark arrow slits they scaled. If there had been alert guards inside the spire, perhaps then the climbers would have been detected. Yet there sounded no alarm and in darkness they ascended.

Climbing in virtual silence, soon they were more than

halfway to the top. Then nearly three-quarters. Of a sudden Aiko stopped, and in the starlight and dim cast of torch Egil could see her pointing down and away. As the others paused as well, Egil set his fingers hard into the crevice, and then he turned his head, his gaze to follow Aiko's outstretched arm. Down in the cove below, and by the torchlight at the pier, he could see the *Brise* moored next to the dhow at Ordrune's dock. Egil silently groaned, for not only had the Foul Folk dragged Alos here, they had brought the sloop to Ordrune's doorstep as well, and he knew they needed a ship to escape from the Wizard's lair. Yet how could they get to the *Brise* undetected and slip away unseen?

Aiko began to climb again, and Egil set the problem aside and followed after, the rest now ascending as well.

Finally Aiko reached the level of the windows atop. She began to sidle toward the western aperture, moving toward a place where she would be exposed should any warder look up. Egil climbed to the same level and then followed her, Burel coming after. Slowly Aiko moved out from the darkest shadows and into dim torchlight, and she paused and set her fingers, then leaned out slightly to scan beyond the girth of the tower and down at the length of the western banquette. Satisfied that no sentry was looking, she edged on toward the window.

In a step or two she reached the side of the dark gape. Now she listened carefully and finally risked a glance. At last she drew a sword and then stepped across and onto the sill and then disappeared within.

Egil followed, and without hesitating at the window he stepped in after her.

Aiko had lit her hooded lantern, and a thin slit of light shone dimly in the circular chamber, though not enough to glow outside. Egil found her closing the drapes on the other windows as planned, and he joined her as Burel squeezed through the gap. Then Delon entered, followed by Arin and finally Ferret.

Delon unsnapped the rope between himself and Arin, then quickly closed the last drape across the window they had entered, and now all were covered. Aiko and Burel with weapons in hand took a stand beside the stairwell door, and Egil opened the shutter of the lantern a bit wider to look for the chest, quickly finding it.

Then Egil and Delon drew their weapons and moved to join Aiko and Burel, while Ferret, with Arin at hand, squatted beside the ironbound box with its three locks. Using her lantern, Ferret carefully examined the whole of the chest without touching it, seeking traps and trips and alarms. Finding none, Ferret glanced up at Arin. "Dara, use your special sight and see if this is charmed."

Arin nodded and gazed at the chest and attempted to <see>. "A faint aura surrounds the box, Ferai."

"What does it mean?"

"I do not know."

Ferret drew in a deep breath and slowly let it out. "Well, alarm or not, trap or not, we've got to get inside. Watch it closely for any change."

Ferret then looked at the three locks, scrupulously investigating them as well. Finally she unrolled a leather-wrapped set of lockpicks, and selecting one, she looked at Arin and then touched the rightmost latch.

"No change."

Now Ferret inserted the lockpick within, and again there was no shift in the aura.

Ferret began probing within the keyhole.

Time eked by.

click!

Ferret glanced at Arin. The Dylvana shook her head.

Ferret set the shackle aside, then moved to the leftmost lock, this time selecting a different pick.

Once more time crept, and the only sounds to be heard were the soft susurration of breathing and the tiny scritching of brass within steel.

click!

Again Arin shook her head.

Now Ferret moved to the center lock and peered long at the peculiar keyhole. Finally she sighed softly and selected two picks, inserting both within.

Time passed and time more, and in the distance they heard a call and the tramp of feet, the sounds muted by the heavy drapes. Egil looked at Aiko and murmured, "The change of guard?"

"Perhaps," she replied.

"What does your tiger say?"

"She is greatly agitated, and has been so ever since the fortress came into view, though the closer we got, the more disturbed she became. Right now she is yowling that peril is at hand."

Egil took a deep breath and then let it out. "Even so, Aiko, we can do nothing but wait."

Still time eked past. Finally Ferret took up a third pick and prodded it into the clasp past the other two. She hissed through her teeth, as if in great effort, and muttered nearly inaudibly to herself.

click!

Releasing a gust of air, Ferret looked up at Arin. The Dylvana murmured, "No." Ferret set the third lock to the floor, then ran her hands about the lid of the chest, and cautiously, carefully, she raised it a crack.

Arin gasped. "The aura shifted color."

"A trap? An alarm?"

"I do not know."

They listened carefully, but no alarum sounded without.

Finally, holding her breath, Ferret raised the lid an inch and then stopped.

"No change," said Arin.

Then Ferret raised the lid steadily, until at last the chest stood gaping.

She waited.

Nothing happened.

Peering inside, she said, "*Merde!* Nothing but papers."

Now Arin moved forward. "*Vada!* They all glow."

With Ferret's help, Arin began examining the scrolls within. One by one they unwrapped them; some they cast aside immediately, others they paused to read. And those Ferret could not cipher she gave over to Arin. The floor about the two became littered with parchment. Of a sudden, Arin hissed, "Listen to this:

"Here I have hidden the green stone, a jadelike talisman of power, now chained by the Kraken Pool in a chest of Dwarven-made silver. The pool itself lies deep inside the rock of Dragons' Roost, with but two ways in. One entrance leading down to the chest stands on the great ledge, a shelf the Dragons jealously guard, for it is their crossing point to the Dragonworld of Kelgor. Straight down the sheer stone from the ledge the other entrance lies, just under the churning surface of the Boreal Sea. Underwater a crevasse splits deeply down a mile or more, a great crack cleaving back into the mountain stone, and through this chasm and outward hurtles a powerful current, a flow so strong no swimmer can brave, driven, I deem, by the Great Maelstrom spinning in the distance nearby. From this underwater entrance a pathway leads a furlong or so back to the Kraken Pool where the chest of the Dragonstone is chained; at high tide, the path is submerged nearly the full of its length, but at low tide only the outermost hundred feet lies underwater, though none can swim in against the current."

Arin looked up from the parchment. "This is the one!"

In that moment soft laughter sounded, and a voice said, "I wondered what brought you here."

Glass shattered.

An odor filled the room.

As Egil's mind spun down toward darkness, light filled the chamber, and stepping forth from an impenetrable cast of arcane shade at the side of one of the tall cabinets, a dark-robed Mage emerged.

"Ordrune, you bastard," choked Egil, and he feebly raised his axe, but it fell from his numbing fingers to clank upon the floor, to Egil's ears the sound deafening, clanging like a great bell of doom in the absolute blackness that engulfed him whole.

CHAPTER 64

Egil's own pulse hammered through his skull with thunderous pain. He was lying in something damp and a sour odor filled his nostrils and he came near to gagging. Groaning, he rolled onto his back, a dank squash accompanying his movement. He opened his eyes to flickering torchlight. Dark stone met his sight. He raised a trembling hand to his head, pounding with the aftereffects of whatever vapor the Mage had used. Wincing, he levered himself to a sitting position and looked about, his gaze falling on stone walls, stone ceiling, stone floors, stone pillars, and iron bars embedded in stone. He was in a cell, and ranging to the left and right were adjacent cells, with another row across the way. At one end of the corridor stood an iron-clad door with an iron grille over a small warder window. He sat on damp, rotting straw, and just beyond the bars of his cage stood a rope-handled bucket, while just inside sat a wooden bowl with a wooden spoon, both crusted with long-dried porridge. He did not need to ask where he was, for he had been here before, long past: these were Ordrune's foul mews.

In a cell opposite he saw faint movement in the shadows. His heart plunged into the depths of despair, for he could see that it was Arin, the Dylvana yet unconscious, she, too, a prisoner of the monster Ordrune.

The worst of his nightmares come true, in wretched desolation Egil stood, and the moment he gained his feet, to the right and in a far cell someone began to hiss and weep.

It was Alos.

"Egil," he wailed. "Egil." But then his voice broke into great howling sobs, and although he tried to speak, his words were lost among the blubberings and yowls and gasps.

In individual cells between Egil and Alos, lay Burel and Delon, those two yet rendered senseless by Ordrune's foul gas, though they were beginning to stir. Aiko and Ferret were caged across the way in cells next to Arin. Ferret was completely stripped, her clothing strewn about the cell. As Egil watched, Aiko rolled onto her back.

Egil stepped to the bars of his cell and looked into the bucket. Water. He kneeled and reached through to take up a handful. As he remembered, it was foul-smelling; even so, he splashed it onto the back of his neck to ease his aching head. It gave no noticeable relief.

Now Aiko was afoot, and she, too, moved to the bars of her cell. Impassively, she glanced across at Egil, then turned her gaze toward Alos, the old man yet howling. Then her sight swept across her environs, a baleful look in her eye.

"Oh, Egil, do not take blame," pled Arin. "If any is at fault, then 'tis I, for I should have scanned the chamber with my <sight>. I would have located Ordrune hiding behind his shadow cast."

Aiko touched her own breast. "Dara, it was I who failed, for my tiger yowled that danger was at hand, yet I did nothing."

"Unh," groaned Delon, holding his head. "As I once heard someone say, we must fix the problem and not the blame."

Dressed once again, Ferret reached down and took up the encrusted wooden spoon from her food bowl. After a moment she cast it down, saying, "This is worthless." She looked across at Delon and said, "They took all my lock-picks, even the ones from my hair."

Delon turned up his hands and shrugged. "That's because Ordrune watched as you opened his chest . . . and this time I have no belt buckle to—"

His words were cut shy by a clank at the door. The warder window opened and a Drôkh peered in. With a clatter, a key rattled into the lock to clack it open. The door swung wide and, accompanied by a squad of armed and armored Drôkha, inward stepped Ordrune.

The Mage paused at the first occupied cell to peer in. Alos shrieked and scrambled to the back of his cage and cowered down sissing and whimpering, but all the other prisoners stood defiantly. Sneering, Ordrune moved onward to stop before Aiko; she casually dropped her hand to her waistband. Ordrune laughed. "No, my dear, the star you feebly cast at me in my sanctum went astray, and the others are no longer with you."

Aiko did not reply.

Ordrune moved onward, pausing in turn before the remainder of the prisoners. He came to Egil last and glanced at the red eye patch, a slight frown on his face. But then a look of enlightenment crossed his features. "Well, Captain, you surprise me. I did not think you could find this place again." Ordrune smiled. "Perhaps it is pleasant memories which bring you back, eh? Tell me, Captain, have you been sleeping well?"

Egil's hands gripped the bars, his knuckles white.

"Yes now you are back," said Ordrune. "Perhaps it is because you did not learn your lesson fully the last time." Then he gestured toward the other cells. "It is of no moment, for I have here more than enough to add to your pleasant slumbers, the stuff from which dreams are made."

Egil howled a wordless yell and lunged forward, hands and arms plunging outward between the bars in an attempt to grasp Ordrune, but the Mage was beyond reach. And in that same moment—*crack!*—a Drôkh lashed a quirt down across Egil's arms. Ordrune snarled something in Slûk, and the Drôkh drew back. "I want this one unharmed," added Ordrune, smiling at Egil.

Now the dark Mage turned and started for the iron-clad door, and again he uttered commands in the Slûk tongue. Alos's cage was flung open, and kicking and shrieking, the old man was wrenched out from his cell.

"Perhaps, Captain," called Ordrune over his shoulder, "perhaps we can sit down to a fine meal once again."

"Ordrune, you bastard!" Egil shouted. "Leave the old man alone!"

The plated door slammed shut and the warder window banged to, cutting off the sounds of Alos's squeals and Ordrune's sinister laughter.

Fallen into despair, Egil slumped to the stone floor and whispered, "Ordrune, come back; take me instead."

Aiko squatted and took up her wooden spoon and began grinding the handle against the stone of the floor.

Egil looked up, desperation in his eye. "We've got to get out, else the fate that befell my crew will . . ." His words stuttered to a halt, though all knew what he meant.

"Ferai," called Arin, "canst thou open these locks?"

"I can, given a probe of some sort," said Ferret. "Yet at the moment I am stymied."

Burel turned to Egil. "When does the warder bring food?"

"Are you hungry already?" asked Delon. "For Drôkken fare?"

But Egil replied, "Late. After sundown, I think. At time of their own mess. Then a warder brings food."

"Perhaps he'll have something which Ferai can use as a pick," said the big man.

"Oh," said Delon, enlightened.

"If we get free— No, rather, *when* we get free," said Ferret, "we'll need weapons."

Aiko paused in grinding the wooden spoon against the rough stone block. "When they opened the door"—she gestured at the iron-bound panel at the end of the hallway—"I could see what looked to be a guardroom. Surely there will be weapons there."

"Wait now," said Egil, leaping to his feet. "There is an *armory* just beyond the guardroom . . . or at least there was when last I was here."

"Then if we get out of these cages and through that door," said Aiko, "we have a chance to secure weaponry and make an escape." She resumed her grinding.

"We still have to get past a fortress filled with Drôkha," said Delon.

"And down to the docks where the *Brise* is now moored," added Egil.

"Unless we abandon the ship and fare through the jungle instead," said Burel.

Egil looked across at Arin. "Is it day or night, love?"

"It is a quarter way 'tween sunrise and noon," she replied.

None questioned her answer, for she was a Dylvana with the inborn Elven talent to know at all times where stand the sun, moon, and stars.

Egil grunted and said, "Then we have, I believe, from now till morning to make our escape, for Ordrune slays but a victim a day. He'll not come for another until tomorrow."

"Art thou saying that Alos . . . ?"

"Yes, love. That is Ordrune's way."

"Oh, *chier.*" Arin buried her face in her hands.

Ferret glanced at Arin, and then at Alos's empty cell. Finally she said, "All right, let's not waste his death. Assuming that I can get my hands on something which will free us, what then? What's our next move?" She looked across at Burel. "What choices lie before us, my fatalistic friend? What predestined path will we take?"

Burel grinned wryly, then turned to Egil. "You have been here before, Egil. What would you advise?"

Egil took a deep breath, then said, "Well, assuming we get free and have weapons in our hands, here is what we can do. . . ."

Near sunset by Arin's reckoning, their deliberations were interrupted by a muffled singing from beyond the iron-clad door. The warder window clanked open and a Drôkh peered in, the sound of the boisterous chanty blaring in as well. Then the door was flung wide, and inward came two Drôkha bearing up an old man singing at the top of his lungs:

> "*Old Snorri in a cog*
> *With his three-legged dog*
> *Sailed off on the Boreal Sea.*
> *And the Mystical Maid*
> *At last was well laid,*
> *So she set Snorri Borri's son free.*"

It was Alos.

Drunk.

The Drôkha opened Alos's cage and shoved him within, the oldster reeling forward to collapse facedown in the rot of the sour straw.

Muttering to one another in Slûk, the Drôkha slammed and locked the cell door and withdrew.

"Alos, old man," called Delon, "you're alive!"

Alos rolled over and peered at the ceiling. "Who said that?"

"We thought you were dead," said Ferret.

Alos craned his head up and bleared at the cell. Then he rolled back over and, levering up to hands and knees, he crawled to the bars and rapped a knuckle to one and then hissed, "Oh, no. I'm back in gaol." He began weeping.

"Alos, old man, tell us what happened," called Delon, kneeling at the bars between their cells.

Snubbing and snuffling, the oldster looked over at the bard. "We're trapped, you know," he whined.

In her cell across the way, Aiko turned her back to Alos, but Delon said, "Indeed. Nevertheless, what happened? What did Ordrune do to you?"

"Do?"

"Yes. Where did he take you? What did he do?"

"Why, he gave me some wine. Splendid wine." Alos slumped sideways, then hitched about until he sat with his back to the bars. Then he squinted his good eye and growled, "And he told me who raided the *Solstrále* with his crew of Trolls, the bastard who sunk her down in the chill waters of the Boreal Sea."

Aiko turned. "That's all, Alos? Nothing more?"

Alos frowned in concentration. "It seemed that there might be something else, but—"

". . . Indeed, my friend, it *was* Durlok and his black galley who did the deed, Durlok who thinks to be Gyphon's regent on this world, but it is I, Ordrune, who will be His agent instead. . . ."

". . . Yet tell me, good Alos, just why would a mere seven of you come to my tower? . . ."

". . . A rutting peacock, eh? Why, I would not have guessed. Here, have some more wine. . . ."

". . . Cut off her hand, you say? . . ."

". . . One eye in dark water? What might it mean? . . ."

". . . From the High King's cage with what? Oh well then, that explains how she opened locks I thought beyond any thief's skill to broach. Let me refill your cup. . . ."

". . . They slew Ubrux the Demon? Oh, they are indeed formidable. . . ."

". . . Here, my friend, inhale the fragrance of this vial, and then we'll have some more wine. That's right, just inhale as I tell you in spite of your misgivings, unlike before, you will never again desert your shipmates in their time of need, and you have said nothing of any consequence—yes, yes, inhale—nothing of any consequence at all. . . ."

"—but I am certain that I told him nothing of any consequence."

"You were gone much too long for that to be the whole of it," said Aiko. "What else did you speak of?"

Alos frowned. "The weather. The stifling jungle air. The blood-sucking bugs. Durlok and his black galley Trolls overwhelming the *Solstråle* simply because her captain and crew knew the way into Serpent Cove." He turned and glared at Aiko. "Say, what are you accusing me of?"

"There's more here than meets the eye," hissed Aiko.

It was after sundown when the portal to the outer door was opened and a Drôkh peered in. Then keys rattled in the lock, and a warder entered lugging an iron pot and he kicked the door to behind. He was alone, yet he was cautious and, with snarling gestures, he made each prisoner move to the back of the cell—all but Alos, that is, for the old man was unconscious and slumped down against the bars—before he dipped gruel out of the kettle and into the crusted wooden bowls at each cage.

Aiko glanced at Ferret and received a nod, and when the Drôkh came to Aiko's cell—*"Saté!"* she called.

The guard looked up.

The hurled wooden spoon, its handle sharpened to a cruel point, took him in the throat. The iron pot clanged down on stone, and gargling and clutching at the air, the Drôkh staggered back, crashing into bars behind, where Burel grabbed him and wrenched his chin sideways, breaking his neck.

Aiko reached out and dragged the pot to her and wrested the soft iron bail forward and back, freeing it from the eyelets, then she handed it through the side bars to Ferret.

Ferret set the tip of the iron into a crevice in the stone, bending the nib into a sharp crook. Quickly she inserted the angled end into the lock, and in mere moments—*click!*—the door was open.

Moving from cell to cell, she opened the locks to each, Aiko's first, Alos's last.

The iron-clad outer door was still unlocked. Cautiously they edged it open a crack. The key ring yet dangled from the latch. The guardroom was empty of warders.

Aiko glanced at Egil, a question in her eyes.

"Perhaps they are at mess," sissed Egil.

Silently they slipped through to the armory, and lo! there on a table were arrayed their own weapons and gear.

"Something is not right," growled Aiko.

Arming themselves, Delon went back for Alos, and he came carrying the oldster across his shoulders, Alos dead to the world.

They scooped up as many lanterns as they could find, and following Egil, up a stone stairwell they crept. At the next level they peered out into the courtyard. A crescent moon hung low in the west and in the shadows immediately at hand they saw no one, though up on the torchlit walls warders patrolled.

Again Aiko growled and shook her head, but she said nothing and instead, with Burel, stood guard at the door, while Arin, Egil, and Ferret emptied lantern oil across the wooden floor.

Ferret set it alight, and then they all scurried out into the night, Delon yet bearing unconscious Alos.

As they came into the shadows of the battlements, a

*Rûp*tish horn blatted, and Drôkha cried in harsh alarm, for smoke poured from the building behind. Amid shouts and clamor *Spaunen* rushed down from the parapets, and others came tumbling out from the main building. And in the confusion, none noted the seven who ran the opposite way, up the ramp to the castellations, and then over the wall, Burel now bearing the burden of Alos as he clambered down the rope in the pale moonlight.

Down the switchbacks to the dark, unwarded docks they ran, where, as some made the sloop ready, others set the sails of the moored dhow aflame. And then, in the light breeze now flowing down the cove toward the sea, wing-on-wing the *Brise* fled the conflagration behind.

And from his aerie atop the tower, Ordrune watched as the sloop slipped away in the ruddy light of the flames. Though unforeseen, it was of little or no consequence that the building behind was ablaze and the sails of his ship were on fire, for all was going according to plan.

CHAPTER 65

As shouting Chun battled the blaze in the main building and other Drik and Ghok scrambled down the switchbacks toward the sail-fired dhow, Ordrune strode along the buttressed walls to enter the tower. Inside, the dark Mage made his way to the spiral stairs leading to the chambers below. Down he wound and down, until at last he came into the shadows of a room of manacles and chains and straps and tables and racks and hooks and knives and other such, a room filled with echoes past of agony and terror, a room where astral blazes were wrenched from tortured souls and twisted to malevolent ends.

Crossing this horrific chamber, Ordrune trod toward an iron door barred with three massive metal beams, a door from which emanated the sound of slow monstrous breathing and the stench of carrion. As the dark Mage approached the heavy portal, something massive thundered into the iron, juddering the panel and rattling the bulky hinges and bars . . . and angry skreighs shrieked forth.

Ordrune mouthed a silent word, quelling the sound and fury on the opposite side. Then he raised each of the heavy bars in turn and opened the door and stepped into the reeking fetor beyond.

There he faced a monstrous winged *thing* from elder days, its flailing pinions leathery and black, a single scimitarlike spur jutting forth from the forward bend of each wing, its long beak filled with jagged teeth, the large piercing claws of its feet hooked and clutching and grasping. And it skrawed and clacked and lurched among a litter of bones, bones gnawed and crushed and cracked and splintered for their marrow.

Ordrune looked into one of the creature's glaring yellow eyes and reached up to stroke its long neck. Then the dark Mage smiled and said, "I have a mission for you, my pet."

CHAPTER 66

Down the channel of Serpent Cove fled the *Brise,* her sails spread wide to catch every bit of the following wind. With Alos unconscious in the cabin below, Egil manned the helm, while Ferret and Delon handled the sheet lines. Arin, Aiko, and Burel stood in the stern peering aft, arrows nocked in the event of pursuit, though only Arin could see fully by the light of the thin crescent moon.

"Something is not right," growled Aiko.

Burel glanced at her. "Not right?"

"It was too easy," she replied, "as if Ordrune wanted us to escape."

Burel canted his head. "My sire was slain for merely knowing of the existence of the scroll, and he did not even get to read but a line or two. Yet we know even more, for we heard the whole of the text, the words Dara Arin read. Why would Ordrune kill one with little or no knowledge yet allow others who know its contents in full to escape? It makes no sense, Aiko."

In the pale moonlight Aiko glanced up at the big man. "Even so, Burel, it was as if our way was deliberately kept free of *Kitanai Kazoku.*"

"*Kitanai Kazoku?*"

"Foul Folk."

"Ah."

Delon, holding a line and peering at the enshadowed jungle to either side, said, "Even had Ordrune wanted us free, Aiko, how could he have known of our plans—your sharpened spoon, for instance?"

Egil said, "Perhaps he did not, yet he did know given the opportunity we would attempt escape."

Aiko nodded and added, "Do you think it was pure chance that our weapons were at hand when we fled?"

Delon shrugged, saying, "It was, after all, an armory where we found our gear. Where else would you expect weapons to be stored? I think you look too far to find a plot, Aiko."

Arin said, "Could it not simply be that Fortune turned Her smiling face our way?"

Aiko looked from Delon to Arin yet said nought, her gaze impassive . . .

. . . And down Serpent Cove sailed the *Brise,* the strengthening wind blowing toward the distant sea.

The moon set, leaving but the glimmer of the spangle overhead to light the way. Arin moved to the fore and used her Elven sight to guide them. Time edged past, along with the slow miles, as night gradually wheeled toward the dawn. Stars above shone down, like silent observers watching desperate life unfold below. And still the *Brise* sailed onward.

It was dark when they slipped past the town in the throat of Serpent Cove, dawn but a faint glimmer in the east. And though the tide was in full ebb and low, they had no choice but to run the fangs in the blackness, for to delay risked discovery by the Rovers.

"As we did before," called Egil, "strike all sails but the main and jib." Working together, Delon, Burel, Aiko, and Ferret took down the jib top, fore stay, square, and the gaff top and stowed them below. Arin took station on the starboard wale to give Egil directions at the tiller, while the others took up lines for the difficult run ahead. And though they fared on but two of her sails, still the *Brise* ran fleet, for the offshore wind blew strongly and bellied the sails full.

"Stand ready on the jib; stand ready on the main," called Egil above the surge of waves as they began their run true northeast toward the striated guide-rock.

"Trim starboard a bit, Egil, half a point," cried Arin, leaning out over the rail and peering ahead. "That's good. That's good. True her up now."

The *Brise* cut a foaming white wake in the water, the churning trail faintly luminous as the sloop ran at an angle toward the jagged Serpent's Fangs, the rocks jutting taller now that the tide was low and ebbing.

"Remember, all," cried Egil, "we will jibe starboard a full ten points to square up on the next guide. Stand ready."

Now the ship fled in among the fangs, the inner guide-rock yet ahead. But even as jagged stone slid by, Arin cried, "Oh, no!"

"What is it, love," shouted Egil, spray showering over the *Brise* in the darkness as her bow churned through the waves.

"Another ship, a dhow, has begun a run inward toward the fangs. 'Tis a Rover craft."

"Damn, damn!" cried Egil. "We can't come about in these rocks. We've no choice but to try to run past her."

"How can they see?" called Ferret. "Have they an Elf aboard?"

Arin did not answer as—*Whoom!*—waves thundered into rock, water leaping to pour over all; instead she called, "Stand by! . . . Stand by! . . . Stand by to make the turn! . . . Now! Now, Egil, now!"

"Now!" shouted Egil. "Jibing now!"

Zzzzzz . . . Wet rope buzzed against cleats as the *Brise* swung rightward 'round the great striated stone to veer sharply starboard, from true northeast by the compass toward a south-southeastern run, Egil hauling the tiller hard over to make the sharp-angled turn, the crew ducking the boom as it slammed 'round from starboard to port as the ship jibed before the wind, the canvas full taut with the sharp-driving air as the sloop on a beam reach slammed her shoulder to the sea and ran through a tangle of deadly fangs for the guide-rock beyond, while crew let line and took up.

And in that same moment the Rover dhow to the east entered the fangs opposite.

Arin quickly moved to the larboard rail to sight on the guide-stone ahead. Billows crashed in against the huge rocks, upflung waves hurtling over the *Brise* and down, drenching ship and sails and crew. Arin shook water from her eyes and stared steadily at an oncoming rock taller than the others.

"Starboard, ease starboard, Egil!" she called. "Now steady as she goes!"

"Hoy now," came a slurred cry, and Alos stumbled topside from the cabin below. "What's all this—?"

"Stand by to jibe larboard a full twenty-eight points," called Egil. "Alos, 'ware the boom!"

"What?" cried Alos, lurching out from the cabin door as the ship sped through the roaring blackness, death to the left and right, her bow crashing, waves smashing, spume flying, water drenching all.

Without turning loose of her line, Aiko kicked the old man's legs out from under him, and just as Alos slammed down to the deck—

"Now, Egil! Now!" shouted Arin.

"Jibing now!" called Egil, haling hard on the tiller.

Zzzzz . . . Again loose ropes buzzed against cleats as strong hands haled hard on the opposite lines. 'Round came the bow of the *Brise,* a tall rock to the larboard looming but an arm's span away. *Wham!* the boom slammed across from port to starboard as the ship heeled over and the stern swung through the wind and the *Brise* came to a larboard beam reach.

Water whelmed into stone and leapt into air as the sloop sped through and onward, while Arin shifted to the starboard rail, stepping over floundering Alos to do so. She leaned out and peered to the fore, where an oncoming Rover dhow loomed.

"Egil!" she screamed. "Trim to starboard now!"

Even as Egil hauled the tiller hard over, a great darkness hulked on the left and—*rrrnnnkkk . . .*—the hull ground against wood, the speeding ship shuddering as the dhow juddered the length of its side, Alos shrieking in fear as the surging water lifted both sloop and dhow, the *Brise* to bang and thud larboard to larboard along the hull of the Rover craft. And in the wind-shadow of the dhow the sloop's sails suddenly fell slack though she yet had momentum, but just as suddenly they were clear of the Rover and the sails snapped taut again, hurling the *Brise* toward disaster beyond.

"Larboard, larboard," cried Arin above the roar of the hammering waves and above Alos's screams. Again Egil hauled on the tiller, and the *Brise* responded, and moments later Arin called out, "Now swing starboard a point and square up."

As the ship flew along its course through fangs and thunder and spray, they could hear loud shouts aft from the scudding dhow, but what the Rovers cried out, none aboard the sloop knew.

"Steady as she goes," called Arin, as whimpering Alos scrambled on hands and knees back into the cabin.

Past her fangs, past her rocks, past her booming surf, out from the mouth of the serpent they sailed, the *Brise* battered but seaworthy still. And as they came into clear water at last, dawn broke on the horizon east.

"Bend on all sail but the square," commanded Egil. "The Rover likely will come after us."

As the crew restored the jib and gaff topsails and the fore staysail, Arin said, "Dost thou think we can outrun them, *chier*?"

Egil looked aft, but the mouth of the cove was now beyond sight 'round a shoulder of land behind. "I know not, love, yet we must try."

In the dawn light the captain of the dhow swung his ship into the cove, then brought her about through the eye of the wind, heading her back toward the Serpent's Fangs to pursue the intruder. He glanced at the rocks and then at the growing light of day, and set aside the potion that briefly allowed him to see by starlight alone. He would not need it for this pass. Besides, he did not wish to risk losing his sight altogether.

Once more he commanded his grumbling crew to set the sails for the run, then true northeast he tacked, his ship picking up speed as he trimmed for the striated rock.

Just as the dhow entered the fangs, something hideous and large and skrawing came swooping from the sky. Men shrieked in fear and cowed down against the deck, and some leapt overboard. And with her crew in panic, the dhow veered and crashed in among the rocks, where the waves battered and bashed her to wreckage against the Serpent's Fangs.

In moments she sank from sight.

And on great dark wings the monstrous *thing* flapped away into the dawn sky above.

CHAPTER 67

"Itell you, Alos, old man, if she hadn't swept your feet
out from under you, you would be dead, bashed overboard by the swinging boom to drown among the rocks."

Alos glared at Delon, then stuck his nose in the air and
sniffed loudly. "Nevertheless, she owes me an apology."

"Ha!" snapped Ferret. "Apology, my left foot! Instead,
you owe her a big thanks for saving your worthless hide."

"Thanks for nearly breaking my elbow?" Alos ruefully
and belatedly rubbed his left arm. "And another thing:
I'm not worthless. There's no better helmsman aboard."

"Yes, but for how long?" said Delon. "You declared in
Sarain that you'd leave us for good once we got free of
the cove. Well, now we're free."

Alos glared at the bard. "I'm going to leave you when
. . . when"—Alos paused, something deep in his memory
nagging at his thoughts, as of a whisper commanding.
Alos shook his head, then said, "Unlike before, I'll not
desert my shipmates in their time of need."

Delon glanced at Ferret, then back to Alos. "Are you
earnest?"

"Of course I am," snapped Alos.

"Then you'll remain until we get the treasure?" asked
Ferret.

Delon cocked an eyebrow at his love. "The time of
need will not be past until the Dragonstone is safely delivered to the Mages."

Ferret looked out to sea and did not reply, and nought
but indigo waters met her gaze.

Kistan lay beyond the horizon some thirty nautical
miles to the west, the *Brise* having sailed directly east and

away from the isle for a quarter of a day before turning to run due north on a beam reach. It was now midafternoon, and Alos, Delon, and Ferret crewed, while Egil and Arin and Aiko and Burel slept below. Their plan was to stay well out to sea and away from the isle and its shipping lanes and run parallel to the eastern marge, hoping to avoid any Rovers, Rovers who ordinarily lurked in the straits far to the north and south and running to the west. Once the *Brise* was free of Kistan some six hundred miles hence, they would head her across the strait, aiming for the coastal waters along the shores of Vancha. From there they would sail to the Weston Ocean, and around Gelen to the Northern Sea, and thence unto the Boreal, for it was on the bounds of those waters where lay their goal: Dragons' Roost. Their journey would cover nearly nine thousand miles altogether, though tacking and hauling as they must, it would be nearly half again as far. There was, of course, a shorter route, one through the channel 'tween Gelen and Jute, but given what Aiko had done to Queen Gudrun the Comely, the waters near Jute were too hostile to fare, and so they avoided that risk by choosing the longer route. And given fair winds and tolerable seas, they would come to Dragons' Roost sometime in the month of May.

It was not until the change of shifts at the dawn of the following day that they began to consider how they would obtain the Dragonstone.

"Here is what we know," said Arin. "The stone is in a cavern in a silver chest chained to rock by a pool."

"The Kraken Pool," appended Egil.

"Do you suppose that means the treasure is guarded by a Kraken?" asked Ferret.

Egil shrugged. "It would be one Hèl of a warder."

"Better than a dog," said Delon, laughing.

"This is no laughing matter," said Aiko, her tone flat.

Delon raised his hands in surrender, then said, "Indeed not. Besides, the 'dog' is on the ledge, guarding the door."

"Dog?"

"Dragon."

Aiko shook her head and sighed.

"There is another door," said Ferret. "The one underwater."

"But the scroll said you can't swim against the current, powered as it is by the Great Maelstrom," said Egil.

"Perhaps Burel could," said Ferret. "He's strong."

Burel shook his head. "I cannot swim. Living in the stone canyons of the labyrinth, I never learned how."

Arin held up a hand. "Let us assume the scroll speaks true. If so, then the only way to reach the pool is to go past the Dragon."

"Ha!" barked Alos. "Not likely. He'd snap us up like morsels before you could say thimblerig."

"We could slip past," said Ferret.

"No you can't," declared Alos. "Dragons *know* when someone is in their domain."

"Why do you say that?"

"Why, it's common knowledge," replied Alos, glaring at Ferret. "Everybody knows that."

"*I* didn't know," rumbled Burel.

Arin held up her hands. "Peace, my friends. Let us not get into an argument over the powers of Drakes." She glanced from one to the other, and then said, "Even so, if we *do* have to win past the Dragon, let us review all we know of them. Mayhap therein we will find an answer to our dilemma."

Alos sniffed and jutted out his chin.

Arin sighed, then said, "This I know of Drakes: they ward the ledge at Dragons' Roost; they sleep four thousand seasons and wake for eight thousand; they are terrible when they raid, though their forays for the most part are to take livestock on which they feed; because of their foraging needs, they live isolated and far from one another and seldom gather but for the time of the mating with Krakens in the Great Maelstrom once every three millennia; the get of these matings are Sea Serpents, which, when their time comes, go to the deeps and enshell in chrysalides, which, when hatched, become Drakes or Krakes, depending upon their gender; Dragons seem to enjoy all that glitters, hence they value treasure, though some claim that Drakes draw power from gold and gems and precious metals, yet how that can be I know not; from the scroll and from the tale told by Arilla at Black Mountain, Dragons come from another Plane, from a world known as Kelgor, and the *in-between* crossing point would seem to be the ledge upon Dragons' Roost, which they guard jealously; Dragons are virtually unkillable, and but for myths I've never heard of a person slaying one, though it is said that they die at times in battle with other Drakes."

Arin fell silent and looked from one to another, finally asking, "Has any aught to add?"

Alos cleared his throat. Arin motioned for him to speak. "Hem," he said. "They can sense when so-called intruders are in their domain, and they can change shape to become anything they wish, at times passing among cities in human guise."

Ferret snorted, but otherwise remained silent.

"They breathe fire," said Aiko. "And in accord with Arilla's tale, I would deem them vain . . . some, at least."

"It is said they like riddle games," added Delon.

"They can see in total darkness," added Burel, "or so Mayam told me when I was but a lad."

"Speaking of that," said Alos, his white eye glaring, "they say that Dragonsight allows them to see things that are hidden, invisible, and unseen. Perhaps that's why they can see in the dark."

Quiet fell, and only the creak of rope and the plash of water along the hull broke the silence. Finally Egil said, "Most of the Dragons are pledged not to raid as long as the Mages guard the Dragonstone."

"Do you think they know that the Dragonstone is, um, mislaid?" asked Delon.

Arin shrugged, then said, "They haven't begun widespread devastation. Hence, mayhap they do not know."

"If so," said Ferret, "then we mustn't give that secret away, especially not to the Dragons."

A murmur of agreement muttered 'round.

"Is there aught else?" asked Arin.

Burel heaved a great sigh. "I have heard from others that Dragons have the power in their eyes to charm a being witless, and that their voices can beguile the wisest of men and women."

"Oh!" exclaimed Ferret. When all eyes turned her way, she said, "Old Nom said that there is a chink in the armor of every Dragon, and if you know where it is, well, you can kill it."

Delon raised a skeptical eyebrow but remained silent.

"Perhaps that's the way Gurd killed the Monster Kram," said Egil to Arin, harking back to the heroic song they had heard while at supper in the Silver Helm in Königinstadt. "Found his chink and did him in."

Arin shook her head. "As with much about Dragons, I think 'tis but a myth Old Nom hath repeated. Even so, let us not overlook the possibility."

Again silence fell upon the group, and no more rumor or fact was forthcoming. Finally Egil said, "Then let us see if we can find a way to get past the Drake on Dragons' Roost."

Ferret took a deep breath and said, "If they value treasure, perhaps we can bribe the Drake to let us enter the cavern and make our way down to the pool."

"I tell y' he'll eat us and just take the tribute for his own," declared Alos.

"Well, perhaps we could hide it—the bribe, I mean—and only tell him where it is after we've got what we came for."

Alos shook his head. "He'd eat us still, and take not only the tribute, but the silver chest and Dragonstone as well."

"Well then," said Delon, "if they like riddles, how about this . . . ?"

They debated until it was nearly noon, discarding plan after plan, until finally Egil said, "We're getting nowhere, and some of us need rest ere it is our turn to crew again. Let us sleep on it."

And so, Arin, Egil, Aiko, and Burel took to the bunks below, while Alos, Ferret, and Delon sailed the *Brise* onward and continued their futile planning.

* * *

Likewise that night, Egil, Arin, Burel, and Aiko debated at length to no resolution. Too, on this night Aiko suddenly took in her breath, then turned to Arin and said, "My tiger growls of distant peril."

Arin stood and scanned the waters all 'round by the light of the silver half moon setting in the west. Finally she said, "I see nought, Aiko."

The Ryodoan shook her head. "Nevertheless, Dara, peril is yon somewhere. I felt it last night as well."

"Is something trailing us, do you think?" asked Burel.

"If so, it comes only at night," Aiko replied.

"Perhaps it's a Rover ship passing by, just beyond the horizon," suggested Egil.

Aiko turned up her hands, for the peril was fading. And none saw the great dark silhouette high in the sky flap away among the stars above.

A week passed, and still the comrades had no viable plan, and still at night peril came and went, or so said Aiko. The *Brise* had now turned on a course across the wide northern strait toward the coastline of Vancha some two hundred miles away. She was making for the port of Castilla on the southern shores of that land, where they planned on restocking the sloop with food and water, and whatever else they might need, should they come up with a scheme.

"Damn, damn!" hissed Egil. "*This* is why that bastard Ordrune hid the chest by the Kraken Pool. There's no way to get in there and steal it back . . . guarded by Dragons and Krakens and a maelstrom-driven current you can't swim against."

"Perhaps we ought to go to the Mages on Rwn and get help," suggested Delon.

"*Take these with thee, no more, no less,*" intoned Ferret. "I don't think the rede permits a Mage to go with us."

"Well, if they can't go with us, there may be a chance that they can suggest something," said Delon. "I mean, after all, Dara Arin sought their help once before."

"Perhaps they can give us a ring of invisibility," said Ferret.

"Ha!" snapped Alos. "Didn't you listen when I said that Dragons can see things hidden, invisible, unseen? Ring of invisibility, indeed. He'd just snap you up and swallow you whole, visible or not."

"Well," said Ferret, nonplused, "if not a ring, then *something* which would help us get into the tunnel past the Drake."

"Not only in, luv, but out, too," said Delon. "Remember, we've got to escape as well."

On the third night in the port city of Castilla, Delon and Ferret sat in the common room of La Estrella Azul, one of the rowdier inns along the waterfront, having tracked down Alos to find him under a table passed out. As they quaffed a brew of their own, Delon laughed and pointed and said to Ferret, "Look."

Gyrating atop the bar was a woman dressed in nought but swirling veils, her hips rolling and turning as she dropped the tissue-thin garments one by one at the behest of a patron with a fistful of coins, the man obviously aroused and paying out copper or bronze for each veil released, depending upon where they were draped. Other men were gathered 'round and whooping and clapping and urging the woman on, their gazes filled with lust.

Suddenly Delon's eyes lit up. "That's it!" he exclaimed.

"What?"

Again Delon pointed. "The man: think of him as a Dragon."

"The man with the coins? How fitting, though 'twould be even more so were he dealing gold. But what does this have to do with us getting the treasure?"

Delon turned to Ferret, his eyes shining. "Think of the dancer as a Kraken."

"Kraken? Look, Delon, though she writhes like one, she hasn't enough arms."

"Yes, yes. But listen, luv, and look: what does the Dragon want?" Delon gestured toward the bar.

Ferret looked once again at the man with the coins; his pants bulged at the crotch. Then she turned to Delon, a glimmer of understanding beginning to dawn in her eyes. "Leave it to you, my love, to think of such a thing."

Delon laughed. "Indeed." He stood and moved 'round the table and dragged Alos out from under and hefted the oldster across his shoulders. He turned to Ferret. "Come, luv, let's go tell the others."

"Offer him what?"

"Love. Offer the Dragon love," replied Delon. "A roll in the hay . . . or in this case, a roll in the sea."

Arin, lying in bed beside Egil, glanced over at him and then turned back to Delon. "How?" she asked.

"Well, look, if there's a Kraken in the pool, we can lure it out for the Dragon."

"Do what?" asked Aiko.

"Lure it out for the Dragon," repeated Delon.

They were all now gathered together, Arin, Egil, Aiko, Burel, Ferret, and Delon. Even Alos was there, though he was on the floor slumped against a leg of a table, dead to the world.

"And just how do you plan on doing that?"

"Look, we can't swim *in* against the current, but we certainly should be able to swim *out*."

"Into the maelstrom? Are you mad?"

"No, no. You see, some will rappel down the cliff and set up ropes or rope webbing or some such so that at low tide, whoever lures the Kraken at the pool can run down the path and draw it after, and dive into the current at the last instant and swim out and be rescued by the ones on the cliff. Then Ferret, here, can unlock the chest and get the Dragonstone. Meanwhile, the Dragon will be entirely out of the way, involved in the arms of the Kraken, making mad passionate love in the whirl of the Great Maelstrom."

Egil looked at Delon. "What makes you think we will even get a chance to talk with the Dragon?"

"They say Dragons are inquisitive," said Delon, "at least when it comes to puzzles and riddles. I think we've a good chance he'll be curious as to why six of us, or seven if Alos goes along, why we might be freely walking into his lair. If so, then I believe we'll make him an offer he'll not refuse."

Egil turned to Arin. "You know, if Delon is right and we *do* get a chance to negotiate with the Dragon before he kills us, this just might work."

"Dost thou think the Dragon will strike such a bargain and permit us access to the Dragonstone?"

Ferret interjected, "Well, we can't tell him that we are going after the Dragonstone, now can we? Instead we'll say we are after the chest . . . tell him that it is an old heirloom or some such."

Burel cleared his throat. "Yes, but Dara Arin has a point: will the Dragon agree to such a bargain?"

"Look," said Delon, "if you could make love but once every three thousand years, wouldn't you seize the chance? Especially if there are no other Dragons about to dispute your claim to the lady in question?"

Burel glanced at Aiko, and for some reason she blushed, though she did not lower her eyes.

"Dost thou think the Kraken will be in season?" asked Arin.

"Perhaps so. Perhaps not," replied Delon. "Yet whether she is in season or is unwillingly ravished by the Drake is of no moment, just as long as we get the stone."

Of a sudden, tears sprang to Ferret's eyes.

"Oh, luv, that was thoughtless of me," said Delon, taking her hand and kissing it gently.

With the heel of her free hand, Ferret wiped the tears away. "It's all right, Delon. I understand what you mean."

Egil looked about the table. "Given that the Drake accepts our offer, we will need to divide: some to rappel down the cliff, others to go to the pool and get the chest."

Delon nodded, then smiled. "And one to be Kraken bait. And since it's my plan, I'll do the honors."

Arin shook her head. "Nay, Delon, thou must deal with the cliff, thou and Aiko and Burel, for only ye three have the skills to rappel down a thousand sheer feet of stone and then climb back up once the deed is done. Egil and Ferai and I will claim the chest, Ferai to free it from its chains, and Egil to bear it. I will be the lure."

The table exploded in argument . . .

. . . But in the end, Arin's scheme prevailed.

CHAPTER 68

"Walk straight into a Dragon's lair? Are you all insane?" His white eye glaring, Alos stared 'round the circle, starting with Delon and ending with him as well. "He'll just snap us up as if we were a half dozen and one sweetmeats."

"Nevertheless, Alos, old man, that's what we intend to do," replied Delon, the bard at the tiller, Castilla over the horizon behind, the coast of Vancha to starboard.

Once again Alos had awakened to find that he was at sea, and when he'd stumbled topside, he'd found his companions sitting adeck in the dawn, the ship well on her way.

And then Delon had told him the gist of the ludicrous plan he had hatched.

"It's stupid, I tell you. Stupid." Alos turned to Arin in silent appeal. "Look, even if he agrees to Delon's insane plan—lets us have the silver chest in return for luring the Kraken out—what makes you think the Dragon'll keep his word?"

"They kept their sworn word to the Mages of Black Mountain," said Delon.

"Yes, but those were *Mages,* and who wouldn't keep a sworn word to a Mage? But we are just common folk. I mean, the Dragon could swear an oath to us, could get what he wants, and then kill us all. Then where would we be? Dead, that's where. No chest, no Dragonstone, just dead. It's insane, I tell you, insane."

" 'Tis all we have, Alos," she said. "Nought else would seem to bear even the slim chance this plan offers."

"Slim chance?" groaned Alos. "No chance, you mean."

Aiko ground her teeth and moved forward and began coiling a line.

"Look, Alos," said Egil, "with fair winds and waves, we have three months, give or take two weeks, before we come to Dragons' Roost. If you hatch a better plan, we'll be most glad to hear it. Until then, though, Delon's scheme seems to be the best at our beck."

Again Alos groaned. Then he looked at the sails and said, "Here, Delon, give me the tiller and trim up those sails, for if you are bound on committing a quick suicide, I'll help you get there, but I won't . . . won't"—a look of confusion spread over the old man's face, and words jerked out of him as if compelled—"unlike before, I'll not desert my shipmates in their time of need."

A week later, in driving rain, the *Brise* cleared the Straits of Kistan and pitched into the heaving waters of the Weston Ocean. All that day she drove through the rolling waves, rounding the shoulder of Vancha. The very next day Egil set a northwesterly course for the western reach of Gelen, and onward they fared.

Every day they reviewed their plan and tried to account for all events, yet much would depend upon the Dragon, and who can predict the whims of such a creature?

And every night, in the depths of the darkness, Aiko sensed distant peril, yet they could find nought to explain the warnings of the red tiger between her breasts: neither ship on the ocean nor creature of the sea did they espy under the sun or moon, and none saw the dark winged *thing* sliding across the stars afar.

"Where will we land, Egil?"

Egil looked up from the chart he had drawn. Then he pointed: "Here is Dragons' Roost at the end of the Gronfangs, where they plunge into the sea. And here churns the Great Maelstrom, between Dragons' Roost on the east and the Seabanes to the west. Here on the southerly approach to Dragons' Roost lies the realm of Gron, a foul land full of Rutcha and such, ruled by a dark Wizard in an iron tower, or so it is said. Here on the north and eastern flanks are the Steppes of Jord, a domain of grass and horses."

"Yes, but, where will we land?" repeated Ferret.

"Not too near the Great Maelstrom, I hope," said Delon. "From what I hear, I wouldn't want to get sucked into that thing."

Alos, at the tiller, shuddered and groaned, but otherwise said nothing.

Again Egil's finger stabbed to the parchment. "Rumor has it that there are perhaps two ways up the mountain to the ledge: one starting in Gron, said to be the easiest to manage; the other beginning in Jord, a more difficult climb, I am told."

Aiko looked up from the map and into Egil's good eye. "Rumor? Is there no accurate description?"

Egil shook his head. "None I know of. Those who have sailed closer than I report such things."

"Has anyone climbed either route?" rumbled Burel.

"If any did," replied Egil, "none has returned to tell the tale."

Alos moaned and looked out to sea, his gaze filling with tears, and he muttered, "Snap us up like sweetmeats all."

"Can we bring the ship nigh enough to see for ourselves?" asked Arin, studying the map.

"The Maelstrom has a long reach, love," replied Egil.

"Even so, can we sail 'tween here and here?" Arin pointed to the channel between the closest two of the Seabane Islands.

Egil turned to Alos. "What do you think, Alos?"

The oldster shuddered, then said in a flat tone, "Shipmates, my shipmates." Egil spread the map before the oldster. Alos wiped the tears from his good eye and stared at the drawing, his breath coming in short gasps. Finally he said, "Perhaps . . . but it will be too perilous, I tell you. I mean, there's a Dragon on the ledge above who can swoop down and swallow us whole, and there's Krakens in these waters who can rise up from out of the depths and drag us under and swallow us whole. And then there's the Great Maelstrom, and if it catches us, ship and all it will swallow us whole."

Arin sighed and looked at the oldster. "If we cannot sail nigh to see for ourselves and must trust to rumor, of the two approaches Egil has named I favor the Jordian side, for a crossing of Gron, no matter how brief, is perilous."

Arin looked up and 'round, receiving nods from all but Alos, who instead peered out to sea, tears again running down his face.

They spent three rainy days in the West Gelen port of Anster, and all the time they were there, Alos was deep in his cups, the oldster trying to drown his fear in drink. Aiko had given up on the task of keeping him sober for, after all, he had safely guided them into and out of Serpent Cove and, other than helming the ship to Jord, there was no part for him to play in the retrieval of the Dragonstone from the Kraken Pool, hence his role in the venture was done. And so she ignored the fact that he was falling-down drunk all the time they were aland, though she was more than fed up with his intemperate blubberings of the doom lying ahead.

On the second night they were in Anster, or rather just before dawn of the third day, as lightning strode across the sky Egil was plagued by a particularly hideous dream, reliving the horror of Miki's face being flayed, the skin being ripped away, the tiny muscles underneath being exposed in wet redness, each muscle then being plucked like individual strings on a grisly, bloody harp, and Miki screaming and screaming and screaming.

Arin held Egil while he wept.

Egil looked up from his plate. "What?"

"I just said, Egil, isn't it dead yet?" repeated Delon.

Egil looked back down. The rasher of bacon was hacked and chopped and torn, as if attacked by a savage beast. Egil slammed his knife to the table and hissed through gritted teeth. "I'm going to kill that bastard."

"Who?"

"Ordrune. When this is over, I'm going back to Serpent Cove and kill him."

"My thoughts exactly," said Burel. "He must pay for my father."

"And my men," added Egil.

"We will need to gather a force," said Aiko. "Enough to throw down his walls or to set siege if necessary."

"And a Mage or two to counter his castings," added Arin.

"That will cost," said Ferret, "yet there should be enough treasure within his walls to pay for all and leave much for us."

"Well then, I take it we know what we will do once this is finished," said Delon. Then he turned to Egil. "But tell me, my friend, why this sudden rage?"

Egil shook his head. "Oh, no, Delon. This rage is not sudden at all, but was forty hideous days in the making and has been tempered for years in the fires of wrath."

"Yes, yes, but why now, this morning?" He looked at Arin to see grief and compassion in her eyes. Enlightenment dawned and he turned back to Egil. "Oh. Another dream, eh? Particularly bad, I take it."

Egil took a deep breath. "Particularly. And I am cursed to relive his monstrous depravities each night."

Burel glanced at Arin and said, "Cannot the Mages at Rwn lift such a curse? If so, why not go there now? According to Egil's charts, the isle is but a week or so away—north and west of here."

Before Arin could reply, Egil said, "No, Burel. Let us first get the Dragonstone and then sail to Rwn. If they can lift the curse, that is the time to try. We've been on this mission for nearly a year—"

"Nearly two," interjected Aiko.

Egil looked at her, then nodded. "Yes. It's been nearly two years since Arin had her vision."

"Two years in July," murmured Arin.

"In July it will be a full year for me," said Egil, then added, "and for Alos. —Regardless, my thinking is that we know not when the doom is set to fall, and the sooner we can get the stone into safe hands, the better for all. After we deliver it to the Mages at the college on Rwn, then and only then should we see if they can lift this hideous curse from my nightly dreams. But whether they can or cannot, I'm going after Ordrune."

"And I will go with you," said Burel, raising his cup to Egil.

And so did they all, all but Alos, who was yet passed out in his room above.

At mid of night on the fourth day after leaving the port of Anster, Arin and her companions stepped out the Elven rite of the vernal equinox, for it was the twenty-first of March— Springday.

On the twenty-third they changed course from a northerly run to head north-northeastward, and late in the day of the twenty-fifth they crossed into the icy waters of the Northern Sea, the *Brise* bound for the wide channel 'tween Thol and Leut.

On April the sixth they came to the marge of the Boreal Sea, and beneath a waxing three-quarter moon they sailed into the broad harbor of Ogan, the port situated on the Long Coast of Thol.

"We'll sail along the shores of Thol and the Jillians and Rian, for it is April, the most unruly of months, and the Boreal's quite fickle this time of year. Should we need shelter from her sudden storms, land will be nearby."

"Well and good, Egil," said Ferret, "but tell me, how many days until Jord?"

Egil looked down at his charts. "Depending on the wind and waves, Ferai, a month, more or less."

"And Dragons' Roost?" asked Aiko.

"Within a day, the same," replied Egil, "for I plan on mooring in Hafen, some thirty, forty miles past. It's the closest port to our goal."

"And that's where we get the horses and cattle?" asked Delon.

Egil nodded.

Alos quaffed the last of his ale and called for another flagon. "Look. Listen. Um." He peered into his empty jack as if seeking his lost train of thought. Then he raised his good eye to Egil. "Do, do, do you truly believe . . . um . . . that the Dragon will prefer cattle to us?"

Egil shrugged, but Ferret said, " 'Tis a tribute we bring to him, Alos. Surely the Dragon will give us a hearing when he sees we bear a gift."

Alos shook his head, and his tongue was thick and slurred. "You think to take him a dinner, but I think we'll be the dinner instead." A sob welled up from within the oldster, momentarily stifled by the arrival of his flagon.

On the eighth day of April, in a light sleet, they set sail from Ogan, heading northeast, heading for the realm of Jord.

They followed the Long Coast of Thol for days, long days and long nights of unremitting sleet and rain and snow, for spring comes late to the bounds of the Boreal Sea. As they approached the waters off the Jillian Tors, the sun finally broke through the overcast, and they sailed for a week in fair weather, coming to the shores of Rian in the last of the April days. Past Rian they sailed, past the end of the Rigga Mountains, and along the marge of Gron, a fog-laden land of cold mists. Here Egil angled outward into the Boreal, aiming the *Brise* for the western-most isle of the Seabanes.

And still during the tail of each and every day, Egil was visited by cursed dreams, and in the mid of each and every night, Aiko sensed peril somewhere lurking.

As they rounded the crags of the Seabanes, to the east and low on the horizon jutted up their ultimate goal—Dragons' Roost—its crest crowned with white snow and glittering ice, the peak winter gripped year 'round. Yet Egil did not aim for this mountain, but swung slightly lar-board instead, bearing for the port of Hafen in Jord. Even so, the mountain grew taller as easterly and north they fared, and they could not seem to take their eyes from that final crest in the arc of the Gronfangs, the chain itself curving away to be lost in the cold mists to the south. Their closest approach came just ere mid of night, a full moon shining down from above, the white pinnacle glittering silver in its light. But onward they sailed north-easterly, leaving the mountain behind.

Just before dawn on the ninth of May, six hundred sev-enty-eight days after Arin had had her vision, they haled into the port of Hafen and made fast to the docks.

As the sun rose they looked south to see their white-capped goal lying but forty miles away—forty miles to Dragons' Roost, forty miles to the Kraken Pool, forty miles to the Dragonstone, forty miles to doom.

CHAPTER 69

[Aye. They do be a path leadin' up,"] said the hostle-keep, eyeing the strange company before him, *[but a man'd ha'e t' be a bluidy fool t' climb them dreaded steeps."]*

Egil nodded and turned to the others and translated the 'keep's words, for he had spoken in the Jordian tongue—oh, not Valur, the battle-tongue of Jord, for that was close-held by the people of this land, reserved for warriors and war. Instead he spoke in the customary Jordian speech, which Egil could clearly understand, for the Jordians and his own Fjordlanders are said to have sprung from the same root stock . . . and their languages had much in common.

Egil turned back to the man. *["We need horses. Cattle, too."]*

The 'keep's eyes flew wide, wider than they had when he had first seen the Dylvana, wider than they had when he'd seen this strange, golden Warrior Maid. *["Ye dunt plan on goin' there, anow, d' ye? Up into Raudhrskal's domain."]*

["We do. Yet we'll allow no others to accompany us."]

[" 'N j'st who d' ye think'd be th' bluidy fool 'r fools who'd want t' go wi' ye, anow?"]

At dawn of the third day after arriving at Hafen, Arin and her companions set out from the port town. A gathering of citizenry watched as these strangers—four males and three females, seven fools altogether—embarked for Dragons' Roost.

That one there, he be th' one-eyed Fjordlander, a raider, no doubt. Aye, but don't ye find it passin' strange that there be *two* one-eyed men among them seven, th' old one wi' a regular evil eye, I'd say; but he be in his cups most o' th' time. Did ye hear that sweet-voiced bard sing, 'n' why do he be along? T' sing t' th' Drake, d' ye suppose? That big man there, he probably be a warrior, 'n' some tell they seen 'im lying flat on th' stones 'n' praying at Elwydd's shrine. Ha! As if prayin' t' Elwydd belike t' save 'im fra th' Drake. That one woman, th' one wi' th' daggers—I heard she be a Gothonian. Ar, but th' other one, th' yellow warrior maid, what land d' ye think she be fra, eh? That Elf, a Dylvana, no less, I'd say she be a sorceress o' great power. 'N' they be all headed f'r Dragons' Roost, 'n' why d' ye think that be? Did ye see all o' them ropes 'n' stuff what they took wi' 'em on th' pack mules? T' get th' treasure, no doubt: th' bard t' sing 'im t' sleep; th' old man t' give 'im th' evil eye; th' sorcerous Dylvana t' charm th' Drake; th' yellow warrior maid t' cut 'im up wi' her magic swords; th' other three t' carry th' gold 'n' jools. But it'll fail, what e're their plan be: cattle 'r no, magic 'r no, swords 'r no, th' Drake Raudhrskal'll j'st burn 'em up wi' 'is fire 'n' be done wi' it. . . .

And thus went the mutter of conversation as seven fools rode out on seven Jordian steeds, driving four head of cattle before them and trailing three laden packmules behind.

"Alos," said Arin, "thou didst not need come with us, but could have stayed in Hafen instead."

Alos shivered as he stared at the white peak ahead, but in a monotone he said, "Unlike before, I'll not desert my shipmates in their time of need."

"Hmm," mused Ferret. "You've said that heretofore, Alos . . . several times, in fact. Tell me, was there a day when you *did* desert your shipmates?"

The oldster looked at her, then glanced across at Arin. The Dylvana smiled. Alos ducked his head, ashamed. "It was in the Boreal," he muttered.

"What?" said Ferret. "I did not hear you."

Alos took a deep breath. "It was in the Boreal," he repeated.

"What was in the Boreal?"

Alos again looked at Arin, his one-eyed gaze pleading, for he had told no one of his cowardice past.

Arin guided her horse next to his. "Thou dost need not speak of aught if it pains thee. Even so, I deem it weighs thee down, yet burdens become lighter when shared."

Tears welled in Alos's gaze. "It was in the Boreal. The Black Mage Durlok and his Trolls boarded my ship, the *Solstråle,* and took all prisoner . . . all but me. I hid in the bilge. Durlok sunk the ship."

"Ah," said Ferret, "now I recall you said something to that effect in Ordrune's gaol."

"And you hid in the bilge," said Aiko, her voice flat.

"I can't help it," said Alos, his chin trembling. "It's the way I am."

Aiko continued to look at him impassively.

Alos could not meet her gaze. "You yourself said that the first rule of life is to live. —Yes, I deserted my ship-mates, but at least I'm alive."

Aiko shrugged slightly. "Is it a life worth living?"

Arin frowned at Aiko, then said to Alos, "But this time, my friend, and unlike before, thou art with us, thy ship-mates, in our time of need."

Alos looked south toward Dragons' Roost looming up in the morning light, his breath wheezing in and out of his gasping lungs, and then he nodded his head and groaned.

Driving the cattle was a laggardly task, for the stolid animals plodded slowly across the grass on the verge of the vast prairie stretching beyond sight to the east, while to the west rolled endless waves across the deeps of the Boreal Sea. South bore the seven companions, south for the flanks of Dragons' Roost some forty miles away, and at the pace they set, it would take the better part of three days to reach the distant slopes.

All day they rode, plodding along, Alos alternately weeping and drinking from one of the flagons of brandy he had slipped into his saddle bags. The sun rode up into the sky and over and down, shedding some warmth in the early spring, the winds yet chill and blowing inland from the brine of the Boreal nearby.

Now and again they would stop along the plentiful

streams to let the animals take on water. Too, they would occasionally pause to feed the horses and mules some grain, and at those times the cattle would graze, the thick grasses now greening with the coming spring. Grass and horses and cattle: these were the riches of Jord, the broad realm itself nought but a vast, lush plain.

As twilight fell they made camp in a coppice, some-what out of the wind. They had come some twelve or thir-teen miles from Hafen, the town just over the horizon behind. In the night they stood watches in turn, all but Alos, that is, for he slept under the influence of brandy and quivered and moaned in his sleep.

As on every night, near mid of night, Aiko on watch felt the presence of peril, peril at a distance. And unseen high in the sky above, *something* slid across the stars, taking care to avoid being silhouetted against the waning gibbous moon.

That night a bleak mist swirled in from the Boreal Sea, turning all dark. The next day found Arin and her band wending slowly southward across the dreary 'scape toward a now obscured goal. Urged forward by the riders, the cattle plodded onward in the still land, moving at their laggardly pace. And although the day brightened as the veiled sun swung up into the drab sky, the coiling fog lin-gered, chilling flesh to the bone.

Alos shivered and blubbered and drank from a second flask. And even though he couldn't see the oncoming mountain, he wept copious tears and swore he would not desert his shipmates in their time of need.

There was no twilight, the gloom merely growing darker with the sinking of the sun, though the mist remained palely luminous from the waning moon beyond. Once again they made camp, this time in a dank swale, the sward wet through and through from the fog. Having no wood they made no fire, and took a cold supper of jerky and tack and water.

As before they stood turns at guard, again excepting Alos, for the old man was beyond redemption in his fear and cried himself to sleep.

* * *

Near mid of night Aiko's tiger again whispered of peril, yet it was a peril that grew and grew. Hastily she awakened the others, hissing, "Something wicked comes."

In the faintly luminous mist, hooded lanterns were lit and made ready for battle, though their light was kept shut for the nonce. And weapons were taken in hand: Egil with his axe, Aiko and Burel and Delon with swords, Ferret with her daggers, and even though Arin loosened her long-knife in its scabbard, she readied her bow, though it was unlikely she would make use of it, for the chill fog yet swirled and coiled 'round. And they stood back to back in a small circle and waited, Alos in the center meeping tiny moans, ready to bolt.

Still the peril grew and grew, and of a sudden something monstrous swept overhead and bellowed an earsplitting roar—*RRRAAAAWWW!*—the comrades all flinching down in the thunderous blare.

The bellow was met by a harsh skreigh, as something screeched high above.

"Waugh!" shrieked Alos, and he threw his blanket over his head and groveled down against the earth.

The others peered upward, yet they could see nought in the dark swirling mist above, but they could hear a mighty swashing, as of huge pinions churning air.

The horses and mules screamed in fear and jerked against tethers staked in the ground, some to get free and gallop away in the dim fog, staves and tethers bouncing behind. The cattle, too, bellowed, and pulled up their own anchors and fled.

RRRAAAAWWWW! came another roar.

Grrrakkk! screeched an answer.

Of a sudden there was a violent blast, and the swirling mist flared red, as if a great gout of fire bloomed above. Again came roars and skreighs and the flap of vast wings, and again the mist above glared red. And now the skreighs dwindled, yet remained overhead, as if whatever *thing* made such shrieks flew higher into the sky.

"What do you—?" began Ferret, but her voice was drowned out by harsh shrieks and a maddened bellowing, and the fog overhead was backlit with furious flames, and moments later there came the sounds of rending, and then something thudded to the ground nearby, and then something else, and again and again, as if huge things were falling from the sky, unseen in the night of pale mist.

Then there came one last vast roar, and a great blooming of fire . . . and the flap of leathery wings heading south.

And as the sound dwindled, so, too, did all peril, or so a red tiger claimed.

CHAPTER 70

Aboard the dhow, mortar and pestle in hand, the dark Mage Ordrune stopped crushing an admixture of black and green crystals and looked up from the arcane blend.

Ah, as anticipated, my fell beast is dead.

Splendid! For it means those fools are nearing their goal.

He hissed a command, and the tongueless Drik leapt up from his station inside the door and raced away topside. Shortly a Ghok came groveling inward.

"Turn east and ready my Hèlsteeds and chariot," commanded Ordrune in Slûk.

The Ghok paused a moment, waiting to see if there were more his master would demand. Yet when Ordrune turned back to his mortar, the Ghok scrambled out and away, shouting his own harsh commands as he gained topside.

In moments there came the sound of rope pulleys in blocks and the whipcrack of canvas in wind, and the dhow heeled over to begin cleaving a new wake across the cold, cold brine.

CHAPTER 71

"A don!" exclaimed Delon. "Look at this."

The others moved toward the bard, misty halos blooming about their lanterns in the fog.

"What *is* it?" asked Ferret, bending down. "A great leather cloak?"

"No, luv. This is no cloak, but part of a wing, I believe."

Ferret sucked in her breath and drew back.

"Wing?" quavered Alos, stepping back as well, then peering over his shoulder as if seeking monsters in the pale night mist. "Wing from what?"

Arin squatted down and touched the leathery membrane. "A fell beast from the elder days, I would imagine, Slain by Raudhrskal."

"Is that what it was, the fight in the sky?" asked Alos, his eye wide with fright.

Arin nodded. "The beast encroached upon the Dragon's domain and was slain for its trespass."

Alos threw back his shoulders and glared at Ferret and said, "See! I *told* you they could sense intruders."

Ferret took a deep breath and said, "If that's true, then it means Raudhrskal can sense us."

The air puffed out of Alos; his triumphant glare collapsed. His face fell and he uttered a small, *"Oo."*

Aiko, squatting on her heels next to Arin, stood. "I think we'll find no more steeds in the dark. The two back at the camp will have to do for rounding up the others in the dawn."

Arin also stood. "As soon as the fog lifts, we'll look. It's not as if the animals can hide from us in this grassland."

Alos looked at Arin beseechingly. "Perhaps we should go back to town and wait until the Dragon gets past his rage. I mean, it would not do to approach him when he's upset, now would it?"

Arin just shook her head, but Egil said, "We are yet two days away from Dragons' Roost, Alos. More than enough time for him to settle."

"We don't know that, Egil," protested Alos, wringing his hands. "It seems to me that a Dragon might hold a grudge a very long time."

Burel looked at the oldster. "And why would the Dragon be vexed with us?"

"Well, we're intruders, for one thing, trespassers," replied Alos, wiping his brow. "And for another thing, perhaps the beast he slew was after us, and that's why it was in his domain."

Aiko's eyes widened, and she touched her breasts where the tiger lay. "Perhaps, *ningen toshi totta,* you have struck upon something. Perhaps the fell creature is what my tiger sensed in the dead of nights past."

"But why would he be following us, my love?" asked Burel.

Aiko shook her head. "Who knows the mind of such a beast?" she replied.

"Nevertheless," said Arin, "whether we led the creature here or no, we will press on for Dragons' Roost as soon as we recover our animals."

At these words, Alos groaned.

The wind from the Boreal shredded the fog and the sun overhead burned the remnants away by midmorn. Aiko and Arin rode the two remaining steeds and rounded up missing horses and mules and cattle, all found placidly munching grass on the open plains.

As they again resumed their journey, they rode past the severed head of the fell beast, its leathery neck torn in twain as if by mighty claws, its glaring yellow eyes now glazed over and dull, its long, fang-filled beak silenced forever.

"Adon," breathed Delon. "Raudhrskal must have ripped the beast apart."

Egil nodded, then said, "Can you imagine how powerful this beast must have been? Look at the size of that beak, and think on its wing as well. And for a creature as powerful as that, think how much mightier a Dragon must be to rend it asunder."

Alos moaned and fumbled in his saddlebags for a flagon of brandy.

On they rode toward Dragons' Roost, the mountain looming ever closer. With hills in the near distance to the fore, the land began to draw upward toward the great slopes ahead. In the sunlight the snow and ice on the peak glittered pearlescent, shining white with glints of blues and greys where frozen crags cast their shades.

And the cattle plodded slowly ahead.

The sun set and darkness fell, but still they pressed on by the light of the gibbous moon, for they wished to make up some of the time they had lost that morning rounding up their scattered animals.

They had gone another two miles or so, when Aiko hissed, "Peril comes on wings," and she pointed toward the crest of Dragons' Roost, where, silhouetted by the moonlight against the white snow, something large and dark with pinions spread wide hurtled toward them.

"Yahhh!" cried Alos, and he leapt from the back of his steed and ran in panic away.

"Dismount!" cried Egil, and, "Take cover!" though there was precious little shelter at hand.

Still, they sprang from their saddles, and Egil and Aiko, pulling on the reins of their steeds, managed to twist the horses' heads back alongside while taking their front legs down as well, each horse grunting as it fell on its side, floundering but unable to rise. Burel, too, got his own horse down, and behind these three steeds the companions flopped to the ground, all but Alos, who fled across the grass northerly.

And amid bawling cattle and scattering horses and mules, in a thunder of wings the Drake swooped down and snatched up a running steed—Alos's. With its mighty pinions churning and a horse in its claws, up into the air flew the great beast, the steed screaming in terror . . . but the Dragon, the Dragon itself seemed to bellow in laughter as back toward the mountain it flew.

CHAPTER 72

As the Drake flew away, Egil and Aiko and Burel kept their downed horses from rising, the steeds grunting and thrashing, yet unable to gain their feet. Finally, the Dragon flew beyond sight, and now the trio allowed the steeds to scramble up, snorting and blowing and sidlestepping, their eyes wide in fear. Yet with soothing words and reassuring touches and strokes, Aiko, Burel, and Egil at last calmed the animals. Burel then gave over his steed to Arin, saying, "Dara, you see best in the night, and our stock is scattered again."

Arin took the reins, then said, "Aiko, I would have thee come with me. Egil, wouldst thou find Alos?"

"Where away?"

"North, I think," said Ferret, pointing.

Egil's gaze followed her outstretched arm, yet he saw nought but prairie in the bright moonlight. Nevertheless, he mounted and rode away northerly, and no more than a hundred yards thither he found the old man lying on his back in the grass, gasping and wheezing in exhaustion.

Egil rode to join Arin and Aiko, and by the time they rounded up the mules and cattle and the remaining horses the moon had moved two hand-widths across the sky.

Arin and Aiko drove the cattle before them, and riding after came Egil, steeds and mules tethered in a line behind. As they arrived where those afoot waited, Aiko looked through the moonlight at Alos now standing with the others, her enshadowed gaze unreadable. Even so, the oldster could not bear the force of her regard, and he turned away and peered toward the Boreal, its waters unseen beyond the dunes to the west.

Without dismounting, Arin said, "Let us move into the shelter of the coppice ahead, a mile, no more. Alos, thou canst ride double with me."

"Double?" Alos looked about. "Say, where is my horse?"

"Taken by Raudhrskal," replied the Dara. "Thou wert fortunate to not be astride at the time."

Alos's knees nearly went out from under him. "The Dragon took my horse," he gasped, his voice tremulous. "And if I'd been in the saddle . . ." He ran a shaking hand across his forehead. "Lord, I need a—" His words jerked to a halt. Then he groaned, "My saddlebags. He got my saddlebags."

They made a small fire and heated water for tea, and as they sat sipping, Alos said, "Why don't we just stake out the cattle and ride back to Hafen, eh?"

"How will that get us the green stone?" asked Ferret.

Alos glared 'round at her. "It won't, but at least the Dragon will be busy eating cattle instead of us."

"Alos, thou canst take one of the horses and ride back to Hafen if thou dost so desire," said Arin. "We'll press on without thee."

Alos moaned and shook his head. "If you are bound to go on, I can do nothing but go with you, for unlike before, I'll not desert my shipmates in their time of need."

"Ha!" snorted Ferret. "Just as you did not desert your shipmates when the Dragon swooped down upon us, eh?"

Alos shook his head and looked into his cup. "I didn't desert you, you know."

"Oh?" Ferret arched her eyebrow. "What else would you call it? Or was that your twin I saw fleeing north?"

"Yes, I bolted, I admit it, but I didn't go far. Found I couldn't, in fact."

Aiko fixed the oldster with a penetrating stare. "How so?"

"I dunno. It seems the farther I got, the harder it was to run, almost as if I were on a steepening hill."

Delon looked out across the level plain. "When was the last time you ran any distance?"

Alos shrugged. "Twenty, thirty years ago."

"Alos, old man, I'd just say your age has caught up with you."

"Think what you will," snapped Alos.

"I do not fault you, Alos," said Egil. "Many would run in fear from a stooping Drake."

Alos looked at the Fjordlander. "I was just heading for a place out of the way, you know."

Delon laughed. "Yes, old man, like all the way back to the safety of town."

Arin shook her head. "But for a Drimmenholt or the like, no place is safe from a Drake." She turned to the oldster. "And neither do I fault thee, Alos, for, as Egil says, any and all may succumb to the dread a Dragon brings."

Alos bobbed his head to the Dylvana, then looked across at Aiko. Yet he received no reassurance from her nor any indication that she agreed with the Dara, for Aiko's dark gaze gave no clue to the thoughts she held inside.

That eve, as Aiko stood watch, contrary to the experience of the past hundred darktides, her red tiger whispered of no peril whatsoever as mid of night came and went.

Perhaps it was the fell beast slain by the Dragon my tiger sensed all along. If so, why would such a creature be lurking on our trail?

The next day they wound upward into the foothills lying against the northern flank of Dragons' Roost. Gradually the land steepened, and the air grew chill. And gradually as well, Aiko's red tiger began to mutter of peril ahead, for the closer they came to that icy pinnacle, the greater the warning of her arcane ward. Still they pressed forward, herding the slowfooted cattle up the cant of the land. Finally, near sunset, they reached a place where they could see that the slope of the terrain lying ahead was simply too steep for the animals to maintain even the slow pace of the past three days.

"Look there," called Arin, pointing forward and to the right.

All hearts beat a bit faster, for where she pointed they

could see the beginnings of the path the folk of Hafen had described: somewhere above lay the ledge, a thousand feet up and three or four miles away, or so the townsfolk had claimed. This was the path they would follow up the mountain flank, hoping to find the place where a fearsome Dragon lay.

Egil looked over at Arin and Alos, the trembling old man sitting behind the rear cantle of her saddle. "I think from here we need to leave the animals behind and go afoot."

Arin scanned the uplift as well, then nodded.

Through his chattering teeth, Alos groaned, then hissed, "Let's turn back. Let's turn back before it's too late."

Arin shook her head. "Nay, Alos, we are going ahead."

"But the Dragon, the Dragon, he won't keep his word. He won't keep his word."

"Nevertheless, Alos, 'tis a risk we must take."

The oldster broke out in sobs.

In the twilight in a grassy box canyon they made a final camp. And they fashioned a simple rope barrier across the choke of the slot, penning the animals within.

That evening they spent sorting the goods they would take with them: ropes, climbing gear, lanterns, food, water, and other such, including weapons, though against a Drake, blades and arrows would be of no use at all. Ferret included her lockpicks, Delon a simple flute, Burel a tabard embroidered with the circle of Ilsitt . . . they all arranged to take something in addition to the gear needed for the planned recovery of the Dragonstone, though none knew what a Drake might find to his fancy or what such a creature might respect—all added something but Alos, that is, for now that his horse was gone, he had nought to bring but his own muttering, trembling, weeping self.

The next morning, just after dawn, they shouldered their considerable gear and began the ascent. Aiko was yet distressed that Arin's role in this mission was to be the lure to draw the Kraken out of the pool and into the sea beyond, out to a place where the Drake could take his pleasure, yet she could think of no reasonable alternative to the plan as conceived: only she and Burel and Delon had the skills to rappel down the long stone of the sheer cliff, and even though someone said that Dwarves claimed the inside of a mountain needed more climbing than an outside ever did, still, Ferret, who also had considerable climbing skills, would lead the team down through the mountain within. Too, Ferret could not be one of the rappellers nor be the Kraken bait, for she had to unlock the chains securing the silver chest. Egil's strength was needed to bear that same silver chest back to the surface, for they could not simply bring the Dragonstone alone, else the Drake above would discover what they had retrieved. Likewise, all three of those on the sheer face of the cliff were needed to increase the chances of a successful rescue, else the Kraken bait would either be snared by the monster if not hauled up swiftly to safety, or would be swept into the Great Maelstrom if they missed her altogether. There were many other reasons why the teams were split as they were, yet those were the prime concerns, and Aiko could think of no acceptable alternatives.

As to Alos, he had no role to play, and why he was along at this juncture was anyone's guess. Yet the old man struggled up the steep pathway, the oldster a whining burden every step of the way, for he had to be helped at even small obstacles and hauled bodily over the larger ones, and soon the freight he carried was shared out among all the others. But although Alos was entirely unweighted of even a minor load, still the old man needed unflagging help as he struggled and gasped and wheezed and whined and wept his way up the steep path, rotely muttering all the while, "Unlike before, unlike before, unlike before . . ." as if it were a mantra . . . or a devoutly held prayer.

Slowly the path wended upward, at times rising, at other times falling, seldom running level. 'Round tall crags and through deep, hemmed-in slots they fared, the way strait, constricting, with frowning, cold stone to left and right. And still the way went onward, over upjuts and downfalls and strews of rubble, the passage hard, and they stopped often to rest. Finally they came to where the path led along a narrow outer ledge, dark stone rising high above to the left, a plunging fall to the right, the somber grey waters of the Boreal hammering against the rocks far below, brine flinging in spray. The path itself clung precipitously to the sheer mountainside, and from somewhere ahead 'round its twists and turns and borne to them on a chill wind, they could hear an unending low rumble, as of ceaseless thunder afar.

They linked themselves together with ropes, Delon in the lead, Burel next and then Aiko, Alos in the center, followed by Egil, then Arin, with Ferret coming last. And onward they went, ineffectual Alos weeping and chanting and clinging to the stone as far from the lip of the precipice as he could get.

They rounded a turn on the pathway, and ahead and below and churning in the sea they could see the wheeling waters of the Great Maelstrom, the spin fully five miles across, a vast twisting funnel, and in the very center gaped a dark rumbling hole, spiraling down and down and down into a black, unplumbed abyss, dragging their hearts down within.

Above Alos's sobbing, Arin remarked, "I once said the green stone was like the eye of a maelstrom, and here I look down upon one."

Ferret took in a deep breath, then said, "Oh, my, speaking of eyes, I just had a thought."

Arin looked back at her. "A thought, Ferai?"

Ferret gestured out at the thundering gape. "Perhaps, Dara, perhaps this is the one eye in dark water."

It was midafternoon when they came to the vast shelf cloven back into the face of the mountain, a great mantel a thousand feet up from the twisting swirl in the ocean below and four miles from where they had started. And as they rounded the final shoulder to come to the wide, stony ledge, a monstrous rust-red Drake turned its flat, scaly head and fixed them with a yellow ophidian eye and hissed, "Why should I not kill you now?"

CHAPTER 73

Babbling incoherently, Alos turned to flee, but he was fastened by rope to Aiko ahead, and Egil stood immediately behind.

In the lead, Delon called out, "Why should you not kill us, O Mighty Raudhrskal? Because we have something to offer, a special gift just for you which will be greatly to your liking, most pleasing, in fact, and we ask but a trifle in return."

Some eighty feet from snout to tail, massive Raudhrskal shifted his weight, his long, saberlike claws scraping against the stone of the ledge, his wicked fangs gleaming. And in a voice sounding like great brazen slabs clanging one on the other, Raudhrskal bellowed, "Pah! Did you think that bringing a few cattle would allow you to trespass into my domain? To actually step here upon this ledge? Imbecile! Cattle are mine to take as I choose. Bah! I am being assailed from *all* sides by fools who surely come seeking death."

The Drake inhaled a deep breath.

Arin clenched her fists. "He readies his flame."

A savage chuff came from Aiko's throat.

Alos fell to his knees and covered his face.

As the others braced for the annihilating fire, Delon straightened his spine and threw back his shoulders and called, "Wait! I demand you hear us out!"

Raudhrskal's eyes flared wide in anger. "Demand? You demand? You who brought a foul beast winging into my domain, you who encroach upon this very ledge, you demand of *me*?"

Delon unclipped the rope at his waist and shrugged out of his pack, then swept low in a deep bow. "O Mighty

Drake, the beast was not of our doing. In that as well as in all other things we are innocent of malice. And yes, we do humbly come into your domain, for there is a boon we would ask, a boon for which we will more than recompense you. O Great Raudhrskal, do you not wish to hear what we have to offer? 'Tis not only cattle we bring—for they are but a minor tribute—but something much greater as well, something more fitting to one of your grand potency."

Now Raudhrskal narrowed his eyes and suspiciously peered through slitted pupils at Delon. "Your voice is most persuasive, man. Is it enhanced in some fashion? Ah, yes, I see. There is a talisman about your neck. Do you attempt to cozen me with a charmed tongue? If so, you will fail."

"Cozen you?" Delon stepped back, aghast. "Nay, O Mighty One, for that would be the height of folly."

"You speak of a grand gift, puny man, yet but for a few paltry coins and gems you and your companions bear, I do not sense any great bounty of treasure. Do you think to ensnare me by guile?"

Delon shook his head. "Ensnare you by guile? Never, Dragonlord, for we know that cannot be done. Nay, we do not bring you common treasure, for it is nought but a material thing; instead we offer you something even more precious, a thing that will pleasure you dearly." The bard glanced back at his companions, then turned once more to the Drake. "May we approach?"

"You pique my curiosity," rumbled Raudhrskal. But then the Drake raised his great head and glared down at the group entire and hissed, "Yet seek to trick me and I'll slay all of you where you stand."

Delon stepped forward, then gestured for the others to follow. Egil raised Alos to his feet, the old man sissing, "Don't look in his eyes, don't look in his eyes, don't look in his eyes, don't, don't," over and again, Alos shuddering and turning his face aside. Egil had to haul him forward, as all followed Delon.

They came out onto the great shelf of smooth dark stone, the mountain to their left rearing up toward snowy heights far above, the precipice to their right falling sheer a thousand feet down to the Boreal Sea below. Two hundred or so paces wide, and just as many deep, the ledge itself cut back into the mountainside, an enormous cavern yawning at the rear. Here and there sat huge boulders, as if deliberately placed in some arcane pattern, but as to the purpose of such an arrangement . . . who could say?

Raudhrskal studied the rest of the band coming onto the ledge—the six yet roped together—his gaze passing over each of them swiftly, all but Arin and Aiko. "You, Elf, there is something strange about your aura. Are you a Mage, perhaps?"

The Dylvana turned up her hands and said, "At times I <see>."

"As I thought: wild magic."

Now the Drake bent his glittering gaze upon Aiko. "I have not seen your kind before, you and your companion."

Aiko glanced at Burel.

"No, no," said the rust-red Drake, "not the fool of a man, but the hidden companion, instead. She paces and lashes as if enraged . . . and now crouches and would leap upon me"—Raudhrskal's laughter boomed—"but changes her mind."

Turning away from Aiko's astonished gape, Raudhrskal glared at Delon. "And now, little man, this boon you would ask, this trade you claim will please me, I would hear your words."

"Honeyed Ogru eye, deliciously aged," declared Raudhrskal, his long forked tongue sliding 'round his wicked fangs. "Have you another?"

Aiko shook her head. "No, Raudhrskal, I do not. Getting that one nearly cost us our lives, my mistress and I. Yet I do have this. . . ." Aiko reached into her pack and pulled out the peacock feather she had carried since finding it in Queen Gudrun the Comely's pool. She presented the iridescent plume to the Drake, saying, "It comes from an exotic bird not found in these parts."

His eyes glittering, Raudhrskal reached out a forelimb and managed to take the lustrous plume from Aiko between two saberlike talons. The Drake held it up in the sunlight and twisted and turned it, the brilliant feather shining in the afternoon rays. "This came from a bird?"

"Yes. 'Tis named peacock."

"When I choose, I shall hunt such a bird for me."

Aiko nodded. "They come from islands south of the Jinga Sea."

Delon cleared his throat. "There's one in the citadel gardens of Gudrun, the Queen of Jute."

Raudhrskal turned his eye to the bard and smiled. "Ah, then, that is much closer. Perhaps I will go there to get my bird."

Delon turned to Aiko and smiled a toothy smile, and she returned his grin, both of their faces filled with guile-less innocence.

"Have you anything else for me?"

Delon shook his head. "No, O Mighty Raudhrskal. Lady Arin and I have sung you our gift of song; Master Burel has invoked the name of Ilsitt on your behalf; Lady Ferai has performed her acrobatics for your pleasure; Master Egil has told the saga as to why Dragonships are so named; and Lady Aiko has given over the honeyed Ogru's eye and the iridescent feather you now hold. In addition, there are four cattle to assuage your hunger when the deed we propose is done."

The Dragon swung his head toward Alos, and as the oldster cringed, Raudhrskal hissed, "What of him? Does this craven bring no tribute? Has he no respect for me?"

Alos moaned and fell to his knees and groveled with his head against the stone.

"O Mighty One, the cattle are his gift," said Delon, then pointed to the rent harness and saddle and saddlebags lying at a distance beyond the Dragon on the stone of the ledge. "And indeed, you took his horse two nights past."

"I took the horse to demonstrate that your fate is mine to determine, and not the other way about."

"Yes, O Raudhrskal, without question what you say is true." Delon glanced at the others, then took a deep breath and risked all. "Yet it is we who offer you that which is perhaps otherwise beyond your grasp." Fire flared in the Drake's eyes, but Delon plunged on: "What of our overture? Will you accept what we would give you in return for what we gain?"

Raudhrskal visibly seethed, for to suggest that *anything* was beyond his grasp was bordering on contempt. Even so, he hissed, "This silver chest, indeed I sense it in the cavern below. What does it hold?"

Delon shook his head. "It is empty, we believe, the chest itself but an old heirloom, precious to none but Lady Ferai and her family. Lost untold years past when the ship went down. Thought to be gone forever until Lady Arin had her vision. Taken, we believe, by Krakens to the cave."

Raudhrskal roared in rage, and all flinched before his fury, Alos shrieking in terror. The Drake fixed a wrathful gaze down upon Delon. "Do you take me for an utter fool, puny man? You would not have come here if the chest is nought but an old heirloom. Now speak the truth!"

Alos moaned, and began to weep, hissing, "He knows. He knows. The Dragon knows."

All the others braced as Delon took a deep breath and lowered his head. "O Raudhrskal, it is clear that we cannot keep our petty secrets from you. Forgive me for not being forthright, but here is the truth"—Delon turned and swept his hand toward Ferret—"Lady Ferai can prove her right to the barony of the Alnawood if she can but recover the chest."

The Dragon grinned wickedly and hissed, "I *knew* there would be greed behind this mission of yours. My question was but a trap, for I have known all along that the chest was empty; I discern nothing within. Ha! If you were expecting it to be filled with treasure, think again. As to Krakens"—Raudhrskal's tail lashed in frustration—"I sense them as well, vexing to one of my potency."

Delon swept a low bow to the Dragon. "You have seen through our subterfuge, O Mighty One. And even though the chest is bare, still it will prove Lady Ferai's claim to the barony. And so, we yet offer our trade: the company of a Kraken for you; an empty chest for us."

The Drake's triumphant gaze swept over them all.

"Very well, I accept. If and when you lure a Kraken out from under, I will cede the silver chest. Yet heed, fail and your lives are forfeit to me."

As the sun lipped the horizon, all but Alos lay on their stomachs peering downward, gazing over the precipice and surveying the sheer drop below; the old man himself remained well back from the fearful fall. But Egil, belly-down, looked over at Delon and whispered, "Well done, Delon. Now I can see why you are a bard, charming a Dragon with nought but your voice."

Ferret, lying at Delon's side, murmured, "The barony of Alnawood, eh? You lie so well, my love. When the Drake demanded you speak the truth I thought we were done for, yet your tongue, sweet Delon, is fast on its feet."

Ferret's mixed metaphor brought a chuckle from all . . . all but Aiko, who pointed downward and said, "Though sheer, there are many cracks and ledges between here and the sea below. We should have no trouble rappelling down, or finding a place to set rescue."

"And the Drake says the crack is directly below where we lay; below this very spot?" asked Ferret.

Burel grunted, "Indeed."

"As Alos would ask, can we trust Raudhrskal's word?"

Delon looked at Ferret. "In this case, I believe so. It's to his interest to tell us the truth, else he will not get what he desires."

"Ah, young love," said Egil, smiling.

Aiko felt her face hotly flush.

Delon and Burel and Aiko spent the eve sorting ropes and loading their climbing harnesses with snap rings and rock-nails and jams, getting ready for their early morning descent, for according to Alos the tide would be at full ebb some eight candlemarks ere noon, and they needed to be well ensconced before then. Likewise did Arin and Egil and Ferret prepare, loading their own climbing harnesses with gear, and adding lanterns as well, for they were going down through the mountain and needed to bear their own light.

That night after all was made ready, they bedded down

on the ledge, though sleep eluded them until the wee marks before dawn. Yet in the few moments he slumbered, Egil had his ill dream, and Arin held him tightly in his throes, for not even the presence of a Drake nearby could stay Ordrune's foul curse.

"Eh, eh," meeped Alos, his face illuminated by the lanternlight in the last candlemark before dawn. "You just can't leave me alone with the Drake. He'll snap me up like a tasty morsel when all of you are gone."

"Stringy morsel, you mean," said Ferret.

Arin turned to the oldster. "Alos, thou canst neither rappel down the face of the stone nor clamber down through the rigors of the mountain. I would have thee stand watch here instead."

"Watch?" groaned Alos. "Stand watch? Watch for what?"

"Should we fail altogether, someone needs to bear word to the Mages."

"Bu-but, Dara, should you fail, the Dragon will kill all the rest of us."

"Nevertheless, my friend, shouldst thou survive, I would have thee bear testament to what we tried here today."

Ferret snapped a last hank of rope to her belt. "What makes you think he won't just run away?"

"Unlike before," quavered Alos, "I'll not desert my shipmates in their time of need."

"Oh, right," growled Ferret. She looked up at the old man, tears streaming down his face. "Ah, Alos, I'm sorry. It's just that I'm a bit nervous, stalking into a Kraken's lair. —Do the best you can, old man."

With a chill wind blowing down from the ice and snow above, dawn came at last, though where they stood in the shadow of Dragons' Roost the light was mostly in the sky. Both teams were set, and with a final embrace of one another, an embrace including weeping Alos, they each turned on their separate courses: Delon, Burel, and Aiko heading for the place marked on the lip of the ledge; Ferret, Arin, and Egil striding past Raudhrskal and into the dark of the vast cavern behind.

As she reached the back of the great cavity and came to the split where a narrow passage led inward and down, Arin turned in time to see Aiko, last in file, her swords fixed across her back, grasp the anchored line and step hindward over the rim.

Then, leaving moaning Alos alone on the ledge, hostage to the rust-red Drake, Arin turned and followed the bobbing light down into the blackness below.

CHAPTER 74

Down she rappelled through the airy silence, but for the distant rumble of the Great Maelstrom afar, down through the shadows of Dragons' Roost, a chill drift of air rolling over the lip of the sheer drop from the icy heights above. The fall of dark stone filled her vision as she footed and fended away, dropping along a slender line down its gloomy face, one gloved hand high, the other at the base of her spine, the rope slipping between. By the time Aiko reached the first ledge and came to a stop near Burel, Delon had already reached the next ledge and Burel was busy lowering fifty-foot hanks of line down to him. As Aiko unclipped her snap-ring from the line above and joined him in this labor, she asked, "Any instructions?"

"None," replied Burel. "The stone above is sound, and so we will continue straight down."

Aiko grunted her acknowledgment and, lowering a hank, peered down at Delon directly below, where he was limned against the dark turning waters of the restless Boreal Sea. The bard received the coils from above and arranged them along the ledge.

Quickly the labor was finished, and then Delon called back up, "We can free-climb this section, so bring the down line with you."

As Delon set a jam into a jagged crack and tested its hold, Burel clipped onto the doubled rope and stepped backward over the ledge, while Aiko behind waited her turn.

Down through the blackness wended the trio, Ferret in the lead, Arin in the center, Egil coming last. Both Ferret and Egil bore lanterns to light the way, but Arin's remained unlit, the Dylvana seeing well by the light of the two. The stone all about them was dark and brooding, and a chill cold enfolded them in an icy grasp, and the lamplight seemed hard-pressed to push back the darkness all 'round.

The steep, downward passage twisted and turned, dropping down slides, wrenching around corners, upjuts and boulders blocking the way, cracks shattering off into blackness. At times the trio edged along precipices, with yawning ravines falling into silent ebon darkness just inches from their feet.

And the deeper they went, the colder the air, until they slid down a slope and stepped 'round a corner to see glittering whiteness ahead.

On the great ledge, Alos huddled shivering in the lee of a boulder, unable to bring himself to crawl to the edge and peer over the terrifying drop to watch his companions rappel down, unable as well to know how the trio in the underground passage fared.

It was not fair, not fair at all, for him to be alone and abandoned as he was, for surely were it the other way 'round he would not have deserted his shipmates, would not have left them in the company of a terrible Drake, would not have forsaken them as he had been.

What was that? A sound. It was Raudhrskal, frightful Raudhrskal, slithering toward the precipice to peer at those below, slithering to watch their progress. Alos, trying to make no sound of his own, scooted on his bottom 'round the boulder, keeping it between himself and the dreadful rust-red monster, a monster who would snap him up and swallow him whole without a second thought.

Tears ran down the old man's face at his unjust plight— abandoned, alone, trapped as he was, no friends, no help, no one to save him, an appalling beast ready to eat him . . .

. . . And then in the shadows of the great cavern at the back of the ledge, Alos saw his stolen saddlebags, left lying unguarded by the creature behind.

* * *

Aiko looked back overhead. Beyond a long stretch of easily climbed stone a length of rope dangled down from above, and higher still, past another stretch, dangled another line—one rope, the top one, was a hundred feet long, the other, fifty. They had not brought enough line to reach all the way down from the lip to the sea, and instead planned on free-climbing part of the way. In only those places found difficult did they leave rope behind.

Aiko turned and looked below. Burel was nearly free of the line, with Delon rappelling down another line farther below. When Aiko's turn came she would slide down this rope, then bring it after.

Again she glanced upward at the long climb above. Going back up would certainly be harder than coming down. And bringing Arin with them would complicate things, for the Dara was untrained in climbing.

As she thought of the Dylvana, Aiko's heart clenched, for the peril her mistress faced was incalculable, and the Ryodoan thought that somehow she should be there, her swords protecting the Dara. Yet Aiko was not at the Dylvana's side but instead prepared for her rescue.

Climbing upward with Lady Arin would be a relief, for it would mean she had survived.

But what if she did not come when the tide was low? Then the climb back up would be long and grievous, for that would mean something had gone dreadfully wrong.

Shaking her head to clear it of these somber thoughts, Aiko looked downward again. Burel was free of the rope and making ready to lower the remaining gear down to Delon below.

Aiko took up the doubled line and backed over the lip of the ledge.

"What is it?" asked Egil, the whiteness casting glints in the lanternlight as he looked out across the enormous crack sliding down at an angle rightward into unplumbed black depths below, a slanting white forming the left-hand slope.

"Ice," called Ferret, her breath blowing white, her voice echoing in the cave.

"Ice? Here underground?"

"From the heights above, I would think," said Arin. "This wide fissure must reach to the very top of Dragons' Roost."

Egil nodded and watched his own breath blow white. "No wonder this cavern is so cold."

Ferret held her lantern high. "The passage continues onward beyond this slope. I can just see it on the other side."

"How do we get across?" asked Egil.

Ferret surveyed the span. "I don't think we can cross on the stone to the right: it's an underhang, and I don't know enough to essay such. It's the ice or nothing."

Egil grunted as he extracted a tool from his small pack. "And here I thought Delon a fool for telling us to take an ice-axe."

Ferret fumbled about her harness belt, finally extracting a rock-nail. Selecting a thin crack, she drove the slender-bladed spike within, then attached a snap-ring to the eyelet and threaded a rope through the ring.

"Anchor me," she said in the chill air, "I'm going to have to chop handholds and footholds as I go."

Egil took up the unbound hank in his gloved hands and arranged it in a coil where he could pay it out. Looping the line over a shoulder and across his back, Egil braced himself against a jut. "When you're ready . . ."

Alos looked back at Raudhrskal. The Drake was fully occupied watching the climbers below. The oldster stealthily pulled a leathern jug from one of the retrieved saddlebags and uncorked the brandy within.

"The stone below is unsound for a stretch," called Delon. "I'm going to move to the left."

Chnk . . . chnk . . . chnk . . . Laboriously, Ferret chopped hand- and footholds in the hard-frozen slope, the ice-axe cutting deeply, silvery shards tumbling away down the slant to be lost in the blackness below. Now and again she would stop to rest, her white breath coming hard, but after a short pause, she would begin chopping again.

P'r-p'r'aps I j'st ought t' walk out of here. I mean, they *were th' ones what wanted t' get this thing.* Alos took another pull on the leathern bottle.

Delon hammered in another rock-nail and fixed it with a snap-ring, the bard leaving behind a trail that would make the ascent easier on their return. He looked above, where Burel and Aiko waited, then lowered himself down to another crack in the cliff face and began to drive in another nail.

"Like the two we left back there spanning the ice," said Ferret, peering down at the lantern dangling below, its yellow light illuminating the vertical shaft dropping away at her feet, "we're going to have to anchor another rope up here and leave it for our return."

"Let's hope we don't run into many more of these, um, barriers," said Egil. "We'll have only three hanks after this."

As Ferret began pounding a rock-nail into a suitable crack, she said, "How do you suppose Ordrune got down here? I mean, I've seen no signs that *anyone* has come this way before—no old rock-nails or rings or ropes . . . nothing whatsoever left behind."

"Mayhap Ordrune has mastered flight," suggested Arin.

Ferret paused in her pounding. "Can anything other than birds fly?"

"Dragons," said Egil. "Bats, fell beasts, insects, and a number of other things."

Ferret grinned ruefully and struck the rock-nail one last time. As she slipped a snap-ring through the eyelet, she said, "I suppose what I meant to ask was, do you really think Ordrune can fly?"

Arin turned up her hands. "He is a Mage, and it is told there are Mages who can move through the air."

Ferret threaded the rope through the ring and tested the anchoring of the rock-nail. "There. It seems sound enough. Let's go."

* * *

N—nope. Can't leave 'em. Unlike before. Shipmates. My shipmates. A sob escaped Alos's wet lips.

As Burel waited, he looked out at the Boreal Sea, out at the vast gurge. The entire turning surface seemed to bend, spiraling down into the distant rumble of the dark, gaping hole.

"I hear water churning," said Arin. "Somewhere ahead."

They clambered over broad shelves of rock, slippery and damp, and scrambled up ledges and leapt over cracks, and slid down rubble-strewn slopes, shards tumbling before them. Soon Egil and Ferret could also hear the swash and surge of water, the sound drifting up the passage.

Great tears rolling down his face, moaning in desolation, Alos pulled another leather bottle from his recovered saddlebags. Uncorking the flask, he lifted it to his brown-stained, gap-toothed mouth and swallowed gulps of the fiery liquid between gut-wrenching sobs of self-pity.

"Do you see it?" called Aiko down.

"No, I do not," replied Delon from below.

"It's got to be there somewhere," rumbled Burel, "or so the Dragon said."

Aiko looked above, sighting on the rope at the very top, there where the Dragon stared over the ledge. "Left!" she called to Delon. "I think it should be somewhat left of where you are."

Delon moved leftward along the ledge, peering down into the churning brine at the foot of the cliff, the bard searching for evidence of the underwater crevice leading to the Kraken Pool within.

"There it is," breathed Ferret, holding her lantern high, the light swallowed up in the darkness of the cavern beyond.

They stood at the entrance of a huge chamber, a short path sloping down to an enormous pool, ebon water upwelling from black depths below. Roughly circular, the grotto itself was perhaps a hundred feet high and two hundred feet across, its far reach lost in dimness to all but the Dylvana's eyes.

Egil put both hands on Arin's shoulders and whispered, "What do you see?"

The Dara's gaze swept the chamber. " 'Round the edge to the right runs a wide pathway, boulder strewn. At the far side it disappears into a wide channel beyond—"

"The treasure," interjected Ferret. "Do you see the treasure?"

Arin nodded and pointed nearly straight away. "Alongside the path just before the entrance to the channel, the silver chest rests up in a small hollow within the wall."

"How long till low tide?" asked Egil.

"Four candlemarks," replied Arin.

Egil pulled Arin to him, and for a while none said ought. But then he sighed and murmured, "Let us hope that Delon and Burel and Aiko are in place and ready."

"Ah, surely they are," said Ferret, gazing in the direction Arin had pointed. "We've come too far and planned too well for anything to go wrong at this stage. And the treasure itself, well, we've almost got it."

But Egil gazed down at the ominous stir of ebony water. "If the scroll is right, then somewhere within is a monster who will dispute that claim."

Arin, too, looked at the dark upwelling, then said, "In four candlemarks we shall know."

CHAPTER 75

Time crept past.

"But what if they *didn't* make it all the way down the cliff, or perhaps couldn't find the underwater exit?"

Arin turned to Egil. "Fear not, *chier* . . . and have faith."

"But we don't know, love. We don't know that all is in readiness. Look, we can return to the ledge above and execute the plan tomorrow. Recall, should low tide come and go without you luring the Kraken outside, the strategy is for them to climb back up. We can meet them atop and know whether all is ready or no."

"Again I say fear not, *chier*. Both Delon and Burel said that given the face of the mountain wall, the descent, though long, would be rather easy and swift. It's the climb back up that will take time."

Egil sighed, and fell silent, and only the rush of water in the cavern beyond broke the stillness.

Finally Ferret said, "Dara, can you tell from here whether or not the treasure has a charm on it?"

Egil growled, "It is not a *treasure,* Ferret."

"Nevertheless, *chier,* she has a good question," said Arin. "I will attempt to <see>." Arin stood and stepped to the cavern entrance. After a moment she said, "Mayhap there is a glow, yet if so, it is too faint to discern from here."

"Oh." Ferret's voice fell.

"Would you rather that it did glow?" asked Egil.

"Oh, no," replied Ferret. "I'd rather that it did not, for who knows what a charm might do? I was simply hoping the Dara could tell whether or not one was present."

* * *

" 'Tis time, *chier,*" said Arin, standing.

Egil looked at her, his heart in his gaze. He tried to speak, but found he could not. Instead, he embraced her, wrapping her small frame in his arms. He kissed her lingeringly, and then with a sigh he released her and stepped back.

Ferret dipped one end of a short section of stiff rope into lantern oil and then lit it. "Your torch to run by, my Lady," she said and handed it to Arin. Then she gave over a lit lantern to the Dara, saying, "And a lantern to leave at the silver chest, should you get the chance."

Egil's heart hammered in his breast as Arin took torch and lantern and nodded her thanks. Yet before she could turn to go, Egil stepped forward once more and took her face in his hands and kissed her one last time and whispered, "I love you."

"Chieran," she replied, then turned and quickly stepped away, blinking back her tears.

Down into the cavern she stepped, and taking a deep breath she began running swiftly along the path to the right and toward the distant goal, while behind, Egil held his breath and gritted his teeth, and Ferret clenched her hands in white-knuckled grips.

Dark waters upwelled in the pool.

Fleetly and lightly Arin ran, rounding the curve of the cavern, dodging past boulders and springing over rocks in her path. Now she came to the final arc, and by the light of the lantern she bore, Egil and Ferret could see a niche in the wall, silver glinting within.

Arin paused, placing the lantern into the hollow, and she called out above the roil of the water, "The chest, 'tis charmed!"

And the black waters of the pool churned and seethed.

Now Arin stepped to the edge of the pool and peered into the moil, waiting. And still the waters welled up, the whole of the flow to race outward toward the sea along the channel at hand.

Nothing.

"Perhaps there is no Kraken whatsoever in the pool," hissed Ferret.

Egil only groaned in response.

Now Arin turned and stepped back to the niche containing the chest, and while watching the pool she reached up and in toward the silver . . .

. . . and touched the charmed metal.

Fwoosh! A great flowing heave exploded upward in the water, huge ropy tentacles bursting forth.

Waves billowed outward toward the walls.

Run! shouted Egil and Ferret together—

—but Arin had already turned to flee, the Dylvana bolting down the path toward the exit a full furlong away, the Great Maelstrom spinning out in the ocean beyond.

And behind her sped a monster, tentacles flowing before it, grasping and snatching at her fleeing form.

"Run! Run!" shouted Egil, as the waves of the creature's emergence crashed into the walls to fling water up in sheeting gouts of spray. And when he could see again, the light of the rope torch had disappeared into the darkness of the channel passage beyond. And Egil whispered, "Run, my love. Oh, Adon, run!"

Arin ran with all of her fleetness, a hurtling wedge of ebon water rushing down the channel behind, a massive flowing heave in the darkness, with great writhing tentacles reaching out after. On Arin sped, hurdling small boulders, leaping over stones, flying before a hideous creature that would rend her in twain should it manage to grasp her.

On came the great wave, a foaming black wake churning behind. And now one massive tentacle reached out to clutch her, but she dodged away. The water roiled with the creature's anger, and it snatched up a great rock and smashed it down at her—*THDD!*—flying stone chips pelting her in the back as she ran.

Thdd! . . . Thdd! . . . There came the sound of a massive pounding, as if a monstrous maul hammered. "Oh, Adon, Adon, what is amiss?" cried Egil, as the strike and beat echoed back through the cavern.

"Now, Egil!" cried Ferret. "While the creature is drawn away. Now is the time to get the treasure, ere the monster returns."

"What?" cried Egil.

"I said, we must move now! Else her effort is like to be in vain," Ferret spat. "Now let's go."

thdd! . . . thdd! . . . The echoes of the hammering diminished, as if becoming more distant.

Egil took a deep breath and then expelled it altogether. He grunted a reply, but what he said, she did not hear. With rage in his face he looked at the dark water and across at the chest, then said, "Wait here, Ferai, until I call you."

She nodded and handed him a twist of rope, one end dipped in oil and lit. He snatched up a lantern and took the torch and stalked out into the cavern.

Ferret watched as he moved toward the chest, one eye on the man, another on the roiling black pool.

At last Egil reached the niche. He set down his lantern and took his axe in hand, and then, as he had seen Arin do, he reached up and touched the silver metal.

Again the pool exploded upward, tentacles boiling forth.

THDD! . . . THDD! . . . THDD! . . . With a great rock maul pounding just inches behind her, Arin fled down the rocky way toward the exit, her feet barely touching stone as she ran. Now she could see the gleam of water ahead and light streaming inward underneath. And just as a huge tentacle swept toward her, she came to the end of the path and made a running dive down into the powerful current sweeping outward.

THDD! . . . Thdd! . . . thdd! . . . Ferret listened to diminishing echoes as Egil fled down the path and away, a monster in pursuit.

Two Krakens. Two. What a hideous trap. And now I am left all alone.

With a rope torch in one hand and the last lantern in the other Ferai stepped out into the cavern.

thdd . . . thdd . . .

As the hammering diminished in the distance, she quickly ran along the path to arrive at the silver chest.

Now she set aside her lantern and wiped her sweating palms on her leathers. Then gritting her teeth, she took a deep breath and stared out at the dark roiling waters . . . and reached out and touched the charmed chest.

CHAPTER 76

Stand ready!" cried Aiko. "Peril comes."

To one side on the ledge, Burel and Delon took up the lines to the rope webbing floating in the water along the outflow from the cavern. Opposite the underwater crevice, Aiko held the third line, and used it to keep the rope mesh positioned correctly in the current below. At the Ryodoan's feet a coiled line lay, ready to cast should Dara Arin miss the webbing altogether.

And loud grew the cry of her silent red tiger as peril came rushing headlong.

Of a sudden, driven by the mighty current, like a shot from a sling the Dara came hurtling through and upward, something huge and dark and deadly speeding after. She nearly missed the floating mesh, but at the very last moment managed to grab on with one hand.

"*Now!*" shouted Aiko, letting go as Burel and Delon hauled with all their might. Sputtering and gasping for air, Arin grabbed hold with her free hand just as she was jerked sideways in the water toward the two men high on the ledge above. Driven onward by the massive flow, the Kraken hurtled straight past the Dara and beyond, its tentacles clutching nought but water where she had been. Even so, its great dark form could be seen turning 'neath the water for another run at its prey.

"Hurry!" shrieked Aiko, the Ryodoan now moving along the ledge, her swords in hand, though when she had drawn them she did not know.

Now Delon and Burel hauled the Dara upward, each man straining to the uttermost, though it was Burel with his great strength carrying most of the burden.

Up she was drawn and up, up and away from the water, a massive dark form speeding toward the cliff below.

Now a huge tentacle whipped out of the brine and snatched at her leg, but Arin jerked aside, and then she was beyond the creature's reach.

Huge tentacles lashed the water in fury and beat against the wall as the monstrous Kraken below clutched upward, only to fall inches short. Again the monster whipped its tentacles in rage, churning the brine into foam.

At last Burel and Delon hauled Arin up to the level of the ledge, and Delon reached out and helped her to stand, while Burel cast the mesh aside.

"Lord Adon," cried Delon, shouting with stress though the danger was past, "but that was close."

Arin stood trembling uncontrollably, though whether it was from cold or fear or from the near brush with death, none could tell. And Burel stepped forward and took her in his wide embrace and murmured, "Be at ease, Dara Arin, for Ilsitt has seen you safe."

But then Aiko cocked her head in puzzlement and looked at the enraged Kraken below, then peered about. "What is it, my love?" asked Burel, still holding the Dylvana in comfort.

"More peril comes," Aiko said. "Whence, I cannot say."

But in that very moment, out from the underwater crevice came hurtling another form, something huge and hideous rushing after.

'Twas Egil and another Kraken, but this time there was no waiting rope net.

Out they hurtled and out, impelled by the massive flow, Egil struggling to the surface, gasping for air, only to be wrenched under by a massive tentacle grasping his leg.

Upward he clawed, his efforts entirely futile, his strength minuscule compared to the monster's. No longer holding an axe, he drew his dagger and desperately hacked at the rope arm, all to no avail, for the edge made no mark whatsoever on the tough hide.

And now with its victim clutched in its underwater grasp, the creature began to swim back toward the entrance, Egil's agonized lungs burning to breathe, his chest heaving spasmodically, his whole being screaming for air.

But there was none to be had, and in the last moments, his mind spinning down into darkness, unable to withstand the demands of his need, Egil drew in great lungfuls of water.

And in that moment in the grasp of a Kraken, Egil began to drown.

CHAPTER 77

*E*gil!" screamed Arin, her eyes wide with horror. "*Egil!*"

She tried to push out from Burel's embrace, but he held her tightly, saying, "Dara, Dara, there's nothing we can do."

Delon kicked off his boots and whipped a rope about his waist and made ready to dive, but Aiko stopped him, saying, "Burel is right, there is nothing we can do."

And they watched as the great creature, Egil in its grasp, swam underwater in silence toward the entrance to the cavern within, the other Kraken turning to join the first. And the only sound to be heard was the quiet weeping of Arin and the far-off rumble of the Great Maelstrom.

Yet suddenly the hush was shattered:

RRRAAAAWWW! From above there echoed a mighty roar, and plummeting down the face of the precipice thundered Raudhrskal, his wings folded back in a stoop. Down he plunged and down, down the sheer fall of stone, his mouth wide and spewing flame, a stream of fire pouring down into the water as he came.

And lo! the Krakens turned and raced toward the place of the fiery blast.

Whoom! Raudhrskal slammed into the water, an enormous wave billowing up and rolling outward, the surge to hammer into the precipice, brine whelming over those clinging to the ledge above.

And still the Krakens raced toward the Drake, as if rivals of one another, each one vying to get there first. And in their wake, in their wake—

"Egil!" shrieked Arin, pointing downward.

There in the water below, the current slowly drawing him into the grasp of the long turn of the sea spiraling toward the Great Maelstrom rumbling afar, just under the surface and abandoned by the Krakens drifted Egil, lifeless, without motion of his own.

"Anchor me," barked Delon, handing Aiko the other end of the line fixed 'round his waist. And then the bard dove from the high ledge and toward the water below, a flurry of rope uncoiling behind. Cleanly he clove down into the brine, a great stream of silvery bubbles showering upward in his wake. And he turned underwater to swim toward the drifting man.

"Stand ready, Burel," called Aiko, handing the end of the line to him. "As soon as he's lashed onto Egil, we'll haul him up."

Moments later Delon reached Egil and, grasping him, swam to the surface. Now the bard undid the line and fixed it about the limp man, and then shouted, "Draw him in!" and hung on as Burel and Aiko pulled both to the cliffside below.

Delon clambered up the stone, free-climbing, and he called, "Don't worry about me, I'm all right. . . . But Egil is dead!"

Arin gasped, but Aiko said, "Draw him up, regardless, Burel. There may yet be a chance."

Now Burel alone hauled the limp body upward, the big man grunting with the strain, Aiko taking up the slack behind.

As Egil was lifted onto the ledge, Arin gritted her teeth. "Roll him onto his stomach," she said, then straddled Egil's waist and pressed down hard on his back.

Water gushed out from Egil's lungs, and again Arin pressed. More water flowed. And once more the Dylvana mashed down. This time only a bare trickle leaked outward, and Arin flopped him over onto his back and brushed his wet hair away from his face, so deathly pale and still. Then she pinched his nose shut and pressed her mouth to his and forced her breath into him, then turned her head and listened as the air escaped.

Once more she breathed into him; once more she turned aside.

And again . . .

And again . . .

And he did not respond . . .

And again . . .

And once more . . .

And still he lay cold . . .

And again she breathed into him . . .

And again . . .

And she hammered on his chest and cried, "Oh, Egil, my Egil, breathe, beloved, breathe . . ."

And again she sealed his lips with hers and breathed into him . . .

Altogether eight times . . .

And of a sudden Egil coughed once, twice, and began breathing on his own—hacking and gagging and spitting up water, but breathing on his own.

Arin covered her face with her hands and burst into wrenching tears.

And in the cold currents of the Boreal Sea, entwined in the tentacles of two fervent Krakens, all three ablaze with lust, Raudhrskal was drawn under and toward the churning whirl of the Great Maelstrom afar.

CHAPTER 78

It was late in the day when Delon reached the rim of the precipice and climbed up over the edge. As soon as he gained the verge, he turned and helped Arin coming after. Then Aiko scrambled onto the lip, following gasping Egil, the Fjordlander spent, weakened by his ordeal, exhausted by the long climb after. He stood bent over, his hands on his knees, and panted for air, now and again coughing, while Delon hauled up the retrieved lines. Last to arrive was Burel.

Their gazes swept across the great ledge. Of Raudhrskal there was no sign, nor was there any sign of Ferret. Near the back of the shelf and behind a boulder they found Alos lying unconscious among several leather bottles, the old man hugging his saddlebags and sleeping in his own vomit.

Delon looked about, worry in his eyes, then glanced at Egil. "Where is Ferai?"

Egil shook his head. "I am sorry, Delon, but she may not have survived. The chest was trapped by a charm. Touching it brought the Krakens."

The blood drained from Delon's face.

"There is another possibility," said Aiko.

With gathering hope in his eyes, Delon looked at her.

The Ryodoan shrugged. "She may be long gone from here, the Dragonstone in her possession."

Delon shook his head. "Oh, no. Not my Ferai. She wouldn't have done that. She wouldn't have stolen the stone and fled."

"I hate to admit it," said Egil, "but Aiko does have a point. Ferret always considered the Dragonstone a treasure, one to be sold to the highest bidder."

"How can you say that?" Delon's words gritted out through clenched teeth. "She has been loyal to the end."

"I'm sorry, Delon," replied Egil, "and if I'm wrong I apologize. But in Pendwyr, if you recall, they named her Queen of All Thieves."

"But she was innocent," protested Delon.

"Or so she said," declared Aiko.

"Mayhap she is injured below and cannot climb back up the way," suggested Arin, pointing toward the crevice at the back of the cavernous hollow in the mountainside.

Delon began gathering up his climbing gear. "I'm going down in."

"I'll go with you," said Burel.

Arin turned to Egil. "I know the way and will go as well, but thou, *chier,* thou shouldst remain and recover from thy trial."

"Hold," hissed Aiko, drawing her blades, "my tiger whispers of peril."

"Where?" asked Egil, grasping his dagger, his axe long lost 'neath the rushing waters of the abyss far below.

"Somewhere near and nearing," replied Aiko, stepping toward the rear of the ledge.

All now held weapons in hand and followed Aiko as she strode toward the entrance to the passage below, the silent hissing of her red tiger growing with each step.

And now from ahead they could hear a scraping, and the gasp of heavy breathing, and from the darkness of the cave there shone a glimmer of lanternlight and came a panting call: "Well, isn't anyone going to help me with this bedamned heavy thing?"

"Ferai!" shouted Delon, running forward, as she came dragging the silver chest out from the crevice. The bard swept her up in his embrace and kissed her soundly, as the others, grinning and laughing, stepped toward her, all but Aiko and Burel.

"The peril, my love!" said the big man, raising an eyebrow.

"Stronger than ever," replied Aiko, peering about in the long shadows of the setting sun.

"Perhaps it is the Dragonstone," he suggested.

Aiko took a prolonged breath and stared at the chest, then looked up at Burel uncertainly.

"Adon, but I'm glad to see you all," said Ferret. Then she turned to Arin and Egil. "Especially you two. I thought you both done for—slain by the Krakens."

"I take it there was no Kraken waiting for you," said Egil.

"No," replied Ferret. "It seems two were enough, or so Ordrunc thought. But I was frightened, let me tell you, and almost couldn't bring myself to touch this charmed silver box. —And another thing: it was damned hard lugging that millstone up all alone . . . especially over the ice—I almost dropped it a dozen times. The farther I went the heavier it got, or so it seemed—it started out 'round seventy pounds but must scale a thousand by now."

"Nevertheless, love, you brought it after all," said Delon, casting Egil and Aiko a significant glance.

"Where's the Dragon?" asked Ferai, looking about.

"In the many arms of his two lovers, luv," replied Delon, gesturing toward the sea.

"Then let's see what's inside," said Ferret, her eyes glittering as she knelt beside the chest and took her lockpicks from her small belt pack. She turned to Arin. "Is it yet charmed?"

Arin looked at the chest, then said, "No. The glow is gone."

"Hmm, it probably went away when I opened the lock on the chain. And by the way, that latch was very tricksy—I had to lock it twice altogether just to get it open."

Ferret carefully examined the chest and the keyhole on its hasp. At last she inserted a pick, and a look of deep concentration fell on her features.

click!

She slid to one side and, using the pick, cautiously raised the hasp and waited. Satisfied, she edged the lid up an inch or so and again waited. Finally she opened it steadily until it lay all the way back.

Aiko gasped. "My tiger. The peril."

Again Burel said, "The Dragonstone?"

"Perhaps." Aiko looked about, sighting no one or

nothing standing near, nought, that is, but enshadowed boulders and Alos beginning to stir and the open chest at hand.

Ferret looked inside, then drew out a leather bag. She set it down and untied the thong wound tightly 'round its neck. Then carefully, cautiously, she reached in and withdrew a large, egg-shaped, melon-sized, translucent, pale green stone, lustrous and faintly glowing with an inner light, and she held it up for all to see.

"Just as in my vision," breathed Arin, reaching out to take it. The Dylvana cradled the jadelike ovoid in two hands and looked at the others. "This, my friends, is the Dragonstone."

Through the bloodred sunlight hurtled a tumbling glitter, and glass shattered at their feet, and a yellow-green gas billowed upward, as from behind there came a sharp command—"*Akoúsete me! Peísesthe moi!* And move not!" Egil tried to turn but found he could not move, his body unable to respond.

"I thank you for recovering my prize," hissed a voice—followed by soft laughter.

And then stepping 'round Arin and taking the stone came stalking the Wizard Ordrune.

CHAPTER 79

Ordrune held the pale jade ovoid to the sky and laughed as the crimson sunset bathed the translucent orb, casting glints to the eye like luminous drops of blood. "At last you are mine once more," cried the Mage, then he whirled 'round in a gleeful dance.

Of a sudden he paused and looked at the ensorcelled band behind, entranced by his arcane words of binding, their resistance lowered by his vaporous concoction. Rage boiled behind their eyes, yet they could not move, for he had so commanded. "Ah, my fools, I thank you for obtaining that which was beyond my grasp. —What's that, you ask? If I hid it in the first place, could I not retrieve it? I suppose since you redeemed it for me, I owe you an explanation before you perish.

"Walk with me and I'll tell you the tale as we stride toward your doom."

Ordrune passed among the six of them, strolling slowly for the lip of the precipice. Completely enslaved and unable to help themselves, woodenly they followed, though their features were filled with fury.

"Heed: long past when Black Kalgalath and Daagor and lowly Quirm stood before me at the portals of Black Mountain, then did I know that I had to possess this most puissant token of power.

"But I knew if I took it then, I would be hounded by the fools cowering inside, hounded by the Mages who ultimately swore the oath.

"And Quirm, ineffectual Quirm, the weakest of the lot, it was he I subverted there before the very gates when the Dragonstone was revealed. It was deep in his mind that I discovered a perfect hiding place for the stone—the place from which you so neatly extracted it."

Ordrune paused in his steps and gazed into the stone, his ensorcelled captives pausing with him.

"Unlike those who were expelled from Black Mountain, I but pretended to swear to the oath of binding, and I bided my time. Then I went on a long sabbatical—to study the world, I claimed. But in truth it was to prepare my strongholt, the one you so foolishly assaulted."

Ordrune took up his stroll once again, and unable to do otherwise, the six trod after, for so their enslavement demanded, and even Aiko, with her red tiger ward, could not break the spell, though low in her chest was a rumble.

"I waited until Quirm stood sentinel here on Dragons' Roost, and I stole back into Black Mountain and took the green stone from the deep vaults within. I knew that when they ultimately discovered it was gone, the fools in that Mageholt would comb the world, and I didn't wish for them to find a trace of the stone within my tower, though the chances of any of those dolts doing so were virtually nonexistent. And for such a token, well, who can blame me?

"I brought it here in its chest of Dwarven silver and passed by Quirm to chain it in the cavern below, and I summoned Krakens as wards—binding two of the creatures so that at least one would always be on guard. It took much astral <fire> to do so . . . yet I spent it willingly, having sacrificed many prisoners to make it so."

Again Ordrune paused and held the spheroid up in the crimson rays of the bloodred sun.

"Isn't it delicious? The Dragons themselves along with their mates were unknowingly guarding that which they feared so." Ordrune turned to the six. "Who else would have been as clever as I? Those idiots in Black Mountain, or those on Rwn? Ha!"

Again he strolled toward the brim of the great ledge, his thralls in a ragged line across, plodding a pace or two behind.

"But then Quirm disappeared—slain by a rival or drowned by a mate, who knows? And with him gone, my access to the stone was eliminated. My own trap kept me from reaching that which I had so cleverly obtained, that which I had so cleverly concealed.

"Though I knew full well where it was, I had almost

given up hope that I would ever see it again, that I would hold it in my hands once more . . . until you fools came along and I discovered that you were driven by a rede, a rede so well explained by that drool lying back there. Because of the rede, there was a chance—albeit a slim one—that you would actually succeed, and so I bound that drunkard to your cause and allowed you to escape, sent my fell beast to track you from above to make certain you didn't take the news of the scroll to my illustrious doltish brethren, those imbeciles at Rwn and Black Mountain."

Ordrune came to the lip of the precipice and stopped, as did the six. He looked out at the Great Maelstrom turning in the distance.

"Pah, the mindless power of that hole in the ocean is as nothing compared to that which I will control, for I will take the stone and unravel the secrets it contains, learn how to command the Drakes, learn . . . but why am I telling you all of this when you are about to plunge to your deaths? Besides, my Hèlsteed chariot awaits below in Gron and I must hasten ere Modru begins to wonder at my business here in his realm."

Ordrune stepped back from the lip, and holding the Dragonstone on high, he said, "Farewell, my unwitting allies. I thank you for retrieving my treasure, and now I believe it is time for all of you to march to your—"

"Yaaaahhhh!" From the shadows nearby, Alos charged at the Mage, the old man shrieking, "Unlike before! Unlike before!" And then Alos slammed into Ordrune, knocking the Dragonstone loose to fall to the ledge as the oldster's charge carried him and the Mage over the rim.

Their eyes wide with horror, the six enspelled companions stood as would statues, unable to move, listening to Ordrune's shrieks interleaved with Alos's screams of "Shipmates . . . shipmates!"

. . . *t–thmp, t–thmp, t–thmp, t–thmp* . . . frantically beat Egil's racing heart . . .

. . . as if marking the passage of frozen time . . .

And slowly, slowly, the green stone rolled toward the lip of the precipice, toward a thousand-foot fall . . .

. . . *t–thmp, t–thmp, t–thmp* . . .

. . . down through the air they tumbled, cloaks fluttering about them, the old man yowling and clawing . . .

. . . *t–thmp, t–thmp* . . .

. . . Ordrune tried to sketch an arcane rune and speak words in the tongue of the Black Mages . . .

. . . *t–thmp* . . .

. . . but Alos's claws raked down the Wizard's face, upsetting the casting . . . .

. . . *t–thmp, t–thmp, t–thmp* . . .

. . . and the green stone rolled . . .

. . . *t–thmp, t–thmp, t–thmp, t–thmp* . . .

. . . and still the comrades could not move . . .

. . . *t–thmp, t–thmp* . . .

. . . in the frantic span of but eighteen racing heartbeats, Alos and Ordrune plummeted from the verge of the precipice to the sea below, spinning and tumbling down through the air, bloodred with the setting sun, the old man clutching and clawing and shouting of shipmates, Ordrune shrieking and trying frantically to cast a spell . . .

. . . *t–thmp, t–thmp* . . .

. . . and then they struck the water . . .

. . . and the companions could move . . .

. . . and the green stone rolled to the edge . . .

Ferret shrieked and dove forward and slid on her stomach across the stone of the great ledge and managed to grab the jadelike ovoid just as it fell beyond the lip, but then, screaming in terror, she, too, slipped over the brim of the thousand foot fall—

—only to be caught by an ankle in the grip of mighty Burel, the big man grunting with the strain.

Now Delon grabbed on, and Egil, too, and they hauled shrieking Ferret back up over the lip and onto the ledge above, the Dragonstone yet held in her white-knuckled, two-handed grip.

T-160	T-120	GX-SILVER	GX-SILVER
T-160	T-120	HGX-GOLD	HGX-GOLD
		XL-HIFI	XL-HIFI

This VHS videocassette is designed for use exclusively with recorders that bear the VHS mark. Cette cassette vidéo VHS est conçue pour être utilisée exclusivement avec les enregistreurs portant le signe "VHS".

PRECAUTIONS
- This videocassette is NOT usable on its reverse side.
- Do not handle the tape with your fingers or attempt to disassemble the cassette.
- Avoid subjecting the cassette to strong shocks.

PRECAUTIONS A PRENDRE
- Cette vidéocassette n'est pas utilisable inversée.
- Ne pas toucher la bande avec les doigts ni démonter la cassette.
- Ne pas soumettre la cassette à des chocs violents.

TO PROTECT RECORDING FROM ACCIDENTAL ERASURE
- To prevent accidental erasure, break off the breakout tab.
- To record again, cover the hole with tape.

PROTECTION CONTRE L'EFFACEMENT INVOLONTAIRE D'ENREGISTREMENTS
- Pour empêcher un effacement accidentel, briser l'ergot de sécurité.
- Pour enregistrer à nouveau, recouvrir la cavité au moyen d'un ruban adhésif.

MOISTURE CONDENSATION
When moisture condensation occurs (for instance, when the cassette is taken from cold outdoors into a heated room), wait until the cassette has warmed up to room temperature before using (about 2 hours). The tape may be damaged when used in a moistened condition.

CONDENSATION DE L'HUMIDITE
Si l'humidité de l'air se condense sur la bande magnétique, attendre (pendant environ 2 heures) que la cassette soit à la température de la pièce avant de s'en servir. La bande magnétique risque un endommagement certain si elle est utilisée dans des conditions de condensation d'humidité.

VIDEOCASSETTE PRODUCTS FULL WARRANTY FOR THE LIFE OF THE PRODUCT
Maxell warrants this product to be free from manufacturing defects in materials and workmanship for the lifetime of the product. *This warranty does not apply to normal wear or to damage resulting from accident, abnormal use, misuse, abuse or neglect.* Any defective product will be replaced at no charge if it is returned to an authorized Maxell dealer or to Maxell Canada, 111 Staffern Dr., Concord, ON Canada L4K 2R2. HOWEVER, MAXELL SHALL NOT BE LIABLE FOR ANY COMMERCIAL DAMAGES, WHETHER INCIDENTAL, CONSEQUENTIAL OR OTHERWISE, ARISING OUT OF THE USE OF, OR INABILITY TO USE, THIS PRODUCT. SOME STATES DO NOT ALLOW THE EXCLUSION OR LIMITATION OF CONSEQUENTIAL DAMAGES, SO THE ABOVE LIMITATION OR EXCLUSION MAY NOT APPLY TO YOU. This warranty gives you specific legal rights, and you may also have other rights which vary from State to State.

GARANTIE COMPLÈTE DES VIDÉOCASSETTES POUR LEUR DURÉE UTILE
Maxell garantit ce produit, pour toute sa durée utile, contre les vices de matières premières ou de fabrication. *Cette garantie exclut l'usure normale et les dommages résultant d'un accident, d'une utilisation anormale de mésusage, d'abus ou de négligence.* Tout produit défectueux sera remplacé sans frais s'il est retourné à un dépositaire Maxell agréé ou à Maxell Canada, 111 Staffern Dr., Concord, ON Canada L4K 2R2. CEPENDANT, MAXELL NE SERA TENUE RESPONSABLE D'AUCUN DOMMAGE COMMERCIAL, QU'IL SOIT ACCIDENTEL, INDIRECT OU AUTRE, OCCASIONNÉ PAR L'UTILISATION OU L'INCAPACITÉ D'UTILISATION DE CE PRODUIT. LA OÙ ELLE EST INTERDITE, L'EXCLUSION OU LA RESTRICTION DES DOMMAGES INDIRECTS NE S'APPLIQUE PAS. Cette garantie vous confère des droits juridiques précis. Vous pouvez avoir d'autres droits, variant selon la province.

Unauthorized recording of copyrighted television programs, video tapes and other materials may infringe the right of copyright owner and be contrary to copyright laws.

L'enregistrement non autorisé des programmes de télévision, des films, de bandes vidéo et de tout autre matériel peut être contraire aux droits de propriété littéraire et artistique des auteurs et constituer une infraction aux lois relatives aux droits de propriété artistique et littéraire.

CHAPTER 80

Shaking with terror, Ferret wept in Delon's arms, the bard stroking her hair, gently rocking, softly humming. Arin and Egil stood at the rear of the ledge, the Dylvana replacing the Dragonstone in its leather bag, preparing to put it once more in the silver chest. Aiko and Burel stood on the lip of the ledge looking down at the Boreal Sea. There was no sign of Alos, nor of Ordrune, nor of the Dragon Raudhrskal, for that matter. Of a sudden, Aiko turned and clutched Burel and began to weep softly.

"What is it, my love?" asked the big man, holding her close.

She looked up at him, tears streaming down her face. "Alos—he was like the man my father became in the year after I was revealed, in the year I awaited banishment. And in that year when he lost all honor, my father became *yadonashi, yopparai.*"

Burel looked down. *"Yadonashi? Yopparai?"*

"Outcast. A drunkard," replied Aiko. "I loathed what he had become. Even so, I loved him still."

"I am sorry, my love. —Oh, not sorry you loved him, but sorry he came to be someone you did not know."

Aiko wiped her eyes with the heels of her hands and looked again down into the sea. "Alos was someone like that . . . someone I did not know. And I think I loved him too, at least a little. He died an honorable death."

They both fell silent and stood gazing out on the moonlit waters, but at last Aiko turned and looked toward Arin and Egil kneeling at the silver chest. "My tiger now does not whisper of peril, though she is uneasy in the presence of the *Ryuishi,* of the Dragonstone, as if she doesn't . . . trust it."

"The stone holds a peril?"

"It is difficult to tell, but obvious peril . . . no."

"Then the peril the tiger sensed earlier must have been Ordrune coming upon us at the very same time Ferret dragged the chest out from the cavern, eh?"

Aiko looked at Burel, her eyes wide in revelation.

"Indeed, my love, you are right."

As twilight fell, they reassembled their packs and prepared to descend that very night. Finally they stood on the precipice one last time, a waning half-moon shining, and they looked out upon the Great Maelstrom rumbling afar.

Ferret peered over the brim at the sheer fall below and said, "I can't believe I nearly lost my life just to save a chunk of jade."

Delon squeezed her hand. "This is no ordinary chunk, luv, but a long-lost token of power. Perhaps now the horrors of Dara Arin's vision will not come to pass."

"Nevertheless . . ." replied Ferret.

"Thou wert a heroine, Ferai, and none shall forget," said Arin.

Egil looked long at the Great Maelstrom, then said, "Alos is the one-eye in the dark water, love, the one of your prophecy."

"Nay, *chier*," replied the Dylvana. "He was but one of the one-eyes in dark water. Thou wert the other."

Ferret laughed. "Don't forget the honeyed Ogru eye and the peacock feather. Without them, Raudhrskal may not have been won over."

"Speaking of Raudhrskal," said Delon, "I suggest we get gone from here ere he returns."

Burel grunted and hefted the silver chest now strapped to the frame of his pack, and they turned to the north and strode across the ledge toward the way down into Jord. And as she reached the end of the shelf, Aiko turned and whispered, *"Dochu heian no inori, Alos, sonkei subeki ningen toshi totta."*

And so, down from Dragons' Roost they went, down by the route they had come, the way eased by lack of having to bear an old man along the difficult path, the way made harder by not having to bear that very same old man.

* * *

Just before midnight, they reached the narrow boxed canyon where the cattle and horses and mules were penned, the animals, especially the horses, glad to see them.

They set no camp, but instead turned the cattle loose to fend on their own on the wide-open lush plains. And they laded one of the balky mules with the silver chest, and saddled the horses, and immediately set off at a goodly pace for the town of Hafen.

It was sunset when they rode into the seaport, and a great stir went 'round, for the strangers were back, all but the one—the old drunk, you see, was missing.

That night the Sea Horse inn was jammed, but the strangers were close-mouthed when it came to answering questions as to where they had been and what they had done. Even so, they *did* indicate that they had been to Dragons' Roost. And they told that the old man had died to save them all. But other than that, there was precious little they revealed. Still, they guarded a canvas-wrapped box they had brought back with them, "... and I shouldn't wonder if it isn't full of Dragon jools," said the barkeep when they'd gone up to their rooms.

Weary with lack of sleep, the six took to their beds. And wonder of wonders, as the morning approached, Egil slept soundly straight through.

"No ill dreams, *chier*?" asked Arin, clasping her love.

"None whatsoever," replied Egil.

"Mayhap they are gone, now that Ordrune is dead."

"Perhaps. But ill dreams or no, the memories remain."

Three mornings later, after provisioning their ship, they set sail in their sloop. Many villagers came down to the docks to see them off, for after all, they had been to Dragons' Roost and had survived.

It was the twentieth day of May when the *Brise* left at the turn of the tide, heading west, but where bound was anyone's guess.

Westerly through the Boreal they fared, and into the Northern Sea, and finally into the Weston Ocean where lay their goal, the weather fair and foul by turns as onward they sailed.

At last, on June the twenty-second, the day of the summer solstice, at the mid of day they arrived at Kairn, the City of Bells in the west on the Isle of Rwn.

Water thundered down into the sea from the Kairn River flowing through the heart of the city and over the hundred-foot precipice above, but the sloop did not reach this flow, for they came to the docks from the north.

And as the six made their way up the cliff and to the city atop, the air was filled with the sounds of bells marking high noon.

Shortly thereafter they were ferried across to the small river isle upon which sat the Academy of Mages, five towers arranged in a pentagram, with a sixth tower in the center.

An apprentice led them to the central tower for their audience with the regent—Mage Doriane, recently returned from Vadaria, or so the apprentice said. He led them to the chamber on the first floor, and after a short pause, they were admitted in.

Black-haired Doriane stood to greet them, her pale blue eyes widening slightly at the sight of the Ryodoan and the Dylvana.

Burel set the burden he bore down on a table nearby, and after the introductions, when Doriane asked what brought them here, he unwrapped the canvas to reveal the untarnishable silver chest.

Although she didn't know it at the time, Doriane would receive no other visitors for the rest of the day.

"Oh, my, but what a tale," said Doriane. She looked at the Dragonstone, the pale green ovoid sitting on her desk. "We thought it gone forever, but this is indeed the genuine stone."

"How can you tell?" asked Ferret.

"Why, Dara Arin could have verified that it was the true Dragonstone."

Arin glanced up at the regent. "How so?"

Doriane smiled. "Simply look at it, my dear, and attempt to <see>."

Arin turned her gaze toward the stone, then gasped, "It's gone! I <see> nothing whatsoever."

Doriane laughed. "Exactly so, Dara, for it is the mysterious Dragonstone: it defies all scrying and seems to have a hold over the Drakes themselves. That you were able to have a vision of the stone defies all we know of it. I can only attribute it to the 'wild magic' you hold."

Arin turned to the Mage. "Wild magic or no, it *is* the stone of my vision. But what I want to know is, now that the stone is back in the safety of Magekind, will the vision come true?"

Doriane frowned. "That, my dear, I cannot say. All I can promise is that the stone will be safely locked in the vaults below, and this time none shall steal it, for we will set deadly wards all 'round."

At the late meal, Doriane said in response to Delon's question, "As to the fate of the Drake Raudhrskal, I think he did not survive, for two Krakens are too many for *any* Dragon—even Black Kalgalath, even Daagor."

Delon grinned and turned to Ferret. "See, luv, this is why a man should never have more than one lusty mate, for one is more than enough to kill us dead."

Aiko looked at Burel, her face turning red.

That eve in the City of Bells, as mid of night came, peals rang across the town. Only four times in a given year did the midnight bells sound: on the equinoxes and on the solstices. This night they signified that the summer solstice had come again.

And in a grove on the Isle of Rwn, Arin and her comrades celebrated the event. The dark of the moon fell on this day as well, yet whether this signified something ominous or instead a new beginning, Arin did not know.

But dark of the moon or no, she and the others glided through the rite, females and males stepping in point and counterpoint—Arin and Aiko and Ferai, Egil and Burel and Delon . . . Arin singing, Delon singing, the others joining in roundelay, harmonies rising on harmonies . . . step . . . pause . . . step . . . shift . . . pause . . . turn . . .

step. Slowly, slowly, move and pause. Voices rising. Voices falling. Step . . . pause . . . step. Ladies passing. Lords pausing. Step . . . pause . . . step . . .

. . . the dance of life goes on.

Epilogue

After delivering the Dragonstone to the Academy of Mages on the Isle of Rwn, Arin and her comrades went their separate ways:

Aiko and Burel of course went back to Sarain to deal with the Fists of Rakka, and the results of their campaign are well recorded and will not be repeated here.

Delon and Ferret took to the road, he singing, she performing escape tricks, and they seemed to accumulate wealth at a rate not accounted for by their showmanship rewards alone. Too, much to Ferai's surprise, she did indeed become the Baroness of the Alnawood—as Delon had told Raudhrskal she would, if they but recovered the silver chest—for Delon was heir to that barony all along. When his father died, Delon and Ferai returned to the 'wood to manage the wide-flung estate; their son, in turn became a bard, and quite a trickster too, but of course the legends of Fallon the Fox are sung throughout the land, and again, I will not overburden you with such well-known tales.

As to Egil and Arin: it was true that with Ordrune's demise Egil's nightmares ceased, for the curse had been lifted with the Black Mage's death. Too, over time, Egil's stolen memories returned, though slowly and not all at once. When Egil and Arin returned to Fjordland, they discovered that the Fjordlanders and the Jutes were at bitter war, occasioned by Queen Gudrun the Comely declaring that the loss of her hand clearly was the Fjordlanders' fault. Egil, however, sought to make peace, in keeping with his pledge to Arin long past when, following in the steps of another, he, too, had declared, "Let it begin with me." But the war raged on in spite of his efforts, though he did win over converts, men and women who traveled across the many lands preaching lasting peace. Throughout the remainder of his life, Egil was unswerving in this cause, though now and again he did take up his axe and Arin took up her bow when there was no other choice. Long did Egil live, but at last age took him, weary and feeble and ill, an infirm old man yet loved by his precious Arin, who remained young and vibrant and bright, Arin who wept bitterly on that cold morn and mourned for many long years after.

Concerning Alos's sacrifice: what is clear is that the oldster awakened from his stupor in time to see his shipmates in peril, and being bound to their cause he could not desert them, could not run away and hide . . . unlike before. Scholars still debate what Alos would have done had Ordrune not laid a curse upon him, a curse they believe the Mage cast merely to keep Arin's band all together. It just may be that Ordrune sealed his own doom by binding the oldster to Arin's quest. Regardless, scholars agree that Alos's last act was heroic, indeed.

As to the others involved in that tale, the most notable event in this time of trouble was the retribution for the Felling of the Nine. Perin, Biren, Vanidar, Rissa, Melor, and Ruar all bore messages concerning the doom of the green stone to many kingdoms in the land, yet none knew what to do, other than stand vigilant. Thus it was that finally those six Elves came together to join the host of Coron Aldor and High King Bleys as they sought out the strongholts of Foul Folk throughout the Grimwall Mountains, strongholts where they displayed the remains of those who had hewn down the nine Eld Trees. At times they fought pitched battles. At other times the *Spaunen* blustered but withdrew in fear. Yet never again in the days thereafter did any Foul Folk fell a precious Eld Tree.

Regarding the Dragonstone: some scholars now speculate that the stone itself was responsible for Dara Arin's vision. It was, after all, a token of power, and tokens of power have ways of fulfilling their own destinies. In any event, after Arin and her companions gave over the stone to Doriane, it was indeed taken to the deep vaults below and a deadly net of spells was cast about it as it was locked away. And when Rwn was destroyed some three hundred twenty-two years after, the stone was thought lost forever. Yet some eight millennia later, and a half a world away, in the Jinga Sea after an all-day struggle a fisherman in a small boat single-handedly landed a great fish. When he finally got back to his village that night and gutted his dark-eyed catch, in its belly he found a peculiar green stone, egg-shaped and jadelike and the size of a melon. This very same day in Moku, after an all-day travail of labor to give birth, a peasant woman was delivered of a child with a peculiar Dragonlike mark on its forehead. The midwives fell down in worship. Some twenty years passed ere the green stone found its way into the hands of this child . . . and of course we all know what happened then.

Finally, concerning free will versus predestination: Ferai and Burel never settled their debate . . . and neither has anyone else.

"The first rule of life is to live."

Acknowledgments

Throughout the tale, I have used diverse historical and current languages to represent several of the foreign tongues involved. Hence, I would like to thank the following people for their expert help with the various adaptations: Shoshana Green, Early Hebrew; Daniel Mc-Kiernan, Ancient Greek; Hiroko Snare, Japanese; Judith Tarr, Latin; Meredith Tarr, German; John Vizcarrondo, Spanish. The other languages used (including French, Norwegian, some of the Japanese, and miscellaneous other tongues) and conversions involved are of my own making, and any errors in usage, translation, or errors in recording the words of my colleagues, are entirely mine.

Coming in September 1997,
Into the Forge,
the first book of the
Hel's Crucible duology.
For the first time ever,
Dennis L. McKiernan tells
the story of the Great War of the Ban,
and how two Warrows changed
the land of Mithgar forever. . . .

Thd! Thd!

"Beau! Beau! Wake up!"

Again came the hammering on the cottage door and a rattling of the latch—*Thd-thmp-clk-clttr!*—followed by another call: "Beau! Blast it!" *Thd-thd!*

In the chill dark, Beau Darby groaned awake.

Thd!

"Ho—" croaked Beau, then, "Hold it! Are you trying to wake the dead?" Striving to not touch the floor at all, the buccan—"Ow, oh"—gingerly tiptoed across the cold wood to the door.

Thd! "Bea—!" the caller started to yell just as Beau clacked back the bar and flung open the portal. An icy waft of air drifted in. "Oh, there you are, Beau. Get dressed; grab your satchel. There's trouble afoot. I've a wounded man at the mill."

In the starlight and moonlight, Beau saw his friend of nearly two years—the only other Warrow living nigh Twoforks—standing on the doorstone of the cote, his bow in hand. They were nearly of the same age, these two, Tipperton a young buccan of twenty-three, Beau at twenty-two, though often in Twoforks they were treated as children simply because of their size.

"What is it, Tip?"

"I said, I've a wounded man at my mill."

"Wounded?"

"Aye. Rûcks and Hlôks. He's bleeding badly."

"Bleeding?"

"Yes, yes. That's what I said, bucco, bleeding." Tipperton pushed past Beau and limped into the cottage and began searching for a lantern. "They killed his horse.

Tried to kill him, too. One even came at me. But he slew them all. Right there at the mill. Seven, eight Rûcks and a Hlôk." Tipperton caught up a lantern and lit it.

In the soft yellow light Tipperton looked across at Beau, that Warrow yet standing dumbstruck, his mouth agape, as was the door.

"Well, come on, Beau. Time's wasting."

Beau closed his mouth as well as the door and sprang across the room even as he pulled off his nightshirt. "Rûcks and such? Here? In the Wilderland? Near Two-forks? Fighting at the mill?" He threw the garment on the rumpled bed and looked at Tipperton, his amber eyes wide with wonder. "What were they doing at the mill? And are you all right? I thought I saw you limping."

"Cut my foot on a piece of glass. My own fault. You can look at it when we've seen to the man. And as to what they were doing at the mill, I haven't the slightest idea. Happenstance, I would suppose."

Beau slipped into his breeks. "Why would Rûcks and such be after a man, I wonder?"

Tipperton shrugged. "Who knows? And mayhap it was the other way about: him after them, I mean. But I'll tell you this: No matter the which of it, they're all dead and he's not . . . at least I don't think so. He was alive when I left him, but bleeding. Oh yes, bleeding. He took a lot of cuts, what with that mob and all. I bandaged him the best I could."

Tipperton agitatedly paced the room as Beau pulled his jerkin over his shoulder-length brown hair and slipped his arms into the sleeves. "Don't worry, Tip. I'm sure that if you bandaged him, we can save him."

"But what if those Rûck blades were poisoned? I mean, I've heard that they slather some dark and deadly taint on their swords."

Beau pulled on his boots and stood and stamped his feet into them. "All the more reason to hurry." He slipped into his down jacket and snatched up his medical satchel and turned to his friend. "I'm ready. Let's go."

Tipperton took up his bow and said, "Quash the light and leave it behind. The man said there were more Rûcks and such out there."

Beau's eyes widened, then he nodded and blew out the lantern. In the darkness, Tipperton stepped to the door and peered out. "All clear," he hissed, and slipped outside and through the shadows and across the clearing and into the woods, this time with Beau on his heels. And beneath the wheeling stars and the waning quarter moon nearing its zenith, two Warrows moved swift and silent among the trees.

"Wait a moment," hissed Tipperton. "Something's not right."

They crouched in the woods and peered across the clearing at the enshadowed mill as moonlight and starlight faded in the predawn skies.

Beau took a deep breath and tried to calm himself, tried to slow his rapidly beating heart. "What is it? I don't see anything."

"I left the door closed. Now it's open."

"Oh, my."

Still they crouched in the gloom of the trees, and then Beau asked, "The man, could he have opened the door? Perhaps he left."

"Perhaps, though I don't think so. He was cut to a faree-thee-well and quite weak."

They watched long moments more, but saw no movement of any kind. At last, Tipperton said, "If we delay any longer then the man will most certainly bleed to death. You wait here, Beau. I'll see what's what. If I whistle, come running. If I yell, flee."

Before Beau could reply, Tipperton glided away, circling 'round to the left.

Time eked by.

The skies lightened.

At last Beau saw a shadow slip across the porch.

Within heartbeats, lantern-light shown, and Tipperton reemerged from the mill and whistled low, then stepped back inside.

Beau snatched up his satchel and trotted across the clearing, past the dead horse and the slain Rûcks. As he came through the door and into the mill, Tipperton grimaced and gestured toward the man and said, "I'm afraid there's nothing you can do, Beau. His throat's been cut."

The man lay in a pool of blood, his dead eyes staring upward, his neck hacked nearly through. His leathers had been completely stripped from his body and strewn about, and his helm and boots and gorget were missing, and the chamber itself looked to have been ransacked—with an overturned table and ripped apart bedding and drawers pulled out and their contents scattered on the floor. Beau moved past Tipperton and knelt by the man, and then sighed and reached down and closed the man's eyes. "You're right, Tip. Nothing I or anyone less than Adon can do at this time. What do you think happened?"

Tipperton's jaw clenched. "The man said there were more Rûcks out and about. They came when he was helpless and slew him." Tip slammed a fist into an open palm. "Damn Rûcks!"

Beau nodded, and as if talking to himself, said, "Back in the Bosky, my Aunt Rose, bless her memory, claimed that each and every Rûck—in fact everyone from Neddra—is born with something missing: a heart. She said they only thought of themselves. Called them 'Gyphon's get.' She thinks He deliberately created them that way—flawed, no compassion, empathy, or conscience whatsoever, seeking only to serve their own ends. This cutting of a helpless man's throat wouldn't have surprised her one bit." As if coming to himself, Beau's eyes widened, and he raised his gaze to Tipperton, then glanced toward the open door. "Oh, my, Tip, do you think any of them are still about? If so—"

Tip shook his head and raised a hand to stop Beau's words. "No, Beau"—he gestured outward—"there's a large track beating westward, across the river and toward the Dellins. The weapons of the slain Rûcks and such are missing, taken, I think, by the others. The man's sword and helm and gorget and boots are gone as well. And as far as I could tell without actually going out there to see, a haunch has been hacked off the horse; rumor has it that's what Rûcks like best: horseflesh. No, I think they're gone for good."

Beau blew out a breath of pent-up air, and his shoulders

slumped as he relaxed. "You're right about the horse, Tip: A haunch *has* been hacked from the steed, and the saddle and saddlebags are hacked up as well. I didn't see a bedroll." Beau stood and peered 'round at the disarray and finally again at the man. "Why did they ransack your mill? And rip off his clothes? And tear up the saddle and bags? What were they searching for?"

Tipperton shook his head, but suddenly his gemlike eyes flew wide. He reached down into his shirt and pulled on the leather thong until the coin came dully to light. "Perhaps this."

"And just who is Agron?"

"I don't know, Beau. The man merely said, 'East, go east, and take this to Agron.' I would have questioned him, but I thought it more pressing to get aid."

"But east? Hoy, now, there's nothing to the east but Drearwood . . . and the Grimwall. Awful places. Deadly. Filled with Rûcks and such." Beau's amber eyes widened. "Say, now, likely where these Spawn came from."

"Nevertheless, Beau, that's what he said—east. Besides, I hear that there's Elves somewhere 'tween here and the Grimwall. And of course, beyond, there's all sorts of lands."

Beau cocked an eyebrow and looked at the token again. "Well I don't see how this coin could be significant. I mean, huh, it seems to be made of common pewter and of little worth. It's competely lackluster . . . and without device of any kind—no design, no figure, no motif. It's even got a hole in it." Beau shook his head and handed the drab disk and thong back to Tipperton.

"Well, it meant something to the man. And it'll probably mean something to the Agron, whoever he or she may be." Tip peered about at the disorderliness and sighed. "Perhaps you are right, Beau, and the coin held no significance to the Rûcks and such. Perhaps the Spawn were simply searching for loot."

Beau shrugged, then looked at the corpse. "We need to put him to rest, Tip. A pyre, I should think, what with the ground being frozen and all."

Tip sighed and nodded and glanced out at the dawn

skies. "We'll build one in the clearing. Burn the Rûcks and the Hlôk as well."

"What about the horse? Cut it up and burn it, too?"

Tipperton pursed his lips and shook his head. "No . . . I think we should leave it for the foxes and other such." Tipperton took up his bow and started for the door. "I'll get an axe and break up some deadwood; you get some billets from my woodpile and build the base for the pyre."

Beau uprighted the table and set his satchel on it, then followed after, finding Tipperton stopped just beyond the porch.

"What is it?" breathed Beau, glancing about for sign of foe but finding none.

Tipperton groaned and pointed northwestward through the gap in the trees where the river ran. "Beacontor. The balefire burns."

"Beacontor?" Beau's gaze followed Tip's outstretched arm. In the far distance atop a high tor glinted the red eye of fire. A signal fire. A balefire. A fire calling for the muster of any and all who could see it throughout the entire region.

Now it was Beau who groaned. "Oh, my. As I said, what with Drearwood just to the east and beyond that the Grimwall, and these Rûcks and such sneaking 'round, I think those of us hereabout are in for some hard times. I mean, look at what happened right here at your mill—the fighting, the dead man, the slain Rûcks and the Hlôk."

Tipperton shook his head. "If Beacontor is lit up, Beau, it means more than just troubles us folk 'round Two-forks've got. Look, you could be right: It might be a skirmish against raiders or such—Rûcks and the like, or not. But if the alarm came from elsewhere—down chain from the north, or up from the Dellin Downs, well then—"

"Oh, Tip—regardless of this, that, or the other, it spells woe."

Tipperton turned to his comrade. "Well, Beau, if the warning *did* come from upchain or down, it'll signify war as well."

Beau's eyes flew wide. "War? With whom?"

Tip gestured about. "Mayhap with Rûcks and Hlôks and other such."

"No, no, Tip"—Beau shook his head—"I mean, if it's war, who's behind it? And what would they hope to gain?"

Tipperton turned up his hands. "As to who or what would be the cause . . ." Tip's words came to a halt and he stood and gazed at the glimmer of the balefire. Finally, he turned to Beau. "All I can say is that fire on Beacontor not only spells woe, but it might spell wide war as well."

The blood drained from Beau's face, and dread sprang into his amber eyes. "Oh, my. Wide war. I wouldn't like that at all—ghastly wounding and maiming, to say nothing of the killing."

"Nevertheless, Beau, that may be what's afoot, in which case it's your skills that will be needed more than mine."

Beau glanced at Tipperton's bow and arrows, then he looked back through the door toward his own satchel containing his healer's goods. "You may be right, Tip—about there being a war and all, what with Beacontor lit—but I pray to Adon that you're wrong."

Tip's gaze softened, and he threw an arm across his friend's shoulder. "It could be just a false alarm, Beau, and perhaps by the time we take care of the pyre and then get to the town square, someone will know."

Glumly, Beau nodded, then said, "Speaking of the pyre, mayhap the balefire has something to do with our dead man."

Tipperton looked 'round at the slain Rûcks. "Or with these Spawn," he added. Then he eyed the distant balefire and said, "Well, let's get cracking, Beau. The sooner we finish, the sooner we might know."